LARSEN

ORCS!™

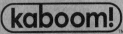

ORCS! Volume 1, November 2021. Published by KaBOOM!, a division of Boom Entertainment, Inc. ORCS! is ™ & © 2021 Christine Larsen. All rights reserved. Originally published in single magazine form as ORCS! #1-6. ™ and © 2021 Christine Larsen. KaBOOM!™ and the KaBOOM! logo are trademarks of Boom Entertainment, Inc., registered in various countries and categories. All characters, events, and institutions depicted herein are fictional. Any similarity between any of the names, characters, persons, events, and/or institutions in this publication to actual names, characters, and persons, whether living or dead, events, and/or institutions is unintended and purely coincidental. KaBOOM! does not read or accept unsolicited submissions of ideas, stories, or artwork.

BOOM! Studios, 5670 Wilshire Boulevard, Suite 400, Los Angeles, CA 90036-5679. Printed in China. First Printing.

ISBN: 978-1-68415-671-9, eISBN: 978-1-64668-156-3

ORCS!™

CREATED BY **CHRISTINE LARSEN**

WRITTEN & ILLUSTRATED BY
CHRISTINE LARSEN

SPECIAL THANKS TO H.E. GREGORY, FOR FLATS

COVER BY
CHRISTINE LARSEN

DESIGNER
CHELSEA ROBERTS

EDITOR
SOPHIE PHILIPS-ROBERTS

ASSISTANT EDITOR
KENZIE RZONCA

SENIOR EDITOR
SHANNON WATTERS

PRAISE DROD, GREAT ORC ADVENTURER AND WARRIOR, WHO - IN DAYS LONG SPED - DID MARK THE HILL AND VALE OF THIS KNOWN WORLD.

NOTHING LIKE THE WIND IN YOUR FACE AND THE SEA BENEATH YOU.

IN THOSE ERSTWHILE TRAVELS, SHE CAME UPON A MYSTERIOUS SHORE. NO STRANGER TO PERIL, DROD PRESSED ON.

THIS PLACE LOOKS PROMISING.

HEH! CREEPY.

DINK DINK DINK

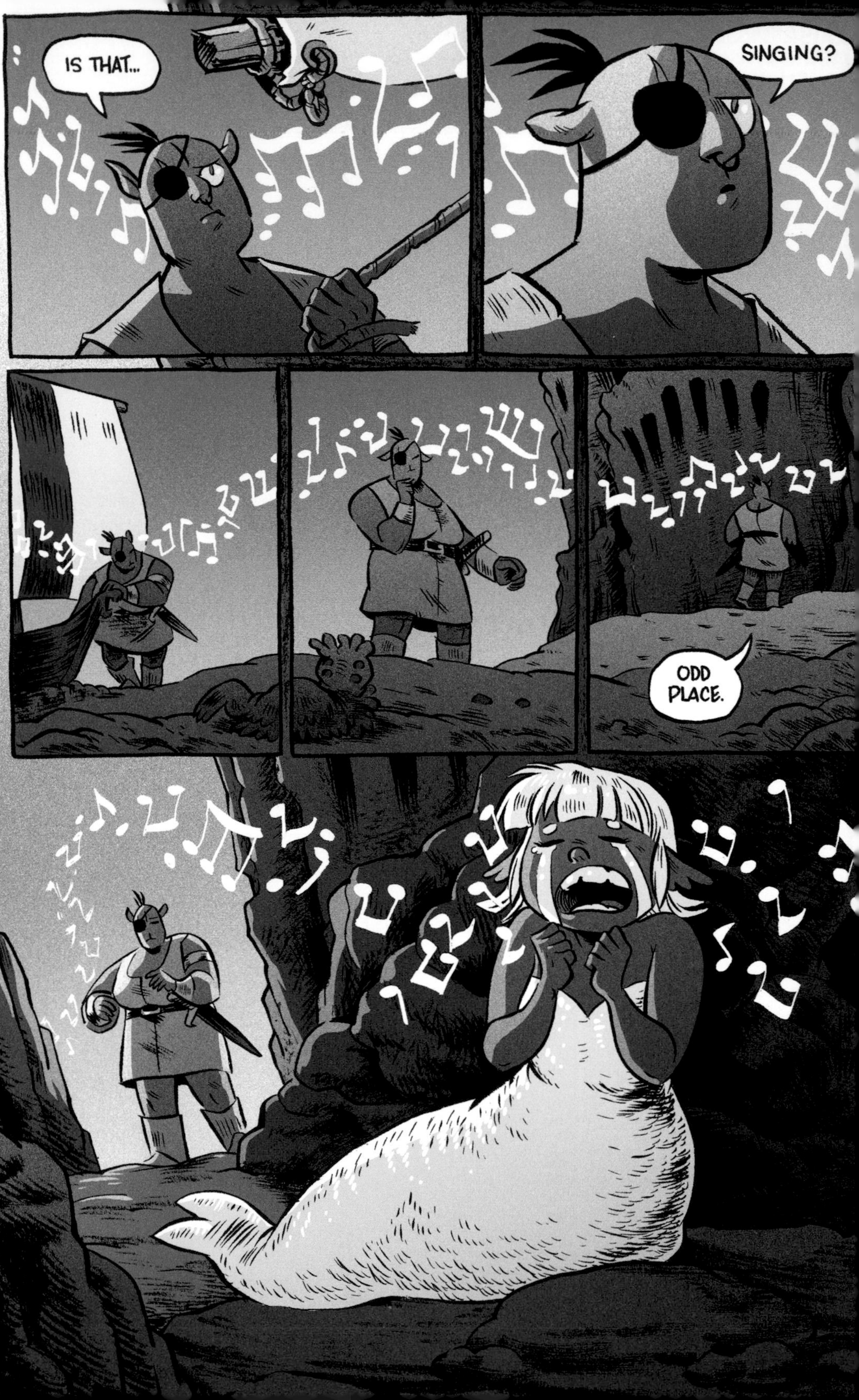
IS THAT...
SINGING?
ODD PLACE.

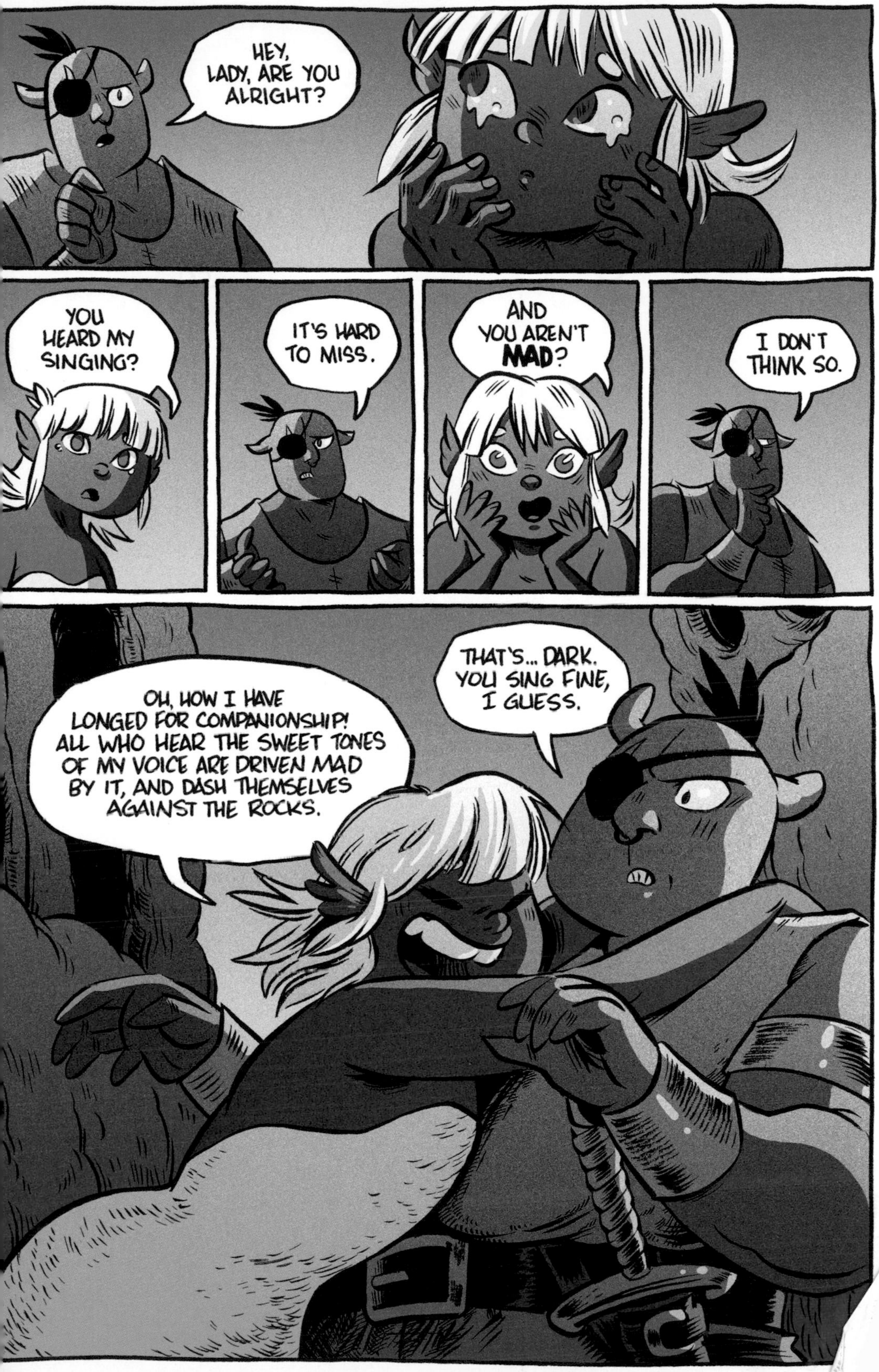
HEY, LADY, ARE YOU ALRIGHT?
YOU HEARD MY SINGING?
IT'S HARD TO MISS.
AND YOU AREN'T MAD?
I DON'T THINK SO.
OH, HOW I HAVE LONGED FOR COMPANIONSHIP! ALL WHO HEAR THE SWEET TONES OF MY VOICE ARE DRIVEN MAD BY IT, AND DASH THEMSELVES AGAINST THE ROCKS.
THAT'S... DARK. YOU SING FINE, I GUESS.

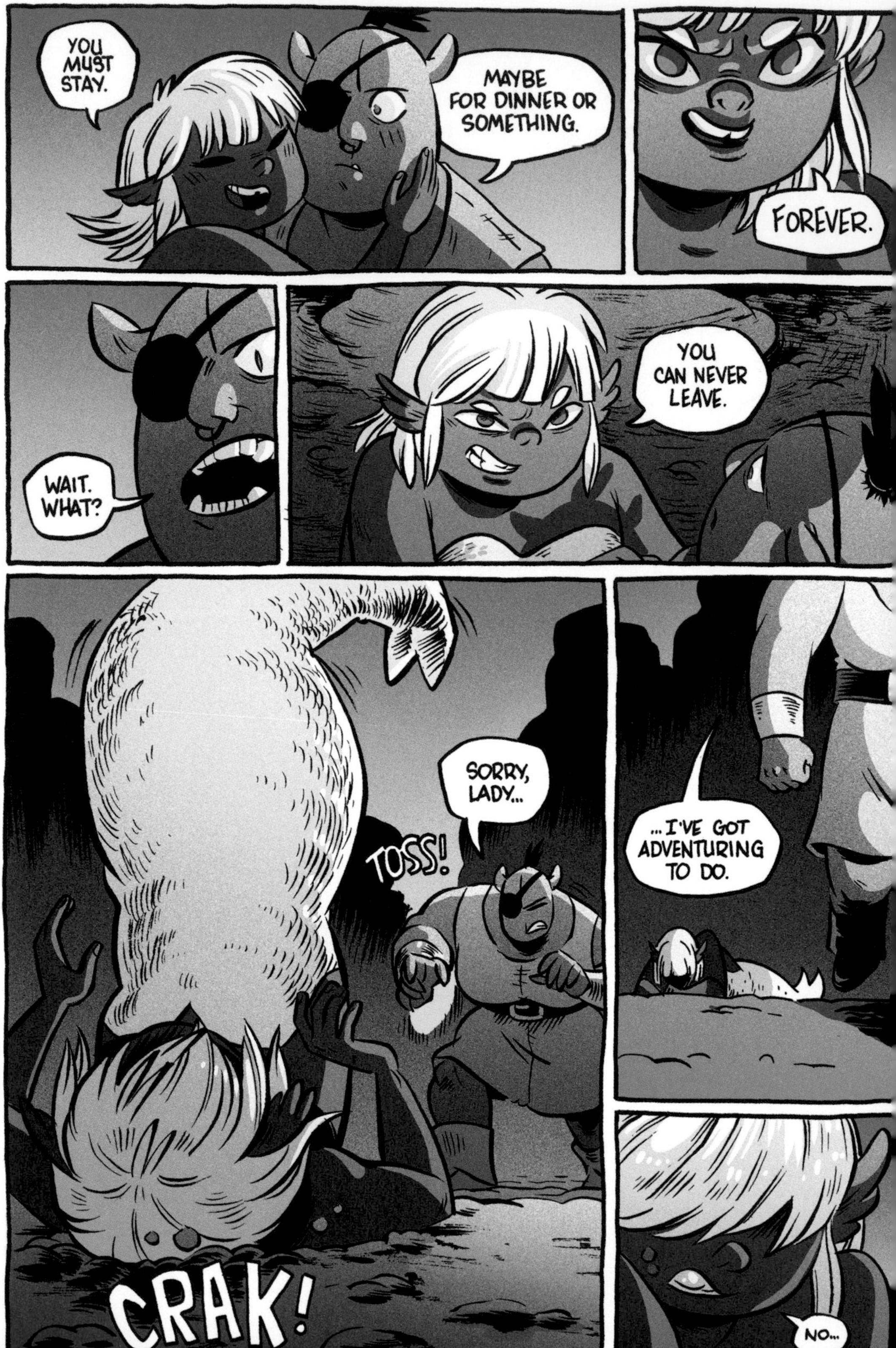
YOU MUST STAY.
MAYBE FOR DINNER OR SOMETHING.
FOREVER.
WAIT. WHAT?
YOU CAN NEVER LEAVE.
SORRY, LADY...
TOSS!
...I'VE GOT ADVENTURING TO DO.
CRAK!
NO...

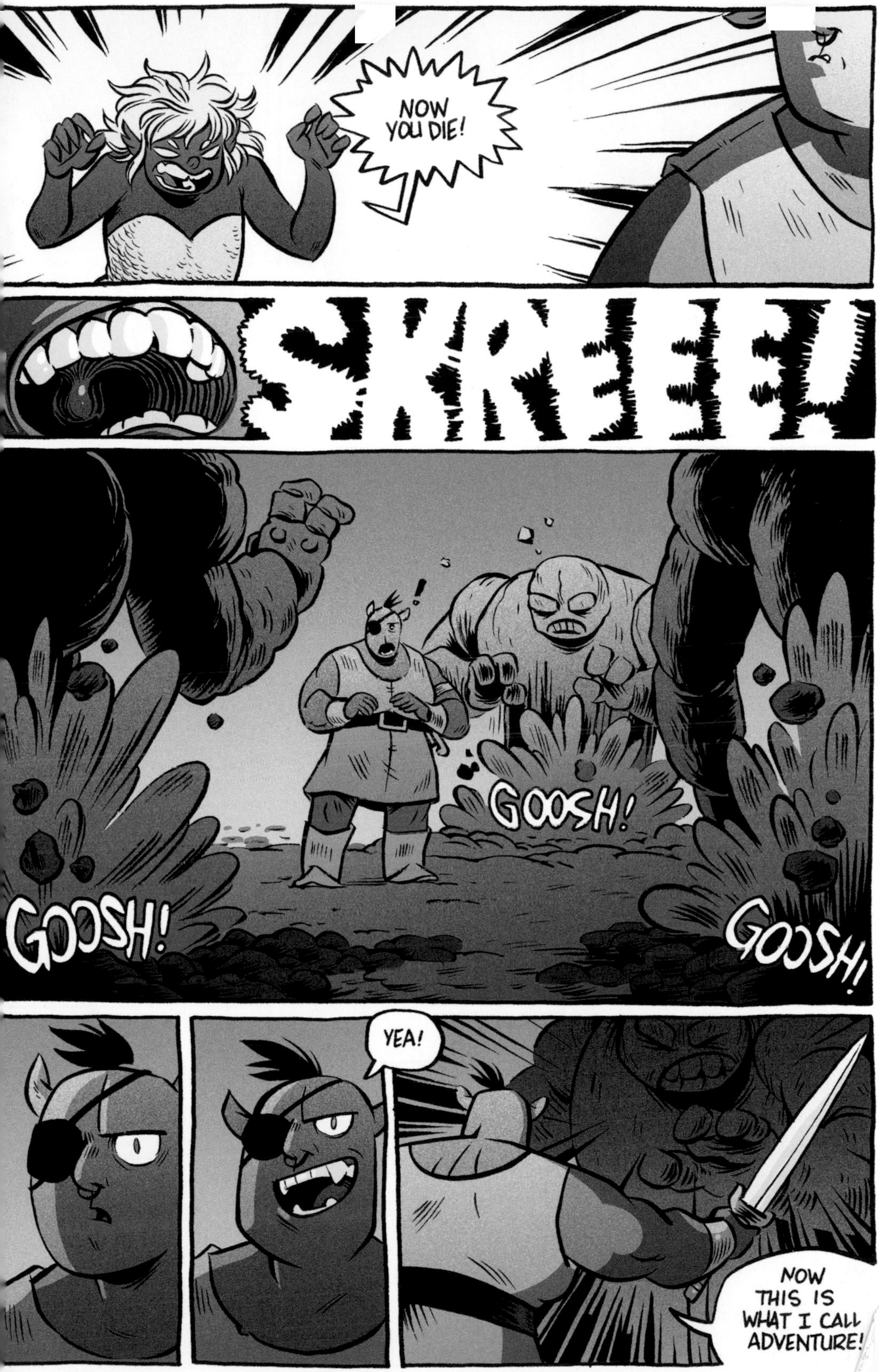
NOW YOU DIE!
SKREEEH
GOOSH!
GOOSH!
GOOSH!
YEA!
NOW THIS IS WHAT I CALL ADVENTURE!

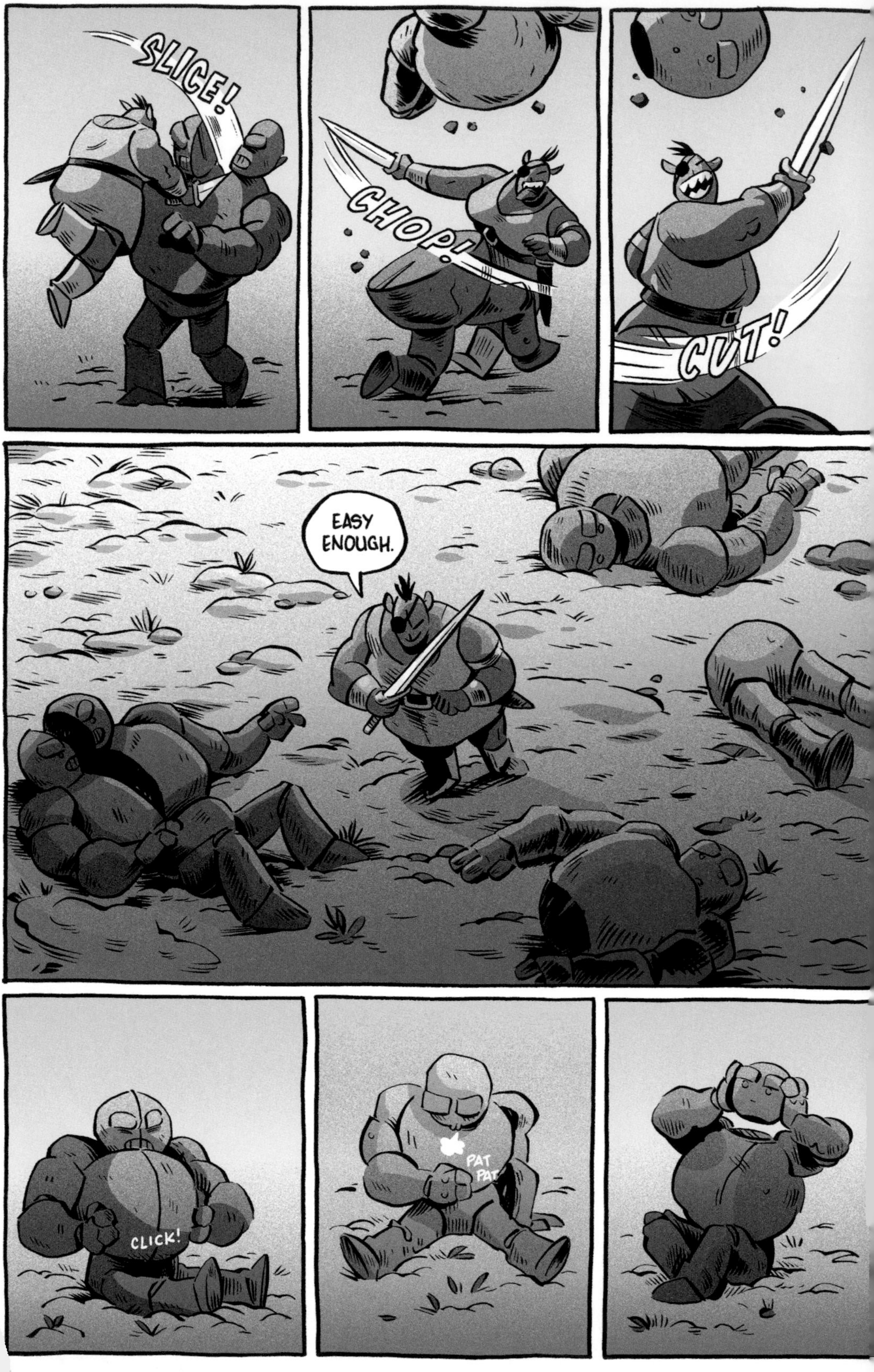
SLICE!
CHOP!
CUT!
EASY ENOUGH.
CLICK!
PAT
PAT

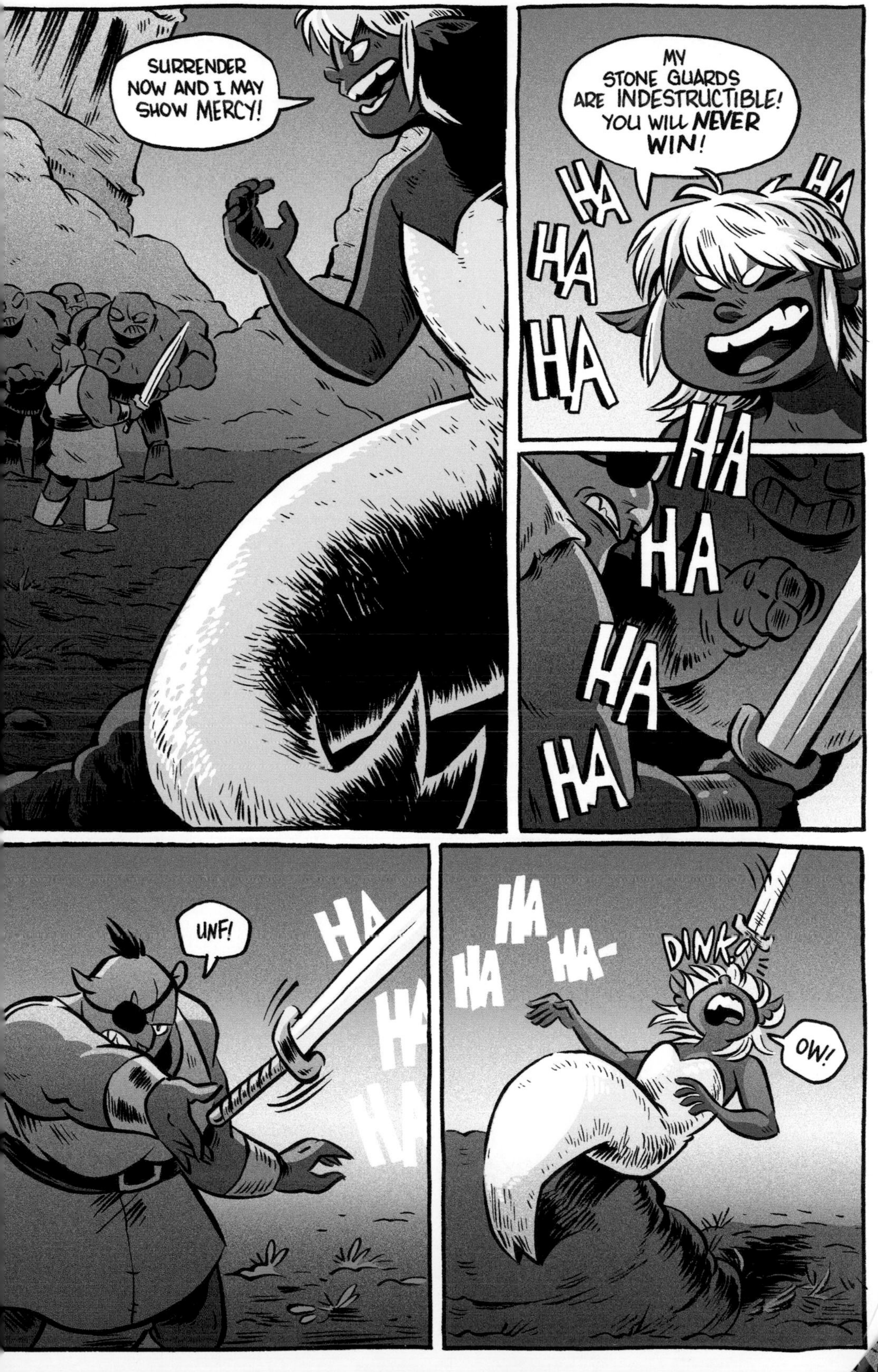
SURRENDER NOW AND I MAY SHOW MERCY!
MY STONE GUARDS ARE INDESTRUCTIBLE! YOU WILL NEVER WIN!
HA HA HA HA HA
HA HA HA HA
UNF!
HA HA HA
HA HA HA HA-
DINK!
OW!

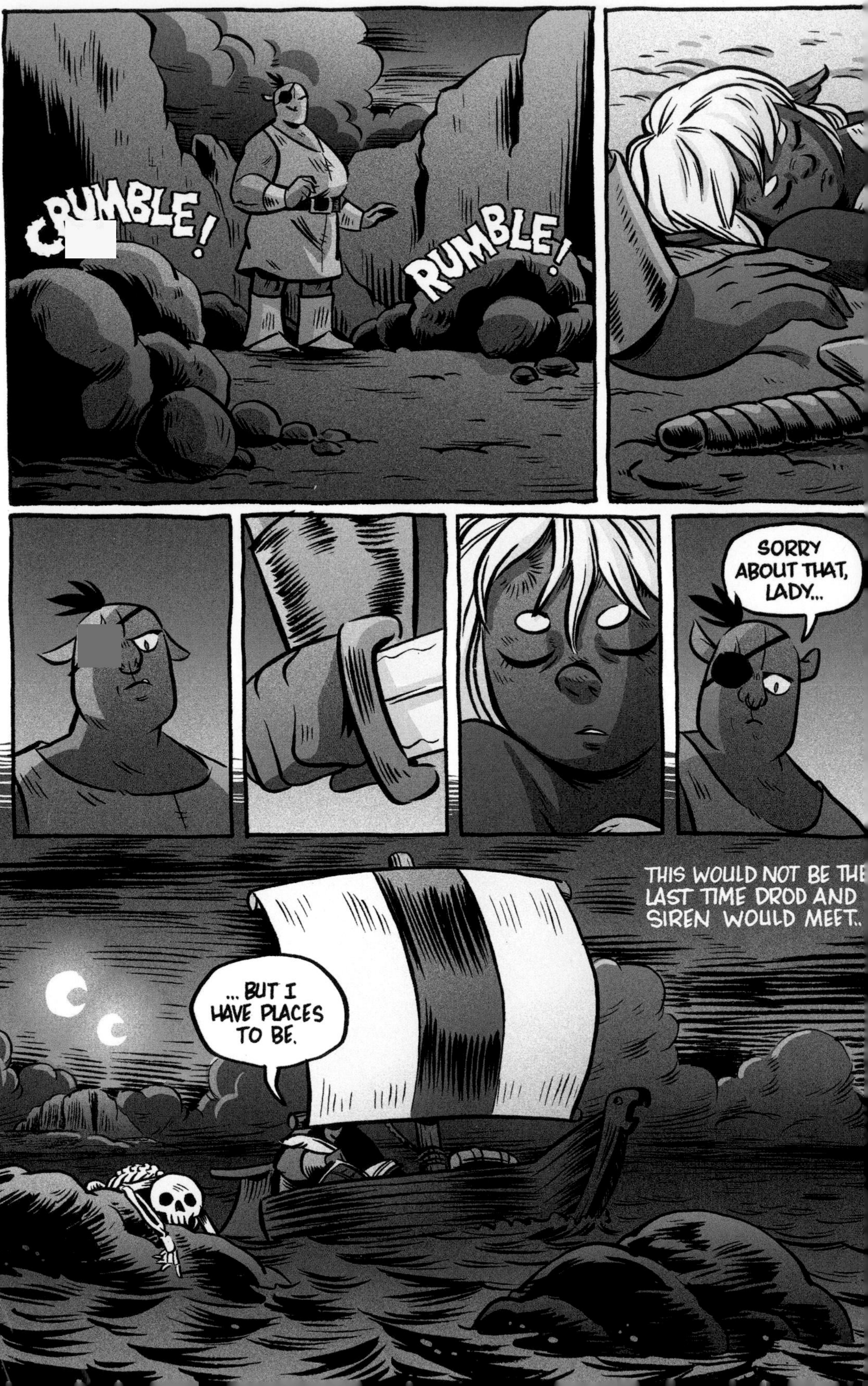
CRUMBLE!
RUMBLE!
SORRY ABOUT THAT, LADY...
... BUT I HAVE PLACES TO BE.
THIS WOULD NOT BE THE LAST TIME DROD AND SIREN WOULD MEET...

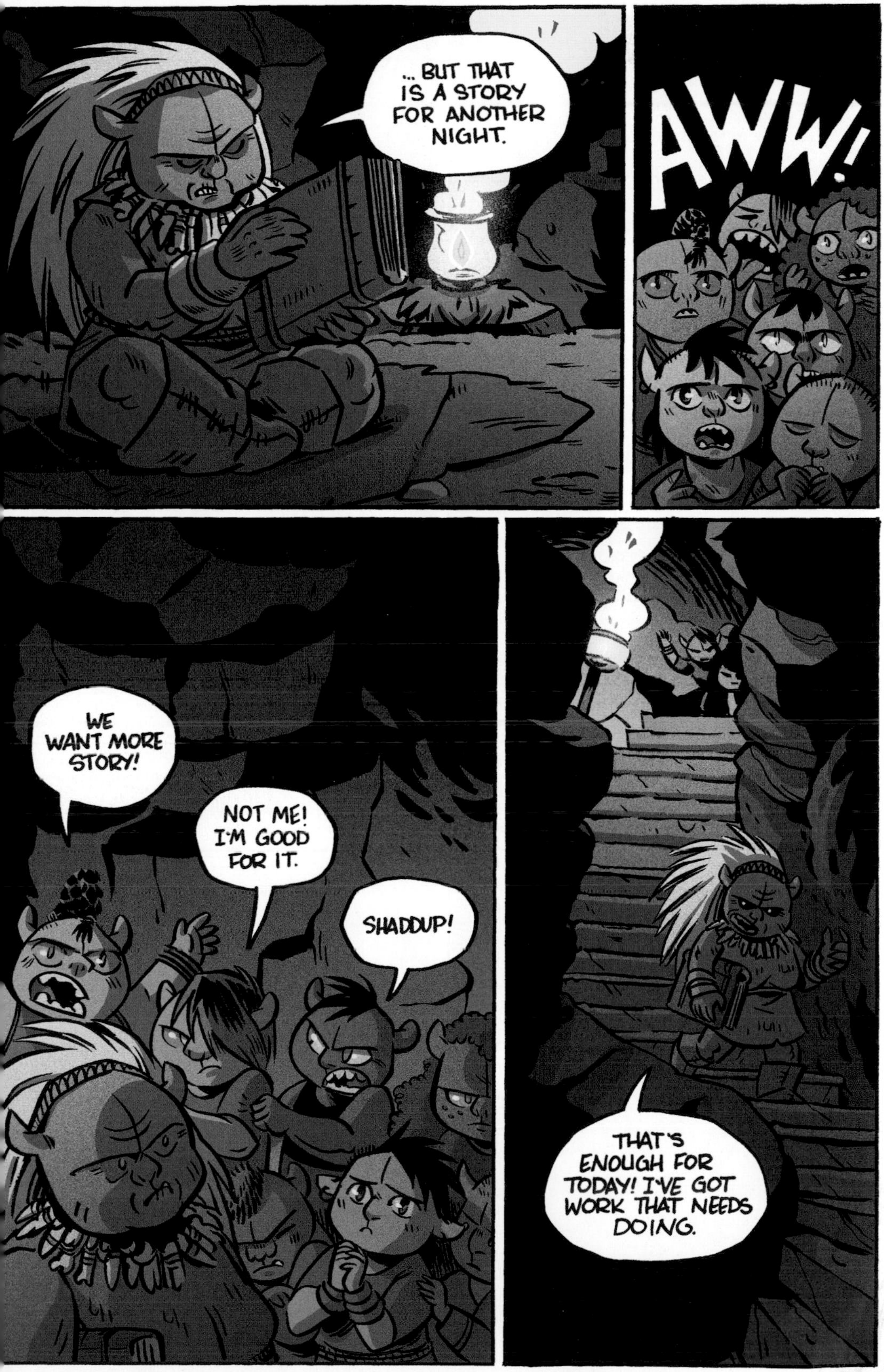
... BUT THAT IS A STORY FOR ANOTHER NIGHT.
AWW!
WE WANT MORE STORY!
NOT ME! I'M GOOD FOR IT.
SHADDUP!
THAT'S ENOUGH FOR TODAY! I'VE GOT WORK THAT NEEDS DOING.

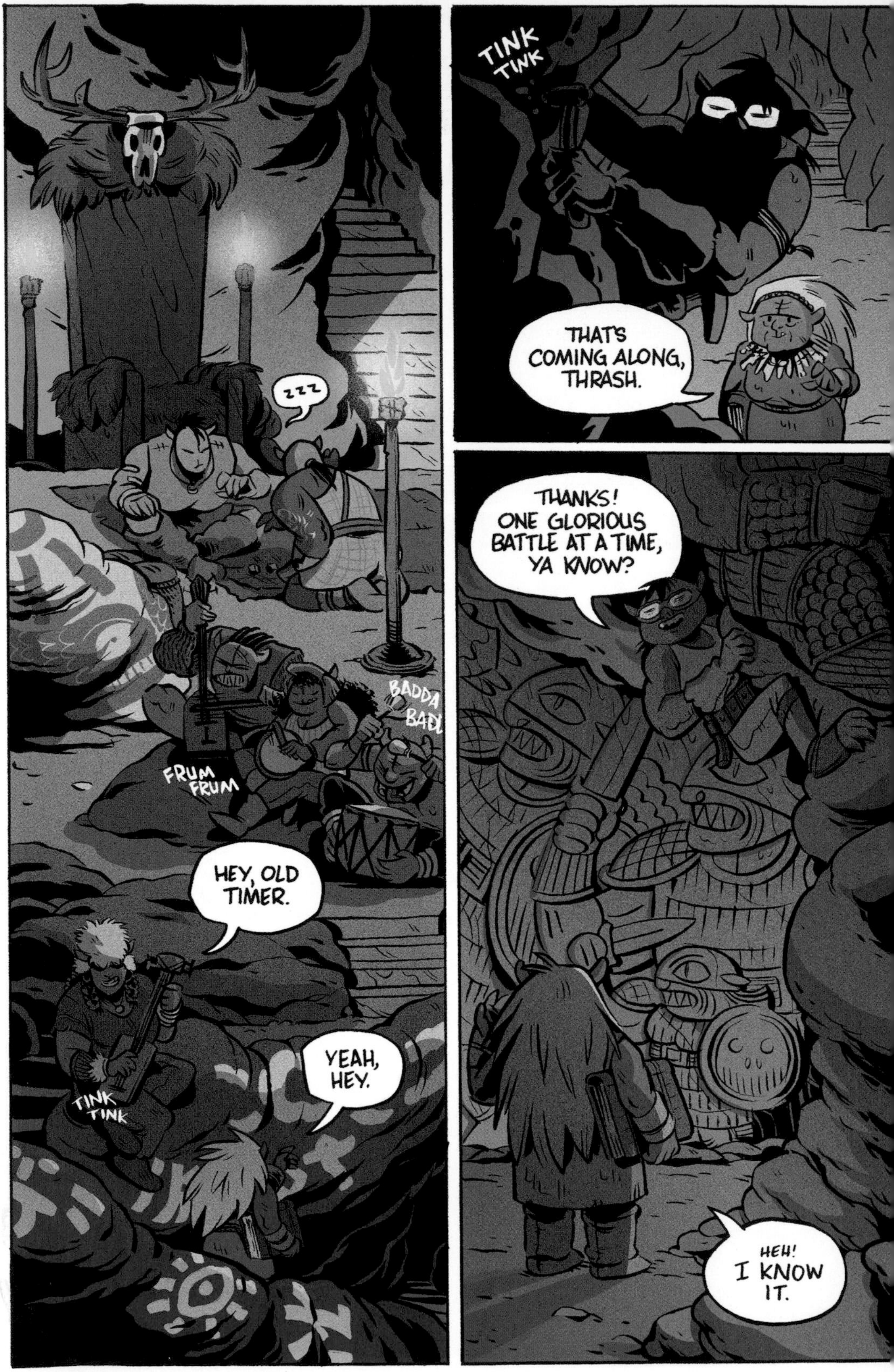
zzz
BADDA BADL
FRUM FRUM
HEY, OLD TIMER.
TINK TINK
YEAH, HEY.
TINK TINK
THAT'S COMING ALONG, THRASH.
THANKS! ONE GLORIOUS BATTLE AT A TIME, YA KNOW?
HEH! I KNOW IT.

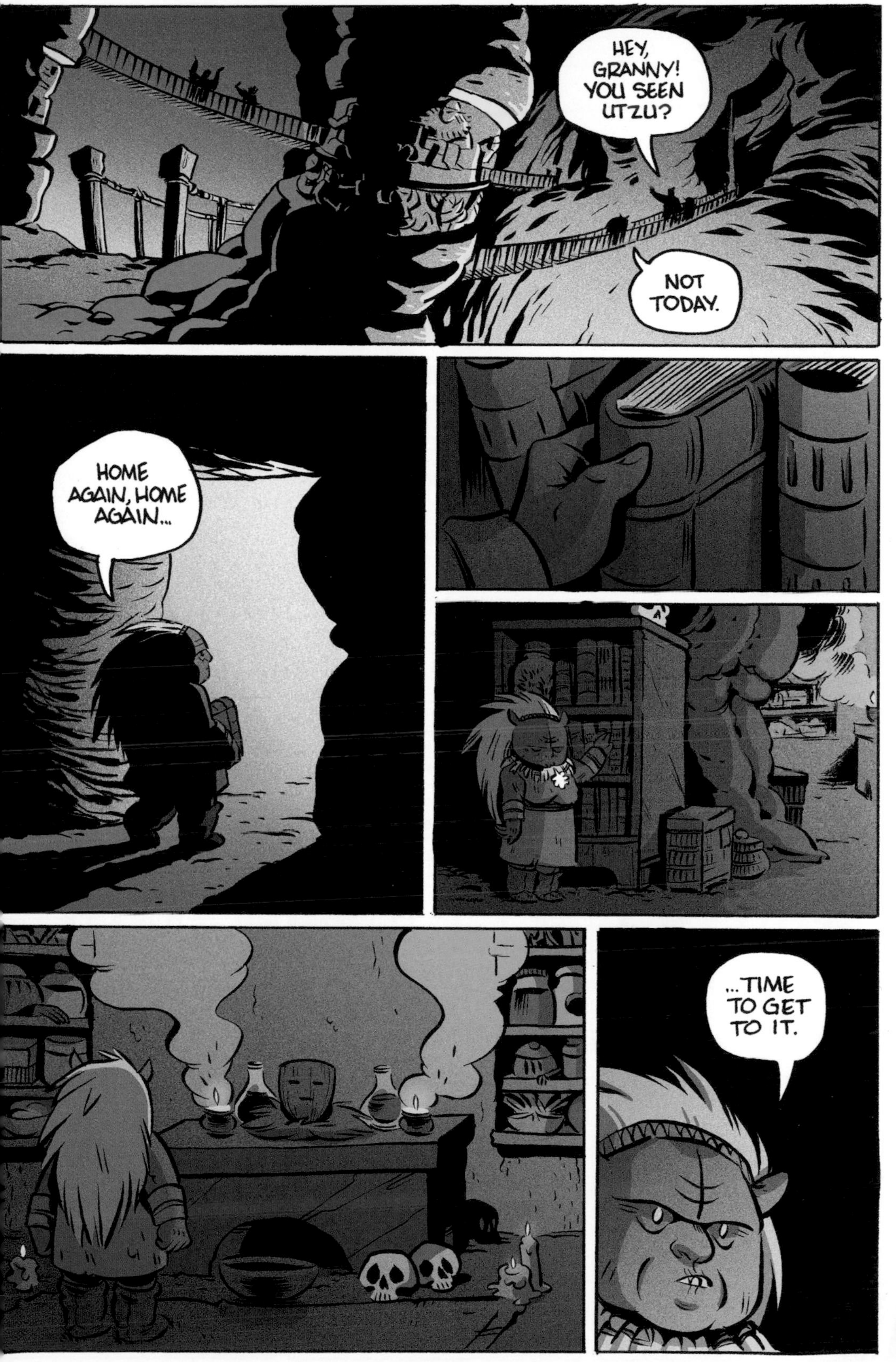
HEY, GRANNY! YOU SEEN UTZU?
NOT TODAY.
HOME AGAIN, HOME AGAIN...
...TIME TO GET TO IT.

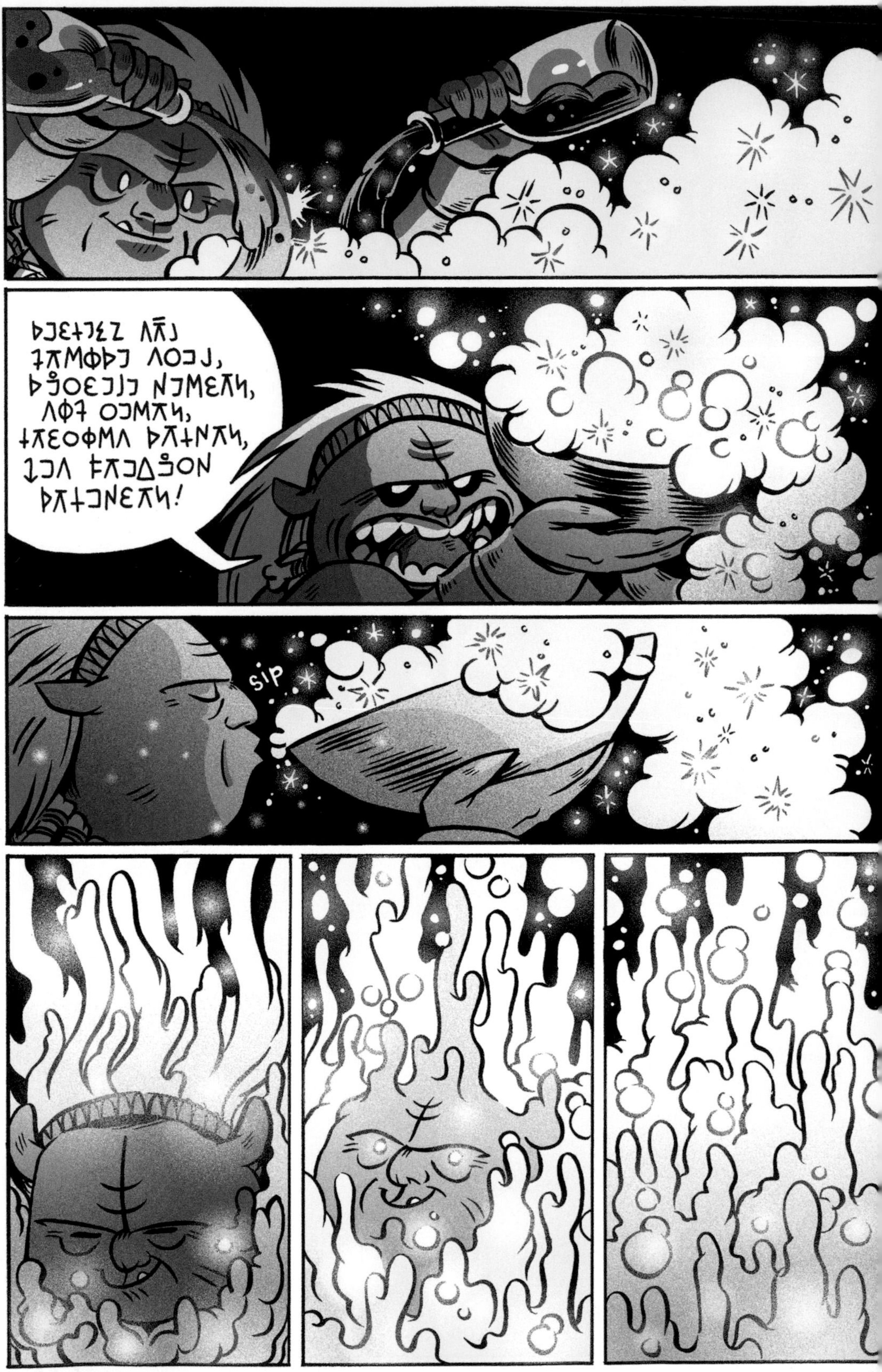
sip

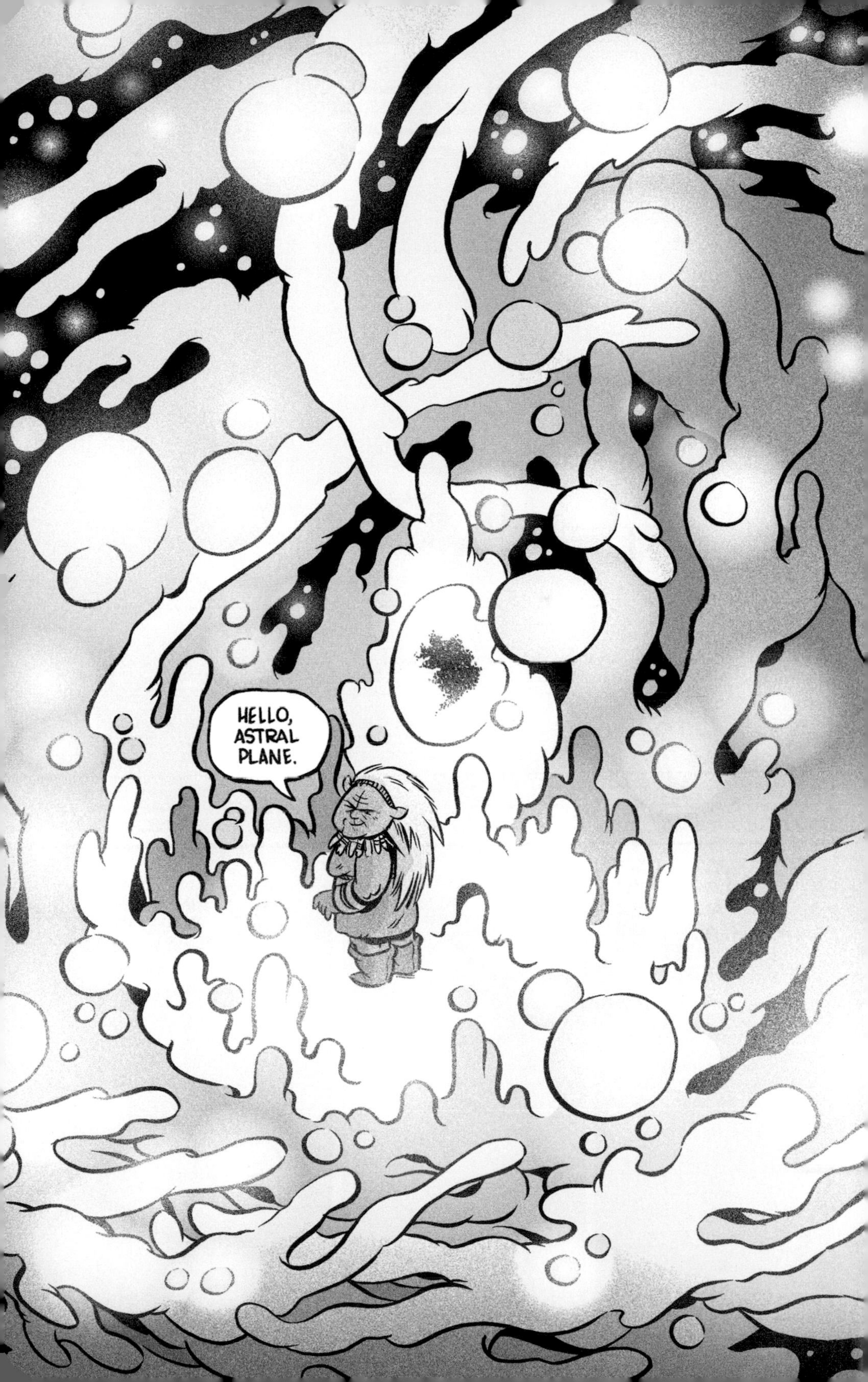
HELLO, ASTRAL PLANE.

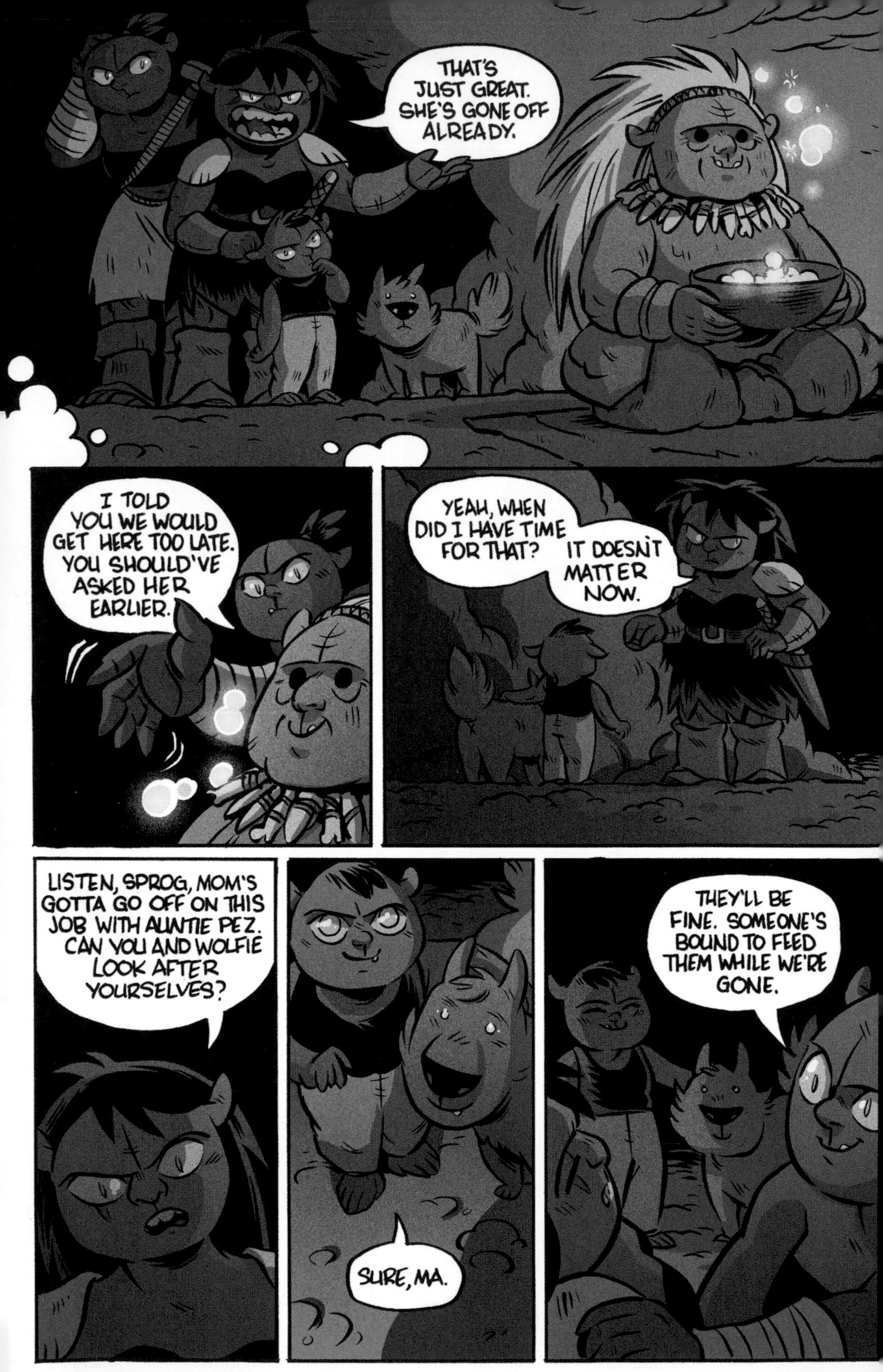
THAT'S JUST GREAT. SHE'S GONE OFF ALREADY.
I TOLD YOU WE WOULD GET HERE TOO LATE. YOU SHOULD'VE ASKED HER EARLIER.
YEAH, WHEN DID I HAVE TIME FOR THAT?
IT DOESN'T MATTER NOW.
LISTEN, SPROG, MOM'S GOTTA GO OFF ON THIS JOB WITH AUNTIE PEZ. CAN YOU AND WOLFIE LOOK AFTER YOURSELVES?
SURE, MA.
THEY'LL BE FINE. SOMEONE'S BOUND TO FEED THEM WHILE WE'RE GONE.

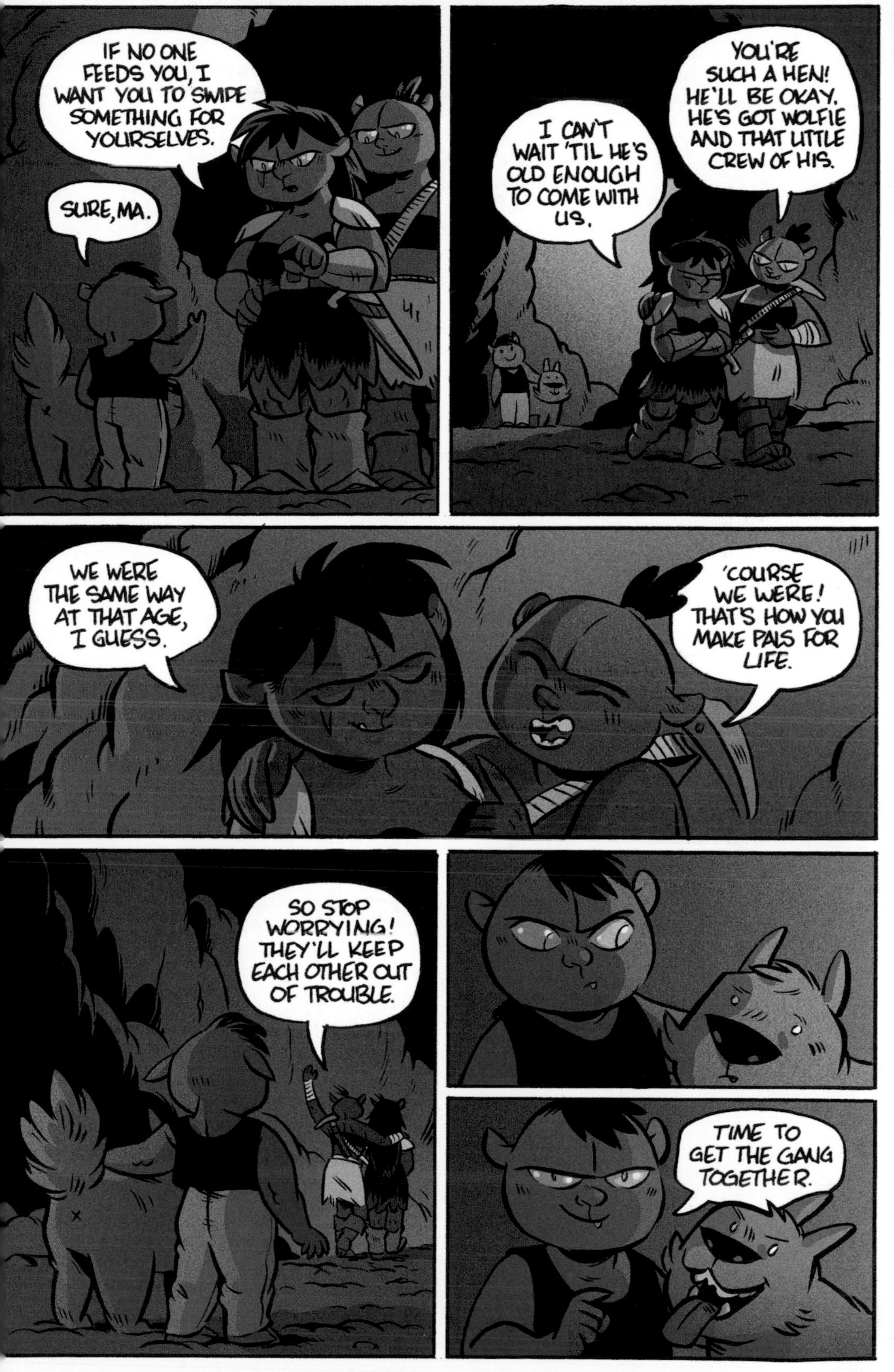
IF NO ONE FEEDS YOU, I WANT YOU TO SWIPE SOMETHING FOR YOURSELVES.
SURE, MA.
I CAN'T WAIT 'TIL HE'S OLD ENOUGH TO COME WITH US.
YOU'RE SUCH A HEN! HE'LL BE OKAY. HE'S GOT WOLFIE AND THAT LITTLE CREW OF HIS.
WE WERE THE SAME WAY AT THAT AGE, I GUESS.
'COURSE WE WERE! THAT'S HOW YOU MAKE PALS FOR LIFE.
SO STOP WORRYING! THEY'LL KEEP EACH OTHER OUT OF TROUBLE.
TIME TO GET THE GANG TOGETHER.

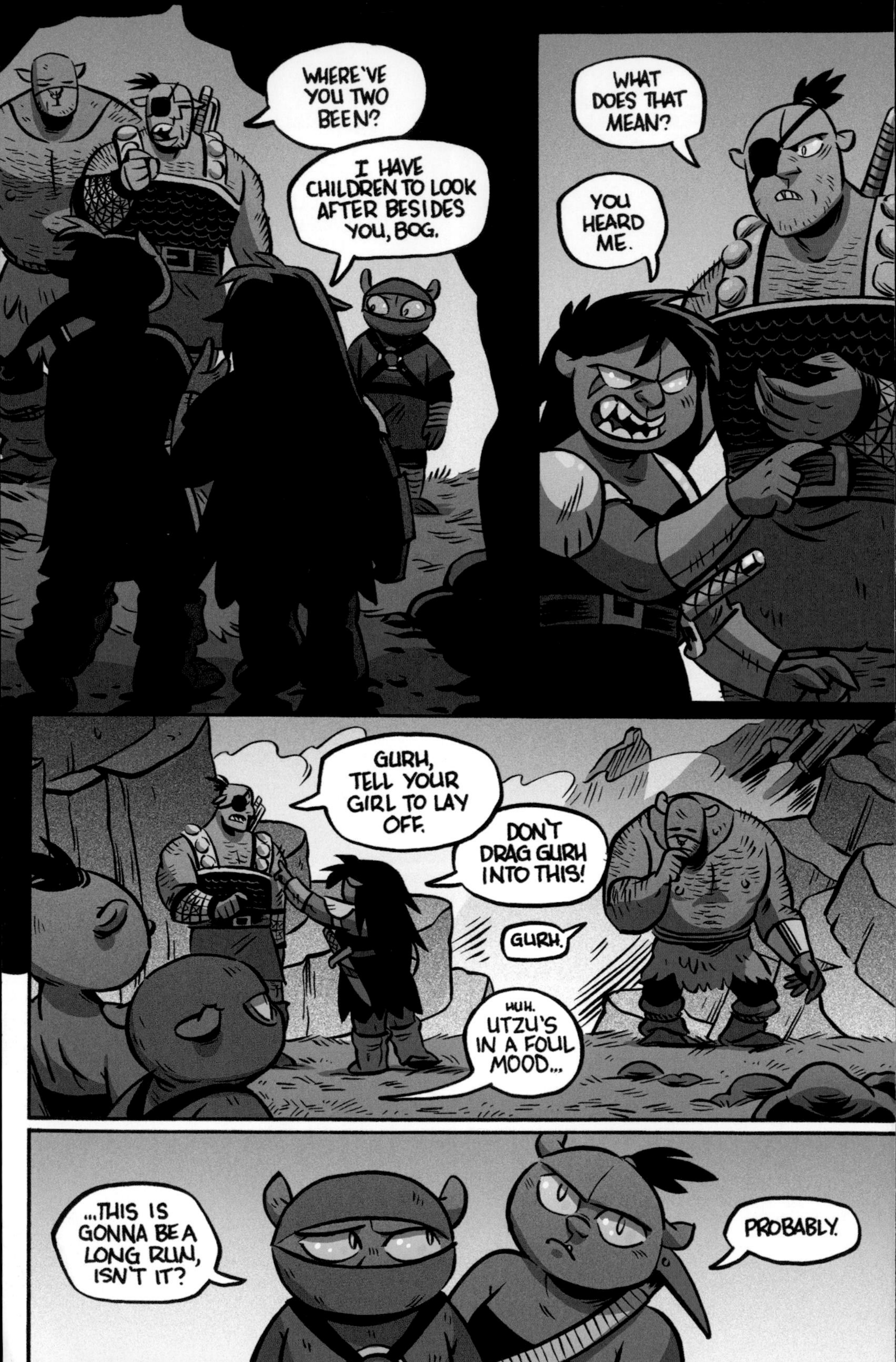
WHERE'VE YOU TWO BEEN?
I HAVE CHILDREN TO LOOK AFTER BESIDES YOU, BOG.
WHAT DOES THAT MEAN?
YOU HEARD ME.
GURH, TELL YOUR GIRL TO LAY OFF.
DON'T DRAG GURH INTO THIS!
GURH.
HUH. UTZU'S IN A FOUL MOOD...
...THIS IS GONNA BE A LONG RUN, ISN'T IT?
PROBABLY.

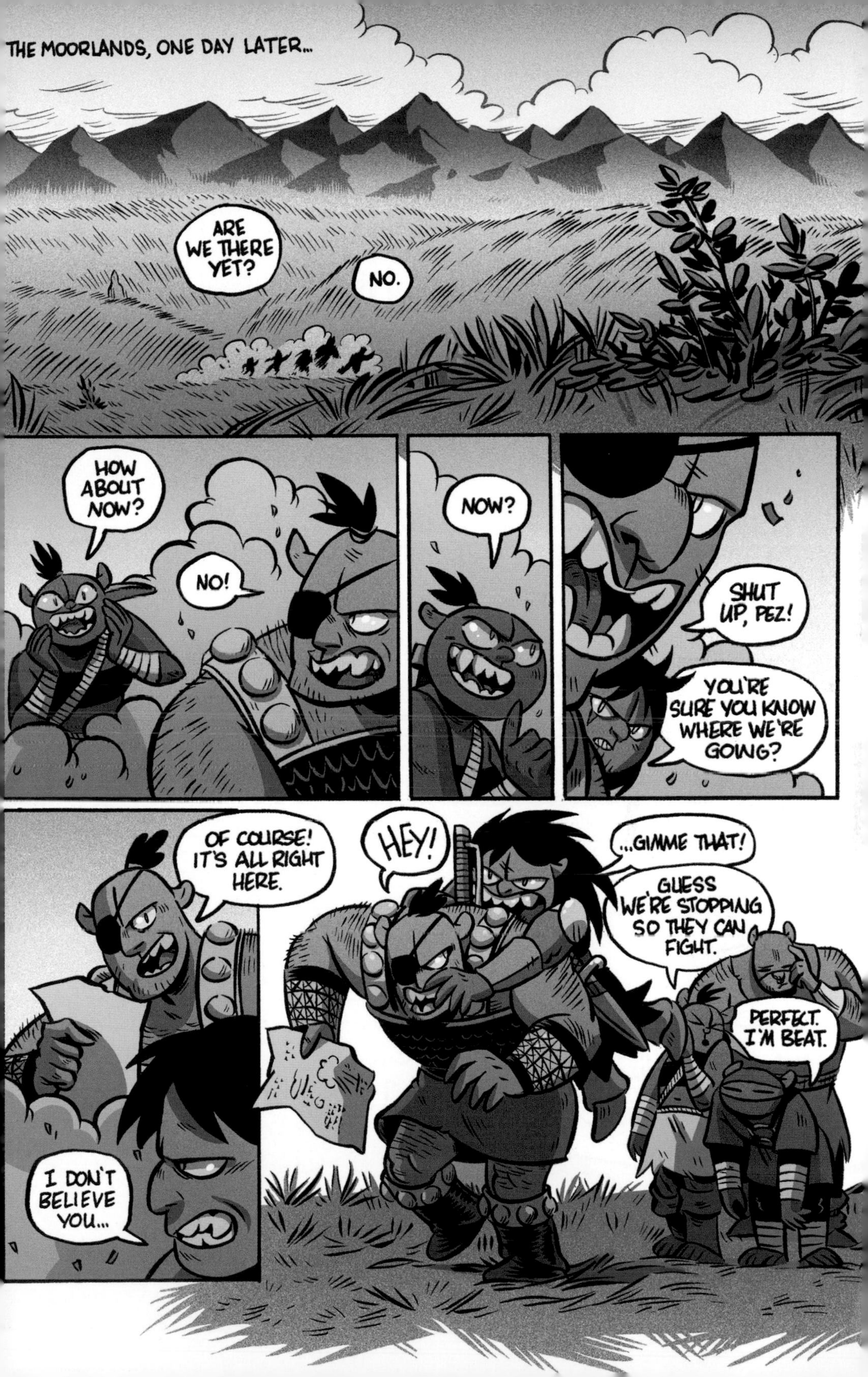
THE MOORLANDS, ONE DAY LATER...
ARE WE THERE YET?
NO.
HOW ABOUT NOW?
NO!
NOW?
SHUT UP, PEZ!
YOU'RE SURE YOU KNOW WHERE WE'RE GOING?
OF COURSE! IT'S ALL RIGHT HERE.
I DON'T BELIEVE YOU...
HEY!
...GIMME THAT!
GUESS WE'RE STOPPING SO THEY CAN FIGHT.
PERFECT. I'M BEAT.

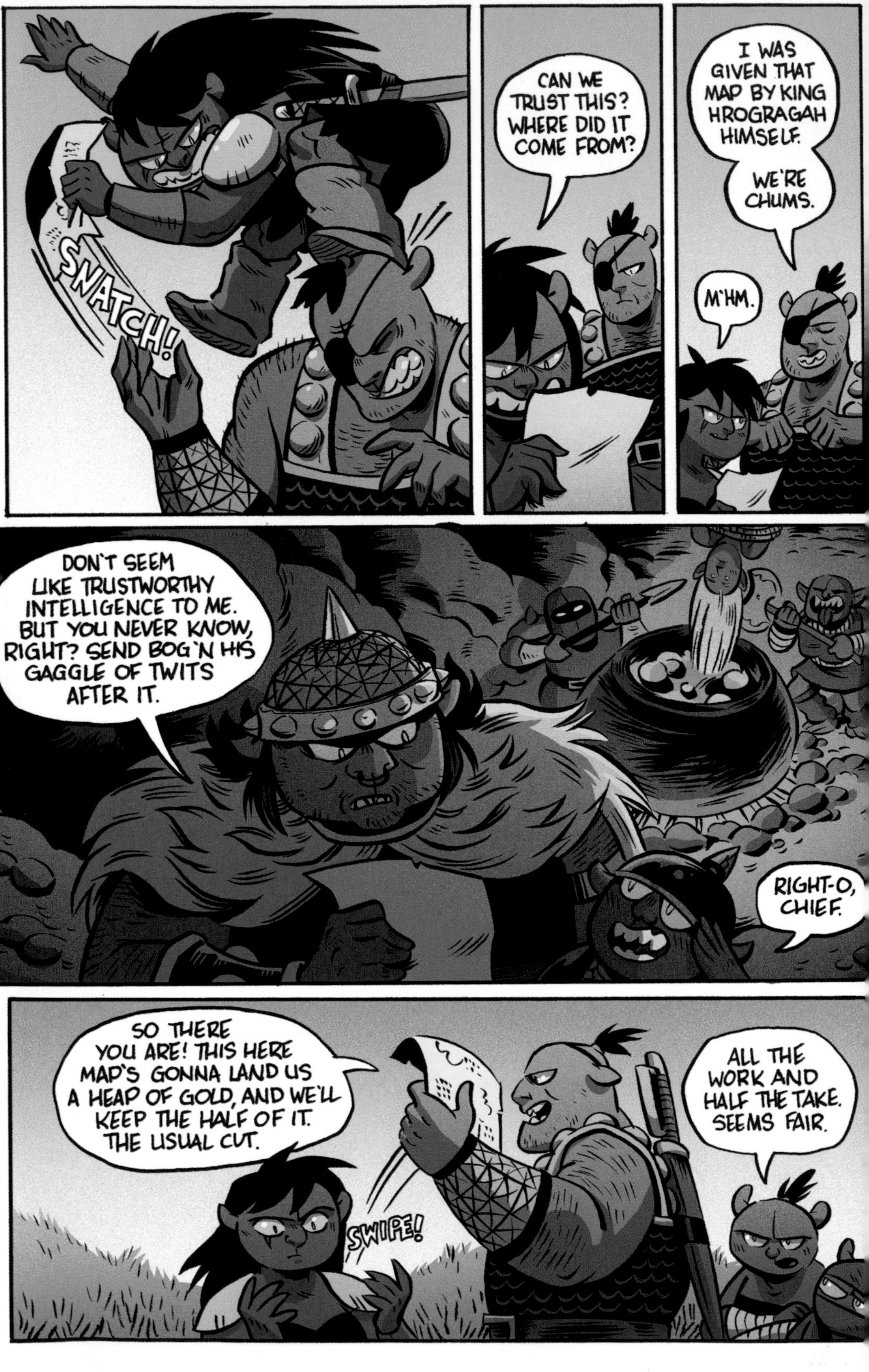
SNATCH!
CAN WE TRUST THIS? WHERE DID IT COME FROM?
I WAS GIVEN THAT MAP BY KING HROGRAGAH HIMSELF.
WE'RE CHUMS.
M'HM.
DON'T SEEM LIKE TRUSTWORTHY INTELLIGENCE TO ME. BUT YOU NEVER KNOW, RIGHT? SEND BOG 'N HIS GAGGLE OF TWITS AFTER IT.
RIGHT-O, CHIEF.
SO THERE YOU ARE! THIS HERE MAP'S GONNA LAND US A HEAP OF GOLD, AND WE'LL KEEP THE HALF OF IT. THE USUAL CUT.
SWIPE!
ALL THE WORK AND HALF THE TAKE. SEEMS FAIR.

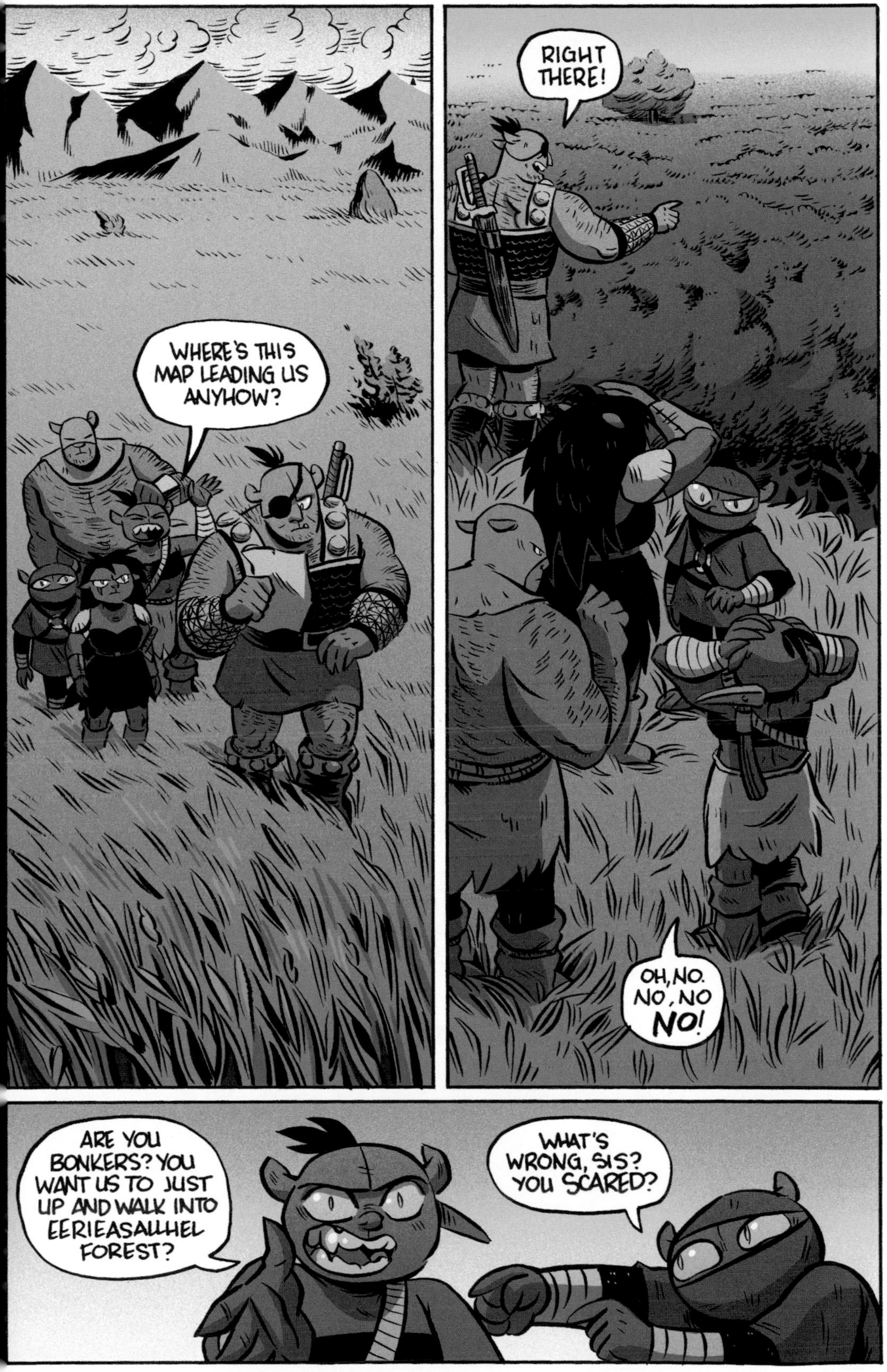
WHERE'S THIS MAP LEADING US ANYHOW?
RIGHT THERE!
OH, NO. NO, NO NO!
ARE YOU BONKERS? YOU WANT US TO JUST UP AND WALK INTO EERIEASALLHEL FOREST?
WHAT'S WRONG, SIS? YOU SCARED?

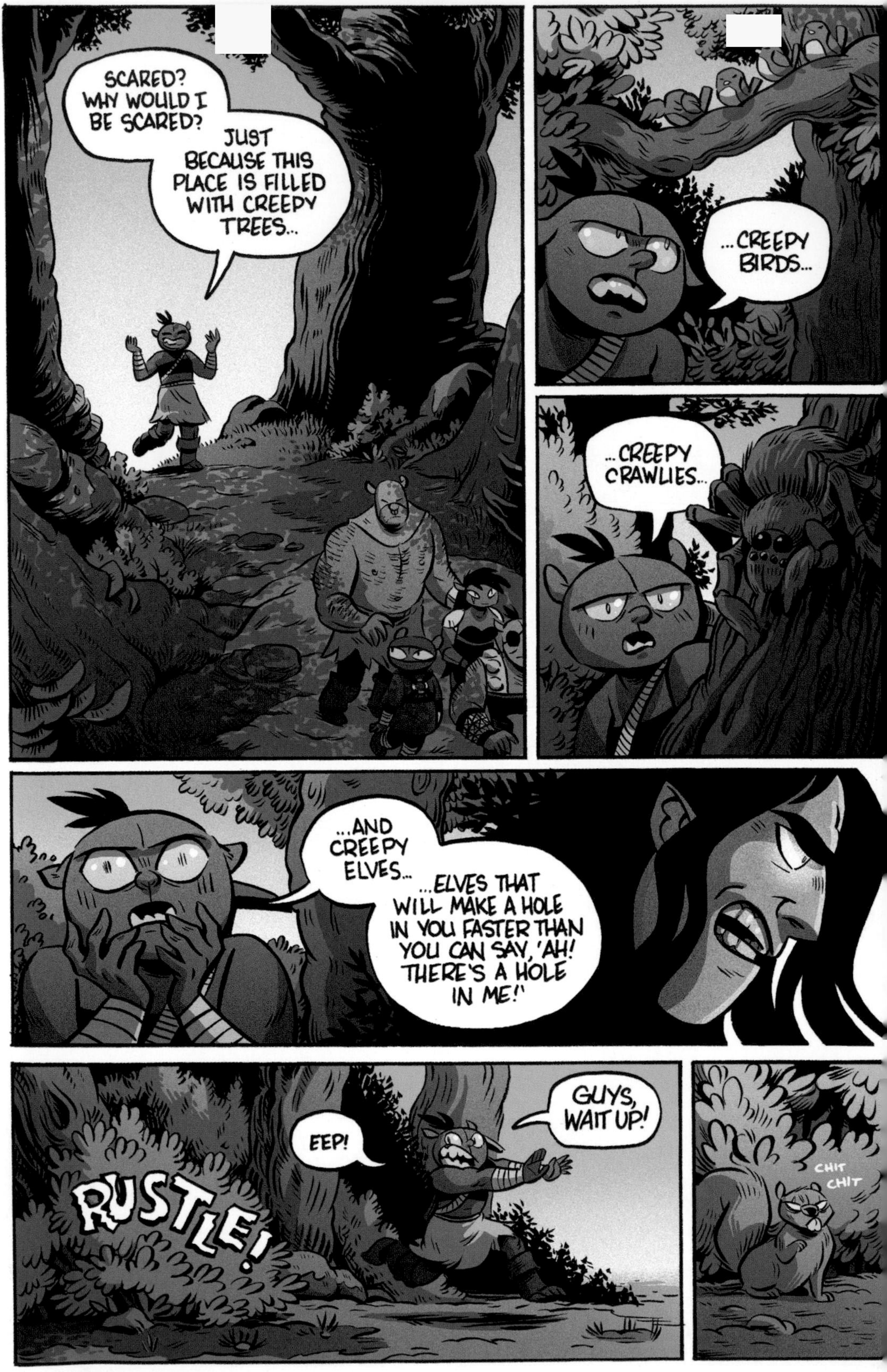

SCARED? WHY WOULD I BE SCARED?
JUST BECAUSE THIS PLACE IS FILLED WITH CREEPY TREES...
...CREEPY BIRDS...
...CREEPY CRAWLIES...
...AND CREEPY ELVES...
...ELVES THAT WILL MAKE A HOLE IN YOU FASTER THAN YOU CAN SAY, 'AH! THERE'S A HOLE IN ME!'
RUSTLE!
EEP!
GUYS, WAIT UP!
CHIT CHIT

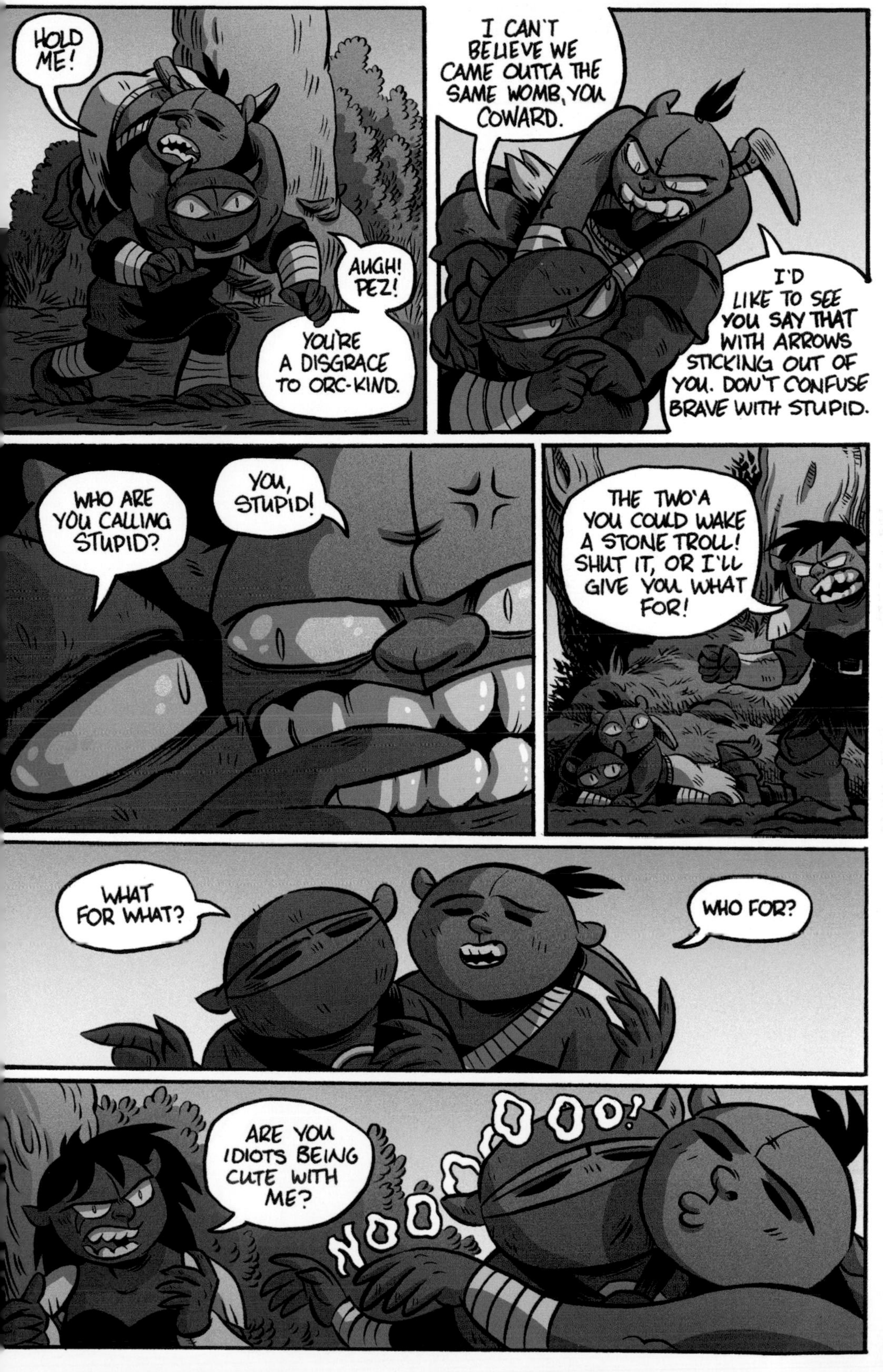
HOLD ME!
AUGH! PEZ!
YOU'RE A DISGRACE TO ORC-KIND.
I CAN'T BELIEVE WE CAME OUTTA THE SAME WOMB, YOU COWARD.
I'D LIKE TO SEE YOU SAY THAT WITH ARROWS STICKING OUT OF YOU. DON'T CONFUSE BRAVE WITH STUPID.
WHO ARE YOU CALLING STUPID?
YOU, STUPID!
THE TWO'A YOU COULD WAKE A STONE TROLL! SHUT IT, OR I'LL GIVE YOU WHAT FOR!
WHAT FOR WHAT?
WHO FOR?
ARE YOU IDIOTS BEING CUTE WITH ME?
NOOOOOOO!

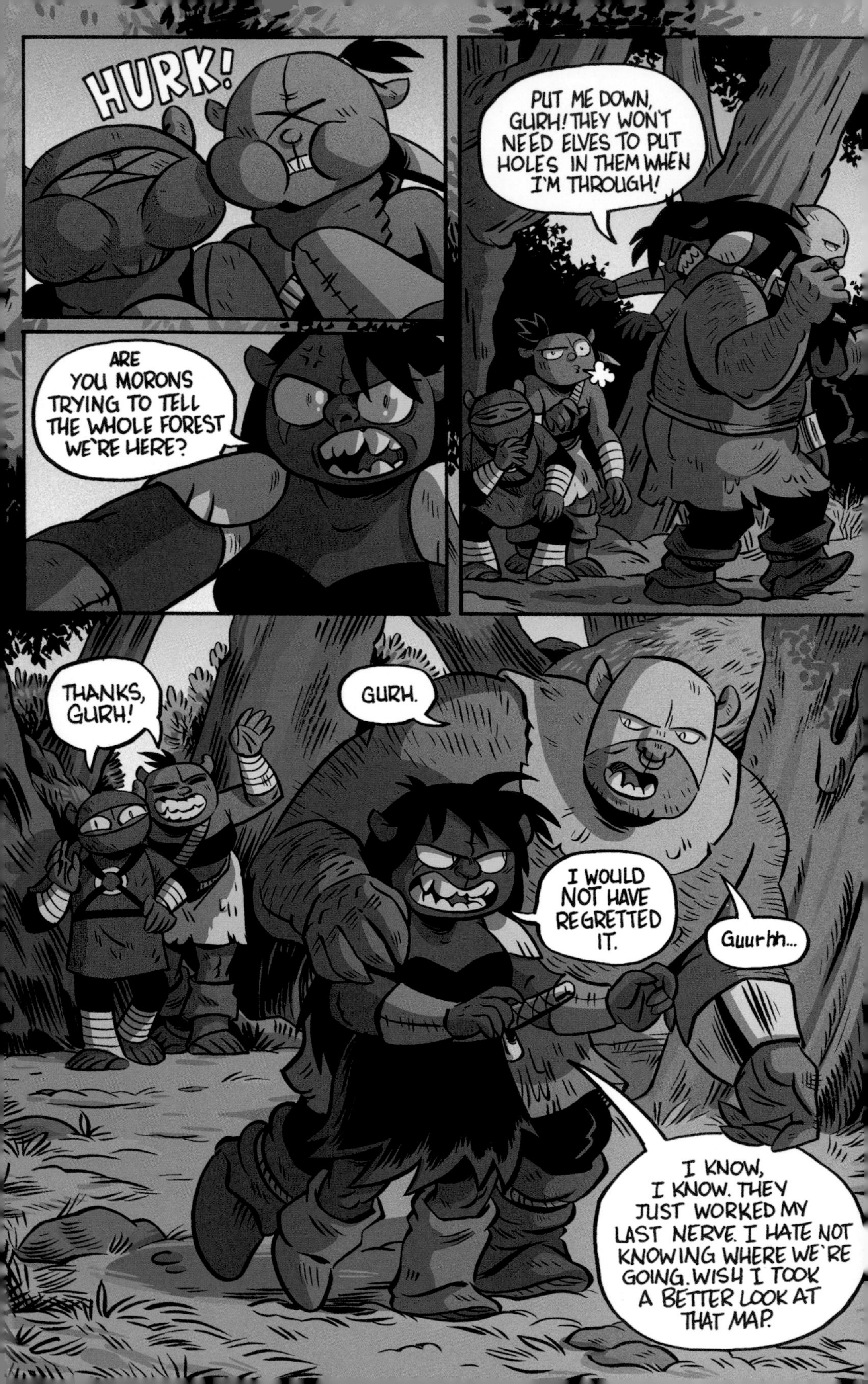
HURK!
PUT ME DOWN, GURH! THEY WON'T NEED ELVES TO PUT HOLES IN THEM WHEN I'M THROUGH!
ARE YOU MORONS TRYING TO TELL THE WHOLE FOREST WE'RE HERE?
THANKS, GURH!
GURH.
I WOULD NOT HAVE REGRETTED IT.
Guurhh...
I KNOW, I KNOW. THEY JUST WORKED MY LAST NERVE. I HATE NOT KNOWING WHERE WE'RE GOING. WISH I TOOK A BETTER LOOK AT THAT MAP.

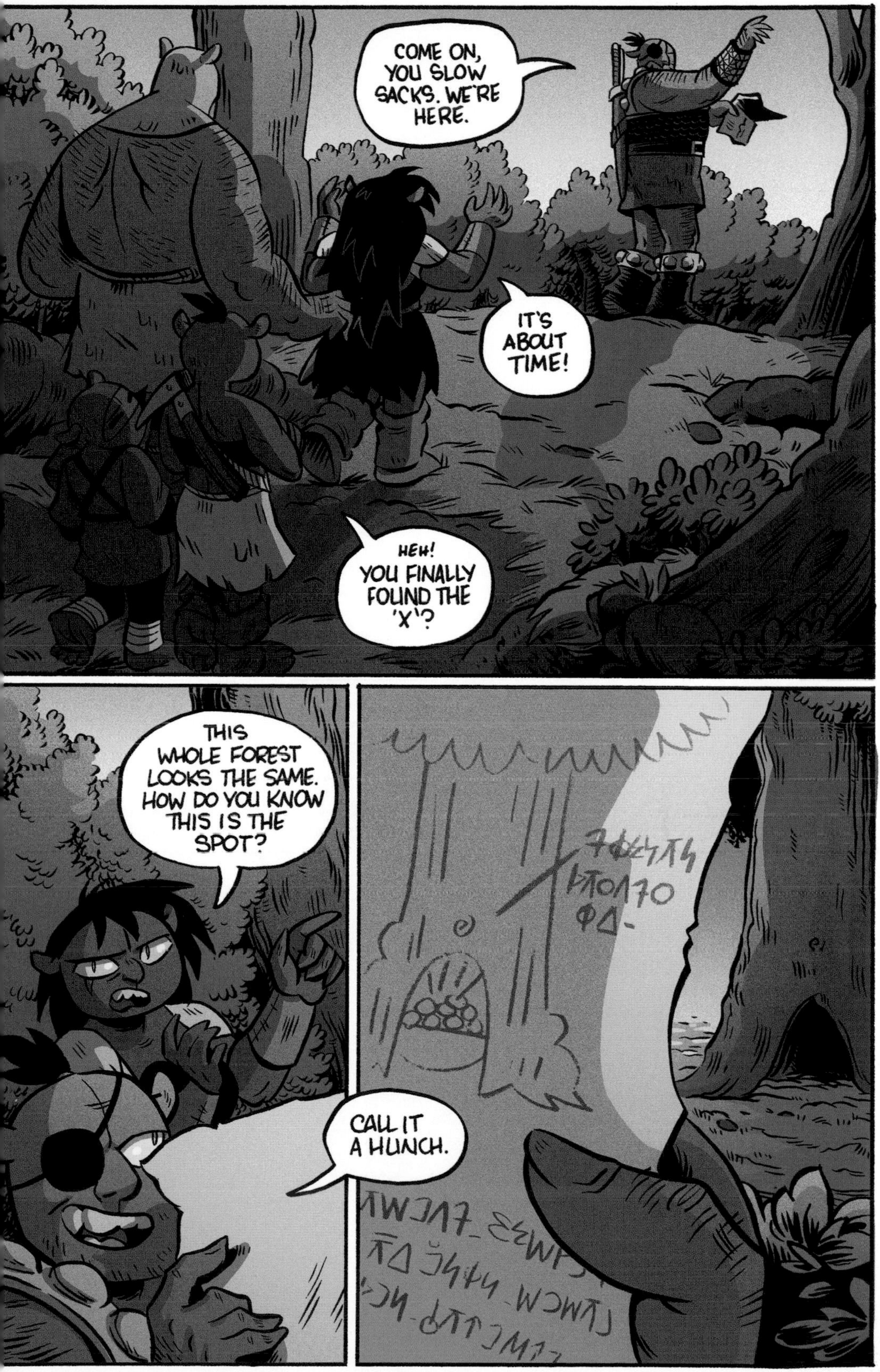
COME ON, YOU SLOW SACKS. WE'RE HERE.
IT'S ABOUT TIME!
HEH! YOU FINALLY FOUND THE 'X'?
THIS WHOLE FOREST LOOKS THE SAME. HOW DO YOU KNOW THIS IS THE SPOT?
CALL IT A HUNCH.

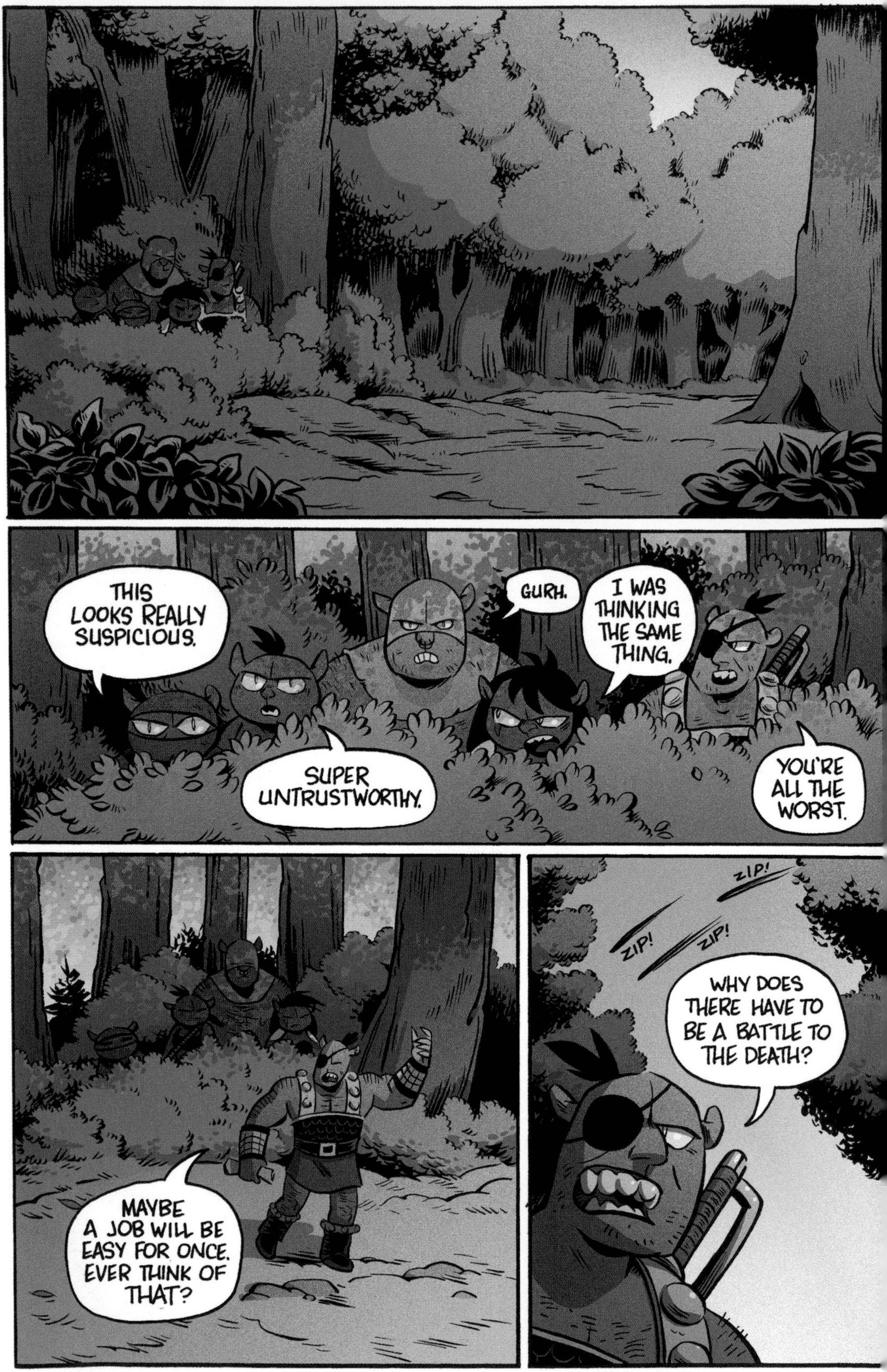
THIS LOOKS REALLY SUSPICIOUS.
SUPER UNTRUSTWORTHY.
GURH.
I WAS THINKING THE SAME THING.
YOU'RE ALL THE WORST.
MAYBE A JOB WILL BE EASY FOR ONCE. EVER THINK OF THAT?
ZIP!
ZIP!
ZIP!
WHY DOES THERE HAVE TO BE A BATTLE TO THE DEATH?

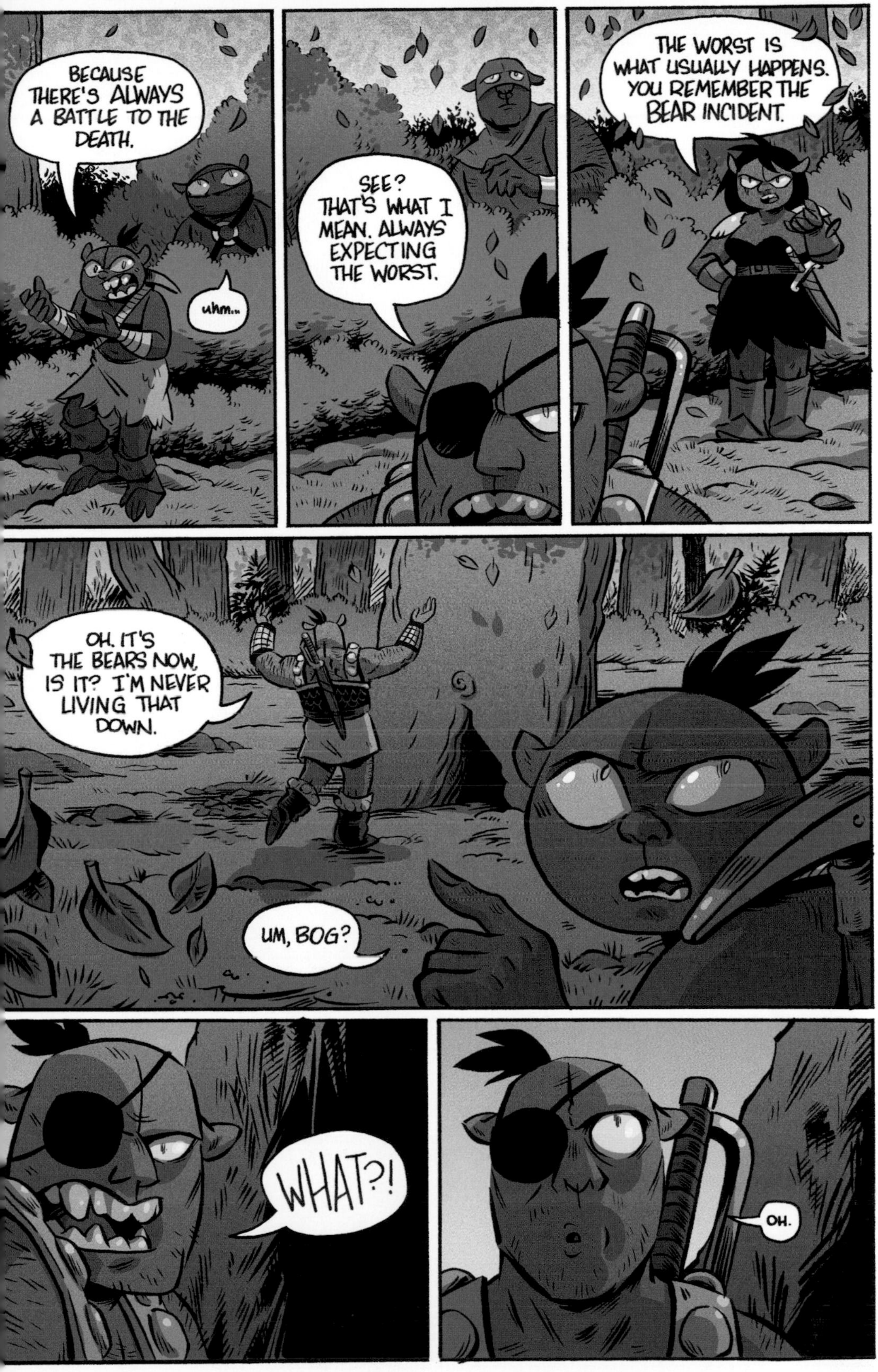
BECAUSE THERE'S ALWAYS A BATTLE TO THE DEATH.
uhm..
SEE? THAT'S WHAT I MEAN. ALWAYS EXPECTING THE WORST.
THE WORST IS WHAT USUALLY HAPPENS. YOU REMEMBER THE BEAR INCIDENT.
OH. IT'S THE BEARS NOW, IS IT? I'M NEVER LIVING THAT DOWN.
UM, BOG?
WHAT?!
OH.

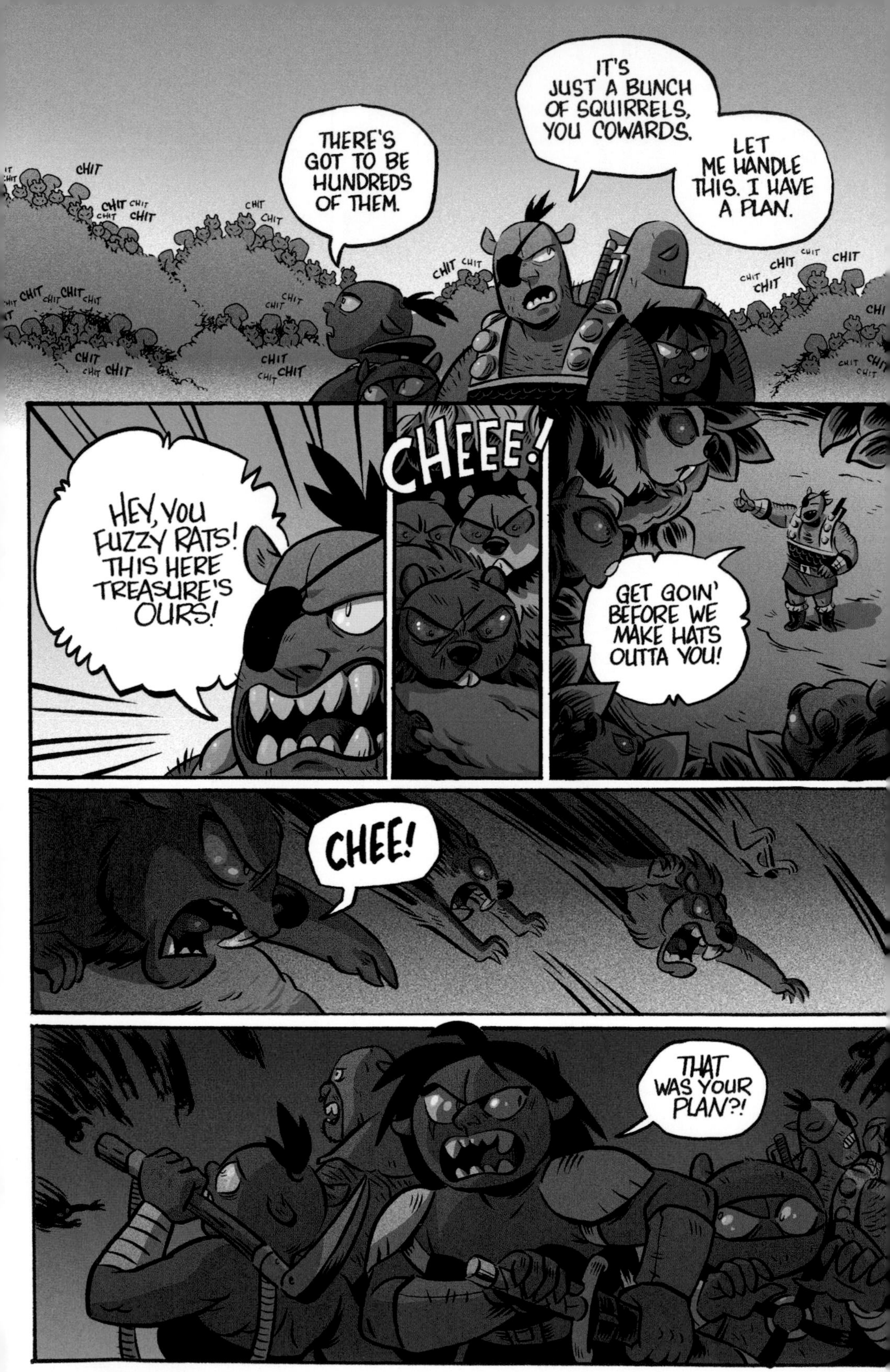
CHIT CHIT CHIT CHIT CHIT
THERE'S GOT TO BE HUNDREDS OF THEM.
IT'S JUST A BUNCH OF SQUIRRELS, YOU COWARDS.
LET ME HANDLE THIS. I HAVE A PLAN.
HEY, YOU FUZZY RATS! THIS HERE TREASURE'S OURS!
CHEEE!
GET GOIN' BEFORE WE MAKE HATS OUTTA YOU!
CHEE!
THAT WAS YOUR PLAN?!

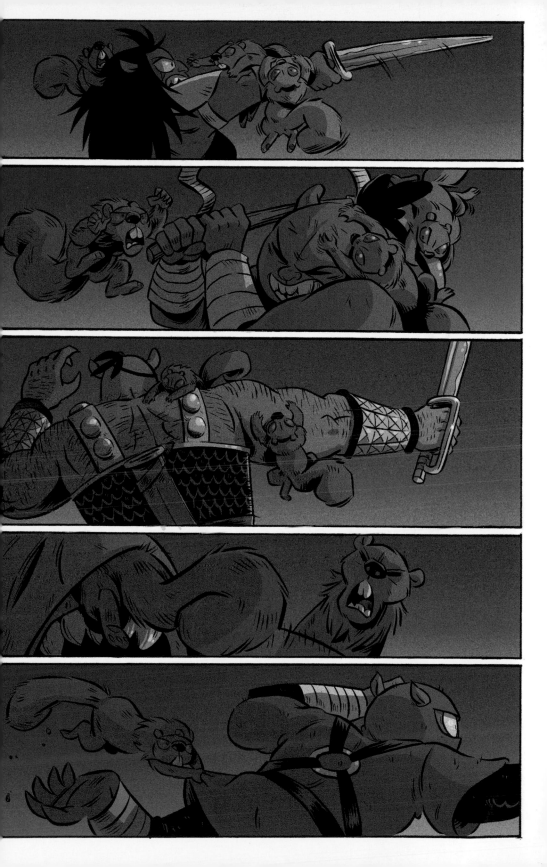

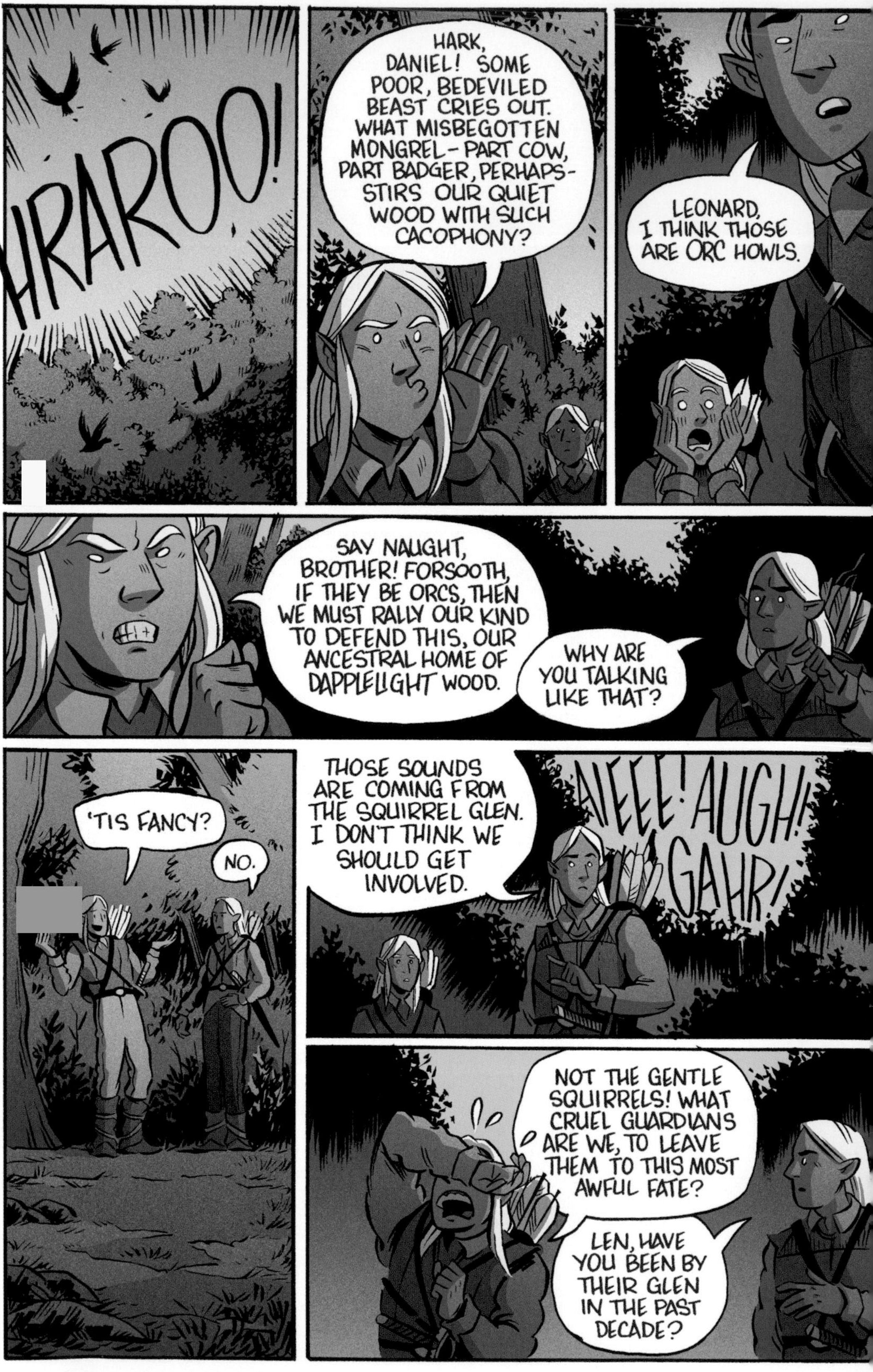
HRAROO!
HARK, DANIEL! SOME POOR, BEDEVILED BEAST CRIES OUT. WHAT MISBEGOTTEN MONGREL - PART COW, PART BADGER, PERHAPS - STIRS OUR QUIET WOOD WITH SUCH CACOPHONY?
LEONARD, I THINK THOSE ARE ORC HOWLS.
SAY NAUGHT, BROTHER! FORSOOTH, IF THEY BE ORCS, THEN WE MUST RALLY OUR KIND TO DEFEND THIS, OUR ANCESTRAL HOME OF DAPPLELIGHT WOOD.
WHY ARE YOU TALKING LIKE THAT?
'TIS FANCY?
NO.
THOSE SOUNDS ARE COMING FROM THE SQUIRREL GLEN. I DON'T THINK WE SHOULD GET INVOLVED.
AIEEE! AUGH! GAHR!
NOT THE GENTLE SQUIRRELS! WHAT CRUEL GUARDIANS ARE WE, TO LEAVE THEM TO THIS MOST AWFUL FATE?
LEN, HAVE YOU BEEN BY THEIR GLEN IN THE PAST DECADE?

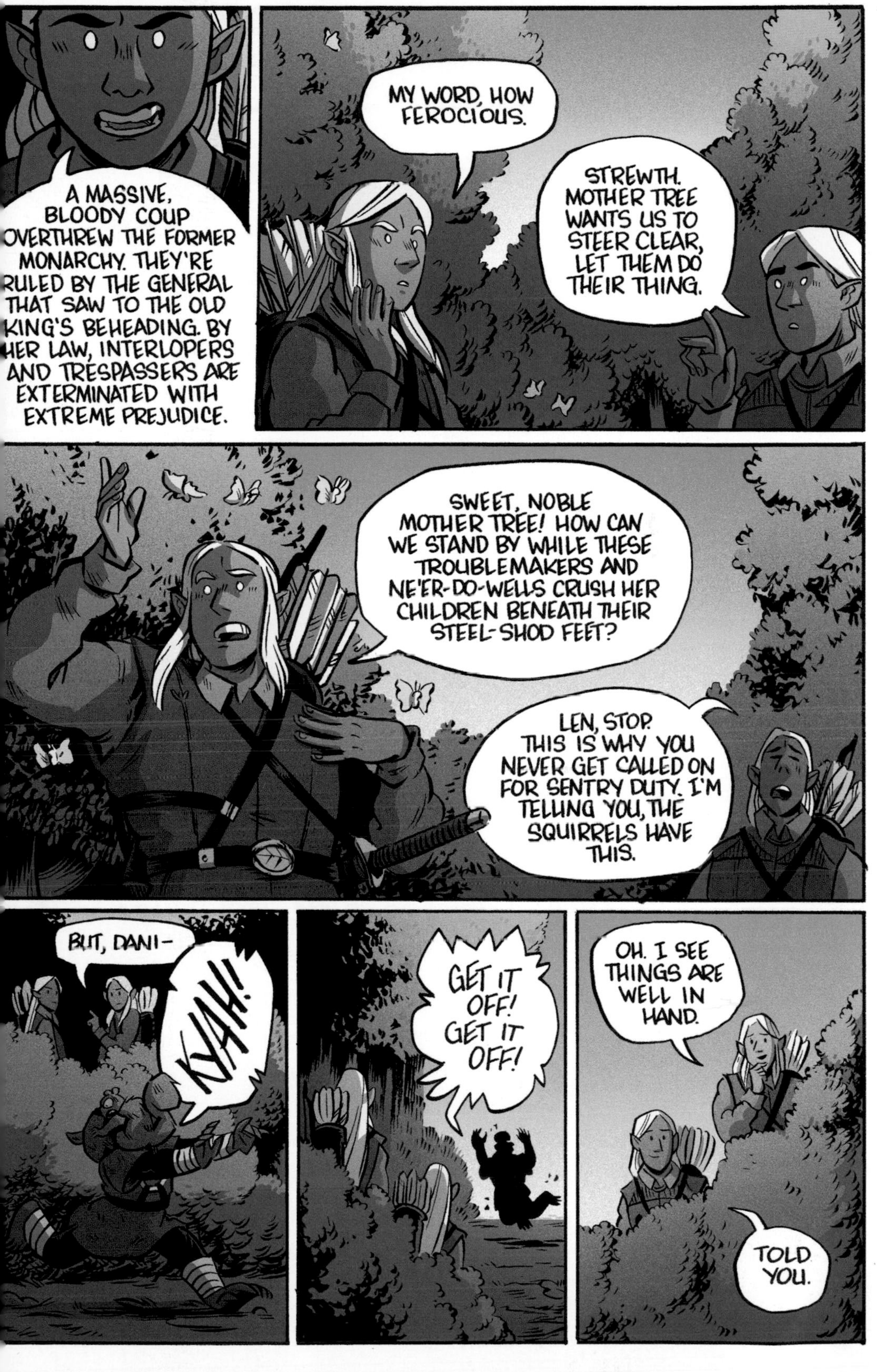
A MASSIVE, BLOODY COUP OVERTHREW THE FORMER MONARCHY. THEY'RE RULED BY THE GENERAL THAT SAW TO THE OLD KING'S BEHEADING. BY HER LAW, INTERLOPERS AND TRESPASSERS ARE EXTERMINATED WITH EXTREME PREJUDICE.
MY WORD, HOW FEROCIOUS.
STREWTH. MOTHER TREE WANTS US TO STEER CLEAR, LET THEM DO THEIR THING.
SWEET, NOBLE MOTHER TREE! HOW CAN WE STAND BY WHILE THESE TROUBLEMAKERS AND NE'ER-DO-WELLS CRUSH HER CHILDREN BENEATH THEIR STEEL-SHOD FEET?
LEN, STOP. THIS IS WHY YOU NEVER GET CALLED ON FOR SENTRY DUTY. I'M TELLING YOU, THE SQUIRRELS HAVE THIS.
BUT, DANI-
KYAH!
GET IT OFF! GET IT OFF!
OH. I SEE THINGS ARE WELL IN HAND.
TOLD YOU.

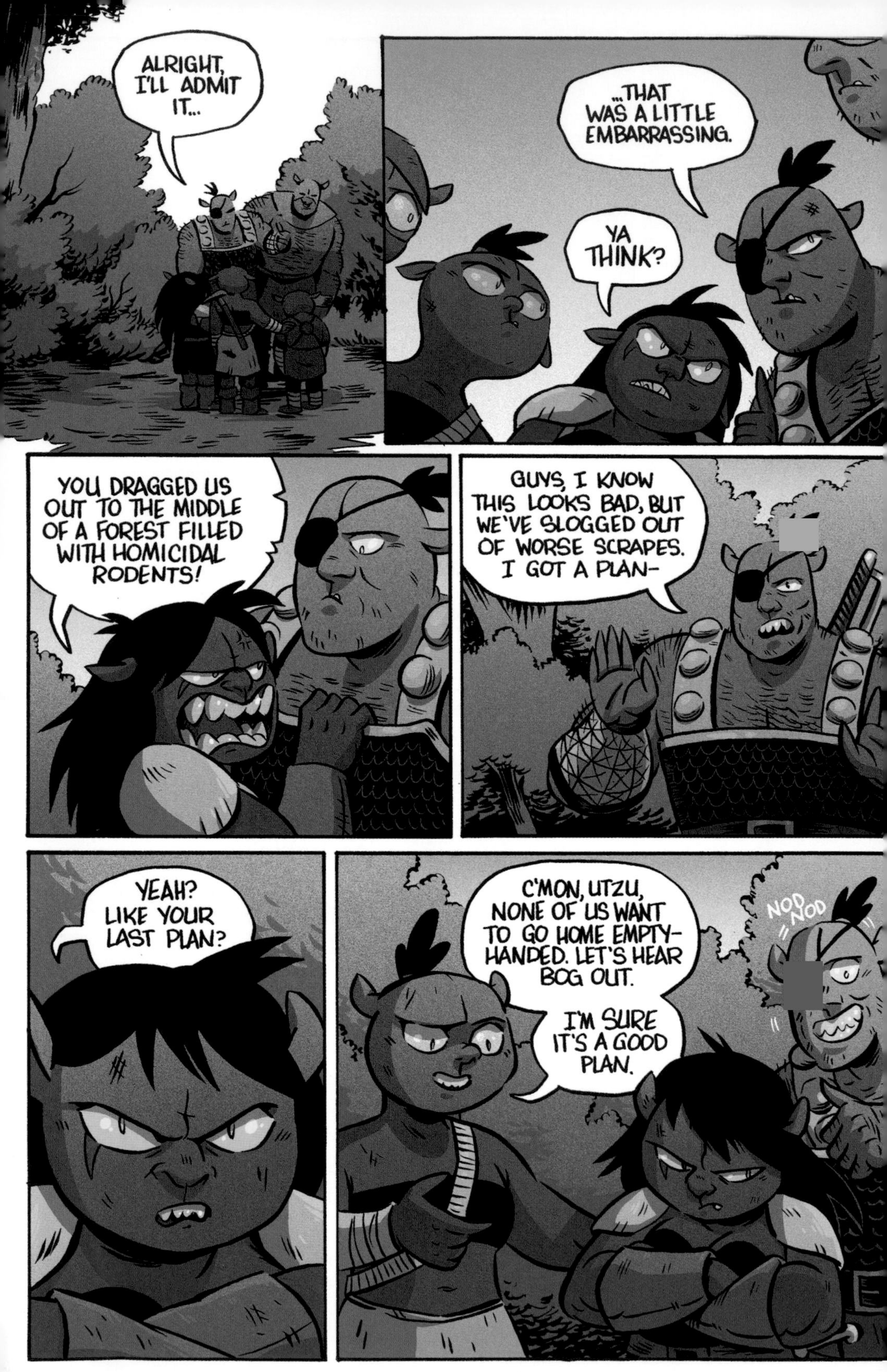
ALRIGHT, I'LL ADMIT IT...
...THAT WAS A LITTLE EMBARRASSING.
YA THINK?
YOU DRAGGED US OUT TO THE MIDDLE OF A FOREST FILLED WITH HOMICIDAL RODENTS!
GUYS, I KNOW THIS LOOKS BAD, BUT WE'VE SLOGGED OUT OF WORSE SCRAPES. I GOT A PLAN–
YEAH? LIKE YOUR LAST PLAN?
C'MON, UTZU, NONE OF US WANT TO GO HOME EMPTY-HANDED. LET'S HEAR BOG OUT.
I'M SURE IT'S A GOOD PLAN.
NOD NOD

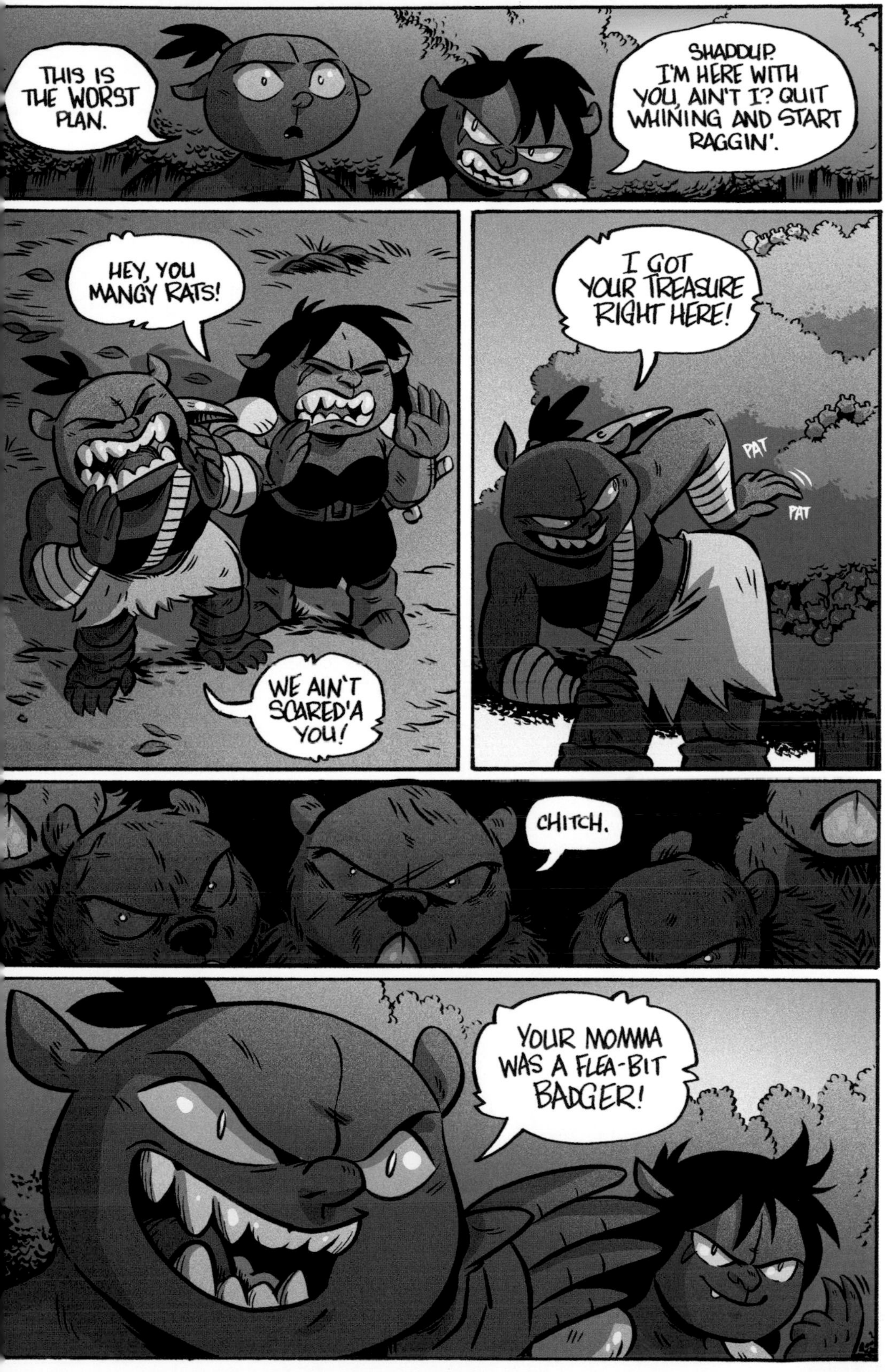
THIS IS THE WORST PLAN.
SHADDUP. I'M HERE WITH YOU, AIN'T I? QUIT WHINING AND START RAGGIN'.
HEY, YOU MANGY RATS!
WE AIN'T SCARED'A YOU!
I GOT YOUR TREASURE RIGHT HERE!
PAT
PAT
CHITCH.
YOUR MOMMA WAS A FLEA-BIT BADGER!

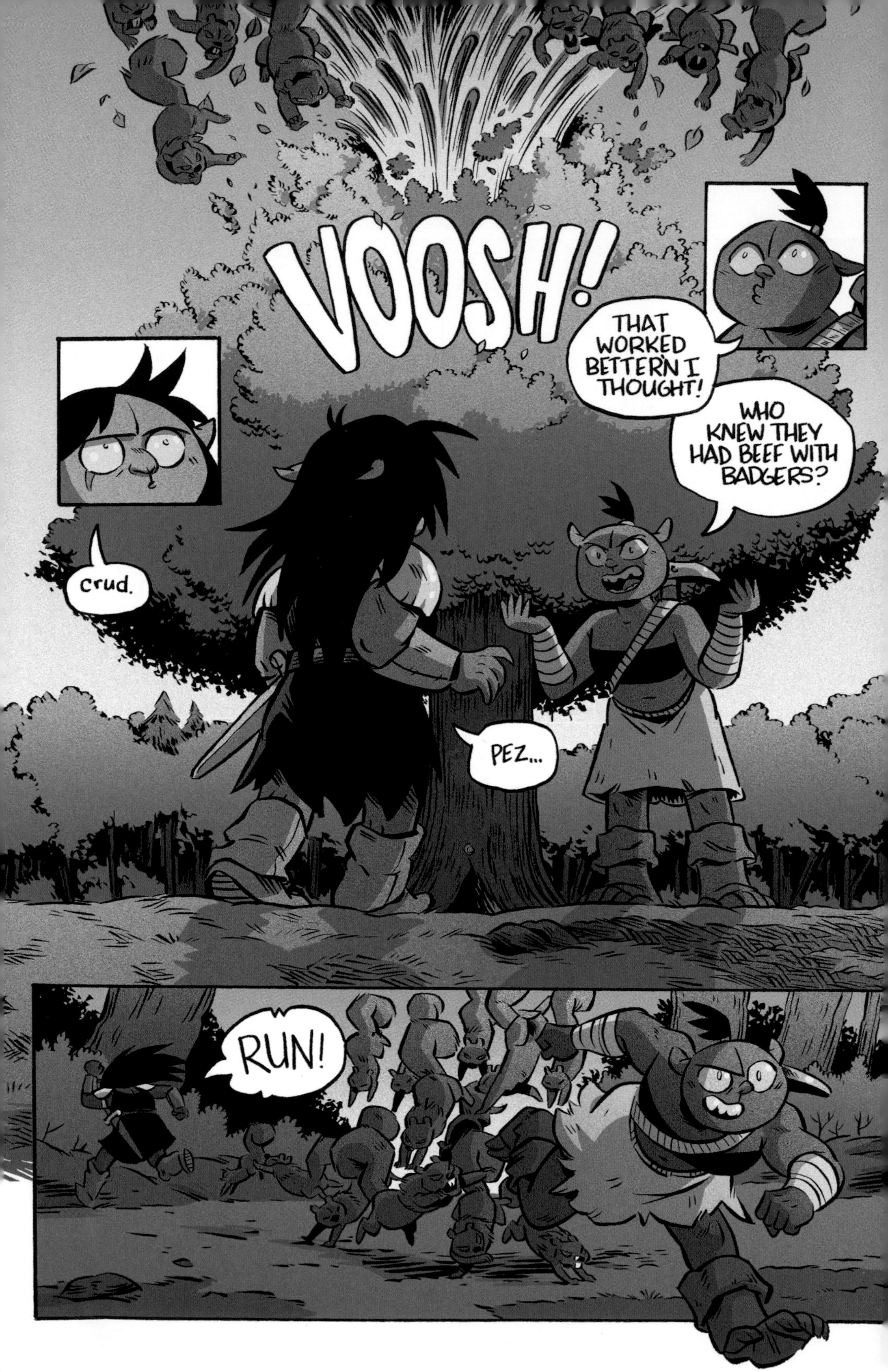
VOOSH!
THAT WORKED BETTER'N I THOUGHT!
WHO KNEW THEY HAD BEEF WITH BADGERS?
crud.
PEZ...
RUN!

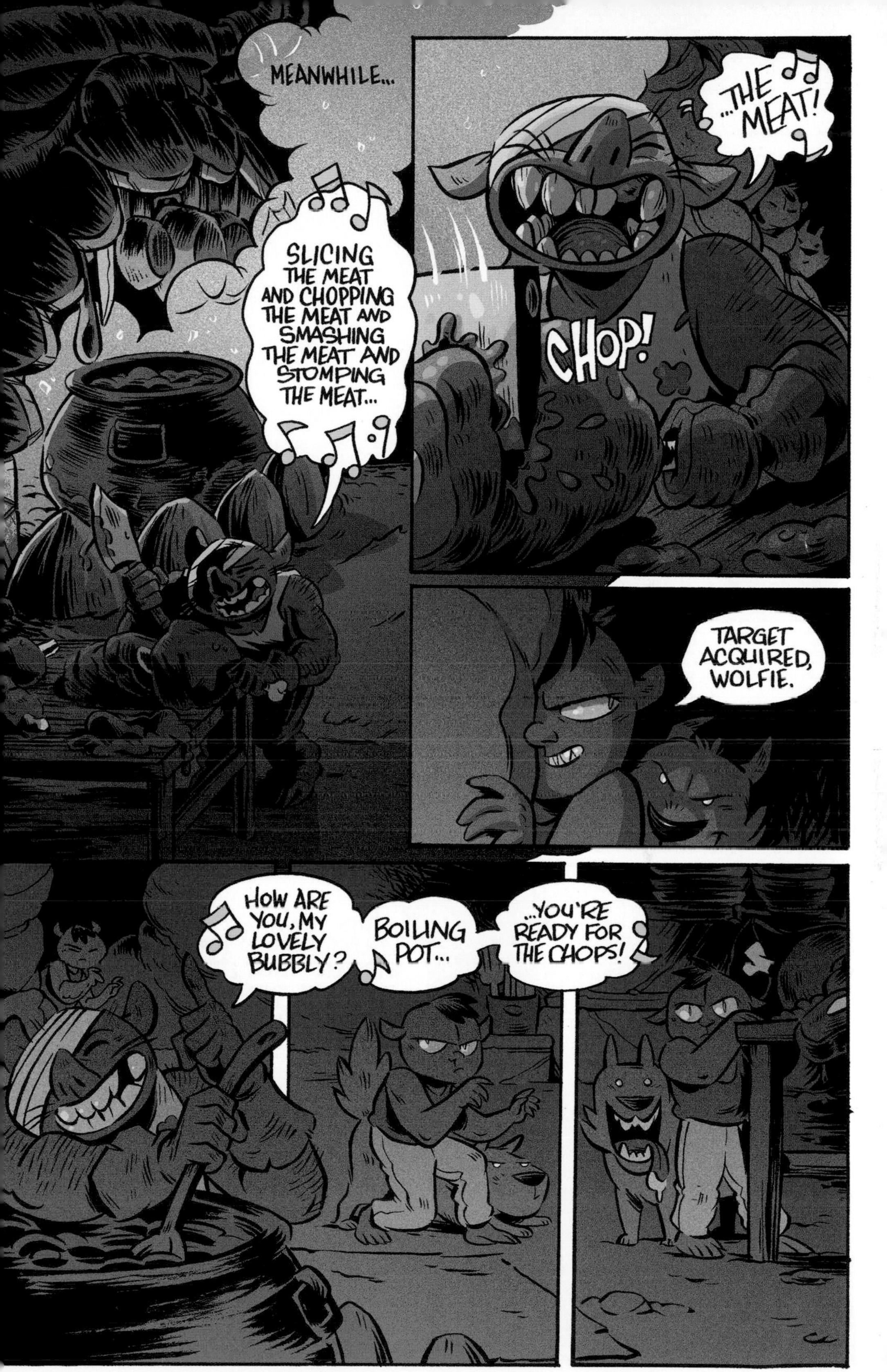
MEANWHILE...
SLICING THE MEAT AND CHOPPING THE MEAT AND SMASHING THE MEAT AND STOMPING THE MEAT...
...THE MEAT!
CHOP!
TARGET ACQUIRED, WOLFIE.
HOW ARE YOU, MY LOVELY BUBBLY?
BOILING POT...
...YOU'RE READY FOR THE CHOPS!

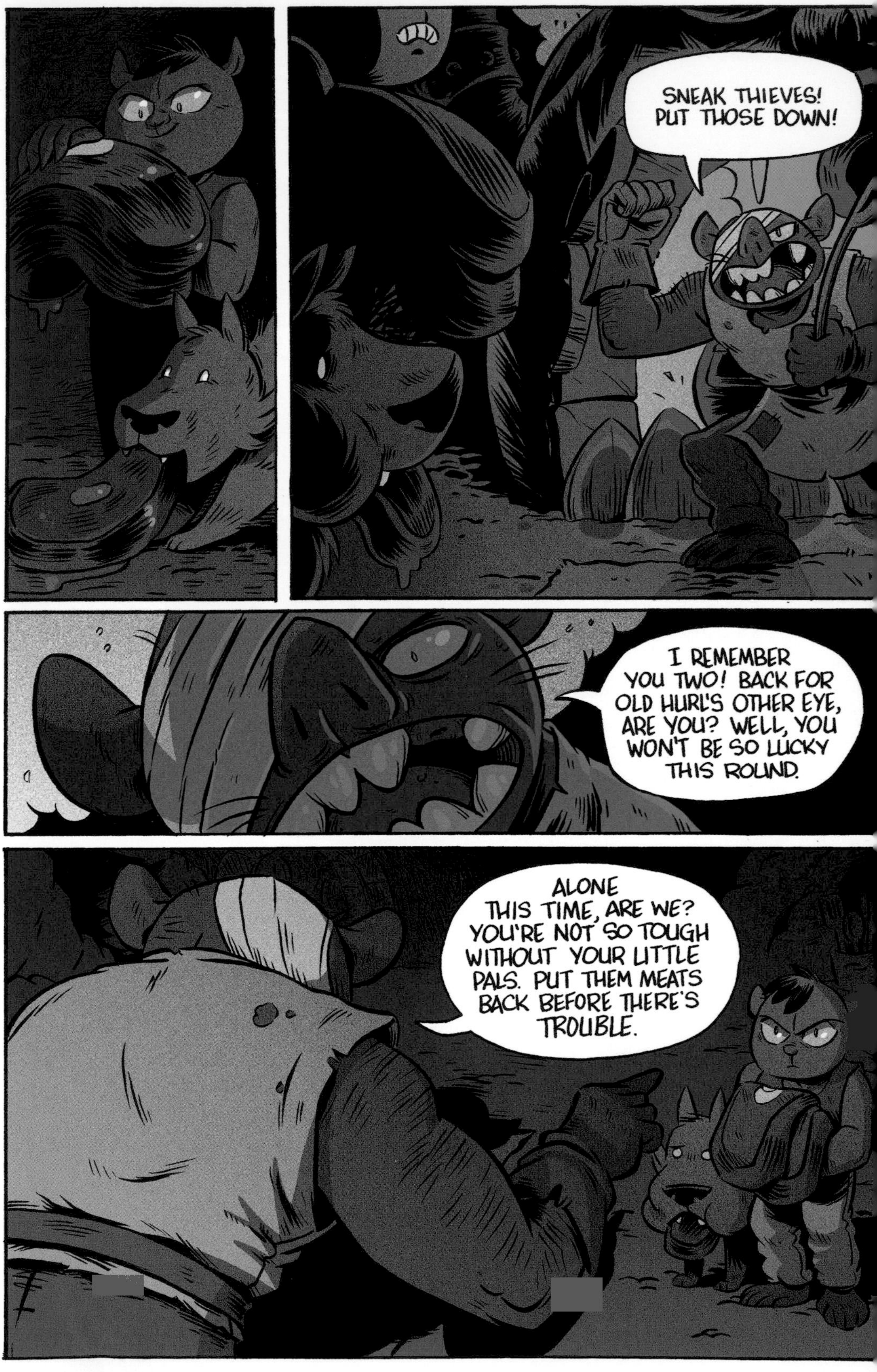
SNEAK THIEVES! PUT THOSE DOWN!
I REMEMBER YOU TWO! BACK FOR OLD HURL'S OTHER EYE, ARE YOU? WELL, YOU WON'T BE SO LUCKY THIS ROUND.
ALONE THIS TIME, ARE WE? YOU'RE NOT SO TOUGH WITHOUT YOUR LITTLE PALS. PUT THEM MEATS BACK BEFORE THERE'S TROUBLE.

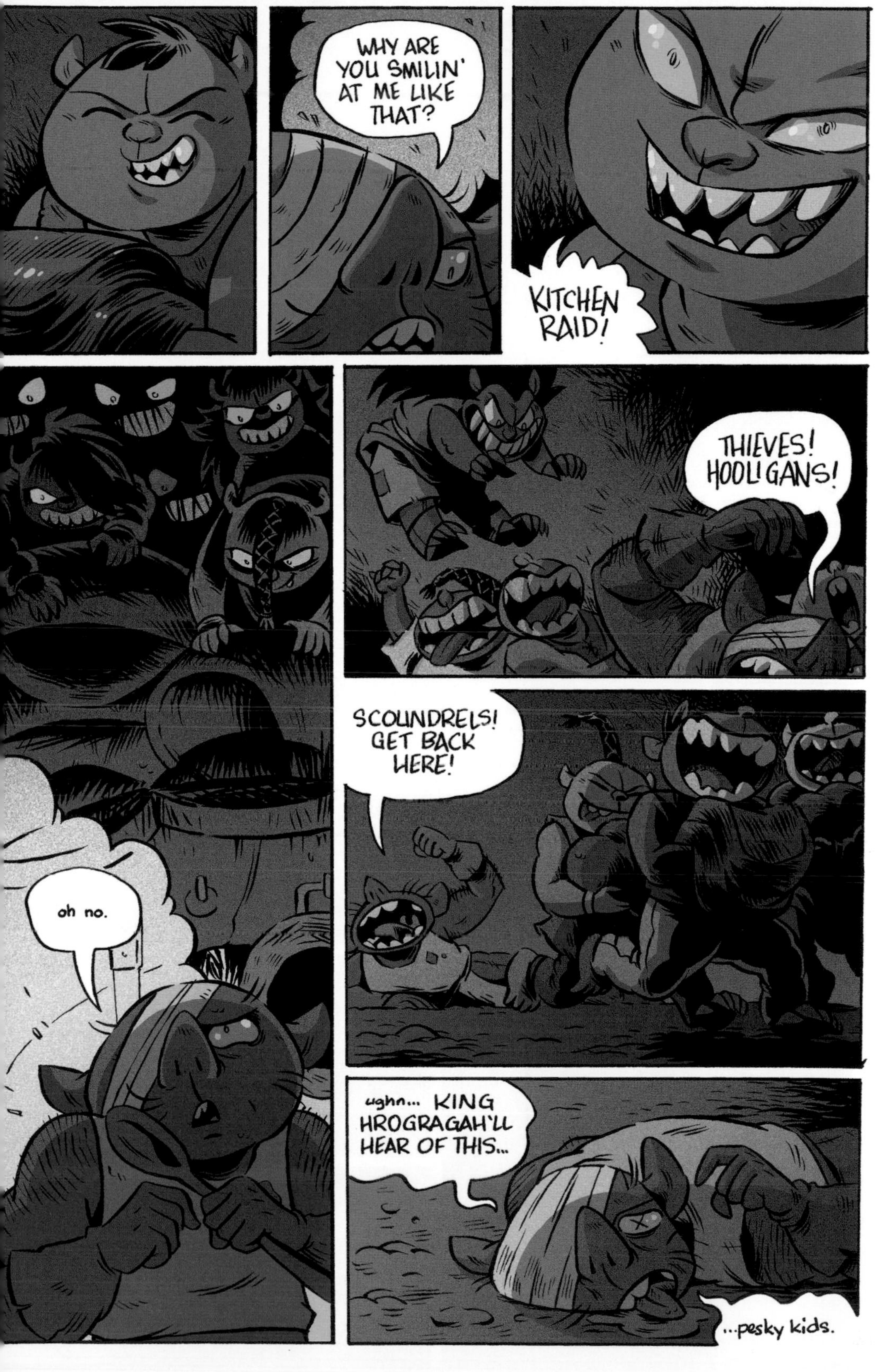
WHY ARE YOU SMILIN' AT ME LIKE THAT?
KITCHEN RAID!
THIEVES! HOOLIGANS!
SCOUNDRELS! GET BACK HERE!
oh no.
ughn... KING HROGRAGAH'LL HEAR OF THIS...
...pesky kids.

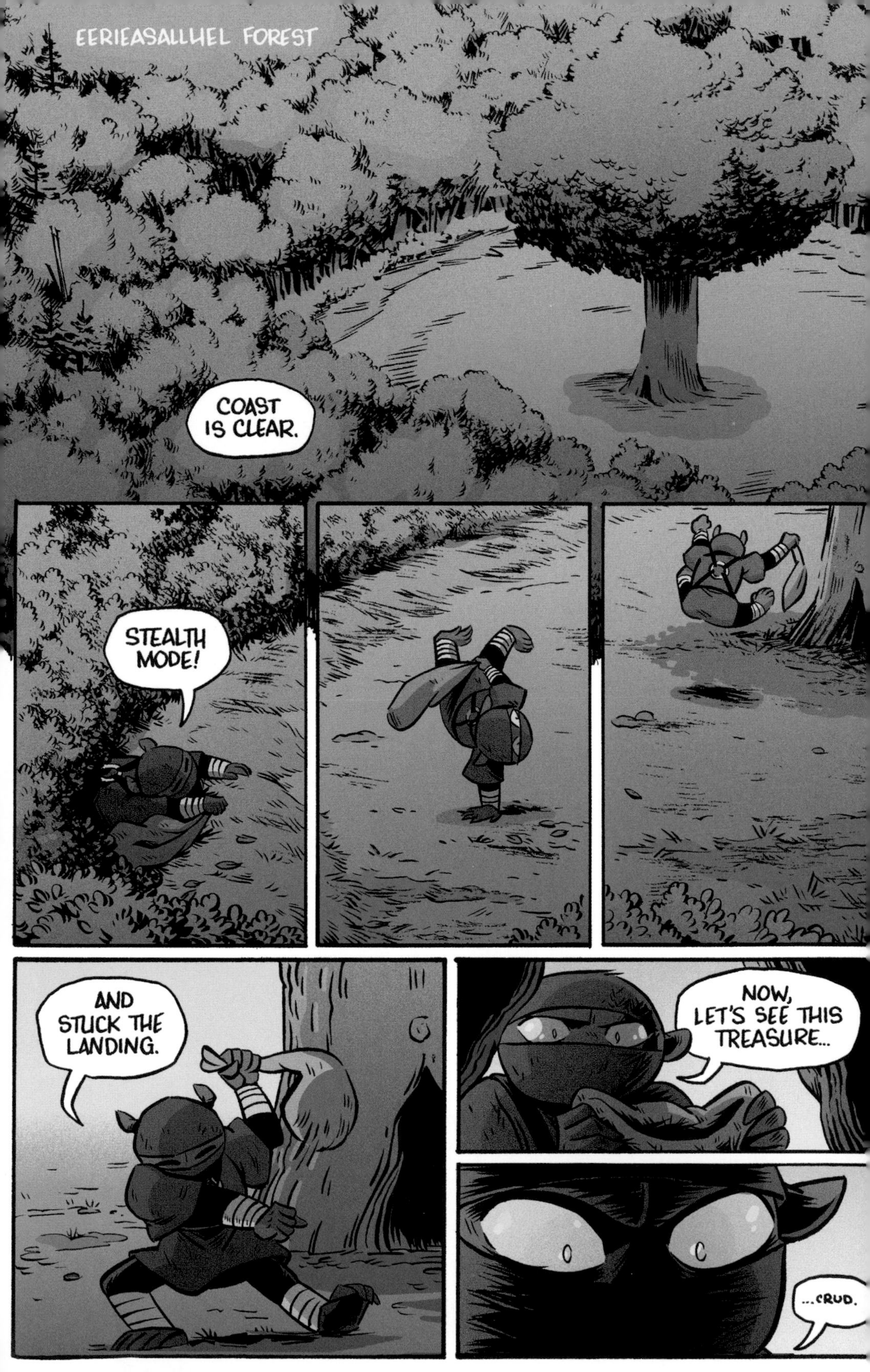
EERIEASALLUEL FOREST
COAST IS CLEAR.
STEALTH MODE!
AND STUCK THE LANDING.
NOW, LET'S SEE THIS TREASURE...
...CRUD.

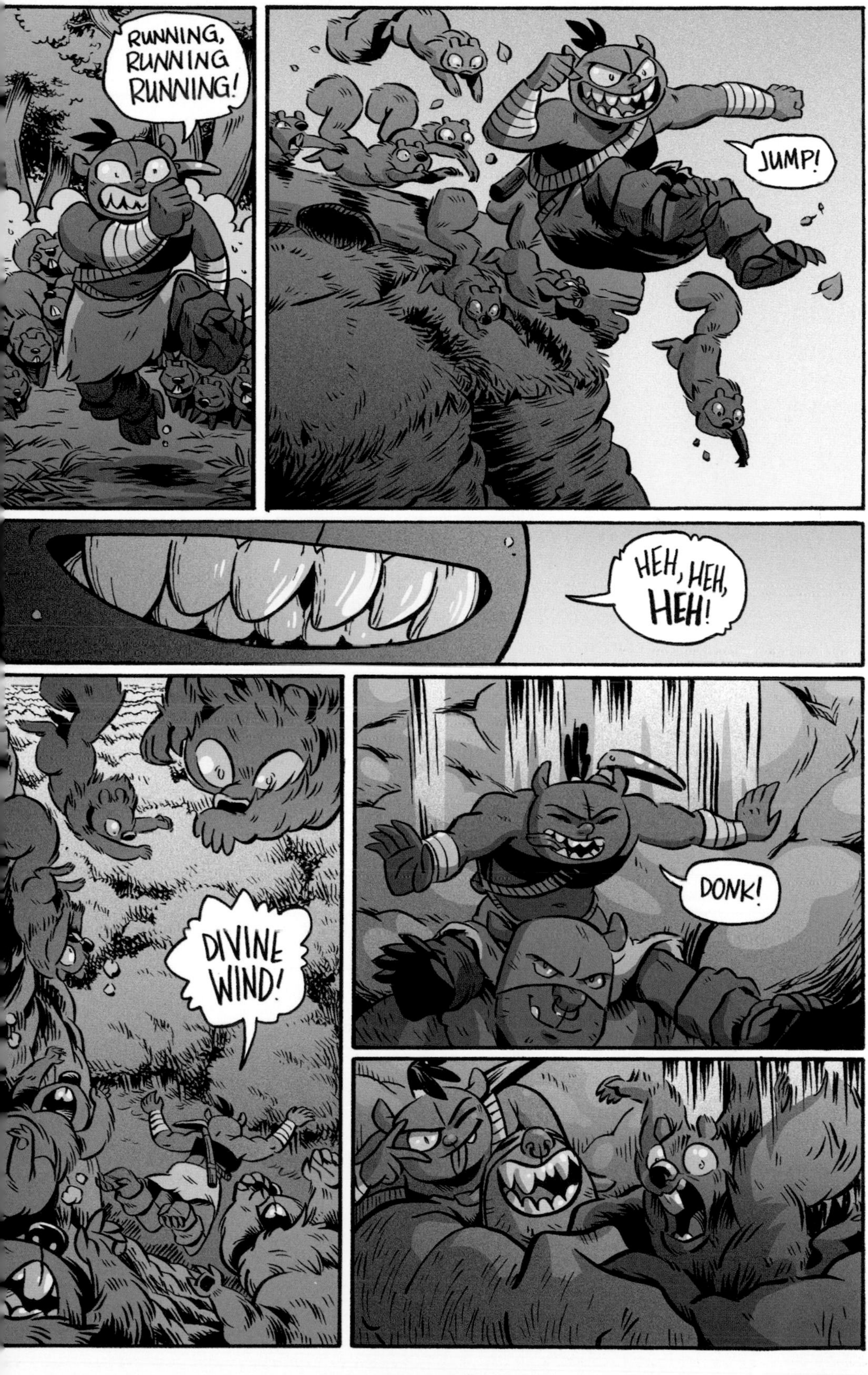
RUNNING, RUNNING RUNNING!
JUMP!
HEH, HEH, HEH!
DIVINE WIND!
DONK!

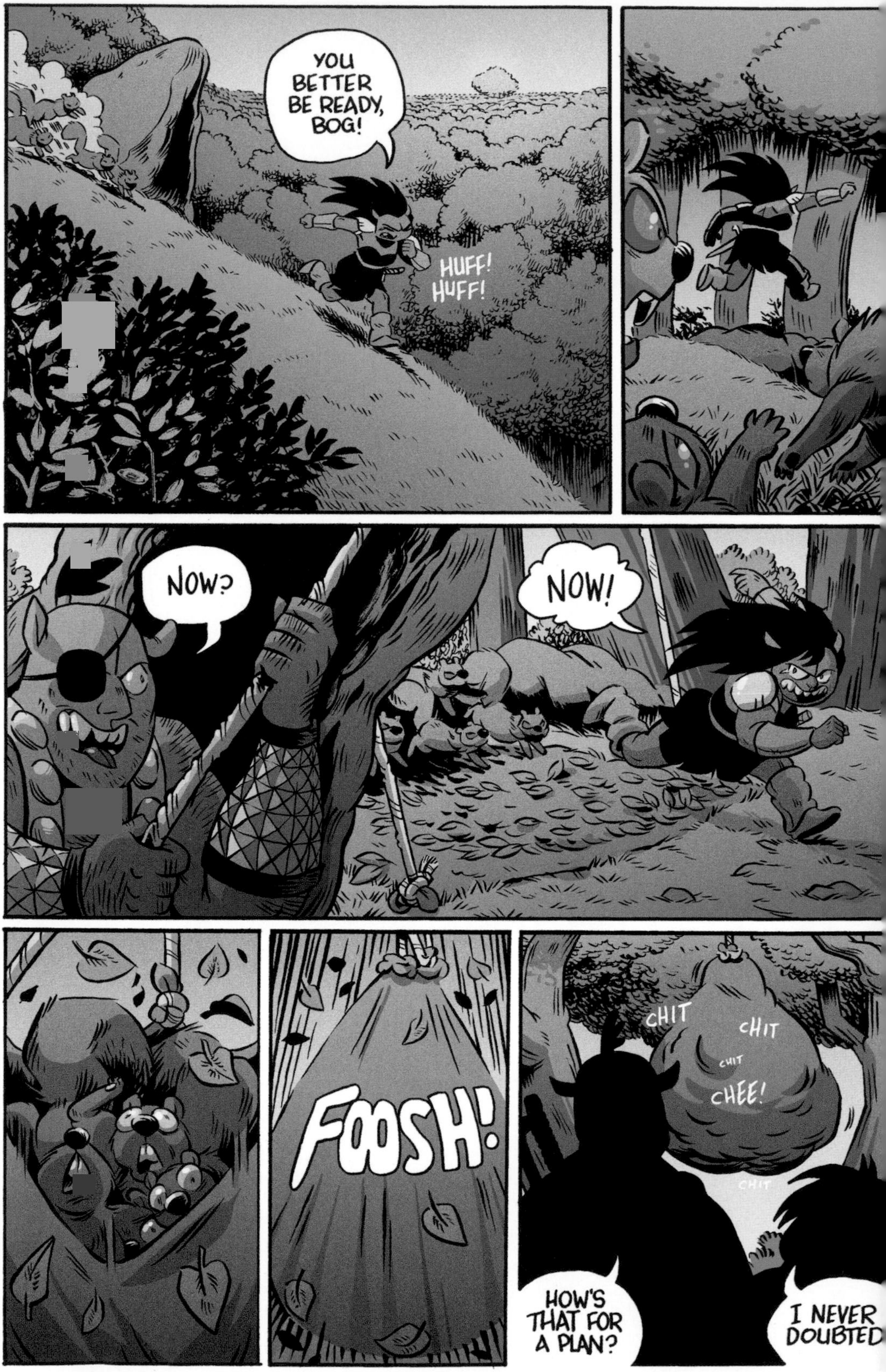
YOU BETTER BE READY, BOG!
HUFF! HUFF!
NOW?
NOW!
FOOSH!
CHIT
CHIT
CHIT
CHEE!
CHIT
HOW'S THAT FOR A PLAN?
I NEVER DOUBTED

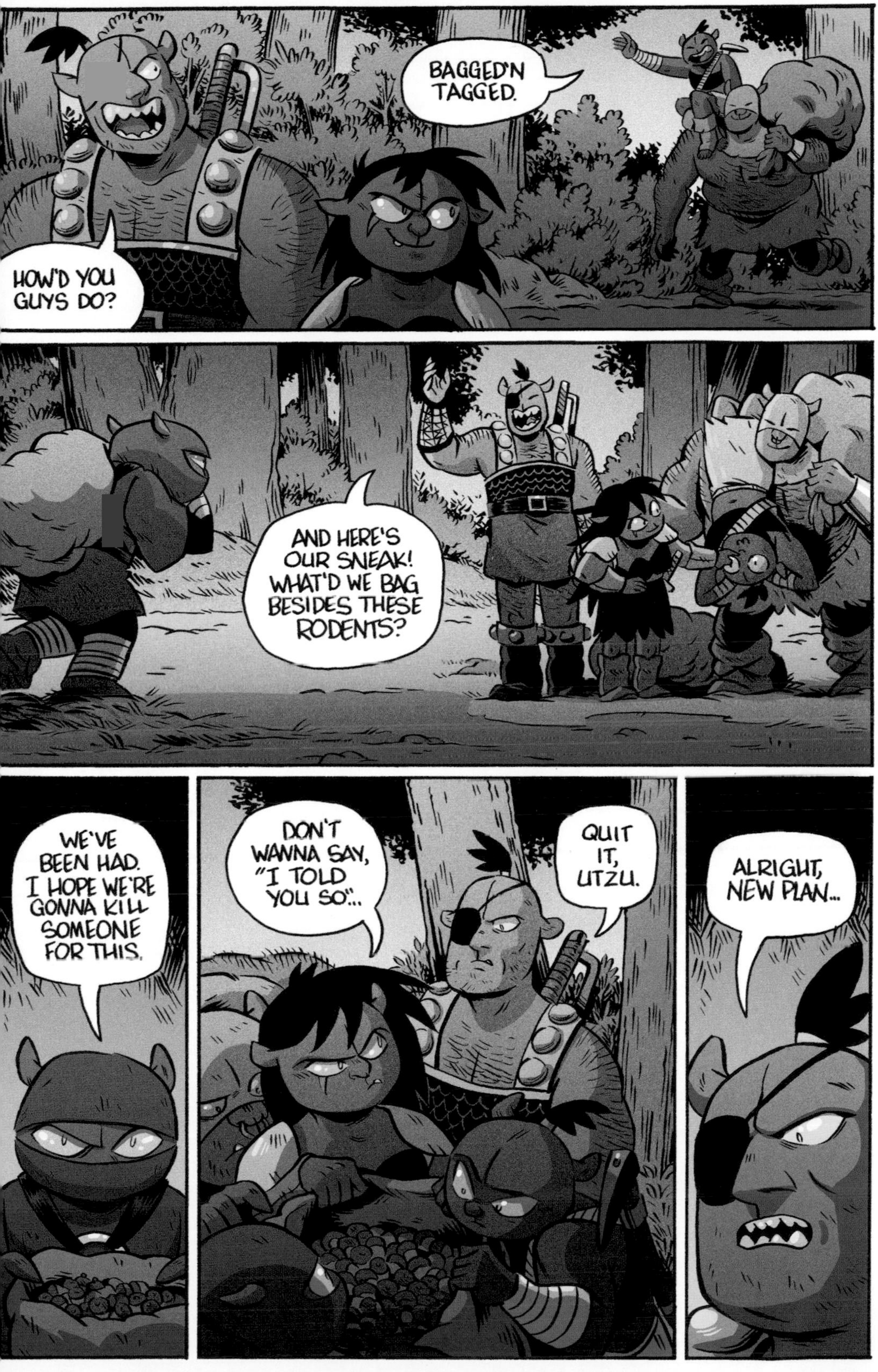
BAGGED'N TAGGED.
HOW'D YOU GUYS DO?
AND HERE'S OUR SNEAK! WHAT'D WE BAG BESIDES THESE RODENTS?
WE'VE BEEN HAD. I HOPE WE'RE GONNA KILL SOMEONE FOR THIS.
DON'T WANNA SAY, "I TOLD YOU SO"...
QUIT IT, UTZU.
ALRIGHT, NEW PLAN...

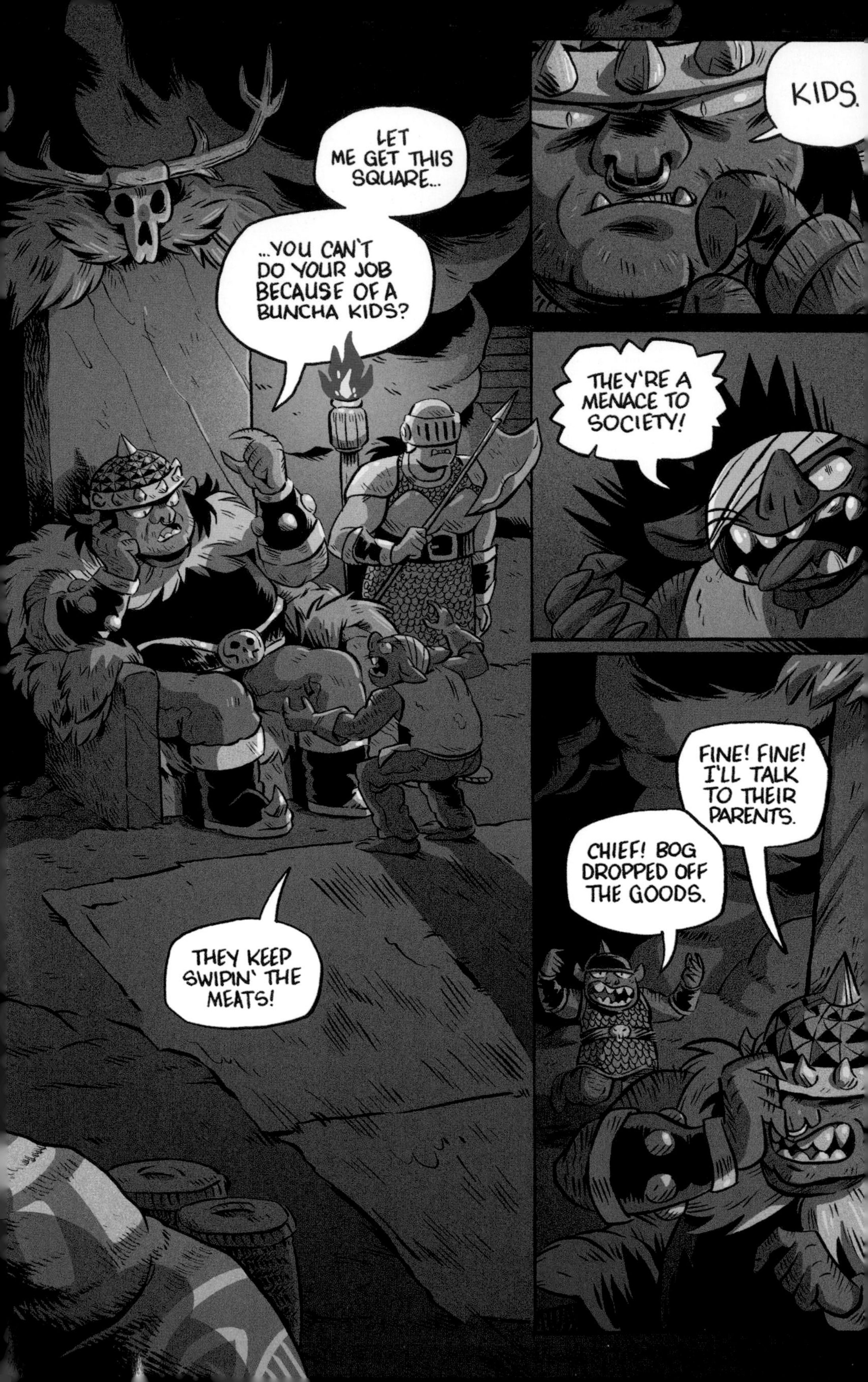
LET ME GET THIS SQUARE...
...YOU CAN'T DO YOUR JOB BECAUSE OF A BUNCHA KIDS?
THEY KEEP SWIPIN' THE MEATS!
KIDS.
THEY'RE A MENACE TO SOCIETY!
FINE! FINE! I'LL TALK TO THEIR PARENTS.
CHIEF! BOG DROPPED OFF THE GOODS.

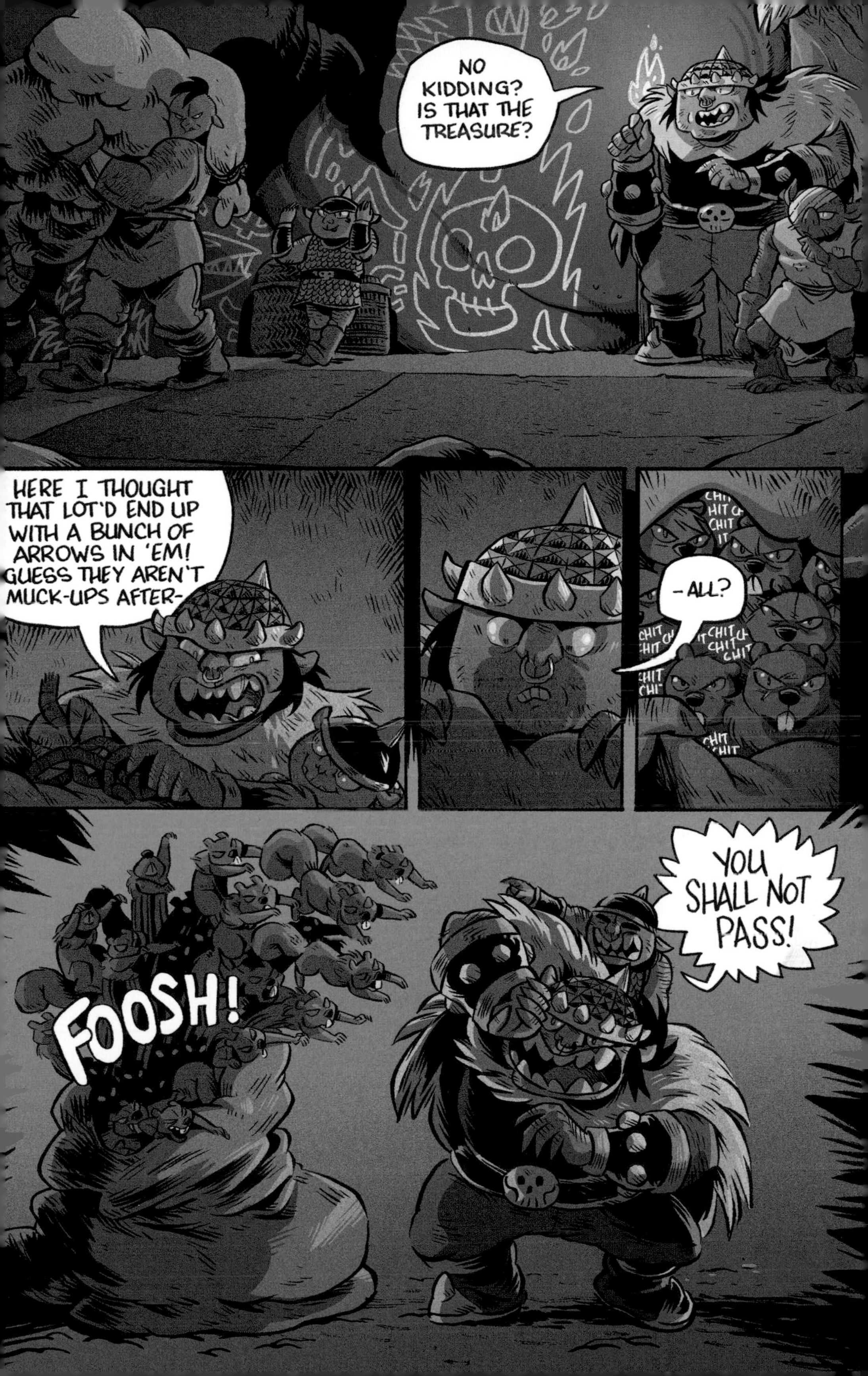
NO KIDDING? IS THAT THE TREASURE?
HERE I THOUGHT THAT LOT'D END UP WITH A BUNCH OF ARROWS IN 'EM! GUESS THEY AREN'T MUCK-UPS AFTER-
-ALL?
CHIT CHIT CHIT
YOU SHALL NOT PASS!
FOOSH!

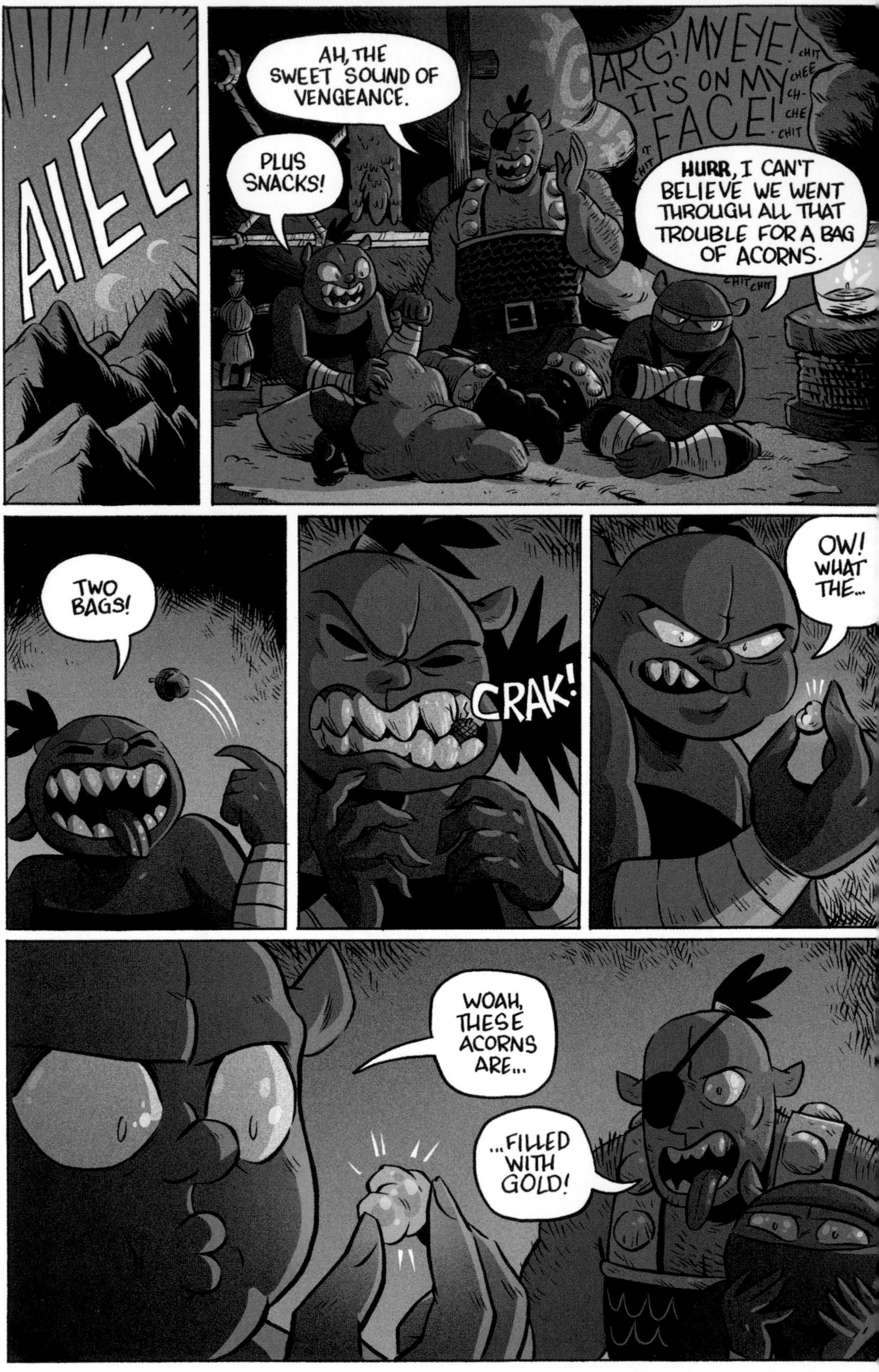
AIEE
AH, THE SWEET SOUND OF VENGEANCE.
PLUS SNACKS!
ARG! MY EYE! IT'S ON MY FACE!
CHIT CHEE CH- CHE CHIT
HURR, I CAN'T BELIEVE WE WENT THROUGH ALL THAT TROUBLE FOR A BAG OF ACORNS.
CHIT CHIT
TWO BAGS!
CRAK!
OW! WHAT THE...
WOAH, THESE ACORNS ARE...
...FILLED WITH GOLD!

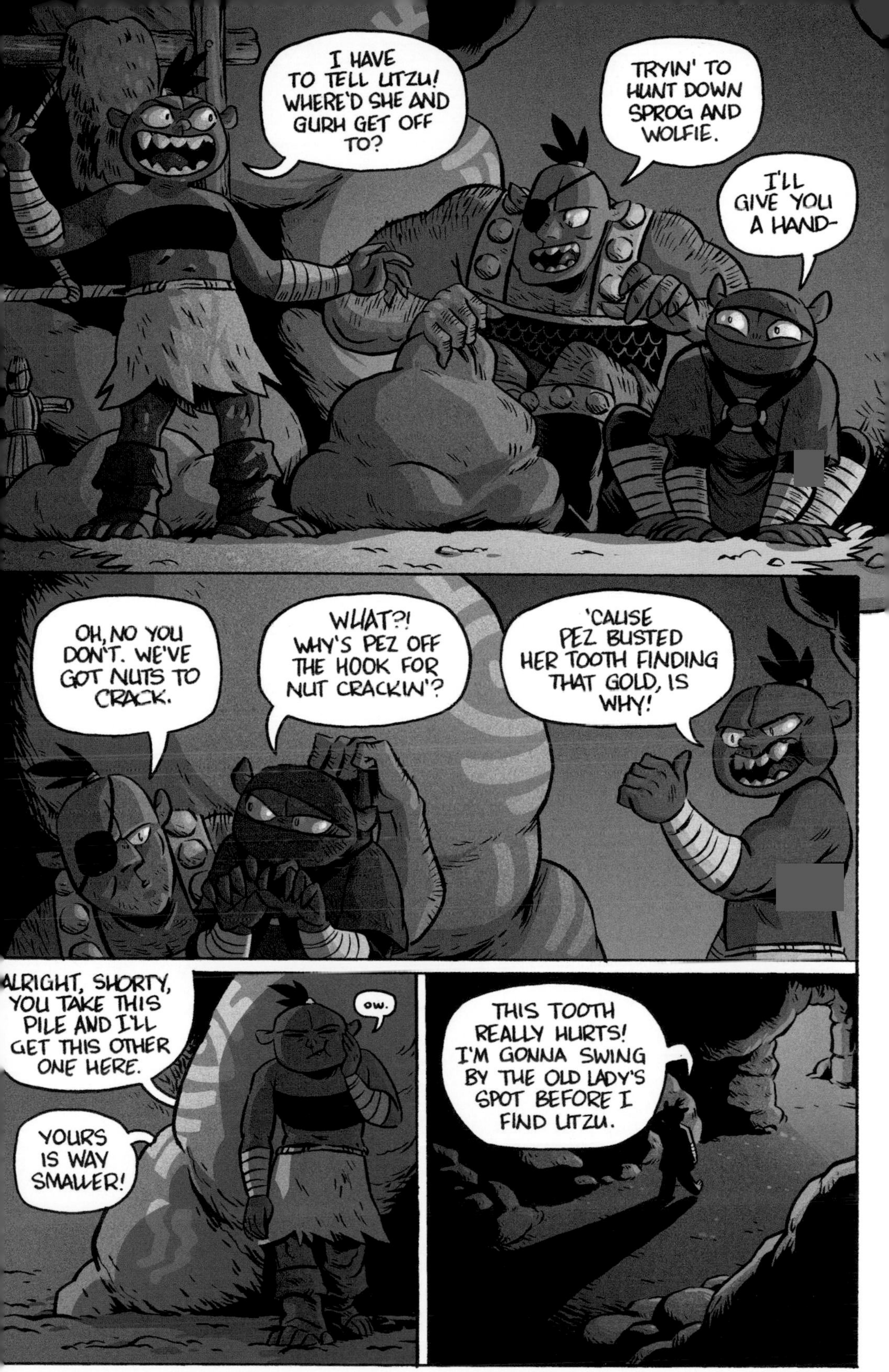
I HAVE TO TELL UTZU! WHERE'D SHE AND GURH GET OFF TO?
TRYIN' TO HUNT DOWN SPROG AND WOLFIE.
I'LL GIVE YOU A HAND-
OH, NO YOU DON'T. WE'VE GOT NUTS TO CRACK.
WHAT?! WHY'S PEZ OFF THE HOOK FOR NUT CRACKIN'?
'CAUSE PEZ BUSTED HER TOOTH FINDING THAT GOLD, IS WHY!
ALRIGHT, SHORTY, YOU TAKE THIS PILE AND I'LL GET THIS OTHER ONE HERE.
OW.
YOURS IS WAY SMALLER!
THIS TOOTH REALLY HURTS! I'M GONNA SWING BY THE OLD LADY'S SPOT BEFORE I FIND UTZU.

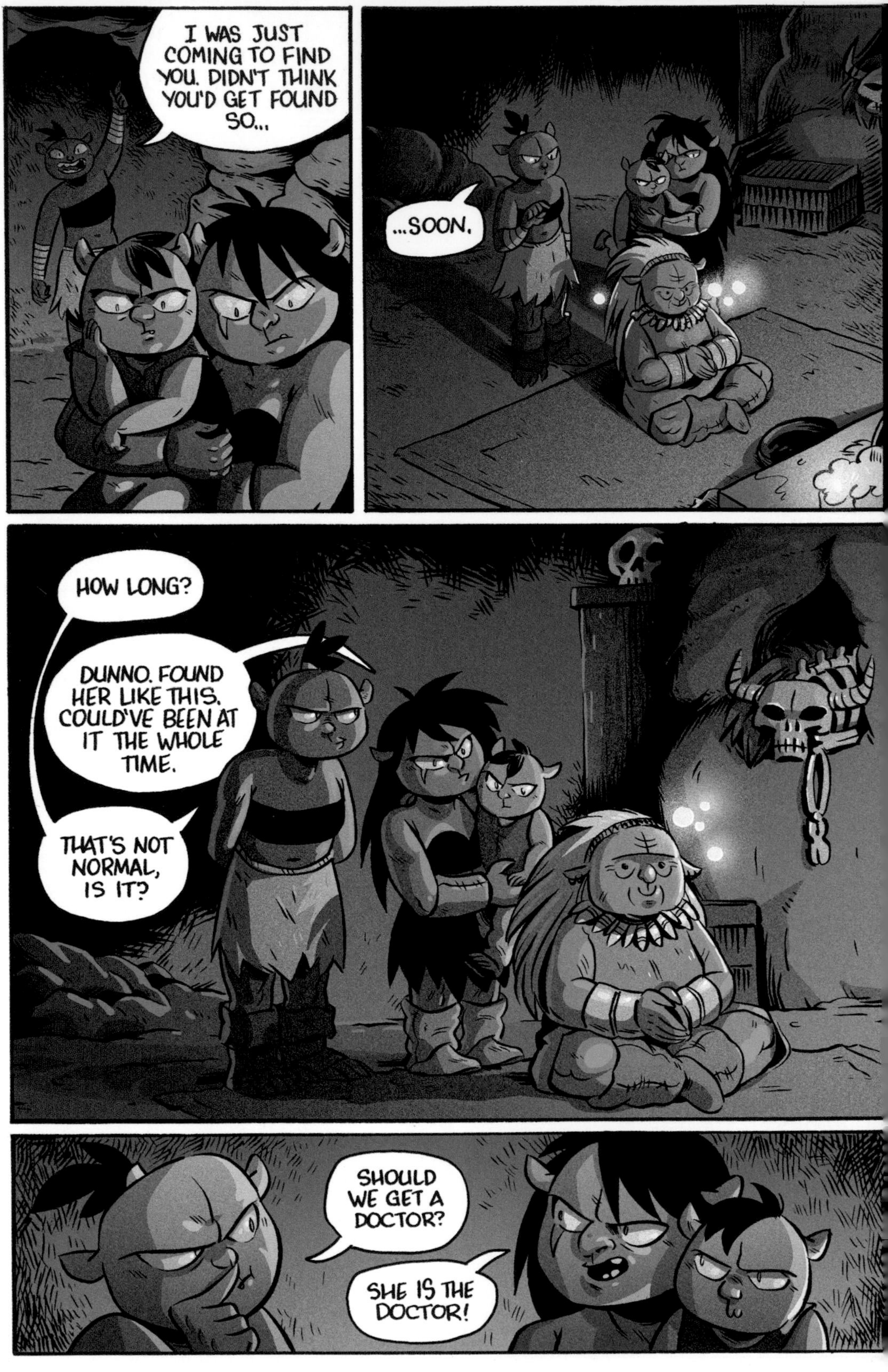
I WAS JUST COMING TO FIND YOU. DIDN'T THINK YOU'D GET FOUND SO...
...SOON.
HOW LONG?
DUNNO. FOUND HER LIKE THIS. COULD'VE BEEN AT IT THE WHOLE TIME.
THAT'S NOT NORMAL, IS IT?
SHOULD WE GET A DOCTOR?
SHE IS THE DOCTOR!

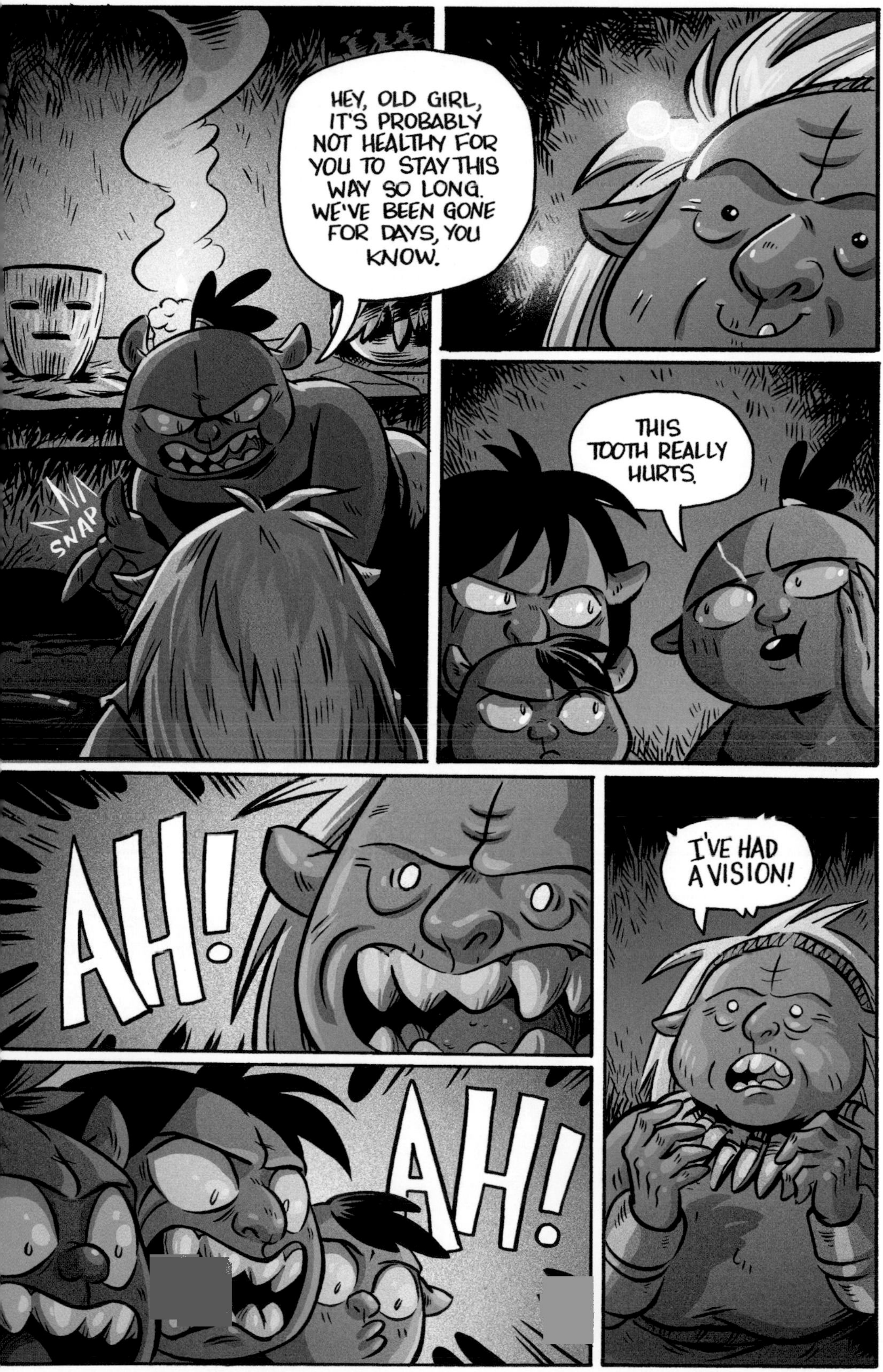
HEY, OLD GIRL, IT'S PROBABLY NOT HEALTHY FOR YOU TO STAY THIS WAY SO LONG. WE'VE BEEN GONE FOR DAYS, YOU KNOW.
SNAP
THIS TOOTH REALLY HURTS.
AH!
AH!
I'VE HAD A VISION!

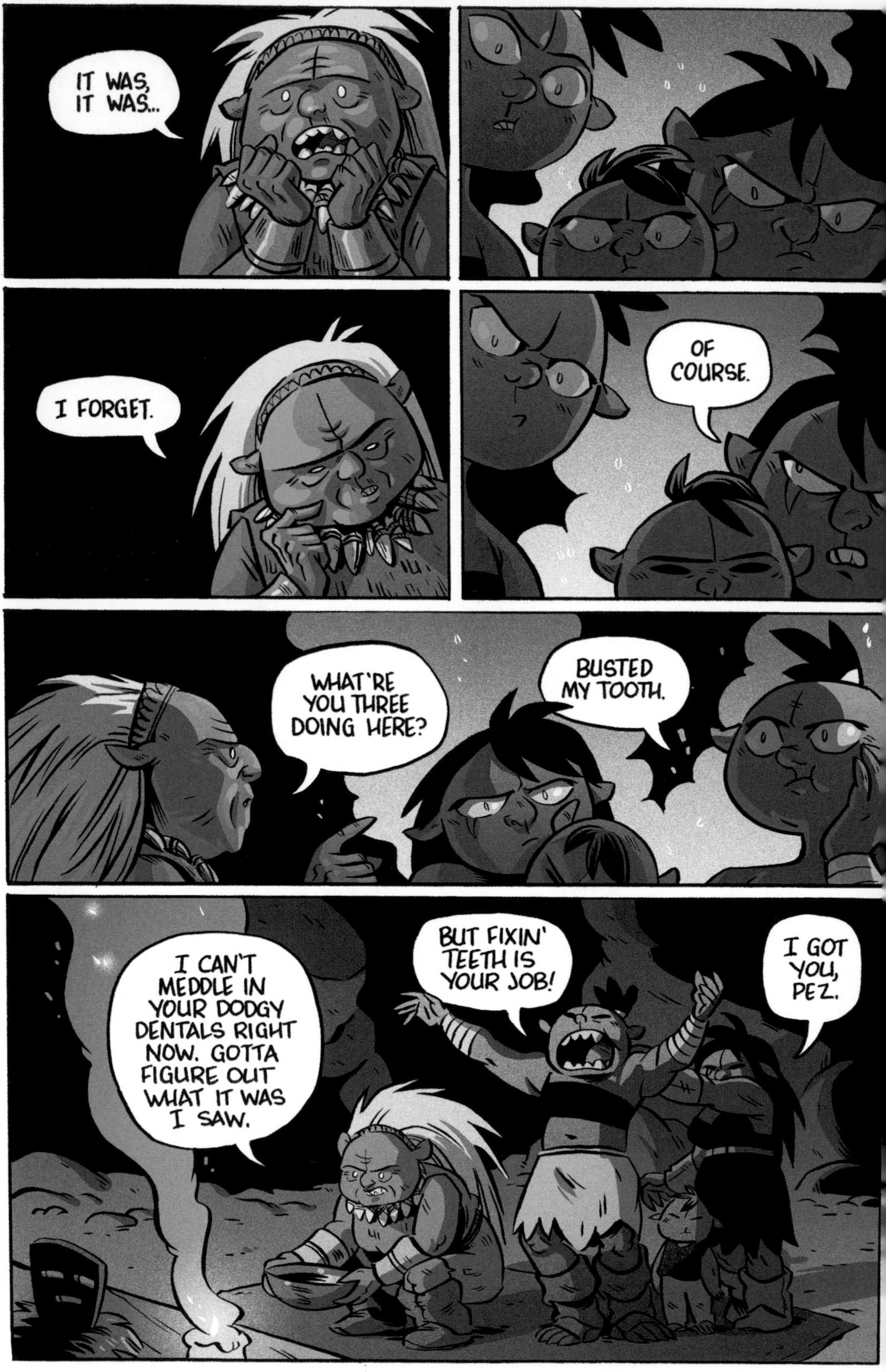
IT WAS, IT WAS...
I FORGET.
OF COURSE.
WHAT'RE YOU THREE DOING HERE?
BUSTED MY TOOTH.
I CAN'T MEDDLE IN YOUR DODGY DENTALS RIGHT NOW. GOTTA FIGURE OUT WHAT IT WAS I SAW.
BUT FIXIN' TEETH IS YOUR JOB!
I GOT YOU, PEZ.

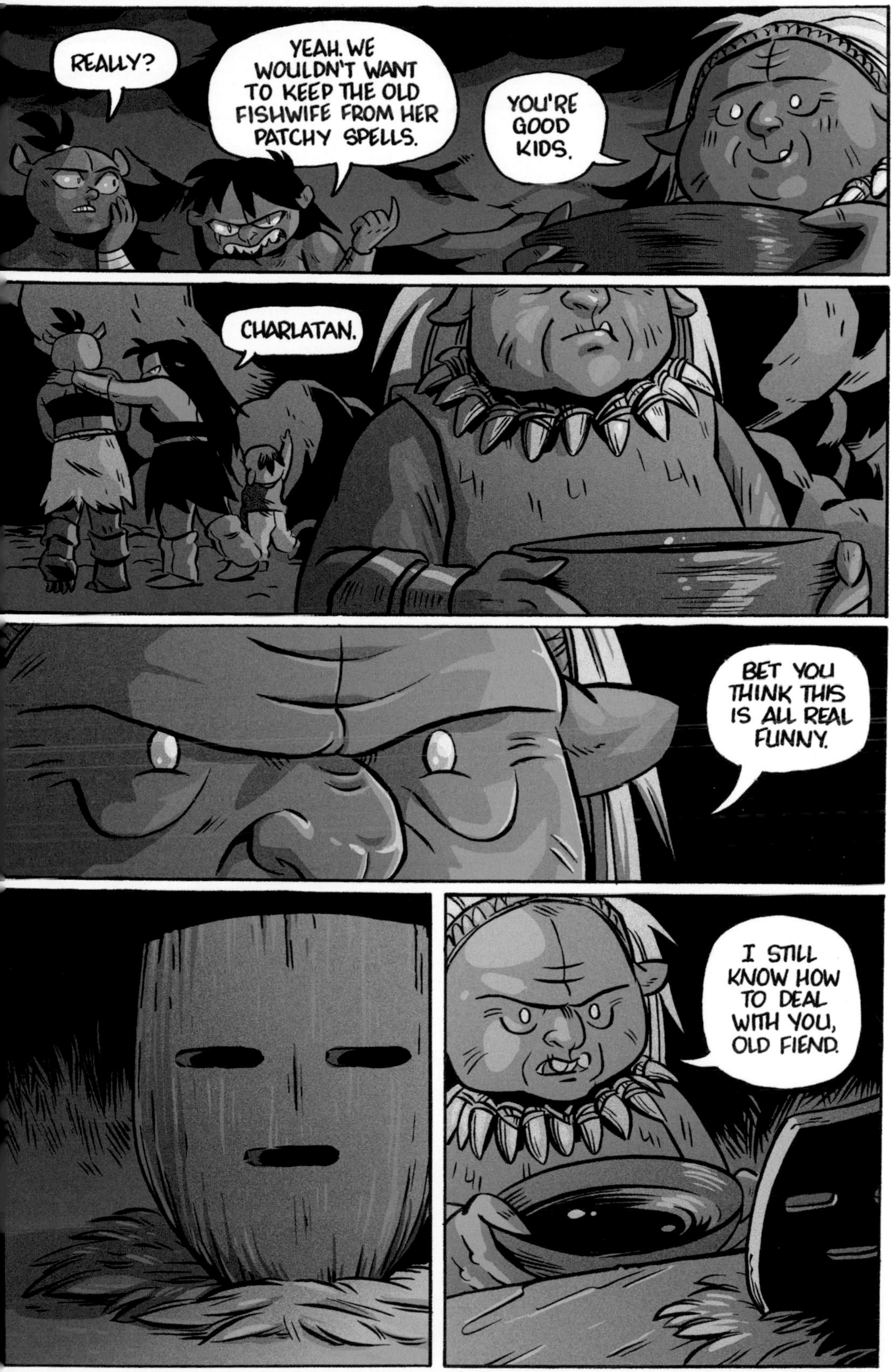
REALLY?
YEAH. WE WOULDN'T WANT TO KEEP THE OLD FISHWIFE FROM HER PATCHY SPELLS.
YOU'RE GOOD KIDS.
CHARLATAN.
BET YOU THINK THIS IS ALL REAL FUNNY.
I STILL KNOW HOW TO DEAL WITH YOU, OLD FIEND.

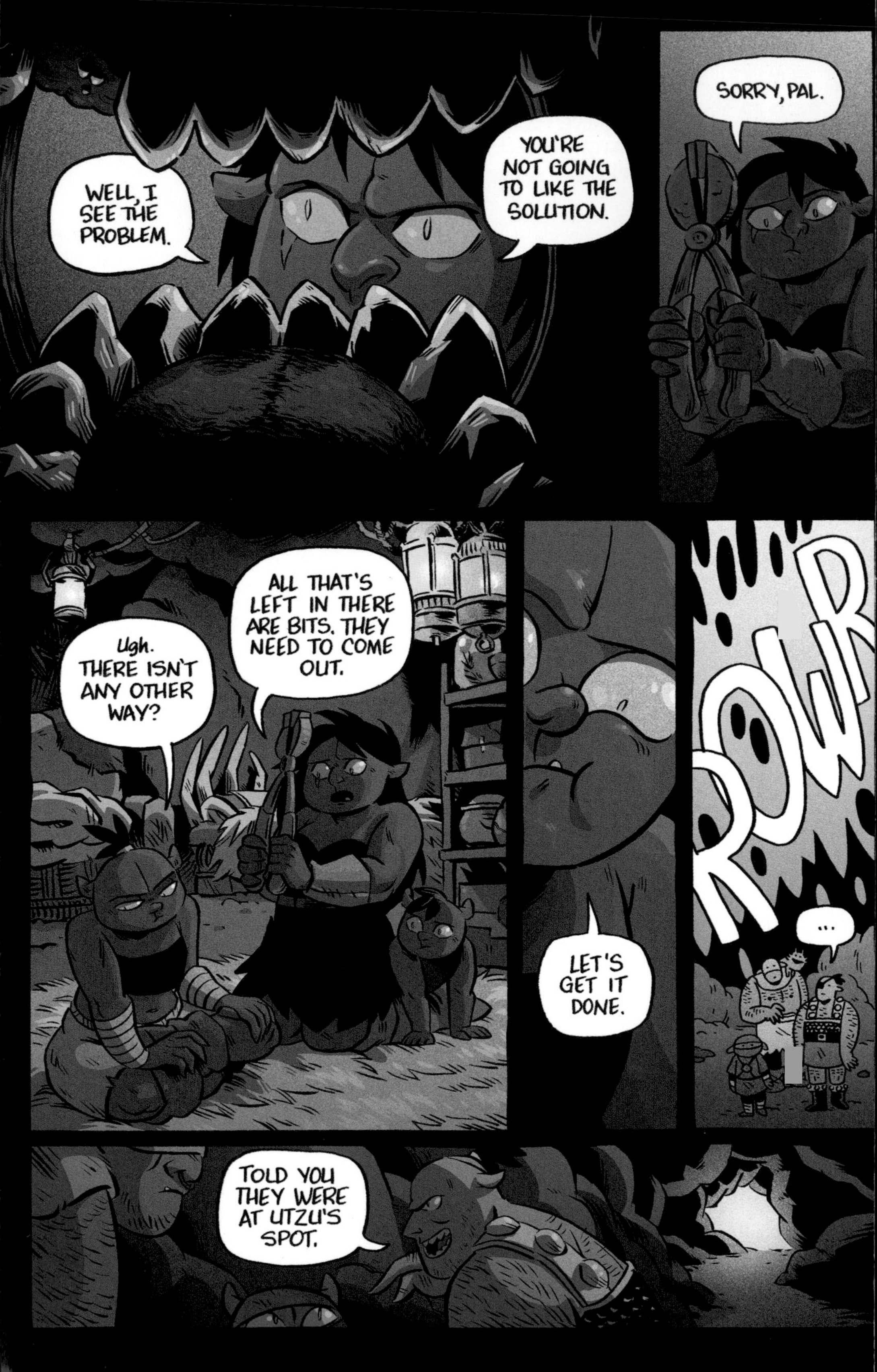
WELL, I SEE THE PROBLEM.
YOU'RE NOT GOING TO LIKE THE SOLUTION.
SORRY, PAL.
Ugh. THERE ISN'T ANY OTHER WAY?
ALL THAT'S LEFT IN THERE ARE BITS. THEY NEED TO COME OUT.
LET'S GET IT DONE.
ROWR
...
TOLD YOU THEY WERE AT UTZU'S SPOT.

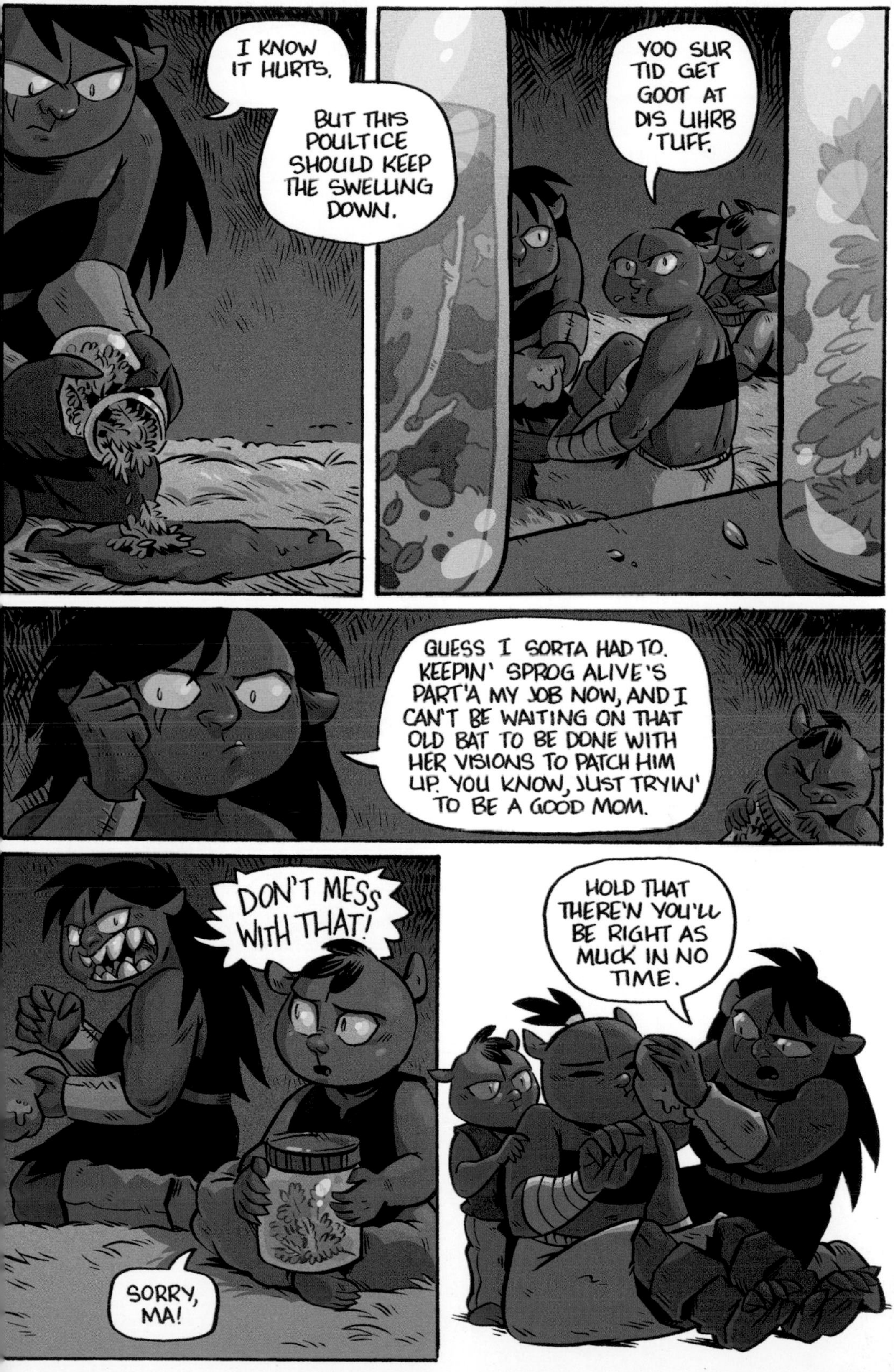

I KNOW IT HURTS.
BUT THIS POULTICE SHOULD KEEP THE SWELLING DOWN.
YOO SUR TID GET GOOT AT DIS UHRB 'TUFF.
GUESS I SORTA HAD TO. KEEPIN' SPROG ALIVE'S PART'A MY JOB NOW, AND I CAN'T BE WAITING ON THAT OLD BAT TO BE DONE WITH HER VISIONS TO PATCH HIM UP. YOU KNOW, JUST TRYIN' TO BE A GOOD MOM.
DON'T MESS WITH THAT!
SORRY, MA!
HOLD THAT THERE'N YOU'LL BE RIGHT AS MUCK IN NO TIME.

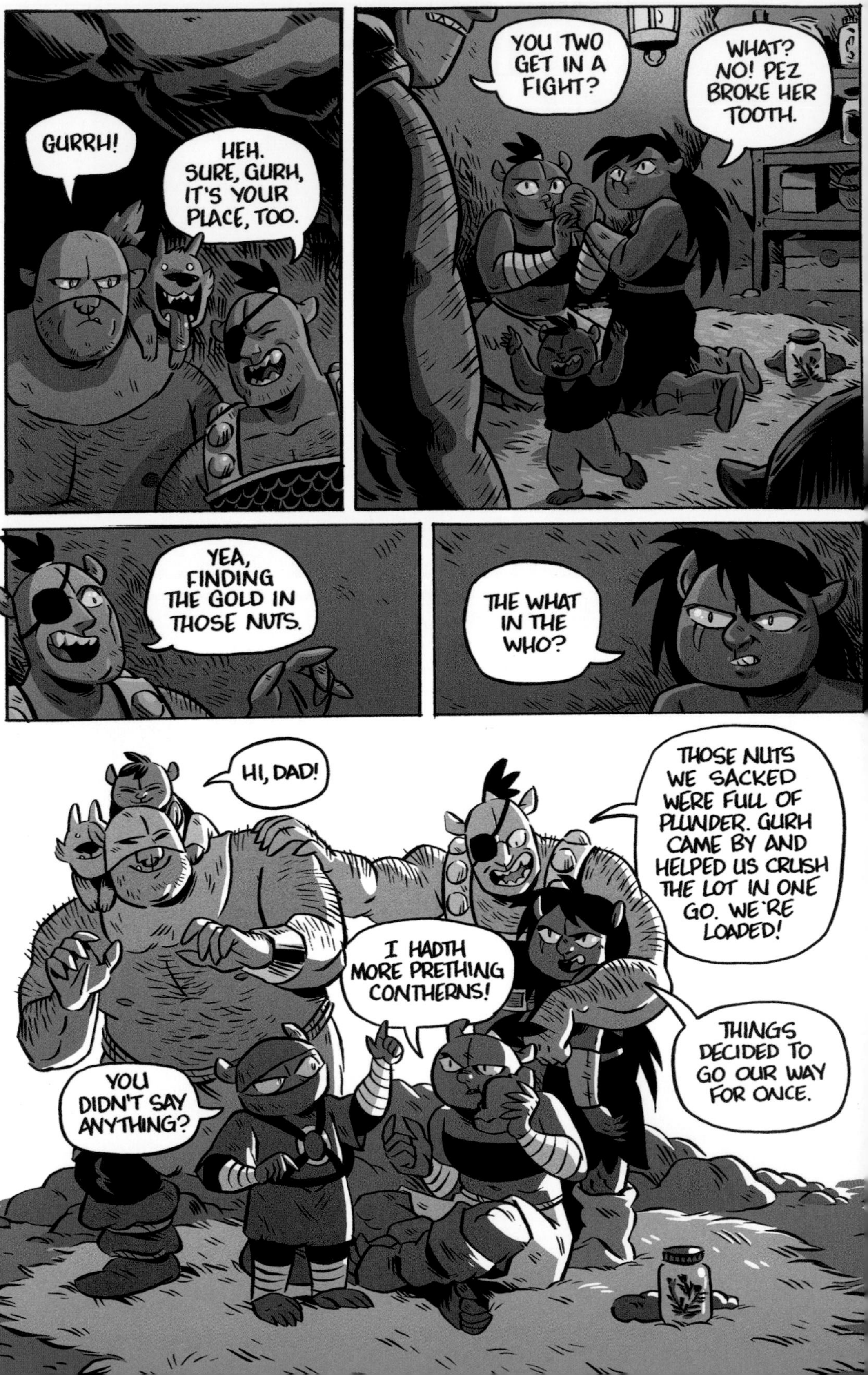
GURRH!
HEH. SURE, GURH, IT'S YOUR PLACE, TOO.
YOU TWO GET IN A FIGHT?
WHAT? NO! PEZ BROKE HER TOOTH.
YEA, FINDING THE GOLD IN THOSE NUTS.
THE WHAT IN THE WHO?
HI, DAD!
THOSE NUTS WE SACKED WERE FULL OF PLUNDER. GURH CAME BY AND HELPED US CRUSH THE LOT IN ONE GO. WE'RE LOADED!
I HADTH MORE PRETHING CONTHERNS!
THINGS DECIDED TO GO OUR WAY FOR ONCE.
YOU DIDN'T SAY ANYTHING?

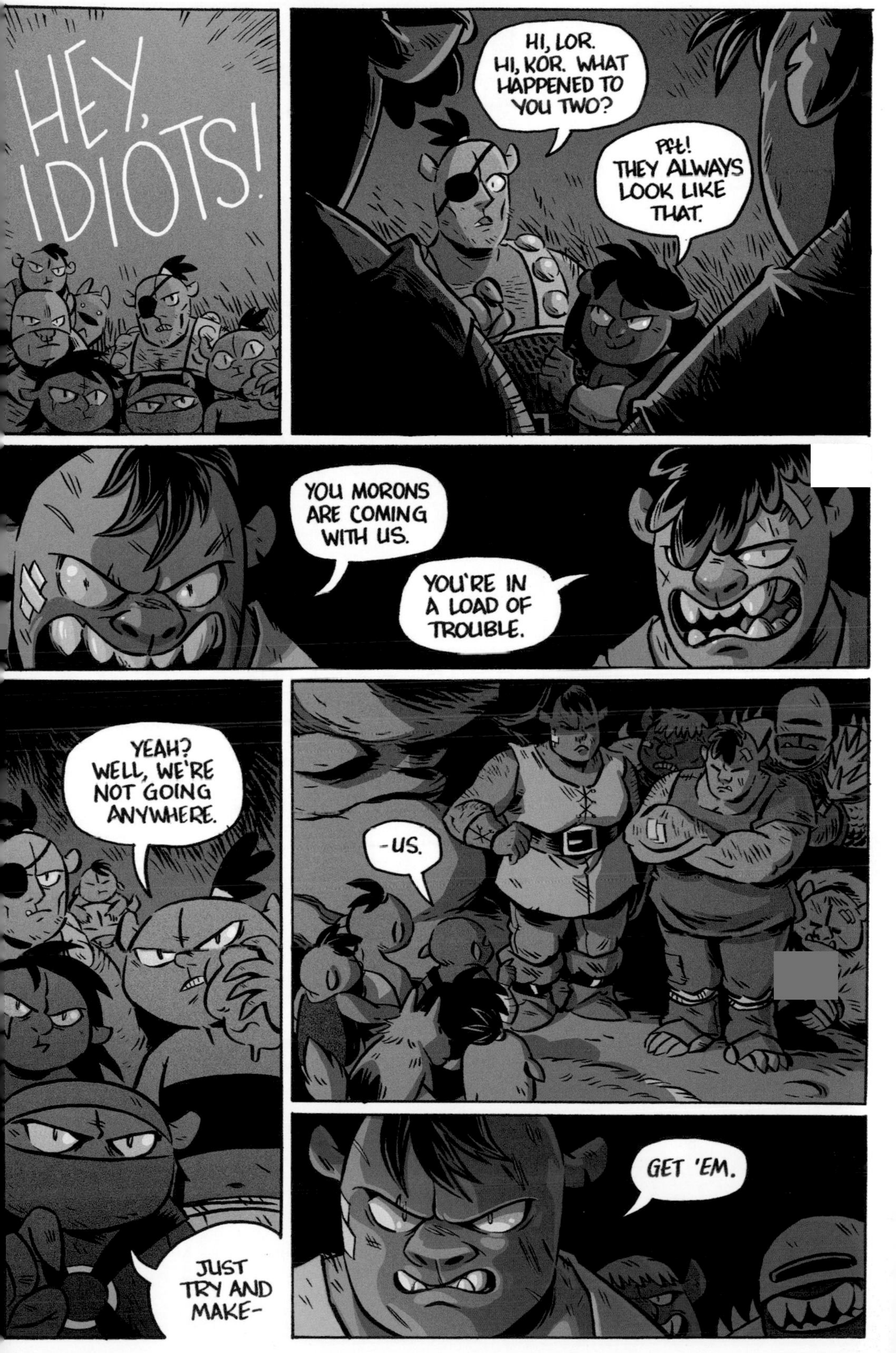
HEY, IDIOTS!
HI, LOR. HI, KOR. WHAT HAPPENED TO YOU TWO?
PFT! THEY ALWAYS LOOK LIKE THAT.
YOU MORONS ARE COMING WITH US.
YOU'RE IN A LOAD OF TROUBLE.
YEAH? WELL, WE'RE NOT GOING ANYWHERE.
JUST TRY AND MAKE-
-US.
GET 'EM.

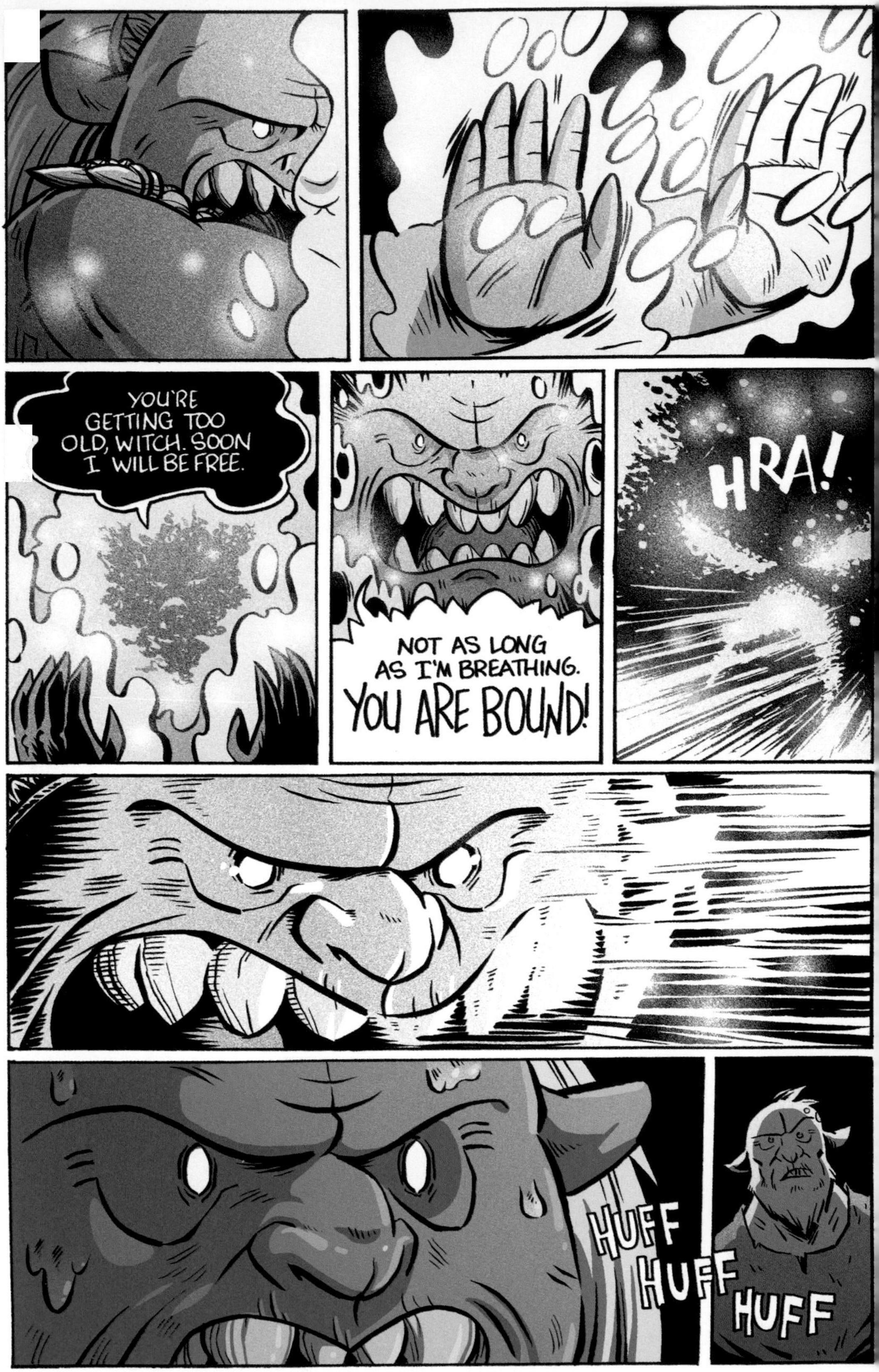
YOU'RE GETTING TOO OLD, WITCH. SOON I WILL BE FREE.
NOT AS LONG AS I'M BREATHING.
YOU ARE BOUND!
HRA!
HUFF
HUFF
HUFF

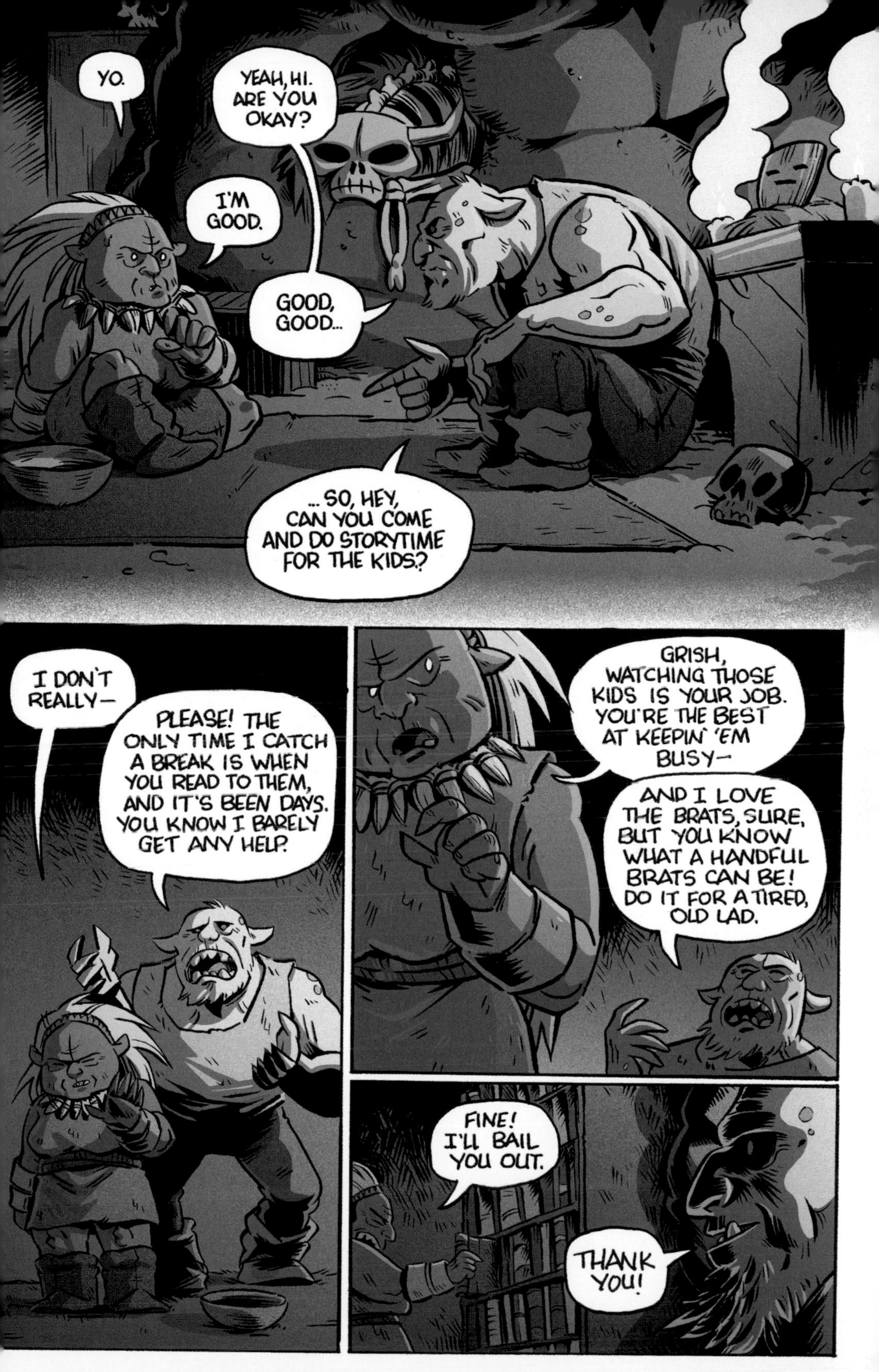
YO.
YEAH, HI. ARE YOU OKAY?
I'M GOOD.
GOOD, GOOD...
... SO, HEY, CAN YOU COME AND DO STORYTIME FOR THE KIDS?
I DON'T REALLY—
PLEASE! THE ONLY TIME I CATCH A BREAK IS WHEN YOU READ TO THEM, AND IT'S BEEN DAYS. YOU KNOW I BARELY GET ANY HELP.
GRISH, WATCHING THOSE KIDS IS YOUR JOB. YOU'RE THE BEST AT KEEPIN' 'EM BUSY—
AND I LOVE THE BRATS, SURE, BUT YOU KNOW WHAT A HANDFUL BRATS CAN BE! DO IT FOR A TIRED, OLD LAD.
FINE! I'LL BAIL YOU OUT.
THANK YOU!

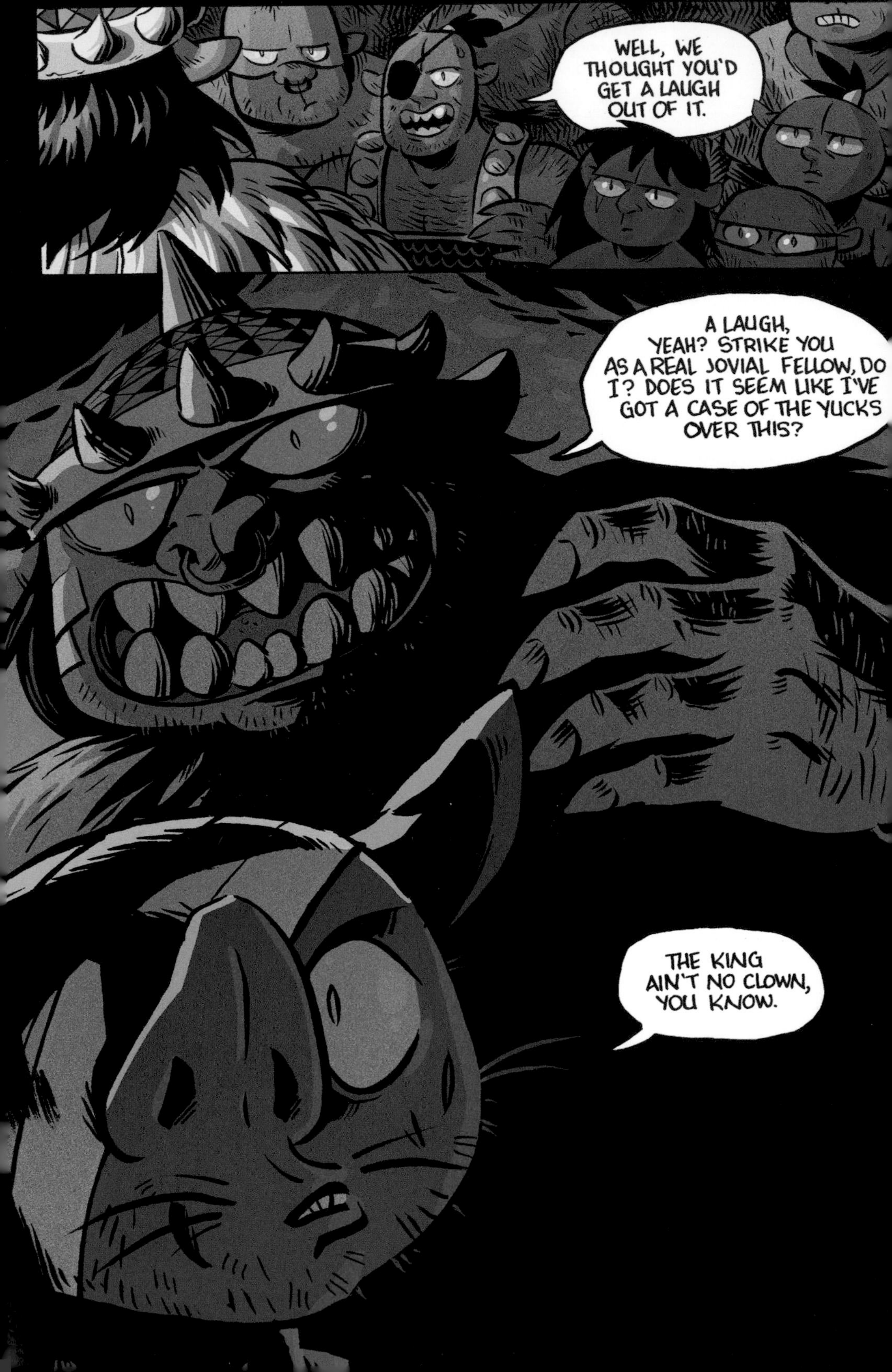
WELL, WE THOUGHT YOU'D GET A LAUGH OUT OF IT.
A LAUGH, YEAH? STRIKE YOU AS A REAL JOVIAL FELLOW, DO I? DOES IT SEEM LIKE I'VE GOT A CASE OF THE YUCKS OVER THIS?
THE KING AIN'T NO CLOWN, YOU KNOW.

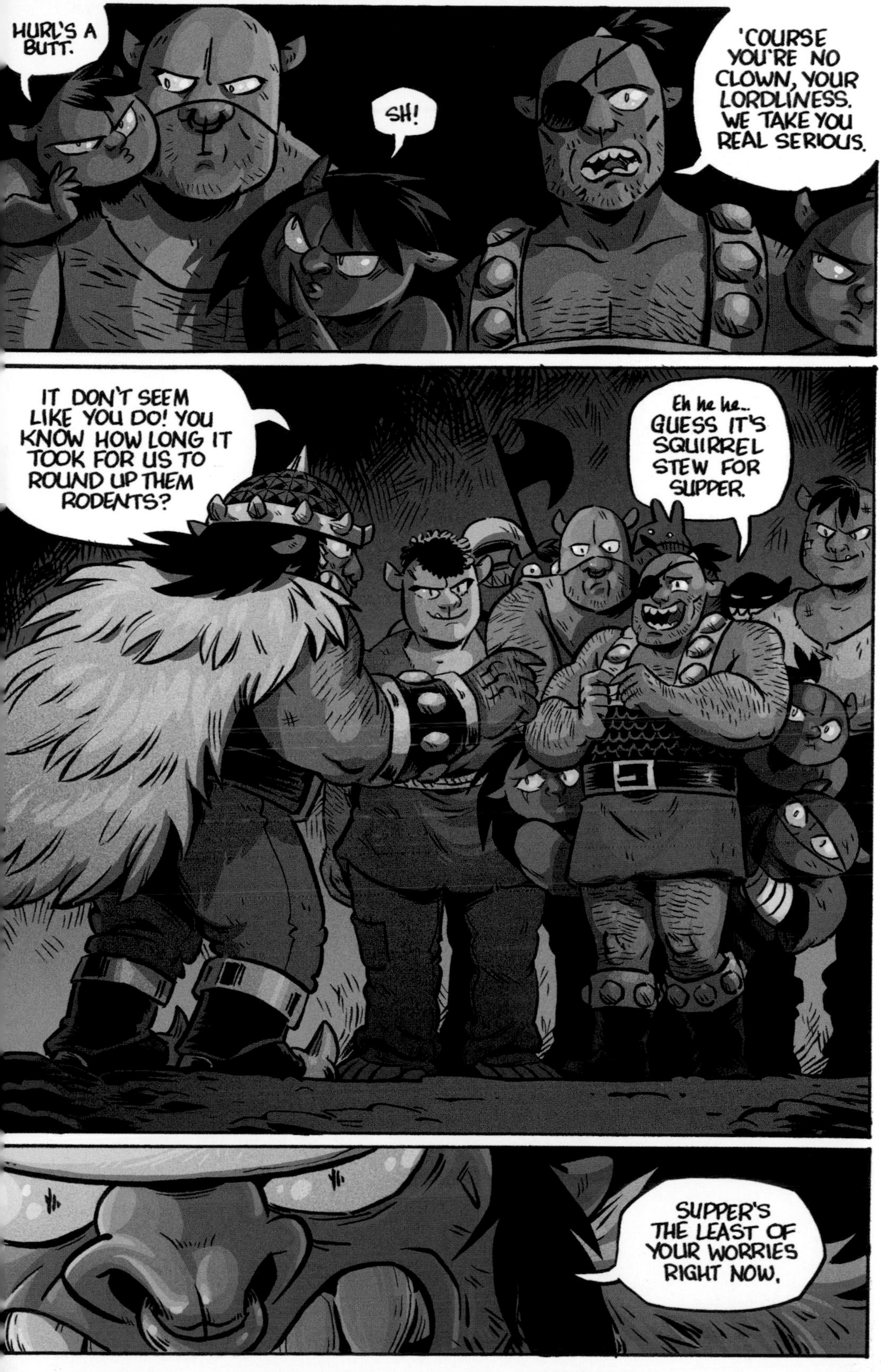
HURL'S A BUTT.
SH!
'COURSE YOU'RE NO CLOWN, YOUR LORDLINESS. WE TAKE YOU REAL SERIOUS.
IT DON'T SEEM LIKE YOU DO! YOU KNOW HOW LONG IT TOOK FOR US TO ROUND UP THEM RODENTS?
Eh he he... GUESS IT'S SQUIRREL STEW FOR SUPPER.
SUPPER'S THE LEAST OF YOUR WORRIES RIGHT NOW.

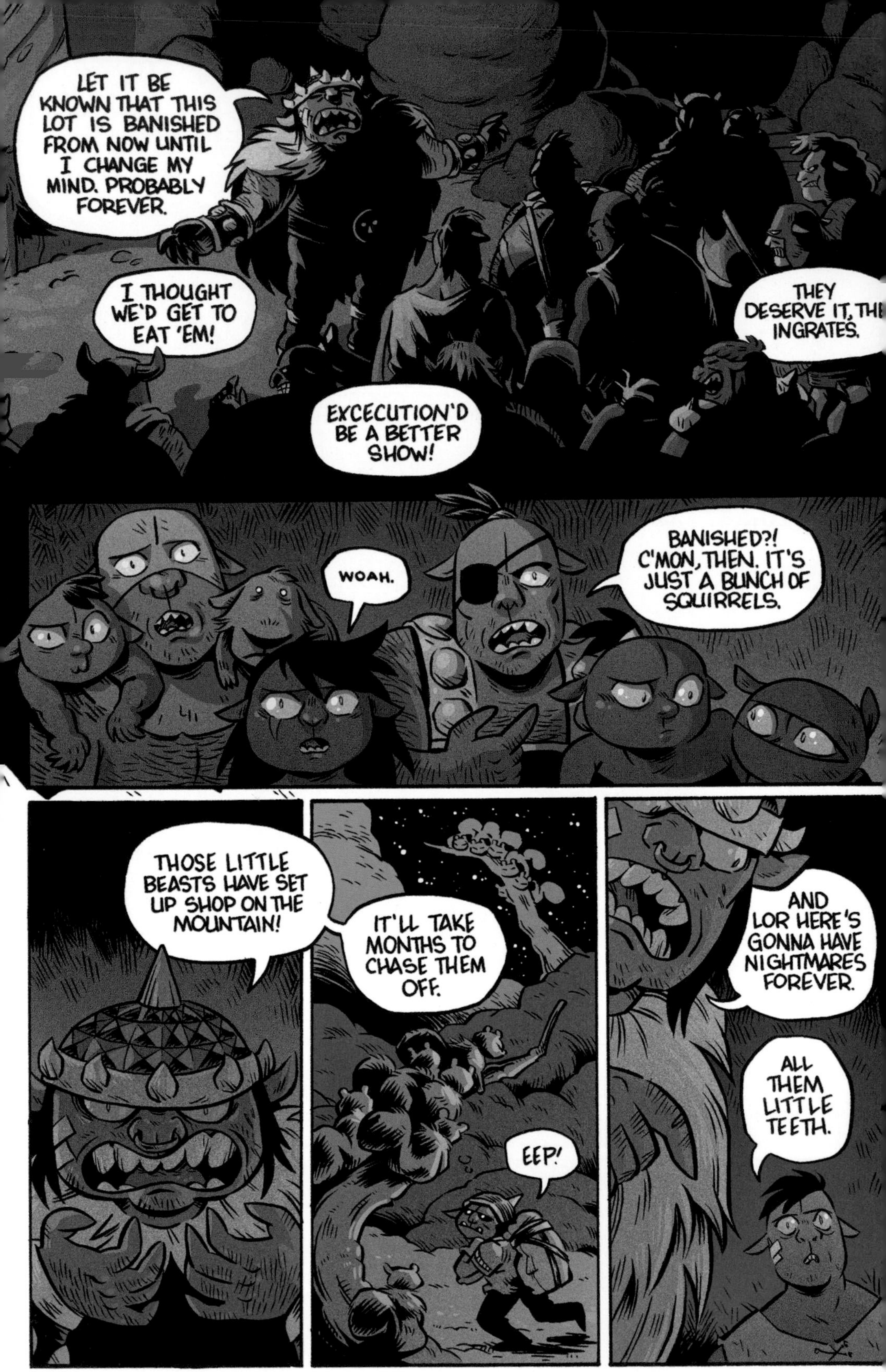
LET IT BE KNOWN THAT THIS LOT IS BANISHED FROM NOW UNTIL I CHANGE MY MIND. PROBABLY FOREVER.
I THOUGHT WE'D GET TO EAT 'EM!
THEY DESERVE IT, THE INGRATES.
EXCECUTION'D BE A BETTER SHOW!
WOAH.
BANISHED?! C'MON, THEN. IT'S JUST A BUNCH OF SQUIRRELS.
THOSE LITTLE BEASTS HAVE SET UP SHOP ON THE MOUNTAIN!
IT'LL TAKE MONTHS TO CHASE THEM OFF.
EEP!
AND LOR HERE'S GONNA HAVE NIGHTMARES FOREVER.
ALL THEM LITTLE TEETH.

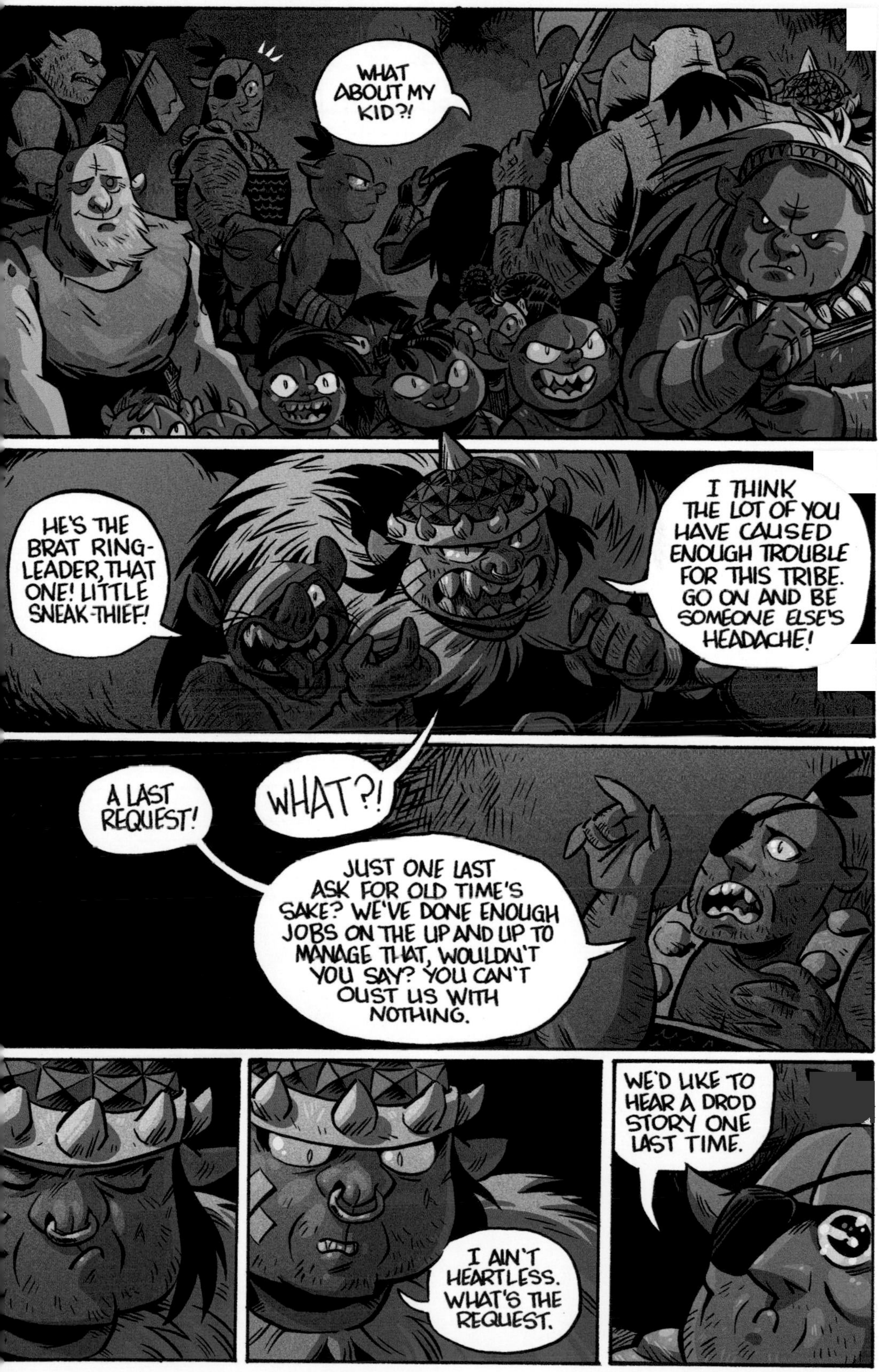
WHAT ABOUT MY KID?!
HE'S THE BRAT RING-LEADER, THAT ONE! LITTLE SNEAK-THIEF!
I THINK THE LOT OF YOU HAVE CAUSED ENOUGH TROUBLE FOR THIS TRIBE. GO ON AND BE SOMEONE ELSE'S HEADACHE!
A LAST REQUEST!
WHAT?!
JUST ONE LAST ASK FOR OLD TIME'S SAKE? WE'VE DONE ENOUGH JOBS ON THE UP AND UP TO MANAGE THAT, WOULDN'T YOU SAY? YOU CAN'T OUST US WITH NOTHING.
I AIN'T HEARTLESS. WHAT'S THE REQUEST.
WE'D LIKE TO HEAR A DROD STORY ONE LAST TIME.

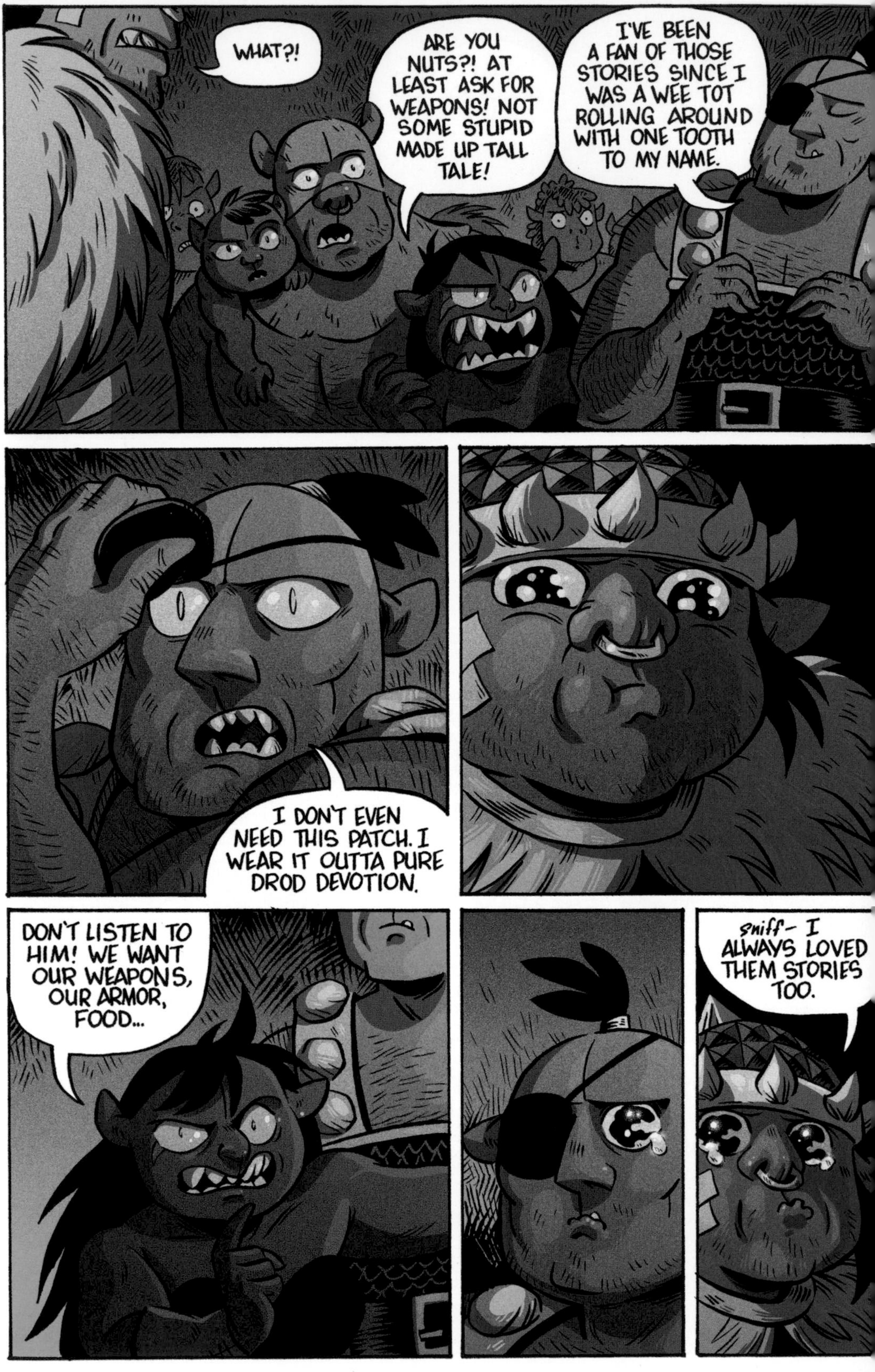
WHAT?!
ARE YOU NUTS?! AT LEAST ASK FOR WEAPONS! NOT SOME STUPID MADE UP TALL TALE!
I'VE BEEN A FAN OF THOSE STORIES SINCE I WAS A WEE TOT ROLLING AROUND WITH ONE TOOTH TO MY NAME.
I DON'T EVEN NEED THIS PATCH. I WEAR IT OUTTA PURE DROD DEVOTION.
DON'T LISTEN TO HIM! WE WANT OUR WEAPONS, OUR ARMOR, FOOD...
sniff- I ALWAYS LOVED THEM STORIES TOO.

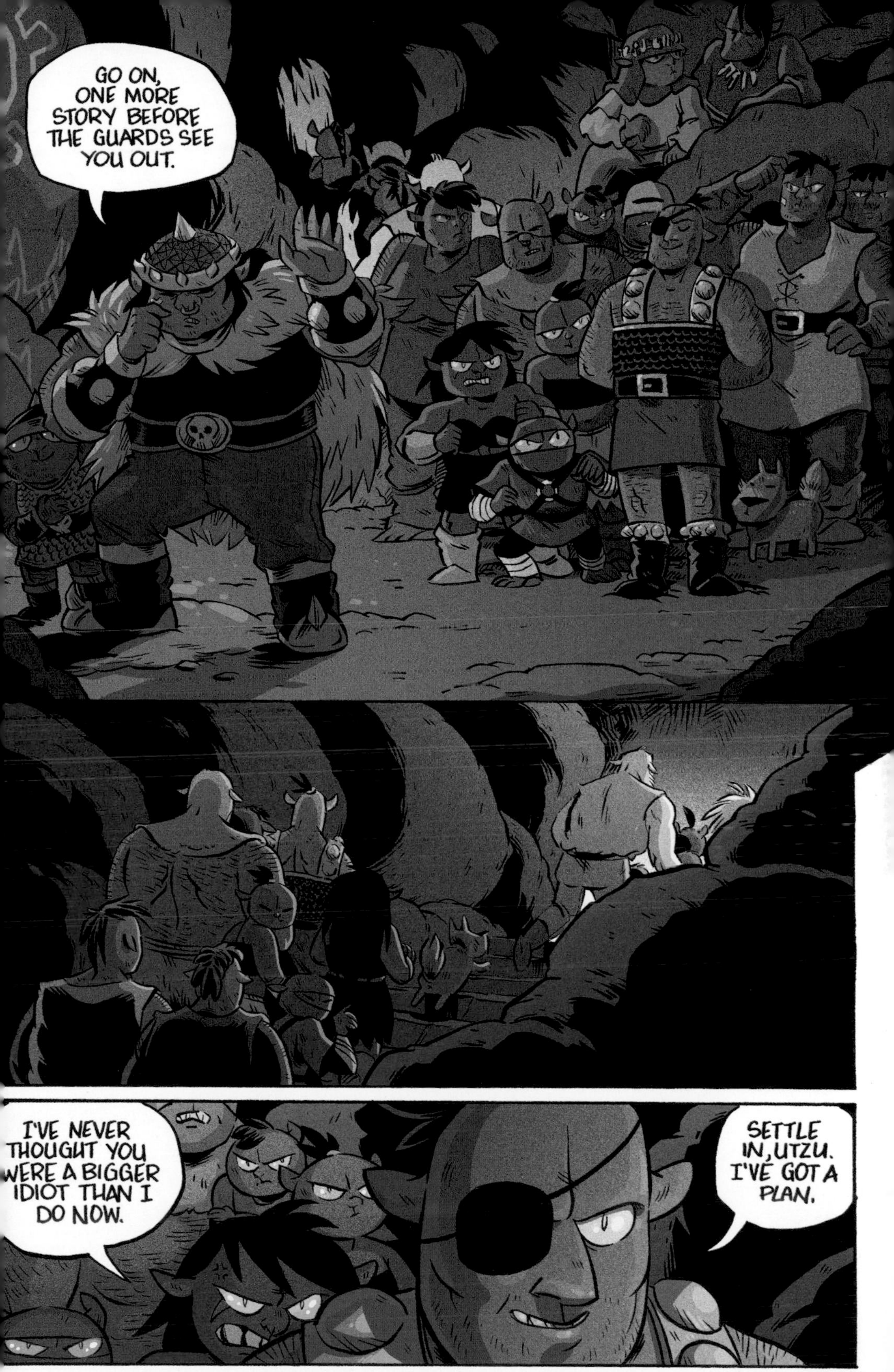
GO ON, ONE MORE STORY BEFORE THE GUARDS SEE YOU OUT.
I'VE NEVER THOUGHT YOU WERE A BIGGER IDIOT THAN I DO NOW.
SETTLE IN, UTZU. I'VE GOT A PLAN.

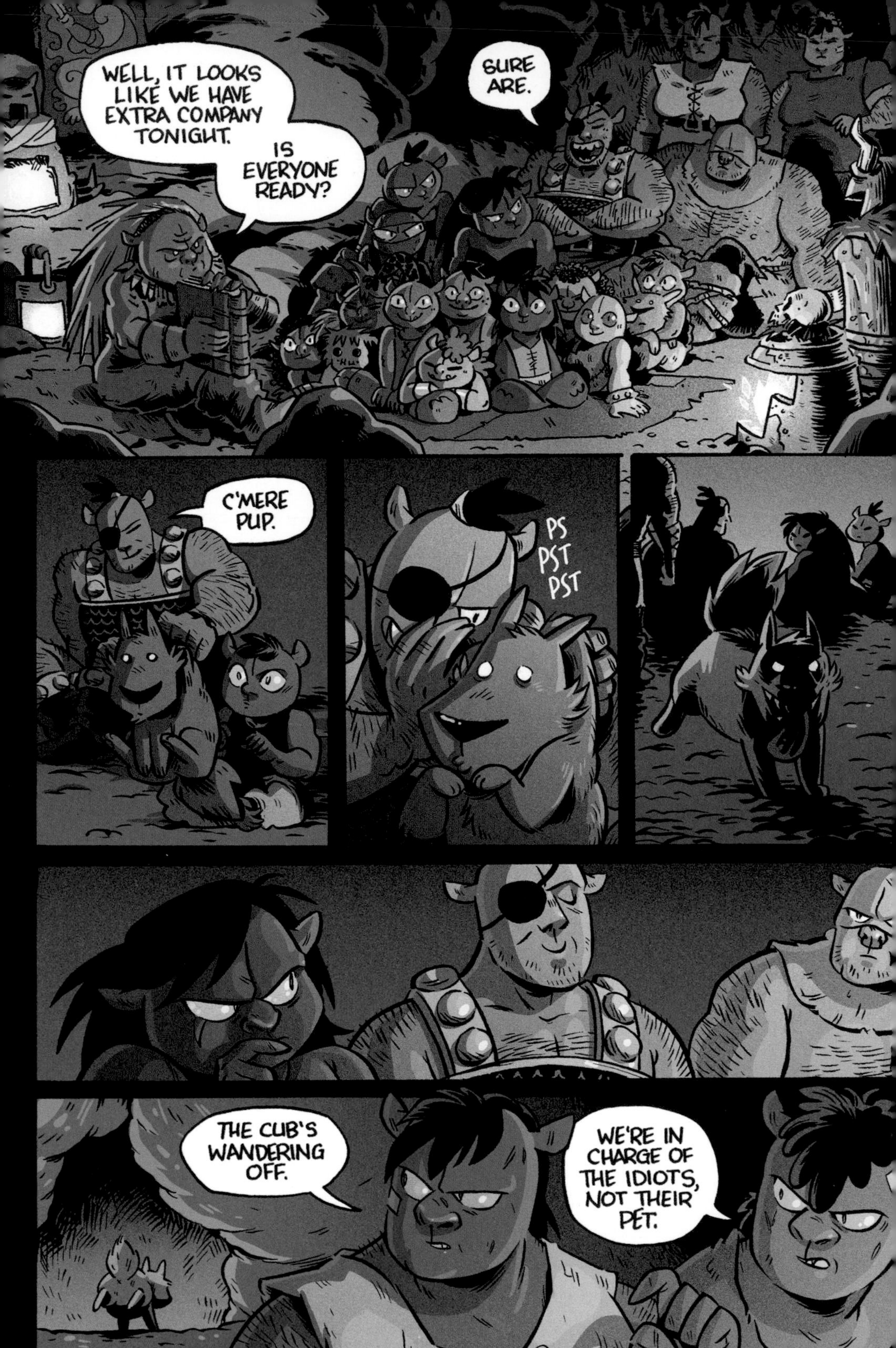
WELL, IT LOOKS LIKE WE HAVE EXTRA COMPANY TONIGHT.
IS EVERYONE READY?
SURE ARE.
C'MERE PUP.
PS PST PST
THE CUB'S WANDERING OFF.
WE'RE IN CHARGE OF THE IDIOTS, NOT THEIR PET.

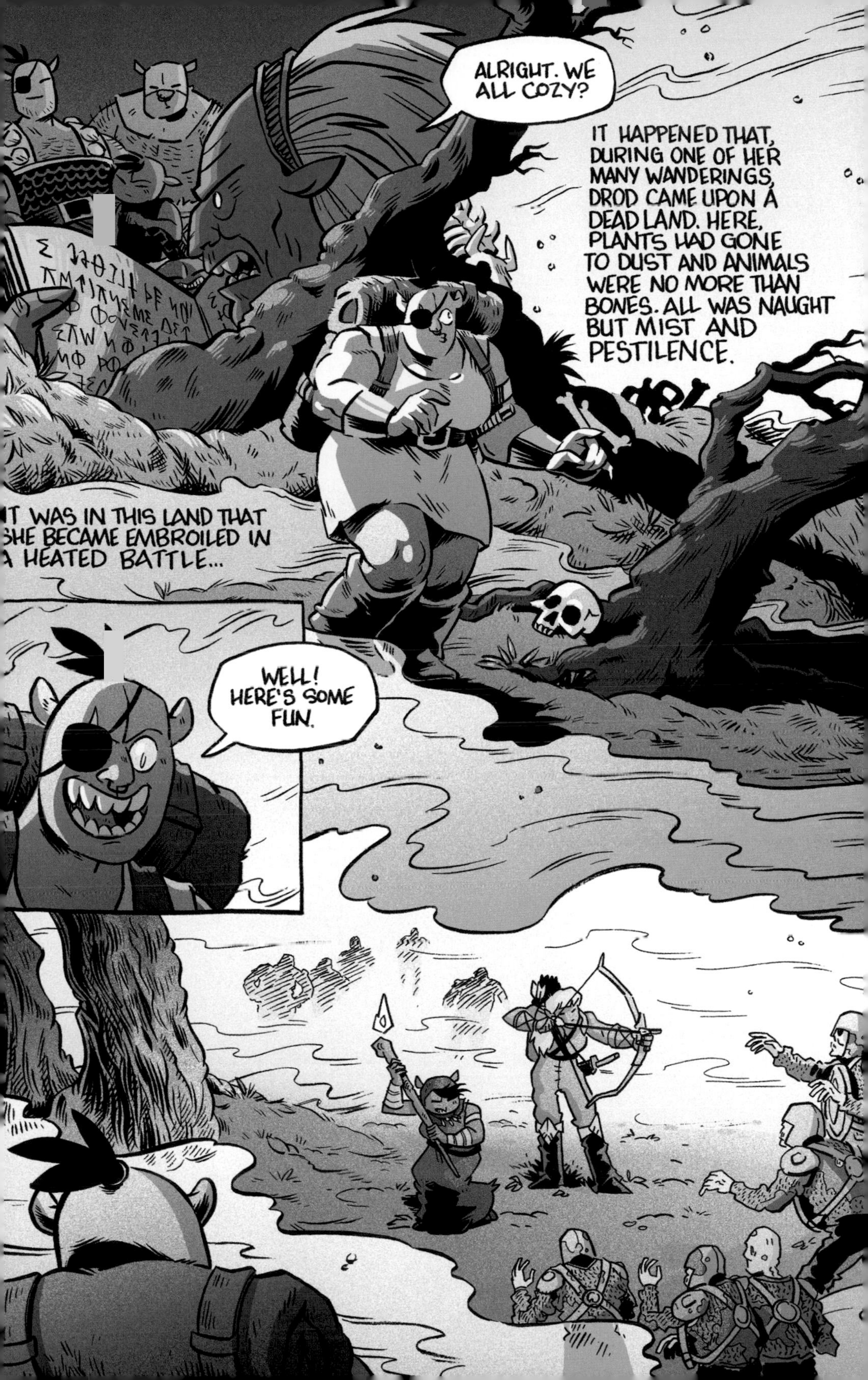
ALRIGHT. WE ALL COZY?
IT HAPPENED THAT, DURING ONE OF HER MANY WANDERINGS, DROD CAME UPON A DEAD LAND. HERE, PLANTS HAD GONE TO DUST AND ANIMALS WERE NO MORE THAN BONES. ALL WAS NAUGHT BUT MIST AND PESTILENCE.
IT WAS IN THIS LAND THAT SHE BECAME EMBROILED IN A HEATED BATTLE...
WELL! HERE'S SOME FUN.

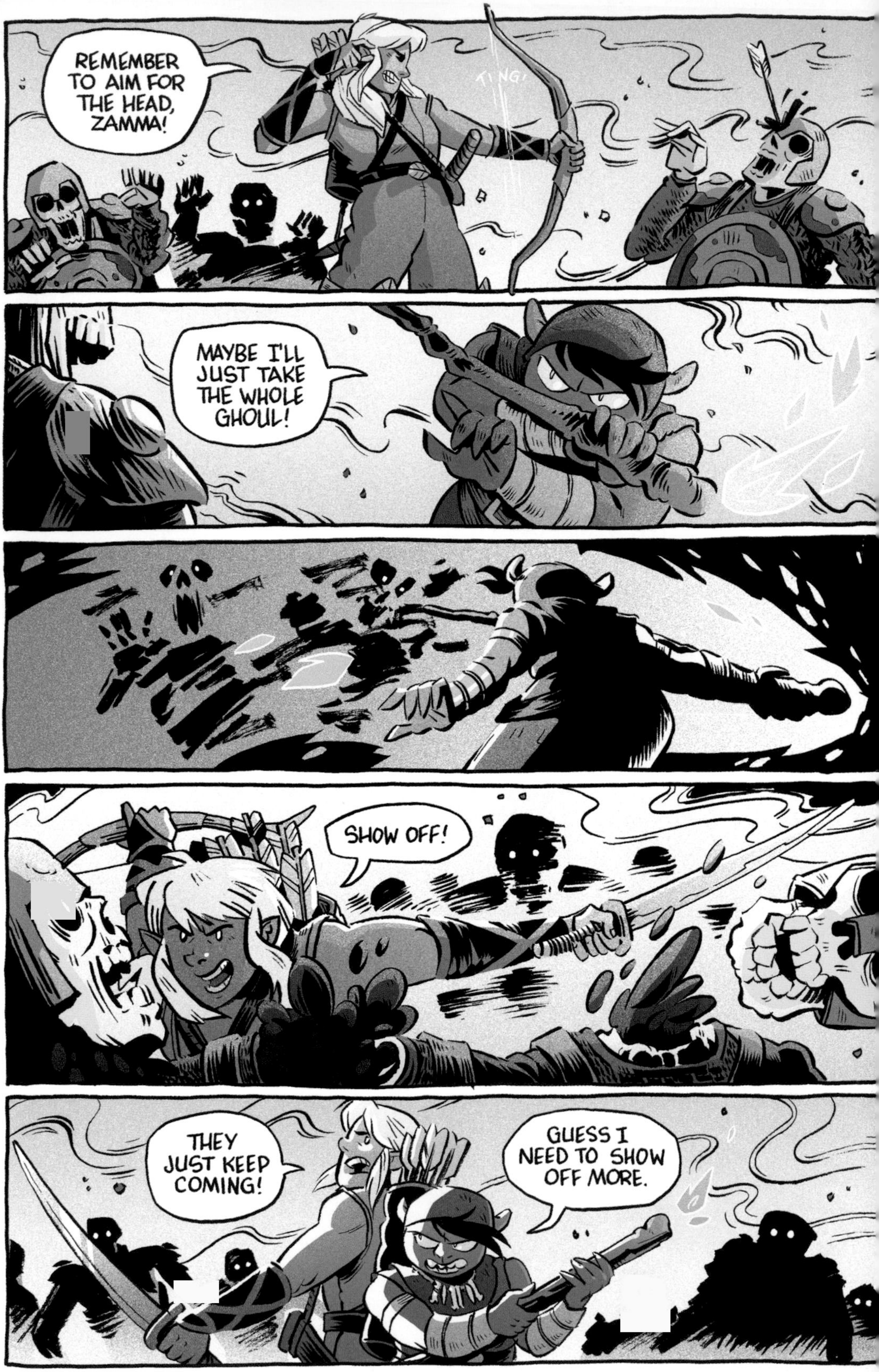
REMEMBER TO AIM FOR THE HEAD, ZAMMA!
TING!
MAYBE I'LL JUST TAKE THE WHOLE GHOUL!
SHOW OFF!
THEY JUST KEEP COMING!
GUESS I NEED TO SHOW OFF MORE.

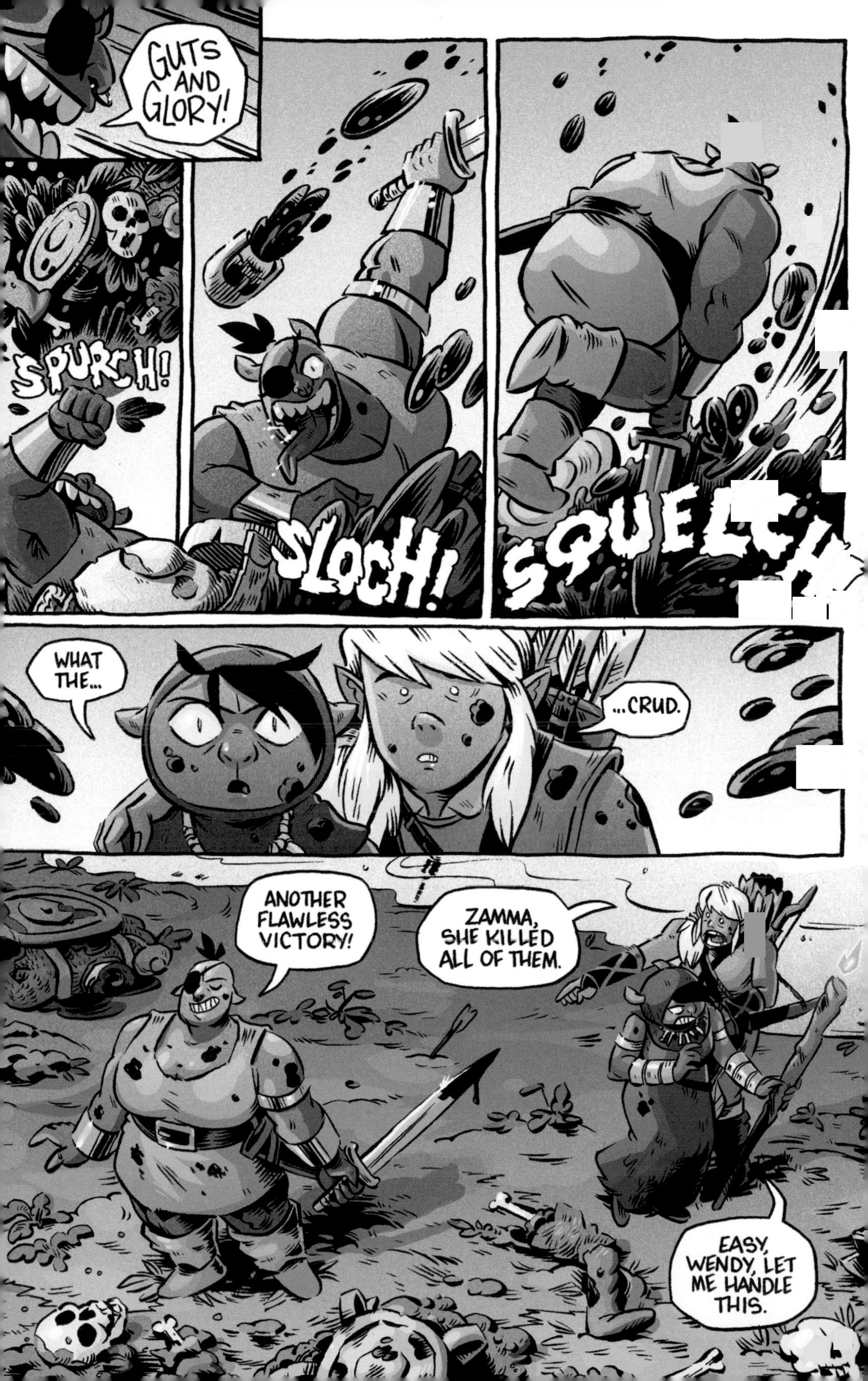
GUTS AND GLORY!
SPURCH!
SLOCH!
SQUELCH!
WHAT THE...
...CRUD.
ANOTHER FLAWLESS VICTORY!
ZAMMA, SHE KILLED ALL OF THEM.
EASY, WENDY, LET ME HANDLE THIS.

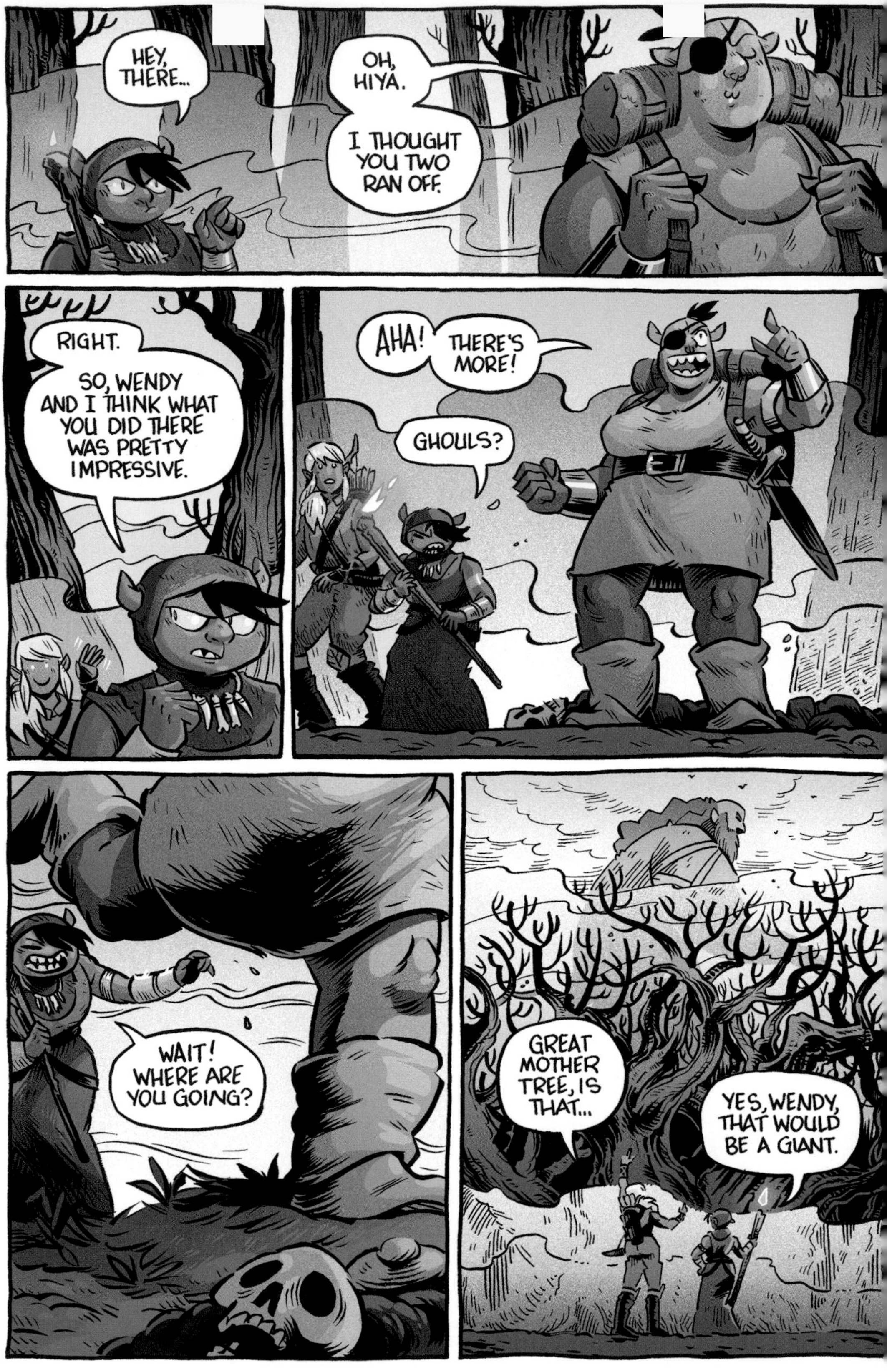
HEY, THERE...
OH, HIYA.
I THOUGHT YOU TWO RAN OFF.
RIGHT.
SO, WENDY AND I THINK WHAT YOU DID THERE WAS PRETTY IMPRESSIVE.
AHA!
THERE'S MORE!
GHOULS?
WAIT! WHERE ARE YOU GOING?
GREAT MOTHER TREE, IS THAT...
YES, WENDY, THAT WOULD BE A GIANT.

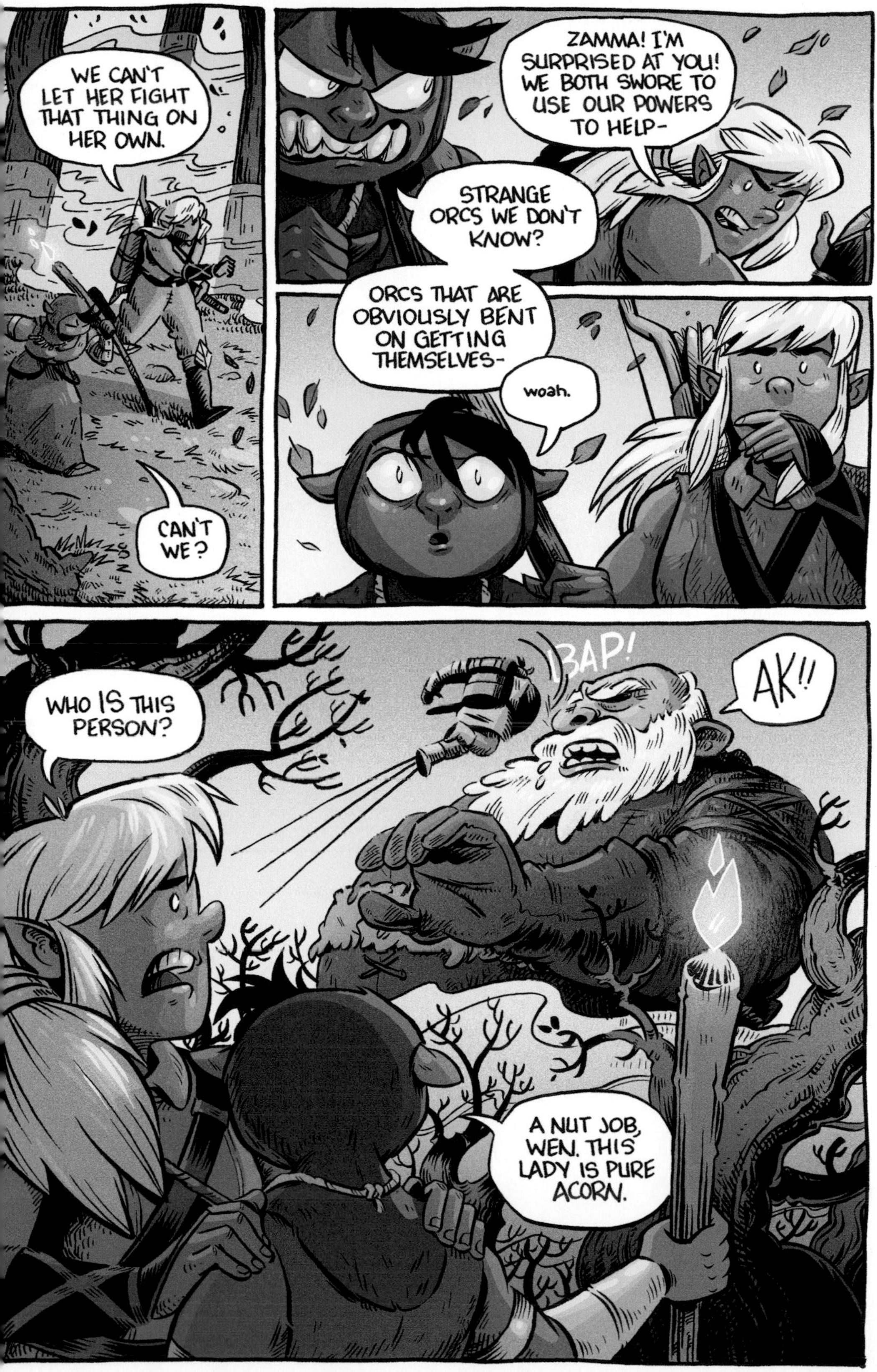
WE CAN'T LET HER FIGHT THAT THING ON HER OWN.
CAN'T WE?
ZAMMA! I'M SURPRISED AT YOU! WE BOTH SWORE TO USE OUR POWERS TO HELP-
STRANGE ORCS WE DON'T KNOW?
ORCS THAT ARE OBVIOUSLY BENT ON GETTING THEMSELVES-
woah.
WHO IS THIS PERSON?
BAP!
AK!!
A NUT JOB, WEN. THIS LADY IS PURE ACORN.

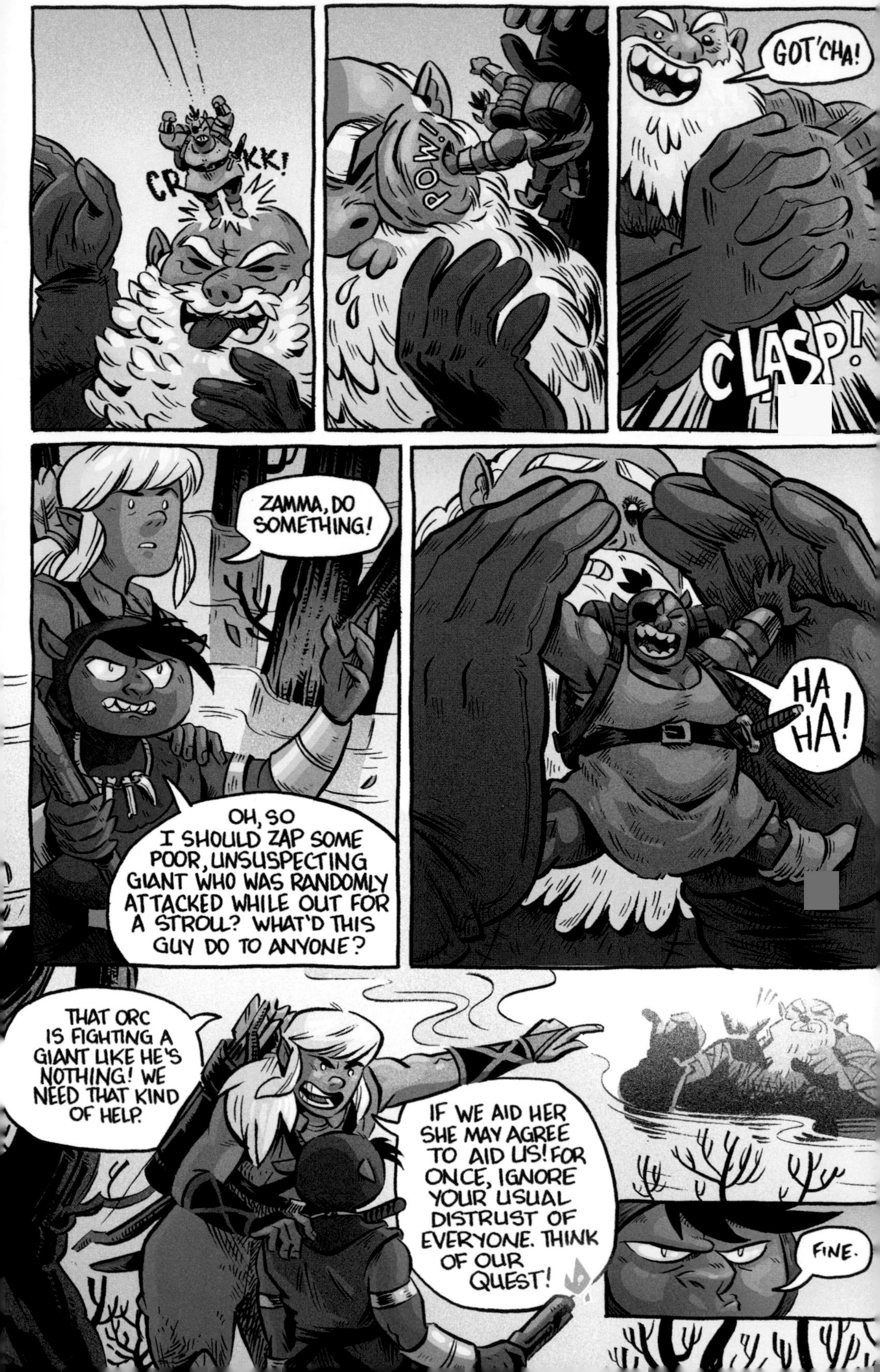
CR
KK!
POW!
GOT'CHA!
CLASP!
ZAMMA, DO SOMETHING!
OH, SO I SHOULD ZAP SOME POOR, UNSUSPECTING GIANT WHO WAS RANDOMLY ATTACKED WHILE OUT FOR A STROLL? WHAT'D THIS GUY DO TO ANYONE?
HA HA!
THAT ORC IS FIGHTING A GIANT LIKE HE'S NOTHING! WE NEED THAT KIND OF HELP.
IF WE AID HER SHE MAY AGREE TO AID US! FOR ONCE, IGNORE YOUR USUAL DISTRUST OF EVERYONE. THINK OF OUR QUEST!
FINE.

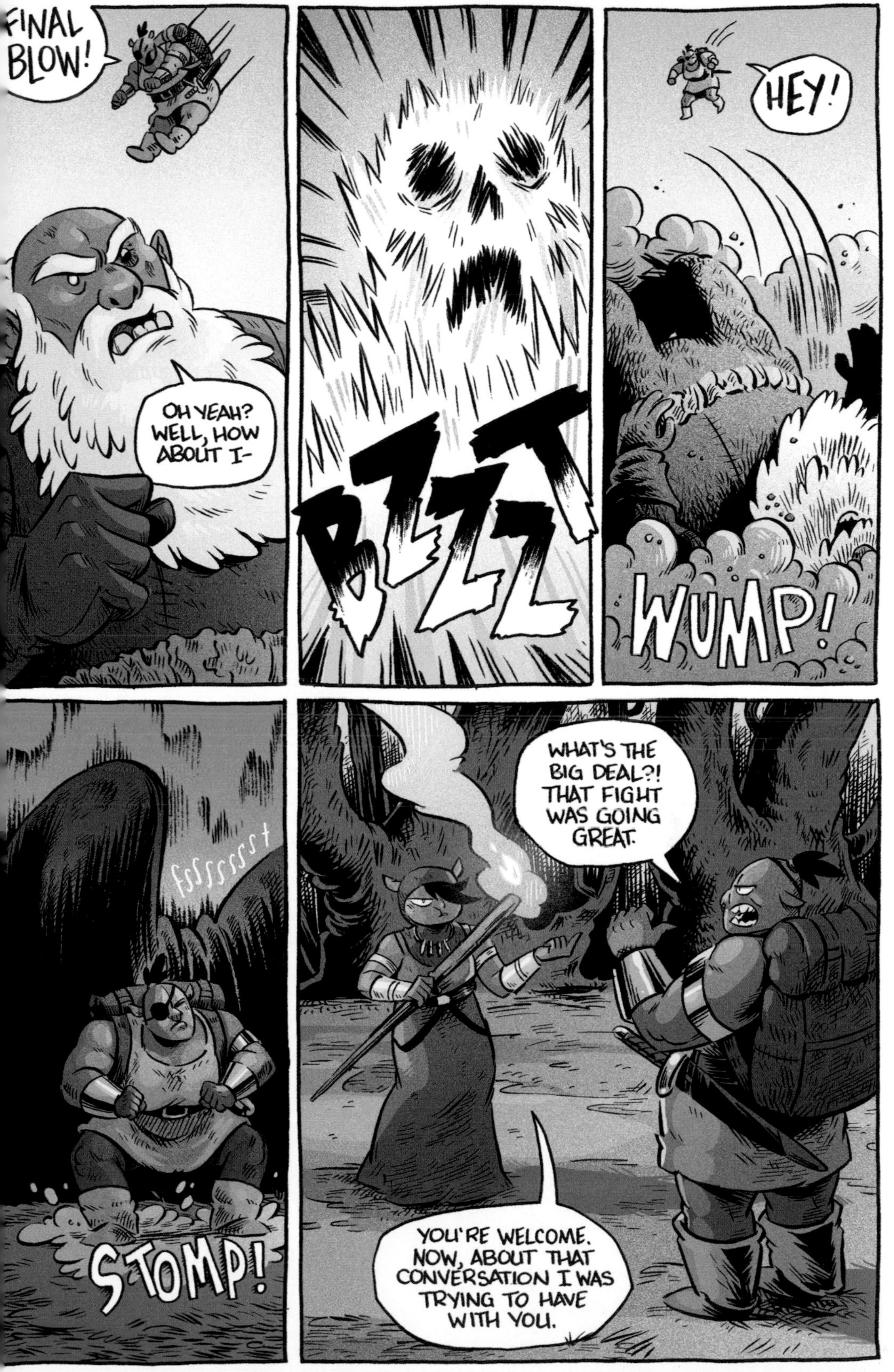
FINAL BLOW!
OH YEAH? WELL, HOW ABOUT I-
BZZT
HEY!
WUMP!
fssssssst
STOMP!
WHAT'S THE BIG DEAL?! THAT FIGHT WAS GOING GREAT.
YOU'RE WELCOME. NOW, ABOUT THAT CONVERSATION I WAS TRYING TO HAVE WITH YOU.

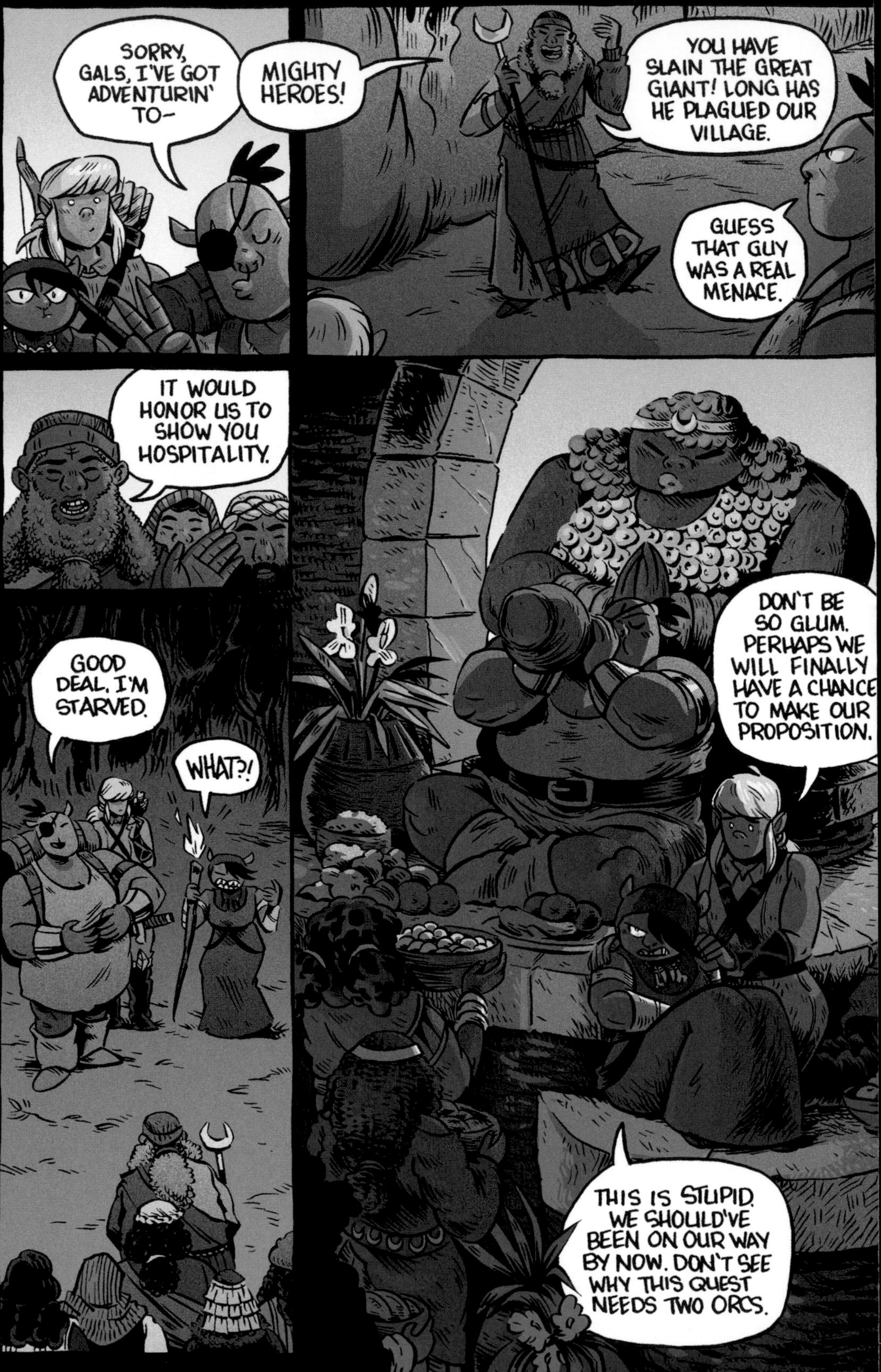
SORRY, GALS, I'VE GOT ADVENTURIN' TO–
MIGHTY HEROES!
YOU HAVE SLAIN THE GREAT GIANT! LONG HAS HE PLAGUED OUR VILLAGE.
GUESS THAT GUY WAS A REAL MENACE.
IT WOULD HONOR US TO SHOW YOU HOSPITALITY.
GOOD DEAL. I'M STARVED.
WHAT?!
DON'T BE SO GLUM. PERHAPS WE WILL FINALLY HAVE A CHANCE TO MAKE OUR PROPOSITION.
THIS IS STUPID. WE SHOULD'VE BEEN ON OUR WAY BY NOW. DON'T SEE WHY THIS QUEST NEEDS TWO ORCS.

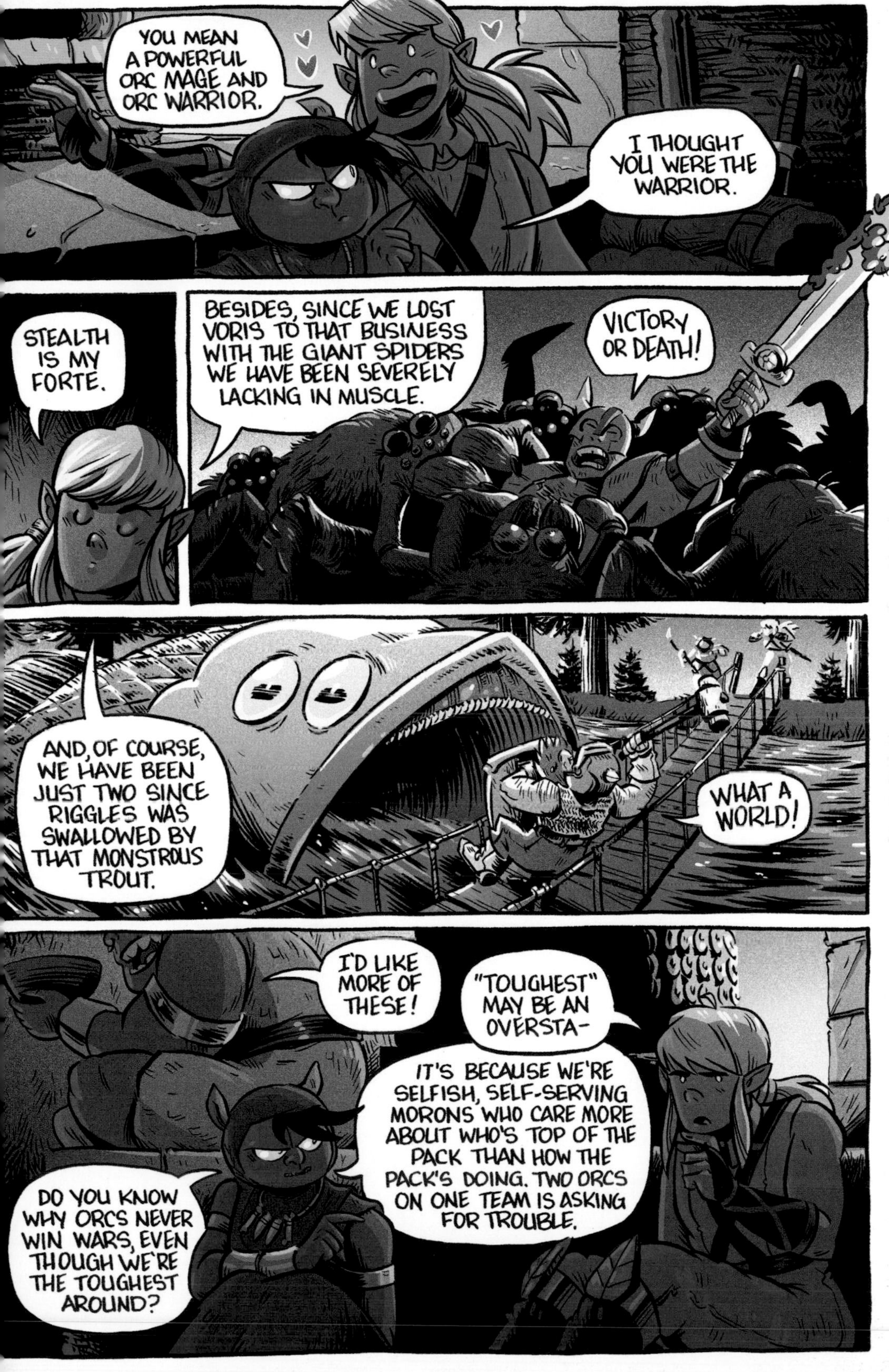
YOU MEAN A POWERFUL ORC MAGE AND ORC WARRIOR.
I THOUGHT YOU WERE THE WARRIOR.
STEALTH IS MY FORTE.
BESIDES, SINCE WE LOST VORIS TO THAT BUSINESS WITH THE GIANT SPIDERS WE HAVE BEEN SEVERELY LACKING IN MUSCLE.
VICTORY OR DEATH!
AND, OF COURSE, WE HAVE BEEN JUST TWO SINCE RIGGLES WAS SWALLOWED BY THAT MONSTROUS TROUT.
WHAT A WORLD!
I'D LIKE MORE OF THESE!
"TOUGHEST" MAY BE AN OVERSTA-
DO YOU KNOW WHY ORCS NEVER WIN WARS, EVEN THOUGH WE'RE THE TOUGHEST AROUND?
IT'S BECAUSE WE'RE SELFISH, SELF-SERVING MORONS WHO CARE MORE ABOUT WHO'S TOP OF THE PACK THAN HOW THE PACK'S DOING. TWO ORCS ON ONE TEAM IS ASKING FOR TROUBLE.

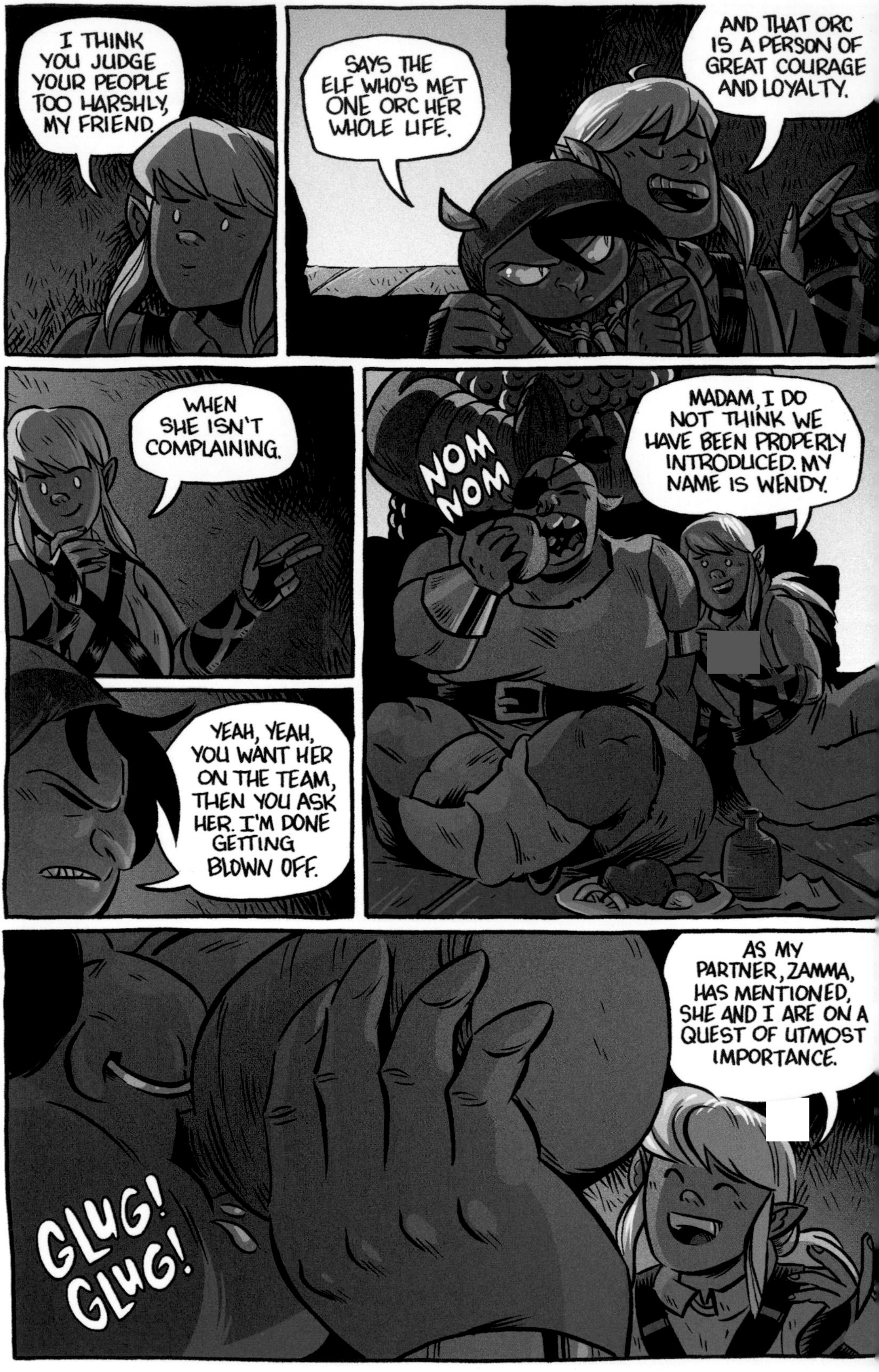
I THINK YOU JUDGE YOUR PEOPLE TOO HARSHLY, MY FRIEND.
SAYS THE ELF WHO'S MET ONE ORC HER WHOLE LIFE.
AND THAT ORC IS A PERSON OF GREAT COURAGE AND LOYALTY.
WHEN SHE ISN'T COMPLAINING.
YEAH, YEAH, YOU WANT HER ON THE TEAM, THEN YOU ASK HER. I'M DONE GETTING BLOWN OFF.
NOM NOM
MADAM, I DO NOT THINK WE HAVE BEEN PROPERLY INTRODUCED. MY NAME IS WENDY.
GLUG! GLUG!
AS MY PARTNER, ZAMMA, HAS MENTIONED, SHE AND I ARE ON A QUEST OF UTMOST IMPORTANCE.

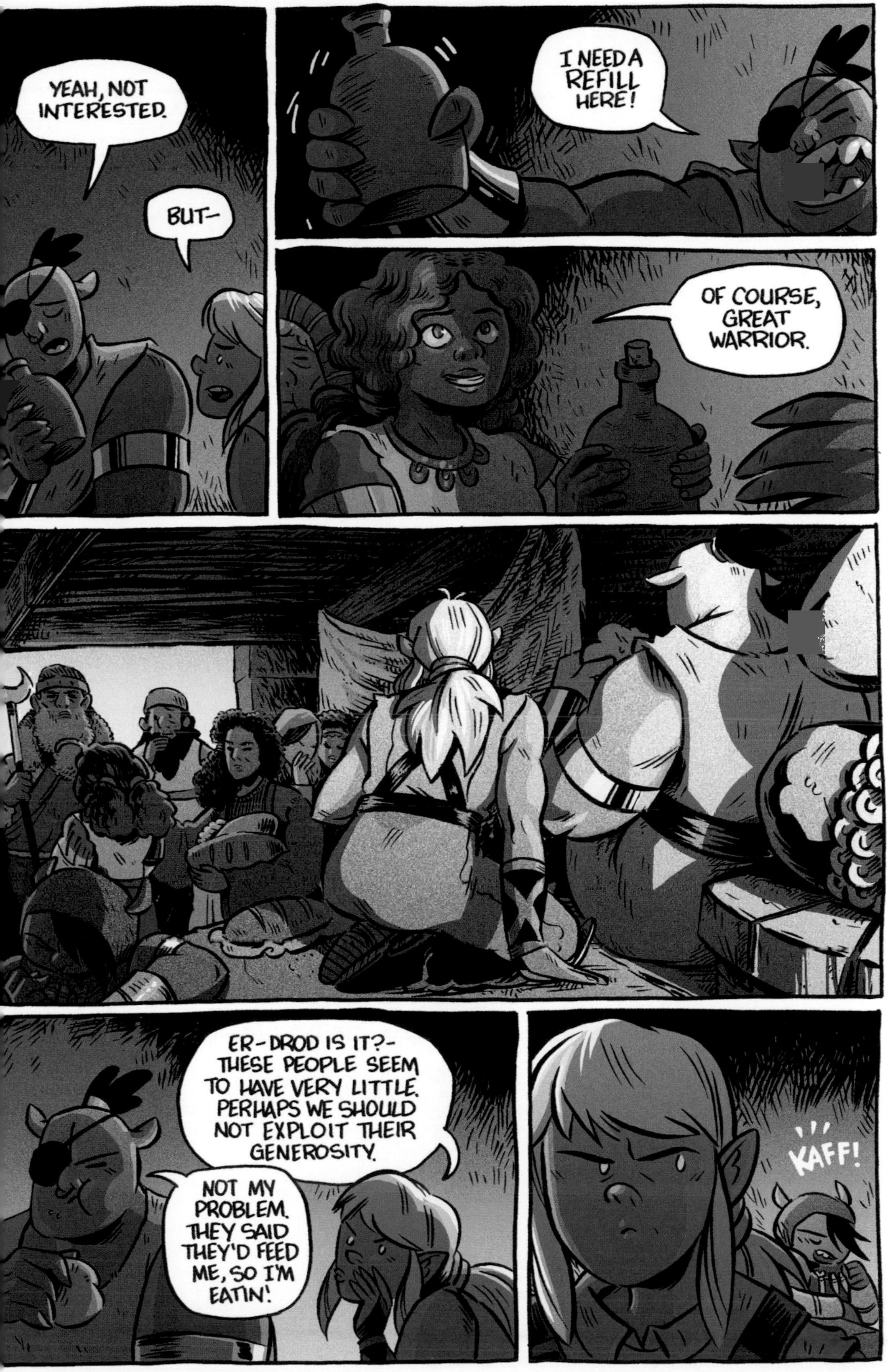
YEAH, NOT INTERESTED.
BUT-
I NEED A REFILL HERE!
OF COURSE, GREAT WARRIOR.
ER-DROD IS IT?- THESE PEOPLE SEEM TO HAVE VERY LITTLE. PERHAPS WE SHOULD NOT EXPLOIT THEIR GENEROSITY.
NOT MY PROBLEM. THEY SAID THEY'D FEED ME, SO I'M EATIN'!
KAFF!

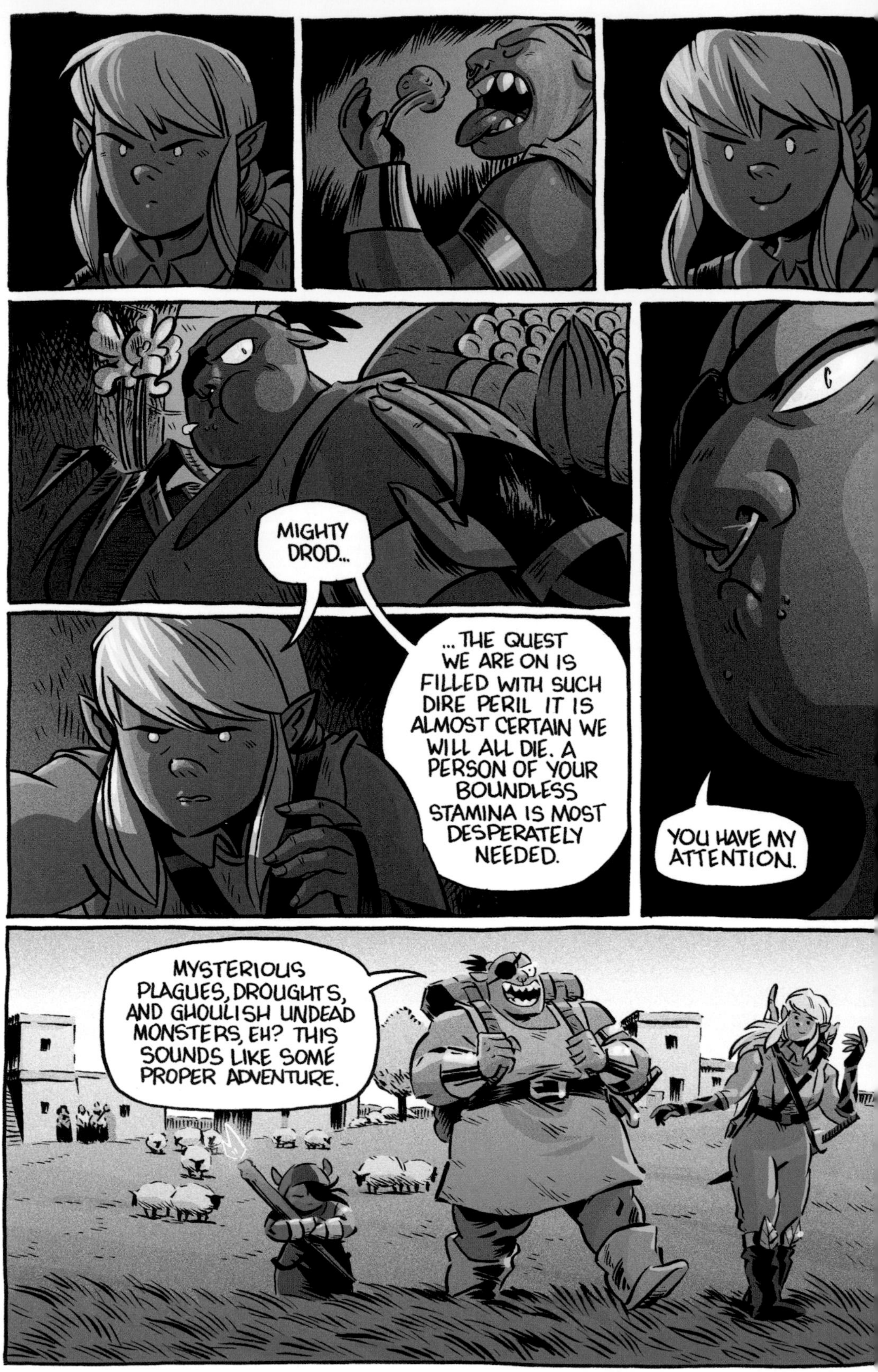
MIGHTY DROD...
...THE QUEST WE ARE ON IS FILLED WITH SUCH DIRE PERIL IT IS ALMOST CERTAIN WE WILL ALL DIE. A PERSON OF YOUR BOUNDLESS STAMINA IS MOST DESPERATELY NEEDED.
YOU HAVE MY ATTENTION.
MYSTERIOUS PLAGUES, DROUGHTS, AND GHOULISH UNDEAD MONSTERS, EH? THIS SOUNDS LIKE SOME PROPER ADVENTURE.

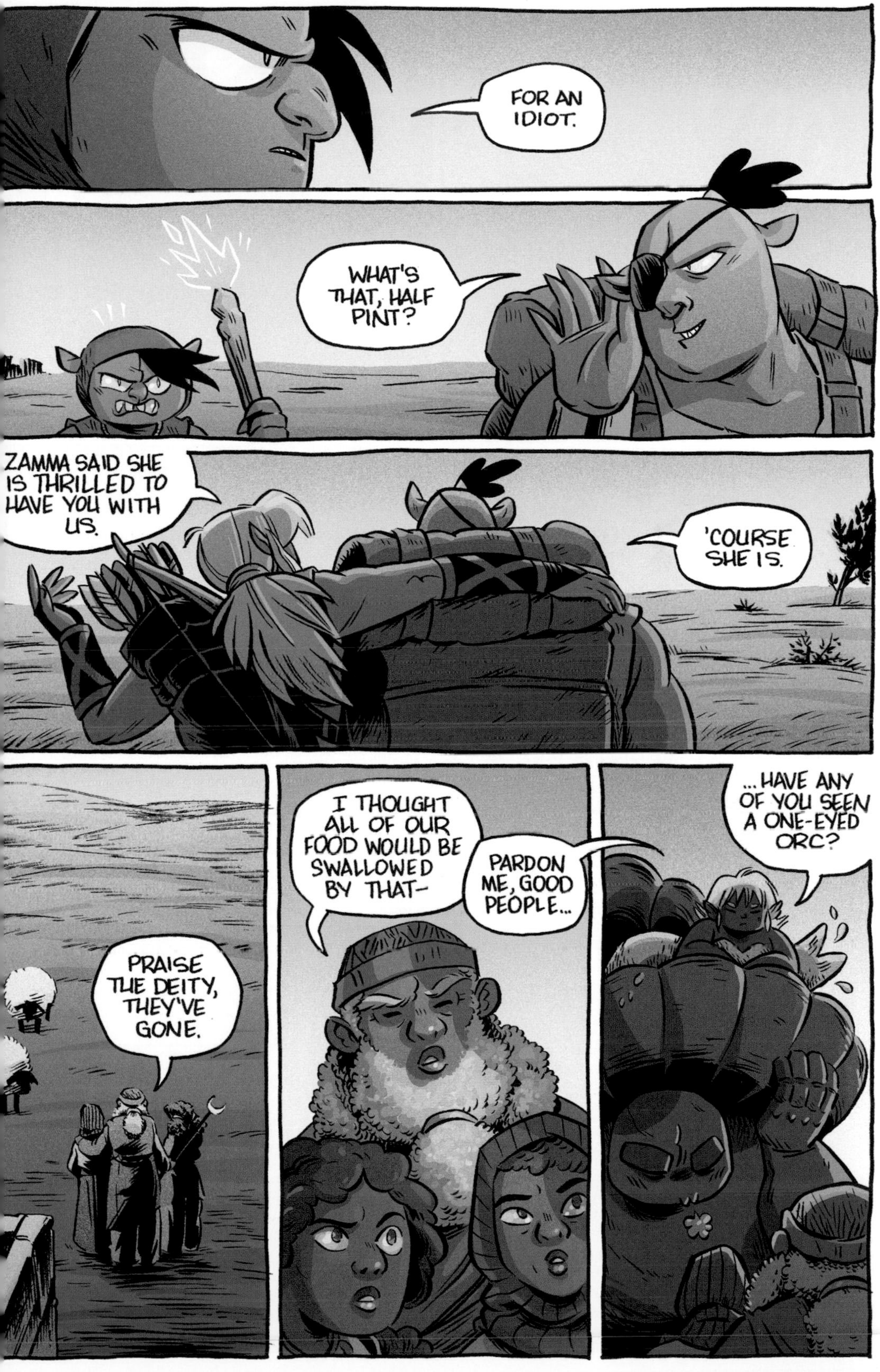
FOR AN IDIOT.
WHAT'S THAT, HALF PINT?
ZAMMA SAID SHE IS THRILLED TO HAVE YOU WITH US.
'COURSE SHE IS.
PRAISE THE DEITY, THEY'VE GONE.
I THOUGHT ALL OF OUR FOOD WOULD BE SWALLOWED BY THAT-
PARDON ME, GOOD PEOPLE...
...HAVE ANY OF YOU SEEN A ONE-EYED ORC?

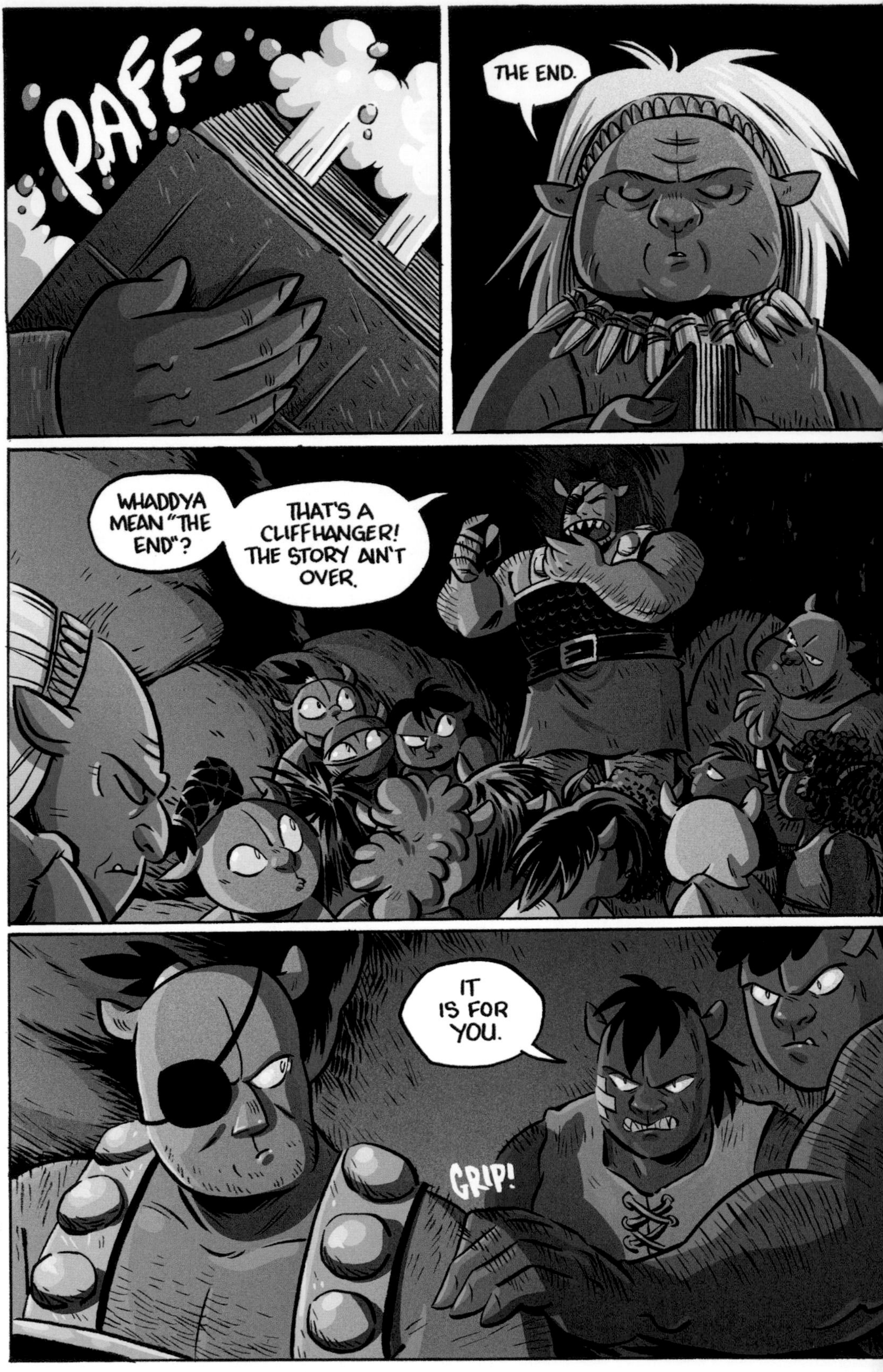
PAFF
THE END.
WHADDYA MEAN "THE END"?
THAT'S A CLIFFHANGER! THE STORY AIN'T OVER.
IT IS FOR YOU.
GRIP!

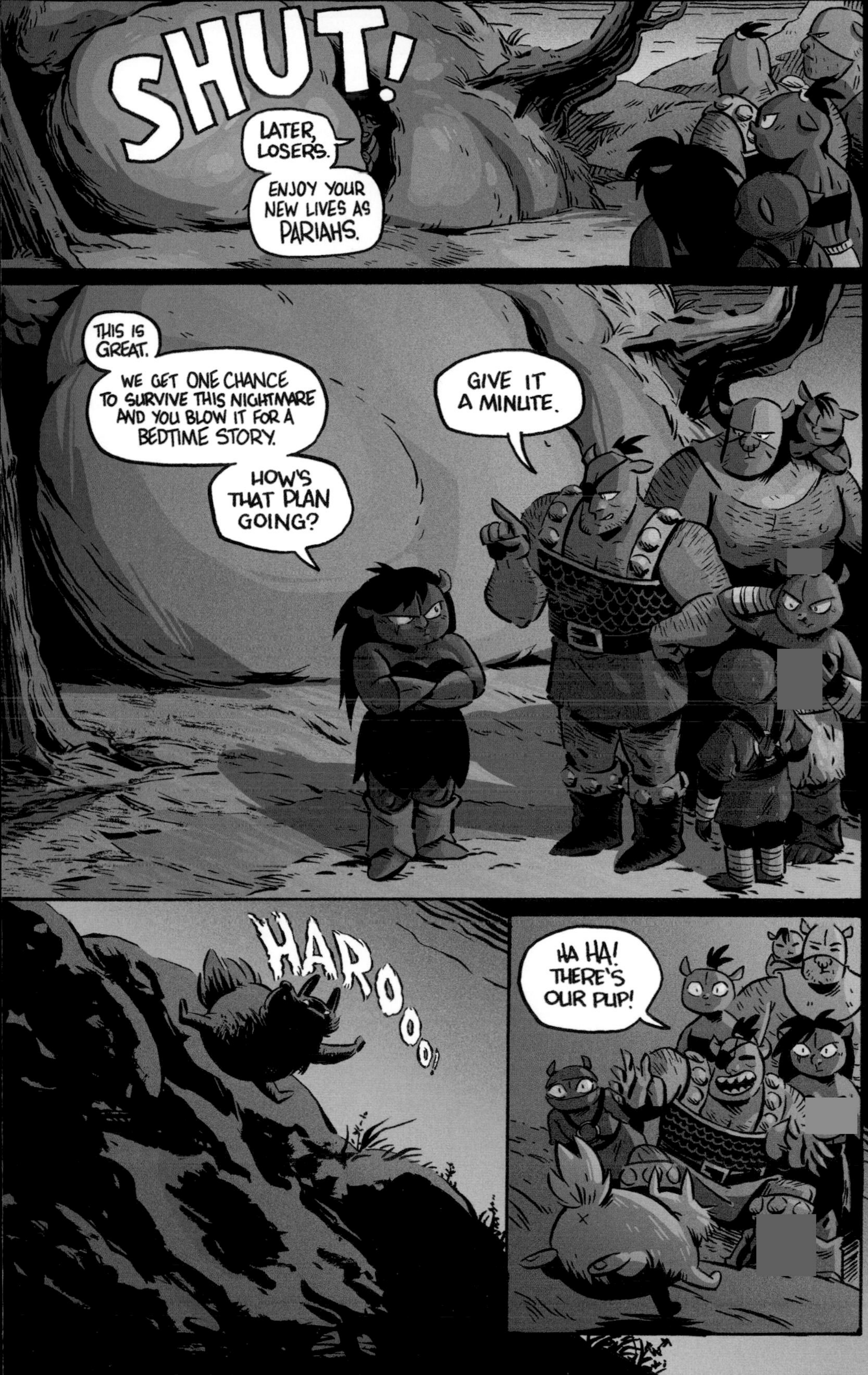
SHUT!
LATER, LOSERS.
ENJOY YOUR NEW LIVES AS PARIAHS.
THIS IS GREAT.
WE GET ONE CHANCE TO SURVIVE THIS NIGHTMARE AND YOU BLOW IT FOR A BEDTIME STORY.
HOW'S THAT PLAN GOING?
GIVE IT A MINUTE.
HAROOOO!!
HA HA! THERE'S OUR PUP!

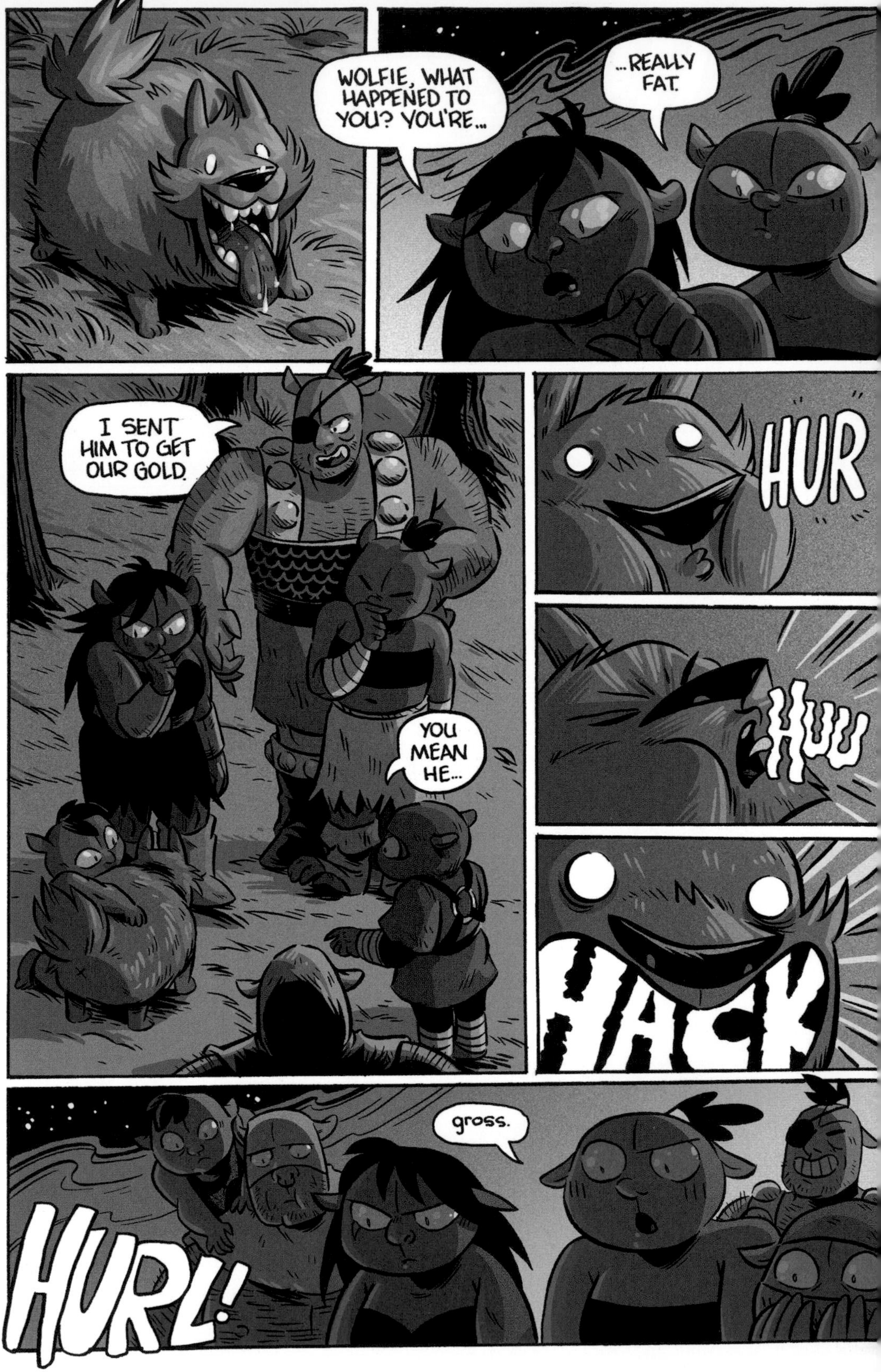
WOLFIE, WHAT HAPPENED TO YOU? YOU'RE...
...REALLY FAT.
I SENT HIM TO GET OUR GOLD.
YOU MEAN HE...
HUR
HUU
HACK
gross.
HURL!

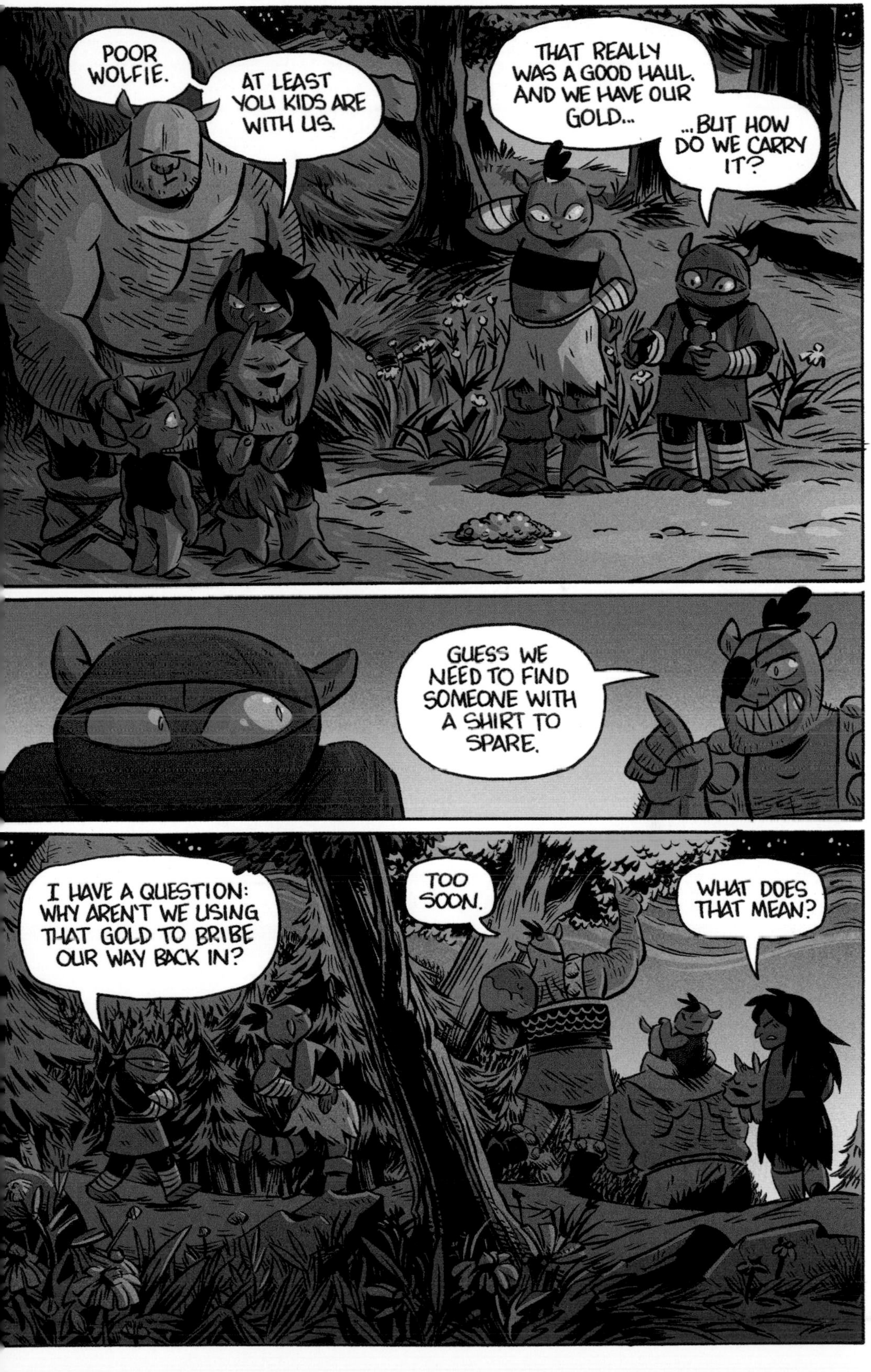
POOR WOLFIE.
AT LEAST YOU KIDS ARE WITH US.
THAT REALLY WAS A GOOD HAUL. AND WE HAVE OUR GOLD...
...BUT HOW DO WE CARRY IT?
GUESS WE NEED TO FIND SOMEONE WITH A SHIRT TO SPARE.
I HAVE A QUESTION: WHY AREN'T WE USING THAT GOLD TO BRIBE OUR WAY BACK IN?
TOO SOON.
WHAT DOES THAT MEAN?

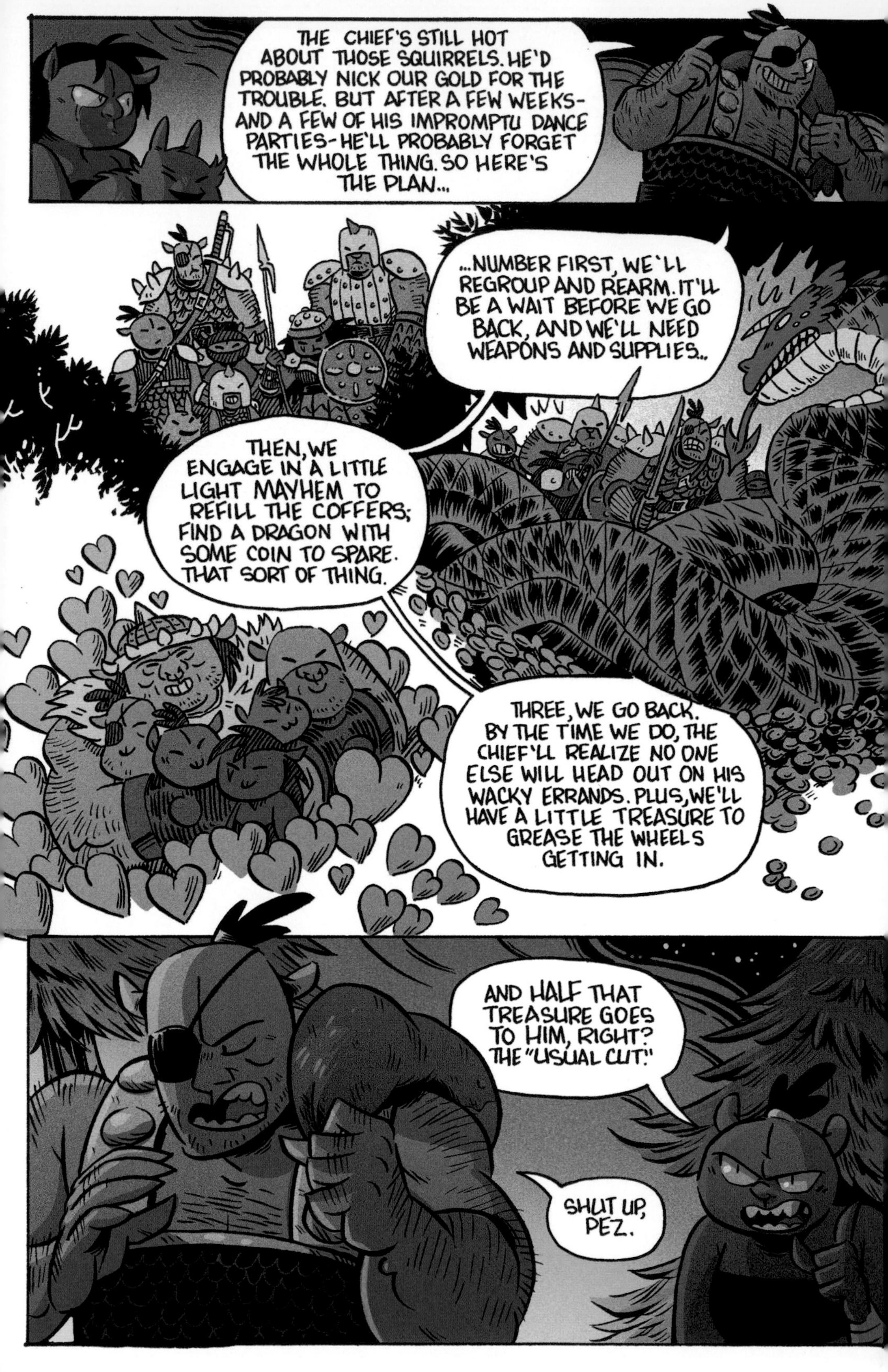
THE CHIEF'S STILL HOT ABOUT THOSE SQUIRRELS. HE'D PROBABLY NICK OUR GOLD FOR THE TROUBLE. BUT AFTER A FEW WEEKS- AND A FEW OF HIS IMPROMPTU DANCE PARTIES- HE'LL PROBABLY FORGET THE WHOLE THING. SO HERE'S THE PLAN...
...NUMBER FIRST, WE'LL REGROUP AND REARM. IT'LL BE A WAIT BEFORE WE GO BACK, AND WE'LL NEED WEAPONS AND SUPPLIES...
THEN, WE ENGAGE IN A LITTLE LIGHT MAYHEM TO REFILL THE COFFERS; FIND A DRAGON WITH SOME COIN TO SPARE. THAT SORT OF THING.
THREE, WE GO BACK. BY THE TIME WE DO, THE CHIEF'LL REALIZE NO ONE ELSE WILL HEAD OUT ON HIS WACKY ERRANDS. PLUS, WE'LL HAVE A LITTLE TREASURE TO GREASE THE WHEELS GETTING IN.
AND HALF THAT TREASURE GOES TO HIM, RIGHT? THE "USUAL CUT."
SHUT UP, PEZ.

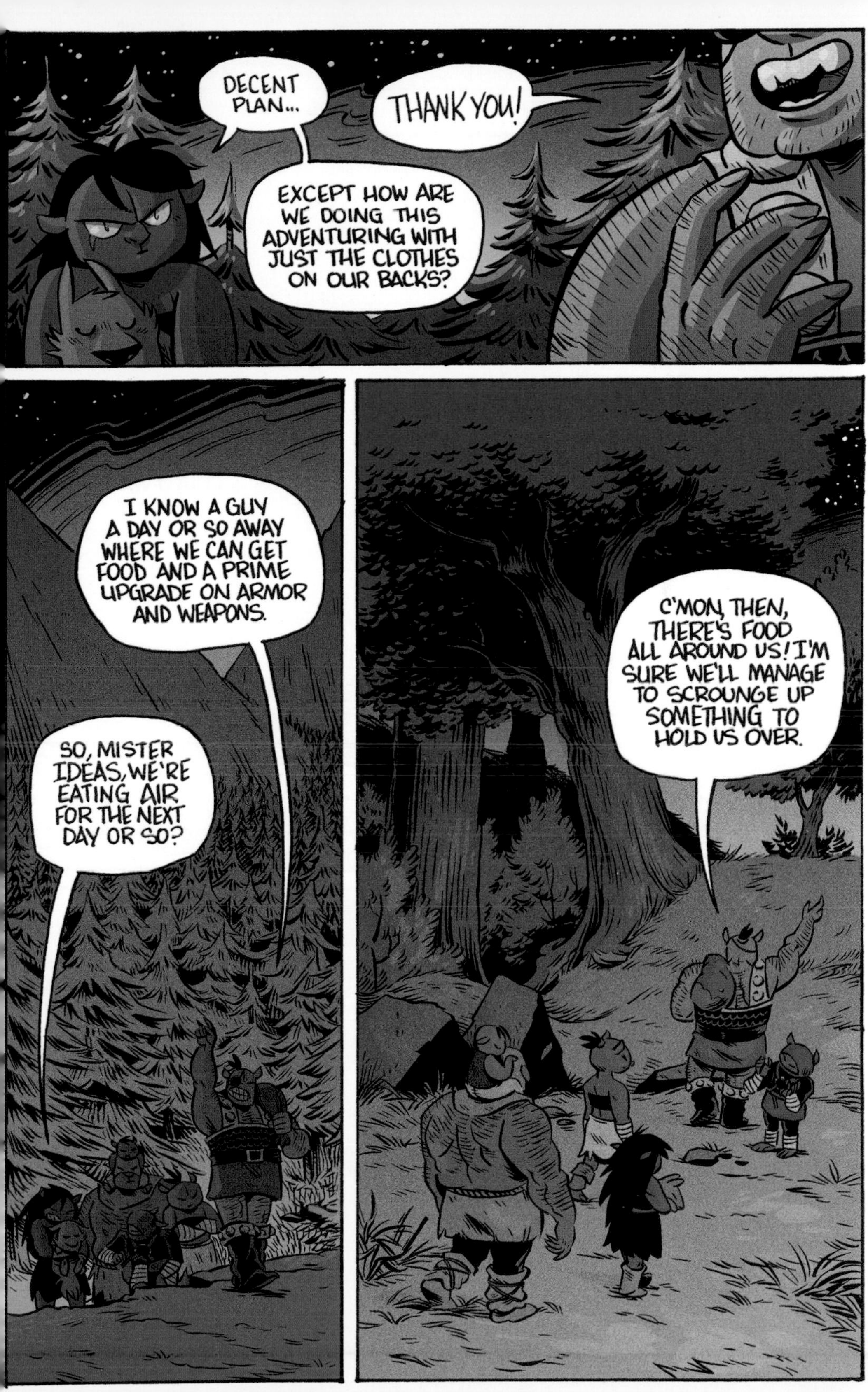
DECENT PLAN...
THANK YOU!
EXCEPT HOW ARE WE DOING THIS ADVENTURING WITH JUST THE CLOTHES ON OUR BACKS?
I KNOW A GUY A DAY OR SO AWAY WHERE WE CAN GET FOOD AND A PRIME UPGRADE ON ARMOR AND WEAPONS.
SO, MISTER IDEAS, WE'RE EATING AIR FOR THE NEXT DAY OR SO?
C'MON, THEN, THERE'S FOOD ALL AROUND US! I'M SURE WE'LL MANAGE TO SCROUNGE UP SOMETHING TO HOLD US OVER.

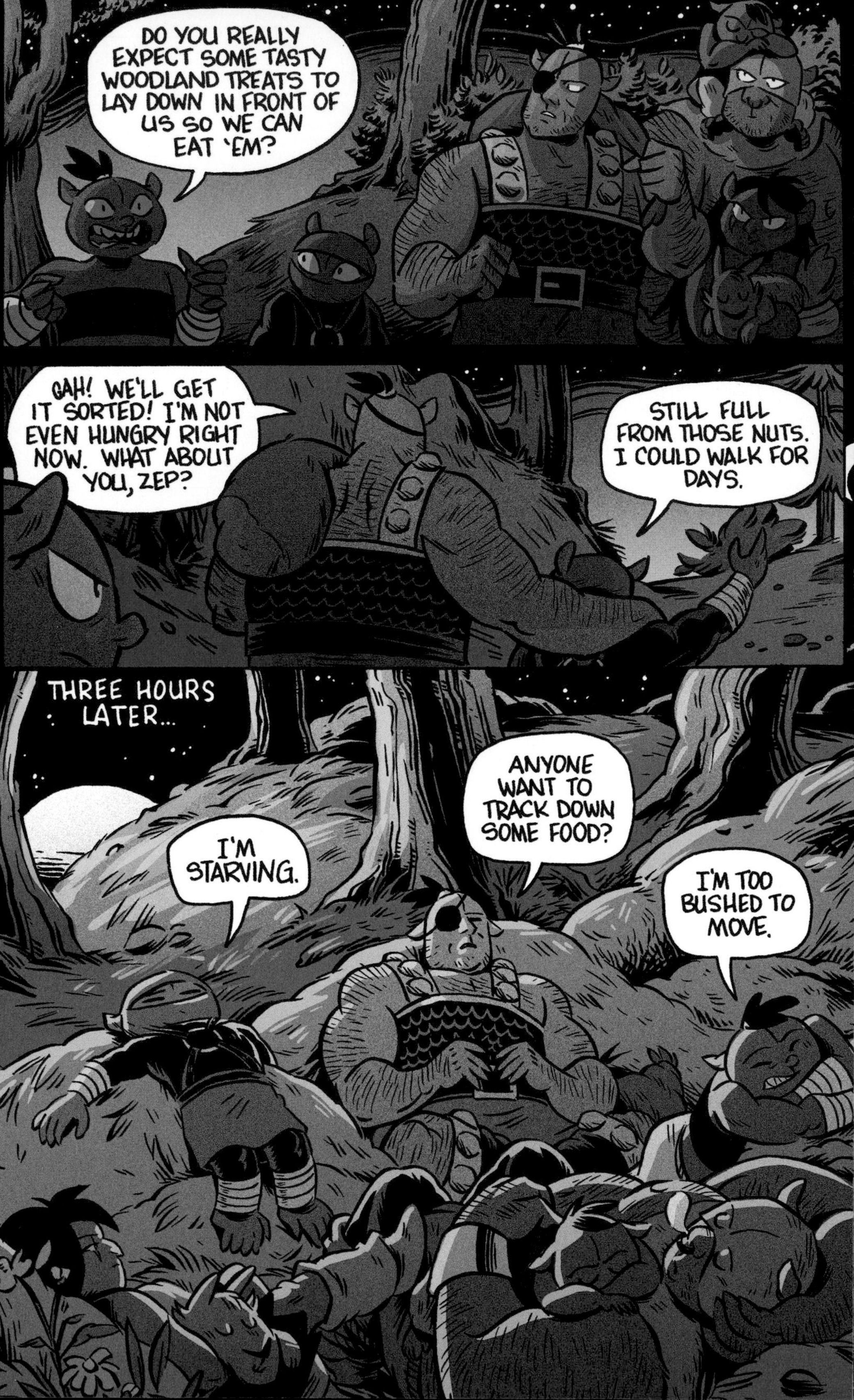
DO YOU REALLY EXPECT SOME TASTY WOODLAND TREATS TO LAY DOWN IN FRONT OF US SO WE CAN EAT 'EM?
GAH! WE'LL GET IT SORTED! I'M NOT EVEN HUNGRY RIGHT NOW. WHAT ABOUT YOU, ZEP?
STILL FULL FROM THOSE NUTS. I COULD WALK FOR DAYS.
THREE HOURS LATER...
I'M STARVING.
ANYONE WANT TO TRACK DOWN SOME FOOD?
I'M TOO BUSHED TO MOVE.

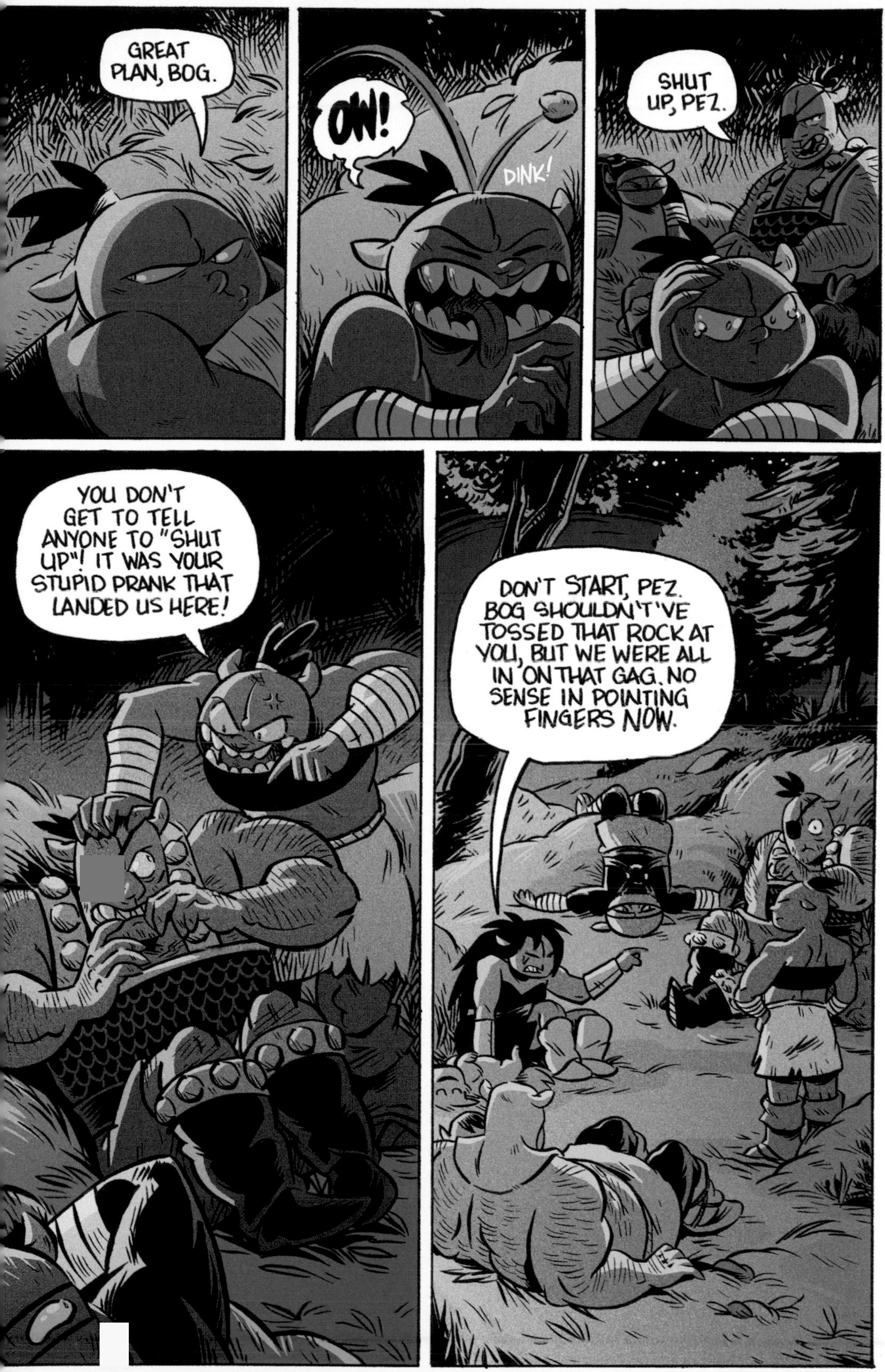
GREAT PLAN, BOG.
OW!
DINK!
SHUT UP, PEZ.
YOU DON'T GET TO TELL ANYONE TO "SHUT UP"! IT WAS YOUR STUPID PRANK THAT LANDED US HERE!
DON'T START, PEZ. BOG SHOULDN'T'VE TOSSED THAT ROCK AT YOU, BUT WE WERE ALL IN ON THAT GAG. NO SENSE IN POINTING FINGERS NOW.

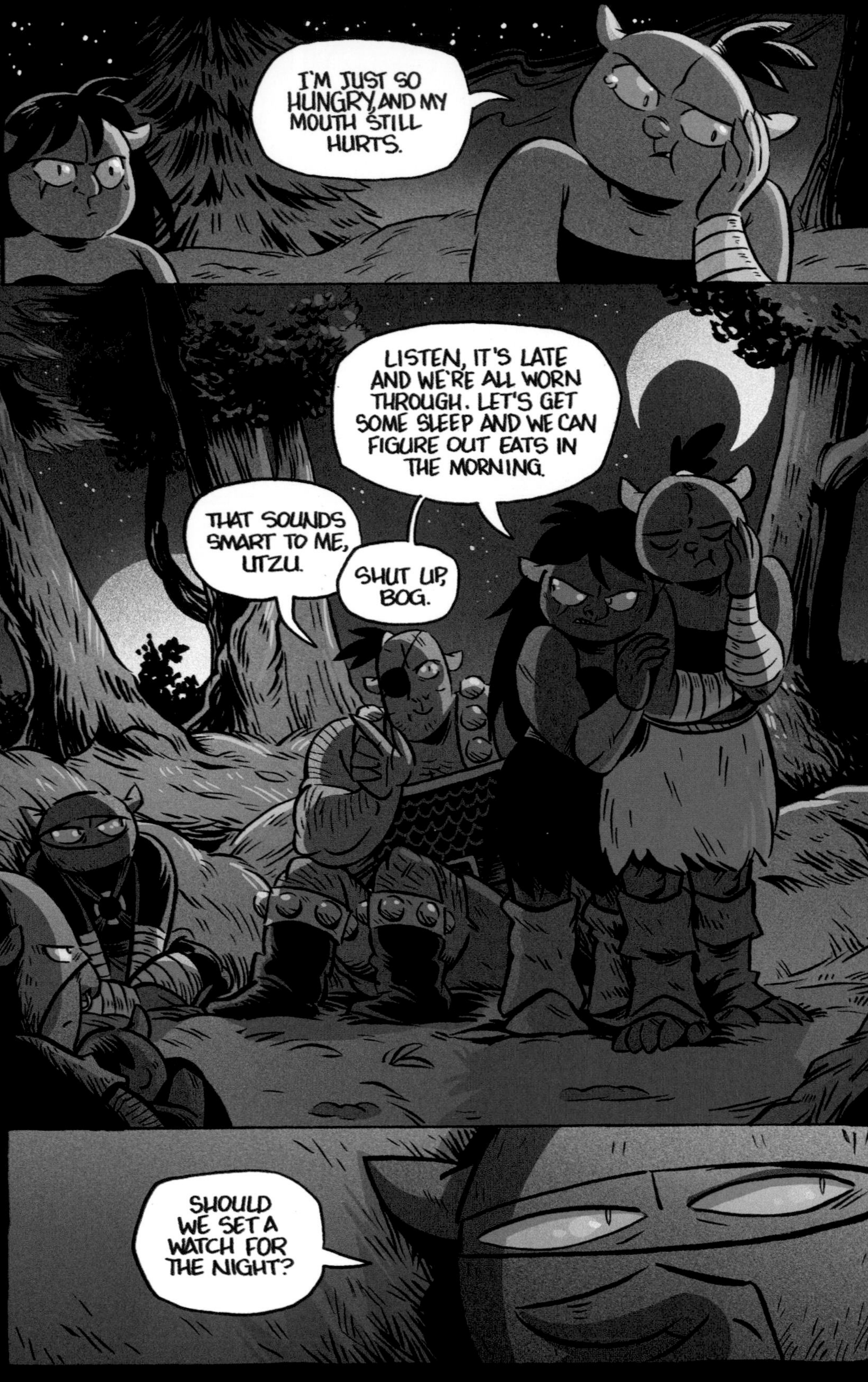
I'M JUST SO HUNGRY, AND MY MOUTH STILL HURTS.
LISTEN, IT'S LATE AND WE'RE ALL WORN THROUGH. LET'S GET SOME SLEEP AND WE CAN FIGURE OUT EATS IN THE MORNING.
THAT SOUNDS SMART TO ME, UTZU.
SHUT UP, BOG.
SHOULD WE SET A WATCH FOR THE NIGHT?

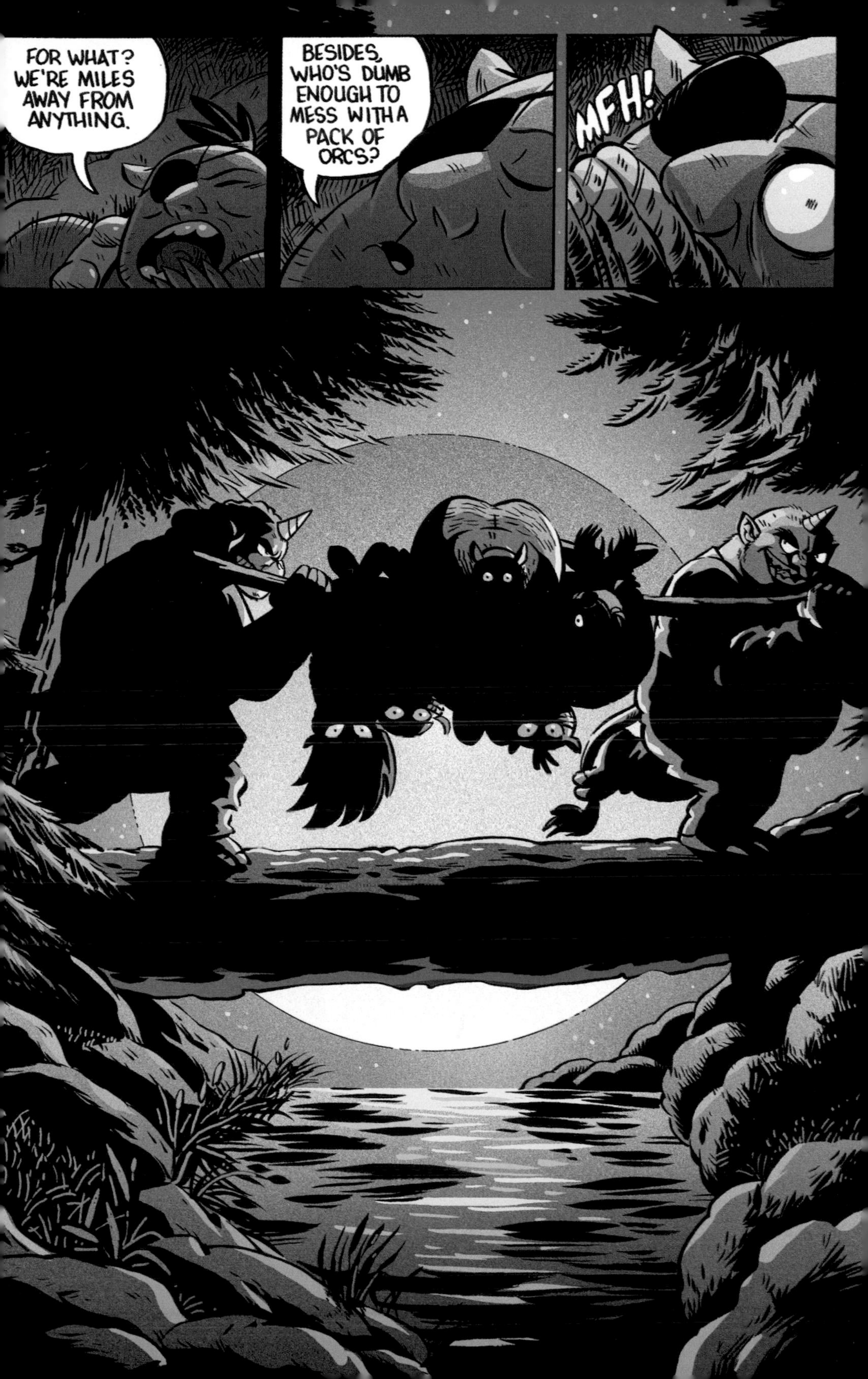
FOR WHAT? WE'RE MILES AWAY FROM ANYTHING.
BESIDES, WHO'S DUMB ENOUGH TO MESS WITH A PACK OF ORCS?
MFH!

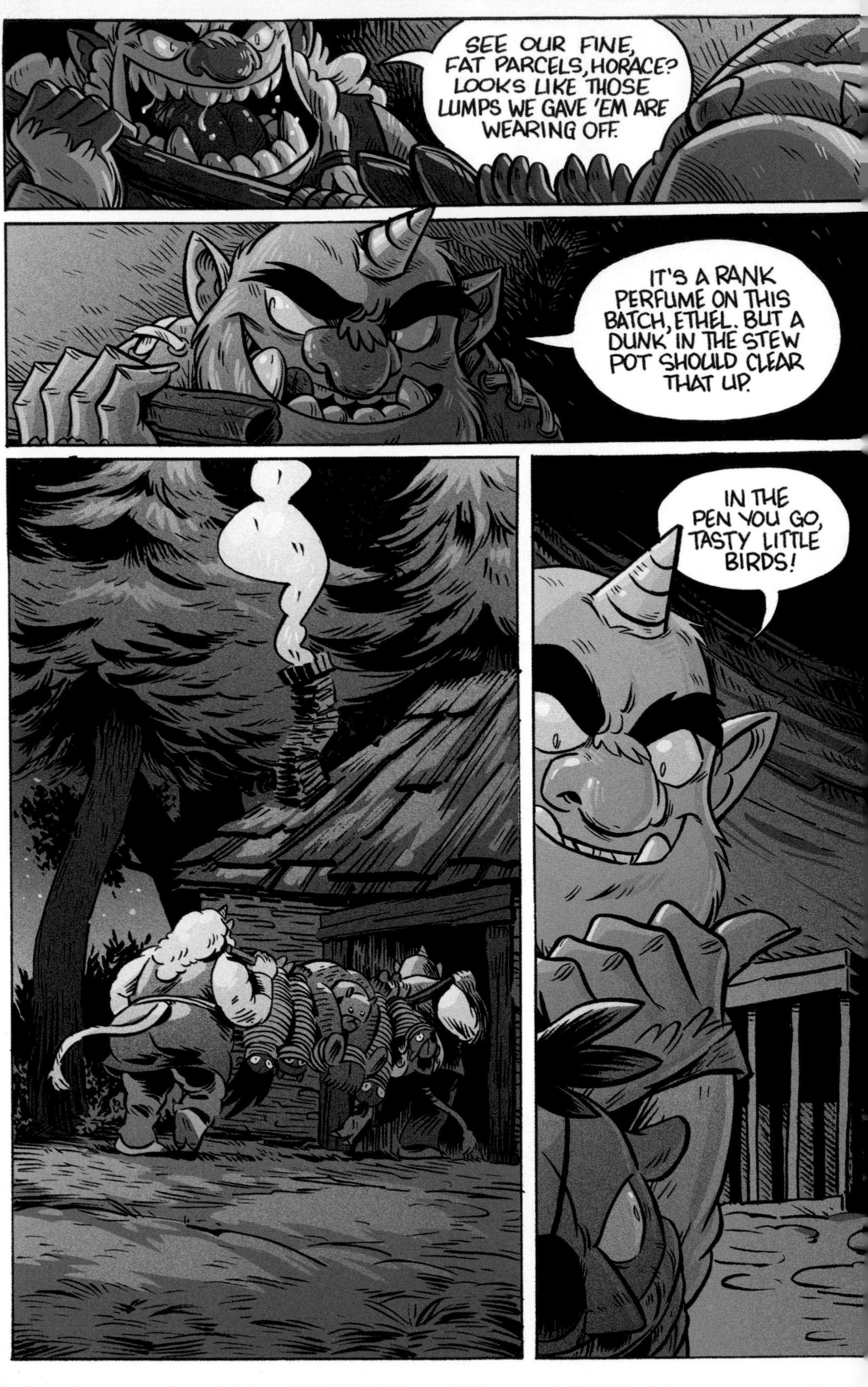
SEE OUR FINE, FAT PARCELS, HORACE? LOOKS LIKE THOSE LUMPS WE GAVE 'EM ARE WEARING OFF.
IT'S A RANK PERFUME ON THIS BATCH, ETHEL. BUT A DUNK IN THE STEW POT SHOULD CLEAR THAT UP.
IN THE PEN YOU GO, TASTY LITTLE BIRDS!

DON'T WORRY, WE'LL GET THE WATER ALL WARM AND BUBBLY FOR YOU.
DRAG!
MPH! MPH!
THINK YOU'RE GONNA EAT US, DO YOU?

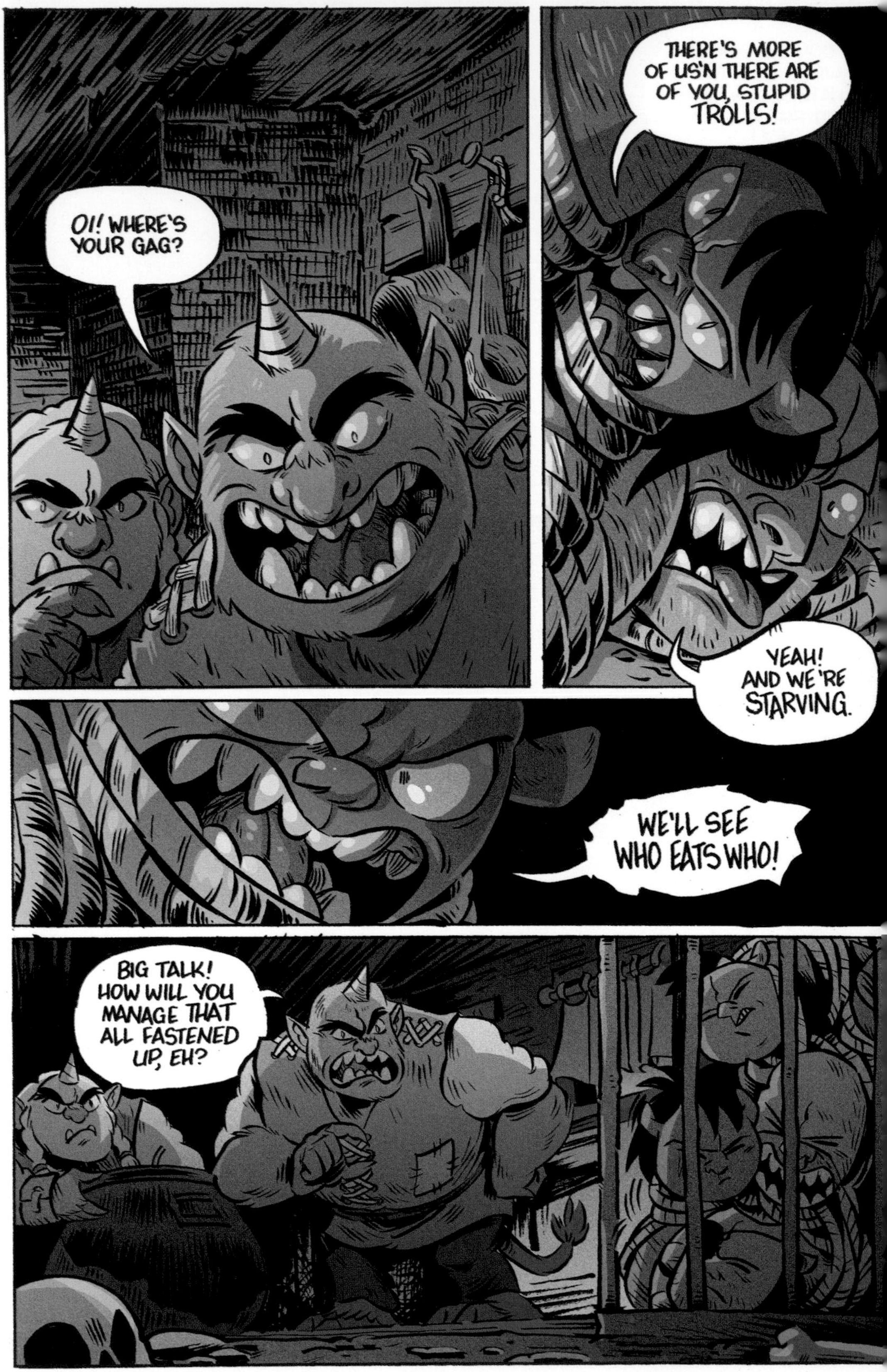
OI! WHERE'S YOUR GAG?
THERE'S MORE OF US'N THERE ARE OF YOU, STUPID TROLLS!
YEAH! AND WE'RE STARVING.
WE'LL SEE WHO EATS WHO!
BIG TALK! HOW WILL YOU MANAGE THAT ALL FASTENED UP, EH?

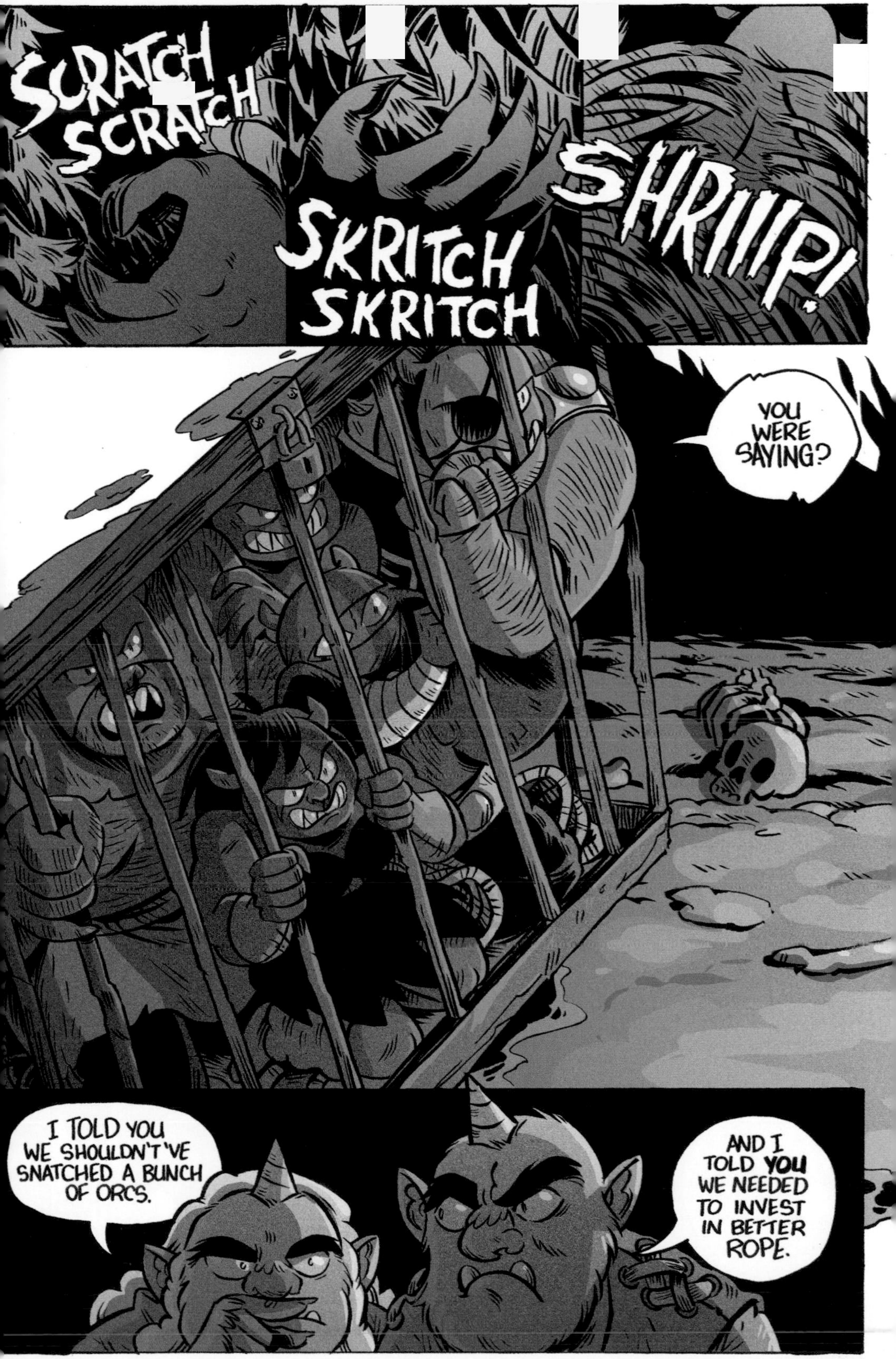
SCRATCH SCRATCH
SKRITCH SKRITCH
SHRIIIP!
YOU WERE SAYING?
I TOLD YOU WE SHOULDN'T'VE SNATCHED A BUNCH OF ORCS.
AND I TOLD **YOU** WE NEEDED TO INVEST IN BETTER ROPE.

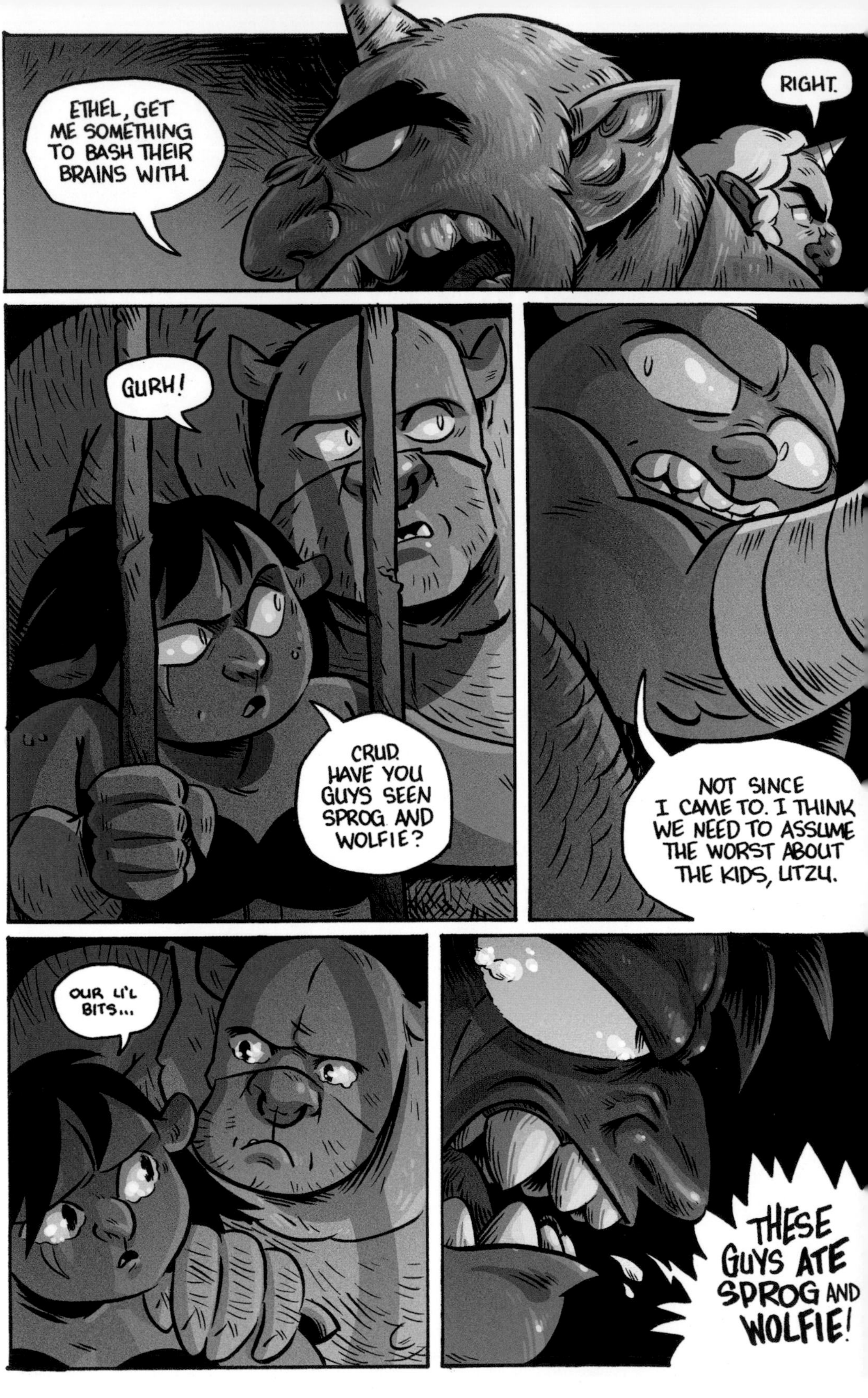
ETHEL, GET ME SOMETHING TO BASH THEIR BRAINS WITH.
RIGHT.
GURH!
CRUD. HAVE YOU GUYS SEEN SPROG AND WOLFIE?
NOT SINCE I CAME TO. I THINK WE NEED TO ASSUME THE WORST ABOUT THE KIDS, LITZU.
OUR LI'L BITS...
THESE GUYS ATE SPROG AND WOLFIE!

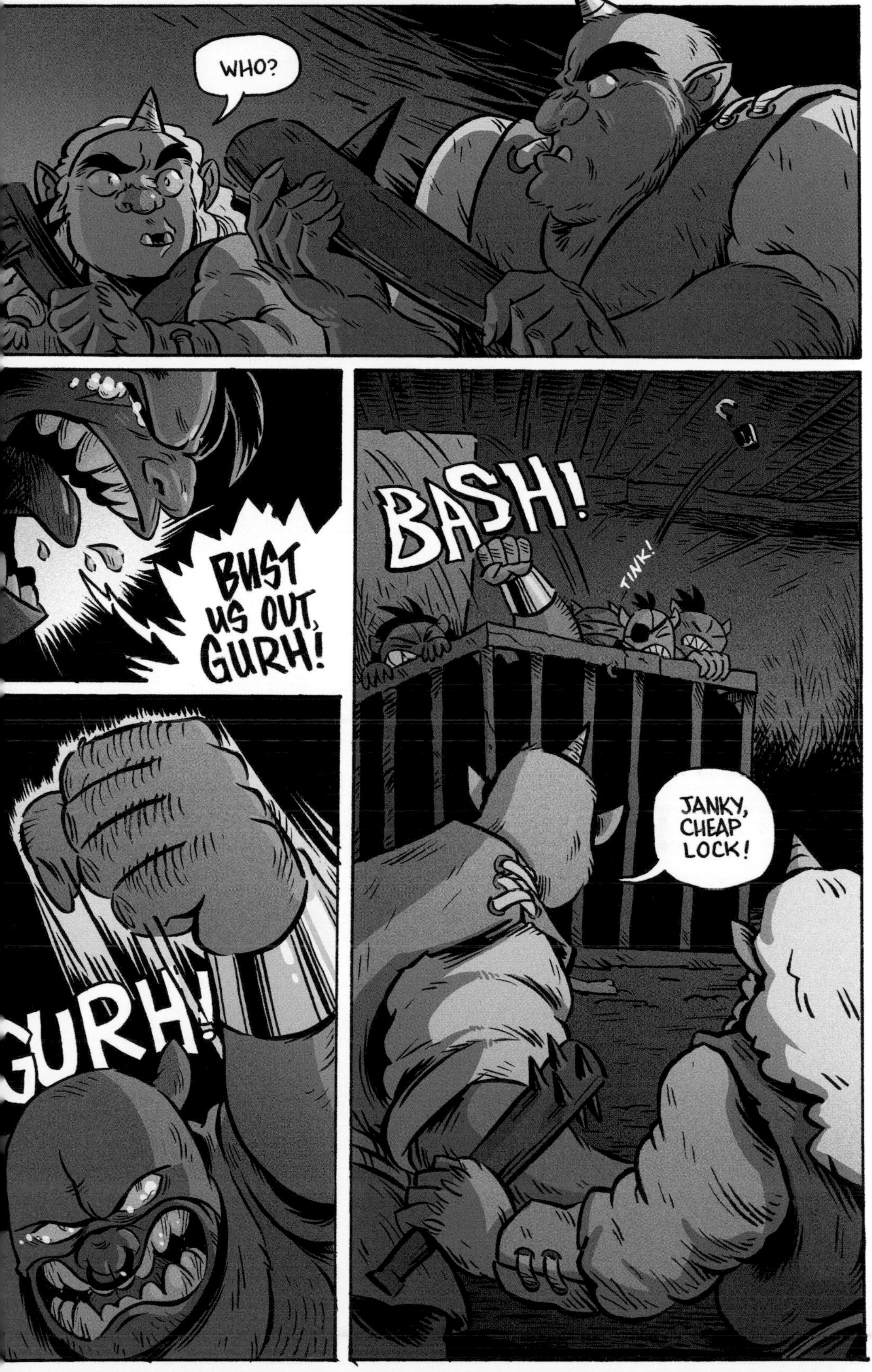
WHO?
BUST US OUT, GURH!
GURH!
BASH!
TINK!
JANKY, CHEAP LOCK!

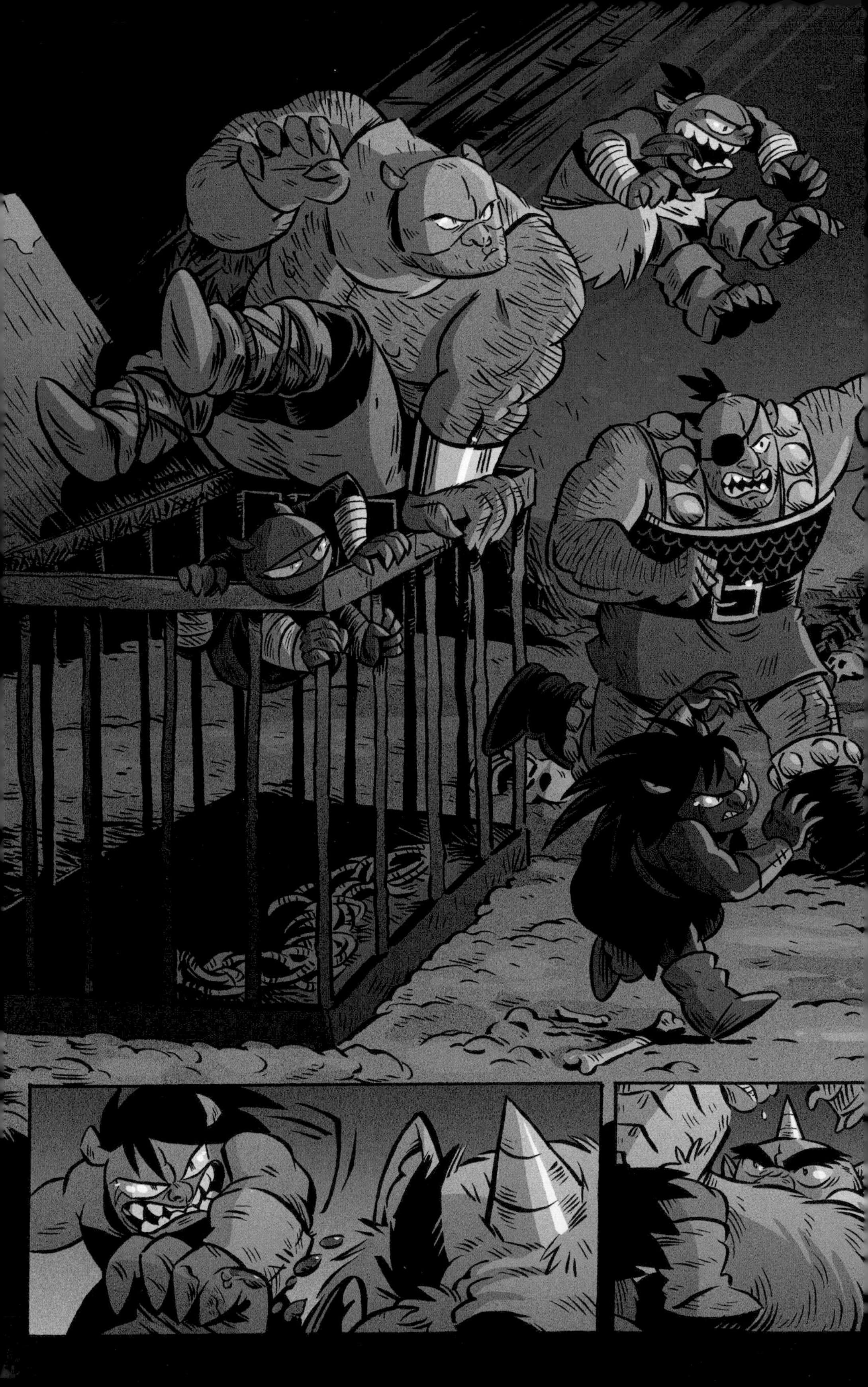

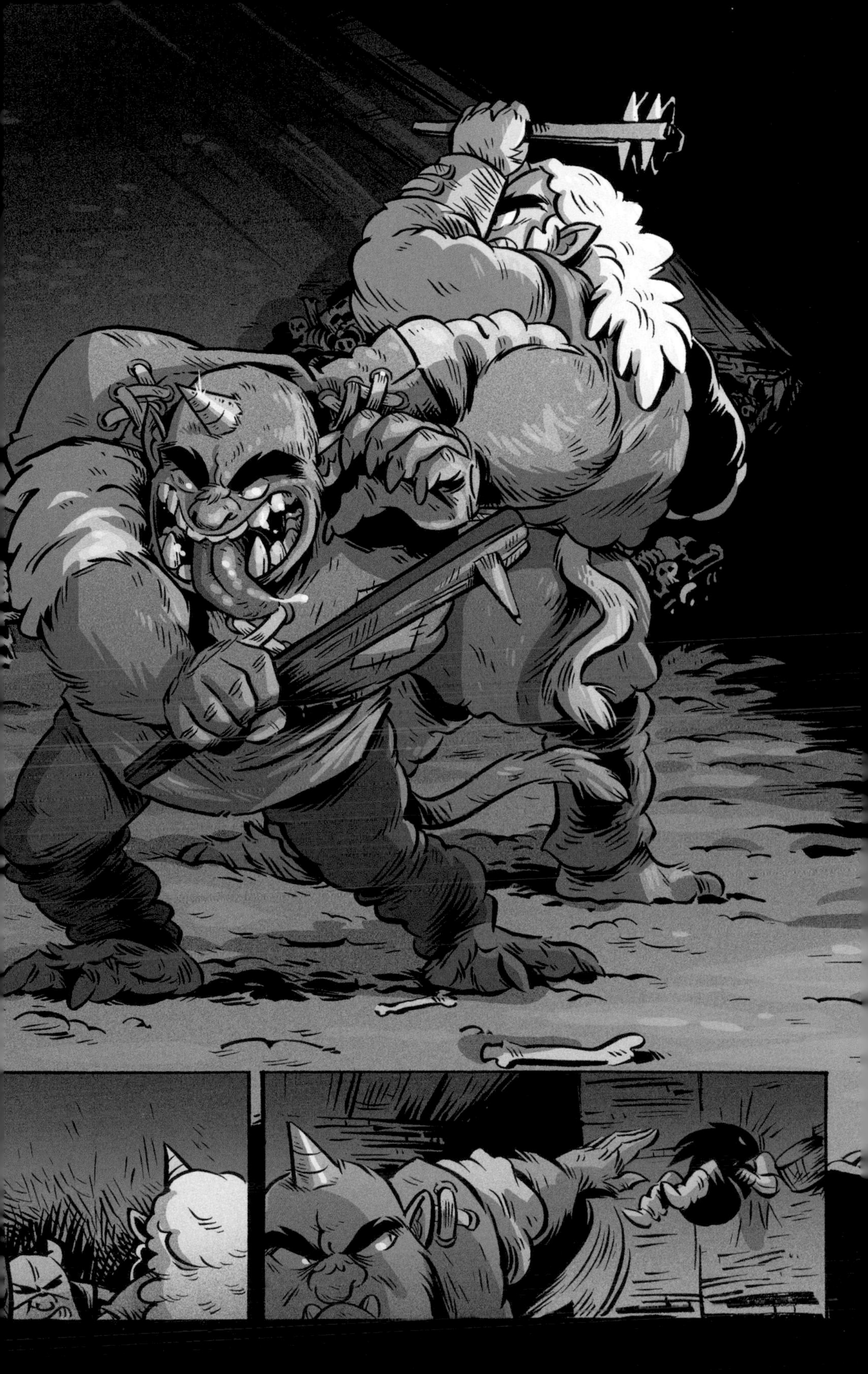

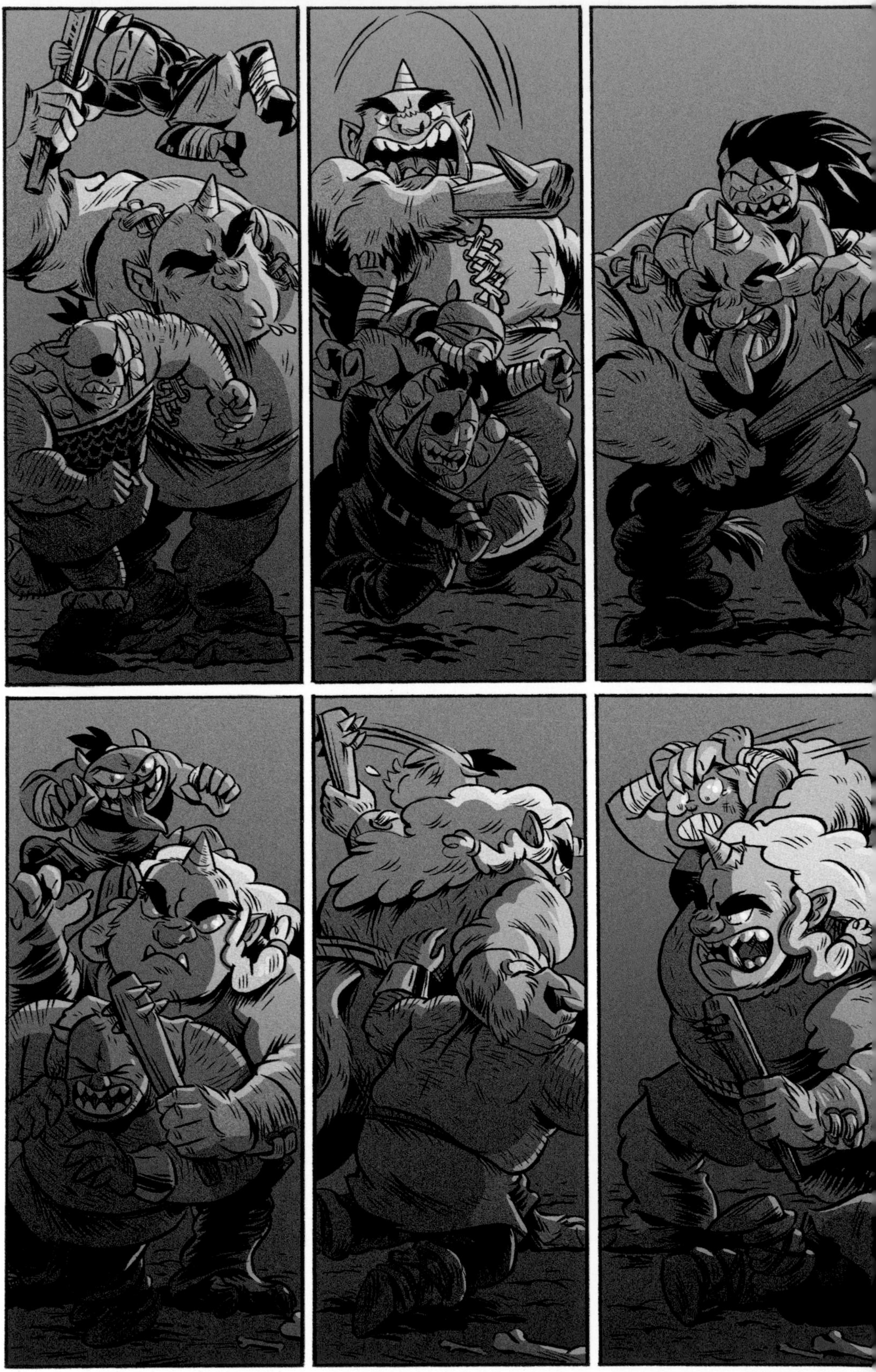

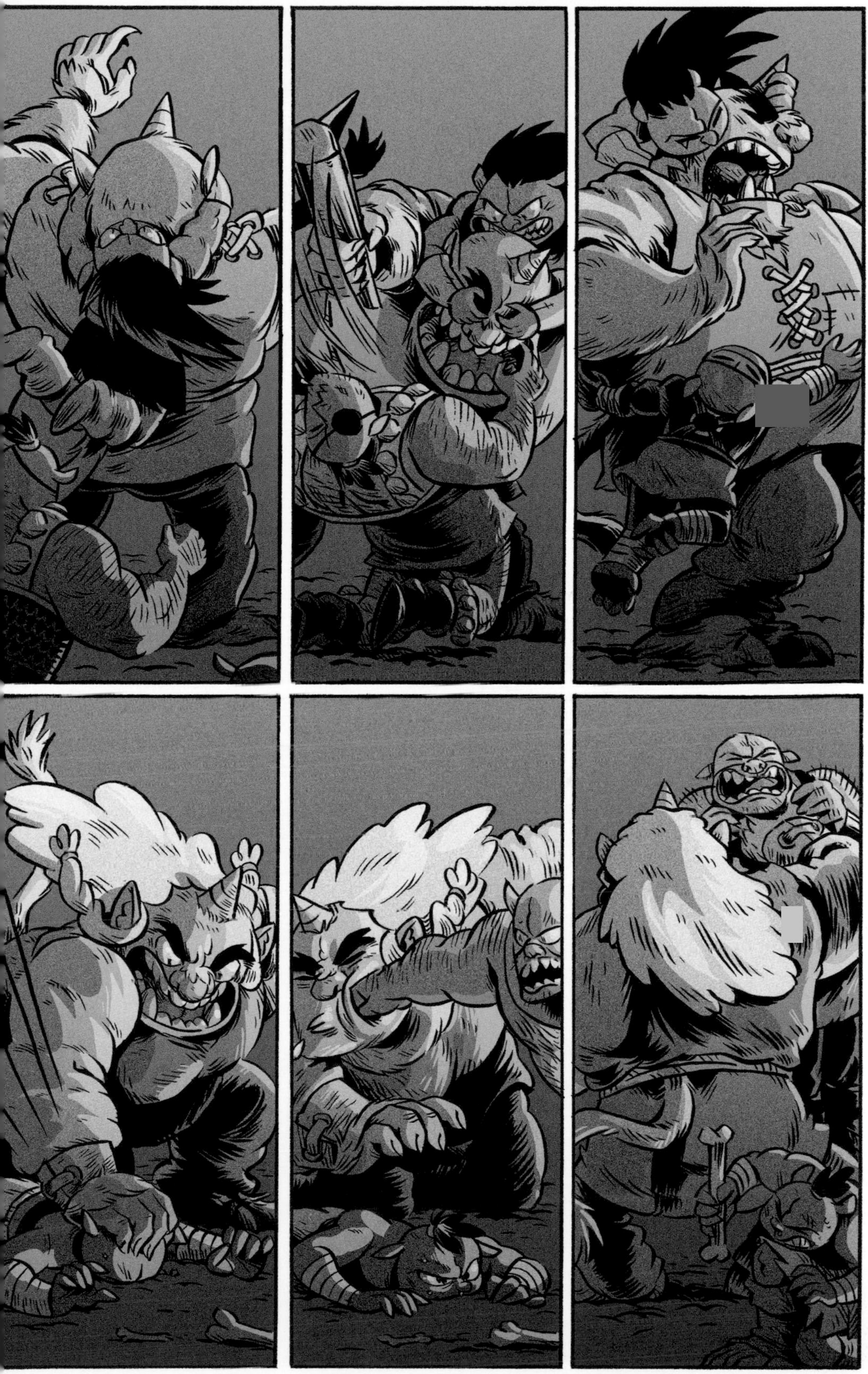

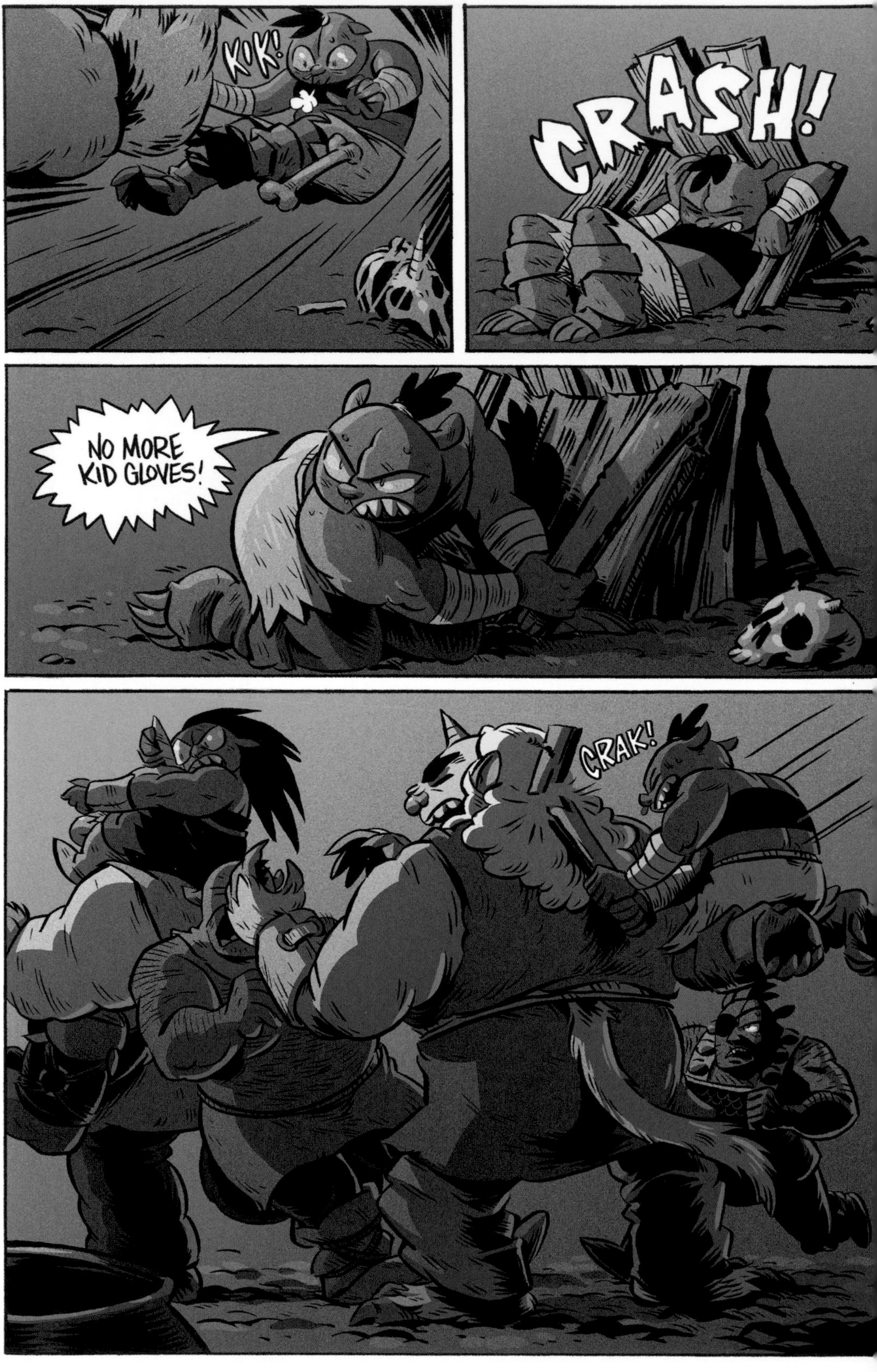
KOK!
CRASH!
NO MORE KID GLOVES!
CRAK!

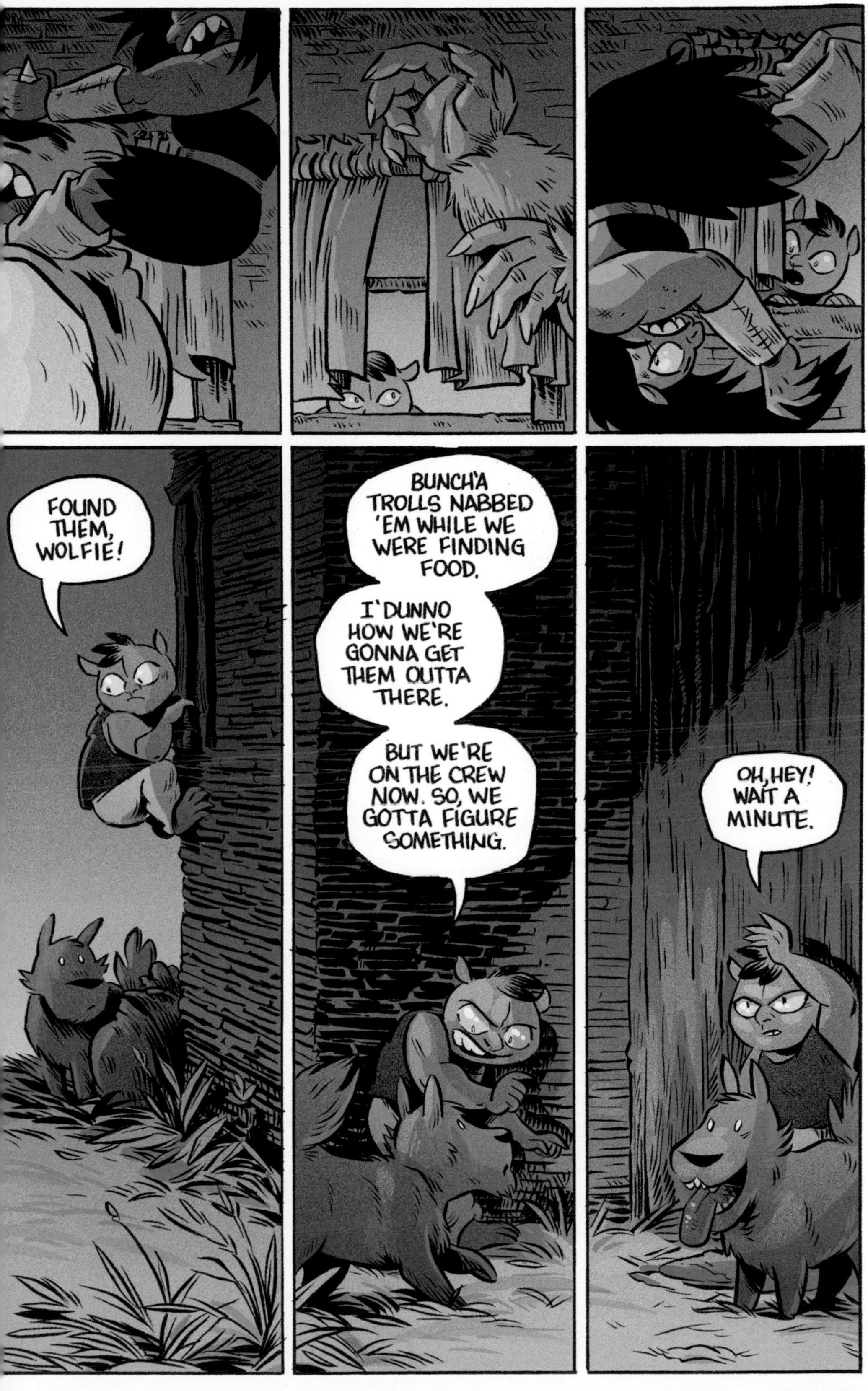
FOUND THEM, WOLFIE!
BUNCH'A TROLLS NABBED 'EM WHILE WE WERE FINDING FOOD.
I'DUNNO HOW WE'RE GONNA GET THEM OUTTA THERE.
BUT WE'RE ON THE CREW NOW. SO, WE GOTTA FIGURE SOMETHING.
OH, HEY! WAIT A MINUTE.

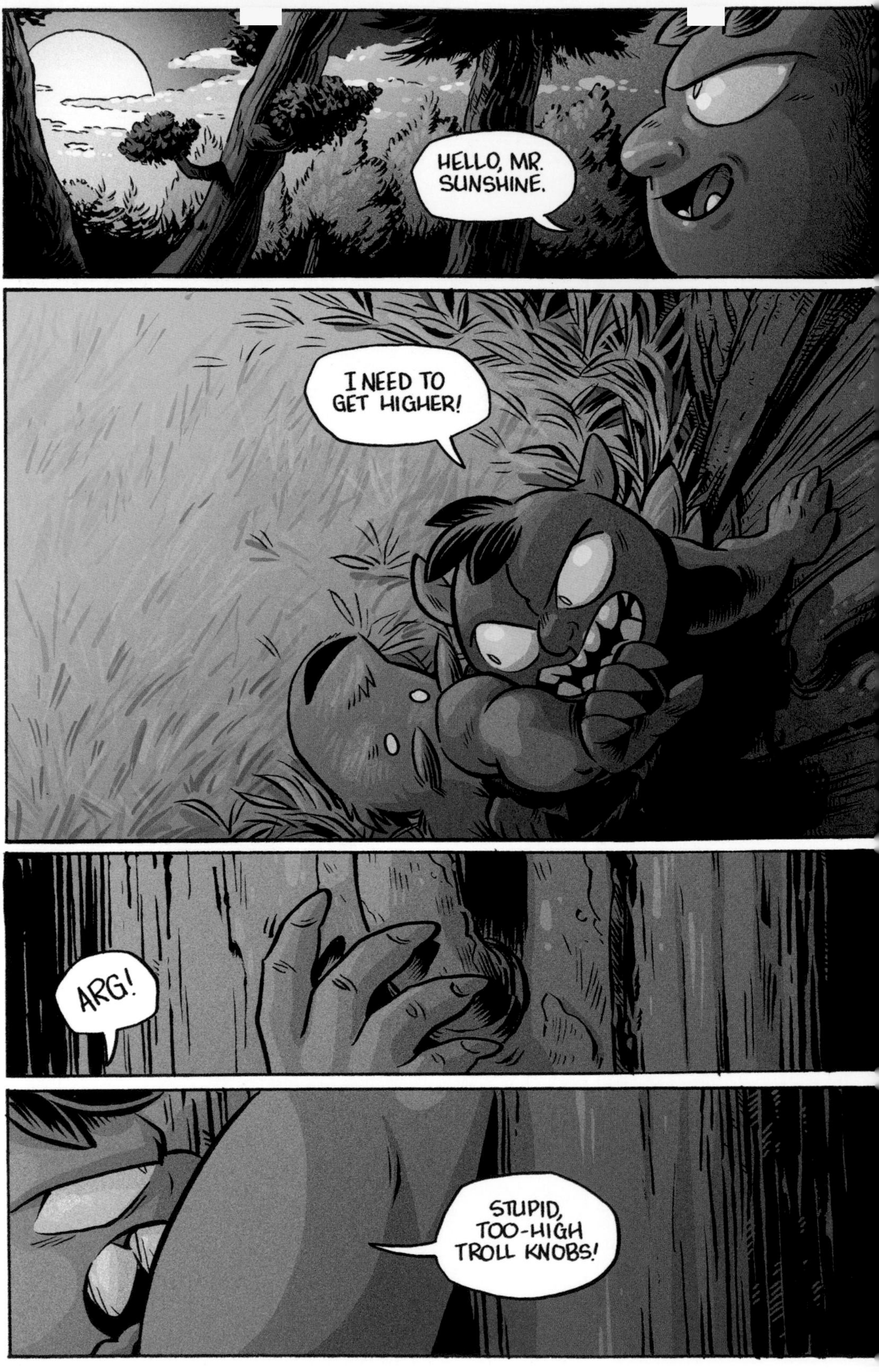
HELLO, MR. SUNSHINE.
I NEED TO GET HIGHER!
ARG!
STUPID, TOO-HIGH TROLL KNOBS!

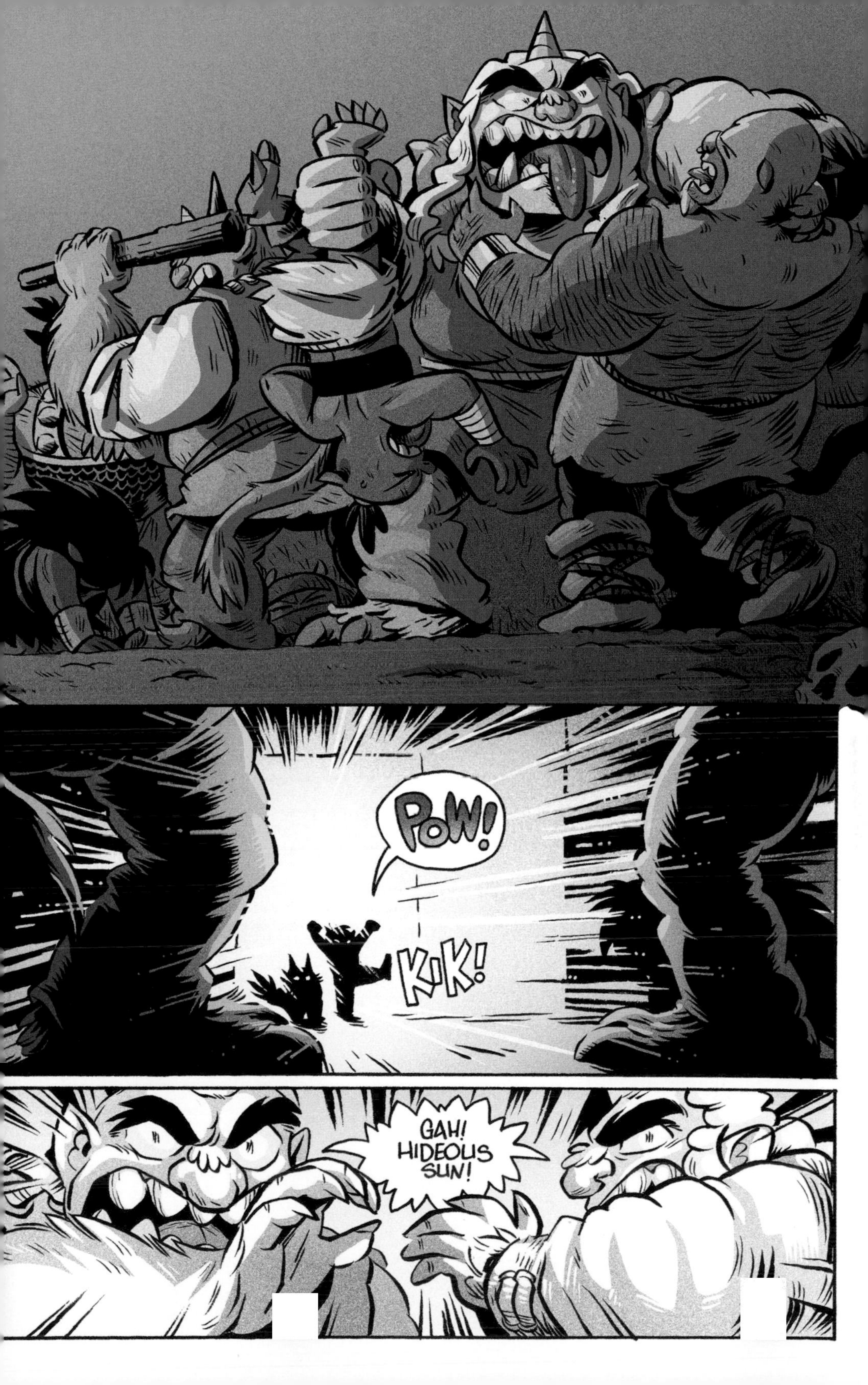
POW!
KIK!
GAH! HIDEOUS SUN!

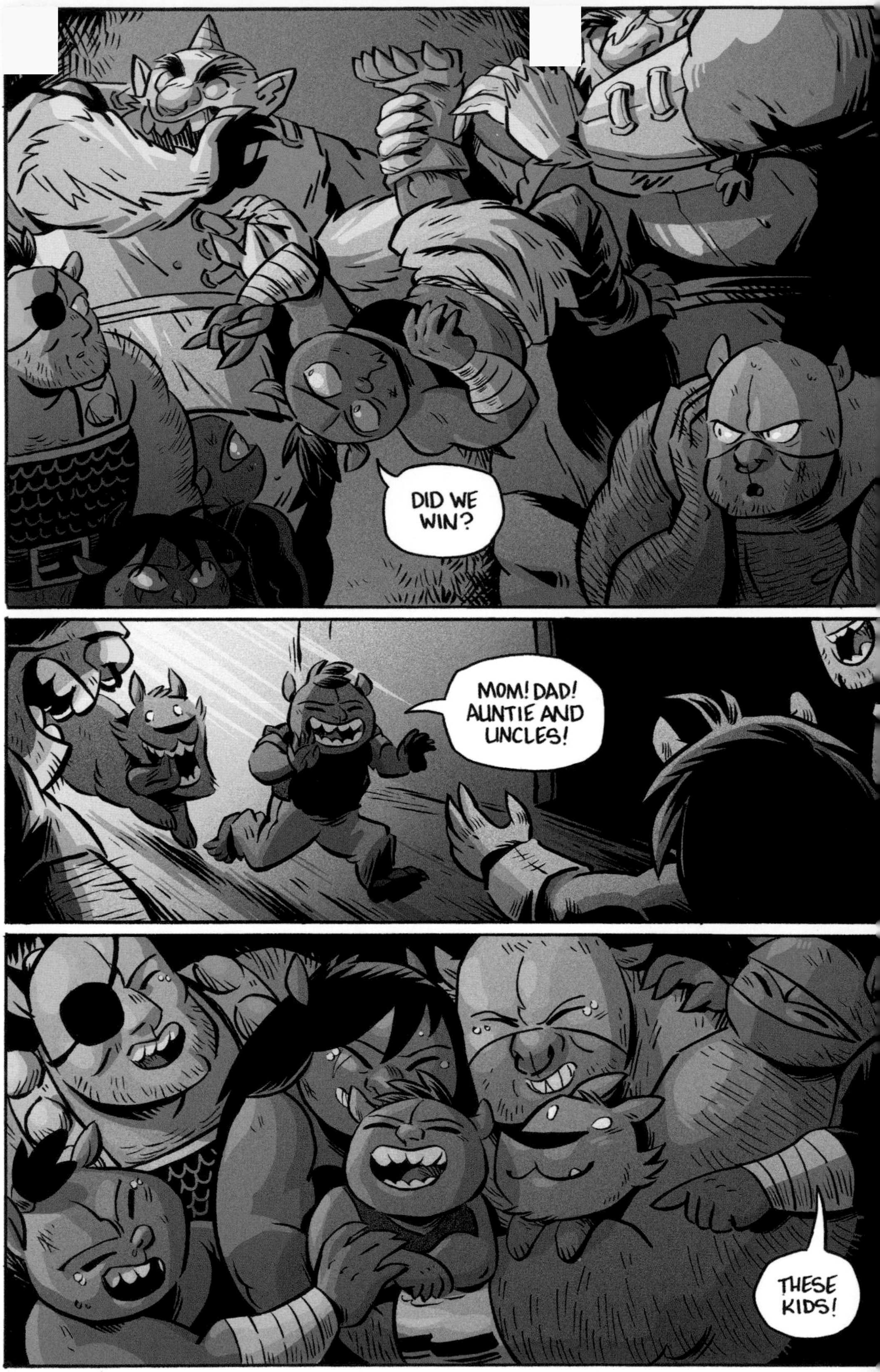
DID WE WIN?
MOM! DAD! AUNTIE AND UNCLES!
THESE KIDS!

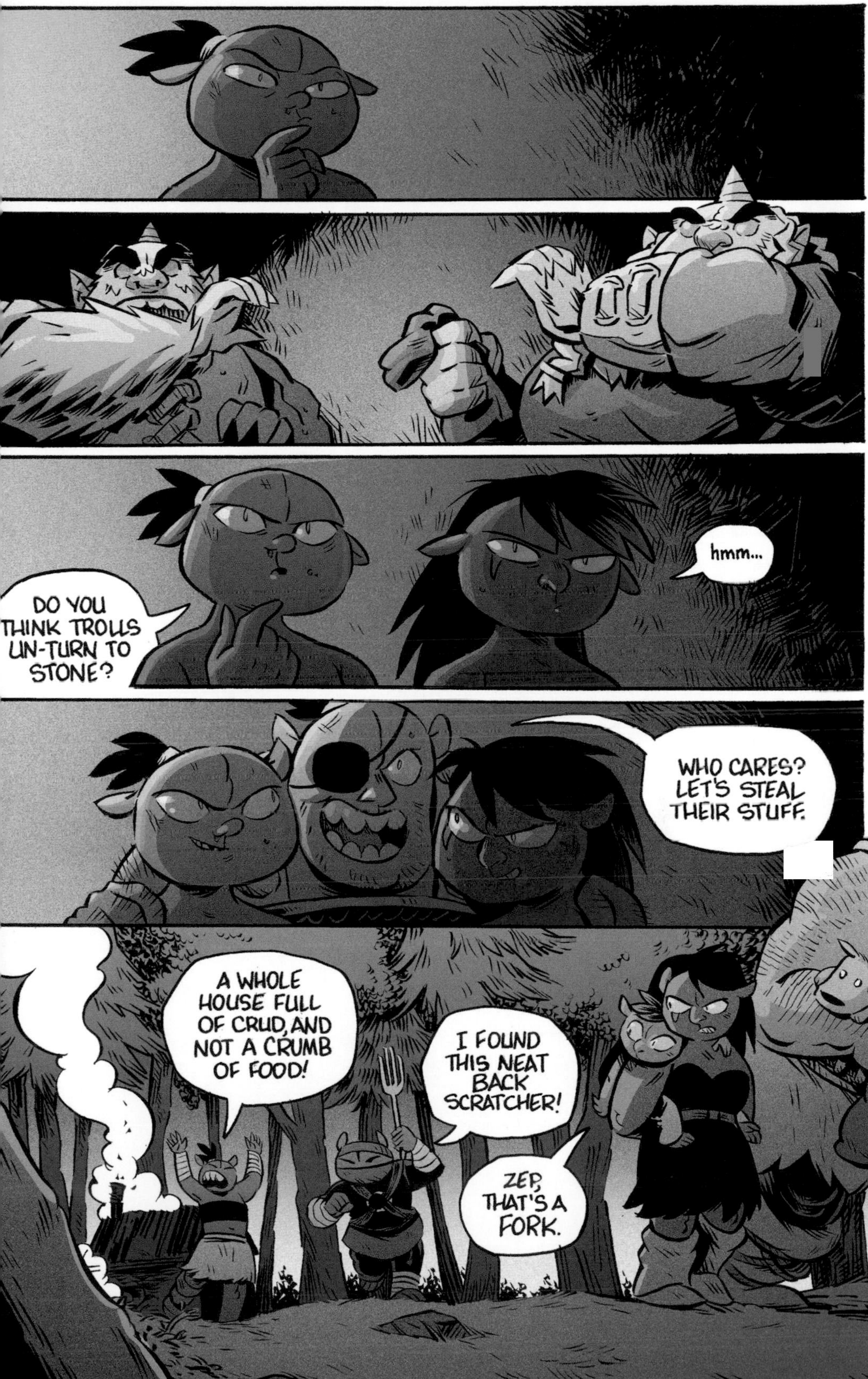
hmm...
DO YOU THINK TROLLS UN-TURN TO STONE?
WHO CARES? LET'S STEAL THEIR STUFF.
A WHOLE HOUSE FULL OF CRUD, AND NOT A CRUMB OF FOOD!
I FOUND THIS NEAT BACK SCRATCHER!
ZEP, THAT'S A FORK.

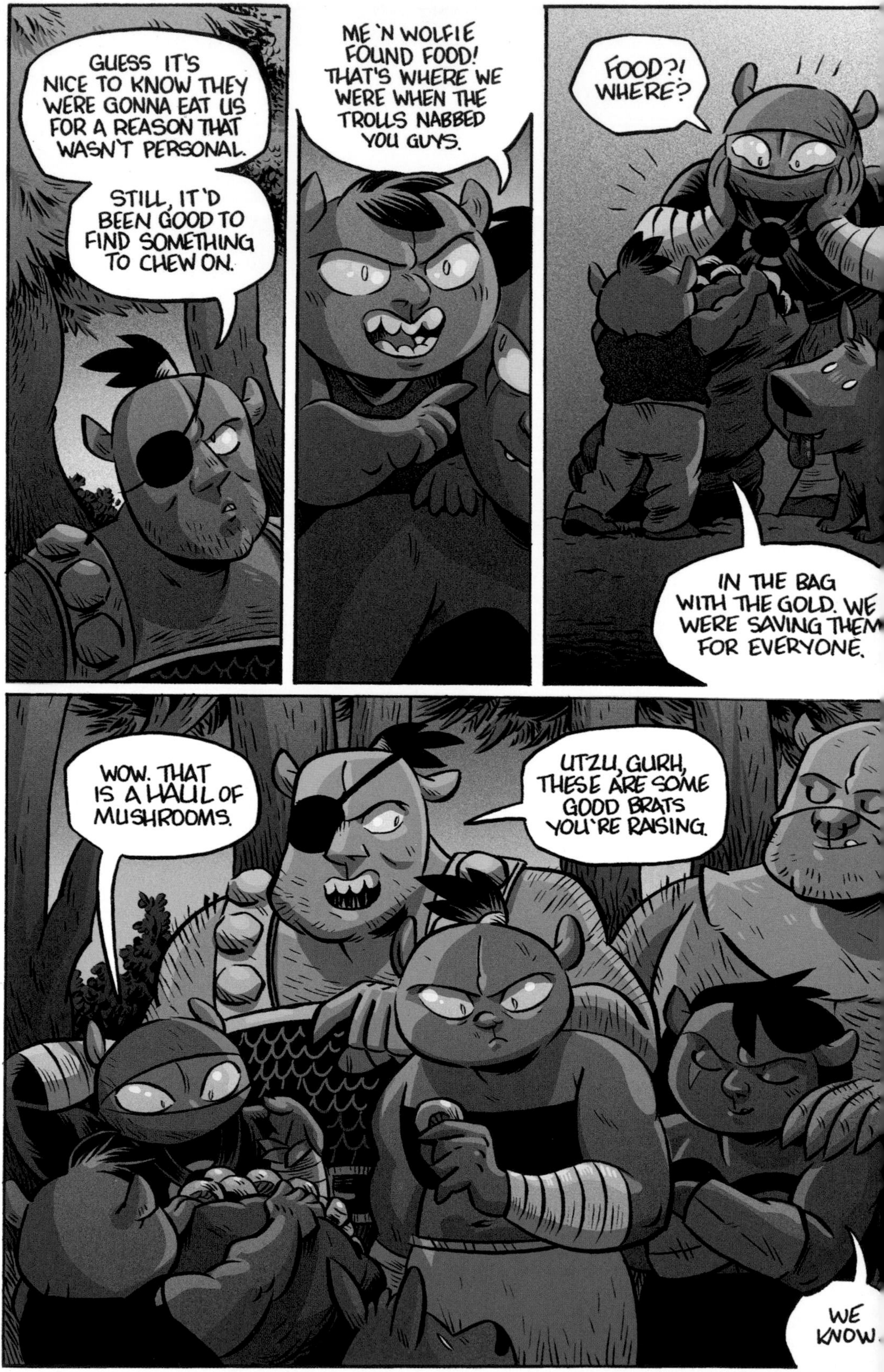
GUESS IT'S NICE TO KNOW THEY WERE GONNA EAT US FOR A REASON THAT WASN'T PERSONAL.
STILL, IT'D BEEN GOOD TO FIND SOMETHING TO CHEW ON.
ME 'N WOLFIE FOUND FOOD! THAT'S WHERE WE WERE WHEN THE TROLLS NABBED YOU GUYS.
FOOD?! WHERE?
IN THE BAG WITH THE GOLD. WE WERE SAVING THEM FOR EVERYONE.
WOW. THAT IS A HAUL OF MUSHROOMS.
UTZU, GURH, THESE ARE SOME GOOD BRATS YOU'RE RAISING.
WE KNOW.

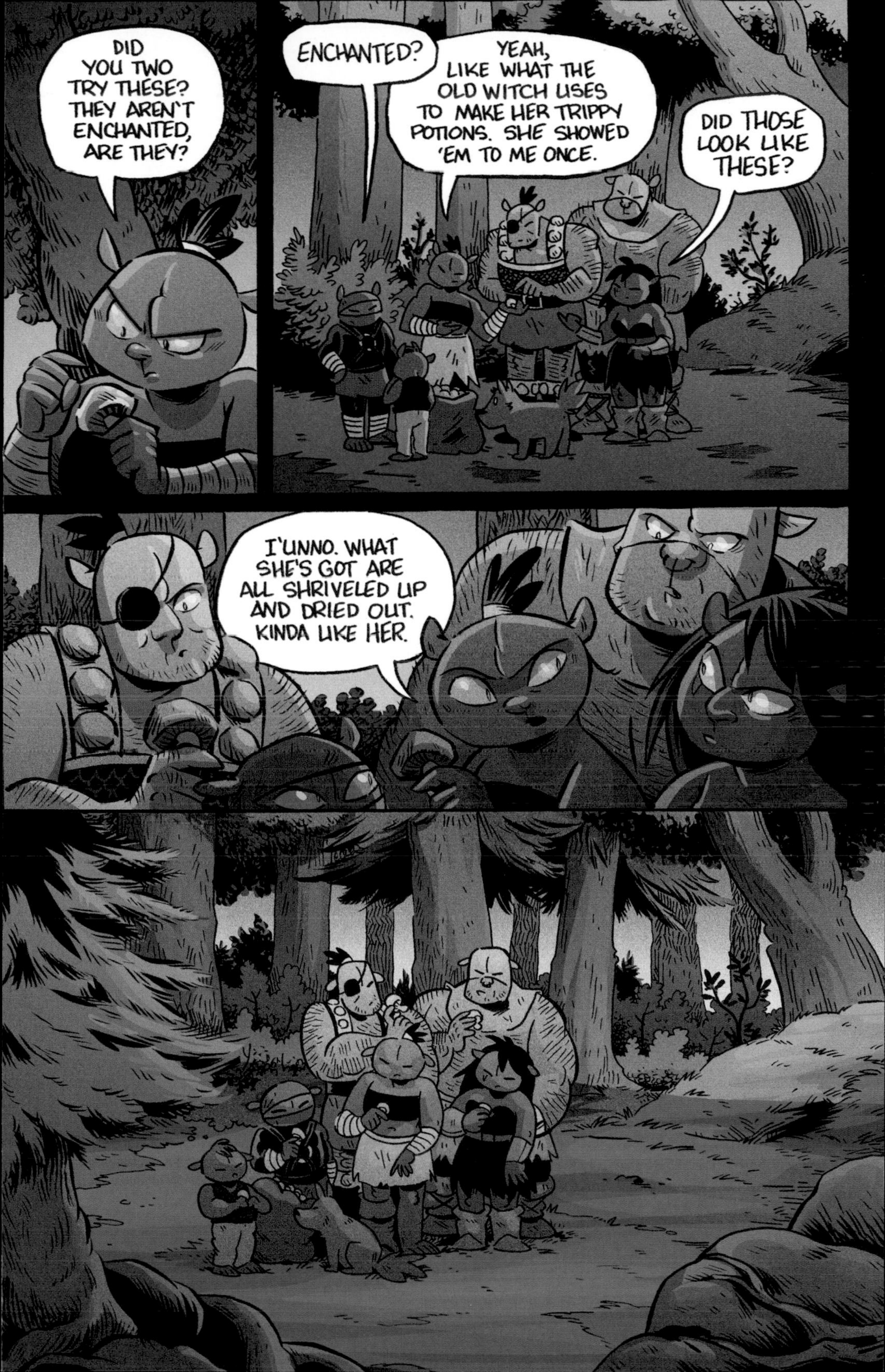
DID YOU TWO TRY THESE? THEY AREN'T ENCHANTED, ARE THEY?
ENCHANTED?
YEAH, LIKE WHAT THE OLD WITCH USES TO MAKE HER TRIPPY POTIONS. SHE SHOWED 'EM TO ME ONCE.
DID THOSE LOOK LIKE THESE?
I'UNNO. WHAT SHE'S GOT ARE ALL SHRIVELED UP AND DRIED OUT. KINDA LIKE HER.

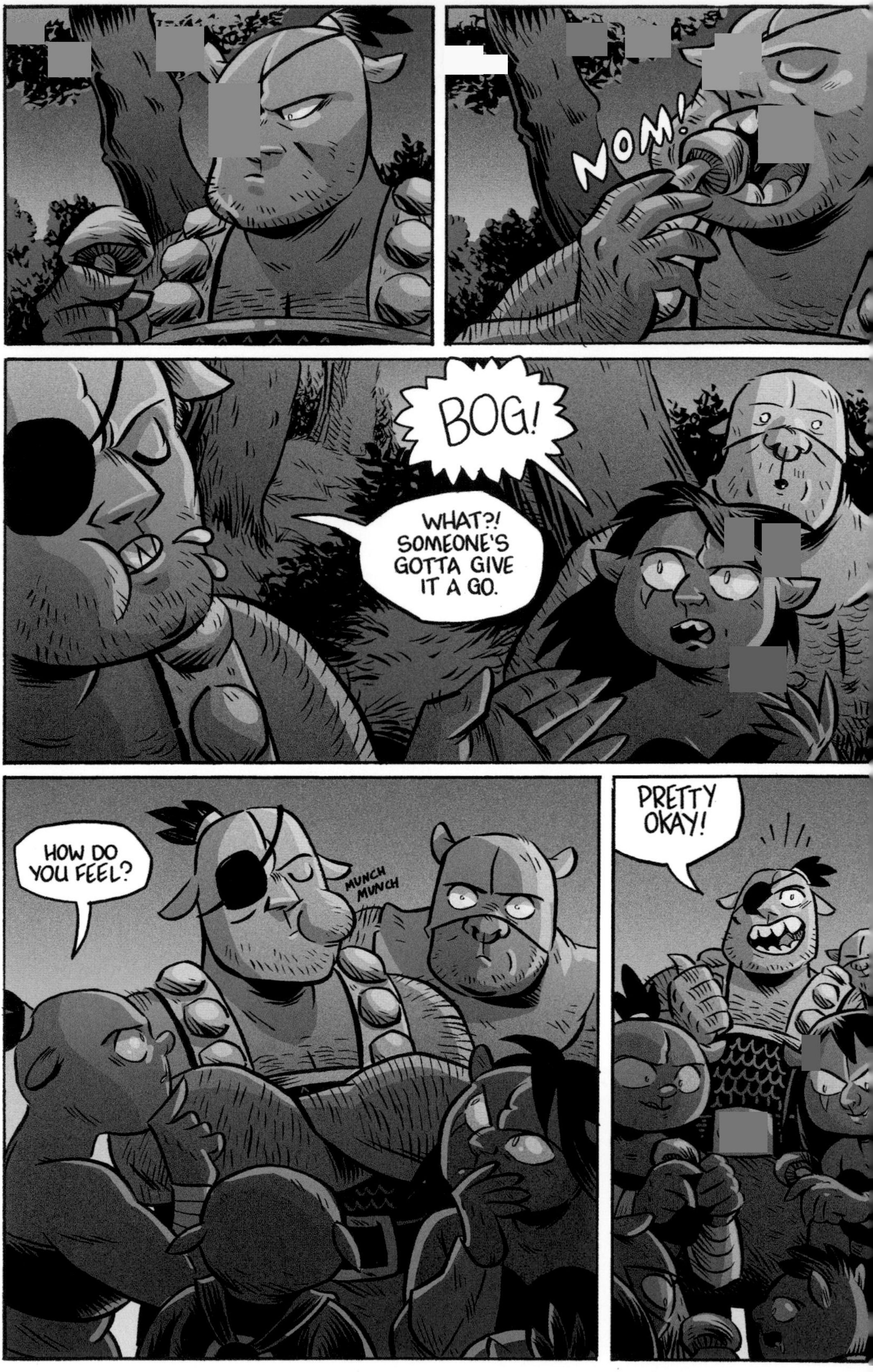
NOM!
BOG!
WHAT?! SOMEONE'S GOTTA GIVE IT A GO.
HOW DO YOU FEEL?
MUNCH MUNCH
PRETTY OKAY!

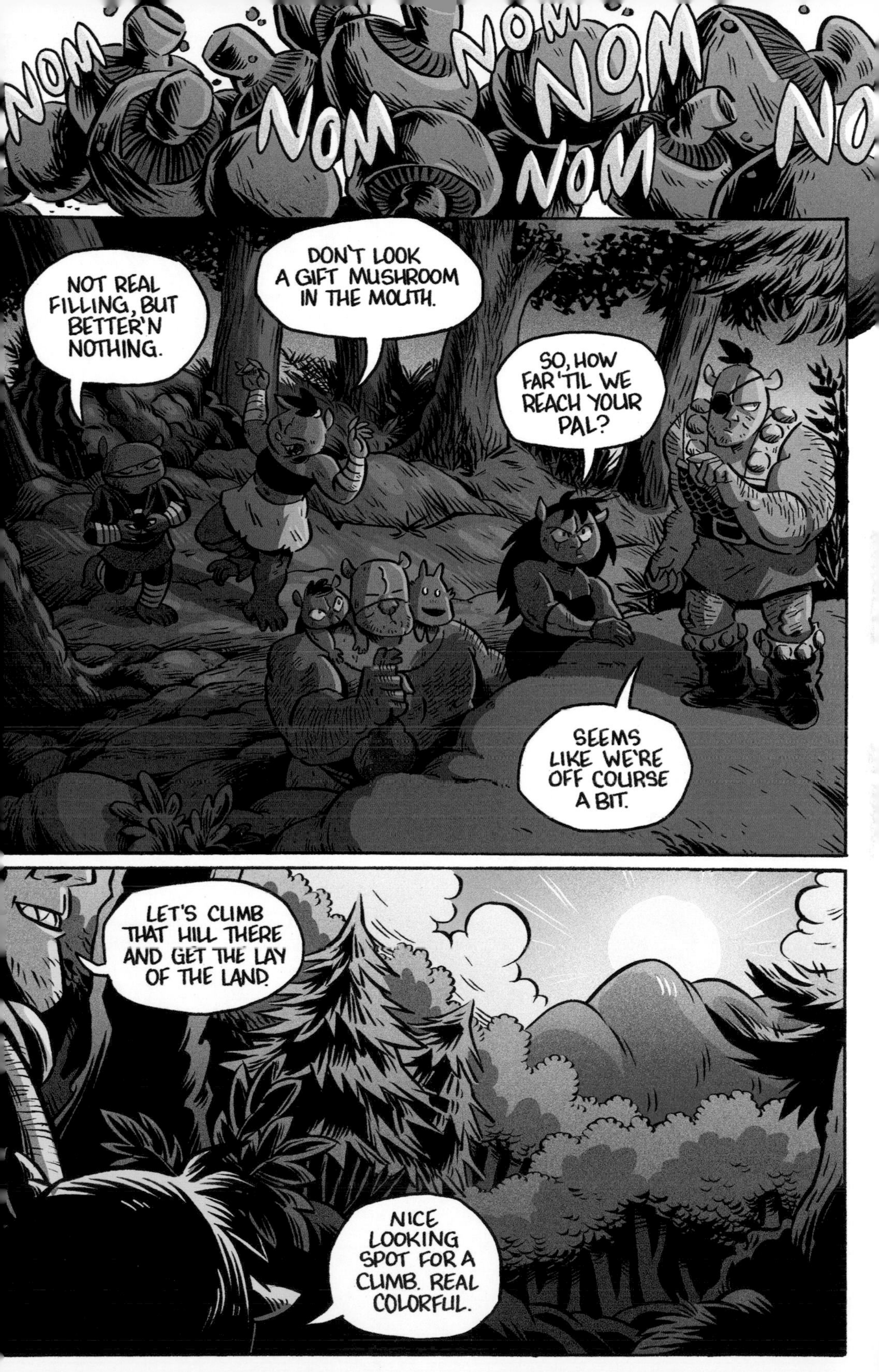
NOM NOM NOM NOM NOM NOM NO
NOT REAL FILLING, BUT BETTER'N NOTHING.
DON'T LOOK A GIFT MUSHROOM IN THE MOUTH.
SO, HOW FAR 'TIL WE REACH YOUR PAL?
SEEMS LIKE WE'RE OFF COURSE A BIT.
LET'S CLIMB THAT HILL THERE AND GET THE LAY OF THE LAND.
NICE LOOKING SPOT FOR A CLIMB. REAL COLORFUL.

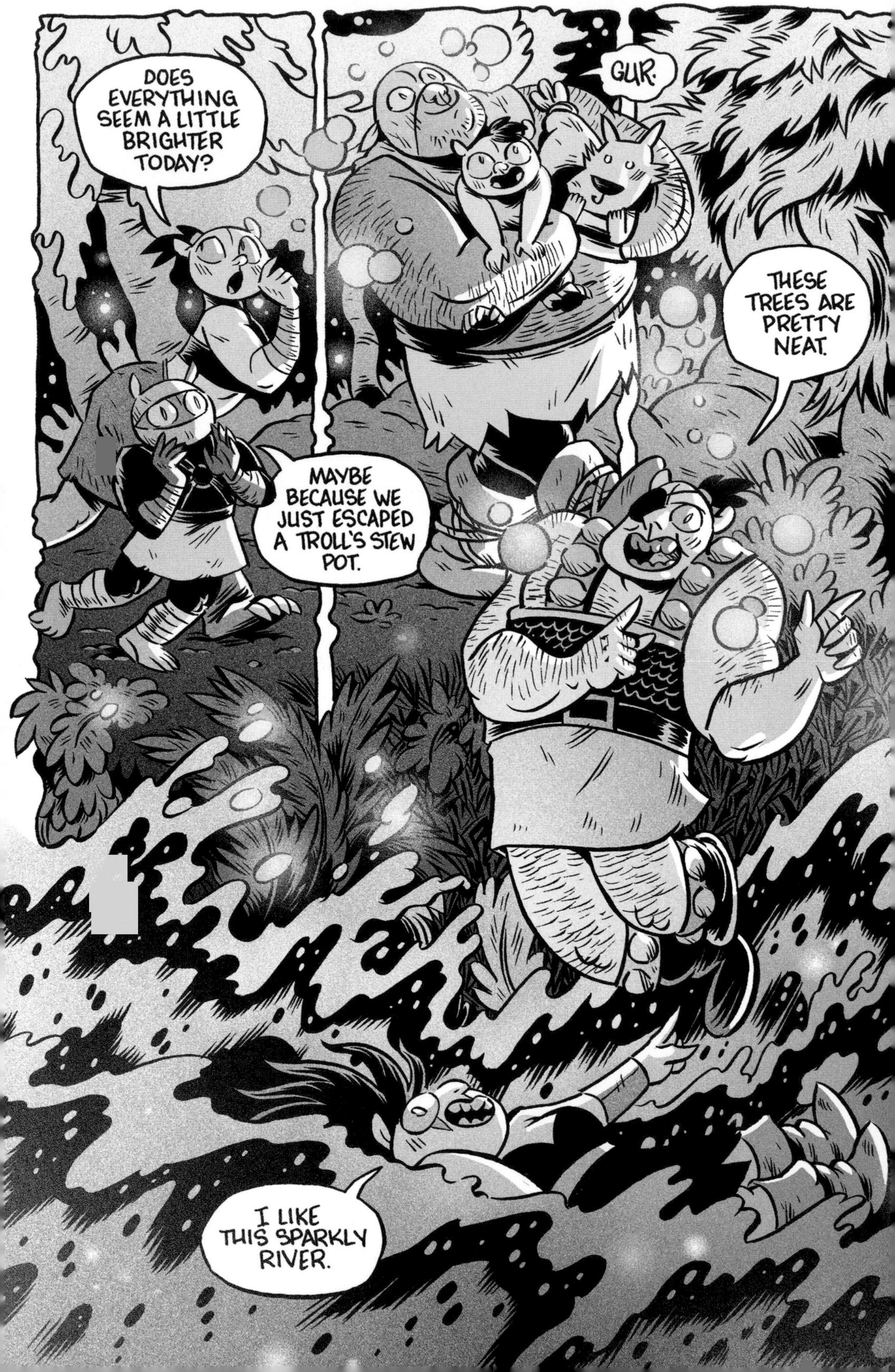
DOES EVERYTHING SEEM A LITTLE BRIGHTER TODAY?
MAYBE BECAUSE WE JUST ESCAPED A TROLL'S STEW POT.
GUR.
THESE TREES ARE PRETTY NEAT.
I LIKE THIS SPARKLY RIVER.

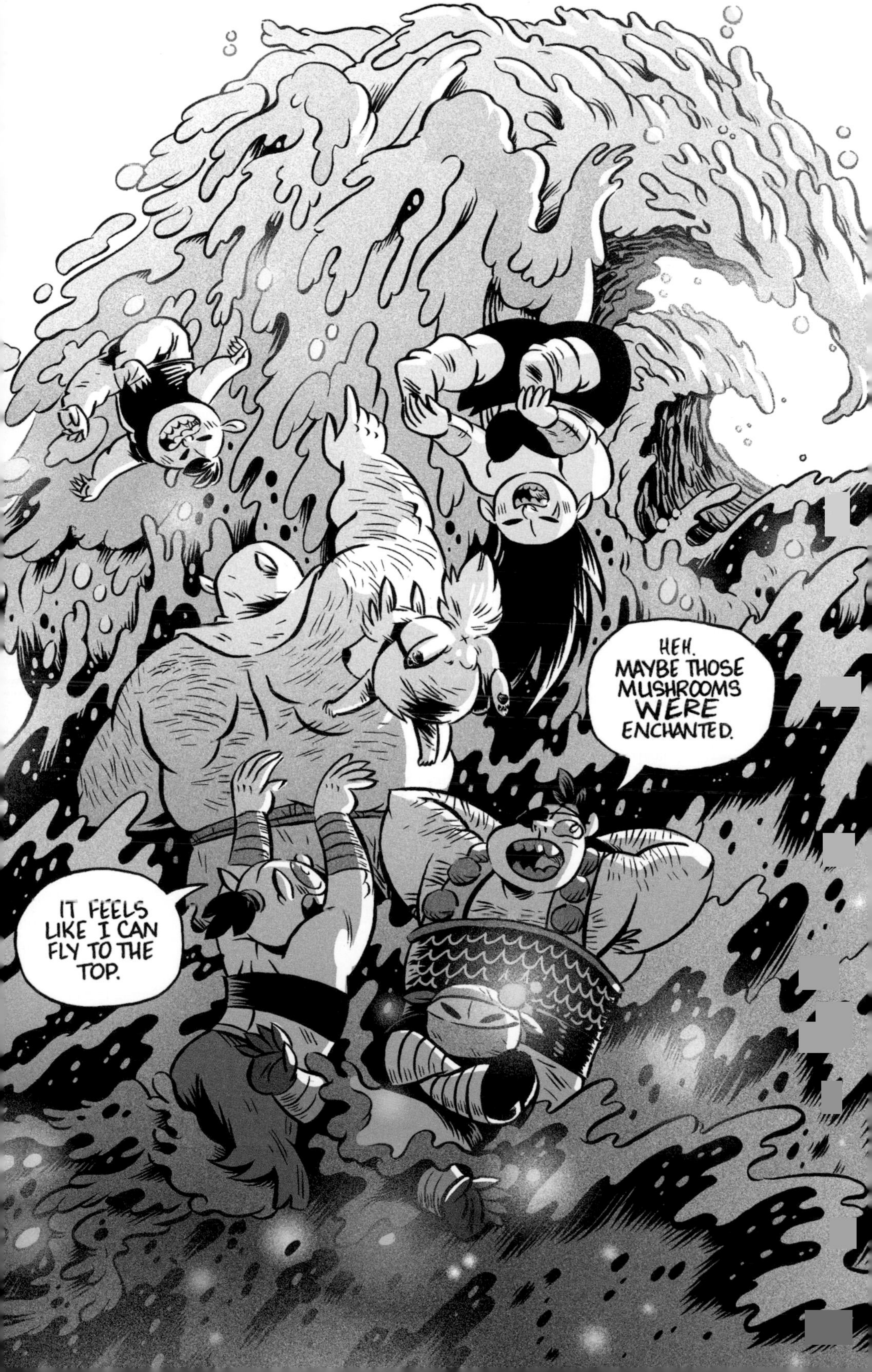
HEH. MAYBE THOSE MUSHROOMS WERE ENCHANTED.
IT FEELS LIKE I CAN FLY TO THE TOP.

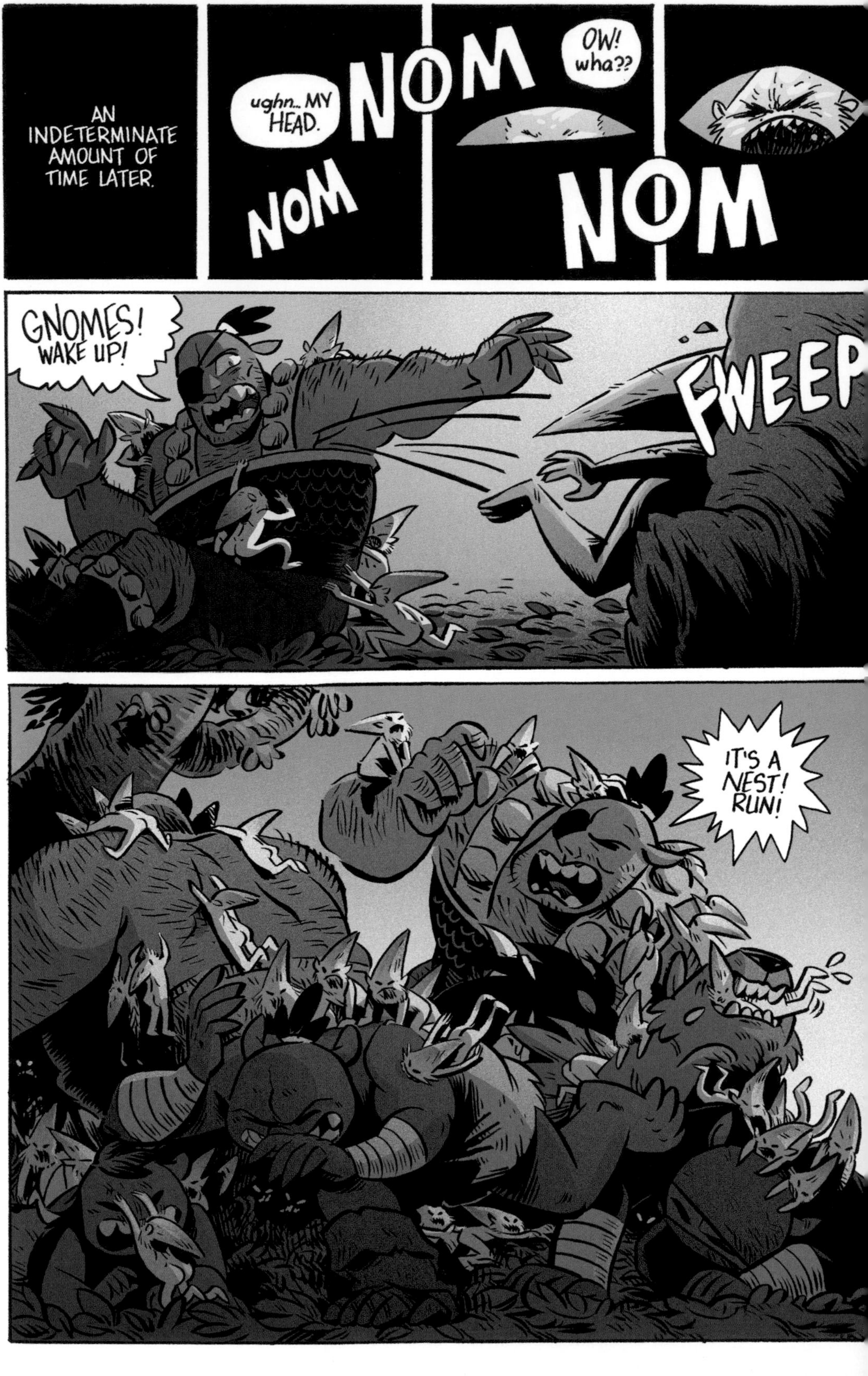
AN INDETERMINATE AMOUNT OF TIME LATER.
ughn... MY HEAD.
NOM
NOM
OW! wha??
NOM
GNOMES! WAKE UP!
FWEEP
IT'S A NEST! RUN!

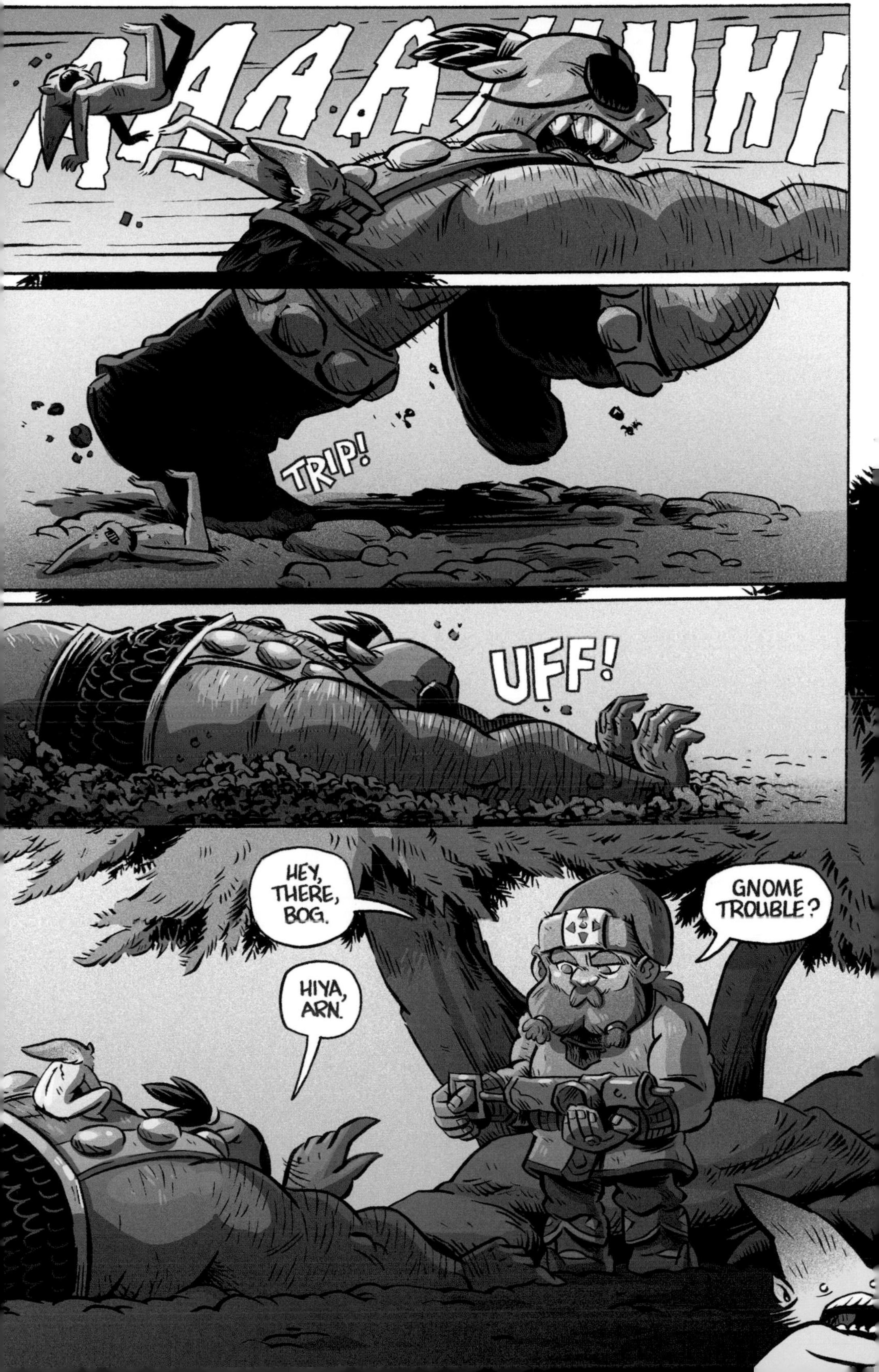
AAAAAHHHH
TRIP!
UFF!
HEY, THERE, BOG.
GNOME TROUBLE?
HIYA, ARN.

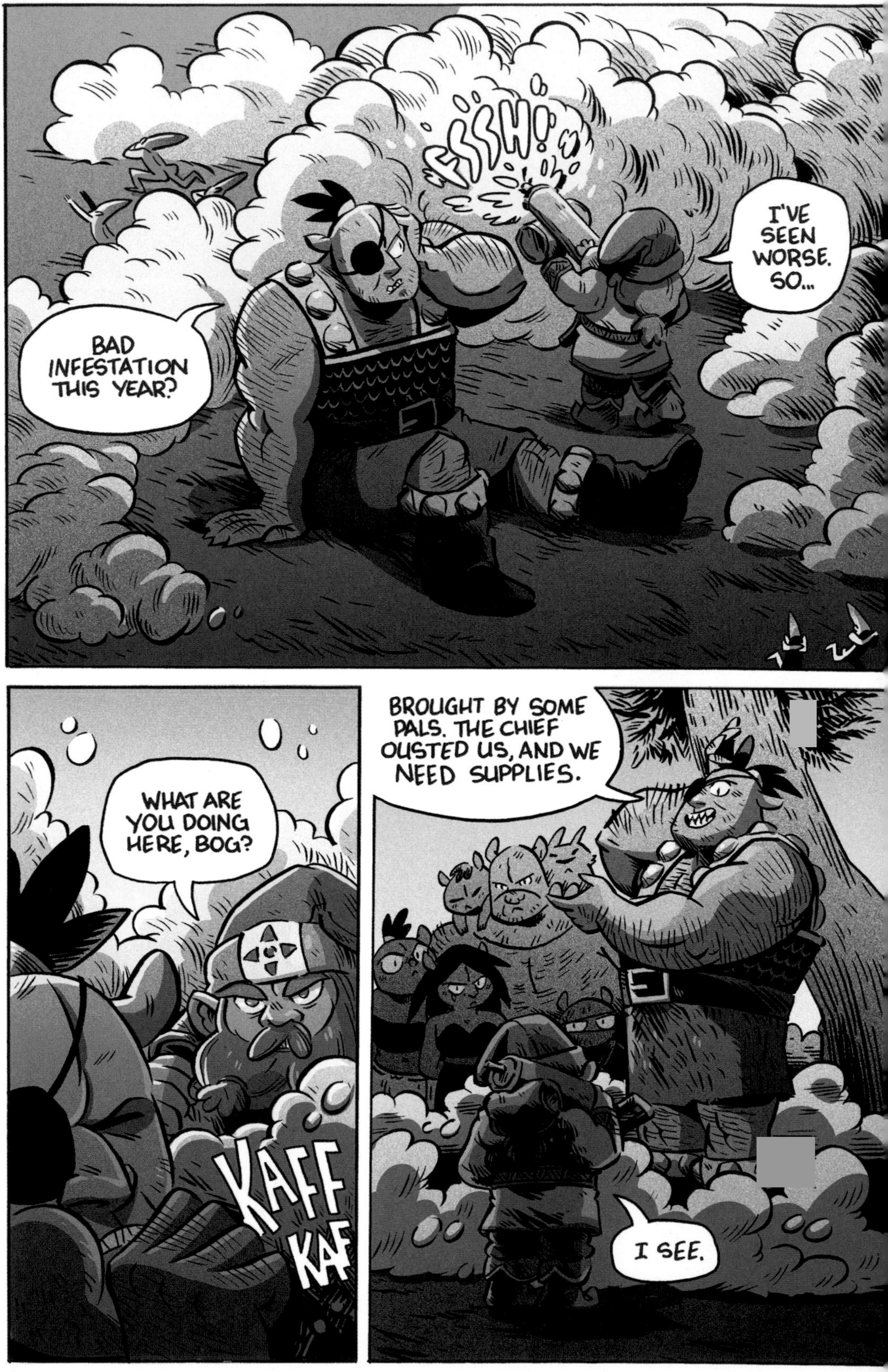
FSSH!
BAD INFESTATION THIS YEAR?
I'VE SEEN WORSE. SO...
WHAT ARE YOU DOING HERE, BOG?
KAFF
KAF
BROUGHT BY SOME PALS. THE CHIEF OUSTED US, AND WE NEED SUPPLIES.
I SEE.

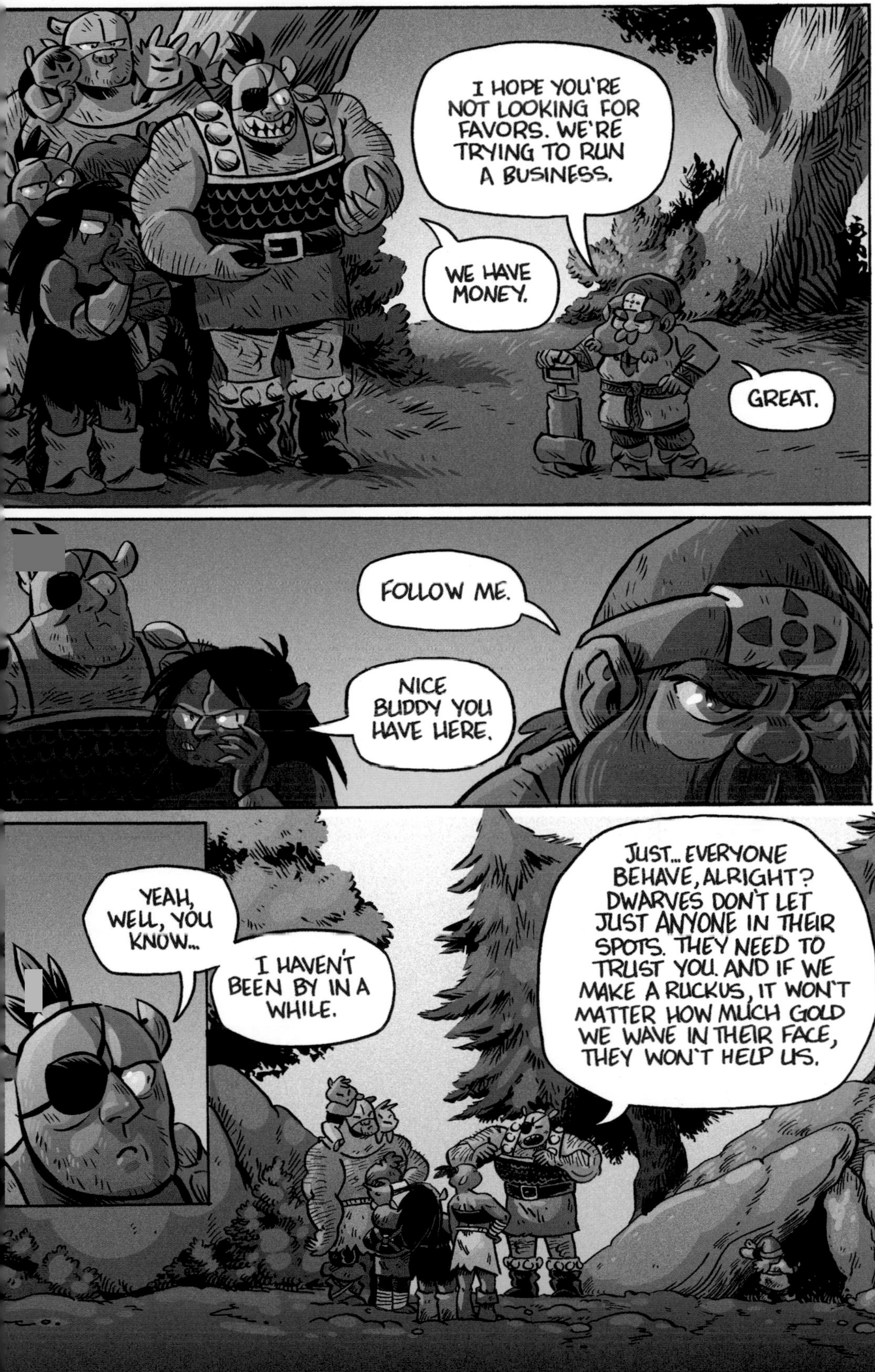
I HOPE YOU'RE NOT LOOKING FOR FAVORS. WE'RE TRYING TO RUN A BUSINESS.
WE HAVE MONEY.
GREAT.
FOLLOW ME.
NICE BUDDY YOU HAVE HERE.
YEAH, WELL, YOU KNOW...
I HAVEN'T BEEN BY IN A WHILE.
JUST... EVERYONE BEHAVE, ALRIGHT? DWARVES DON'T LET JUST ANYONE IN THEIR SPOTS. THEY NEED TO TRUST YOU. AND IF WE MAKE A RUCKUS, IT WON'T MATTER HOW MUCH GOLD WE WAVE IN THEIR FACE, THEY WON'T HELP US.

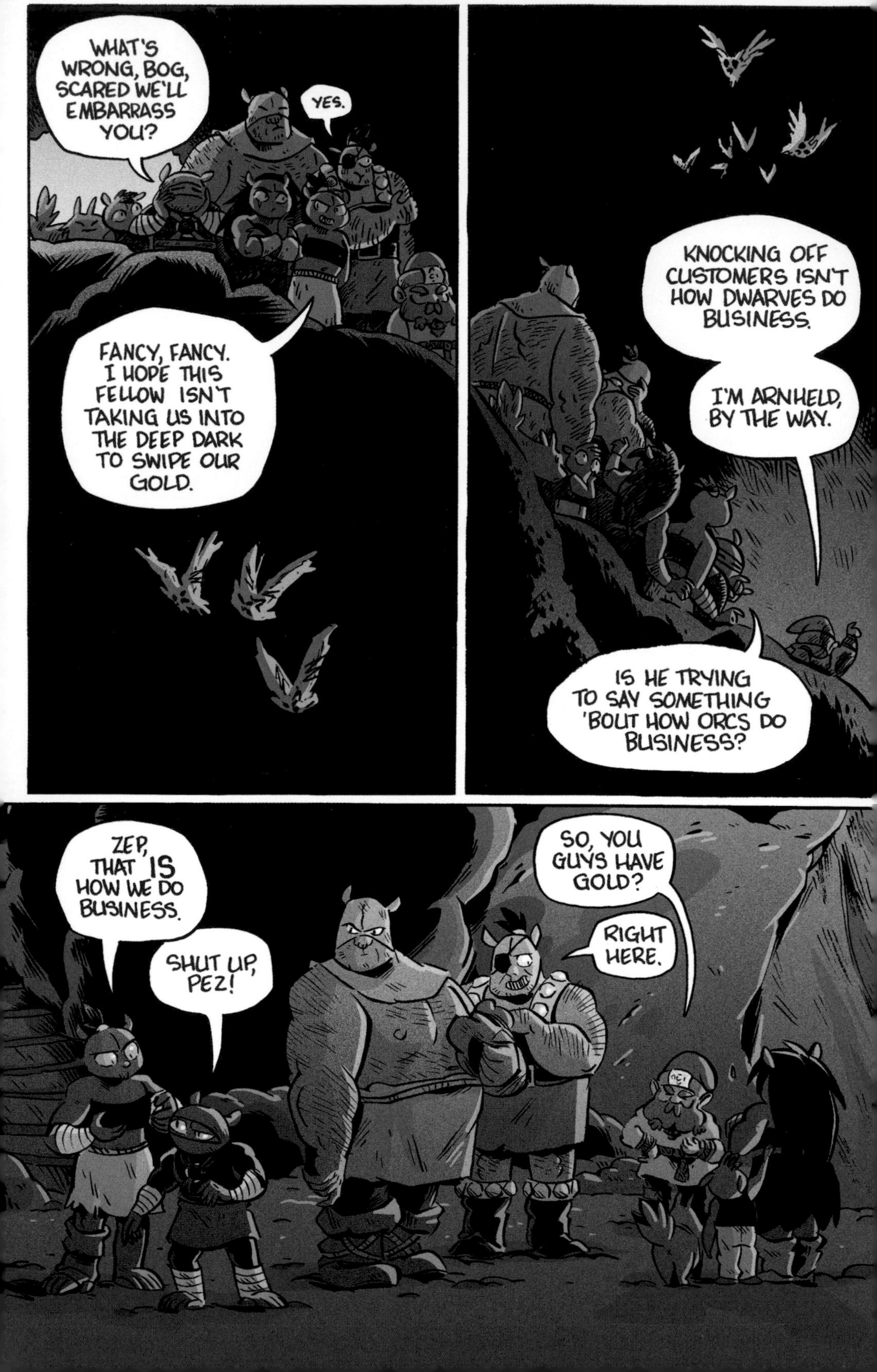
WHAT'S WRONG, BOG, SCARED WE'LL EMBARRASS YOU?
YES.
FANCY, FANCY. I HOPE THIS FELLOW ISN'T TAKING US INTO THE DEEP DARK TO SWIPE OUR GOLD.
KNOCKING OFF CUSTOMERS ISN'T HOW DWARVES DO BUSINESS.
I'M ARNHELD, BY THE WAY.
IS HE TRYING TO SAY SOMETHING 'BOUT HOW ORCS DO BUSINESS?
ZEP, THAT IS HOW WE DO BUSINESS.
SHUT UP, PEZ!
SO, YOU GUYS HAVE GOLD?
RIGHT HERE.

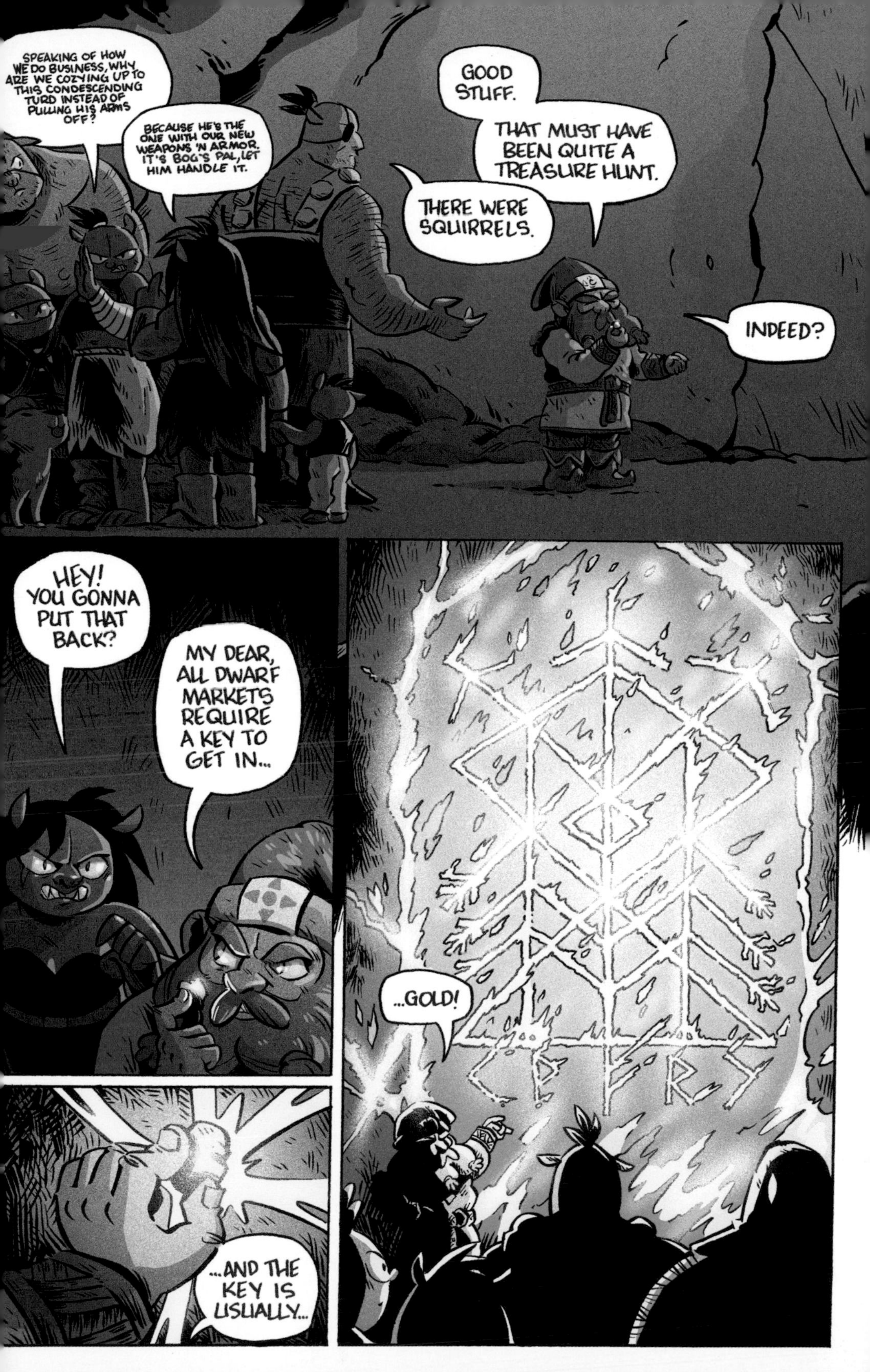

SPEAKING OF HOW WE DO BUSINESS, WHY ARE WE COZYING UP TO THIS CONDESCENDING TURD INSTEAD OF PULLING HIS ARMS OFF?
BECAUSE HE'S THE ONE WITH OUR NEW WEAPONS 'N ARMOR. IT'S BOG'S PAL, LET HIM HANDLE IT.
GOOD STUFF.
THAT MUST HAVE BEEN QUITE A TREASURE HUNT.
THERE WERE SQUIRRELS.
INDEED?
HEY! YOU GONNA PUT THAT BACK?
MY DEAR, ALL DWARF MARKETS REQUIRE A KEY TO GET IN...
...AND THE KEY IS USUALLY...
...GOLD!

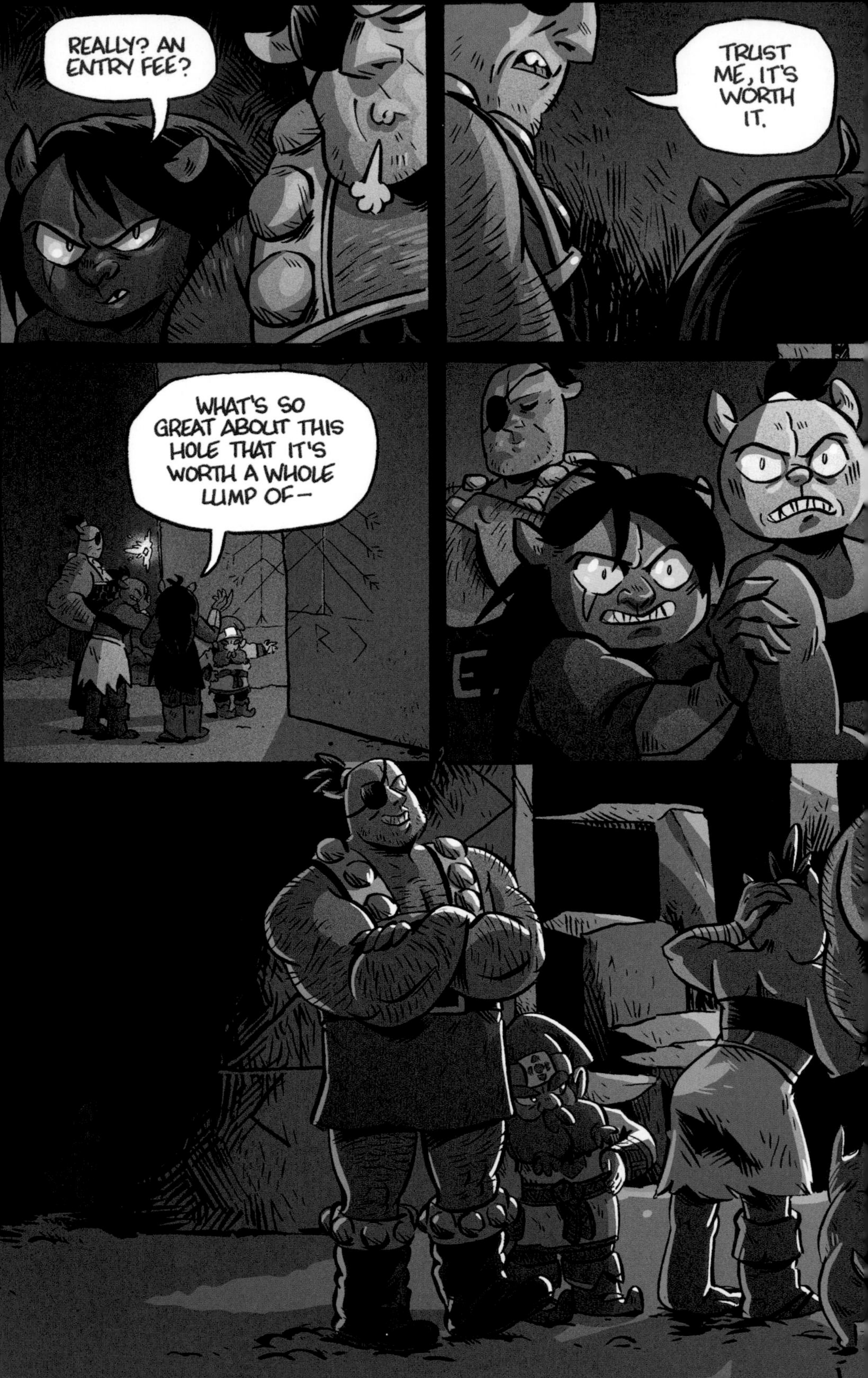
REALLY? AN ENTRY FEE?
TRUST ME, IT'S WORTH IT.
WHAT'S SO GREAT ABOUT THIS HOLE THAT IT'S WORTH A WHOLE LUMP OF—

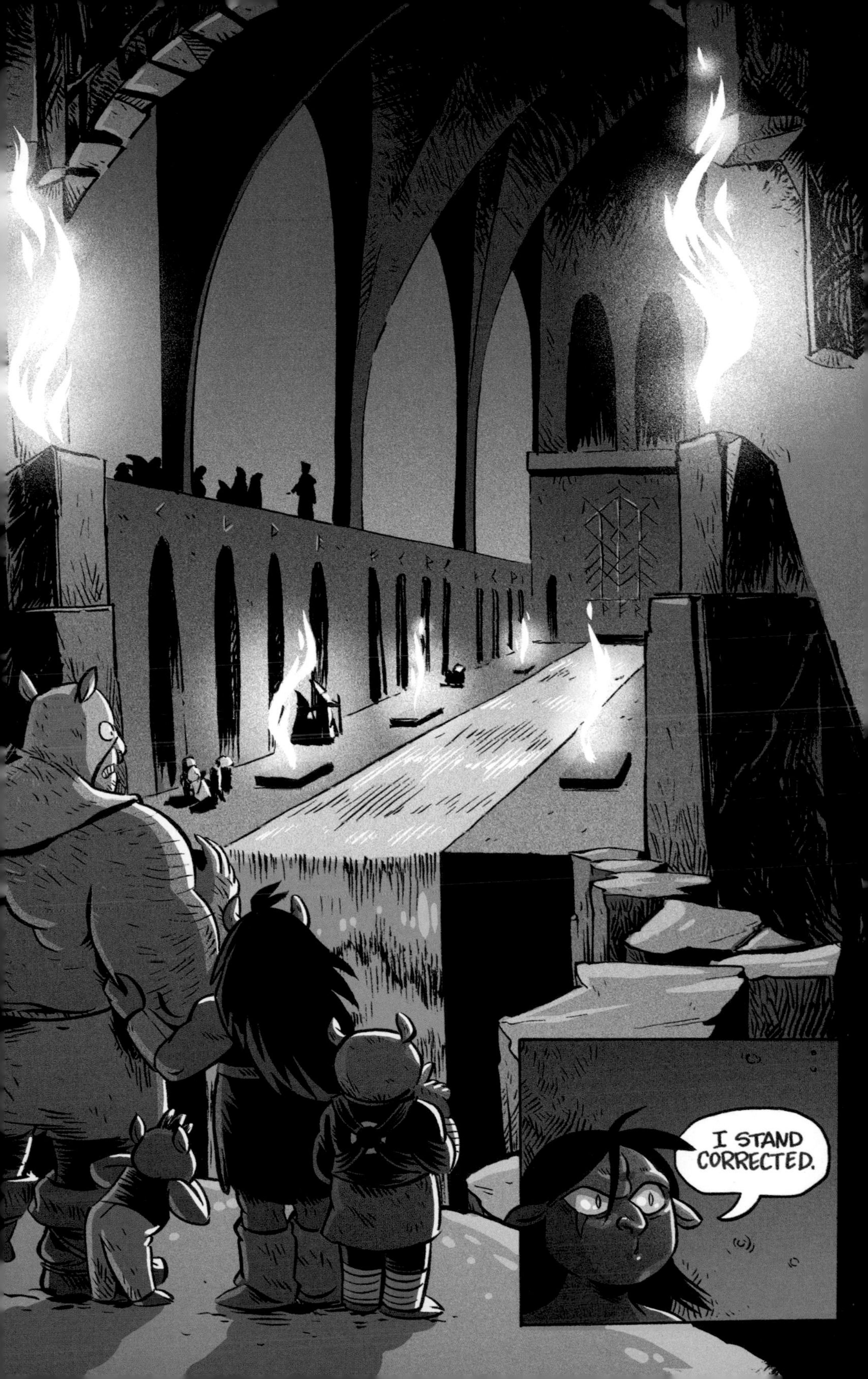
I STAND CORRECTED.

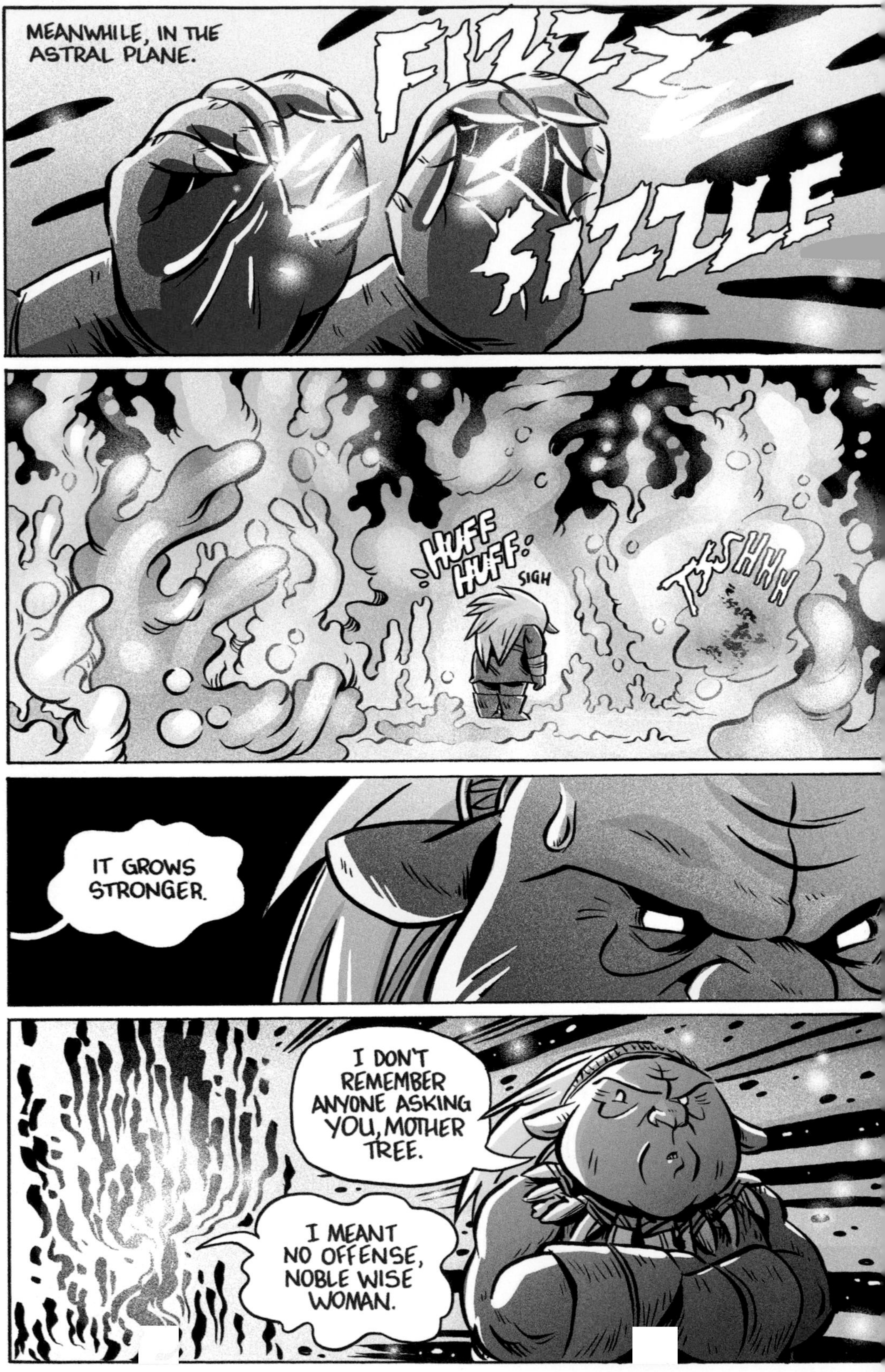
MEANWHILE, IN THE ASTRAL PLANE.
FIZZZ
SIZZLE
HUFF HUFF
SIGH
TSSHHH
IT GROWS STRONGER.
I DON'T REMEMBER ANYONE ASKING YOU, MOTHER TREE.
I MEANT NO OFFENSE, NOBLE WISE WOMAN.

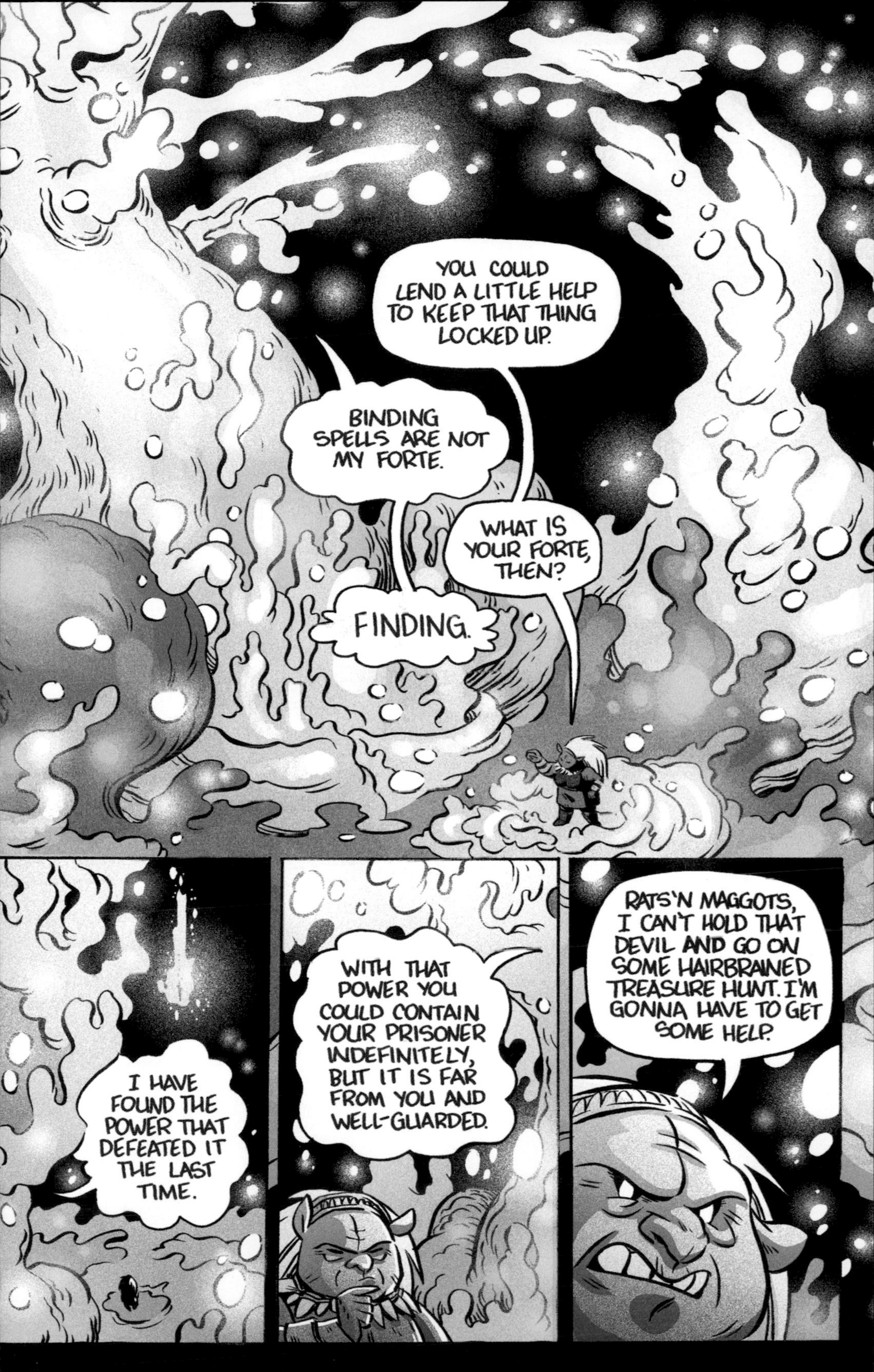
YOU COULD LEND A LITTLE HELP TO KEEP THAT THING LOCKED UP.
BINDING SPELLS ARE NOT MY FORTE.
WHAT IS YOUR FORTE, THEN?
FINDING.
I HAVE FOUND THE POWER THAT DEFEATED IT THE LAST TIME.
WITH THAT POWER YOU COULD CONTAIN YOUR PRISONER INDEFINITELY, BUT IT IS FAR FROM YOU AND WELL-GUARDED.
RATS'N MAGGOTS, I CAN'T HOLD THAT DEVIL AND GO ON SOME HAIRBRAINED TREASURE HUNT. I'M GONNA HAVE TO GET SOME HELP.

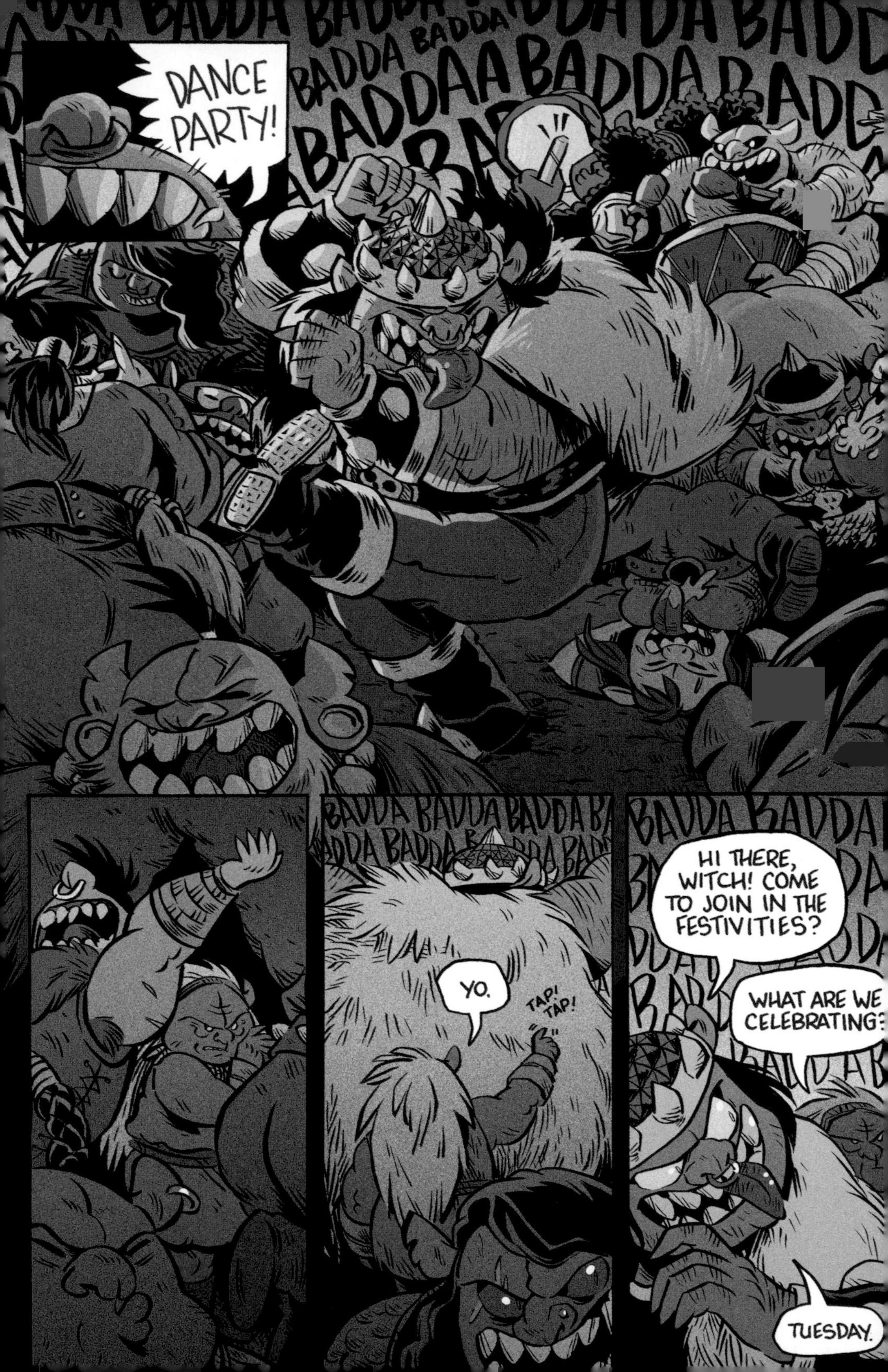
BADDA BADDA BADDA
BADDA BADDA
BADDAA BADDA BADD
BA BA
DANCE PARTY!
BADDA BADDA BADDA BA
BADDA BADDA BADDA BA
YO.
TAP! TAP!
BADDA BADDA
HI THERE, WITCH! COME TO JOIN IN THE FESTIVITIES?
WHAT ARE WE CELEBRATING?
TUESDAY.

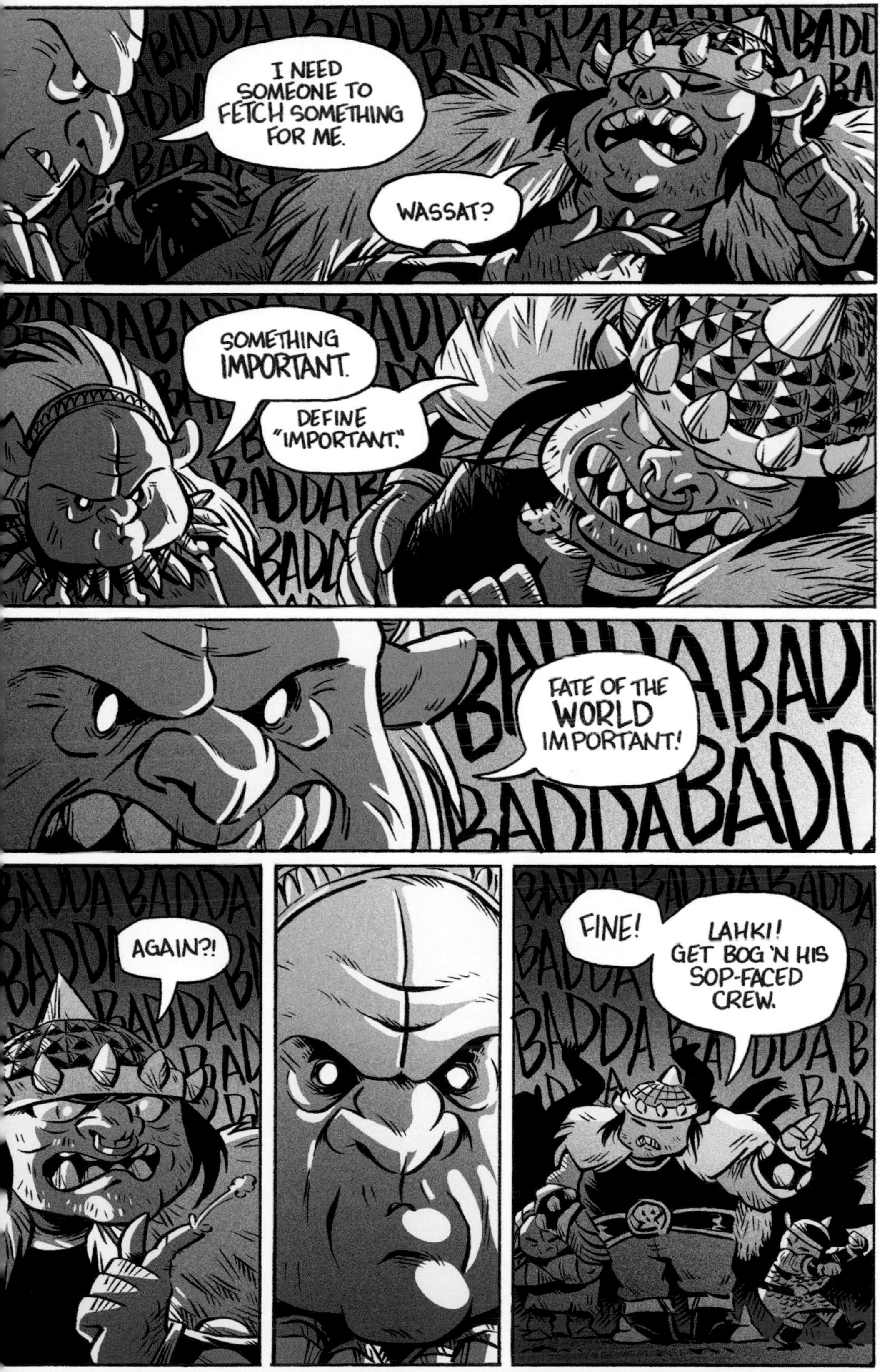
I NEED SOMEONE TO FETCH SOMETHING FOR ME.
WASSAT?
SOMETHING IMPORTANT.
DEFINE "IMPORTANT."
FATE OF THE WORLD IMPORTANT!
AGAIN?!
FINE!
LAHKI! GET BOG 'N HIS SOP-FACED CREW.

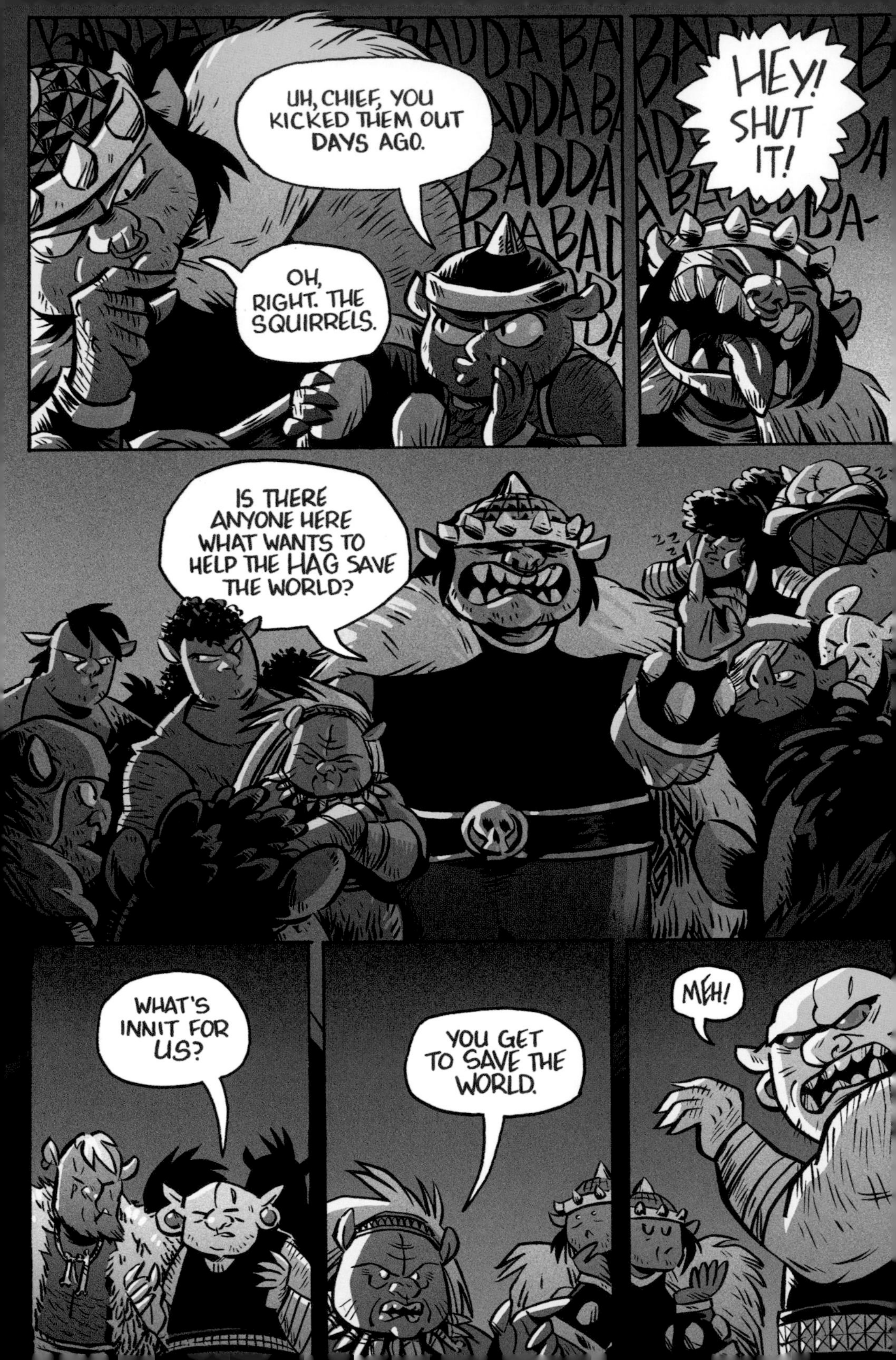
BADDA BADDA BADDA BADDA BA
UH, CHIEF, YOU KICKED THEM OUT DAYS AGO.
OH, RIGHT. THE SQUIRRELS.
HEY! SHUT IT!
IS THERE ANYONE HERE WHAT WANTS TO HELP THE HAG SAVE THE WORLD?
WHAT'S INNIT FOR US?
YOU GET TO SAVE THE WORLD.
MEH!

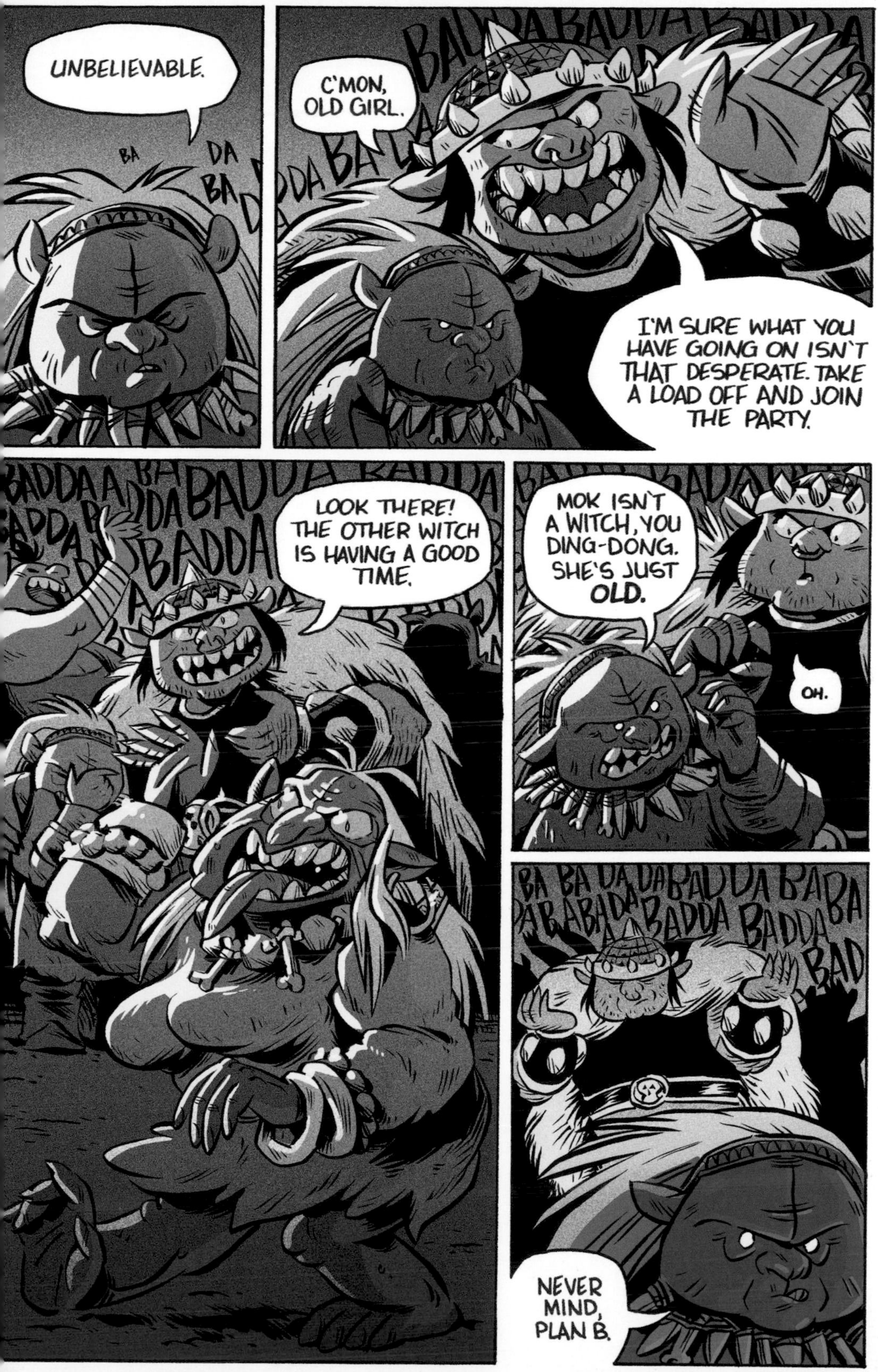
UNBELIEVABLE.
BA
DA
BA
C'MON, OLD GIRL.
BADDA BADDA
BADDA BA
I'M SURE WHAT YOU HAVE GOING ON ISN'T THAT DESPERATE. TAKE A LOAD OFF AND JOIN THE PARTY.
BADDA BADDA
LOOK THERE! THE OTHER WITCH IS HAVING A GOOD TIME.
MOK ISN'T A WITCH, YOU DING-DONG. SHE'S JUST OLD.
OH.
BA BA DA DA BADDA BA BA
BADDA BADDA
NEVER MIND, PLAN B.

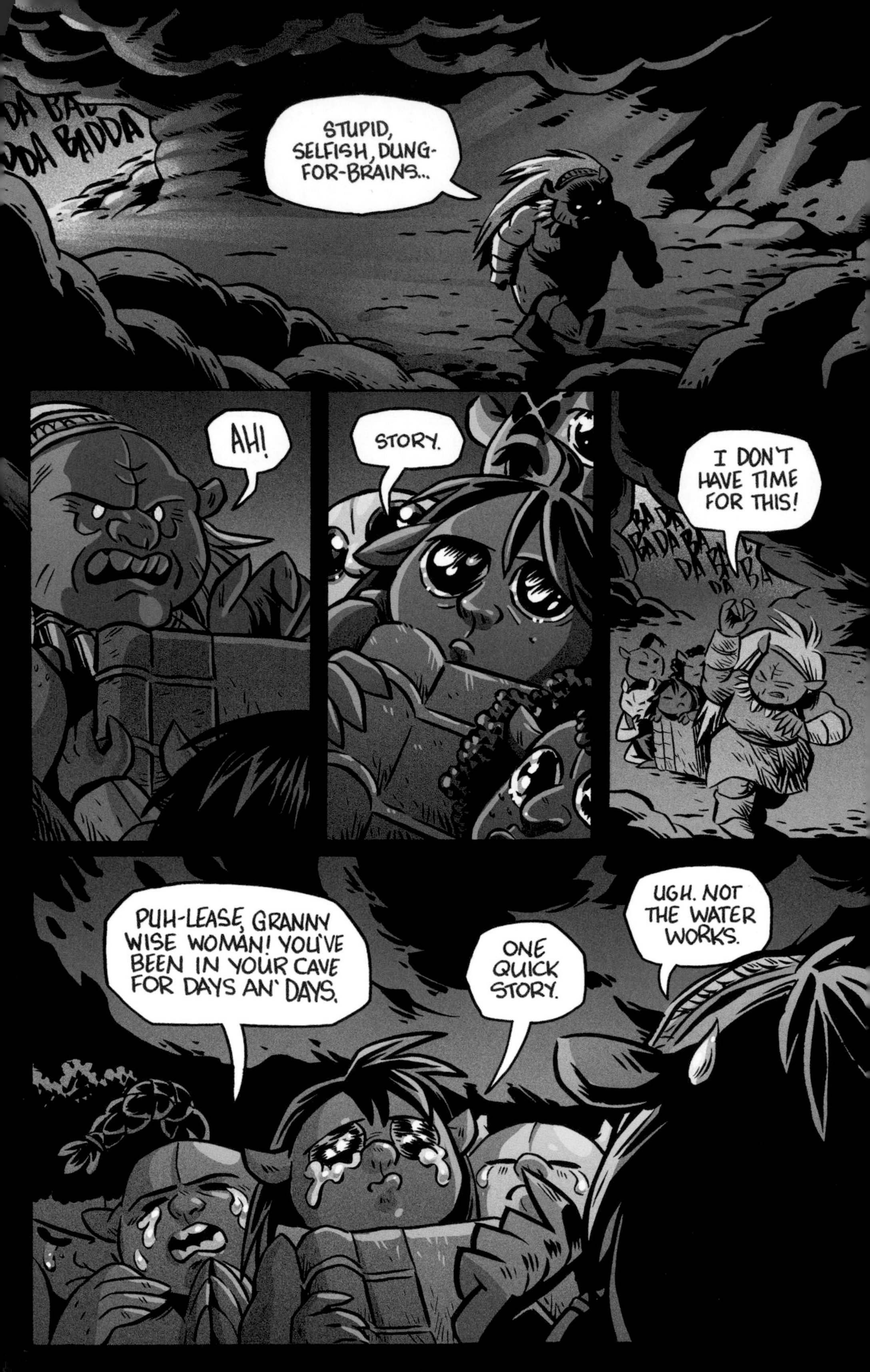
DA BAD
DA BADDA
STUPID, SELFISH, DUNG-FOR-BRAINS...
AH!
STORY.
I DON'T HAVE TIME FOR THIS!
BA DA BA DA BA DA BA DA BA DA
PUH-LEASE, GRANNY WISE WOMAN! YOU'VE BEEN IN YOUR CAVE FOR DAYS AN' DAYS.
ONE QUICK STORY.
UGH. NOT THE WATER WORKS.

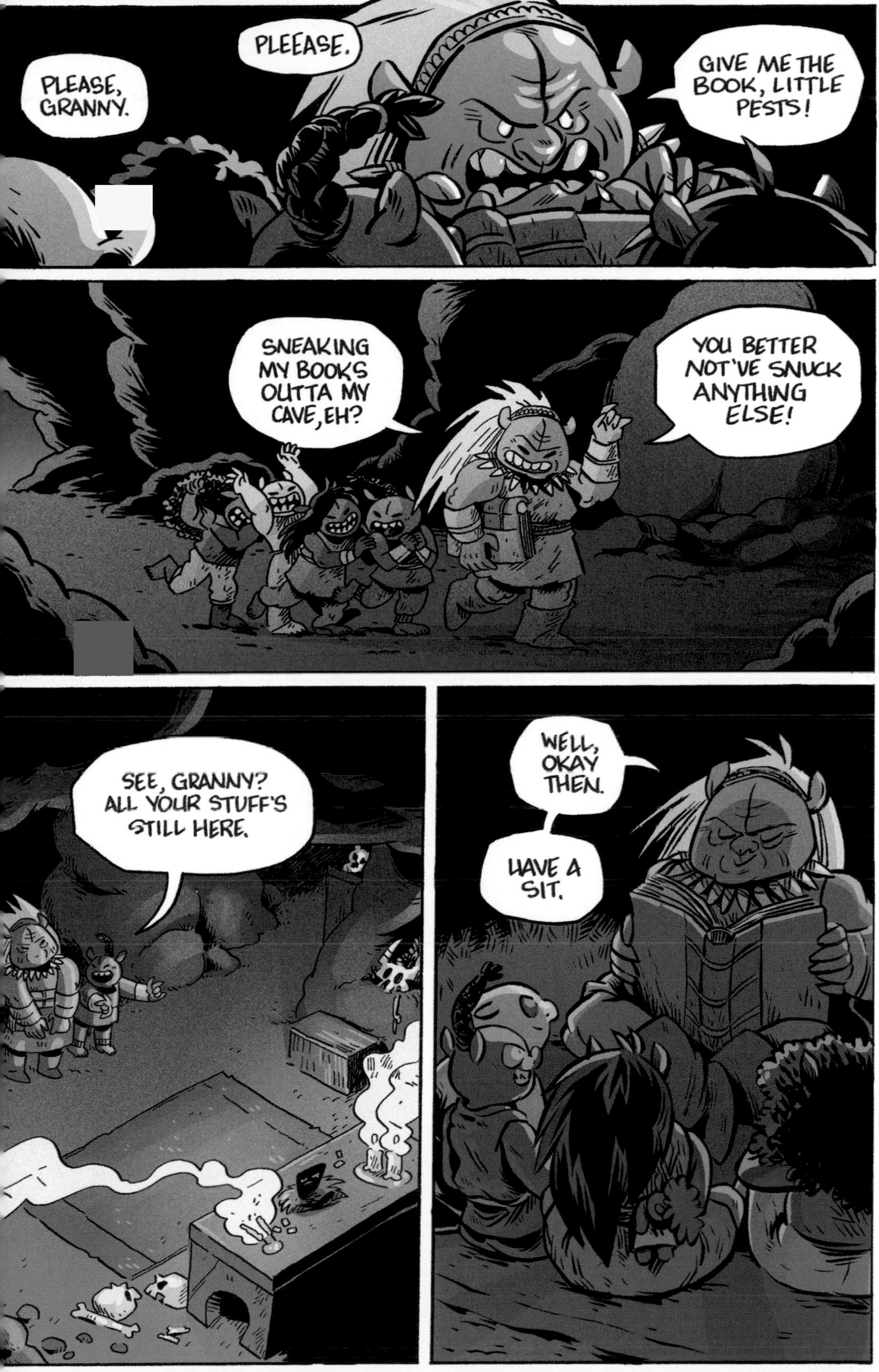
PLEASE, GRANNY.
PLEEASE.
GIVE ME THE BOOK, LITTLE PESTS!
SNEAKING MY BOOKS OUTTA MY CAVE, EH?
YOU BETTER NOT'VE SNUCK ANYTHING ELSE!
SEE, GRANNY? ALL YOUR STUFF'S STILL HERE.
WELL, OKAY THEN.
HAVE A SIT.

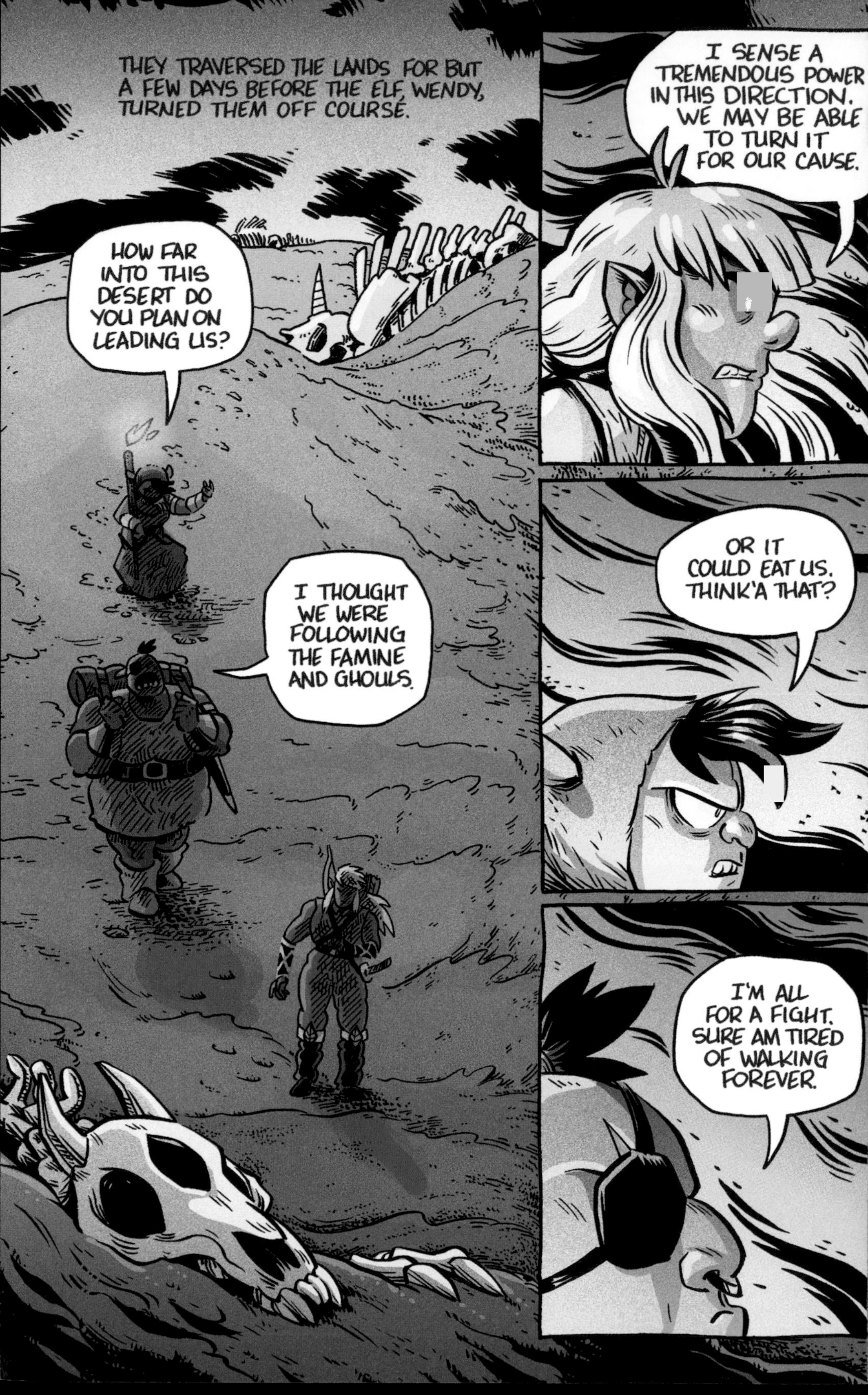
THEY TRAVERSED THE LANDS FOR BUT A FEW DAYS BEFORE THE ELF, WENDY, TURNED THEM OFF COURSE.
HOW FAR INTO THIS DESERT DO YOU PLAN ON LEADING US?
I THOUGHT WE WERE FOLLOWING THE FAMINE AND GHOULS.
I SENSE A TREMENDOUS POWER IN THIS DIRECTION. WE MAY BE ABLE TO TURN IT FOR OUR CAUSE.
OR IT COULD EAT US. THINK'A THAT?
I'M ALL FOR A FIGHT. SURE AM TIRED OF WALKING FOREVER.

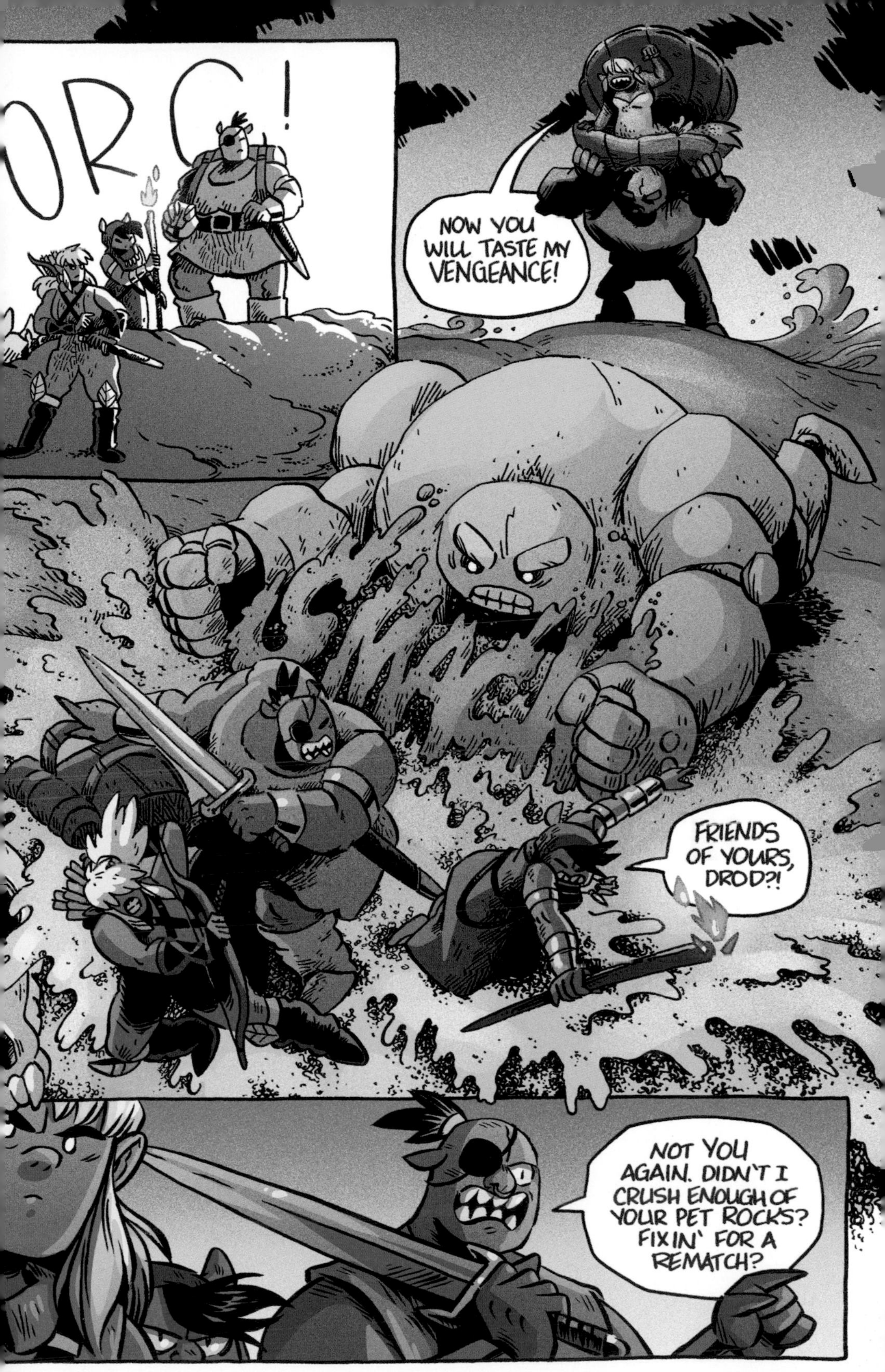
ORC!
NOW YOU WILL TASTE MY VENGEANCE!
FRIENDS OF YOURS, DROD?!
NOT YOU AGAIN. DIDN'T I CRUSH ENOUGH OF YOUR PET ROCKS? FIXIN' FOR A REMATCH?

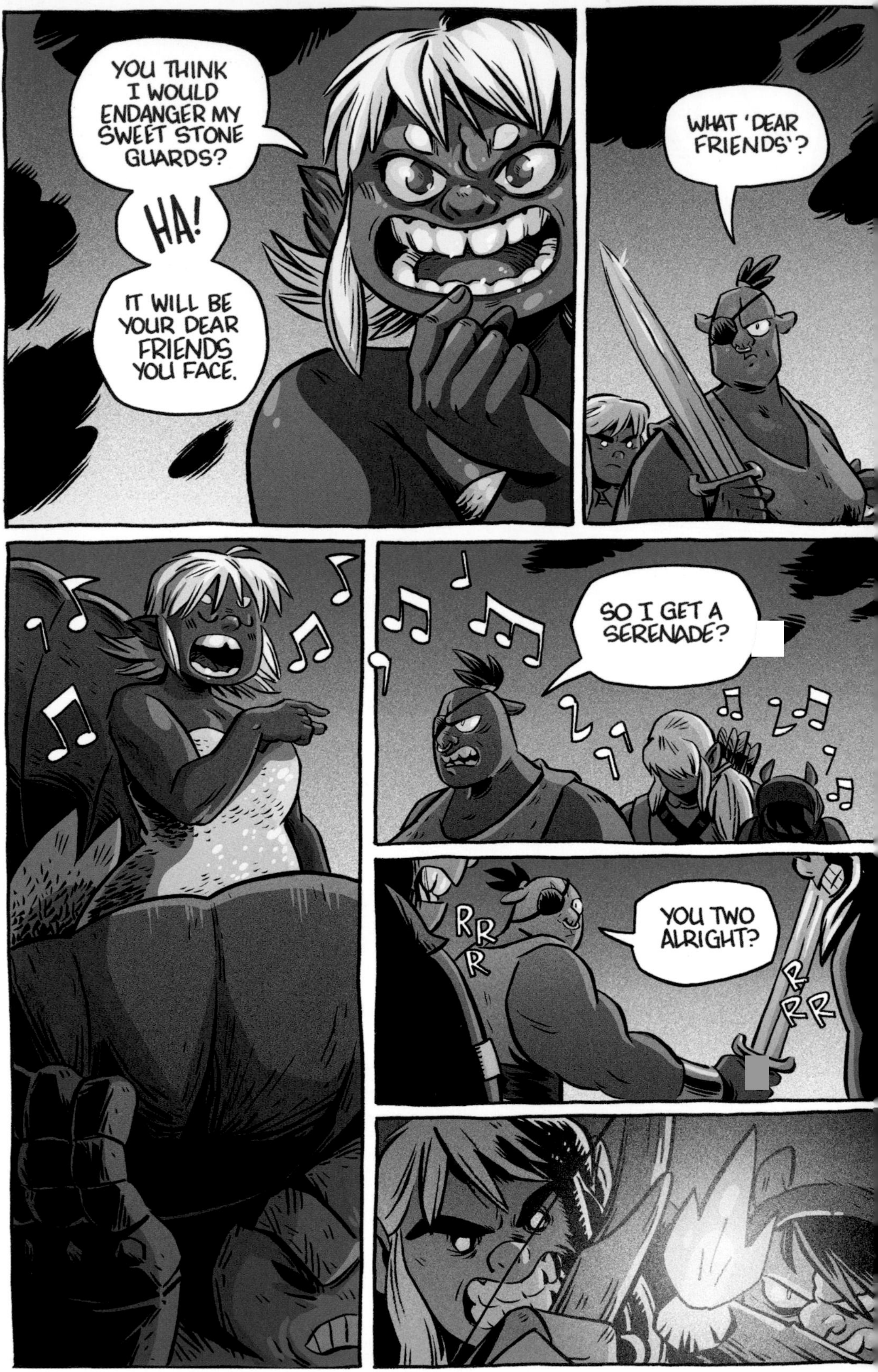
YOU THINK I WOULD ENDANGER MY SWEET STONE GUARDS?
HA!
IT WILL BE YOUR DEAR FRIENDS YOU FACE.
WHAT 'DEAR FRIENDS'?
SO I GET A SERENADE?
RRR
YOU TWO ALRIGHT?
RRR

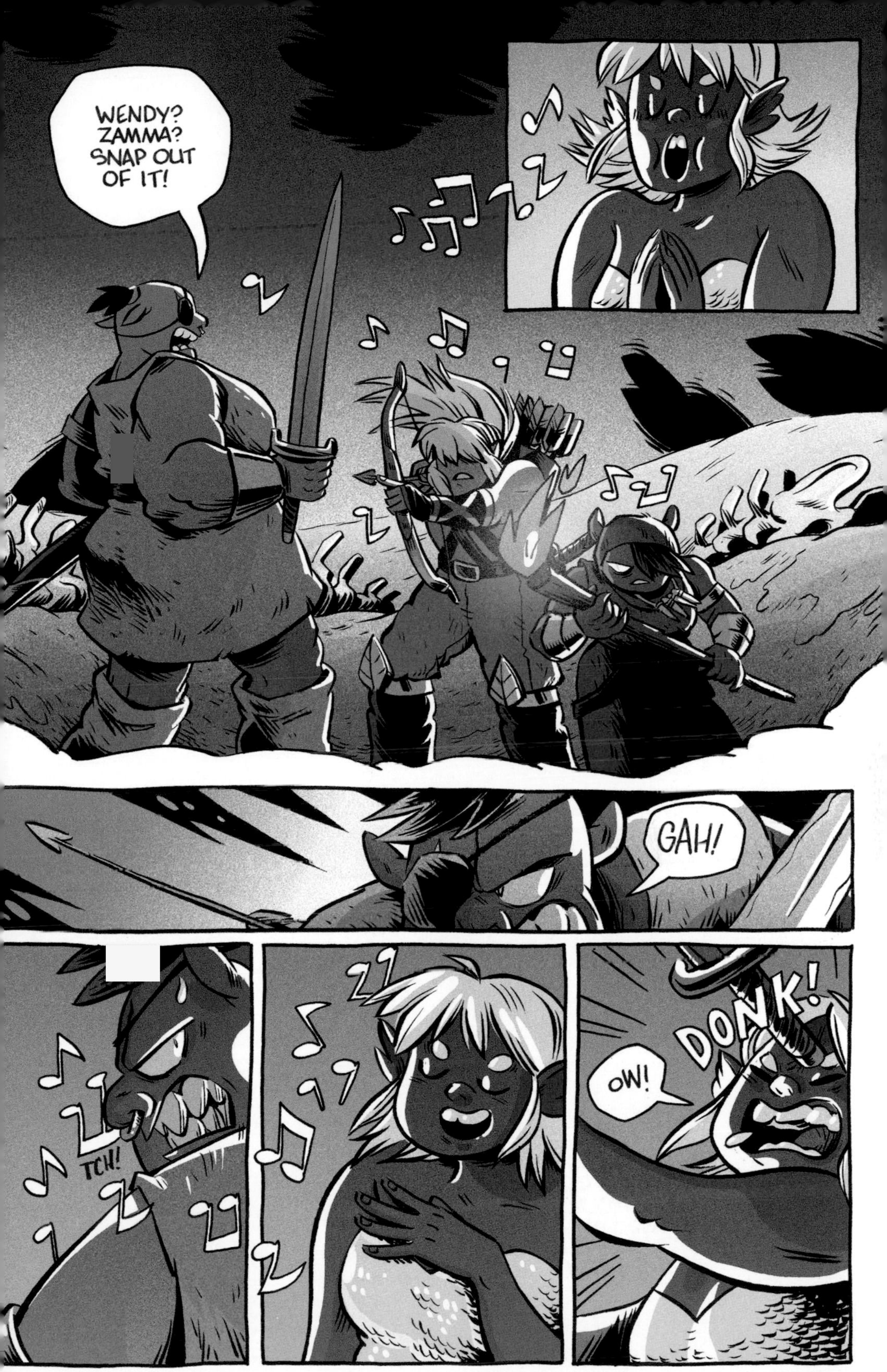
WENDY? ZAMMA? SNAP OUT OF IT!
GAH!
TCH!
OW!
DONK!

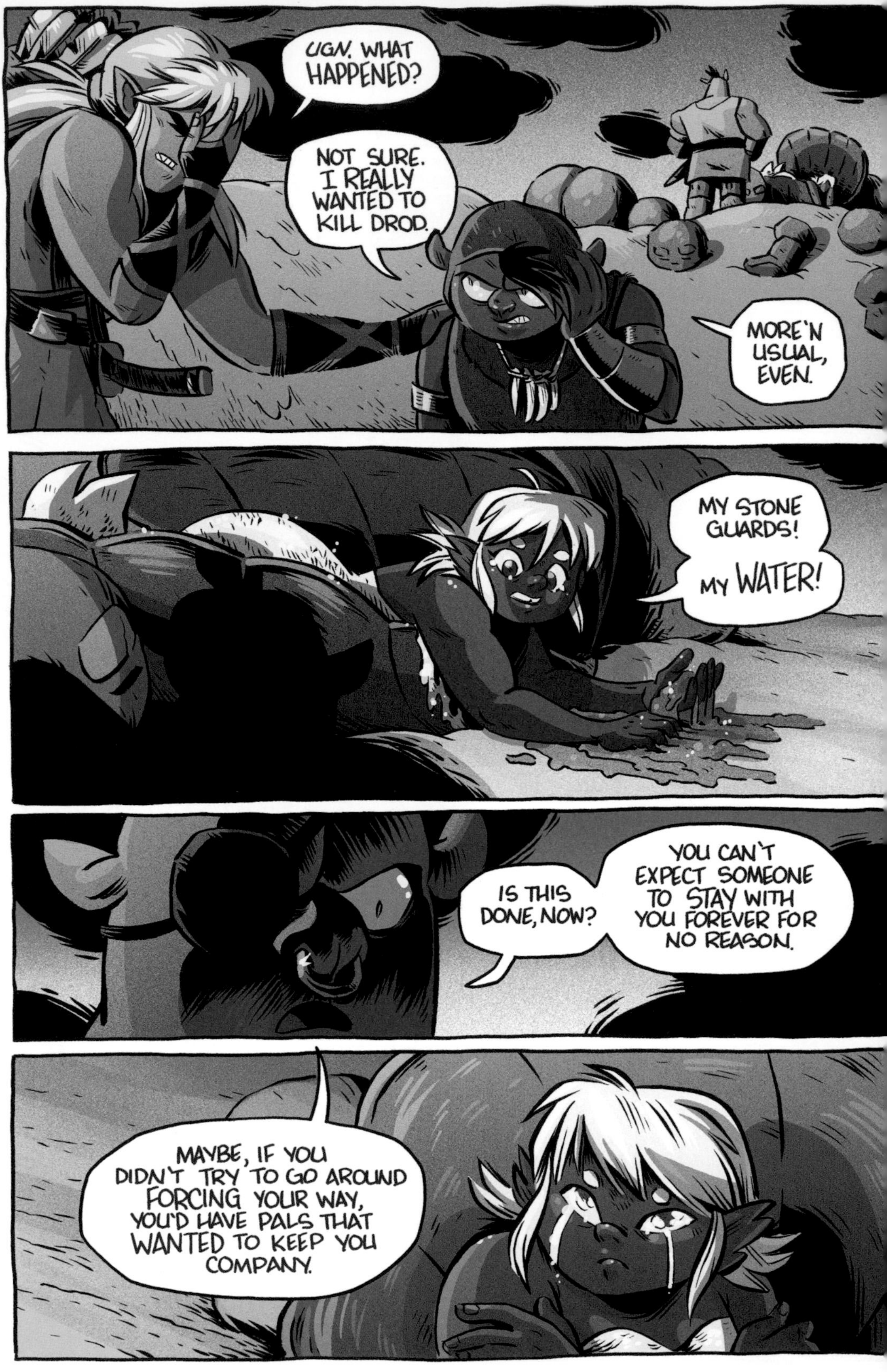
UGN. WHAT HAPPENED?
NOT SURE. I REALLY WANTED TO KILL DROD.
MORE'N USUAL, EVEN.
MY STONE GUARDS!
MY WATER!
IS THIS DONE, NOW?
YOU CAN'T EXPECT SOMEONE TO STAY WITH YOU FOREVER FOR NO REASON.
MAYBE, IF YOU DIDN'T TRY TO GO AROUND FORCING YOUR WAY, YOU'D HAVE PALS THAT WANTED TO KEEP YOU COMPANY.

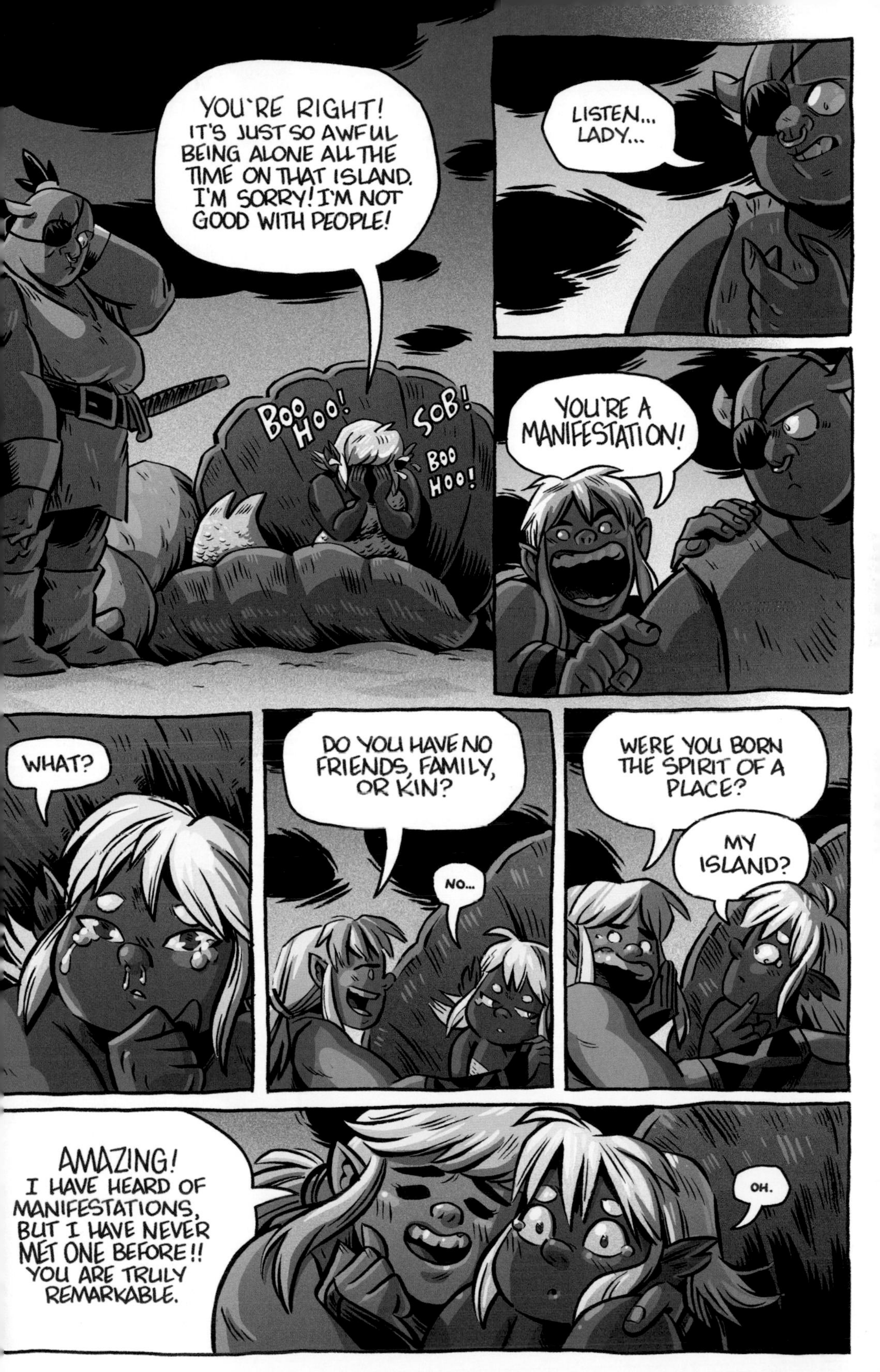
YOU'RE RIGHT! IT'S JUST SO AWFUL BEING ALONE ALL THE TIME ON THAT ISLAND. I'M SORRY! I'M NOT GOOD WITH PEOPLE!
BOO HOO!
SOB!
BOO HOO!
LISTEN... LADY...
YOU'RE A MANIFESTATION!
WHAT?
DO YOU HAVE NO FRIENDS, FAMILY, OR KIN?
NO...
WERE YOU BORN THE SPIRIT OF A PLACE?
MY ISLAND?
AMAZING! I HAVE HEARD OF MANIFESTATIONS, BUT I HAVE NEVER MET ONE BEFORE!! YOU ARE TRULY REMARKABLE.
OH.

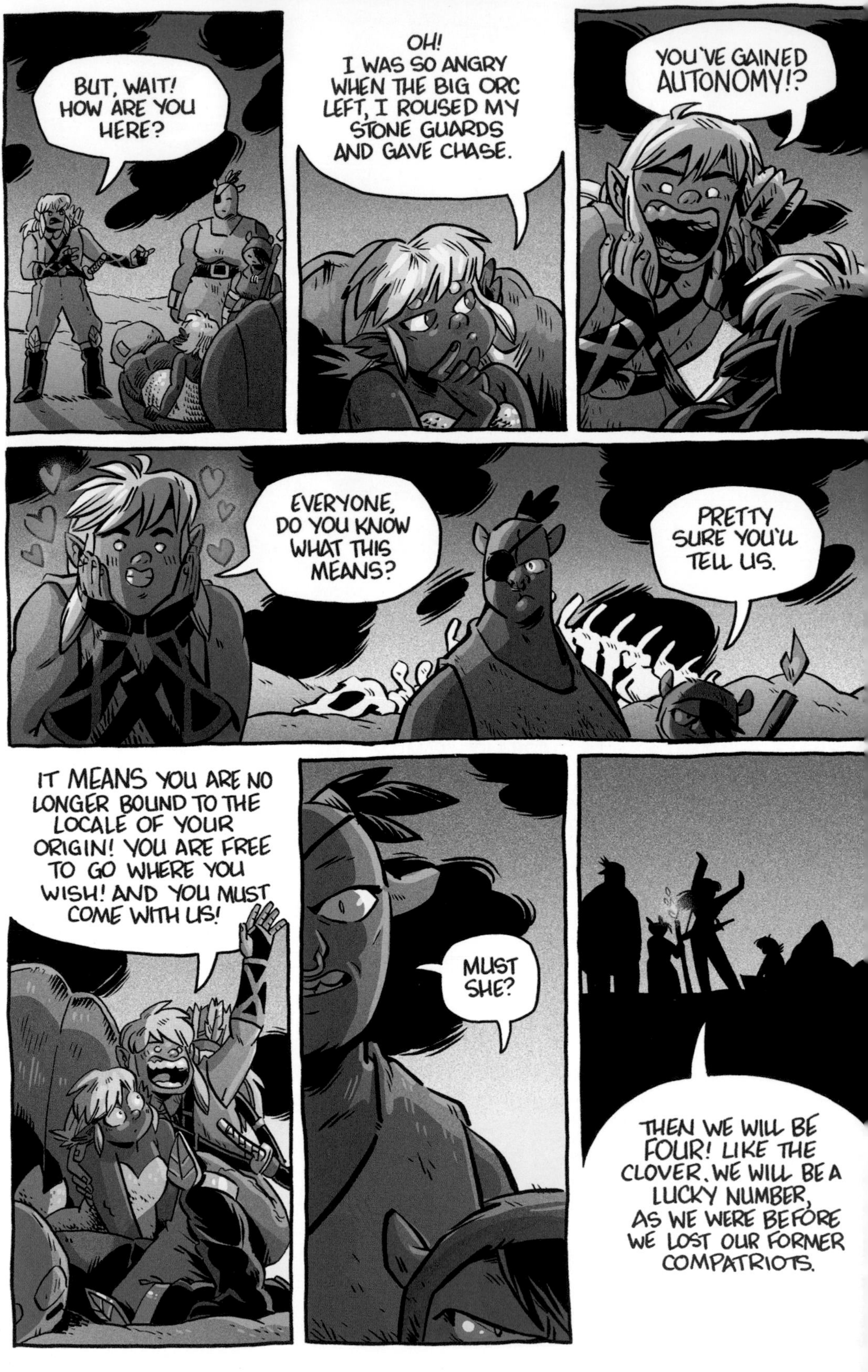
BUT, WAIT! HOW ARE YOU HERE?
OH! I WAS SO ANGRY WHEN THE BIG ORC LEFT, I ROUSED MY STONE GUARDS AND GAVE CHASE.
YOU'VE GAINED AUTONOMY!?
EVERYONE, DO YOU KNOW WHAT THIS MEANS?
PRETTY SURE YOU'LL TELL US.
IT MEANS YOU ARE NO LONGER BOUND TO THE LOCALE OF YOUR ORIGIN! YOU ARE FREE TO GO WHERE YOU WISH! AND YOU MUST COME WITH US!
MUST SHE?
THEN WE WILL BE FOUR! LIKE THE CLOVER. WE WILL BE A LUCKY NUMBER, AS WE WERE BEFORE WE LOST OUR FORMER COMPATRIOTS.

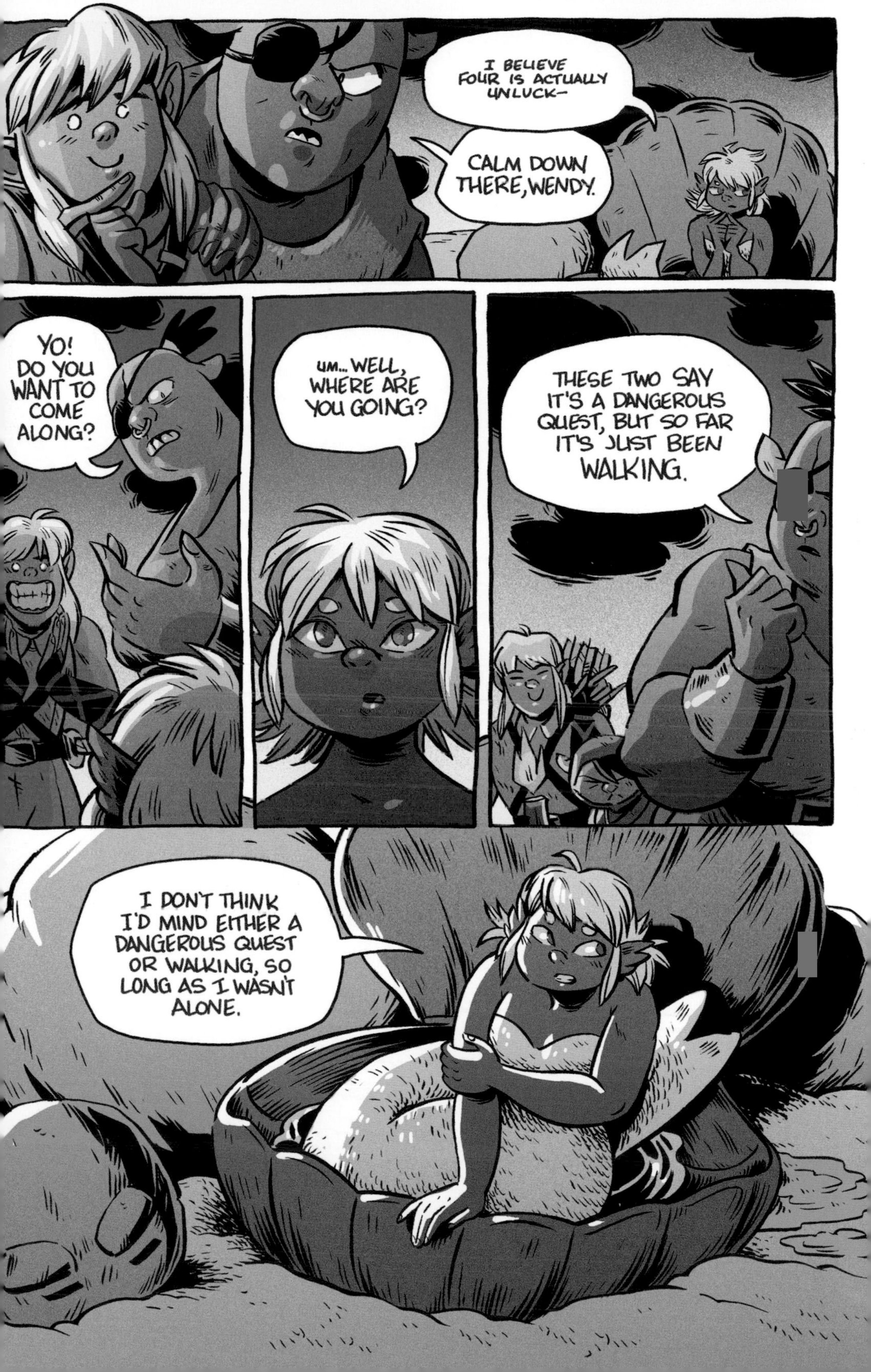
I BELIEVE FOUR IS ACTUALLY UNLUCK—
CALM DOWN THERE, WENDY.
YO! DO YOU WANT TO COME ALONG?
UM... WELL, WHERE ARE YOU GOING?
THESE TWO SAY IT'S A DANGEROUS QUEST, BUT SO FAR IT'S JUST BEEN WALKING.
I DON'T THINK I'D MIND EITHER A DANGEROUS QUEST OR WALKING, SO LONG AS I WASN'T ALONE.

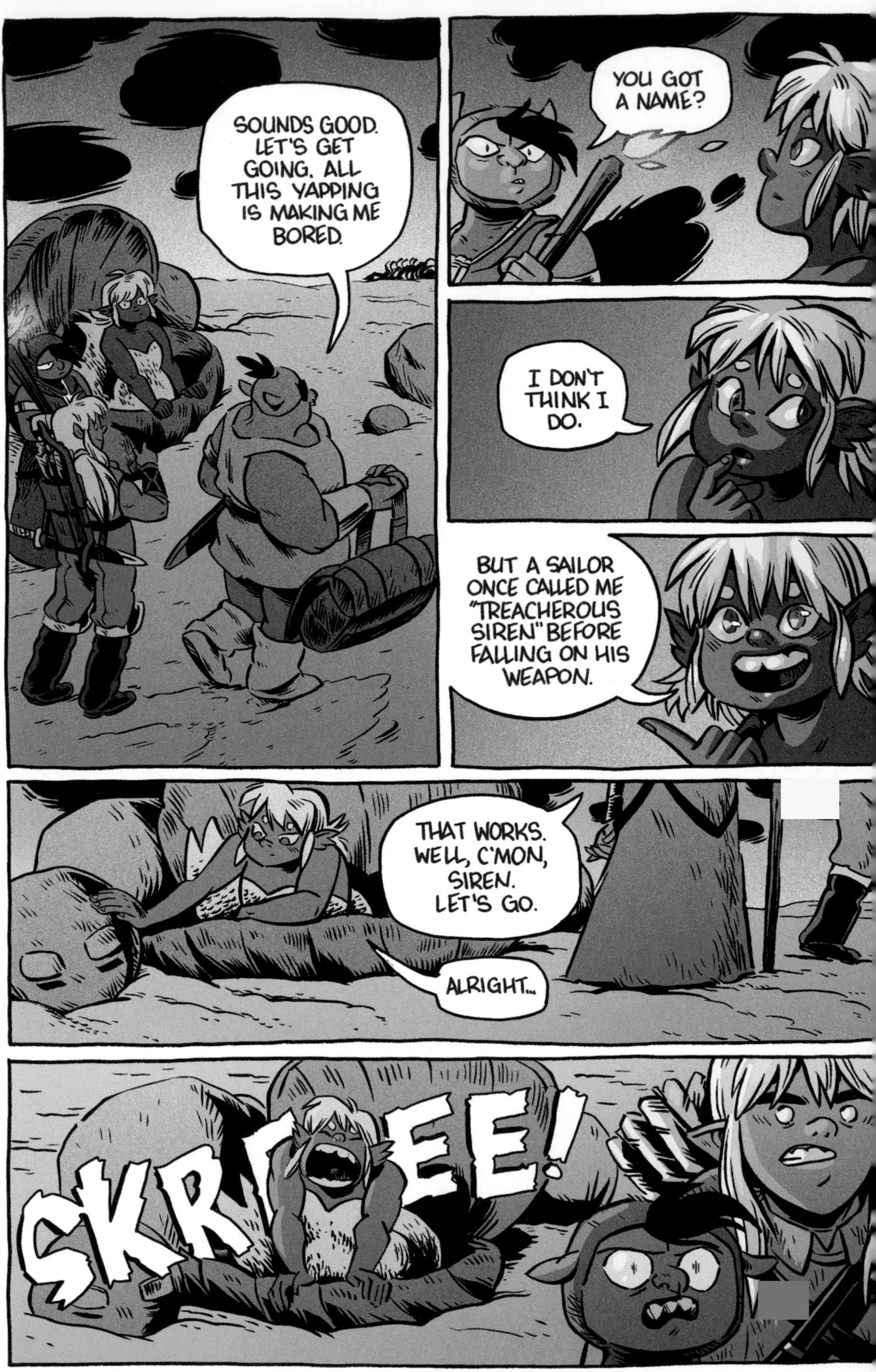
SOUNDS GOOD. LET'S GET GOING. ALL THIS YAPPING IS MAKING ME BORED.
YOU GOT A NAME?
I DON'T THINK I DO.
BUT A SAILOR ONCE CALLED ME "TREACHEROUS SIREN" BEFORE FALLING ON HIS WEAPON.
THAT WORKS. WELL, C'MON, SIREN. LET'S GO.
ALRIGHT...
SKREEE!

WHAT WAS THAT ABOU—

· · ·

DRAG!

CRAK

CLIK!

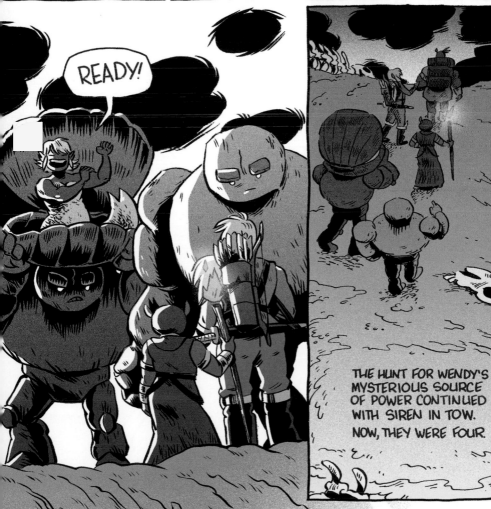

READY!

THE HUNT FOR WENDY'S MYSTERIOUS SOURCE OF POWER CONTINUED WITH SIREN IN TOW. NOW, THEY WERE FOUR.

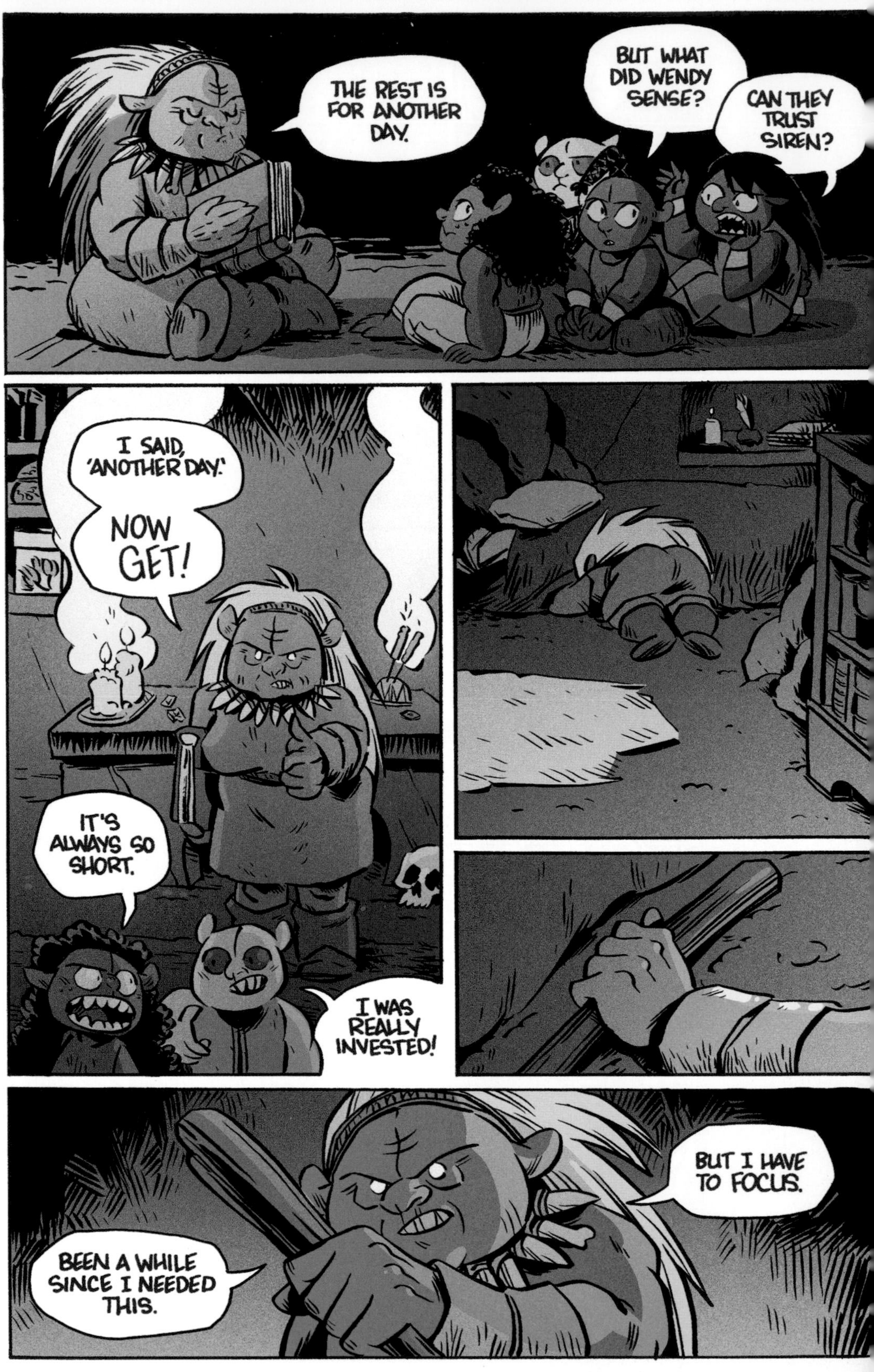
THE REST IS FOR ANOTHER DAY.
BUT WHAT DID WENDY SENSE?
CAN THEY TRUST SIREN?
I SAID, 'ANOTHER DAY.'
NOW GET!
IT'S ALWAYS SO SHORT.
I WAS REALLY INVESTED!
BUT I HAVE TO FOCUS.
BEEN A WHILE SINCE I NEEDED THIS.

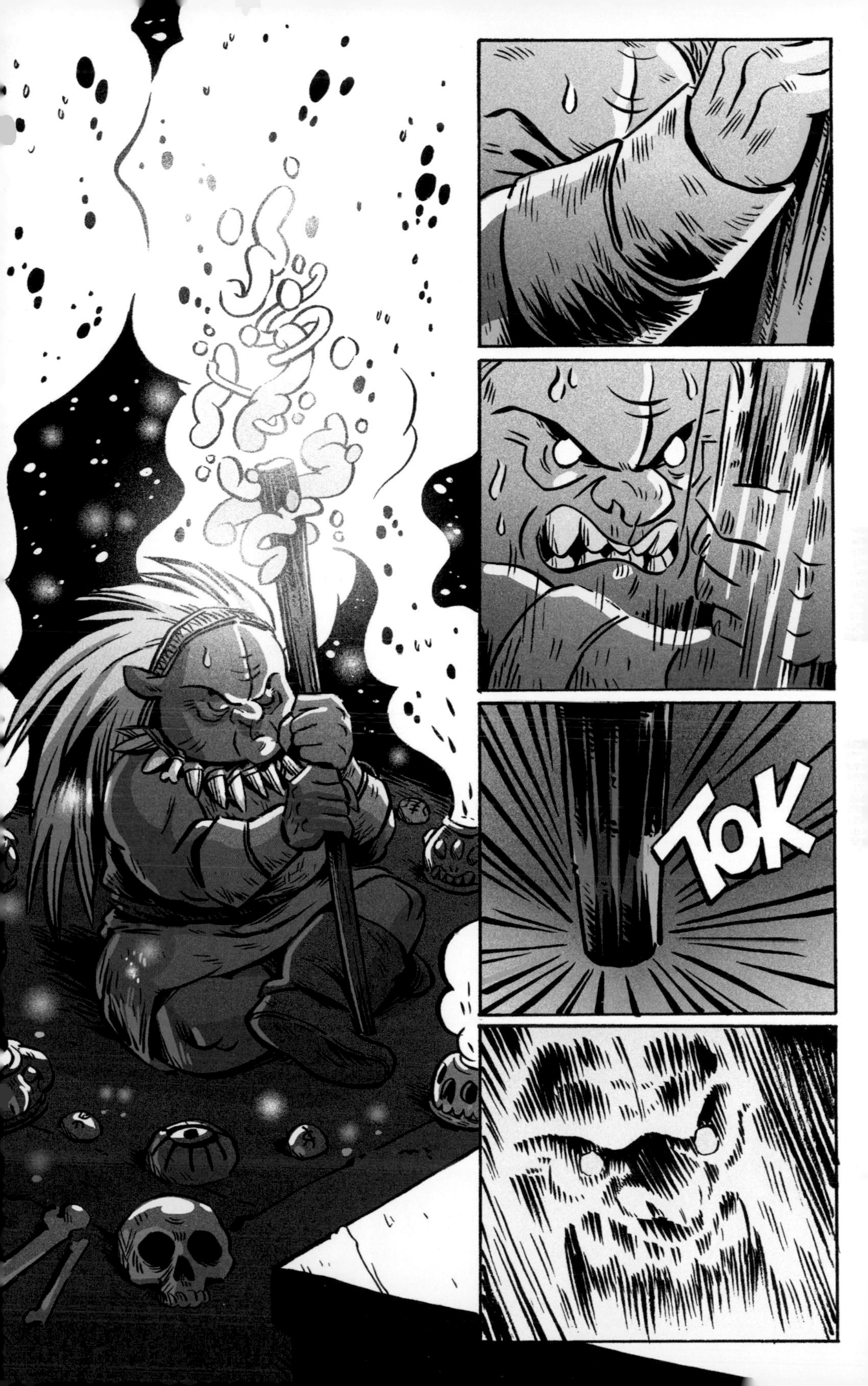
TOK

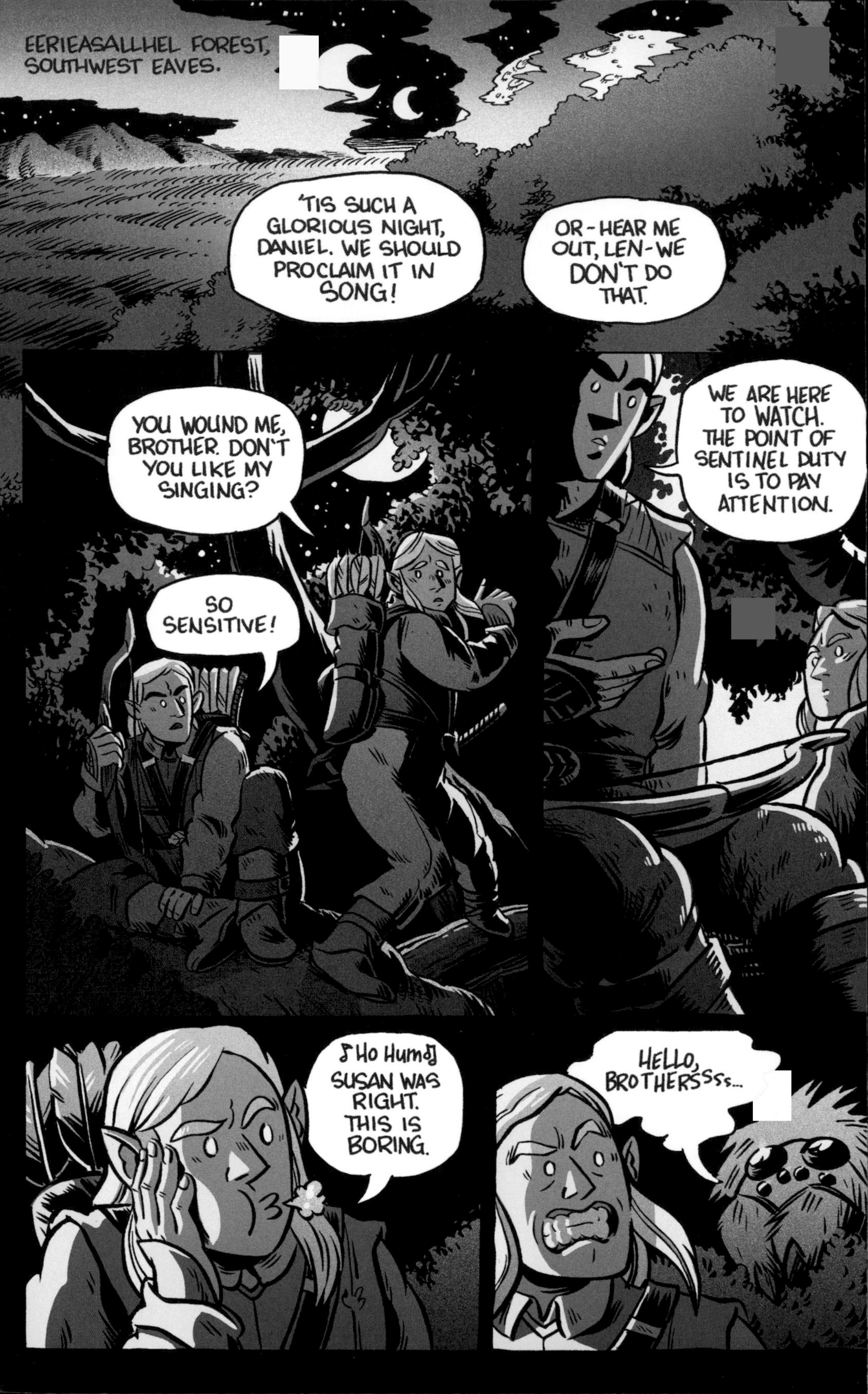
EERIEASALLHEL FOREST, SOUTHWEST EAVES.
'TIS SUCH A GLORIOUS NIGHT, DANIEL. WE SHOULD PROCLAIM IT IN SONG!
OR-HEAR ME OUT, LEN-WE DON'T DO THAT.
YOU WOUND ME, BROTHER. DON'T YOU LIKE MY SINGING?
SO SENSITIVE!
WE ARE HERE TO WATCH. THE POINT OF SENTINEL DUTY IS TO PAY ATTENTION.
♪ HO HUM ♫ SUSAN WAS RIGHT. THIS IS BORING.
HELLO, BROTHERSSSS...

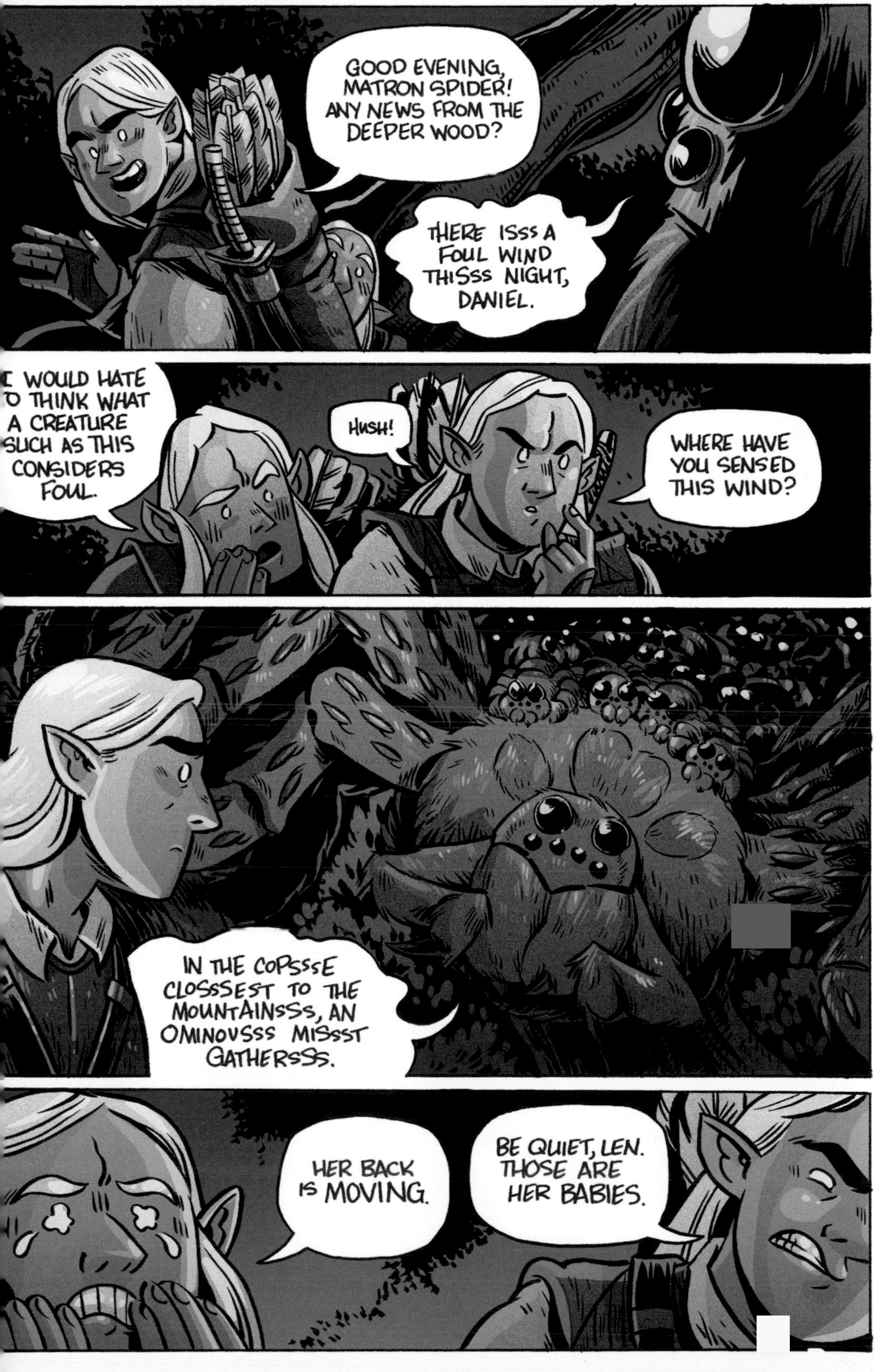
GOOD EVENING, MATRON SPIDER! ANY NEWS FROM THE DEEPER WOOD?
THERE ISSS A FOUL WIND THISSS NIGHT, DANIEL.
I WOULD HATE TO THINK WHAT A CREATURE SUCH AS THIS CONSIDERS FOUL.
HUSH!
WHERE HAVE YOU SENSED THIS WIND?
IN THE COPSSSE CLOSSSEST TO THE MOUNTAINSSS, AN OMINOUSSS MISSST GATHERSSS.
HER BACK IS MOVING.
BE QUIET, LEN. THOSE ARE HER BABIES.

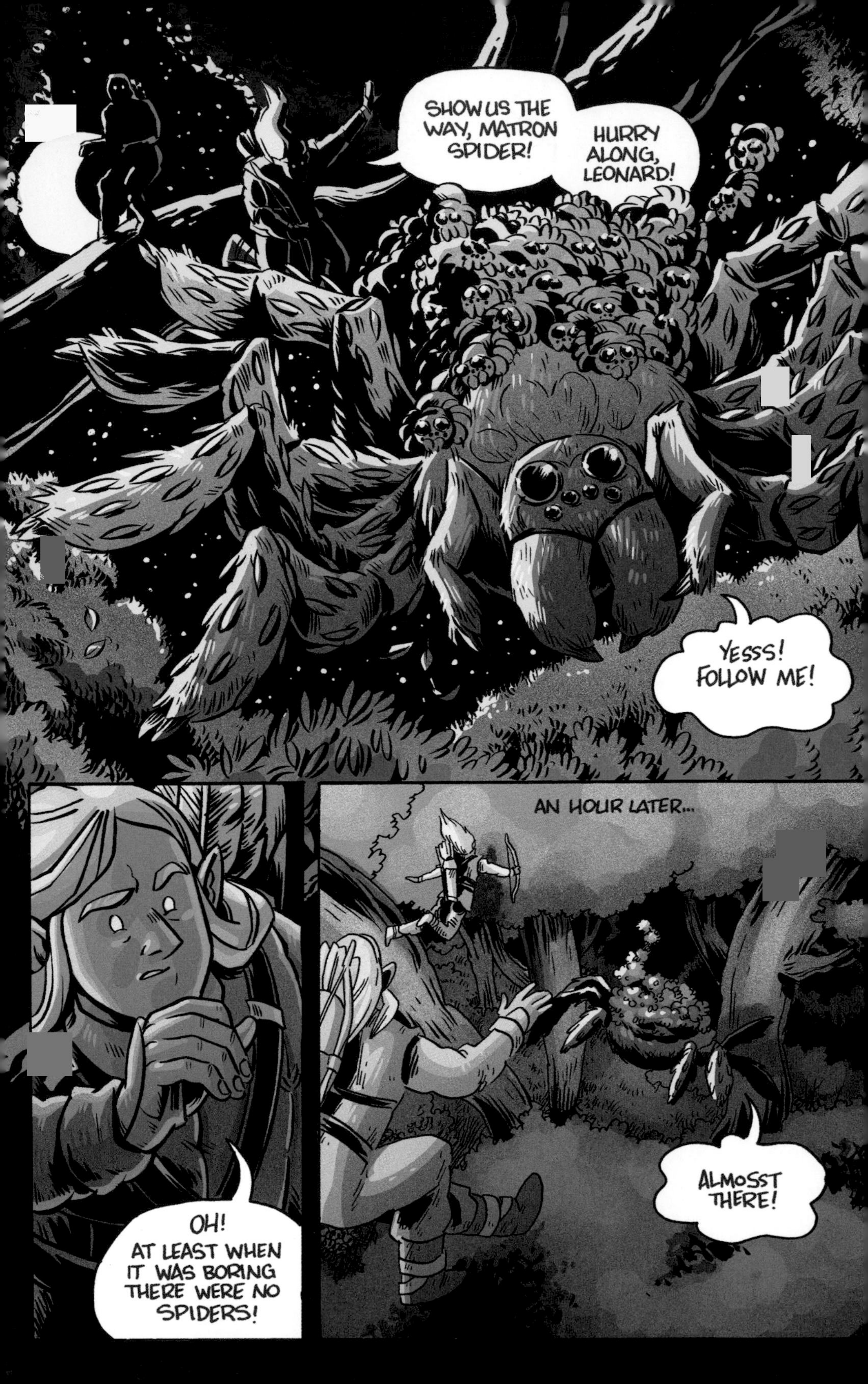
SHOW US THE WAY, MATRON SPIDER!
HURRY ALONG, LEONARD!
YESSS! FOLLOW ME!
OH! AT LEAST WHEN IT WAS BORING THERE WERE NO SPIDERS!
AN HOUR LATER...
ALMOSST THERE!

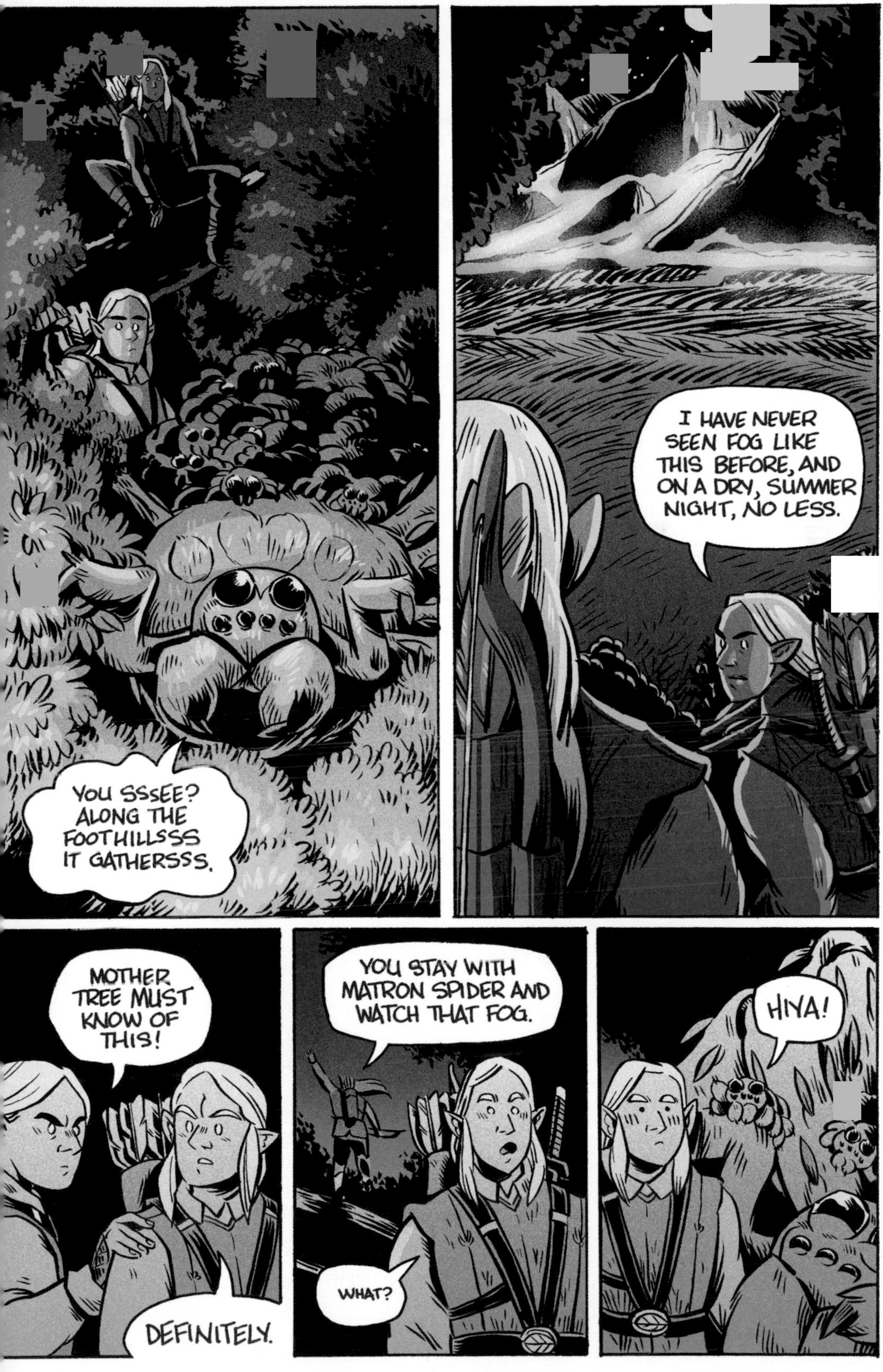
YOU SSSEE? ALONG THE FOOTHILLSSS IT GATHERSSS.
I HAVE NEVER SEEN FOG LIKE THIS BEFORE, AND ON A DRY, SUMMER NIGHT, NO LESS.
MOTHER TREE MUST KNOW OF THIS!
DEFINITELY.
YOU STAY WITH MATRON SPIDER AND WATCH THAT FOG.
WHAT?
HIYA!

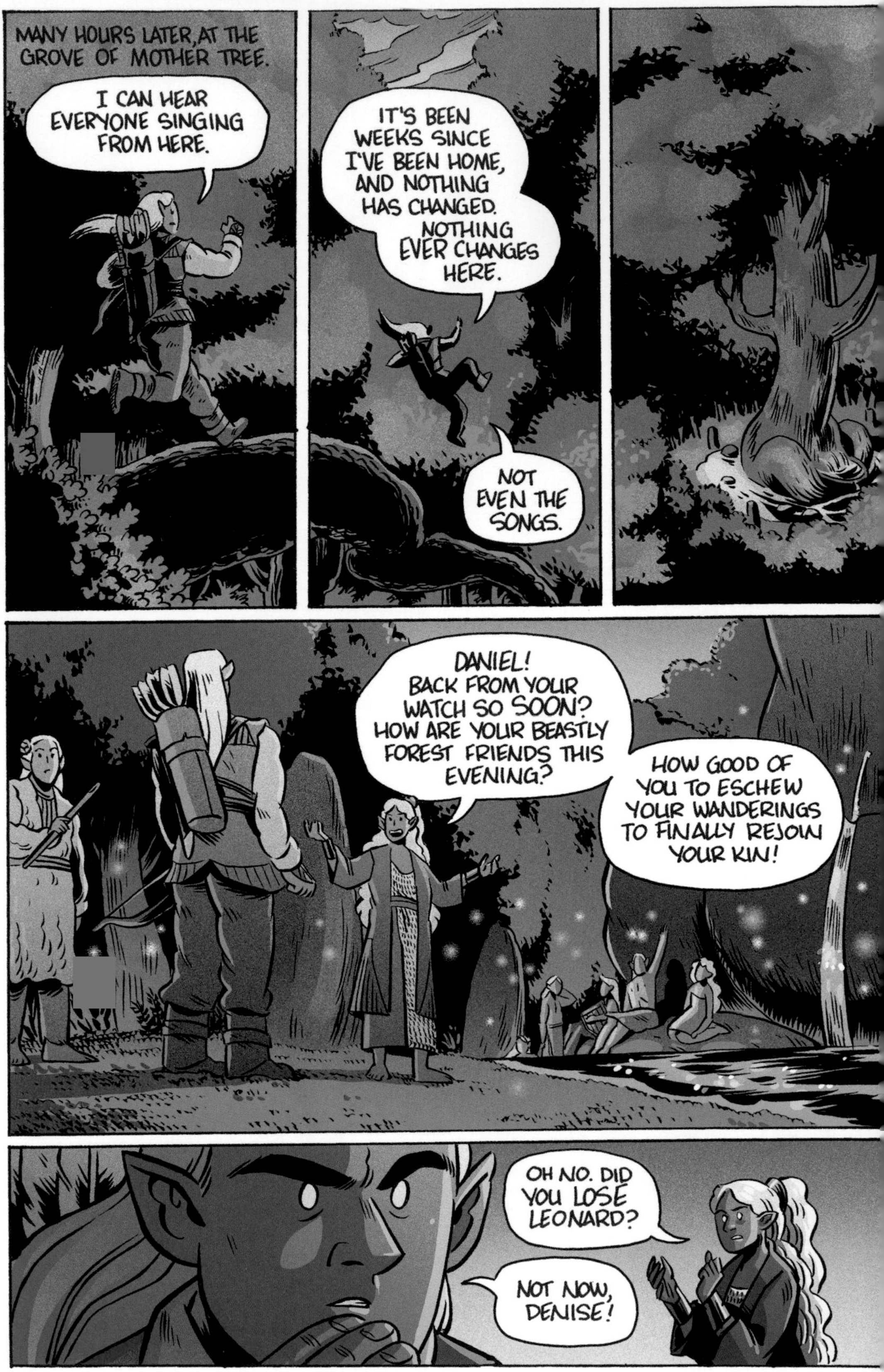
MANY HOURS LATER, AT THE GROVE OF MOTHER TREE.
I CAN HEAR EVERYONE SINGING FROM HERE.
IT'S BEEN WEEKS SINCE I'VE BEEN HOME, AND NOTHING HAS CHANGED.
NOTHING EVER CHANGES HERE.
NOT EVEN THE SONGS.
DANIEL! BACK FROM YOUR WATCH SO SOON? HOW ARE YOUR BEASTLY FOREST FRIENDS THIS EVENING?
HOW GOOD OF YOU TO ESCHEW YOUR WANDERINGS TO FINALLY REJOIN YOUR KIN!
OH NO. DID YOU LOSE LEONARD?
NOT NOW, DENISE!

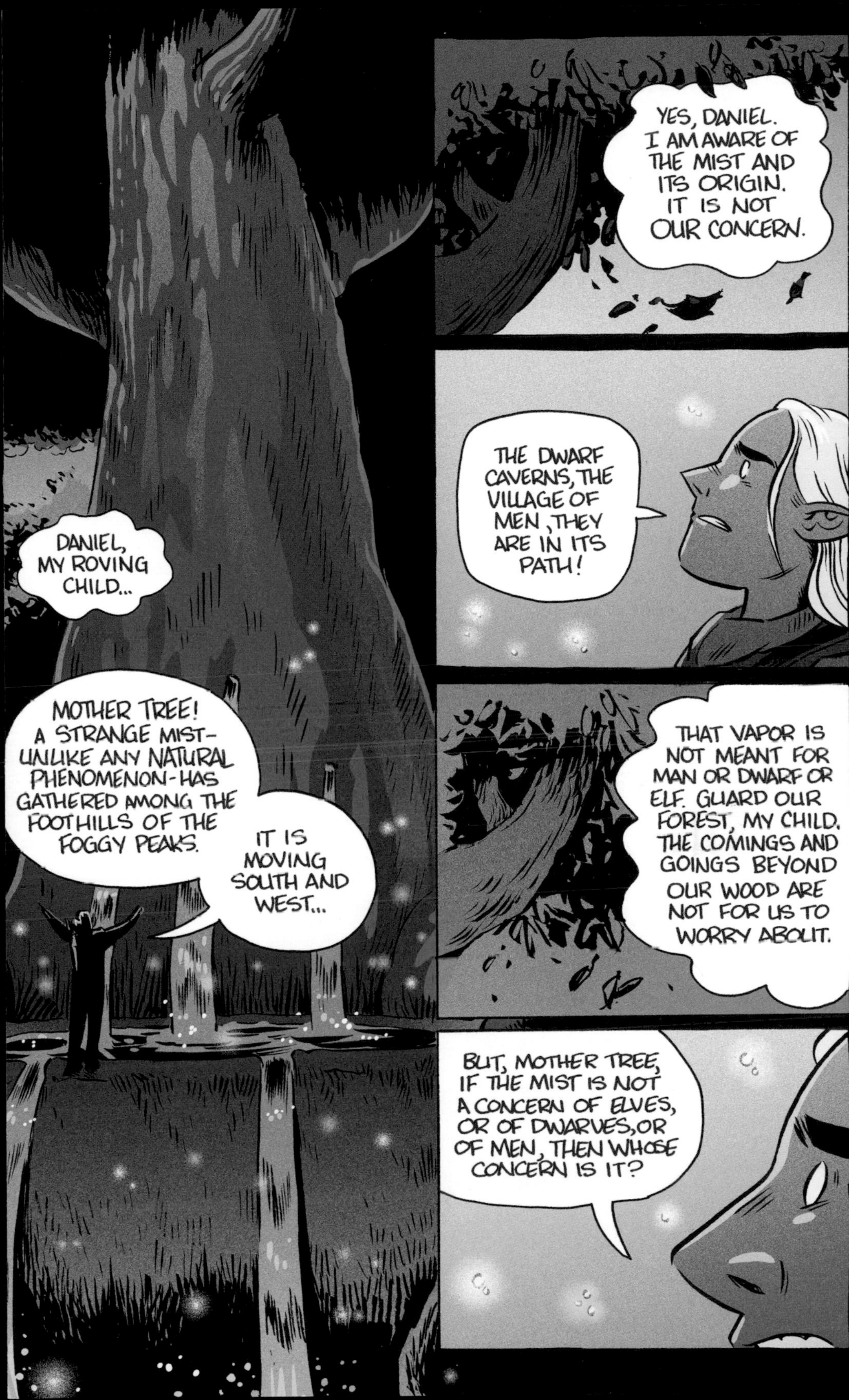
DANIEL, MY ROVING CHILD...
MOTHER TREE! A STRANGE MIST- UNLIKE ANY NATURAL PHENOMENON- HAS GATHERED AMONG THE FOOTHILLS OF THE FOGGY PEAKS.
IT IS MOVING SOUTH AND WEST...
YES, DANIEL. I AM AWARE OF THE MIST AND ITS ORIGIN. IT IS NOT OUR CONCERN.
THE DWARF CAVERNS, THE VILLAGE OF MEN, THEY ARE IN ITS PATH!
THAT VAPOR IS NOT MEANT FOR MAN OR DWARF OR ELF. GUARD OUR FOREST, MY CHILD. THE COMINGS AND GOINGS BEYOND OUR WOOD ARE NOT FOR US TO WORRY ABOUT.
BUT, MOTHER TREE, IF THE MIST IS NOT A CONCERN OF ELVES, OR OF DWARVES, OR OF MEN, THEN WHOSE CONCERN IS IT?

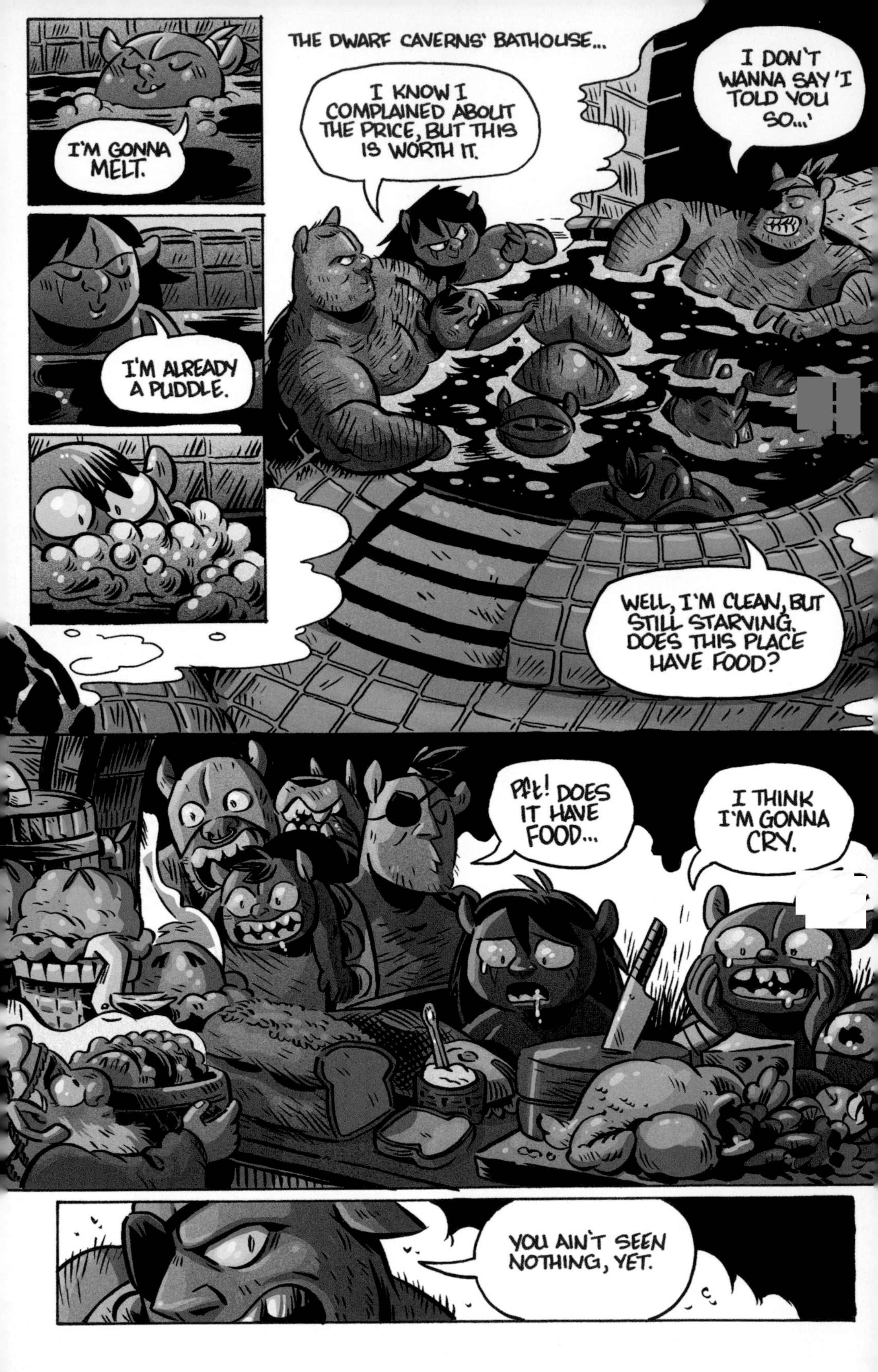
THE DWARF CAVERNS' BATHOUSE...
I'M GONNA MELT.
I KNOW I COMPLAINED ABOUT THE PRICE, BUT THIS IS WORTH IT.
I DON'T WANNA SAY 'I TOLD YOU SO...'
I'M ALREADY A PUDDLE.
WELL, I'M CLEAN, BUT STILL STARVING. DOES THIS PLACE HAVE FOOD?
PFT! DOES IT HAVE FOOD...
I THINK I'M GONNA CRY.
YOU AIN'T SEEN NOTHING, YET.

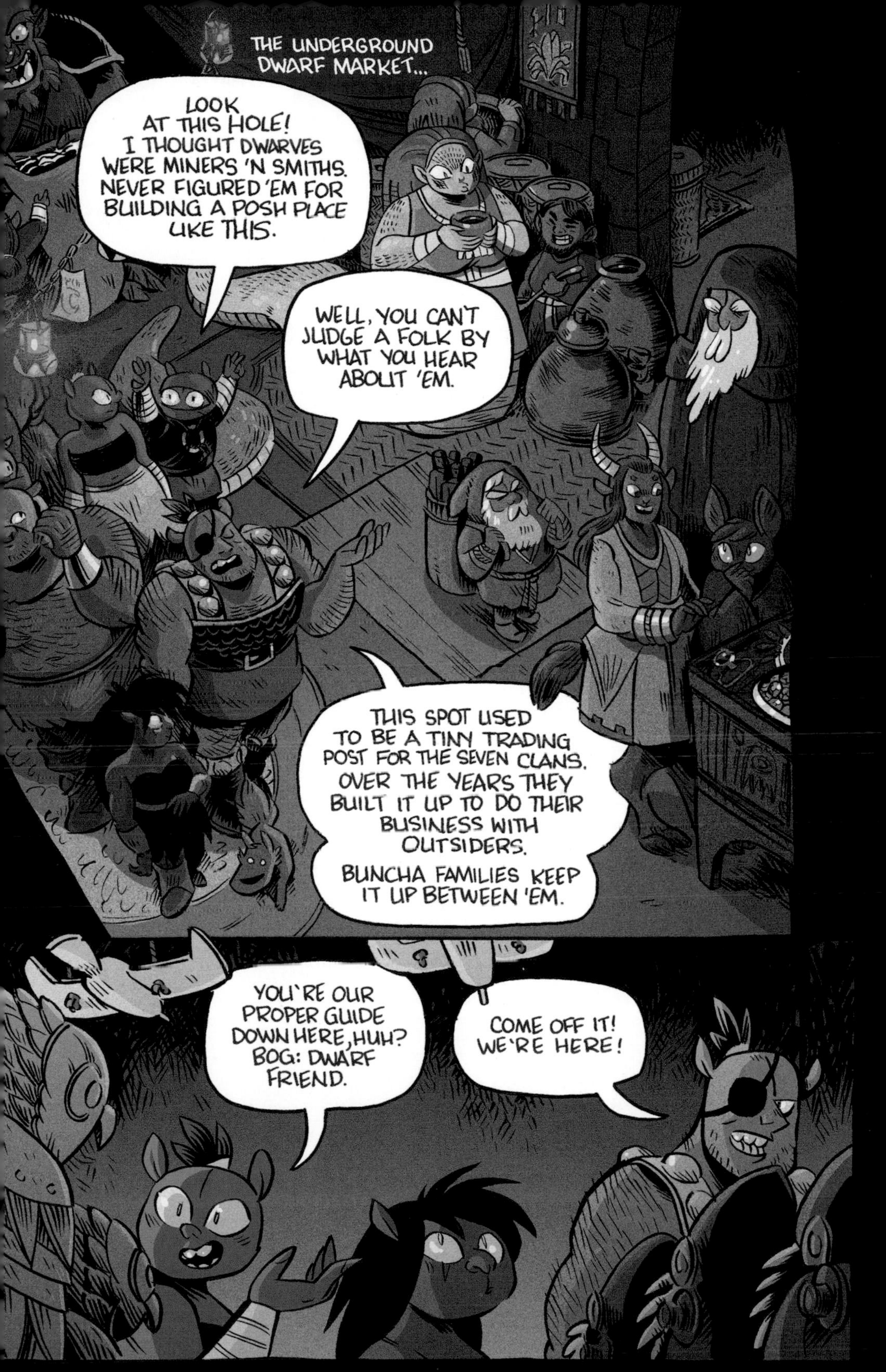
THE UNDERGROUND DWARF MARKET...
LOOK AT THIS HOLE! I THOUGHT DWARVES WERE MINERS 'N SMITHS. NEVER FIGURED 'EM FOR BUILDING A POSH PLACE LIKE THIS.
WELL, YOU CAN'T JUDGE A FOLK BY WHAT YOU HEAR ABOUT 'EM.
THIS SPOT USED TO BE A TINY TRADING POST FOR THE SEVEN CLANS. OVER THE YEARS THEY BUILT IT UP TO DO THEIR BUSINESS WITH OUTSIDERS.
BUNCHA FAMILIES KEEP IT UP BETWEEN 'EM.
YOU'RE OUR PROPER GUIDE DOWN HERE, HUH? BOG: DWARF FRIEND.
COME OFF IT! WE'RE HERE!

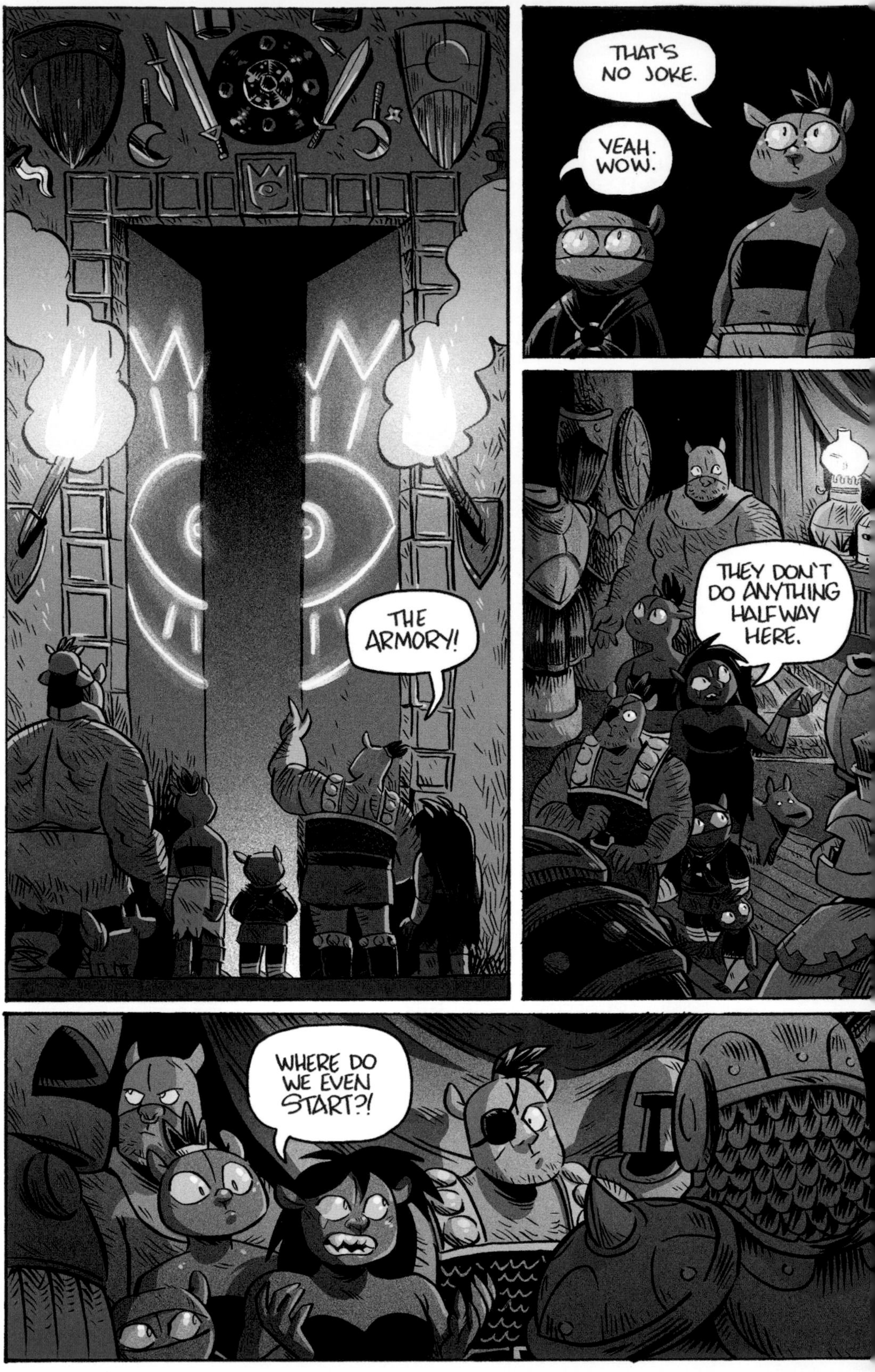
THE ARMORY!
THAT'S NO JOKE.
YEAH. WOW.
THEY DON'T DO ANYTHING HALFWAY HERE.
WHERE DO WE EVEN START?!

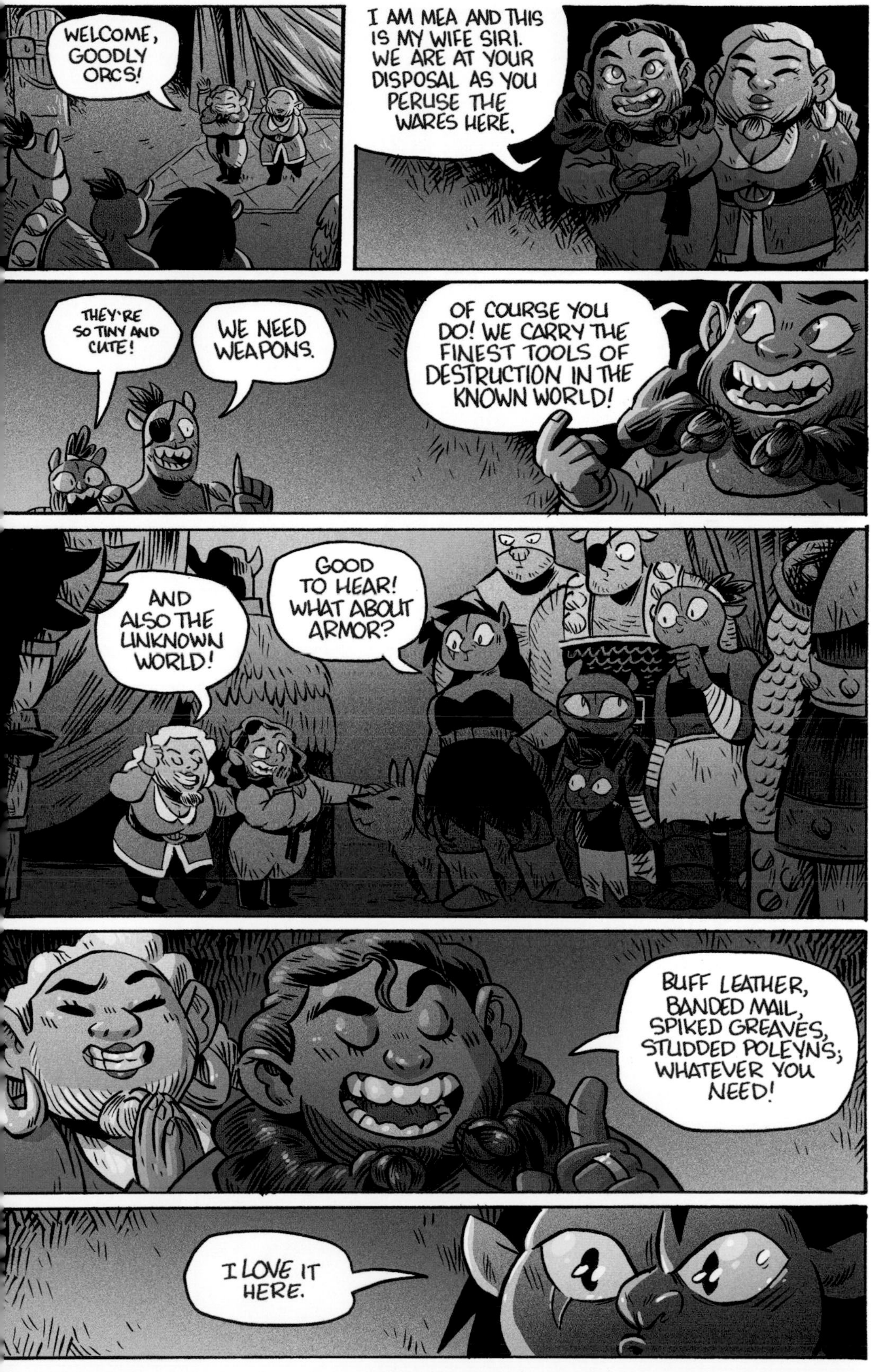
WELCOME, GOODLY ORCS!
I AM MEA AND THIS IS MY WIFE SIRI. WE ARE AT YOUR DISPOSAL AS YOU PERUSE THE WARES HERE.
THEY'RE SO TINY AND CUTE!
WE NEED WEAPONS.
OF COURSE YOU DO! WE CARRY THE FINEST TOOLS OF DESTRUCTION IN THE KNOWN WORLD!
AND ALSO THE UNKNOWN WORLD!
GOOD TO HEAR! WHAT ABOUT ARMOR?
BUFF LEATHER, BANDED MAIL, SPIKED GREAVES, STUDDED POLEYNS; WHATEVER YOU NEED!
I LOVE IT HERE.

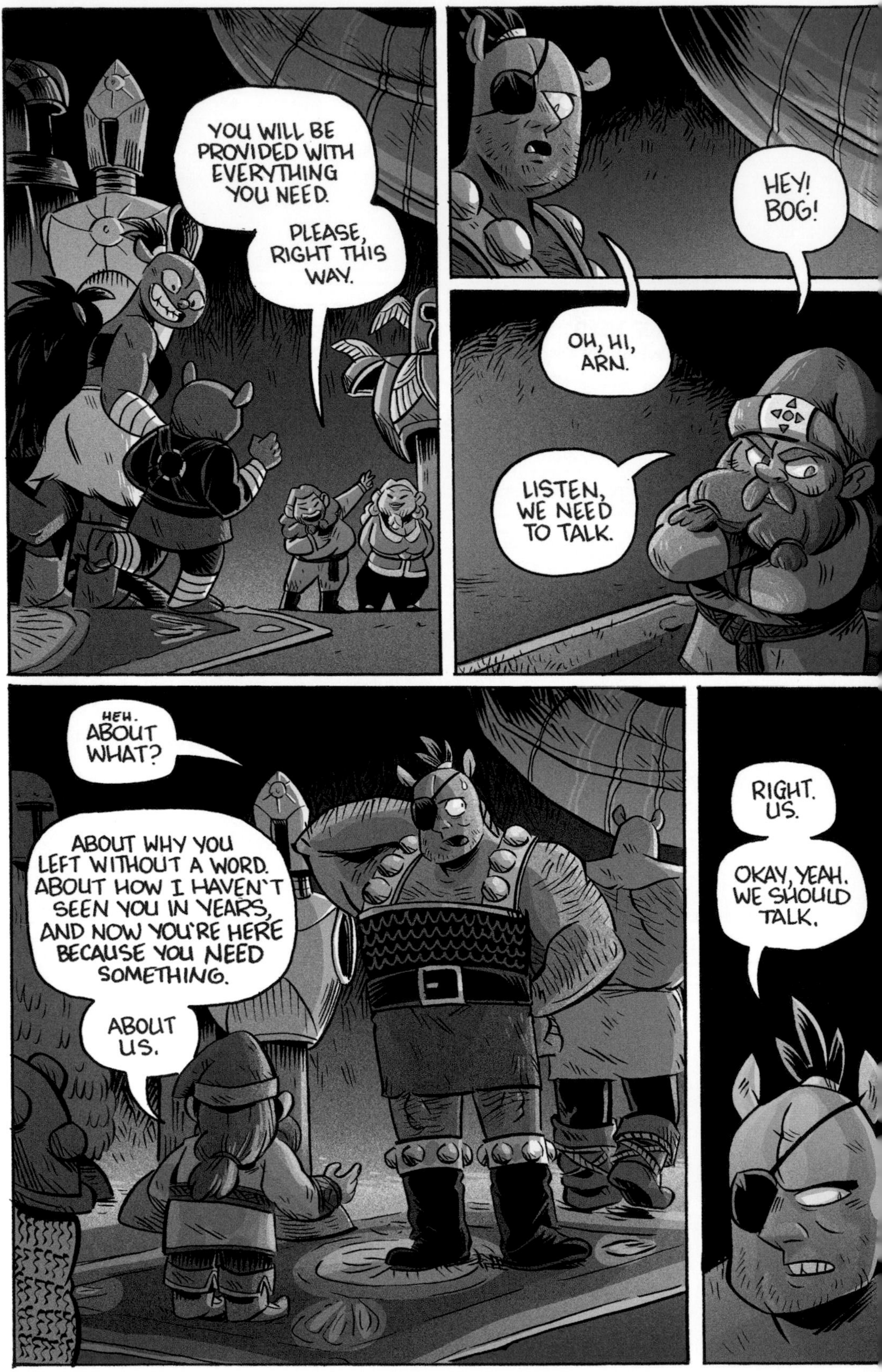
YOU WILL BE PROVIDED WITH EVERYTHING YOU NEED.
PLEASE, RIGHT THIS WAY.
HEY! BOG!
OH, HI, ARN.
LISTEN, WE NEED TO TALK.
HEH. ABOUT WHAT?
ABOUT WHY YOU LEFT WITHOUT A WORD. ABOUT HOW I HAVEN'T SEEN YOU IN YEARS, AND NOW YOU'RE HERE BECAUSE YOU NEED SOMETHING.
ABOUT US.
RIGHT. US.
OKAY, YEAH. WE SHOULD TALK.

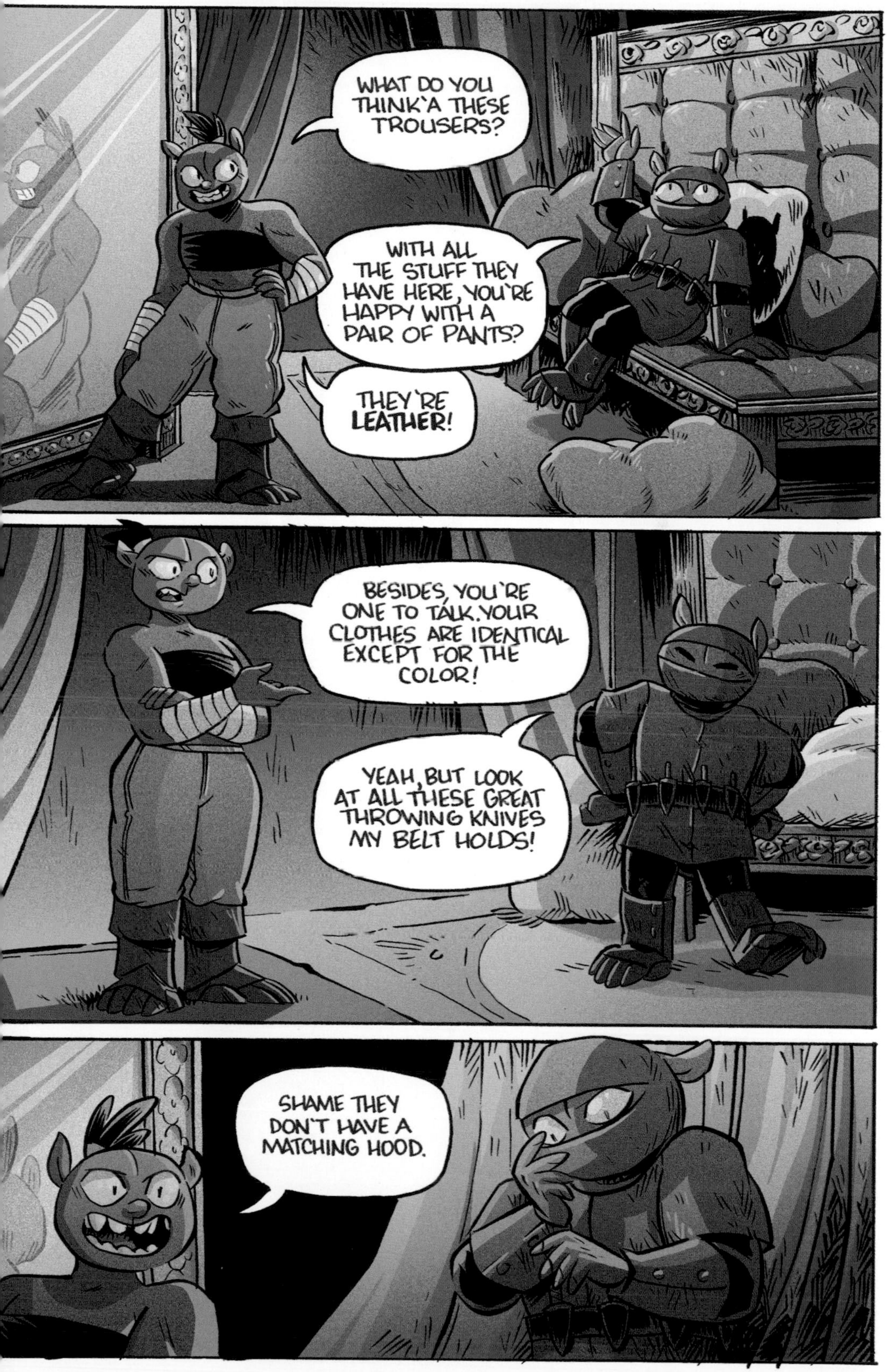
WHAT DO YOU THINK'A THESE TROUSERS?
WITH ALL THE STUFF THEY HAVE HERE, YOU'RE HAPPY WITH A PAIR OF PANTS?
THEY'RE **LEATHER**!
BESIDES, YOU'RE ONE TO TALK. YOUR CLOTHES ARE IDENTICAL EXCEPT FOR THE COLOR!
YEAH, BUT LOOK AT ALL THESE GREAT THROWING KNIVES MY BELT HOLDS!
SHAME THEY DON'T HAVE A MATCHING HOOD.

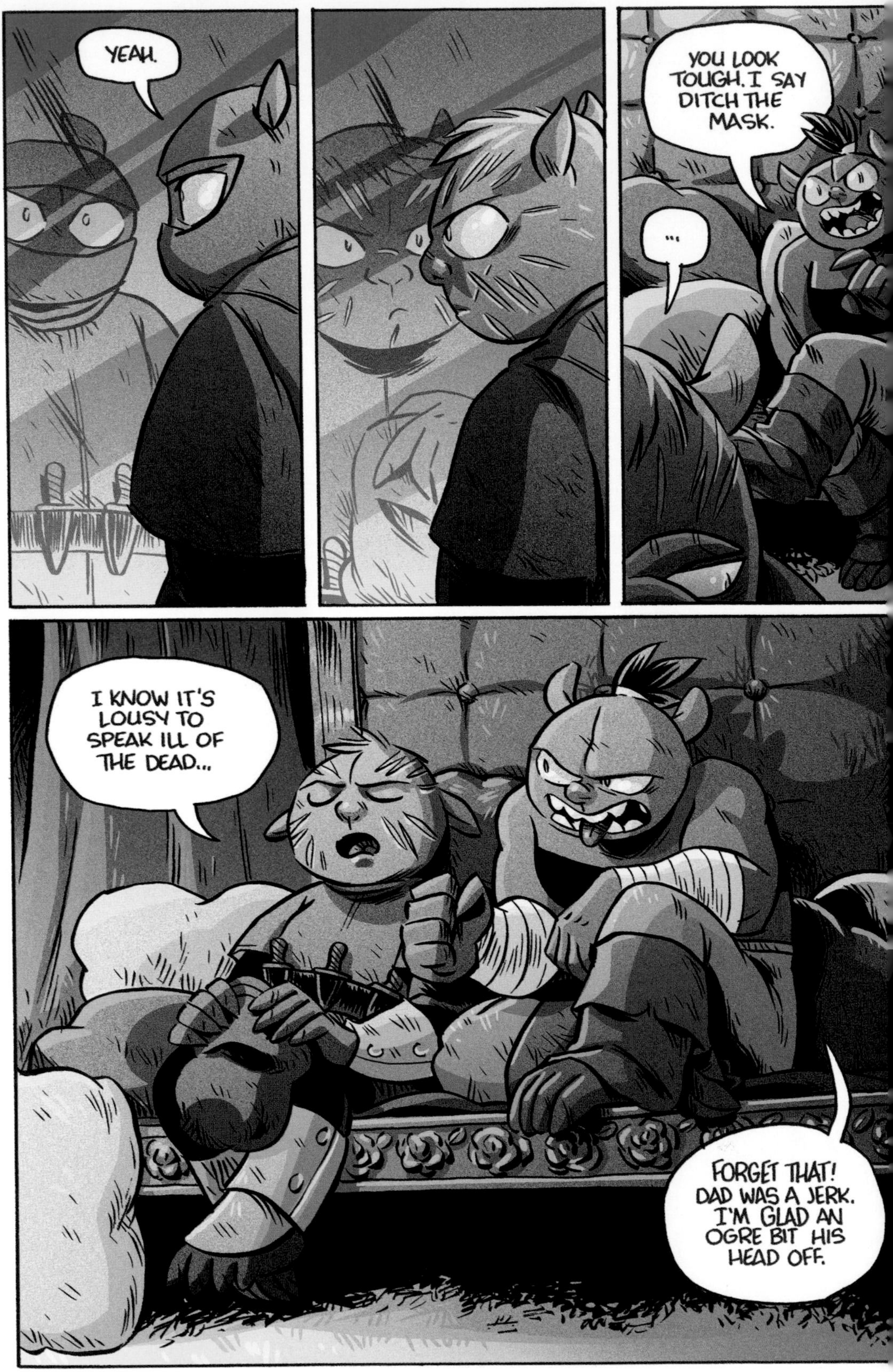
YEAH.
YOU LOOK TOUGH. I SAY DITCH THE MASK.
...
I KNOW IT'S LOUSY TO SPEAK ILL OF THE DEAD...
FORGET THAT! DAD WAS A JERK. I'M GLAD AN OGRE BIT HIS HEAD OFF.

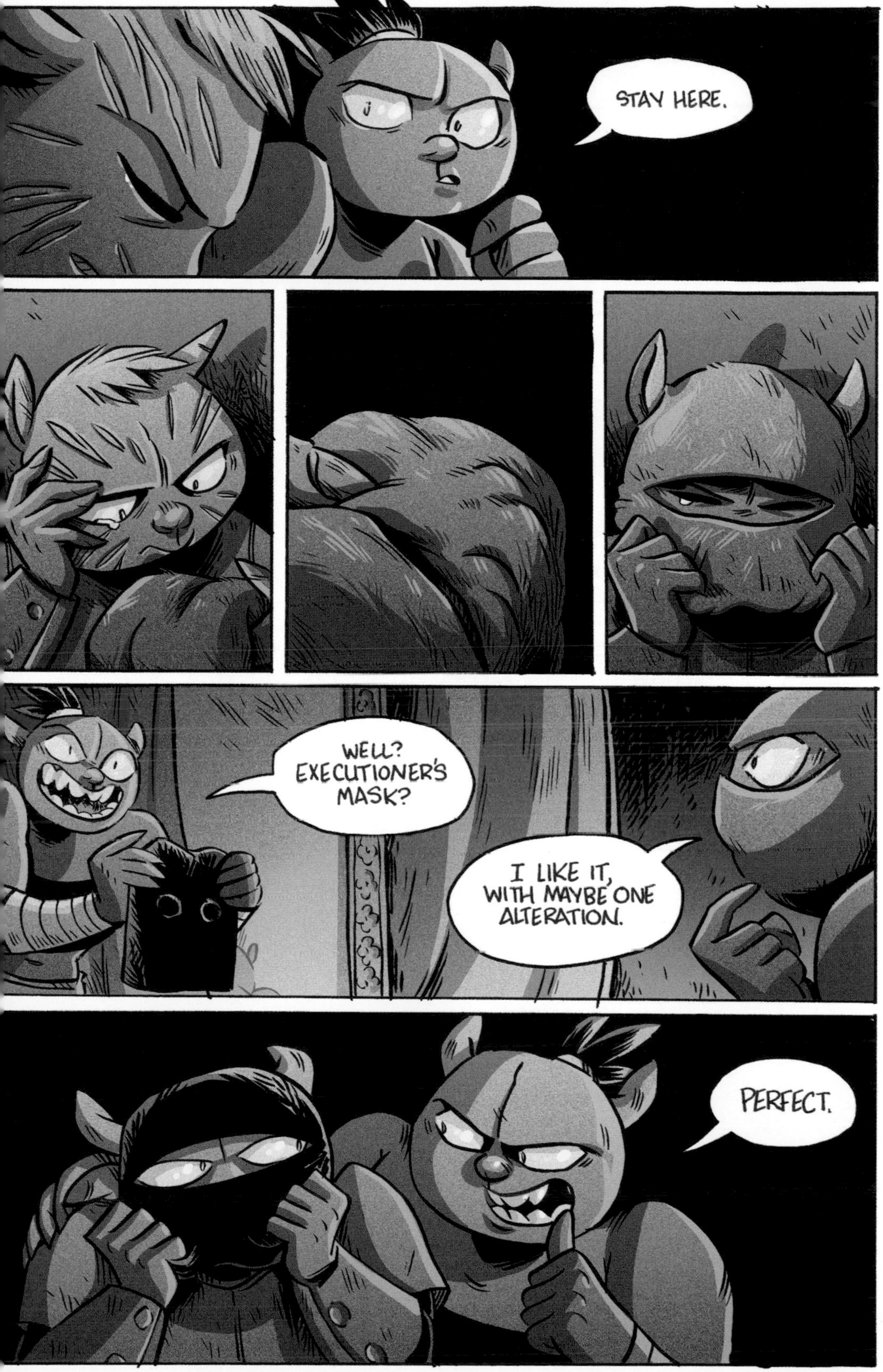
STAY HERE.
WELL? EXECUTIONER'S MASK?
I LIKE IT, WITH MAYBE ONE ALTERATION.
PERFECT.

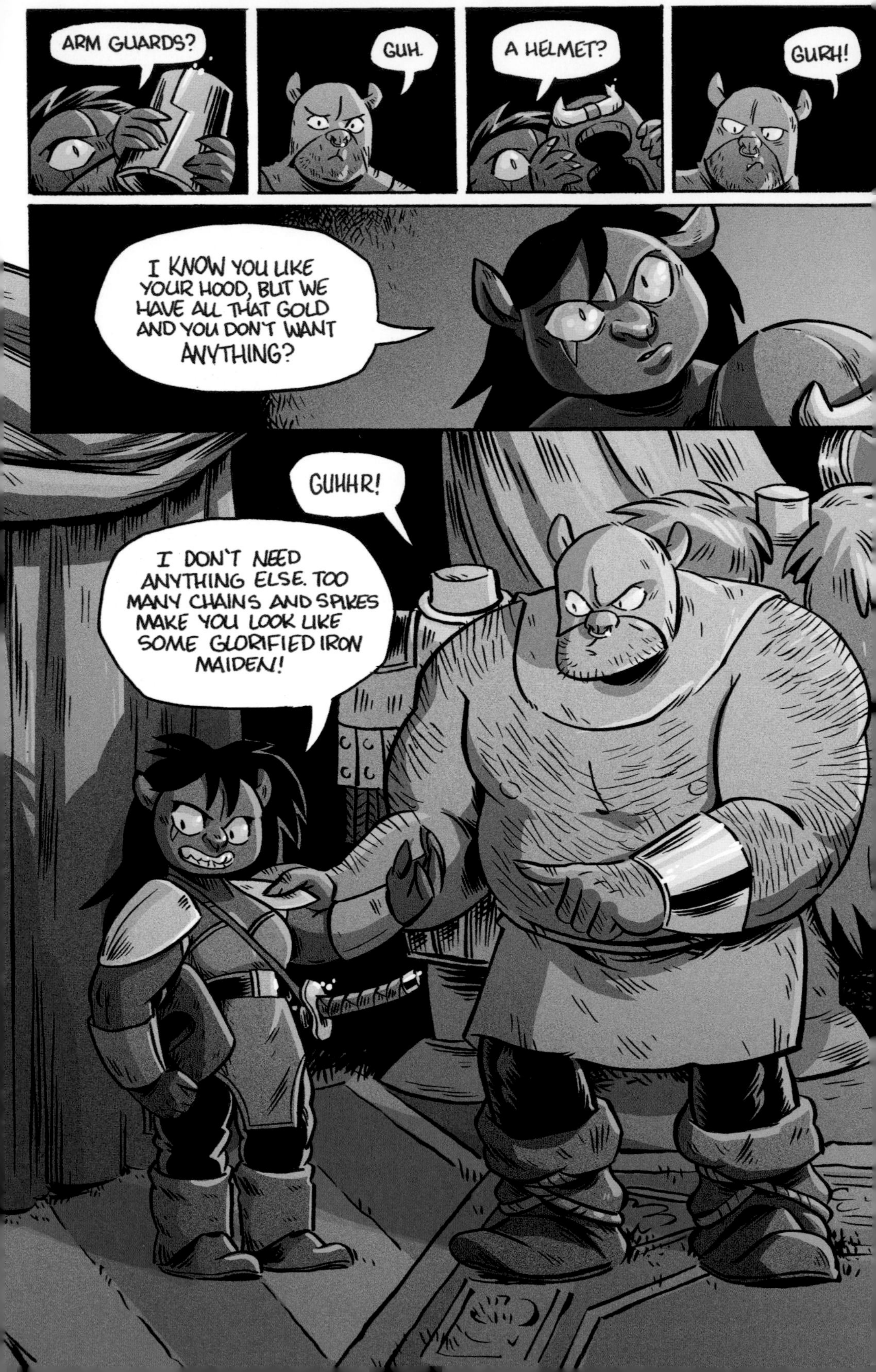
ARM GUARDS?
GUH.
A HELMET?
GURH!
I KNOW YOU LIKE YOUR HOOD, BUT WE HAVE ALL THAT GOLD AND YOU DON'T WANT ANYTHING?
GUHHR!
I DON'T NEED ANYTHING ELSE. TOO MANY CHAINS AND SPIKES MAKE YOU LOOK LIKE SOME GLORIFIED IRON MAIDEN!

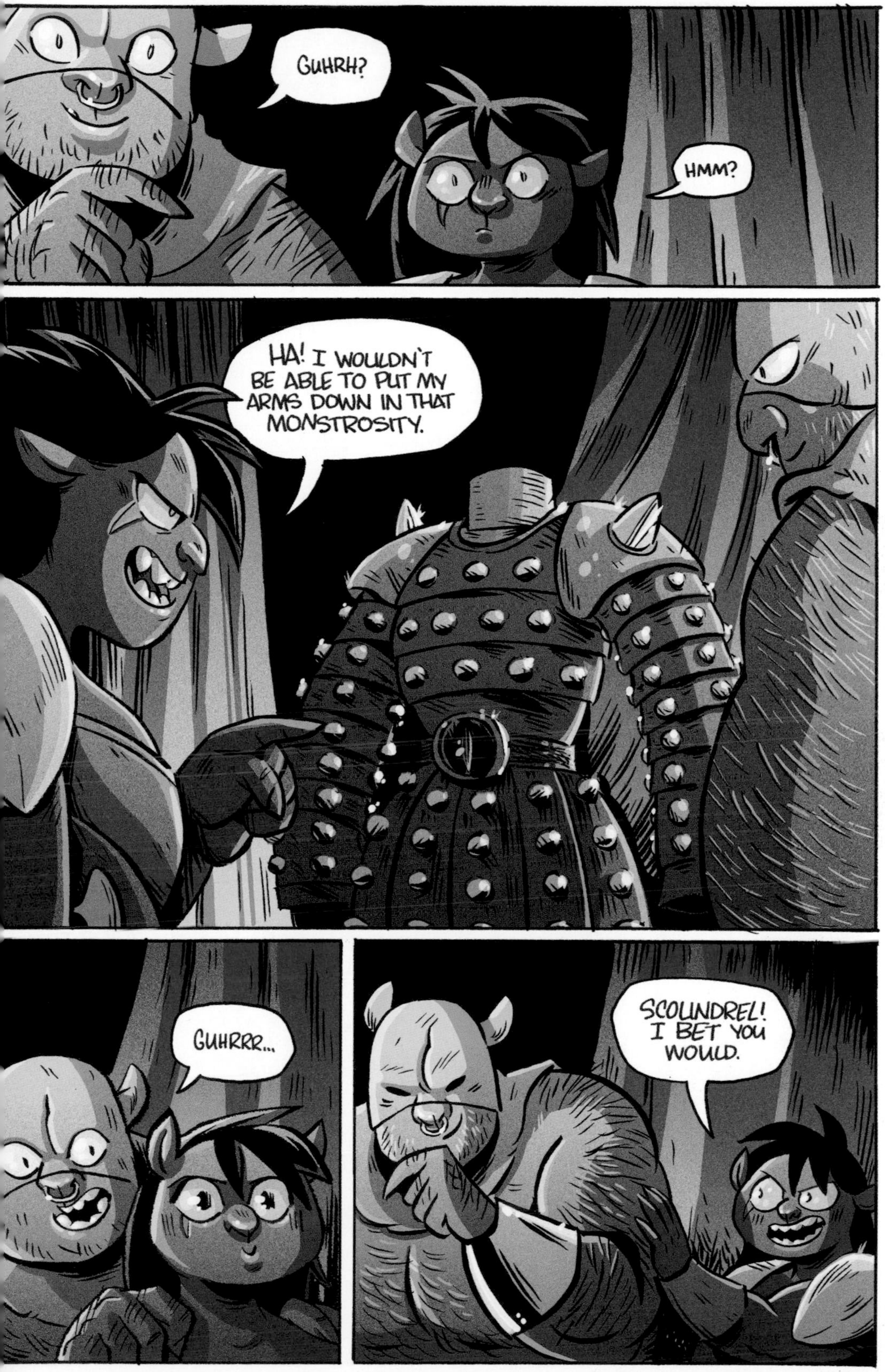
GUHRH?
HMM?
HA! I WOULDN'T BE ABLE TO PUT MY ARMS DOWN IN THAT MONSTROSITY.
GUHRRR...
SCOUNDREL! I BET YOU WOULD.

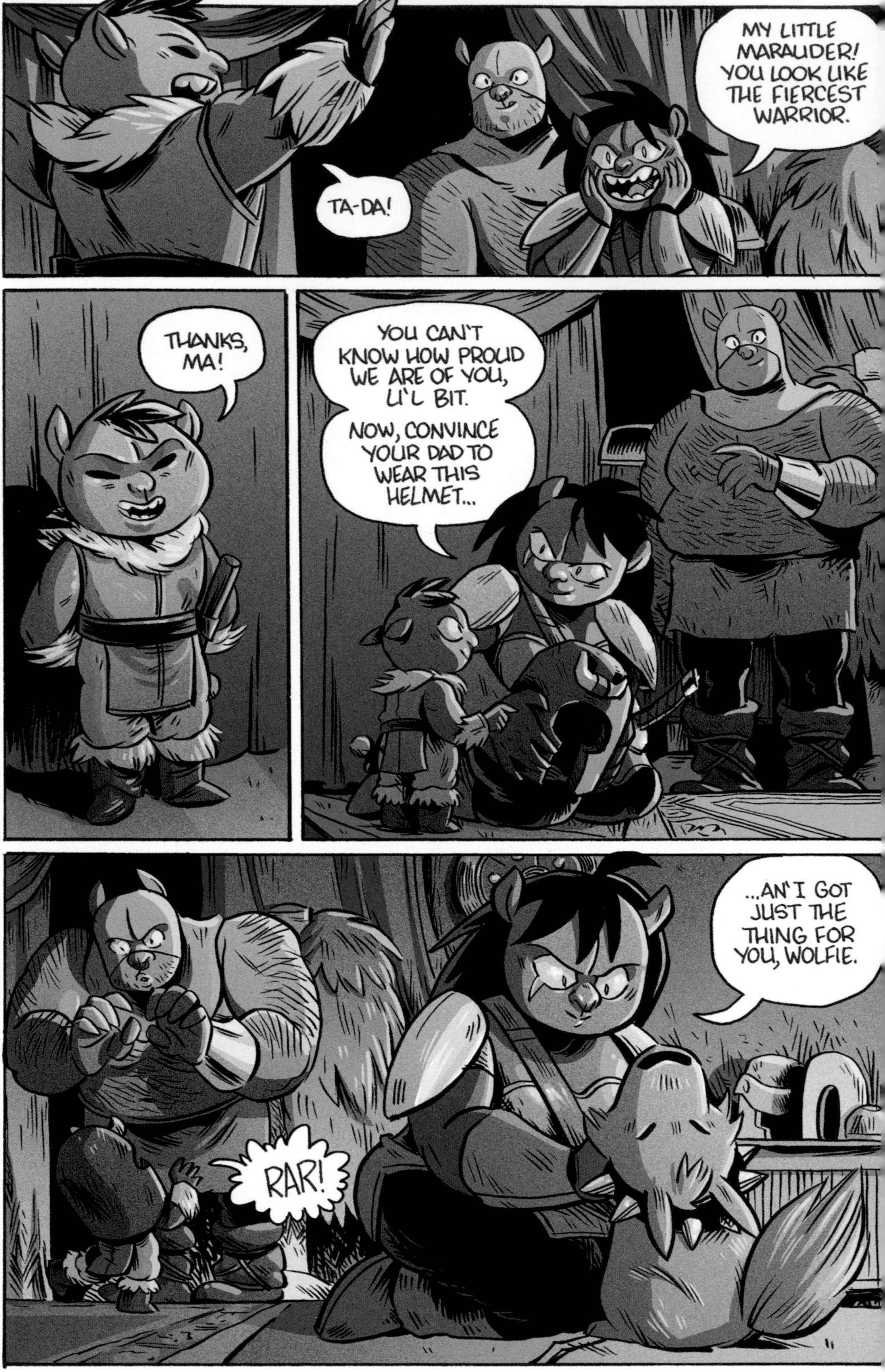
TA-DA!
MY LITTLE MARAUDER! YOU LOOK LIKE THE FIERCEST WARRIOR.
THANKS, MA!
YOU CAN'T KNOW HOW PROUD WE ARE OF YOU, LI'L BIT.
NOW, CONVINCE YOUR DAD TO WEAR THIS HELMET...
...AN' I GOT JUST THE THING FOR YOU, WOLFIE.
RAR!

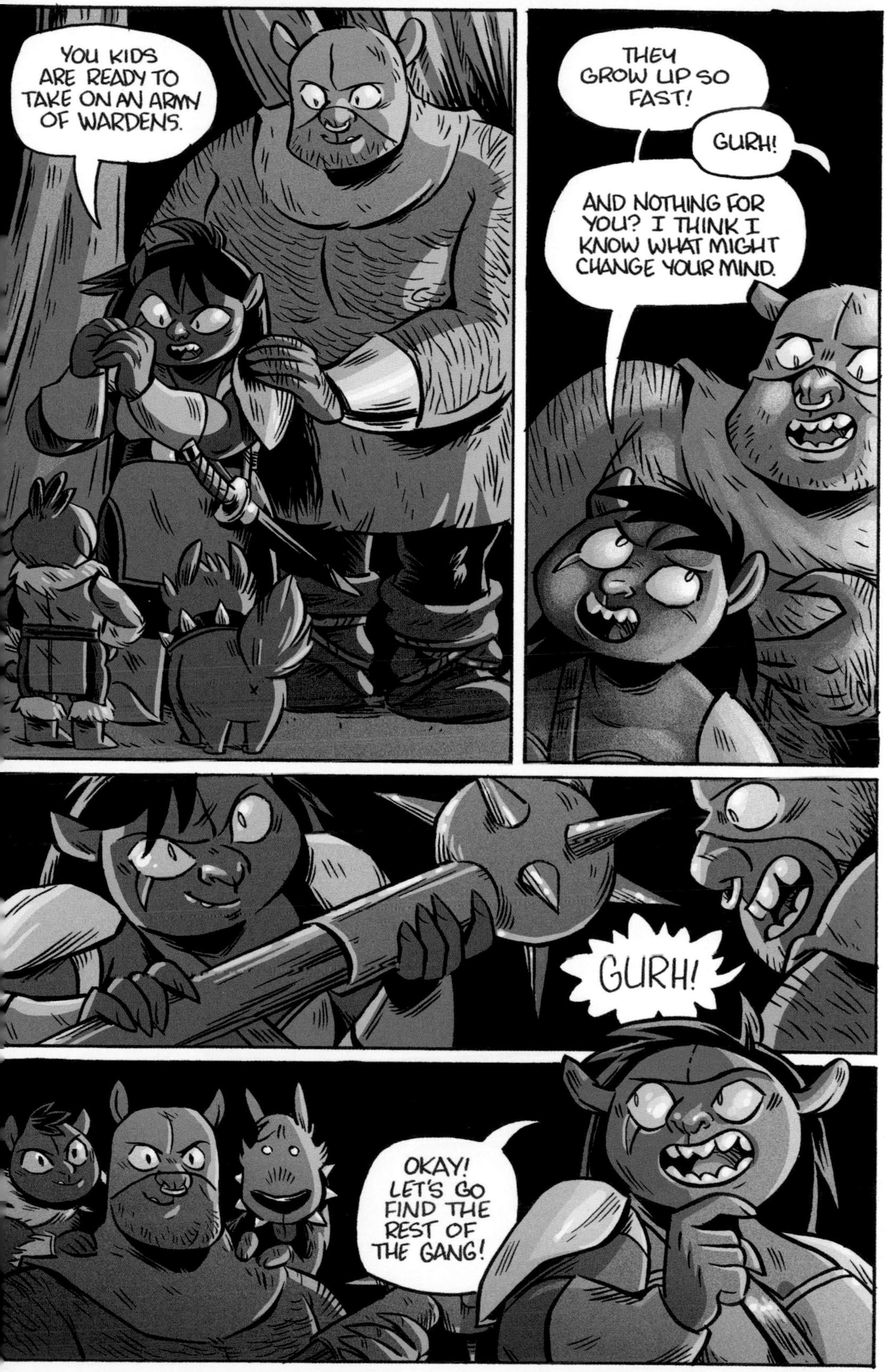
YOU KIDS ARE READY TO TAKE ON AN ARMY OF WARDENS.
THEY GROW UP SO FAST!
GURH!
AND NOTHING FOR YOU? I THINK I KNOW WHAT MIGHT CHANGE YOUR MIND.
GURH!
OKAY! LET'S GO FIND THE REST OF THE GANG!

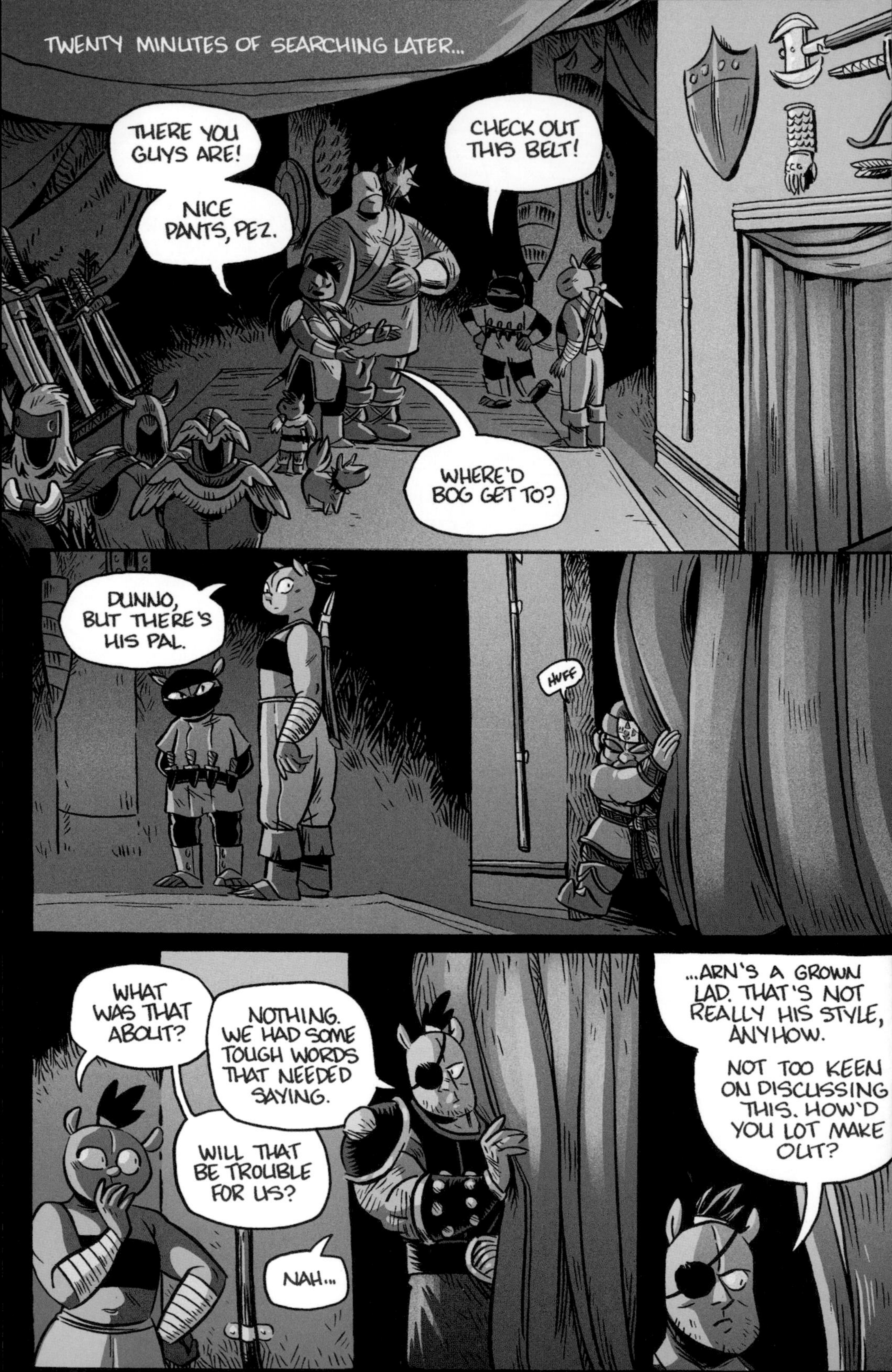

TWENTY MINUTES OF SEARCHING LATER...
THERE YOU GUYS ARE!
NICE PANTS, PEZ.
CHECK OUT THIS BELT!
WHERE'D BOG GET TO?
DUNNO, BUT THERE'S HIS PAL.
HUFF
WHAT WAS THAT ABOUT?
NOTHING. WE HAD SOME TOUGH WORDS THAT NEEDED SAYING.
WILL THAT BE TROUBLE FOR US?
NAH...
...ARN'S A GROWN LAD. THAT'S NOT REALLY HIS STYLE, ANYHOW.
NOT TOO KEEN ON DISCUSSING THIS. HOW'D YOU LOT MAKE OUT?

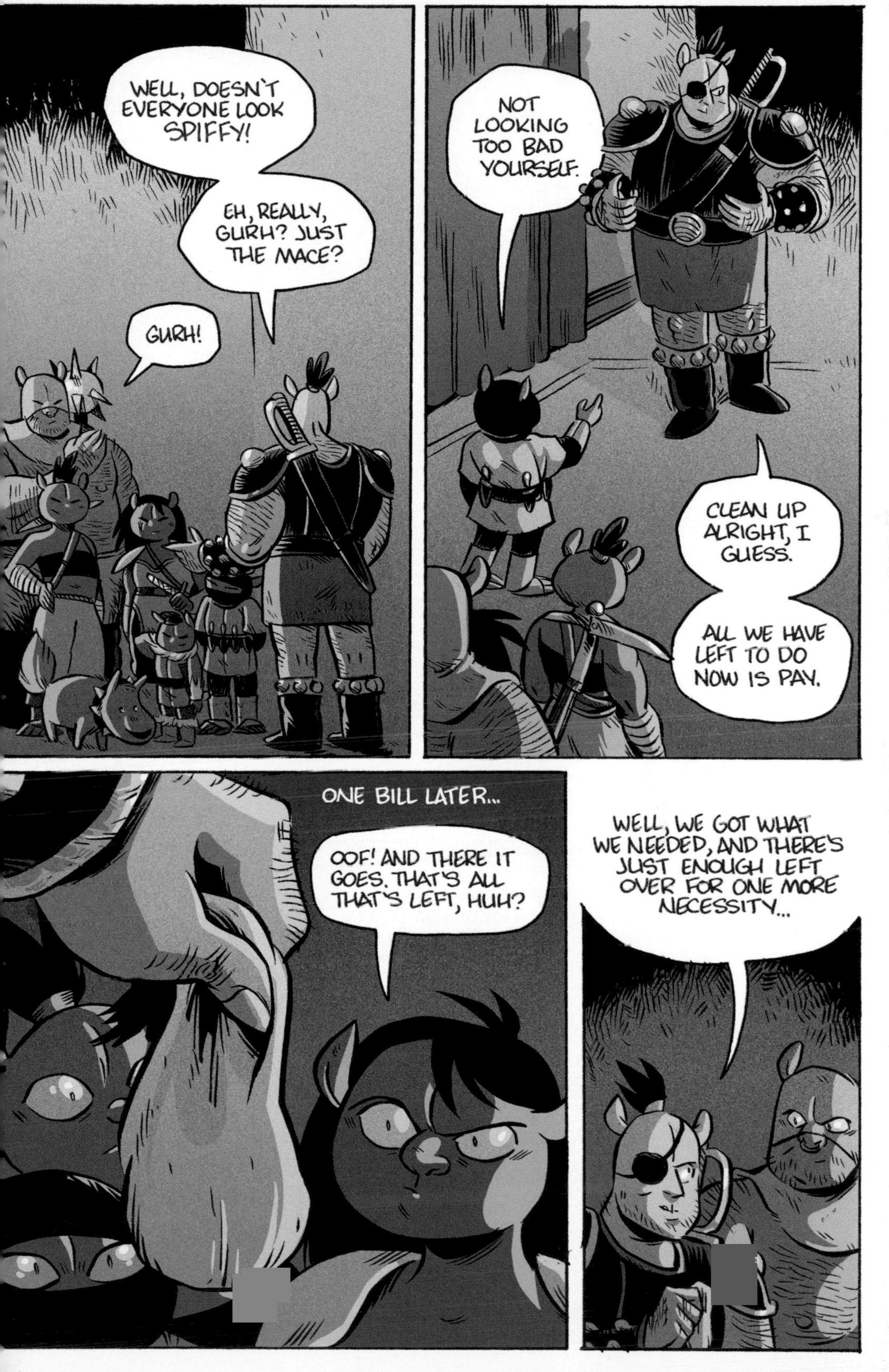
WELL, DOESN'T EVERYONE LOOK SPIFFY!
EH, REALLY, GURH? JUST THE MACE?
GURH!
NOT LOOKING TOO BAD YOURSELF.
CLEAN UP ALRIGHT, I GUESS.
ALL WE HAVE LEFT TO DO NOW IS PAY.
ONE BILL LATER...
OOF! AND THERE IT GOES. THAT'S ALL THAT'S LEFT, HUH?
WELL, WE GOT WHAT WE NEEDED, AND THERE'S JUST ENOUGH LEFT OVER FOR ONE MORE NECESSITY...

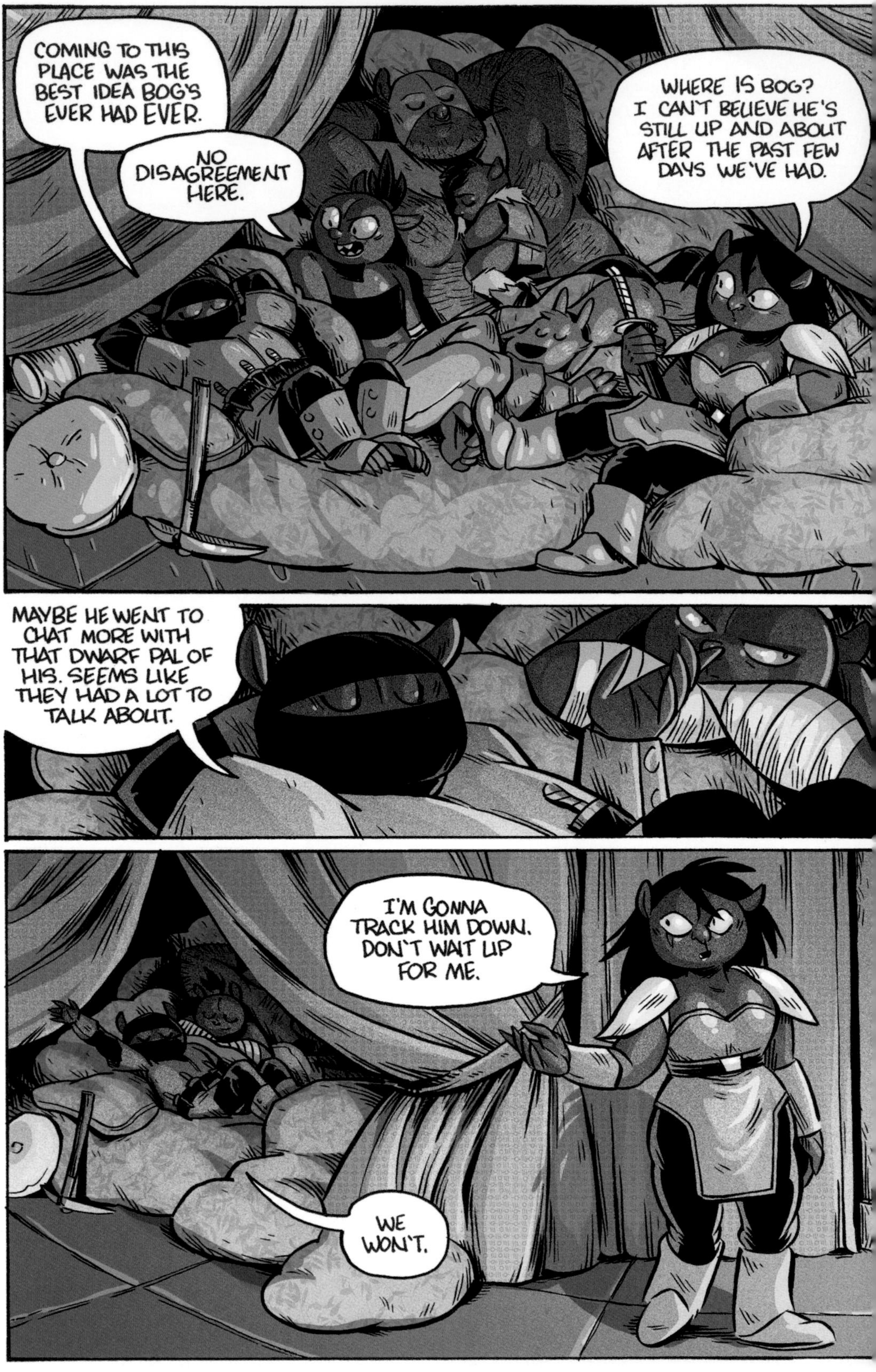
COMING TO THIS PLACE WAS THE BEST IDEA BOG'S EVER HAD EVER.
NO DISAGREEMENT HERE.
WHERE IS BOG? I CAN'T BELIEVE HE'S STILL UP AND ABOUT AFTER THE PAST FEW DAYS WE'VE HAD.
MAYBE HE WENT TO CHAT MORE WITH THAT DWARF PAL OF HIS. SEEMS LIKE THEY HAD A LOT TO TALK ABOUT.
I'M GONNA TRACK HIM DOWN. DON'T WAIT UP FOR ME.
WE WON'T.

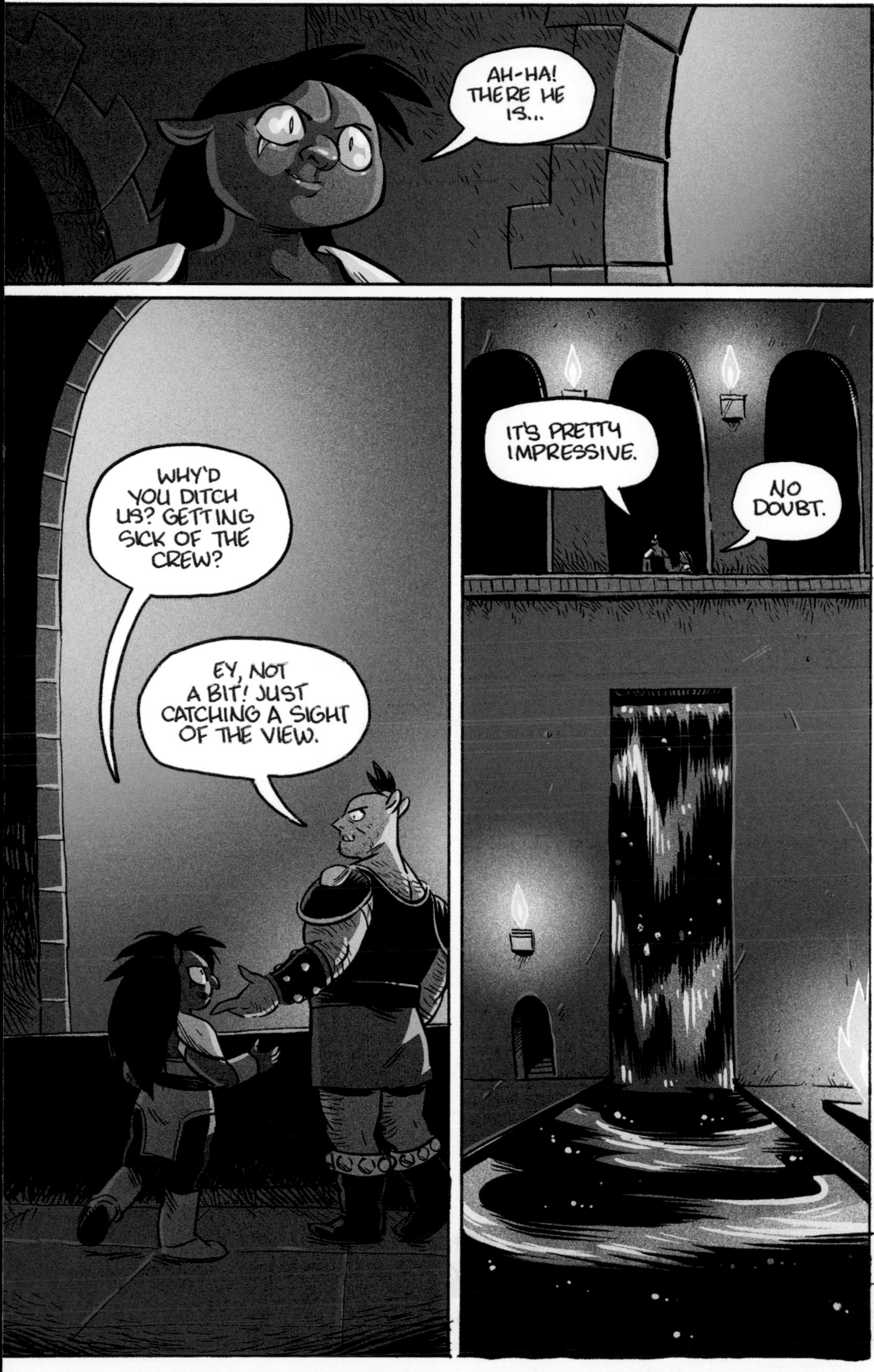
AH-HA! THERE HE IS...
WHY'D YOU DITCH US? GETTING SICK OF THE CREW?
EY, NOT A BIT! JUST CATCHING A SIGHT OF THE VIEW.
IT'S PRETTY IMPRESSIVE.
NO DOUBT.

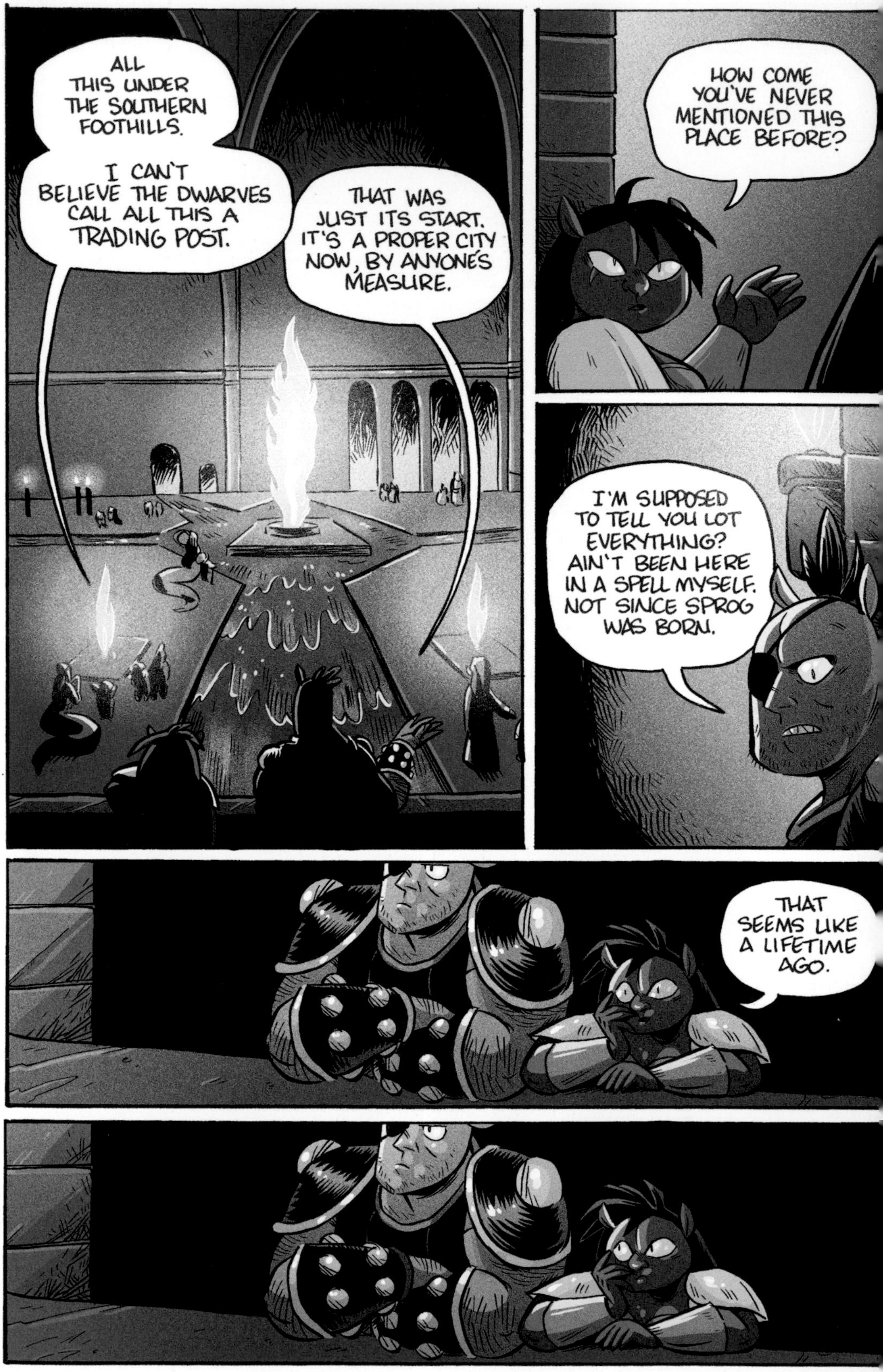
ALL THIS UNDER THE SOUTHERN FOOTHILLS.
I CAN'T BELIEVE THE DWARVES CALL ALL THIS A TRADING POST.
THAT WAS JUST ITS START. IT'S A PROPER CITY NOW, BY ANYONE'S MEASURE.
HOW COME YOU'VE NEVER MENTIONED THIS PLACE BEFORE?
I'M SUPPOSED TO TELL YOU LOT EVERYTHING? AIN'T BEEN HERE IN A SPELL MYSELF. NOT SINCE SPROG WAS BORN.
THAT SEEMS LIKE A LIFETIME AGO.

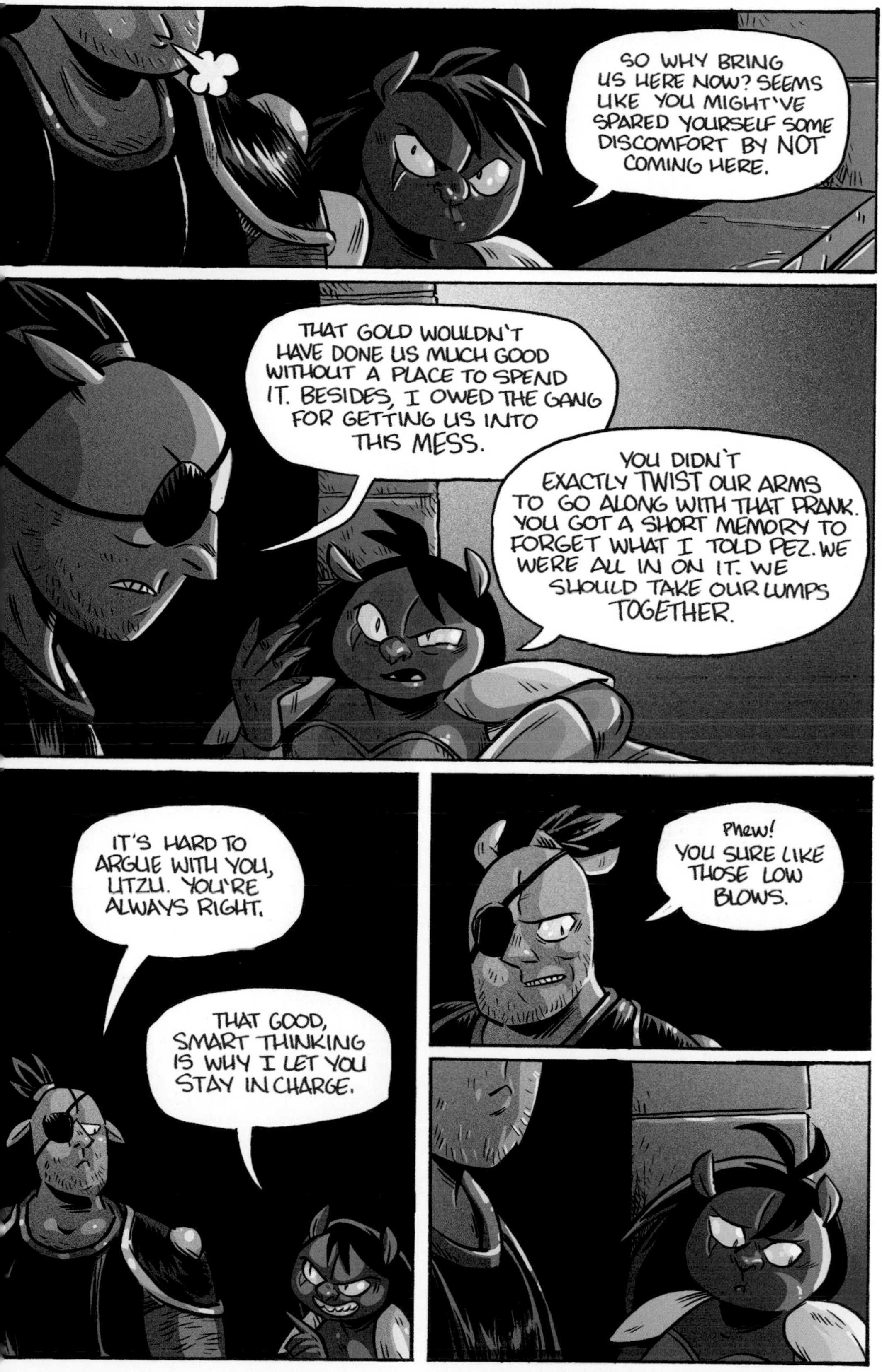
SO WHY BRING US HERE NOW? SEEMS LIKE YOU MIGHT'VE SPARED YOURSELF SOME DISCOMFORT BY NOT COMING HERE.
THAT GOLD WOULDN'T HAVE DONE US MUCH GOOD WITHOUT A PLACE TO SPEND IT. BESIDES, I OWED THE GANG FOR GETTING US INTO THIS MESS.
YOU DIDN'T EXACTLY TWIST OUR ARMS TO GO ALONG WITH THAT PRANK. YOU GOT A SHORT MEMORY TO FORGET WHAT I TOLD PEZ. WE WERE ALL IN ON IT. WE SHOULD TAKE OUR LUMPS TOGETHER.
IT'S HARD TO ARGUE WITH YOU, LITZU. YOU'RE ALWAYS RIGHT.
THAT GOOD, SMART THINKING IS WHY I LET YOU STAY IN CHARGE.
Phew! YOU SURE LIKE THOSE LOW BLOWS.

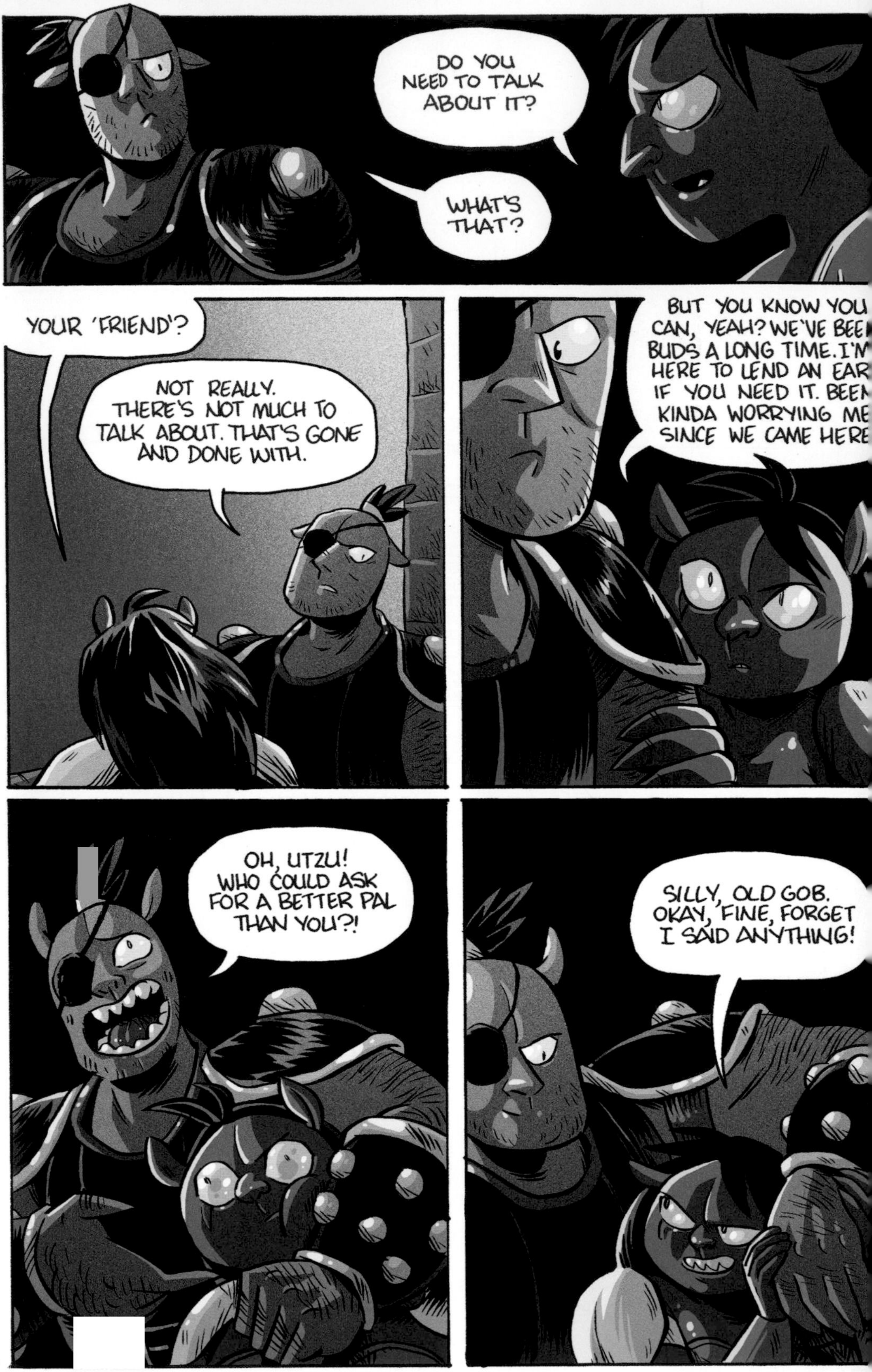

DO YOU NEED TO TALK ABOUT IT?
WHAT'S THAT?
YOUR 'FRIEND'?
NOT REALLY. THERE'S NOT MUCH TO TALK ABOUT. THAT'S GONE AND DONE WITH.
BUT YOU KNOW YOU CAN, YEAH? WE'VE BEE BUDS A LONG TIME. I'M HERE TO LEND AN EAR IF YOU NEED IT. BEEN KINDA WORRYING ME SINCE WE CAME HERE
OH, UTZU! WHO COULD ASK FOR A BETTER PAL THAN YOU?!
SILLY, OLD GOB. OKAY, FINE, FORGET I SAID ANYTHING!

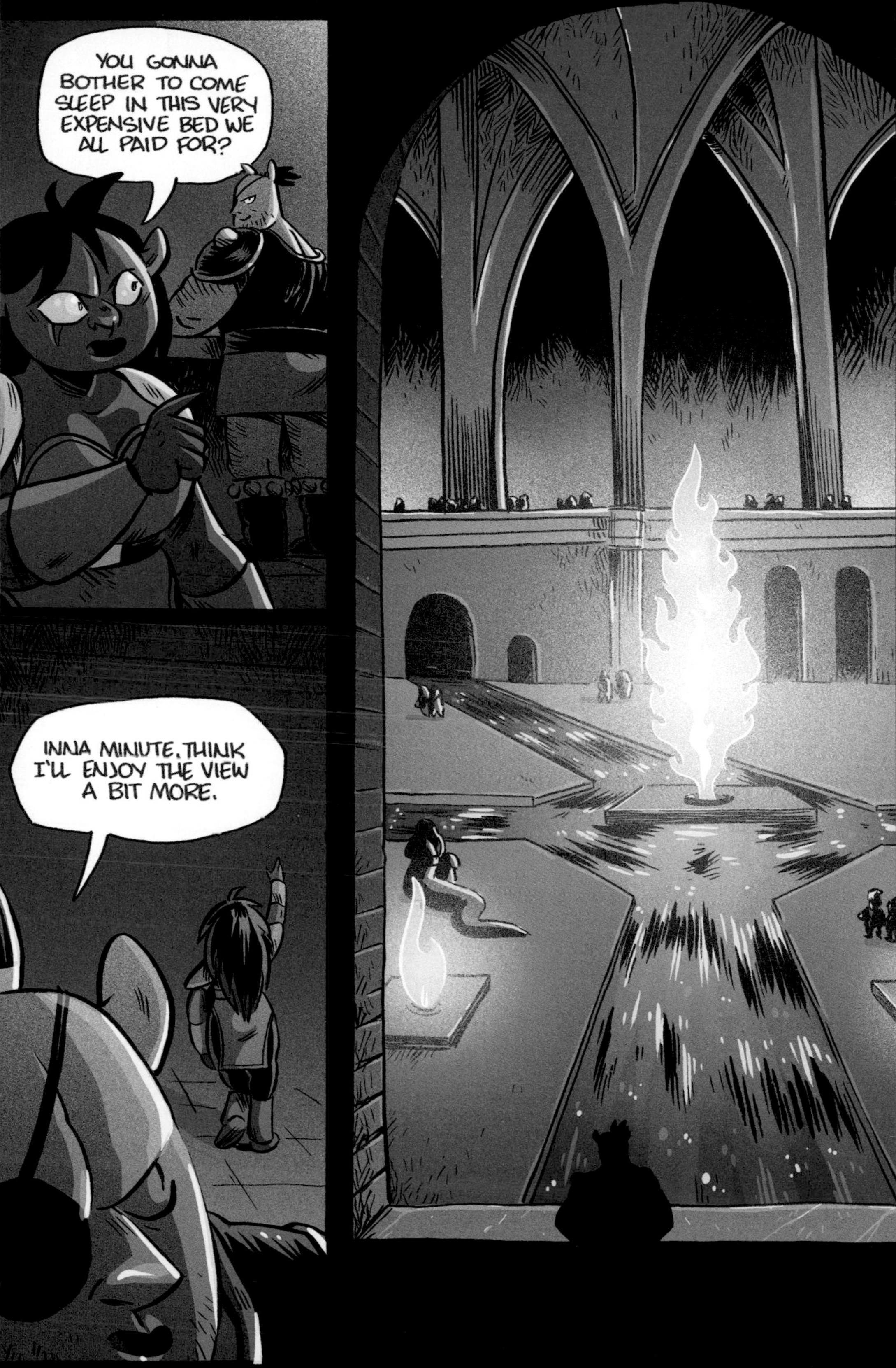

YOU GONNA BOTHER TO COME SLEEP IN THIS VERY EXPENSIVE BED WE ALL PAID FOR?
INNA MINUTE. THINK I'LL ENJOY THE VIEW A BIT MORE.

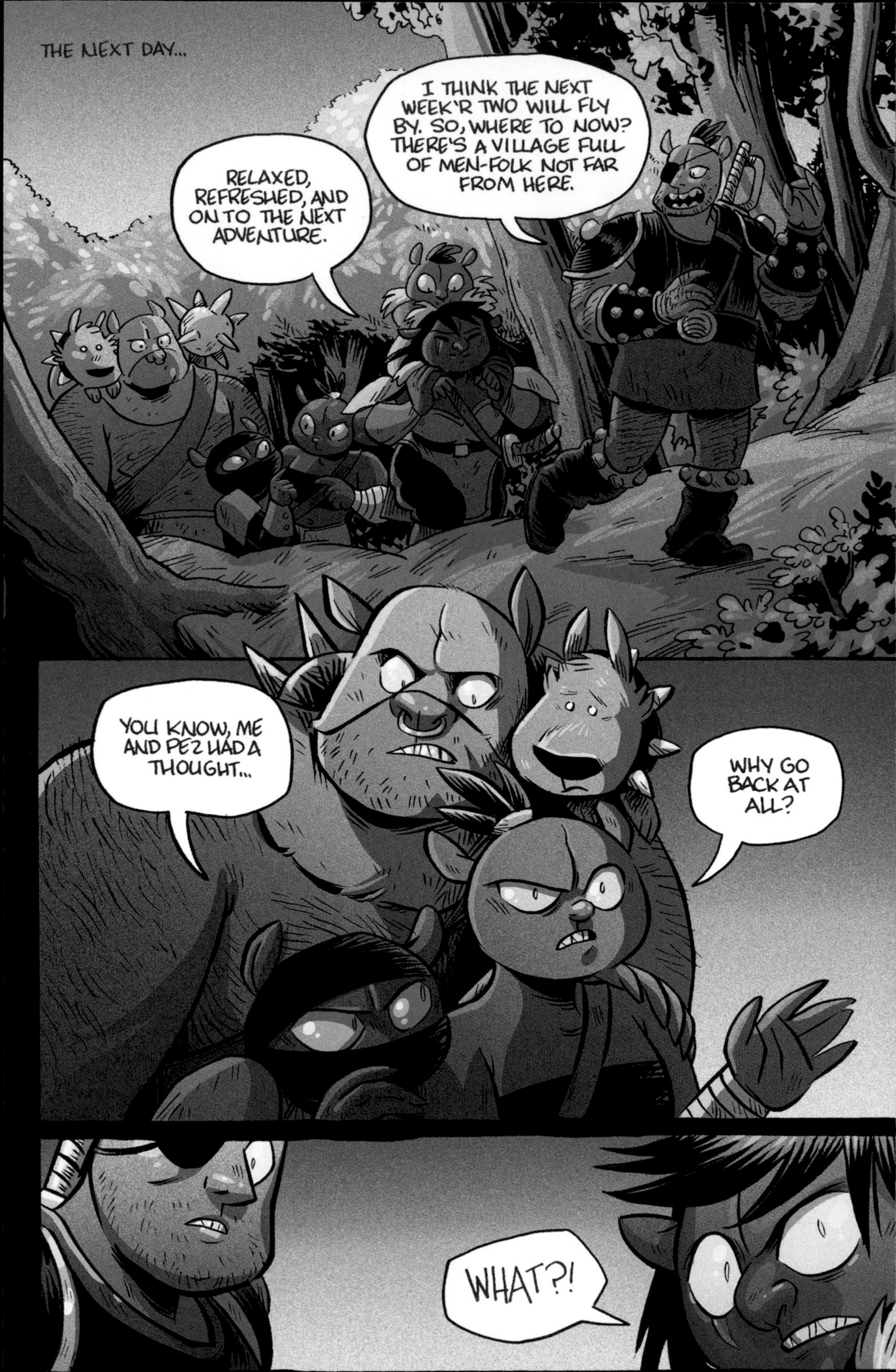
THE NEXT DAY...
RELAXED, REFRESHED, AND ON TO THE NEXT ADVENTURE.
I THINK THE NEXT WEEK'R TWO WILL FLY BY. SO, WHERE TO NOW? THERE'S A VILLAGE FULL OF MEN-FOLK NOT FAR FROM HERE.
YOU KNOW, ME AND PEZ HAD A THOUGHT...
WHY GO BACK AT ALL?
WHAT?!

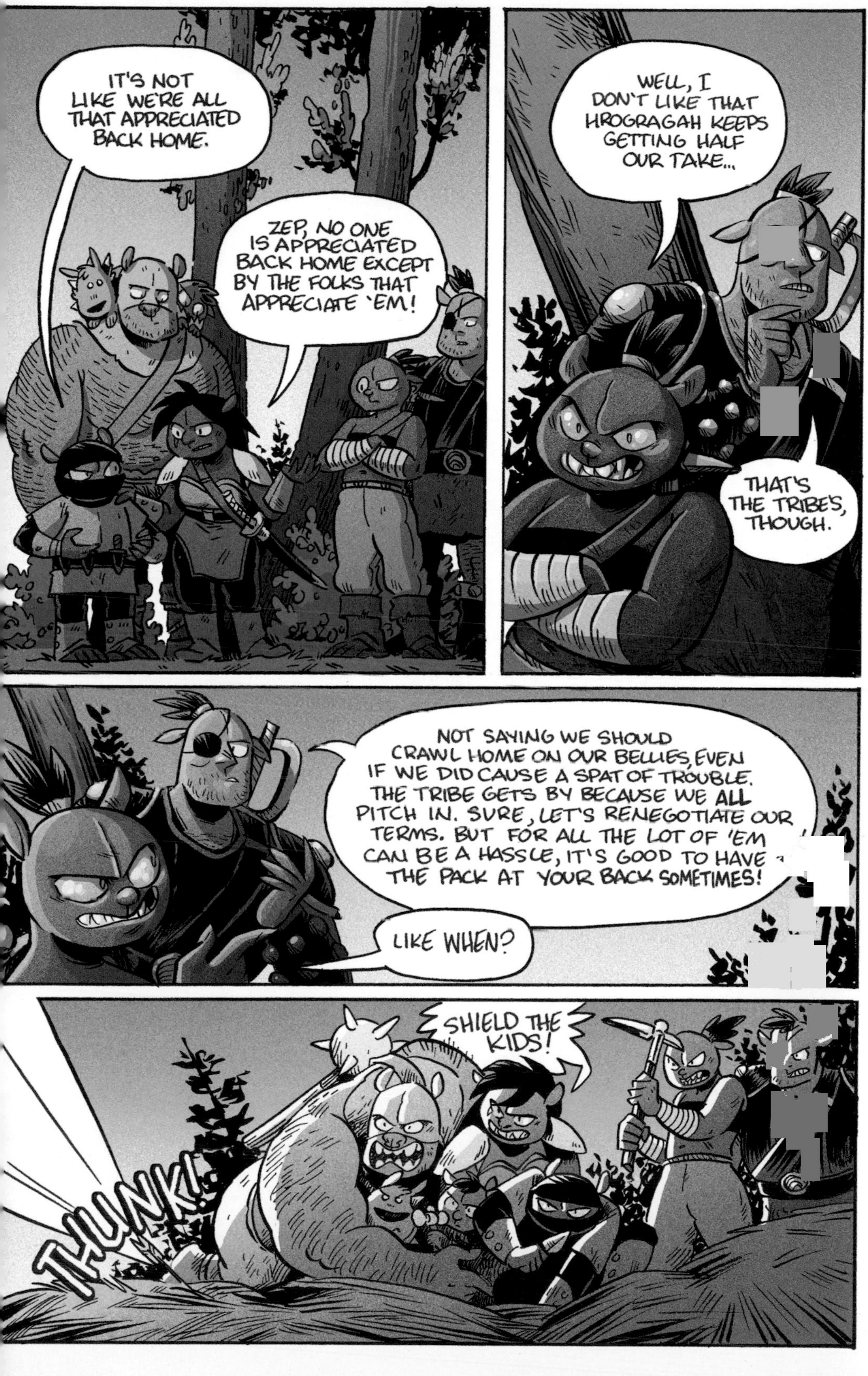
IT'S NOT LIKE WE'RE ALL THAT APPRECIATED BACK HOME.
ZEP, NO ONE IS APPRECIATED BACK HOME EXCEPT BY THE FOLKS THAT APPRECIATE 'EM!
WELL, I DON'T LIKE THAT HROGRAGAH KEEPS GETTING HALF OUR TAKE...
THAT'S THE TRIBE'S, THOUGH.
NOT SAYING WE SHOULD CRAWL HOME ON OUR BELLIES, EVEN IF WE DID CAUSE A SPAT OF TROUBLE. THE TRIBE GETS BY BECAUSE WE ALL PITCH IN. SURE, LET'S RENEGOTIATE OUR TERMS. BUT FOR ALL THE LOT OF 'EM CAN BE A HASSLE, IT'S GOOD TO HAVE THE PACK AT YOUR BACK SOMETIMES!
LIKE WHEN?
SHIELD THE KIDS!
THUNK!

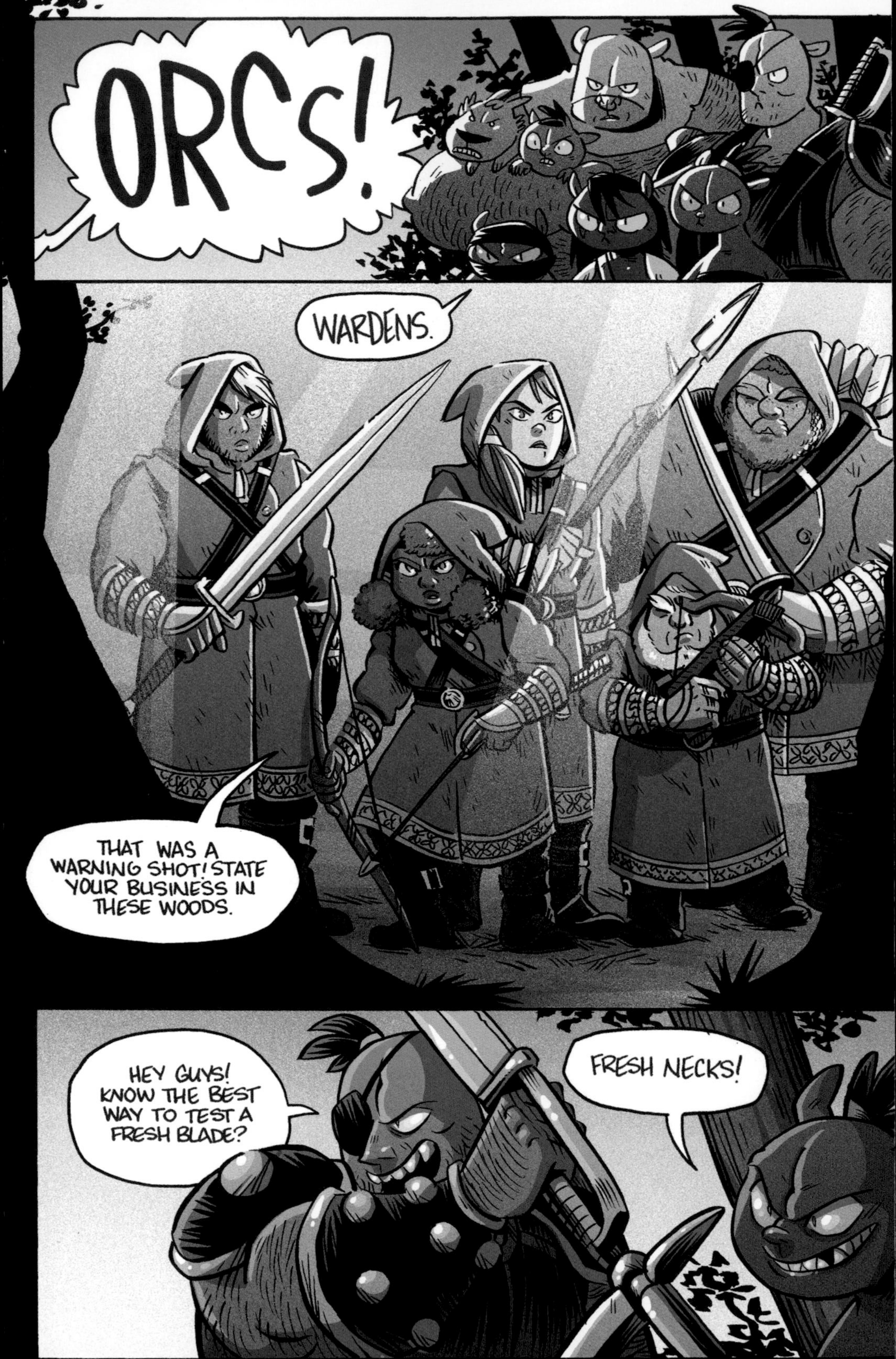
ORCS!
WARDENS.
THAT WAS A WARNING SHOT! STATE YOUR BUSINESS IN THESE WOODS.
HEY GUYS! KNOW THE BEST WAY TO TEST A FRESH BLADE?
FRESH NECKS!

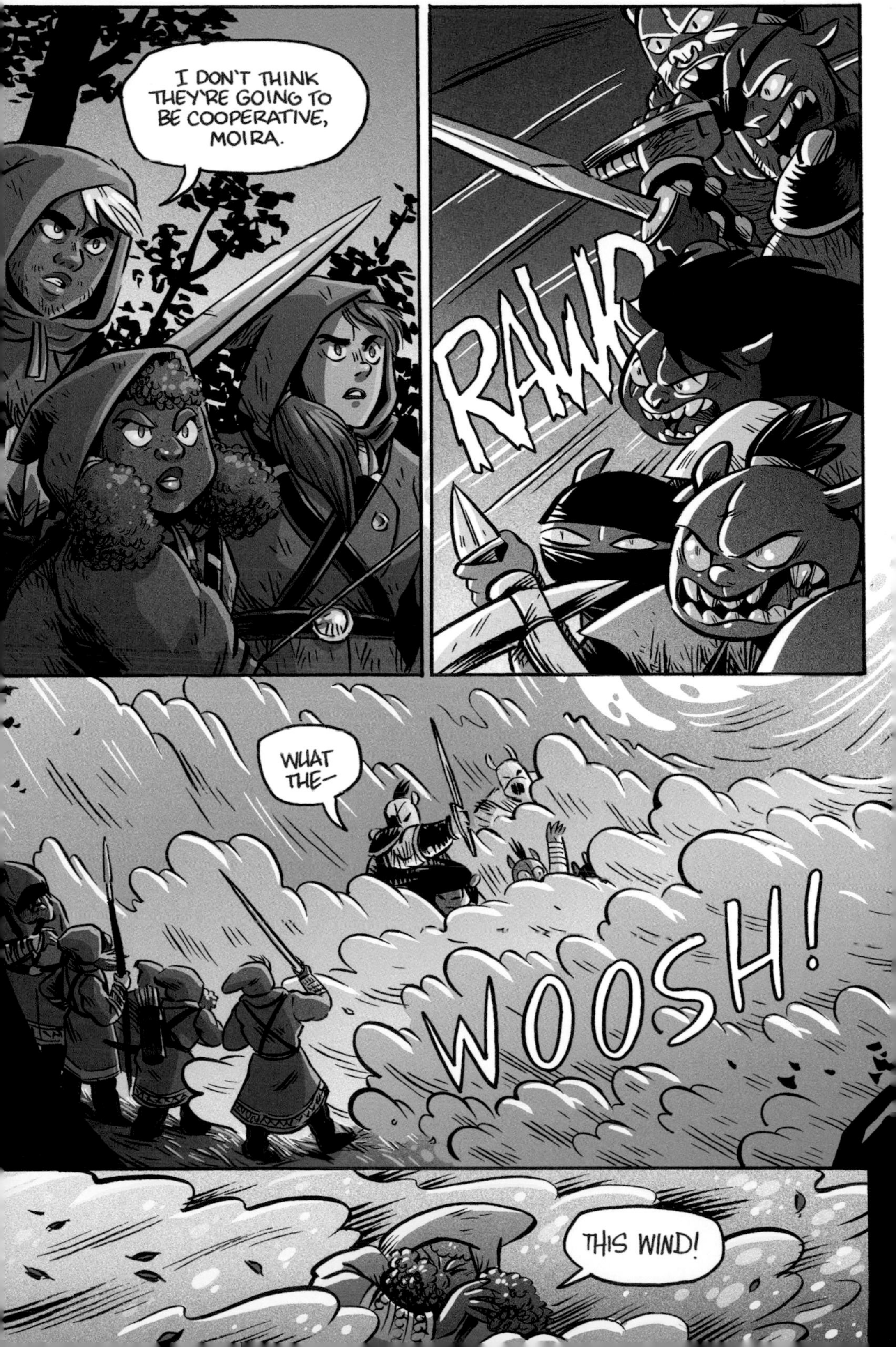
I DON'T THINK THEY'RE GOING TO BE COOPERATIVE, MOIRA.
RAWR
WHAT THE-
WOOSH!
THIS WIND!

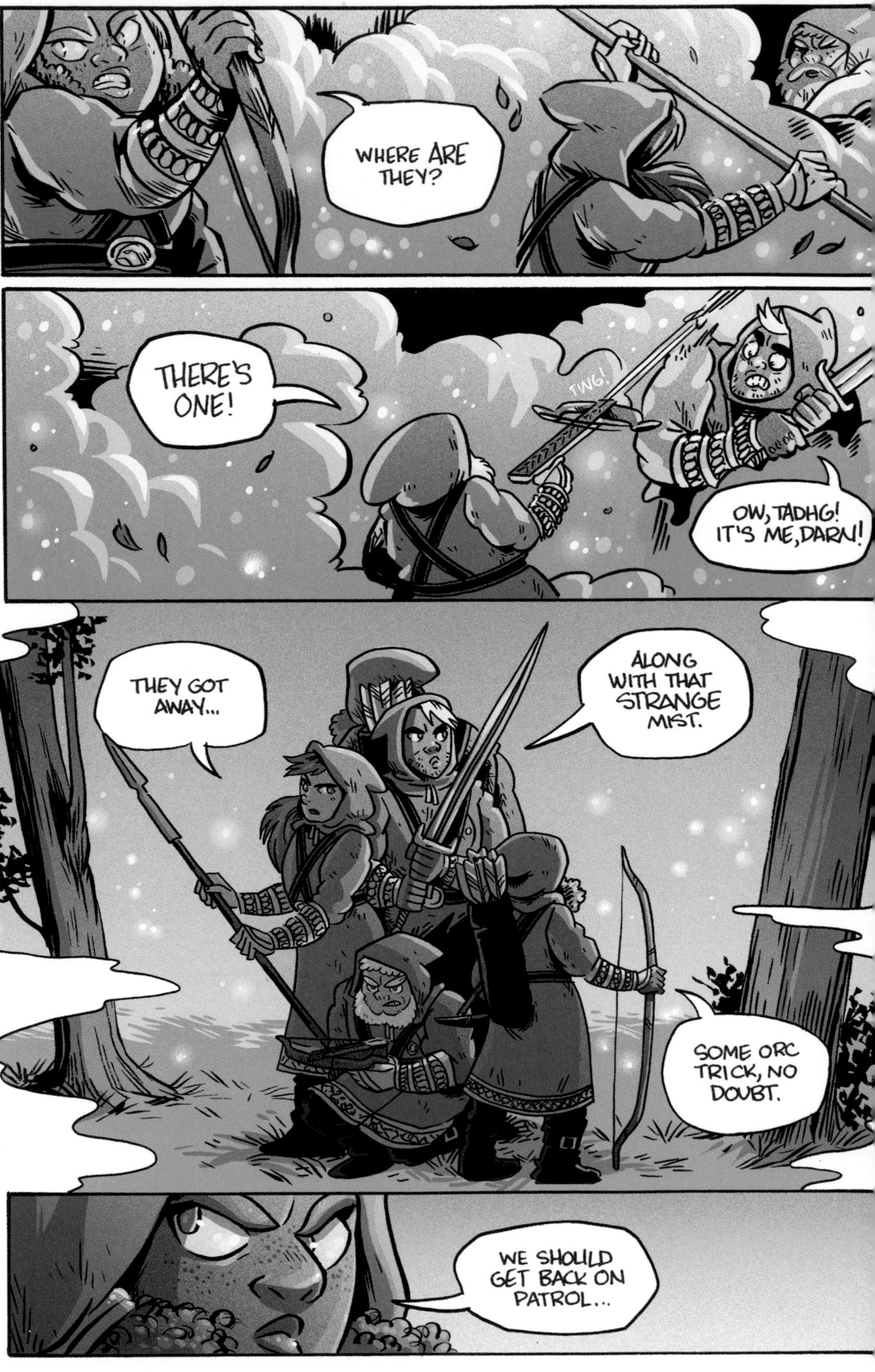
WHERE ARE THEY?
THERE'S ONE!
TING!
OW, TADHG! IT'S ME, DARN!
THEY GOT AWAY...
ALONG WITH THAT STRANGE MIST.
SOME ORC TRICK, NO DOUBT.
WE SHOULD GET BACK ON PATROL...

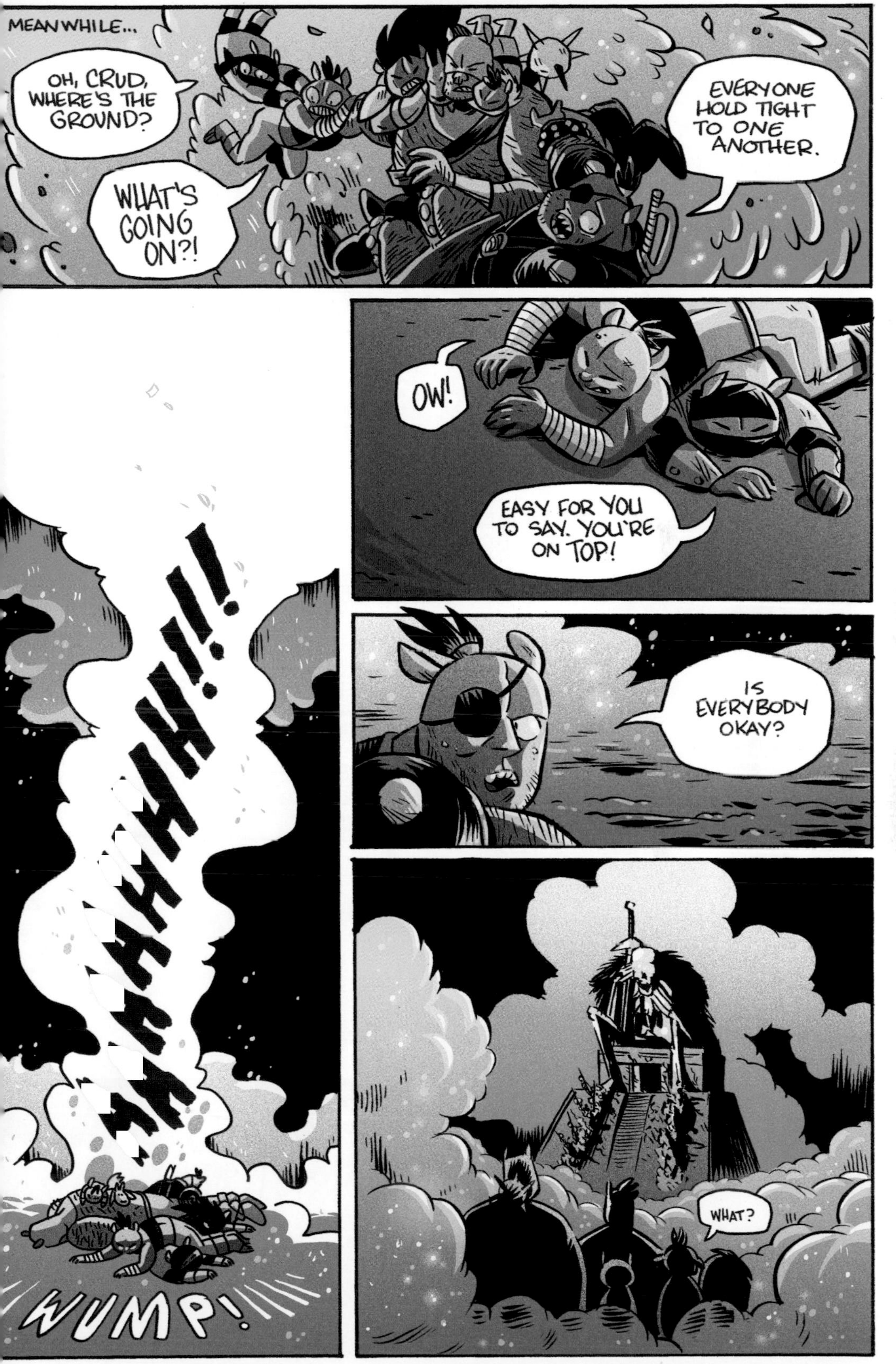
MEANWHILE...
OH, CRUD, WHERE'S THE GROUND?
WHAT'S GOING ON?!
EVERYONE HOLD TIGHT TO ONE ANOTHER.
AAAAHHHH!!!
WUMP!
OW!
EASY FOR YOU TO SAY. YOU'RE ON TOP!
IS EVERYBODY OKAY?
WHAT?

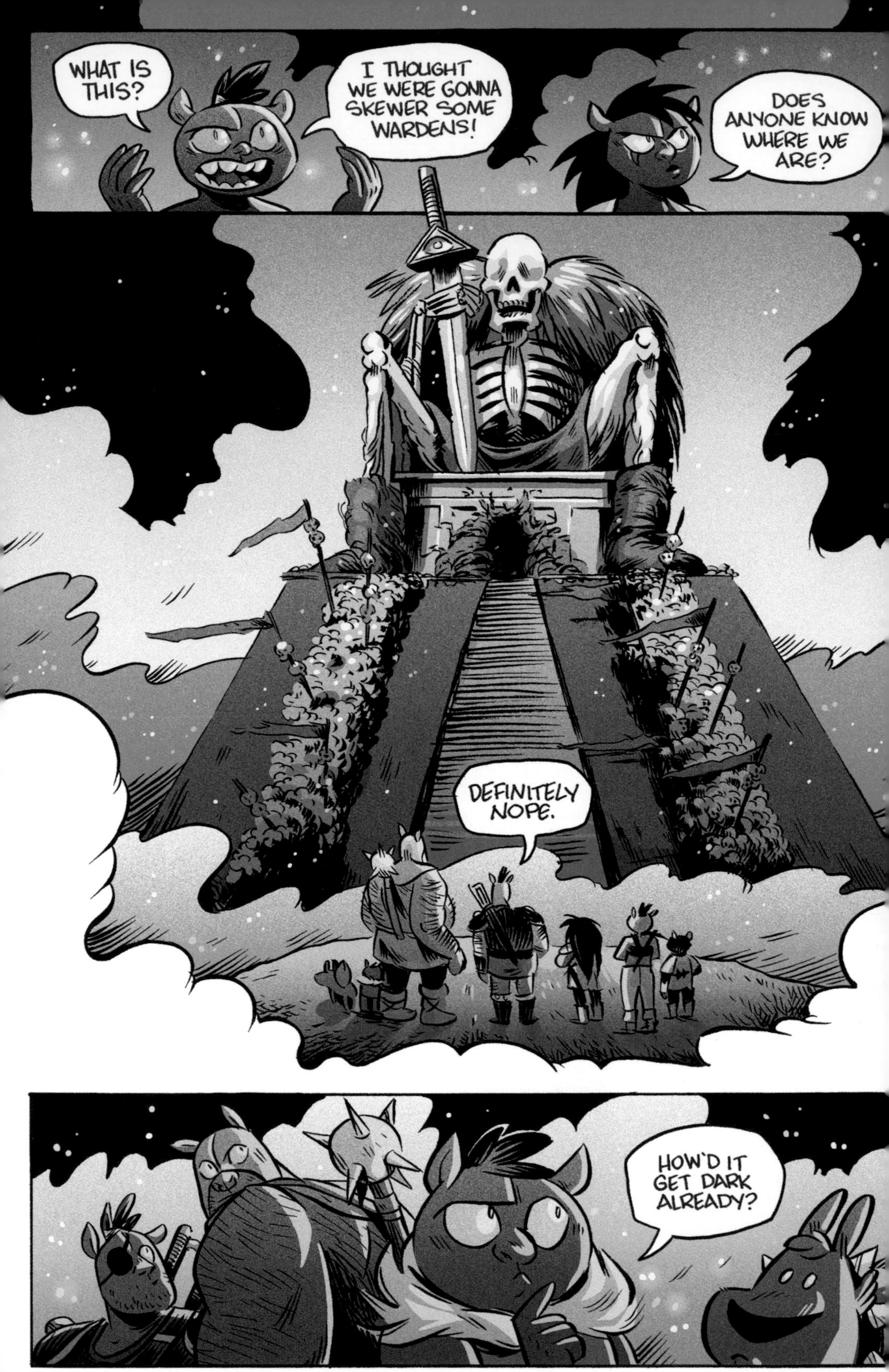
WHAT IS THIS?
I THOUGHT WE WERE GONNA SKEWER SOME WARDENS!
DOES ANYONE KNOW WHERE WE ARE?
DEFINITELY NOPE.
HOW'D IT GET DARK ALREADY?

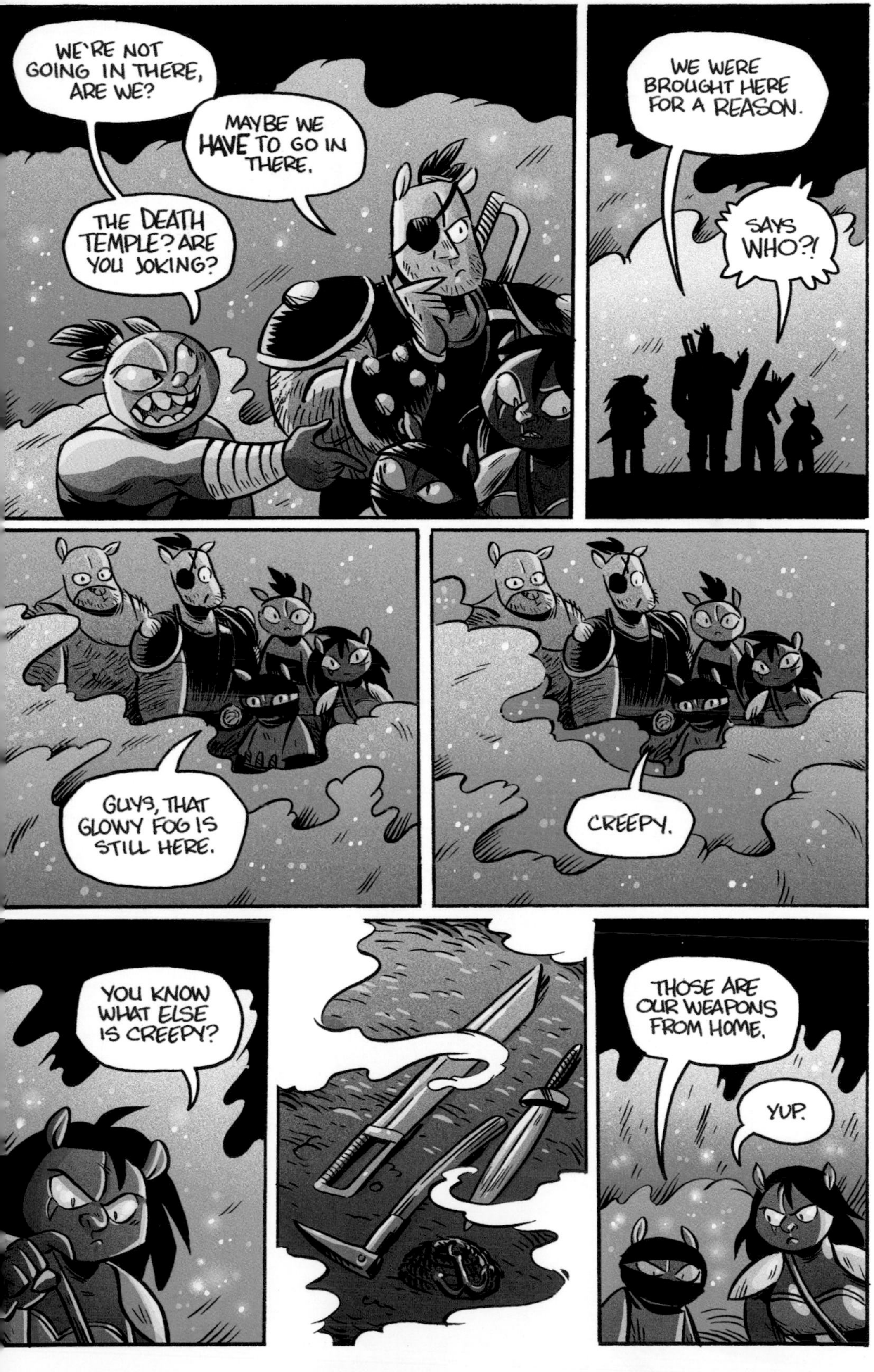
WE'RE NOT GOING IN THERE, ARE WE?
THE DEATH TEMPLE? ARE YOU JOKING?
MAYBE WE HAVE TO GO IN THERE.
WE WERE BROUGHT HERE FOR A REASON.
SAYS WHO?!
GUYS, THAT GLOWY FOG IS STILL HERE.
CREEPY.
YOU KNOW WHAT ELSE IS CREEPY?
THOSE ARE OUR WEAPONS FROM HOME.
YUP.

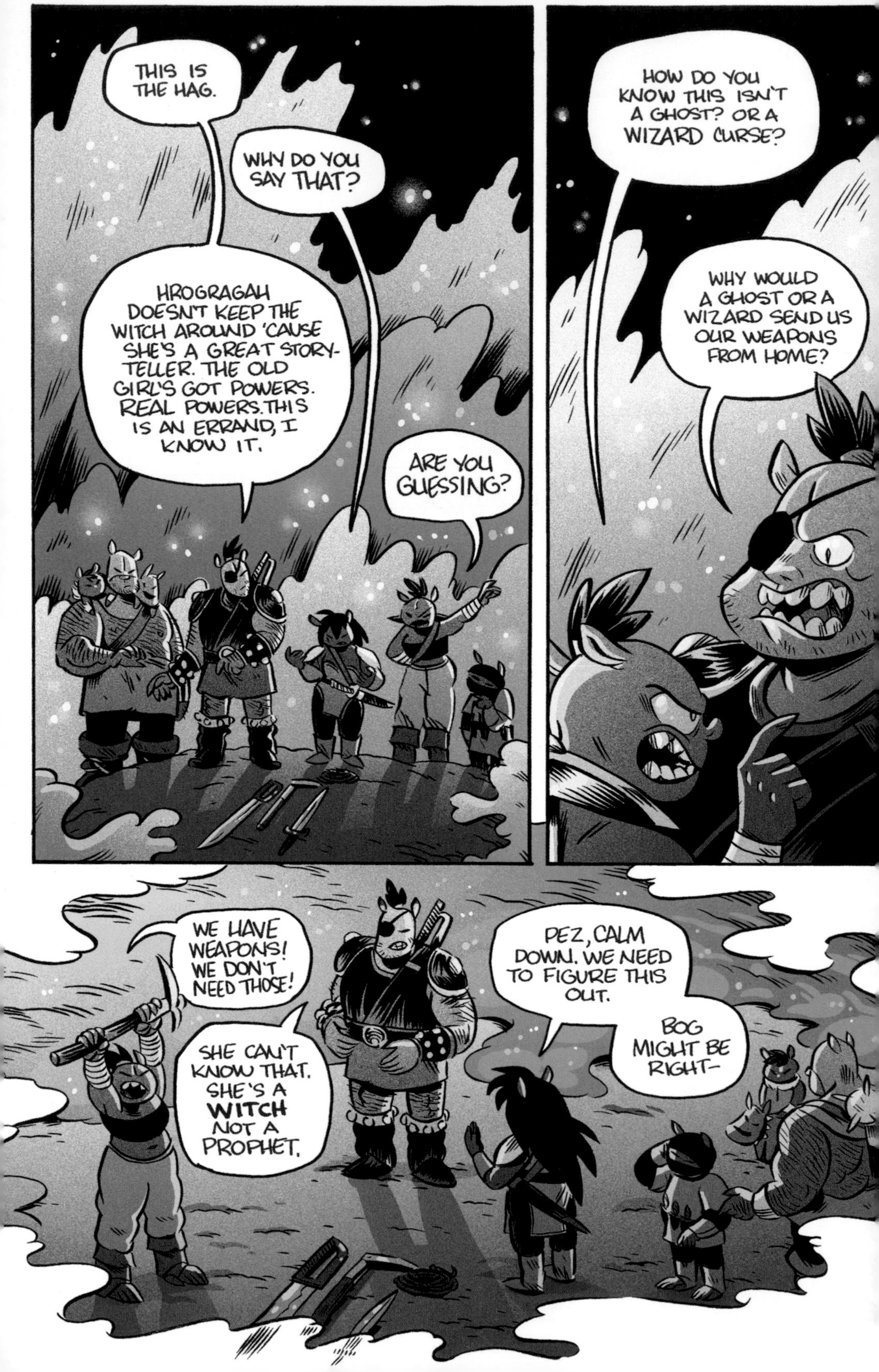
THIS IS THE HAG.
WHY DO YOU SAY THAT?
HROGRAGAH DOESN'T KEEP THE WITCH AROUND 'CAUSE SHE'S A GREAT STORY-TELLER. THE OLD GIRL'S GOT POWERS. REAL POWERS. THIS IS AN ERRAND, I KNOW IT.
ARE YOU GUESSING?
HOW DO YOU KNOW THIS ISN'T A GHOST? OR A WIZARD CURSE?
WHY WOULD A GHOST OR A WIZARD SEND US OUR WEAPONS FROM HOME?
WE HAVE WEAPONS! WE DON'T NEED THOSE!
SHE CAN'T KNOW THAT. SHE'S A WITCH NOT A PROPHET.
PEZ, CALM DOWN. WE NEED TO FIGURE THIS OUT.
BOG MIGHT BE RIGHT-

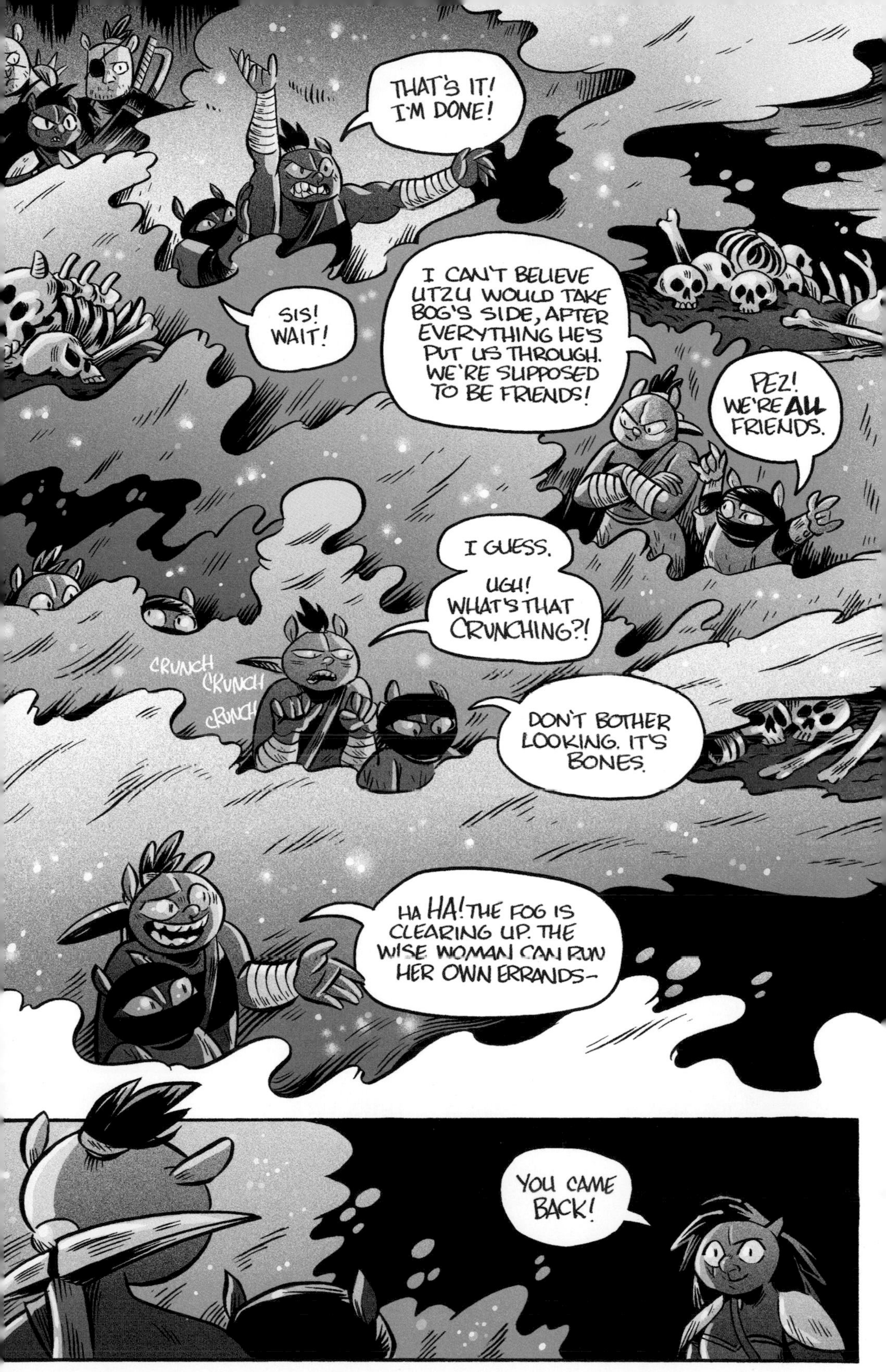
THAT'S IT! I'M DONE!
SIS! WAIT!
I CAN'T BELIEVE UTZU WOULD TAKE BOG'S SIDE, AFTER EVERYTHING HE'S PUT US THROUGH. WE'RE SUPPOSED TO BE FRIENDS!
PEZ! WE'RE ALL FRIENDS.
I GUESS.
UGH! WHAT'S THAT CRUNCHING?!
CRUNCH CRUNCH CRUNCH
DON'T BOTHER LOOKING. IT'S BONES.
HA HA! THE FOG IS CLEARING UP. THE WISE WOMAN CAN RUN HER OWN ERRANDS-
YOU CAME BACK!

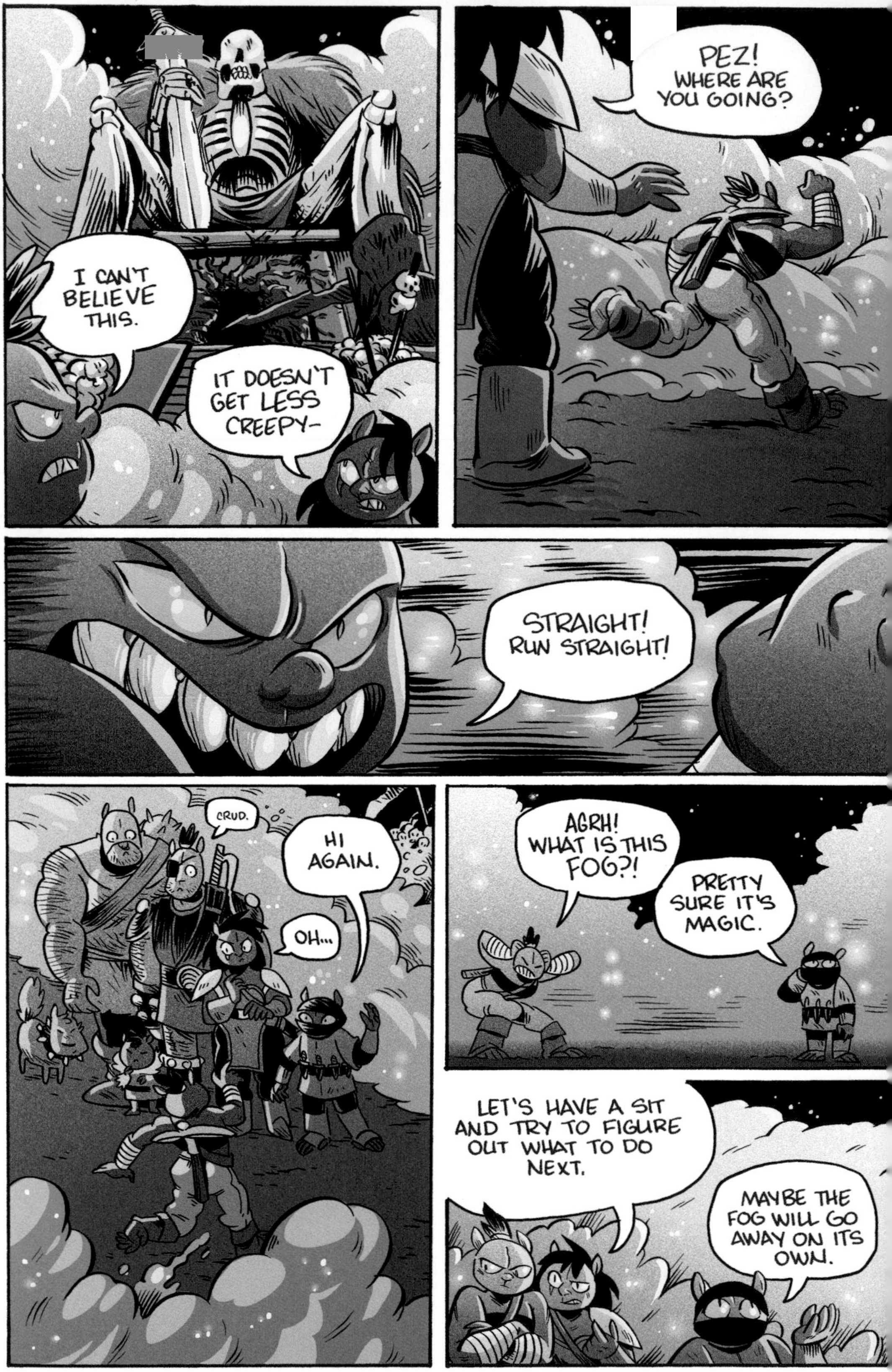
I CAN'T BELIEVE THIS.
IT DOESN'T GET LESS CREEPY-
PEZ! WHERE ARE YOU GOING?
STRAIGHT! RUN STRAIGHT!
CRUD.
HI AGAIN.
OH...
AGRH! WHAT IS THIS FOG?!
PRETTY SURE IT'S MAGIC.
LET'S HAVE A SIT AND TRY TO FIGURE OUT WHAT TO DO NEXT.
MAYBE THE FOG WILL GO AWAY ON ITS OWN.

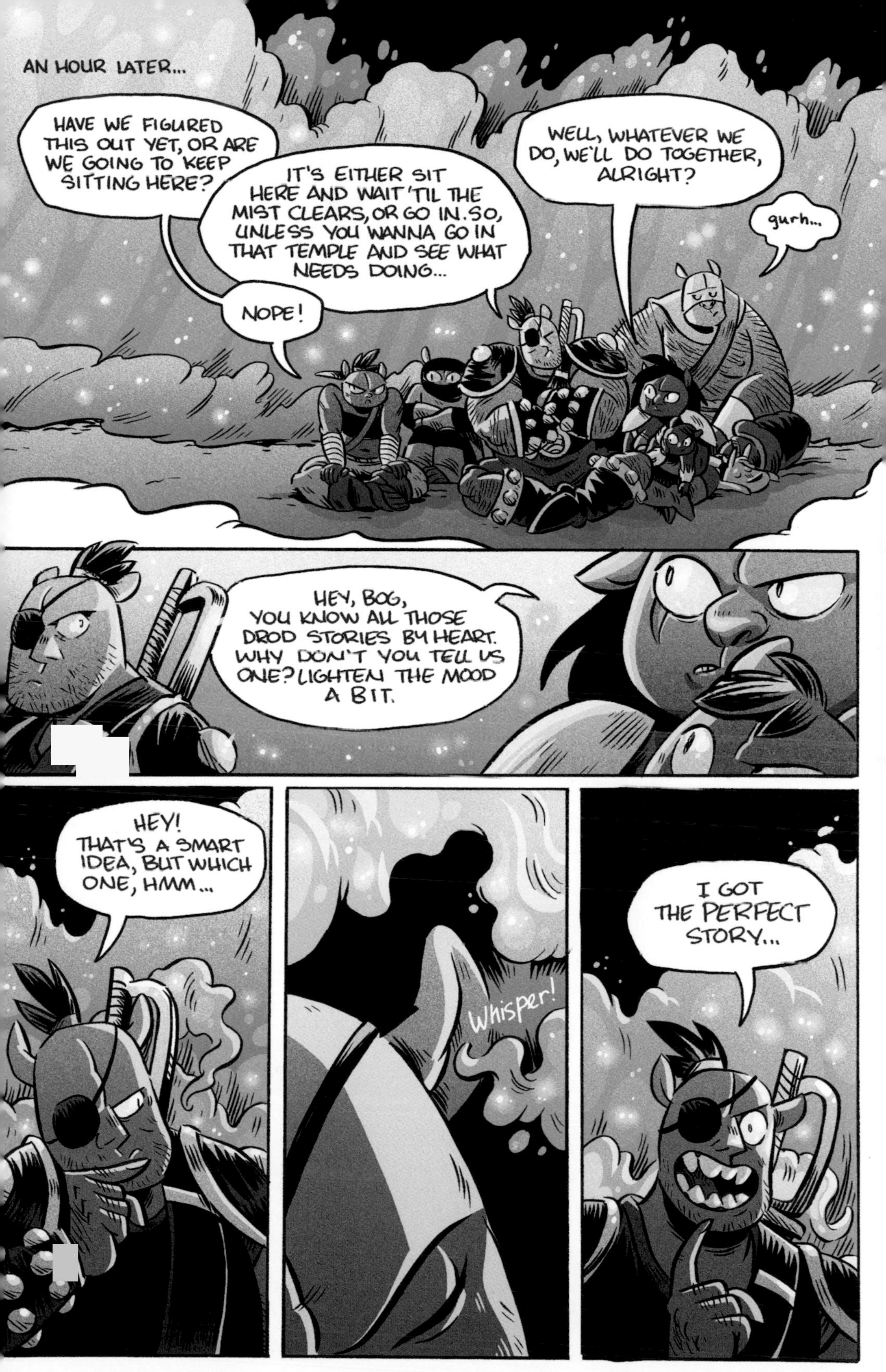
AN HOUR LATER...
HAVE WE FIGURED THIS OUT YET, OR ARE WE GOING TO KEEP SITTING HERE?
IT'S EITHER SIT HERE AND WAIT 'TIL THE MIST CLEARS, OR GO IN. SO, UNLESS YOU WANNA GO IN THAT TEMPLE AND SEE WHAT NEEDS DOING...
NOPE!
WELL, WHATEVER WE DO, WE'LL DO TOGETHER, ALRIGHT?
gurh...
HEY, BOG, YOU KNOW ALL THOSE DROD STORIES BY HEART. WHY DON'T YOU TELL US ONE? LIGHTEN THE MOOD A BIT.
HEY! THAT'S A SMART IDEA, BUT WHICH ONE, HMM...
Whisper!
I GOT THE PERFECT STORY...

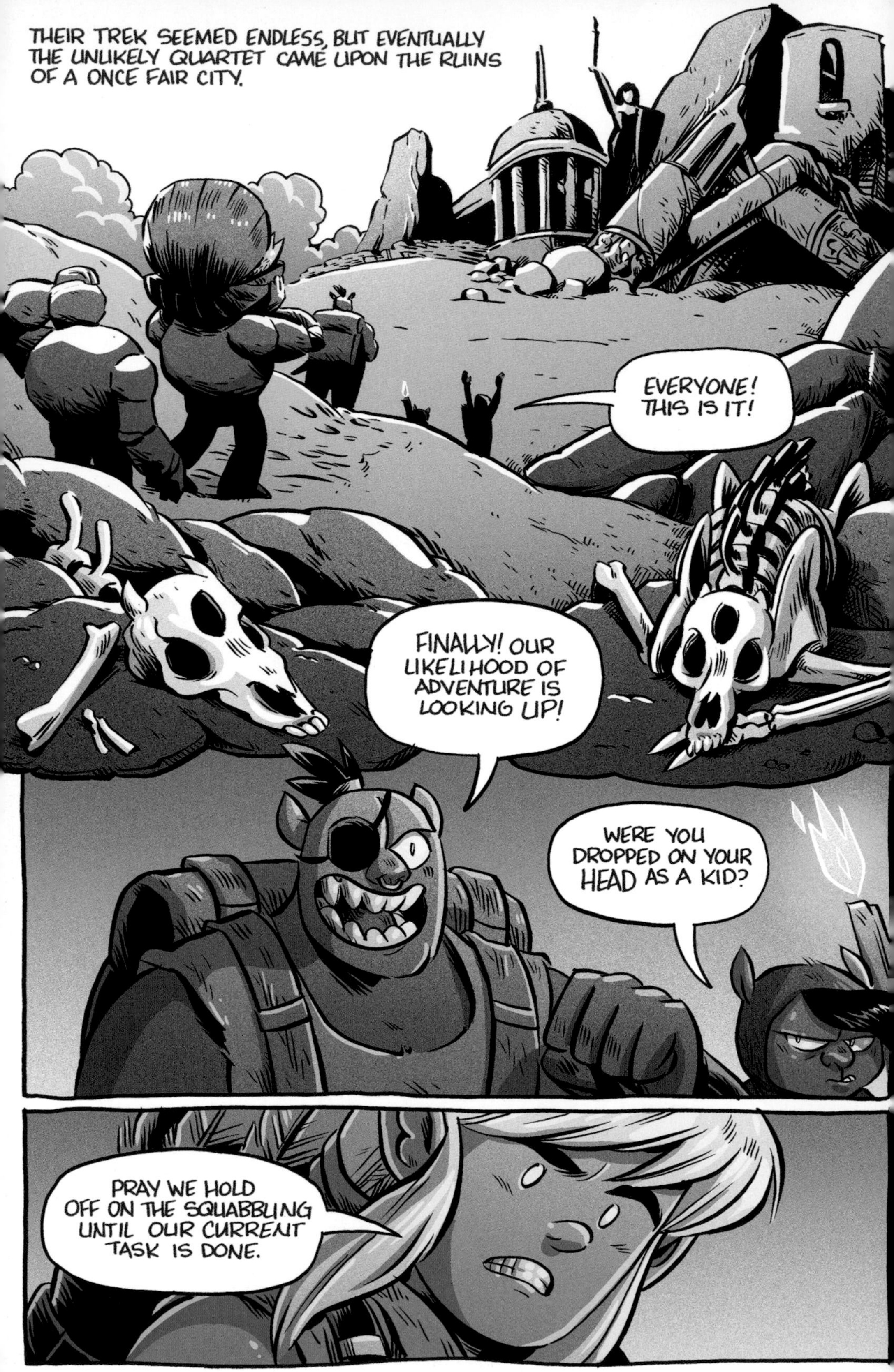
THEIR TREK SEEMED ENDLESS, BUT EVENTUALLY THE UNLIKELY QUARTET CAME UPON THE RUINS OF A ONCE FAIR CITY.
EVERYONE! THIS IS IT!
FINALLY! OUR LIKELIHOOD OF ADVENTURE IS LOOKING UP!
WERE YOU DROPPED ON YOUR HEAD AS A KID?
PRAY WE HOLD OFF ON THE SQUABBLING UNTIL OUR CURRENT TASK IS DONE.

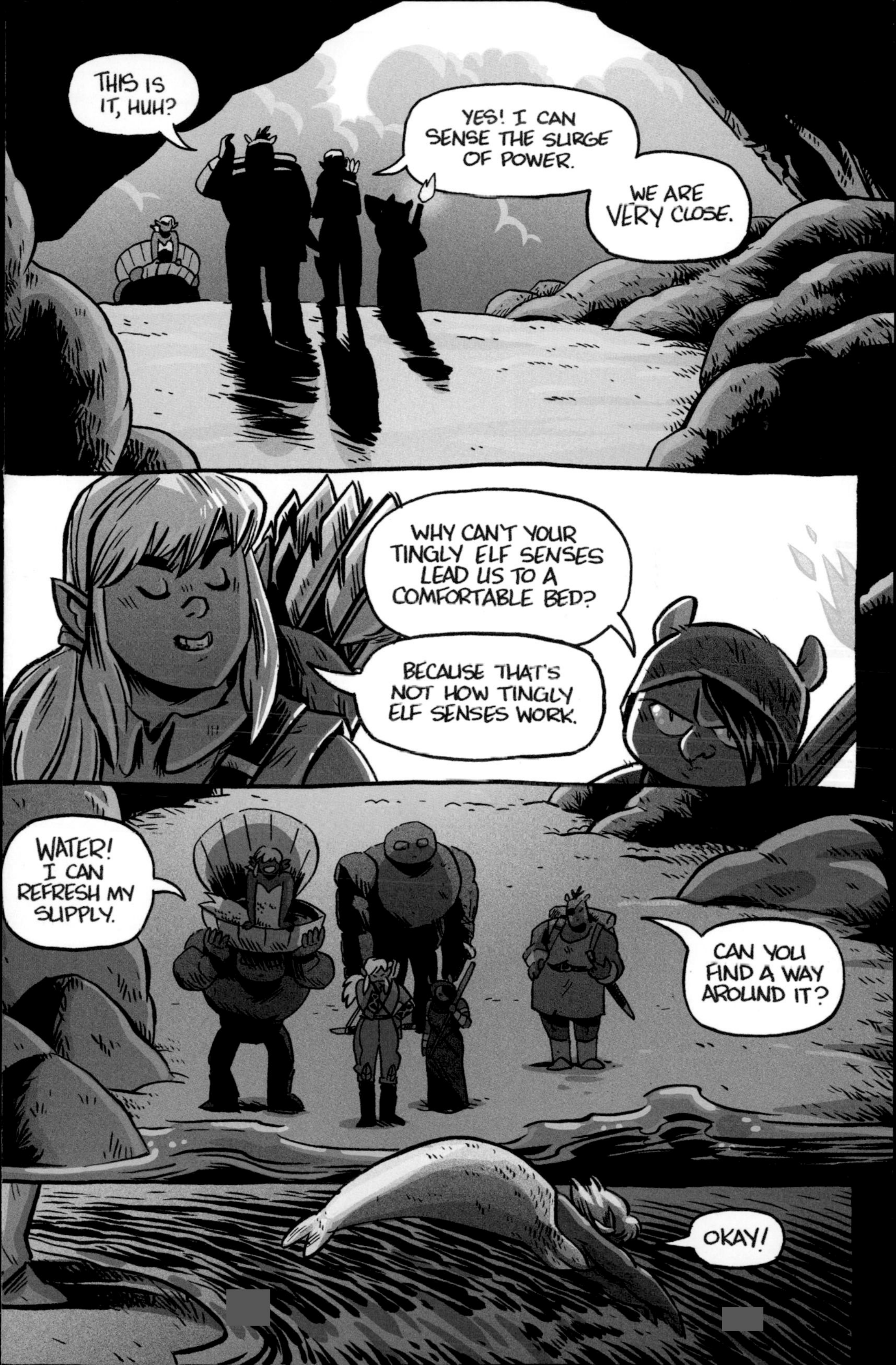
THIS IS IT, HUH?
YES! I CAN SENSE THE SURGE OF POWER.
WE ARE VERY CLOSE.
WHY CAN'T YOUR TINGLY ELF SENSES LEAD US TO A COMFORTABLE BED?
BECAUSE THAT'S NOT HOW TINGLY ELF SENSES WORK.
WATER! I CAN REFRESH MY SUPPLY.
CAN YOU FIND A WAY AROUND IT?
OKAY!

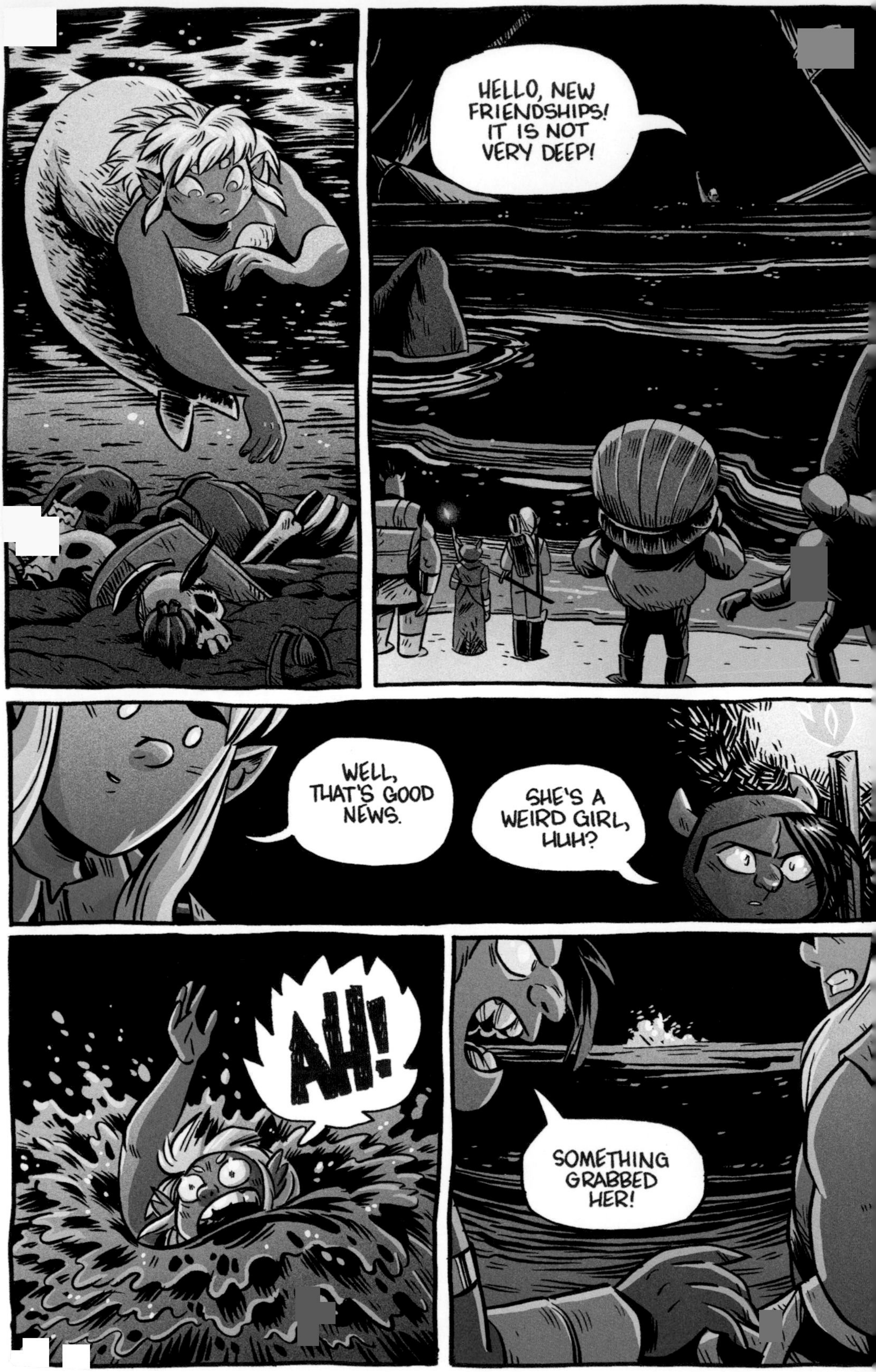
HELLO, NEW FRIENDSHIPS! IT IS NOT VERY DEEP!
WELL, THAT'S GOOD NEWS.
SHE'S A WEIRD GIRL, HUH?
AH!
SOMETHING GRABBED HER!

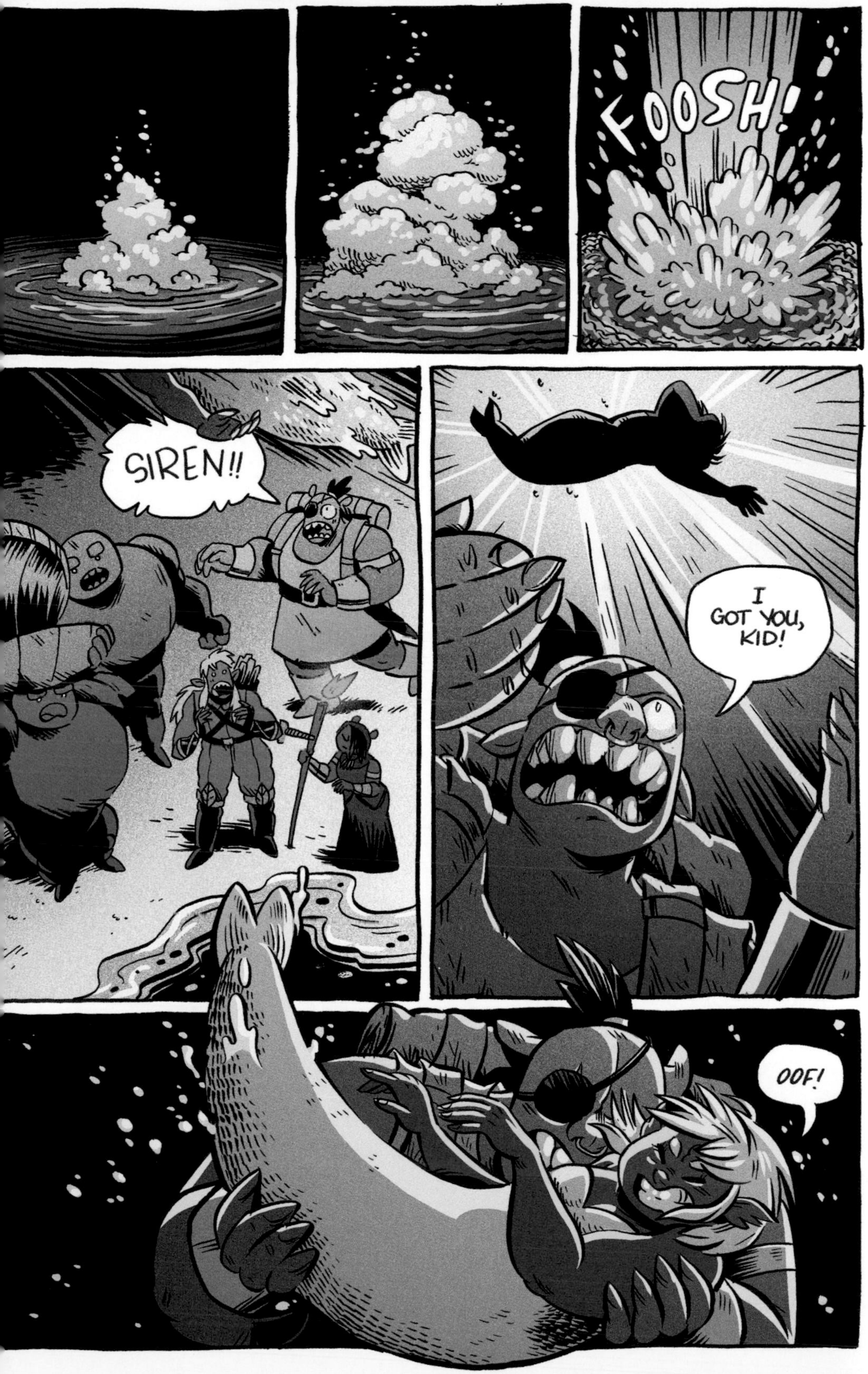
FOOSH!
SIREN!!
I GOT YOU, KID!
OOF!

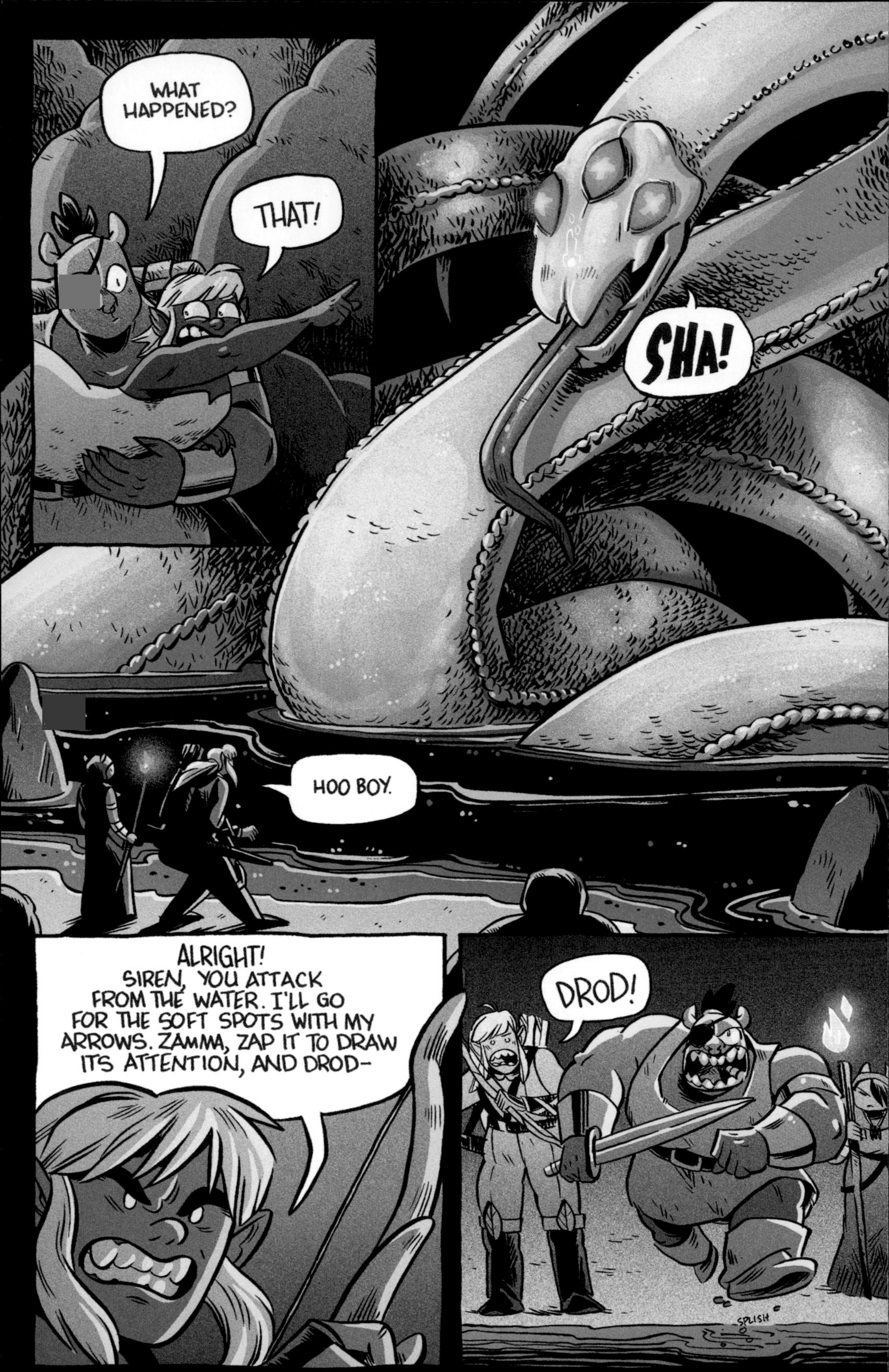
WHAT HAPPENED?
THAT!
SHA!
HOO BOY.
ALRIGHT! SIREN, YOU ATTACK FROM THE WATER. I'LL GO FOR THE SOFT SPOTS WITH MY ARROWS. ZAMMA, ZAP IT TO DRAW ITS ATTENTION, AND DROD-
DROD!
SPLISH

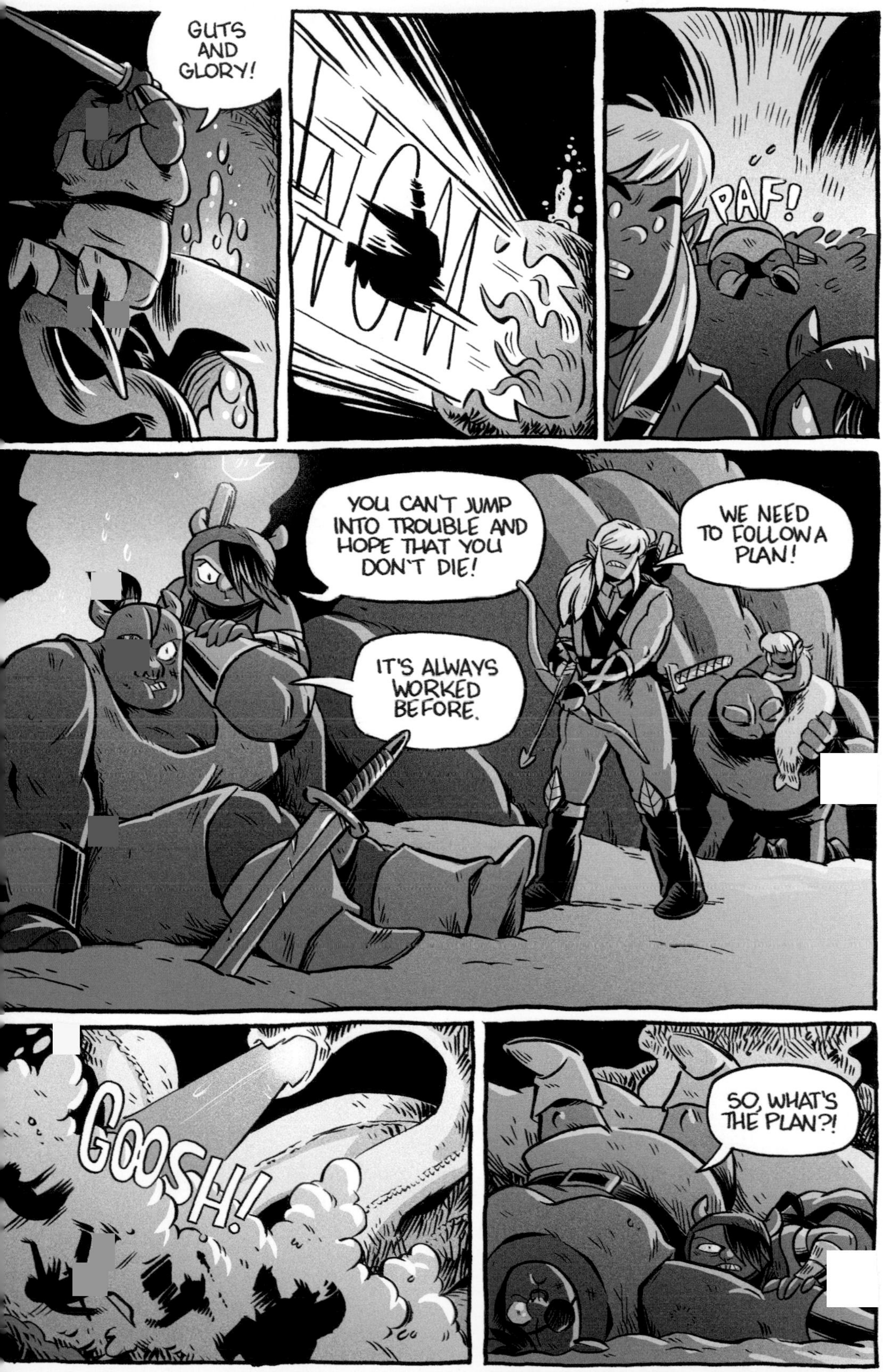
GUTS AND GLORY!
PAF!
YOU CAN'T JUMP INTO TROUBLE AND HOPE THAT YOU DON'T DIE!
WE NEED TO FOLLOW A PLAN!
IT'S ALWAYS WORKED BEFORE.
GOOSH!
SO, WHAT'S THE PLAN?!

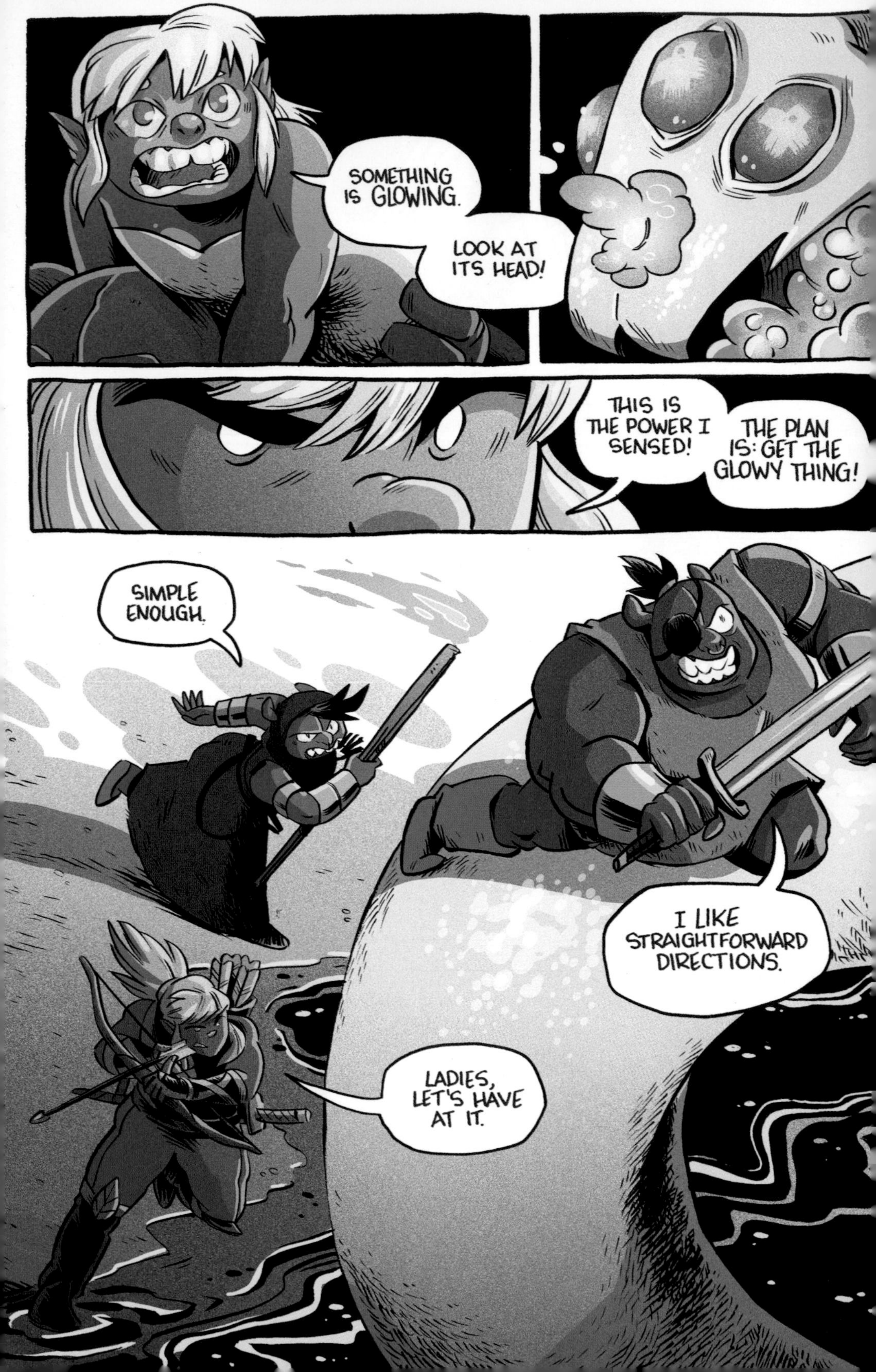
SOMETHING IS GLOWING.
LOOK AT ITS HEAD!
THIS IS THE POWER I SENSED!
THE PLAN IS: GET THE GLOWY THING!
SIMPLE ENOUGH.
I LIKE STRAIGHTFORWARD DIRECTIONS.
LADIES, LET'S HAVE AT IT.

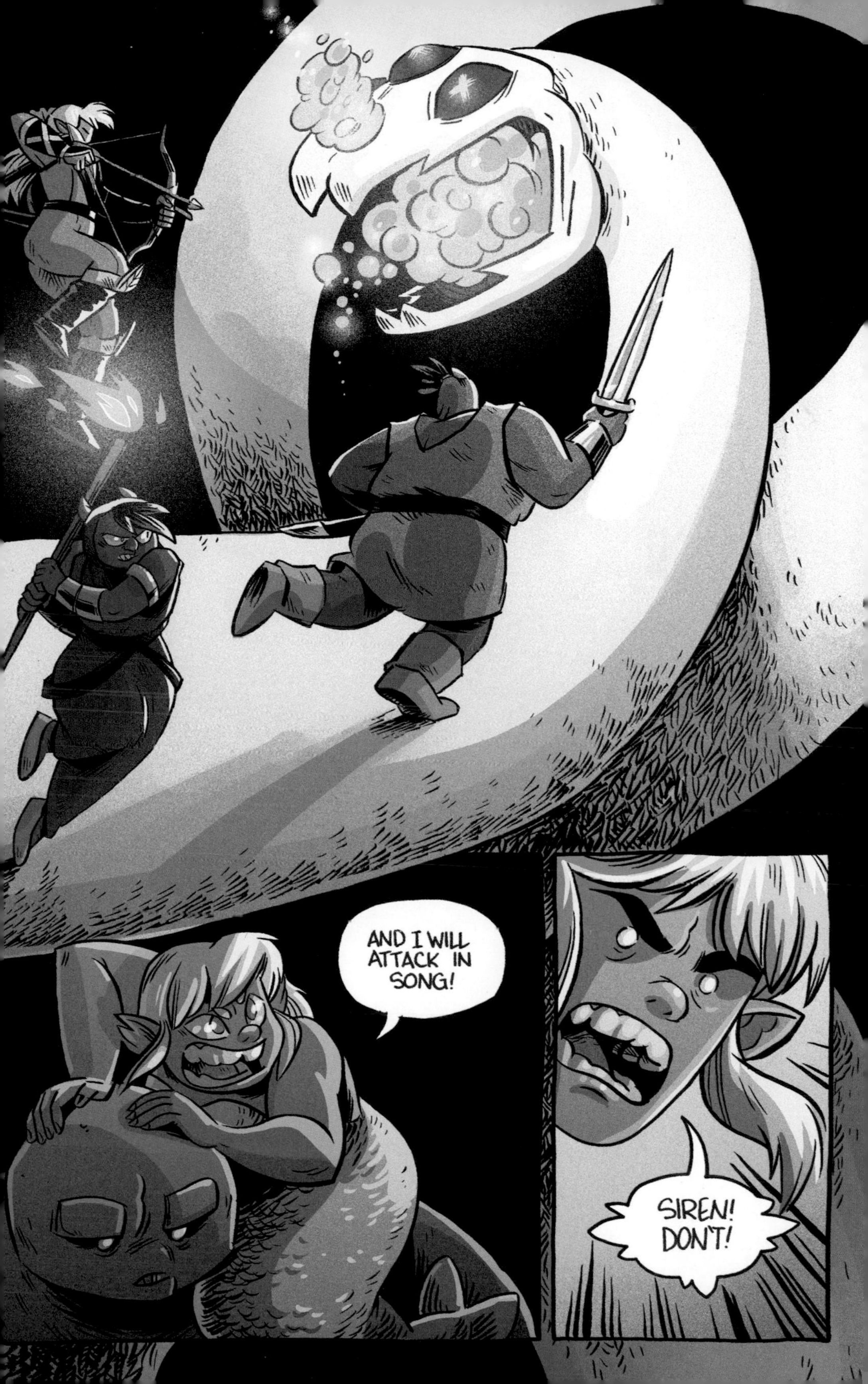
AND I WILL ATTACK IN SONG!
SIREN! DON'T!

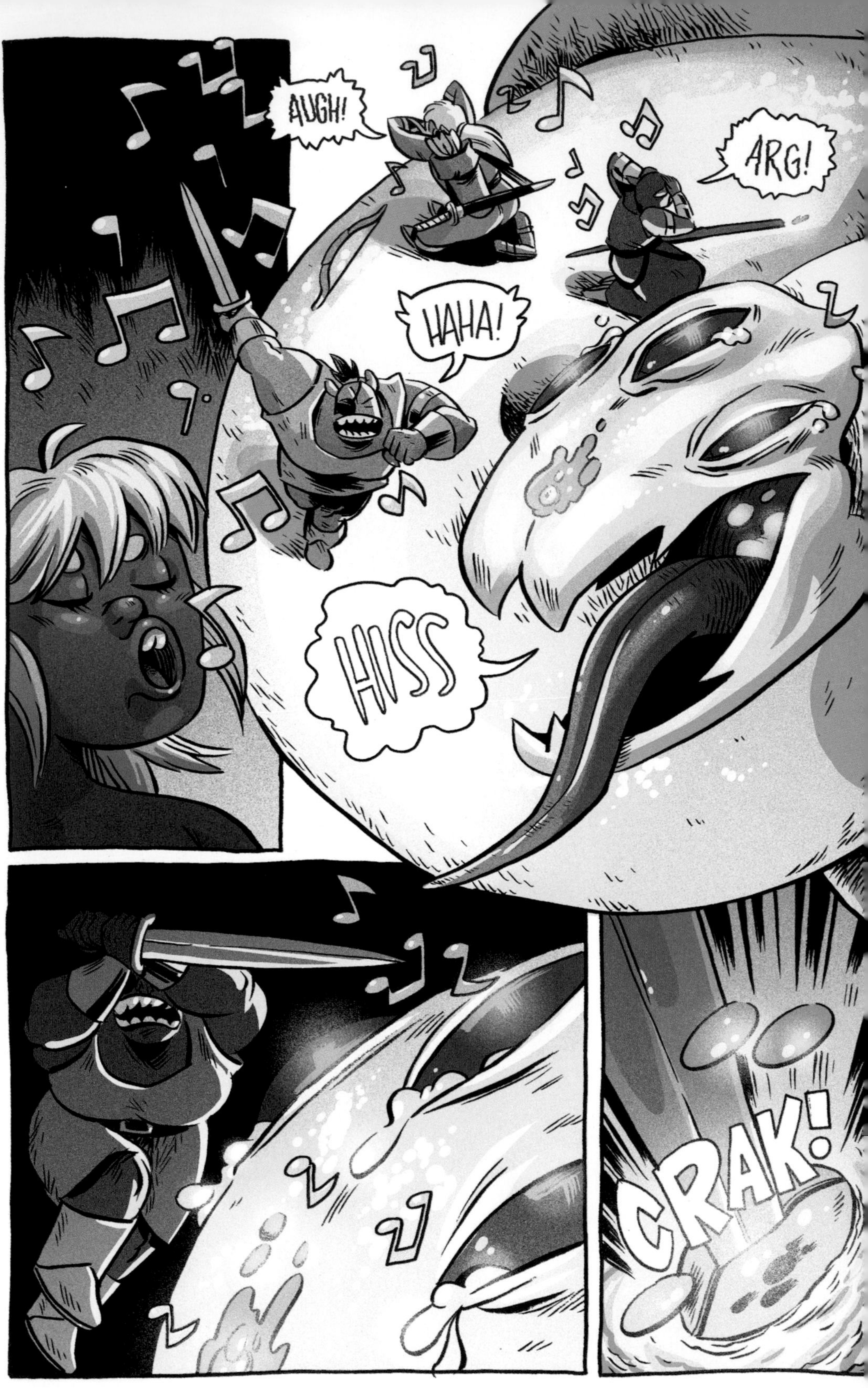
AUGH!
ARG!
HAHA!
HISS
CRAK!

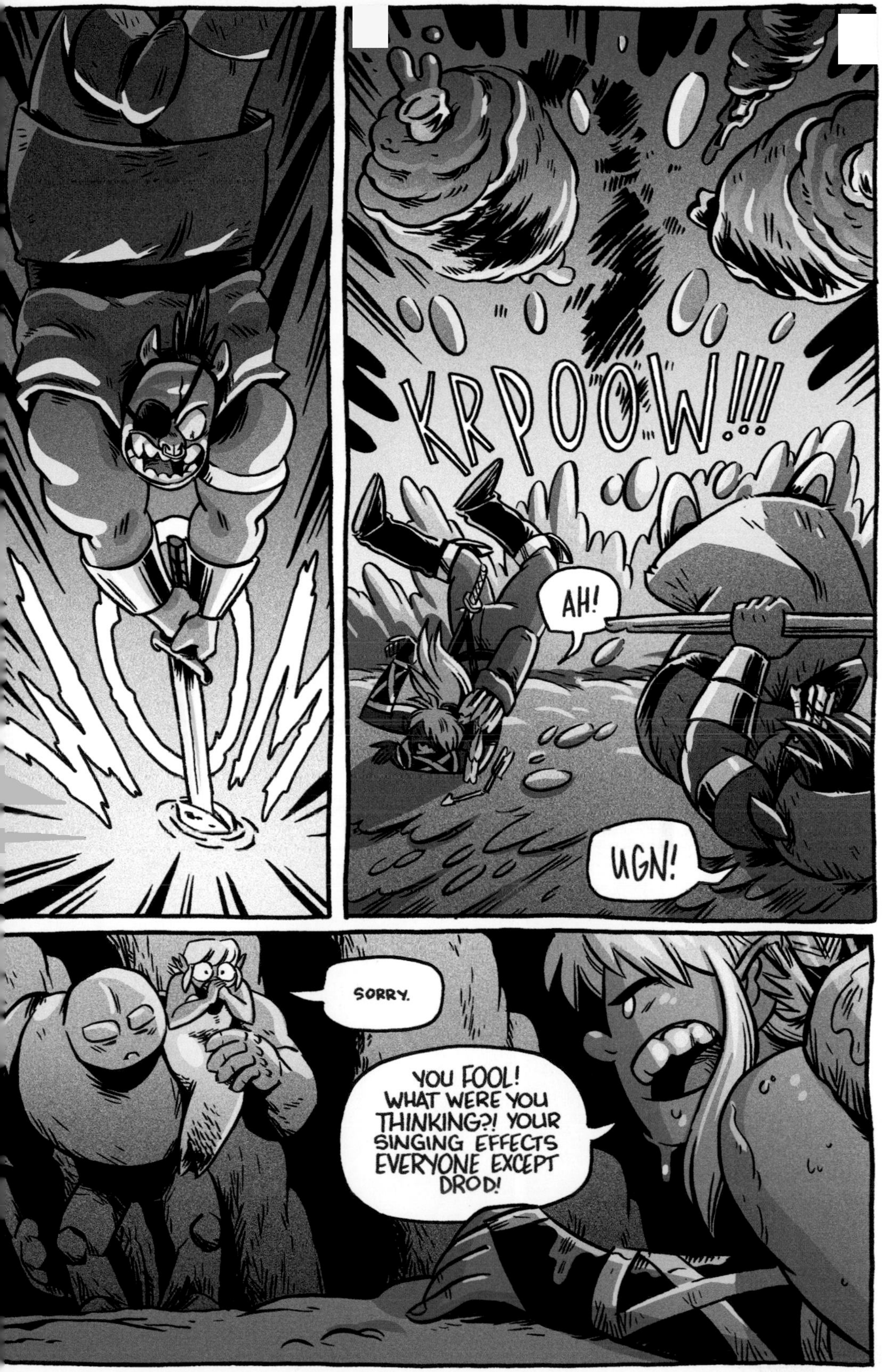
KRPOOW!!!
AH!
UGN!
SORRY.
YOU FOOL! WHAT WERE YOU THINKING?! YOUR SINGING EFFECTS EVERYONE EXCEPT DROD!

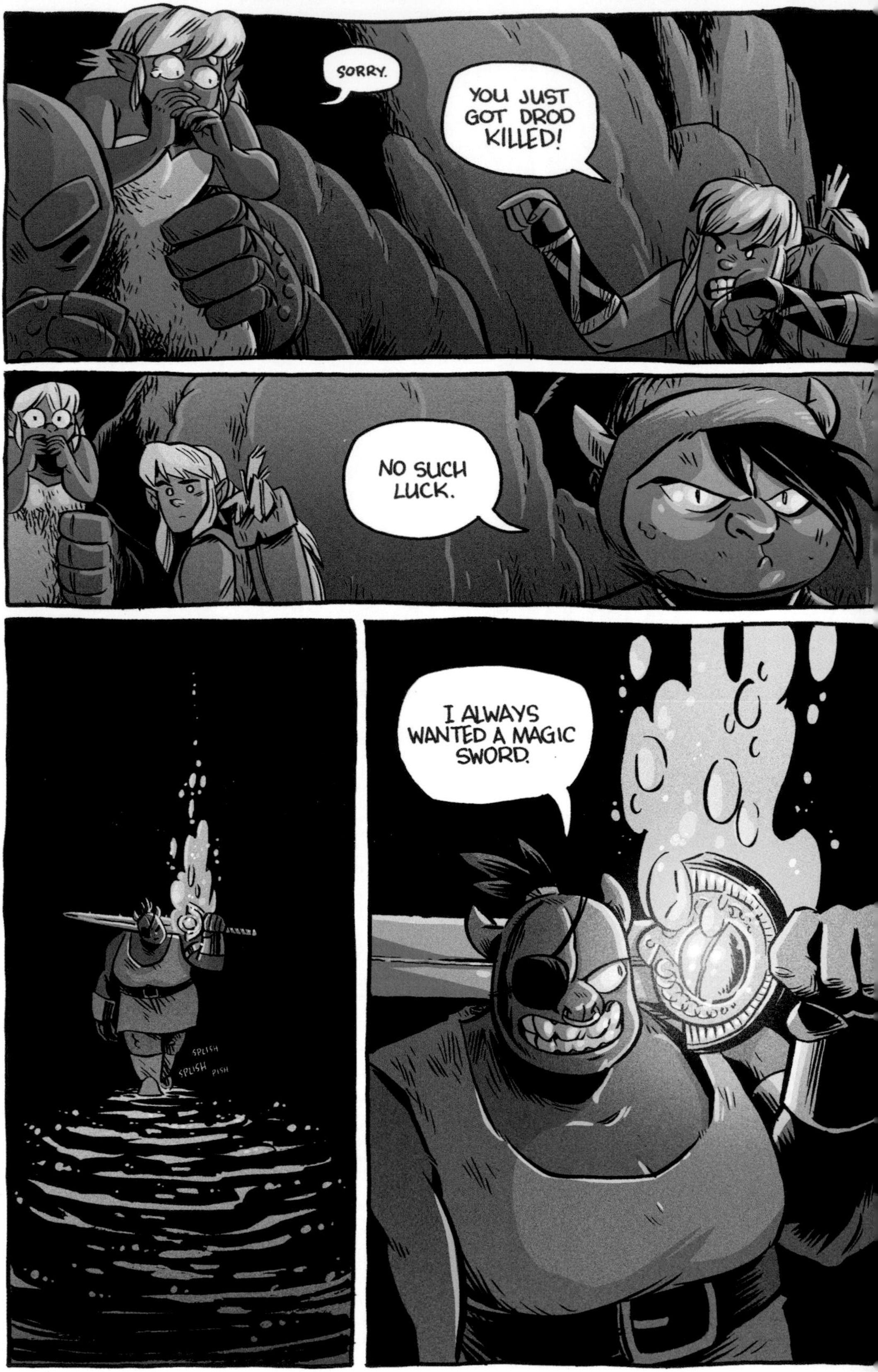
SORRY.
YOU JUST GOT DROD KILLED!
NO SUCH LUCK.
SPLISH
SPLISH
PISH
I ALWAYS WANTED A MAGIC SWORD.

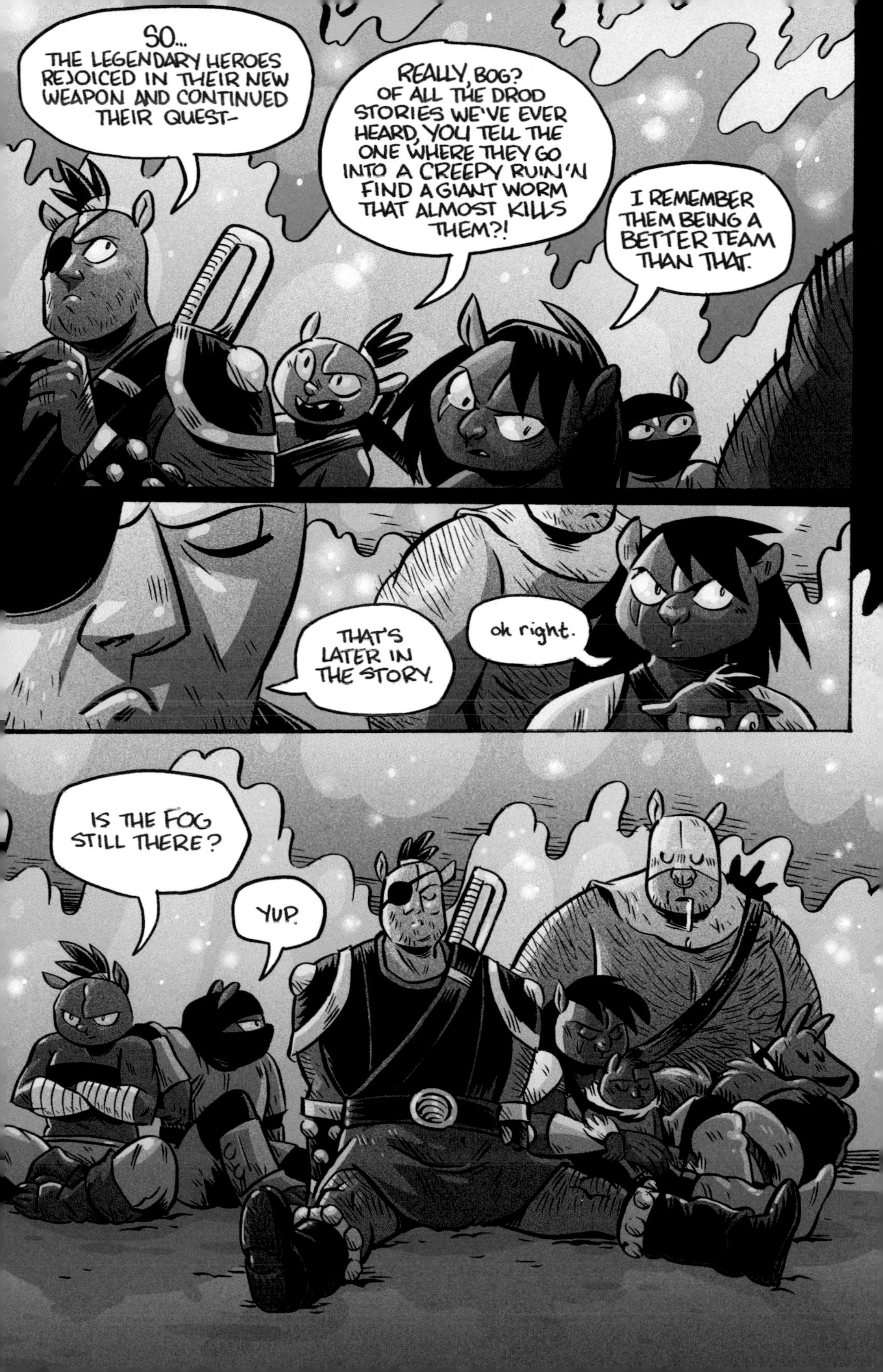

SO...
THE LEGENDARY HEROES REJOICED IN THEIR NEW WEAPON AND CONTINUED THEIR QUEST-
REALLY, BOG? OF ALL THE DROD STORIES WE'VE EVER HEARD, YOU TELL THE ONE WHERE THEY GO INTO A CREEPY RUIN 'N FIND A GIANT WORM THAT ALMOST KILLS THEM?!
I REMEMBER THEM BEING A BETTER TEAM THAN THAT.
THAT'S LATER IN THE STORY.
oh right.
IS THE FOG STILL THERE?
YUP.

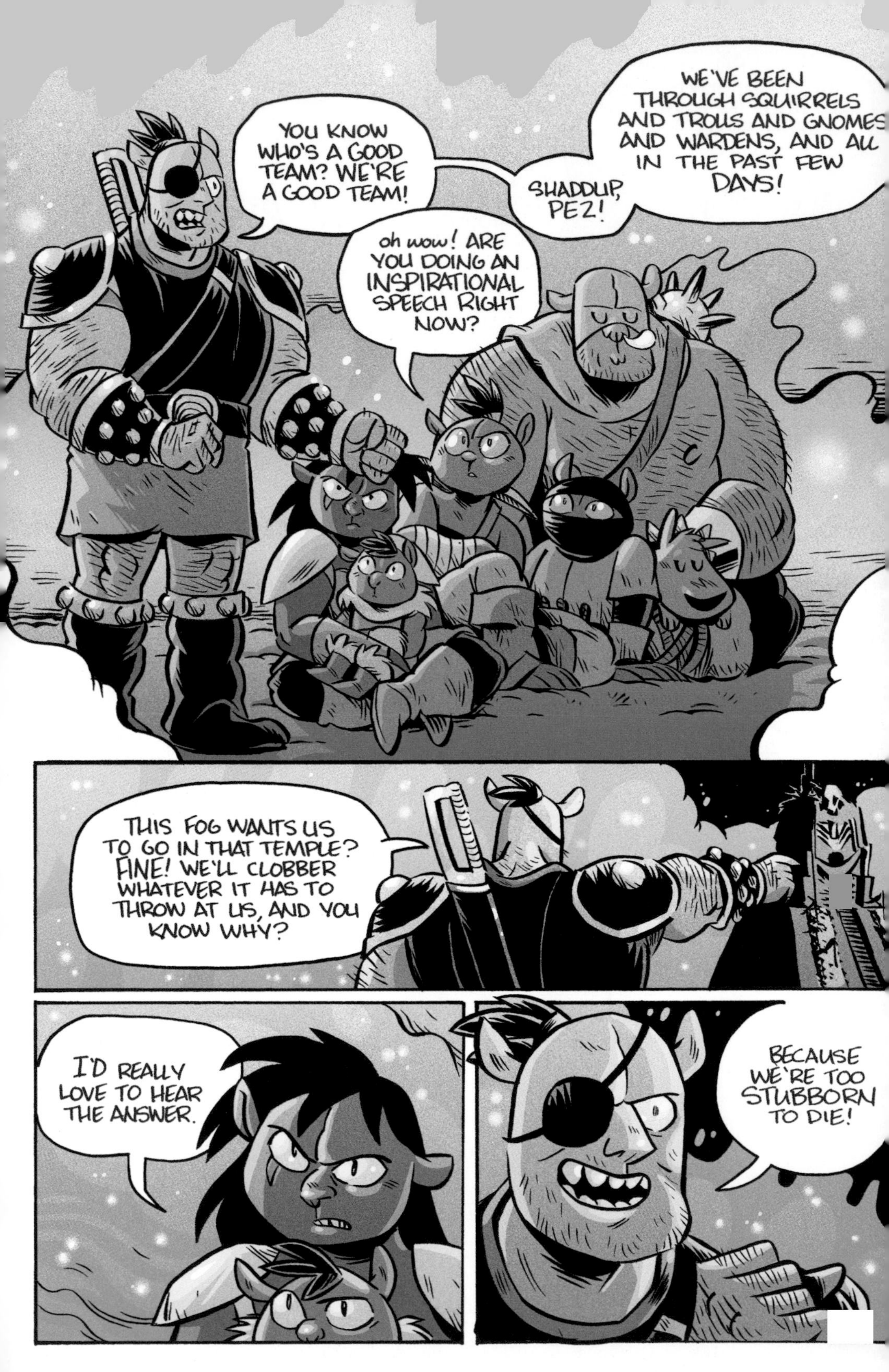
YOU KNOW WHO'S A GOOD TEAM? WE'RE A GOOD TEAM!
WE'VE BEEN THROUGH SQUIRRELS AND TROLLS AND GNOMES AND WARDENS, AND ALL IN THE PAST FEW DAYS!
SHADDUP, PEZ!
oh wow! ARE YOU DOING AN INSPIRATIONAL SPEECH RIGHT NOW?
THIS FOG WANTS US TO GO IN THAT TEMPLE? FINE! WE'LL CLOBBER WHATEVER IT HAS TO THROW AT US, AND YOU KNOW WHY?
I'D REALLY LOVE TO HEAR THE ANSWER.
BECAUSE WE'RE TOO STUBBORN TO DIE!

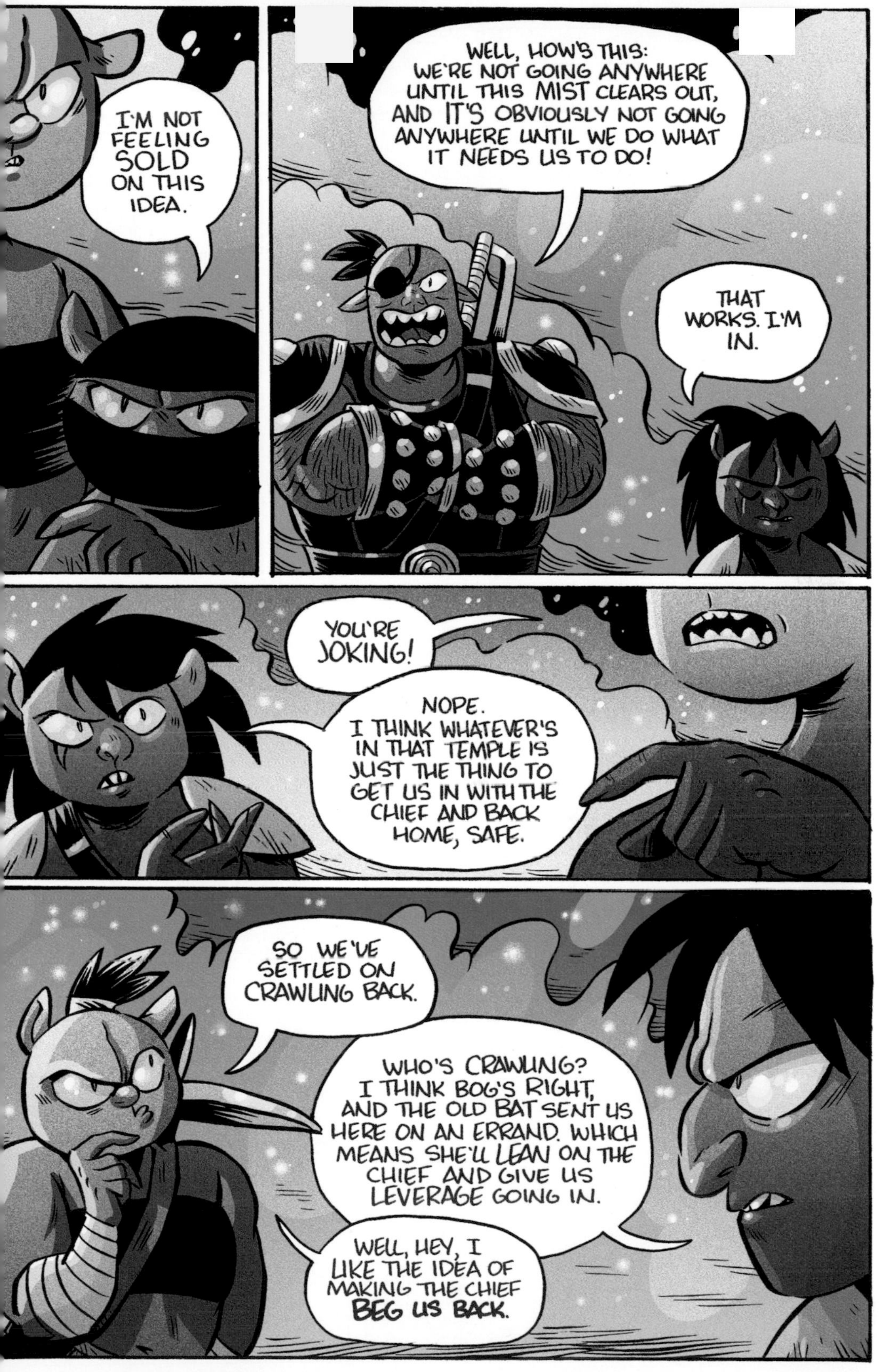
I'M NOT FEELING SOLD ON THIS IDEA.
WELL, HOW'S THIS: WE'RE NOT GOING ANYWHERE UNTIL THIS MIST CLEARS OUT, AND IT'S OBVIOUSLY NOT GOING ANYWHERE UNTIL WE DO WHAT IT NEEDS US TO DO!
THAT WORKS. I'M IN.
YOU'RE JOKING!
NOPE. I THINK WHATEVER'S IN THAT TEMPLE IS JUST THE THING TO GET US IN WITH THE CHIEF AND BACK HOME, SAFE.
SO WE'VE SETTLED ON CRAWLING BACK.
WHO'S CRAWLING? I THINK BOG'S RIGHT, AND THE OLD BAT SENT US HERE ON AN ERRAND. WHICH MEANS SHE'LL LEAN ON THE CHIEF AND GIVE US LEVERAGE GOING IN.
WELL, HEY, I LIKE THE IDEA OF MAKING THE CHIEF BEG US BACK.

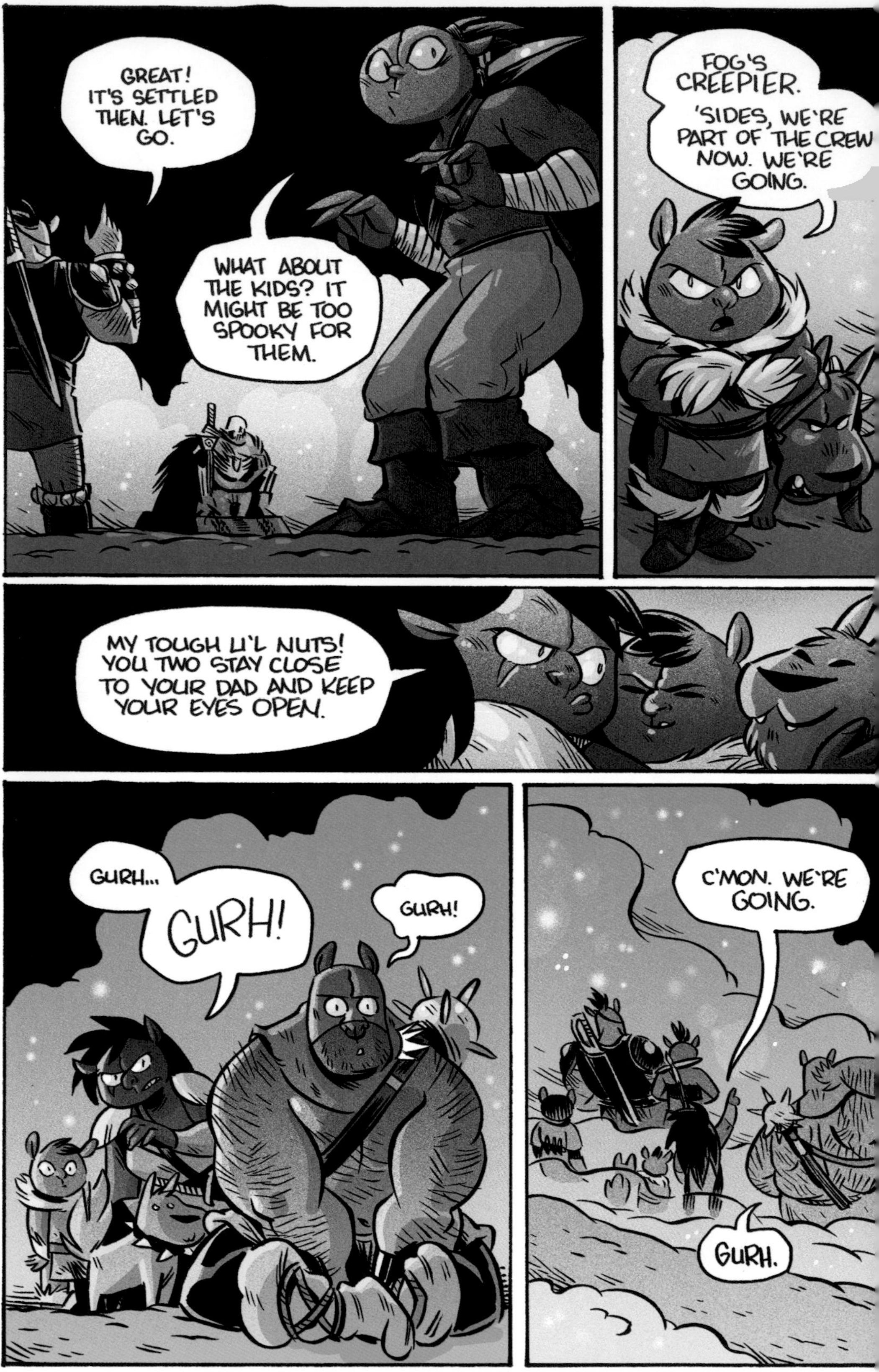
GREAT! IT'S SETTLED THEN. LET'S GO.
WHAT ABOUT THE KIDS? IT MIGHT BE TOO SPOOKY FOR THEM.
FOG'S CREEPIER.
'SIDES, WE'RE PART OF THE CREW NOW. WE'RE GOING.
MY TOUGH LI'L NUTS! YOU TWO STAY CLOSE TO YOUR DAD AND KEEP YOUR EYES OPEN.
GURH...
GURH!
GURH!
C'MON. WE'RE GOING.
GURH.

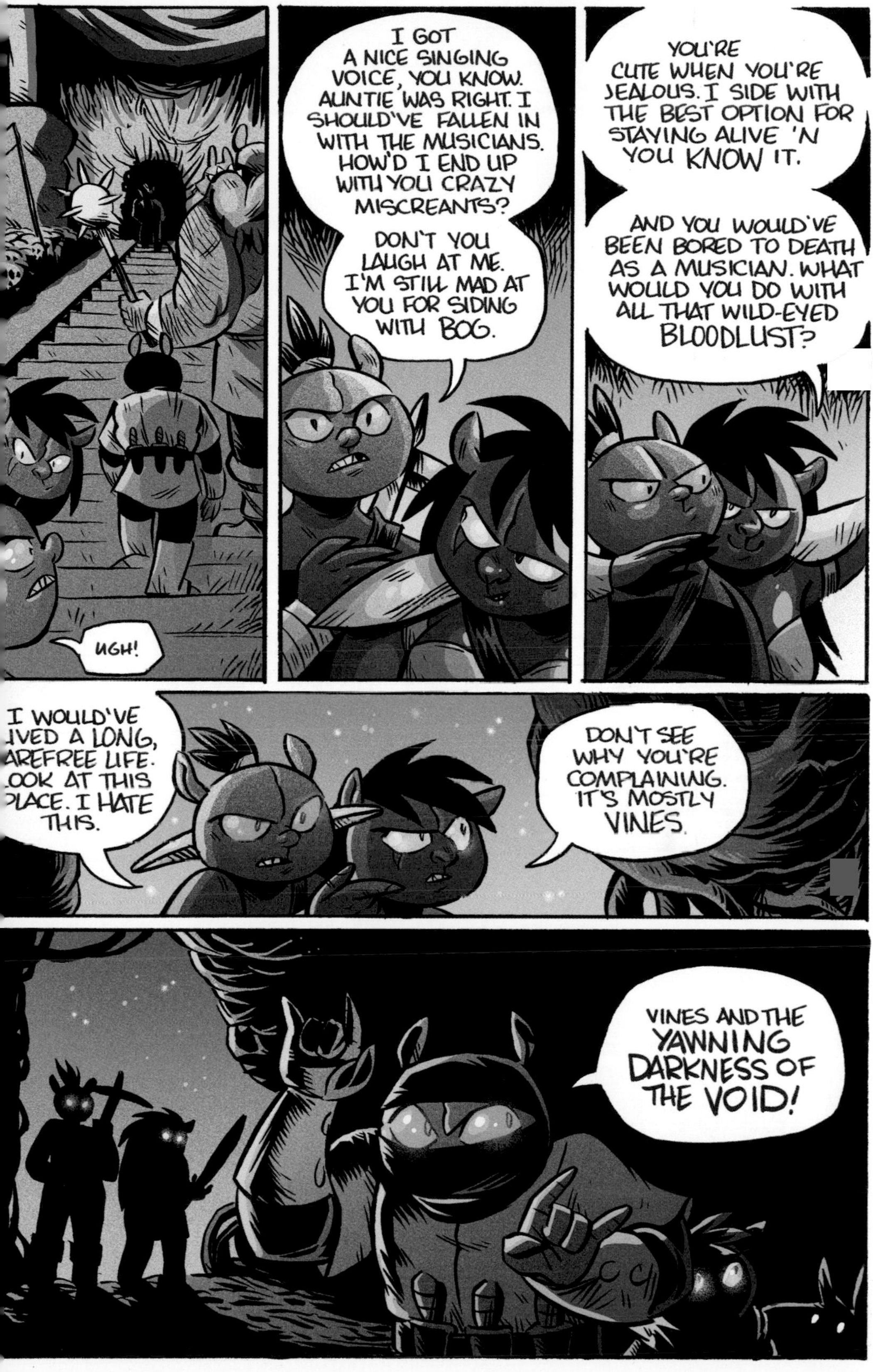
UGH!
I GOT A NICE SINGING VOICE, YOU KNOW. AUNTIE WAS RIGHT. I SHOULD'VE FALLEN IN WITH THE MUSICIANS. HOW'D I END UP WITH YOU CRAZY MISCREANTS?
DON'T YOU LAUGH AT ME. I'M STILL MAD AT YOU FOR SIDING WITH BOG.
YOU'RE CUTE WHEN YOU'RE JEALOUS. I SIDE WITH THE BEST OPTION FOR STAYING ALIVE 'N YOU KNOW IT.
AND YOU WOULD'VE BEEN BORED TO DEATH AS A MUSICIAN. WHAT WOULD YOU DO WITH ALL THAT WILD-EYED BLOODLUST?
I WOULD'VE LIVED A LONG, CAREFREE LIFE. LOOK AT THIS PLACE. I HATE THIS.
DON'T SEE WHY YOU'RE COMPLAINING. IT'S MOSTLY VINES.
VINES AND THE YAWNING DARKNESS OF THE VOID!

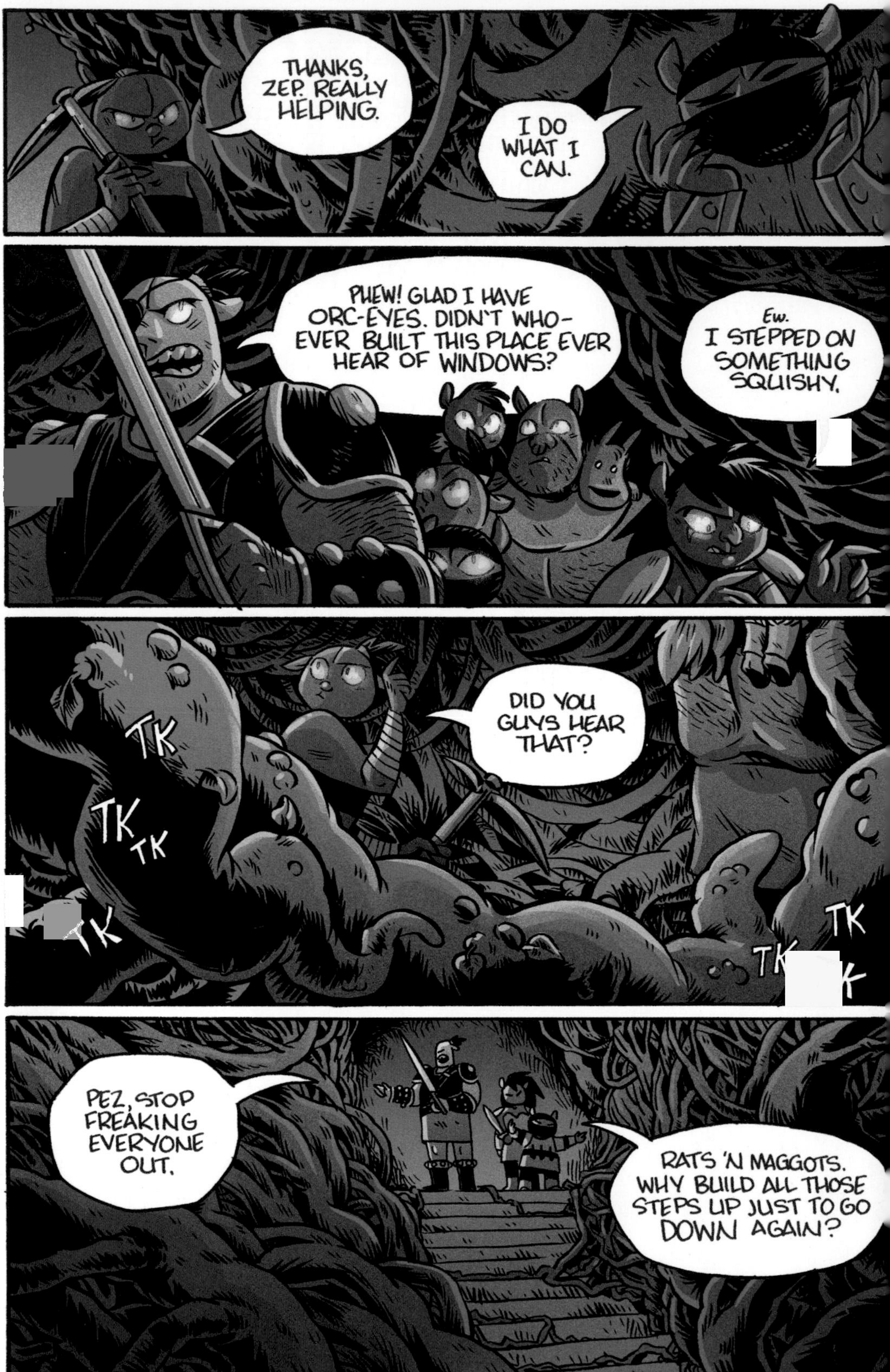
THANKS, ZEP. REALLY HELPING.
I DO WHAT I CAN.
PHEW! GLAD I HAVE ORC-EYES. DIDN'T WHO-EVER BUILT THIS PLACE EVER HEAR OF WINDOWS?
Ew. I STEPPED ON SOMETHING SQUISHY.
TK
TK
TK
TK
DID YOU GUYS HEAR THAT?
TK
PEZ, STOP FREAKING EVERYONE OUT.
RATS 'N MAGGOTS. WHY BUILD ALL THOSE STEPS UP JUST TO GO DOWN AGAIN?

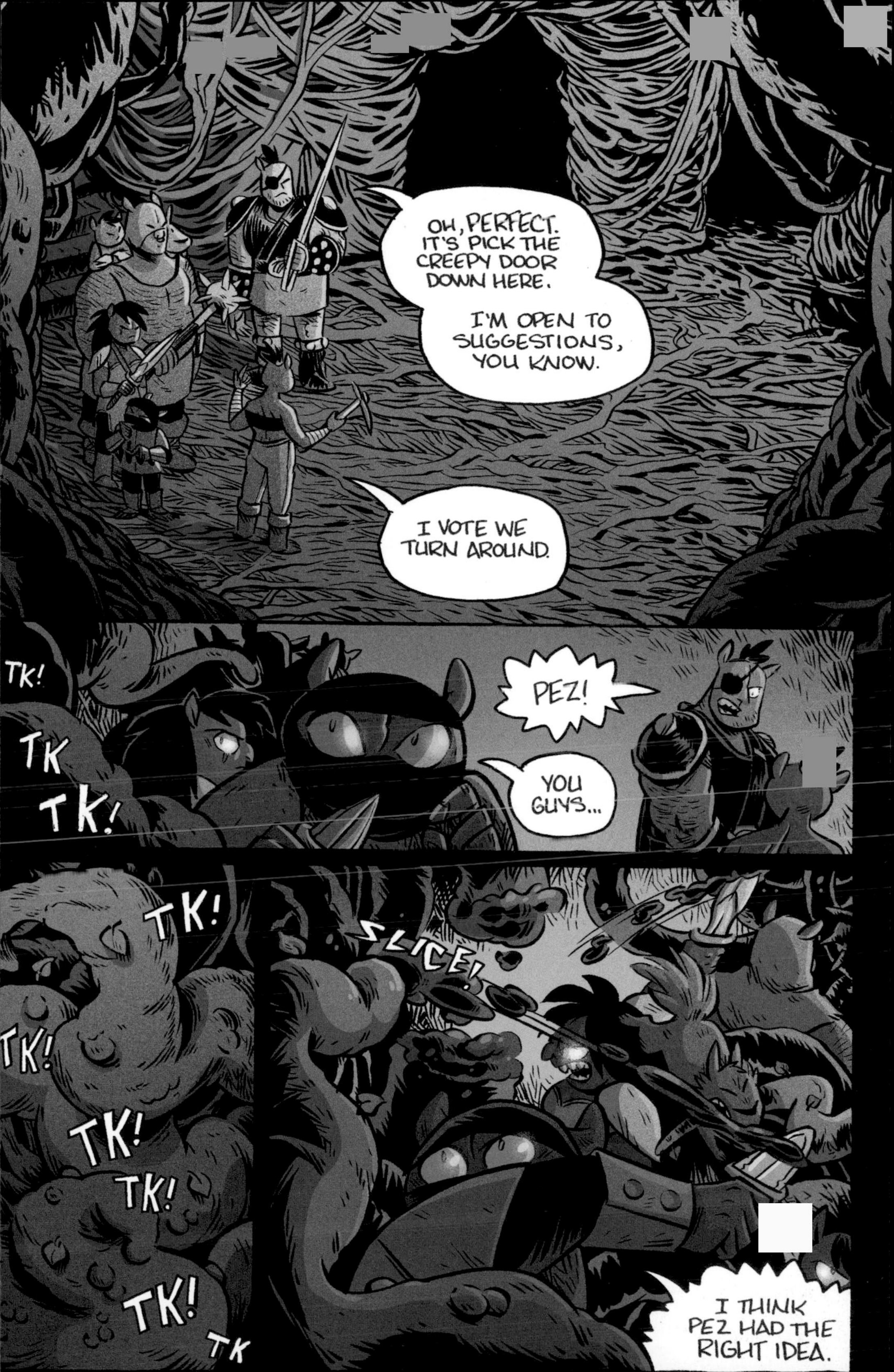
OH, PERFECT. IT'S PICK THE CREEPY DOOR DOWN HERE.
I'M OPEN TO SUGGESTIONS, YOU KNOW.
I VOTE WE TURN AROUND.
TK!
TK
TK!
PEZ!
YOU GUYS...
TK!
TK!
TK!
TK!
TK!
TK
SLICE!
I THINK PEZ HAD THE RIGHT IDEA.

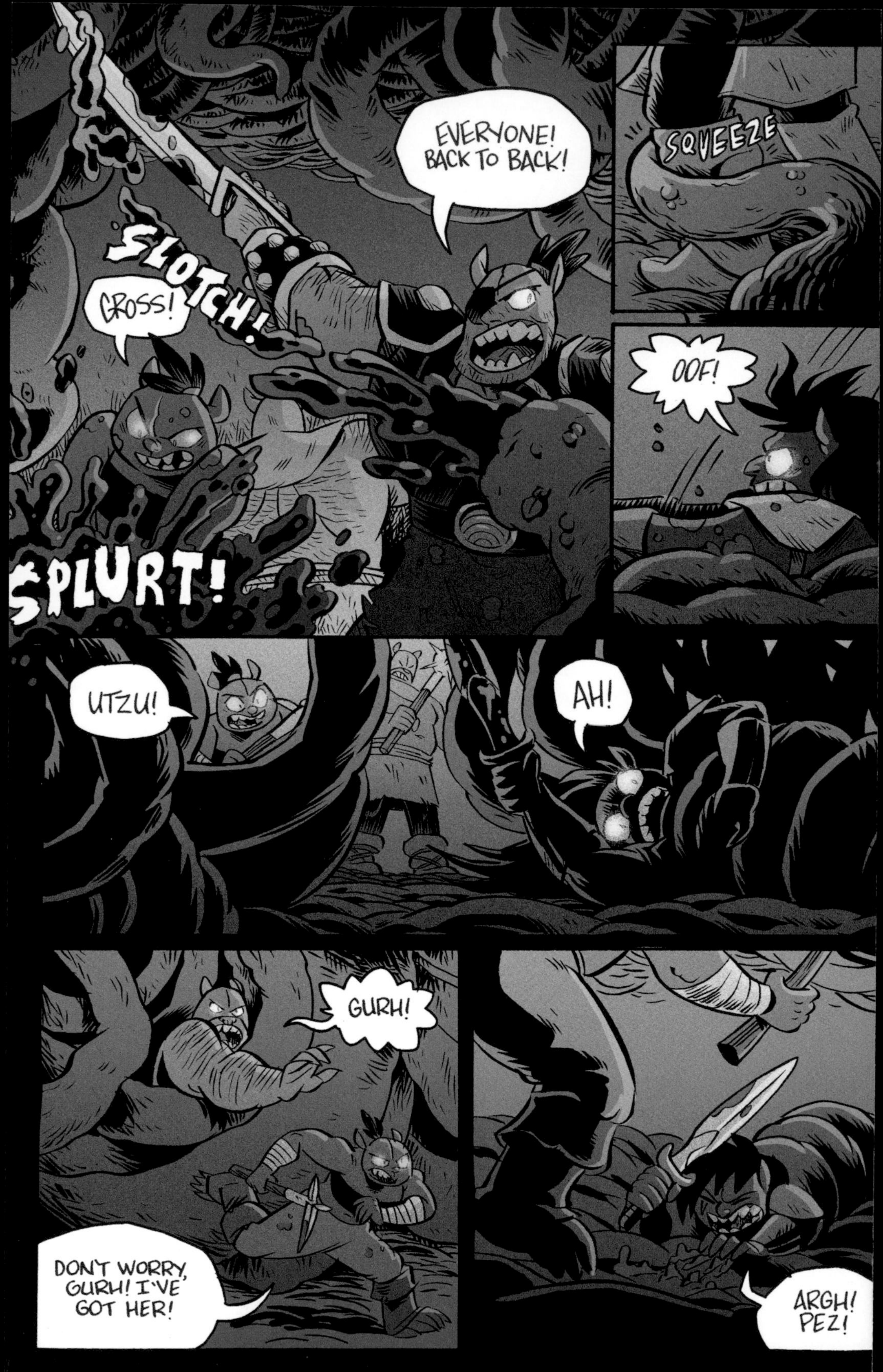
EVERYONE! BACK TO BACK!
SLOTCH!
GROSS!
SPLURT!
SQUEEZE
OOF!
UTZU!
AH!
GURH!
DON'T WORRY, GURH! I'VE GOT HER!
ARGH! PEZ!

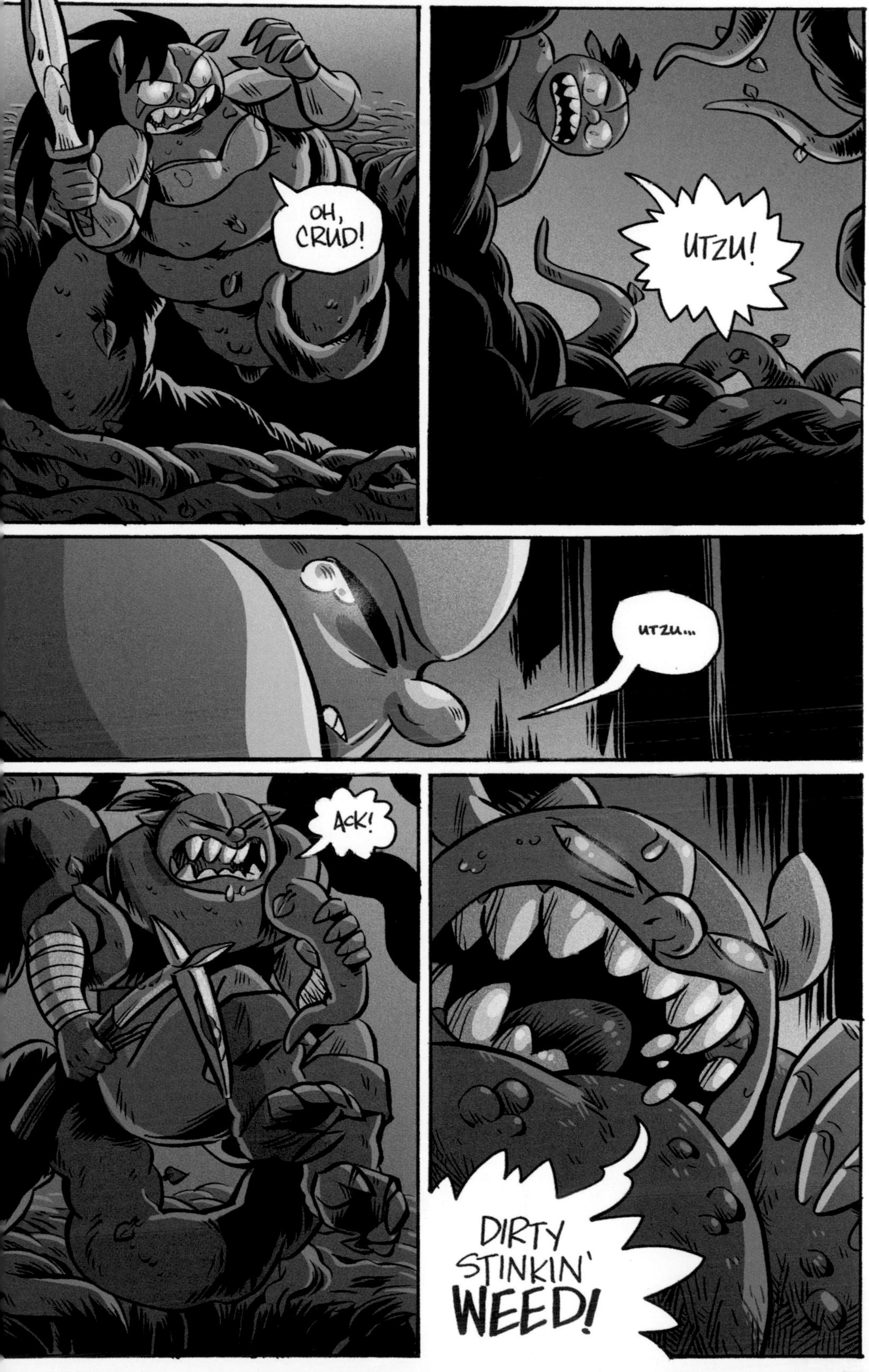
OH, CRUD!
UTZU!
UTZU...
ACK!
DIRTY STINKIN' WEED!

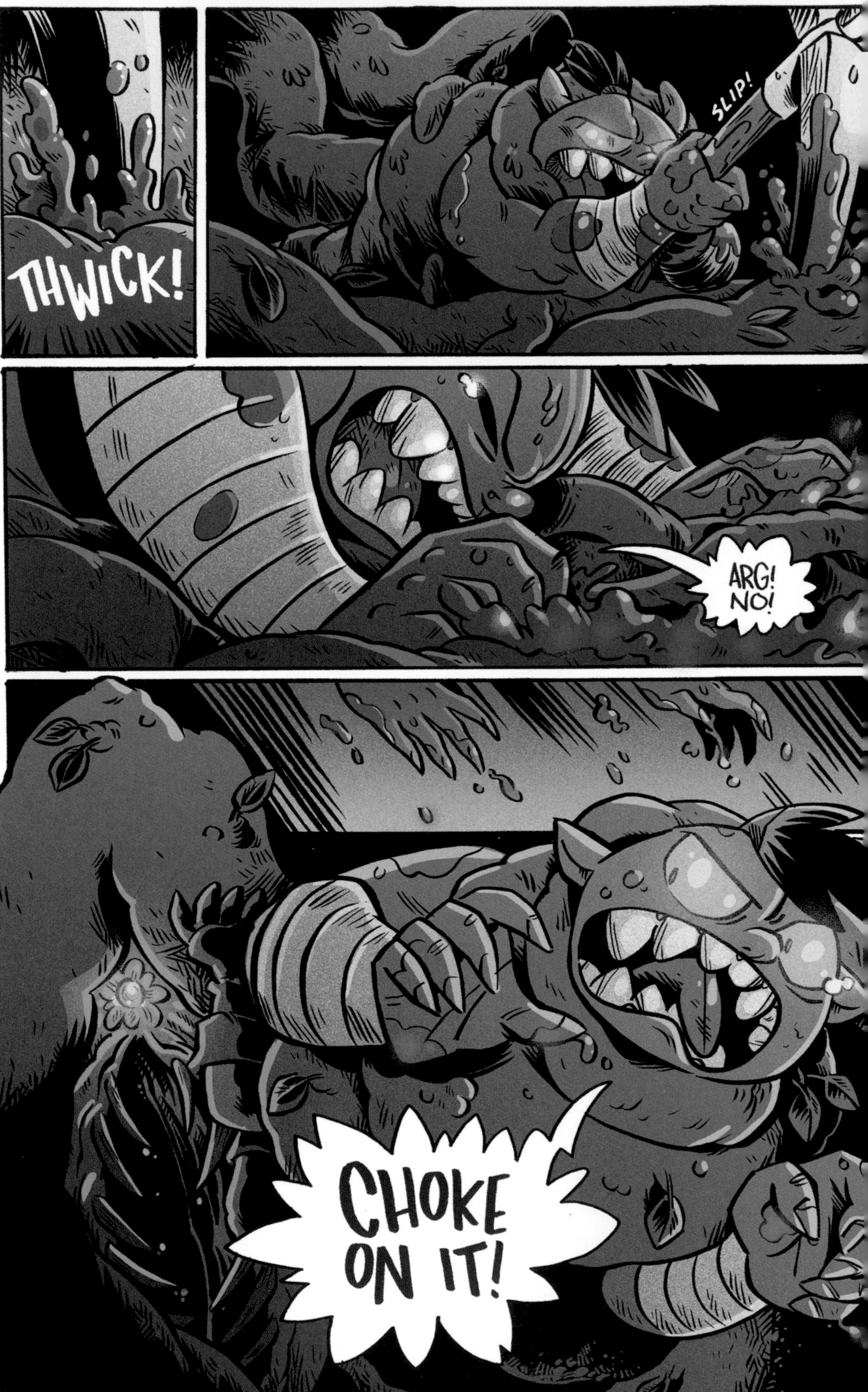
THWICK!
SLIP!
ARG! NO!
CHOKE ON IT!

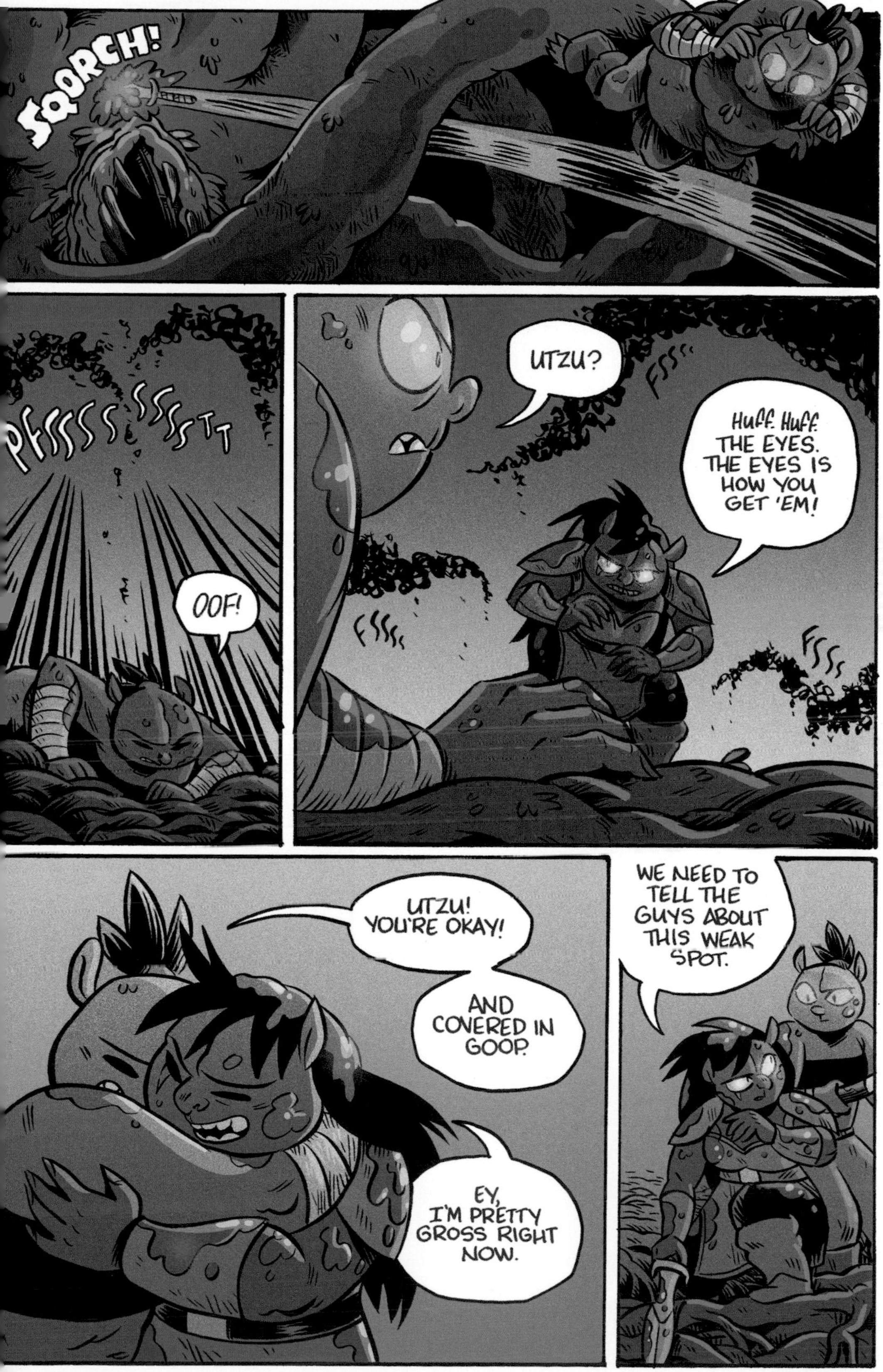
SQORCH!
PFSSSSSSSSSTT
OOF!
UTZU?
FSSS
HUFF. HUFF. THE EYES. THE EYES IS HOW YOU GET 'EM!
FSSS
FSSS
UTZU! YOU'RE OKAY!
AND COVERED IN GOOP.
EY, I'M PRETTY GROSS RIGHT NOW.
WE NEED TO TELL THE GUYS ABOUT THIS WEAK SPOT.

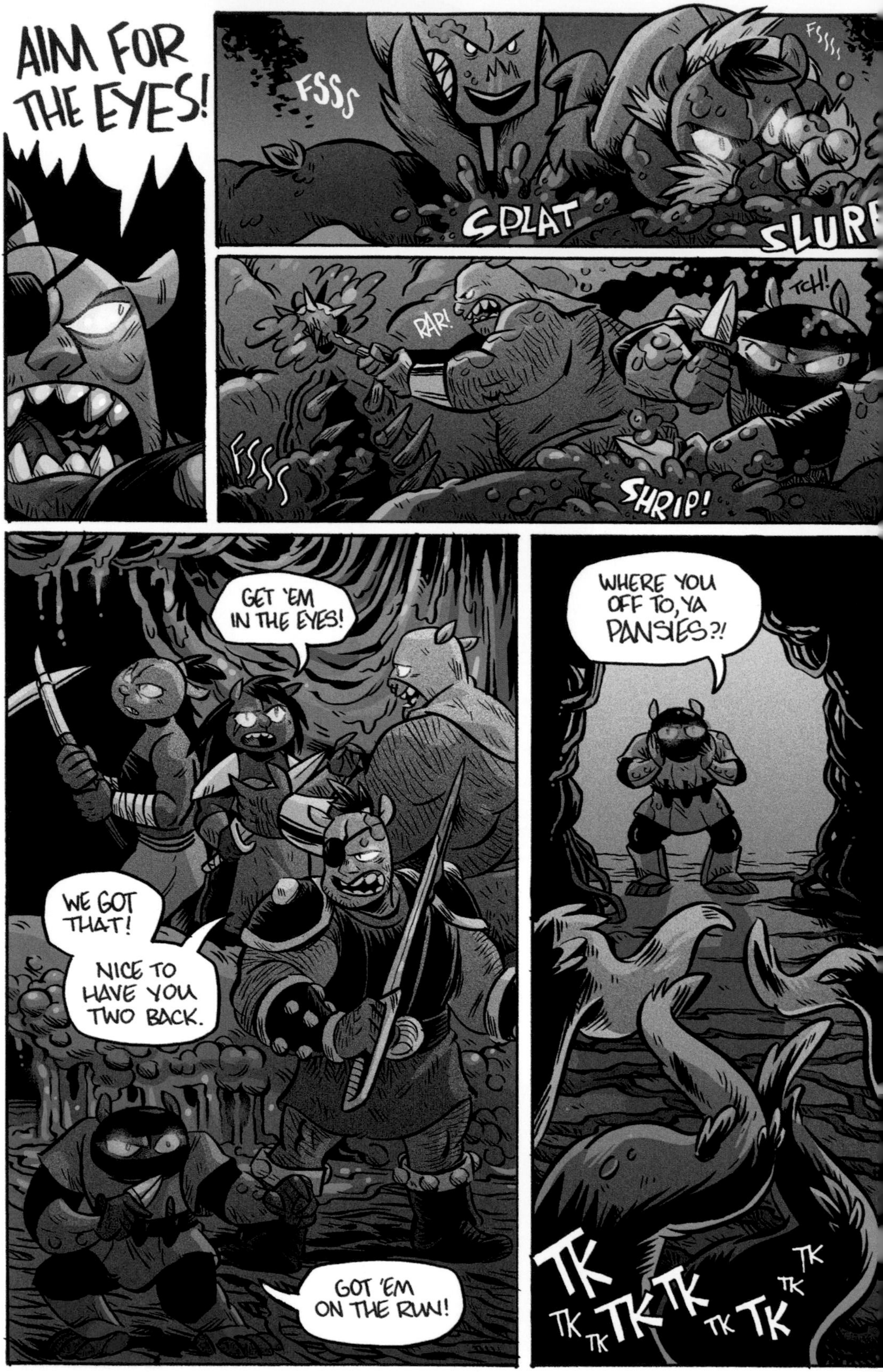
AIM FOR THE EYES!
FSSS
FSSSS
SPLAT
SLURP
RAR!
TCH!
FSSS
SHRIP!
GET 'EM IN THE EYES!
WE GOT THAT!
NICE TO HAVE YOU TWO BACK.
GOT 'EM ON THE RUN!
WHERE YOU OFF TO, YA PANSIES?!
TK TK TK TK TK TK TK TK TK TK TK

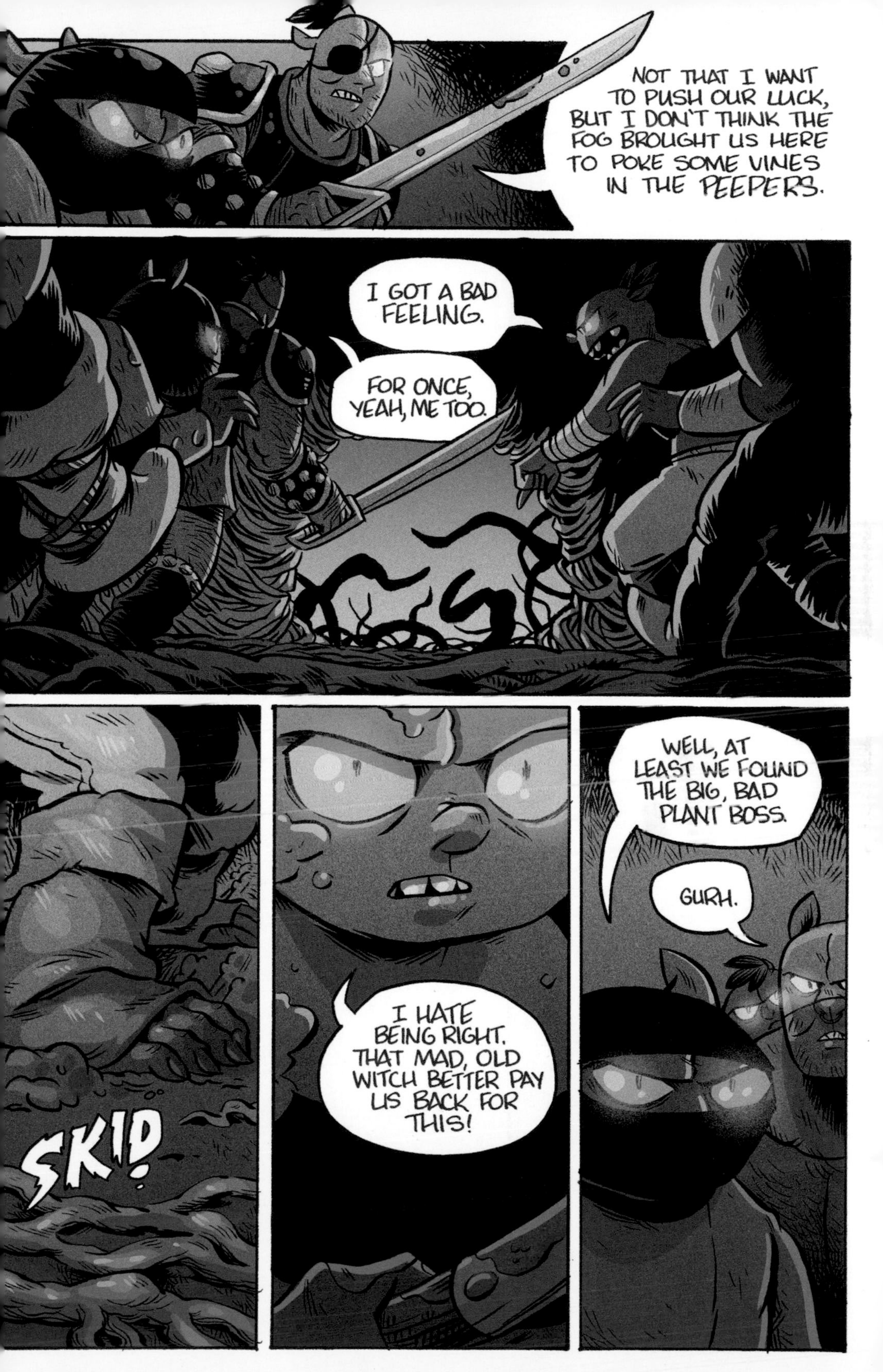
NOT THAT I WANT TO PUSH OUR LUCK, BUT I DON'T THINK THE FOG BROUGHT US HERE TO POKE SOME VINES IN THE PEEPERS.
I GOT A BAD FEELING.
FOR ONCE, YEAH, ME TOO.
SKID
I HATE BEING RIGHT. THAT MAD, OLD WITCH BETTER PAY US BACK FOR THIS!
WELL, AT LEAST WE FOUND THE BIG, BAD PLANT BOSS.
GURH.

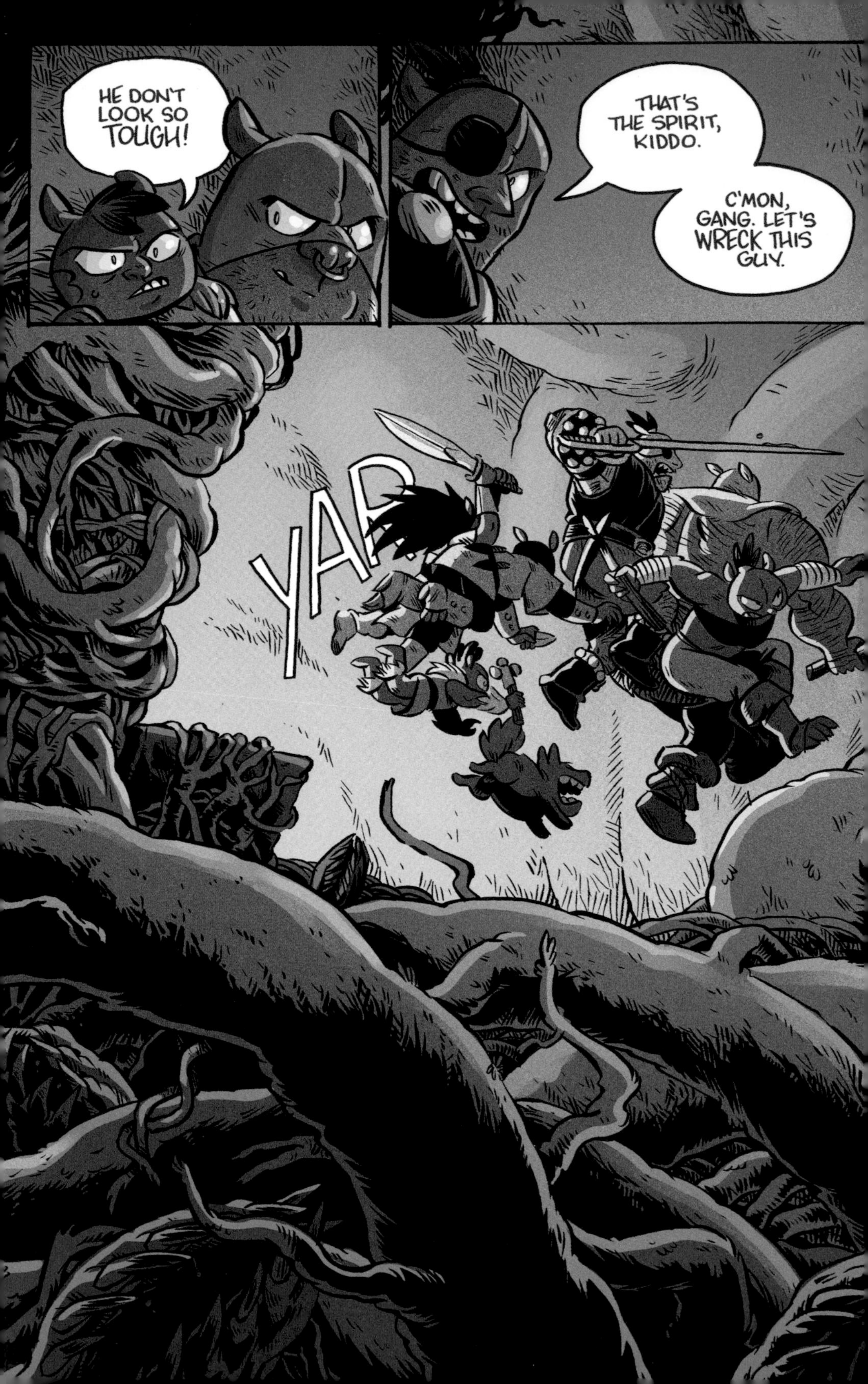
HE DON'T LOOK SO TOUGH!
THAT'S THE SPIRIT, KIDDO.
C'MON, GANG. LET'S WRECK THIS GUY.
YAR!

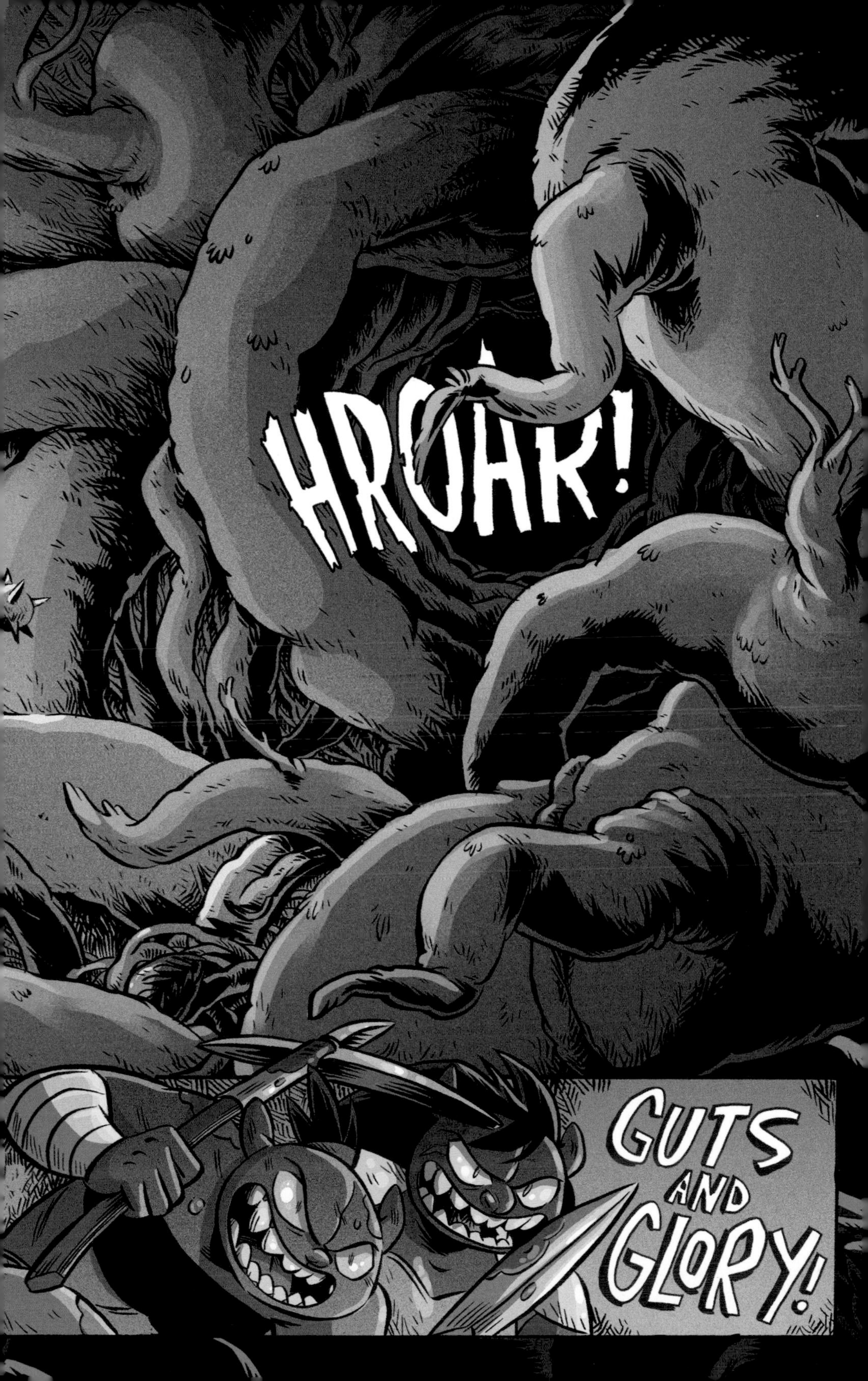
HROAR!
GUTS AND GLORY!

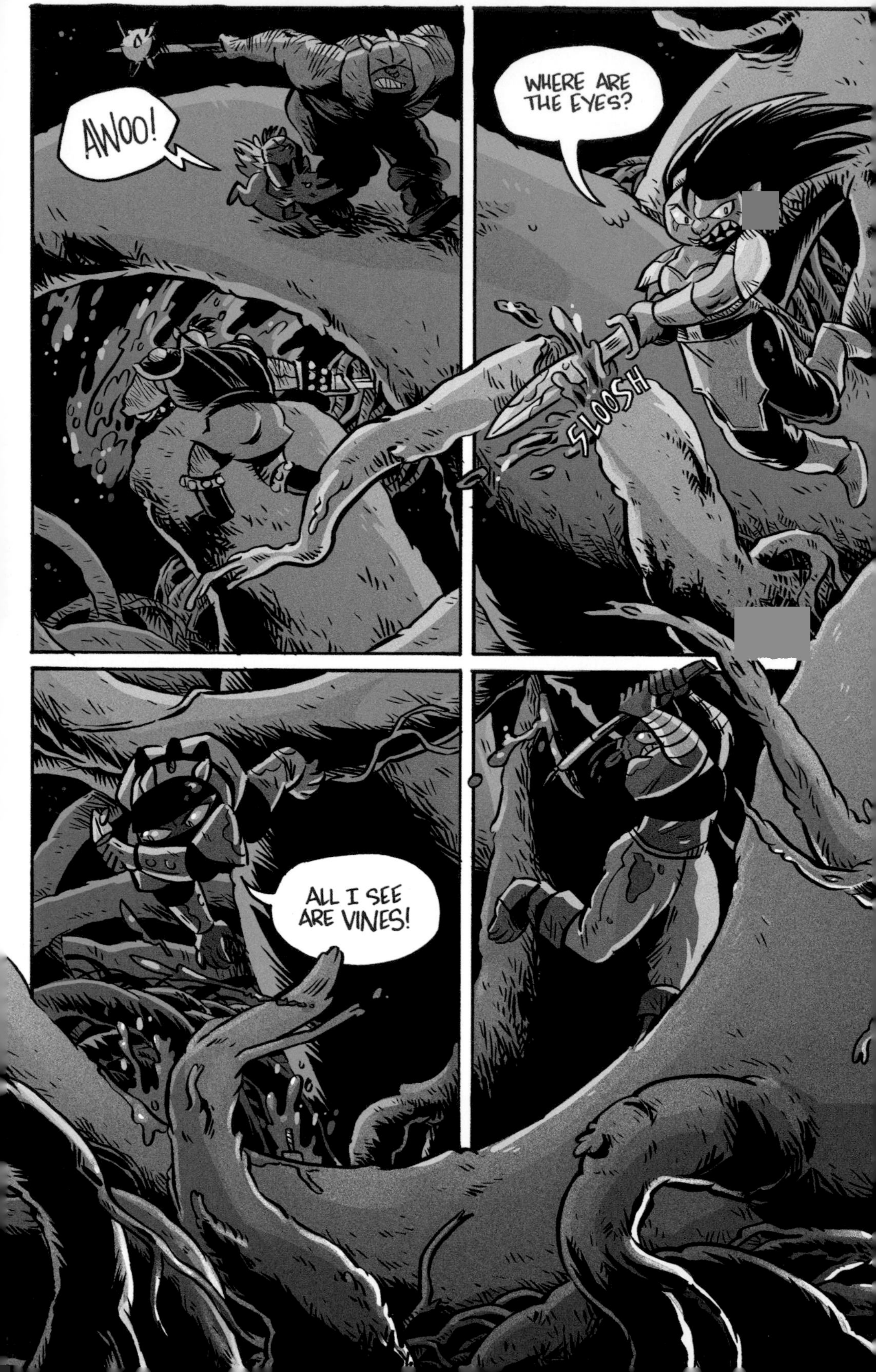
AWOO!
WHERE ARE THE EYES?
SLOOSH
ALL I SEE ARE VINES!

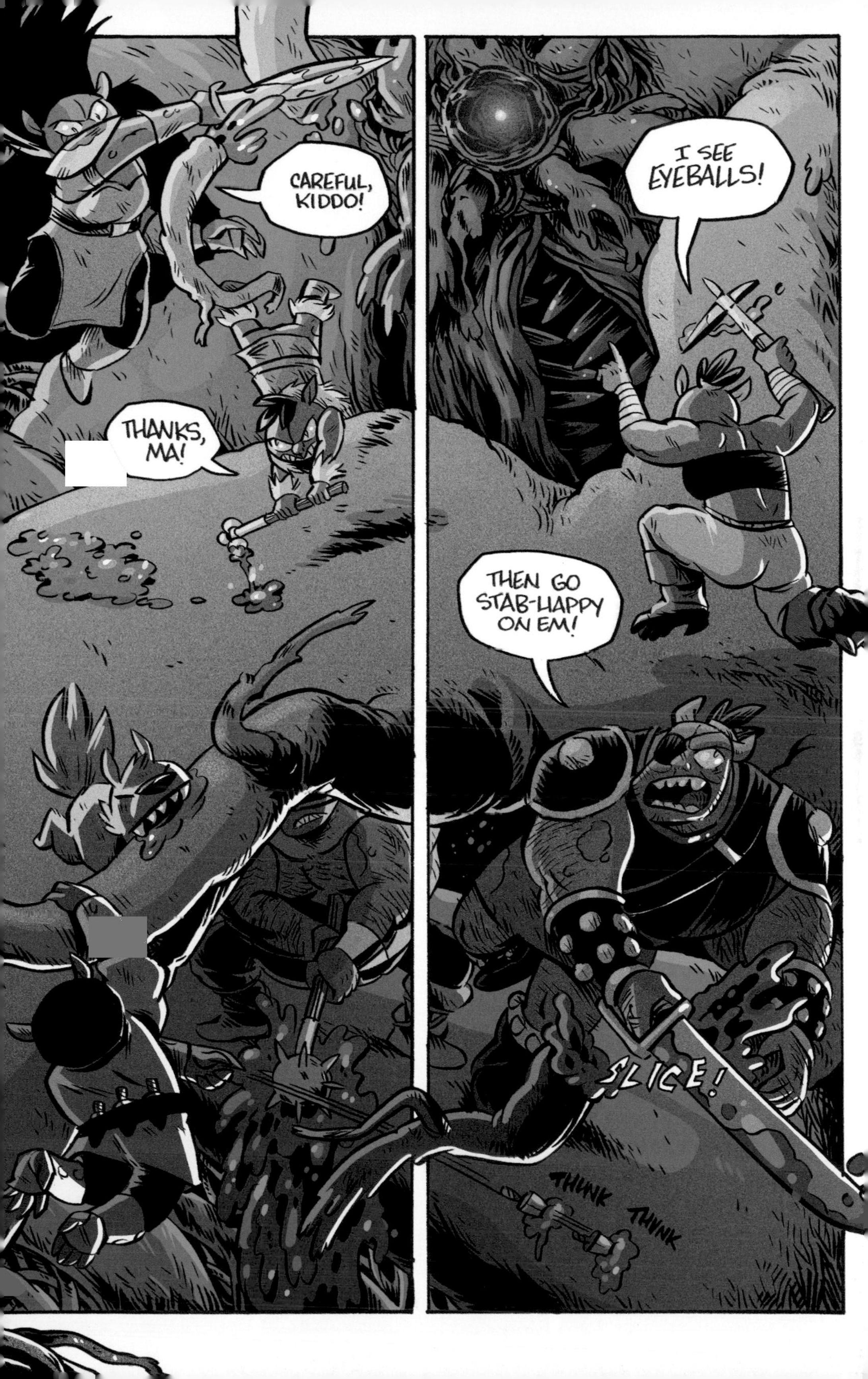
CAREFUL, KIDDO!
THANKS, MA!
I SEE EYEBALLS!
THEN GO STAB-HAPPY ON EM!
SLICE!
THUNK
THUNK

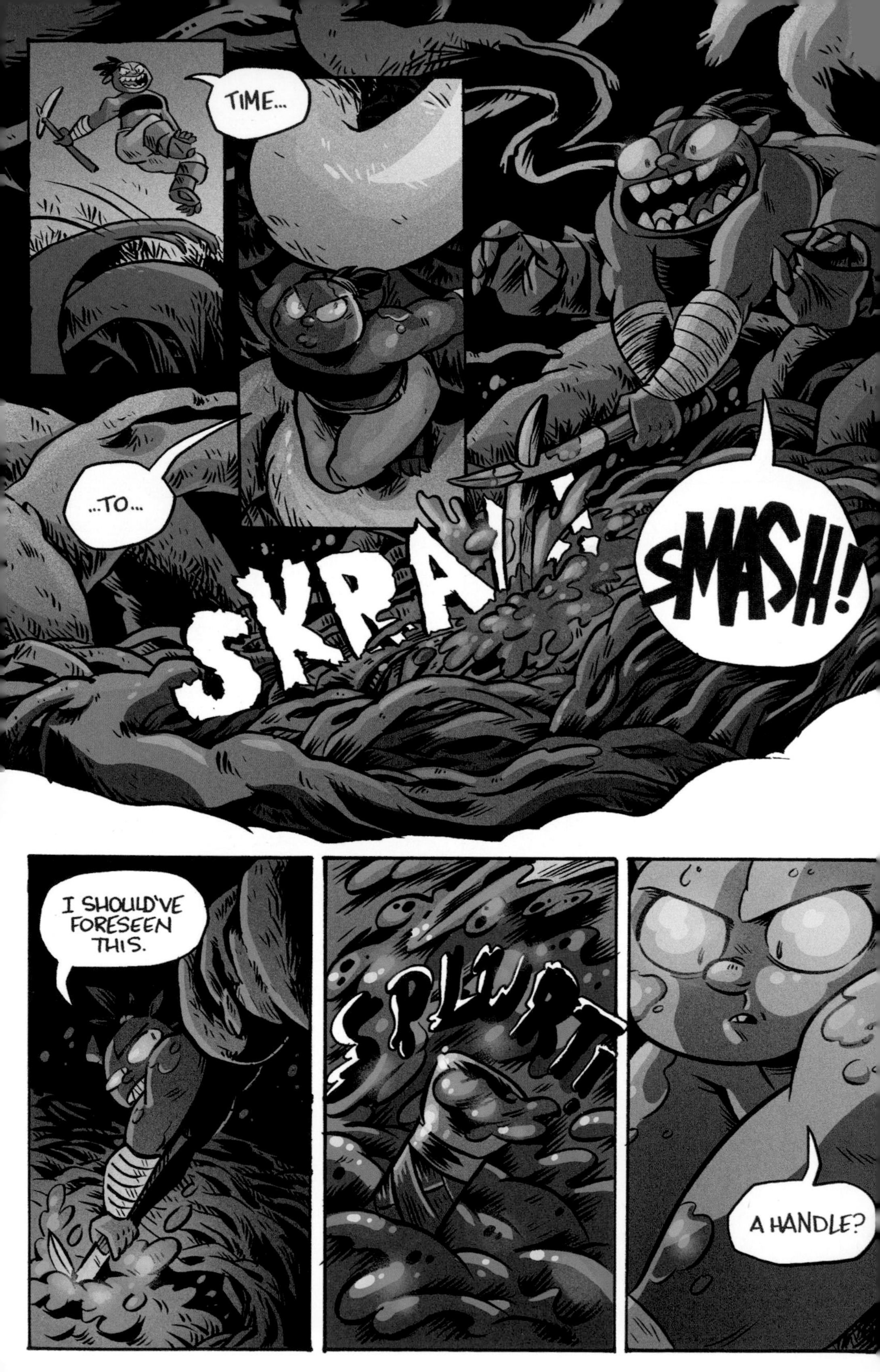
TIME...
...TO...
SKRA
SMASH!
I SHOULD'VE FORESEEN THIS.
SPLURT
A HANDLE?

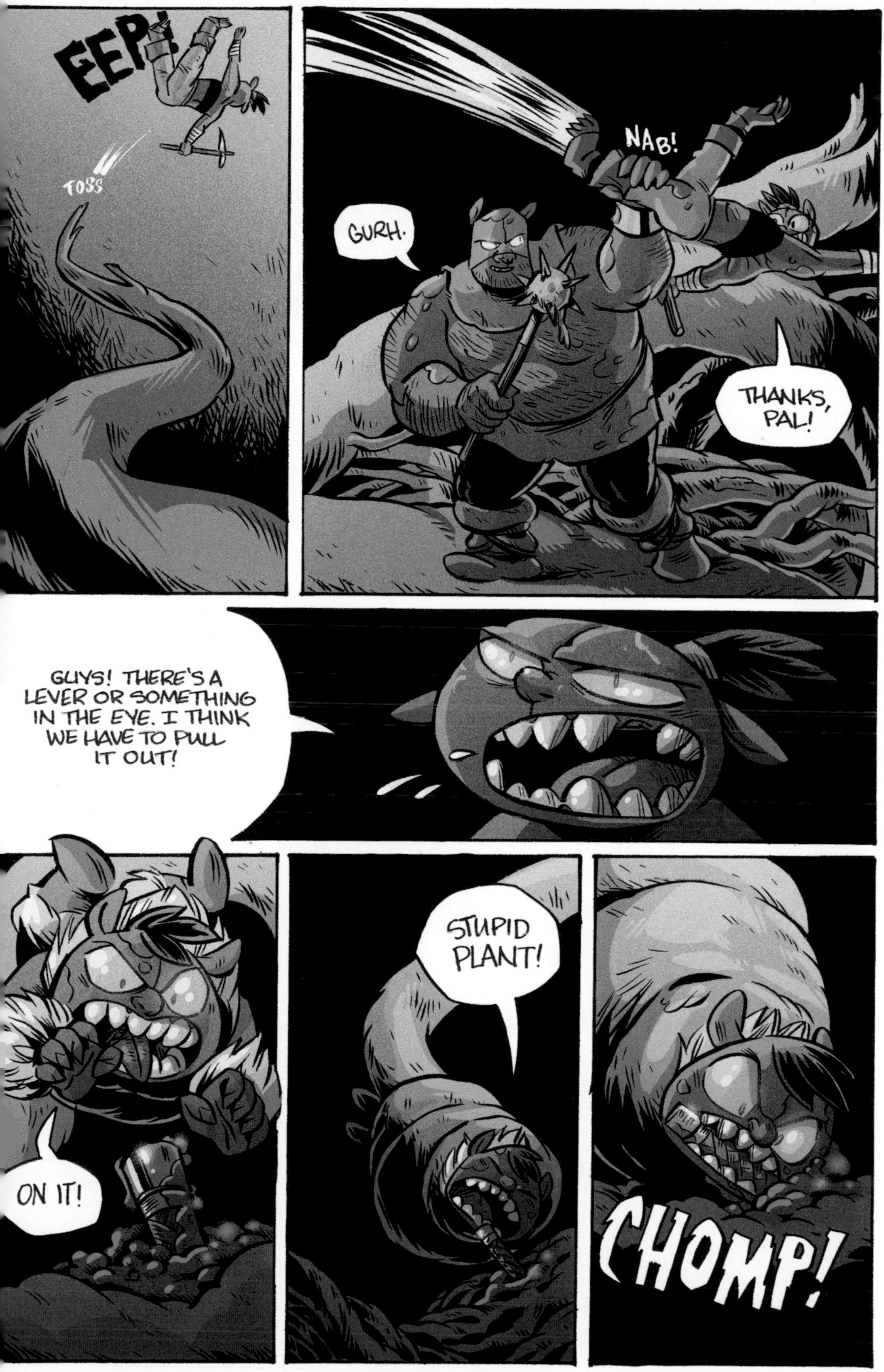
EEP!
TOSS
NAB!
GURH.
THANKS, PAL!
GUYS! THERE'S A LEVER OR SOMETHING IN THE EYE. I THINK WE HAVE TO PULL IT OUT!
ON IT!
STUPID PLANT!
CHOMP!

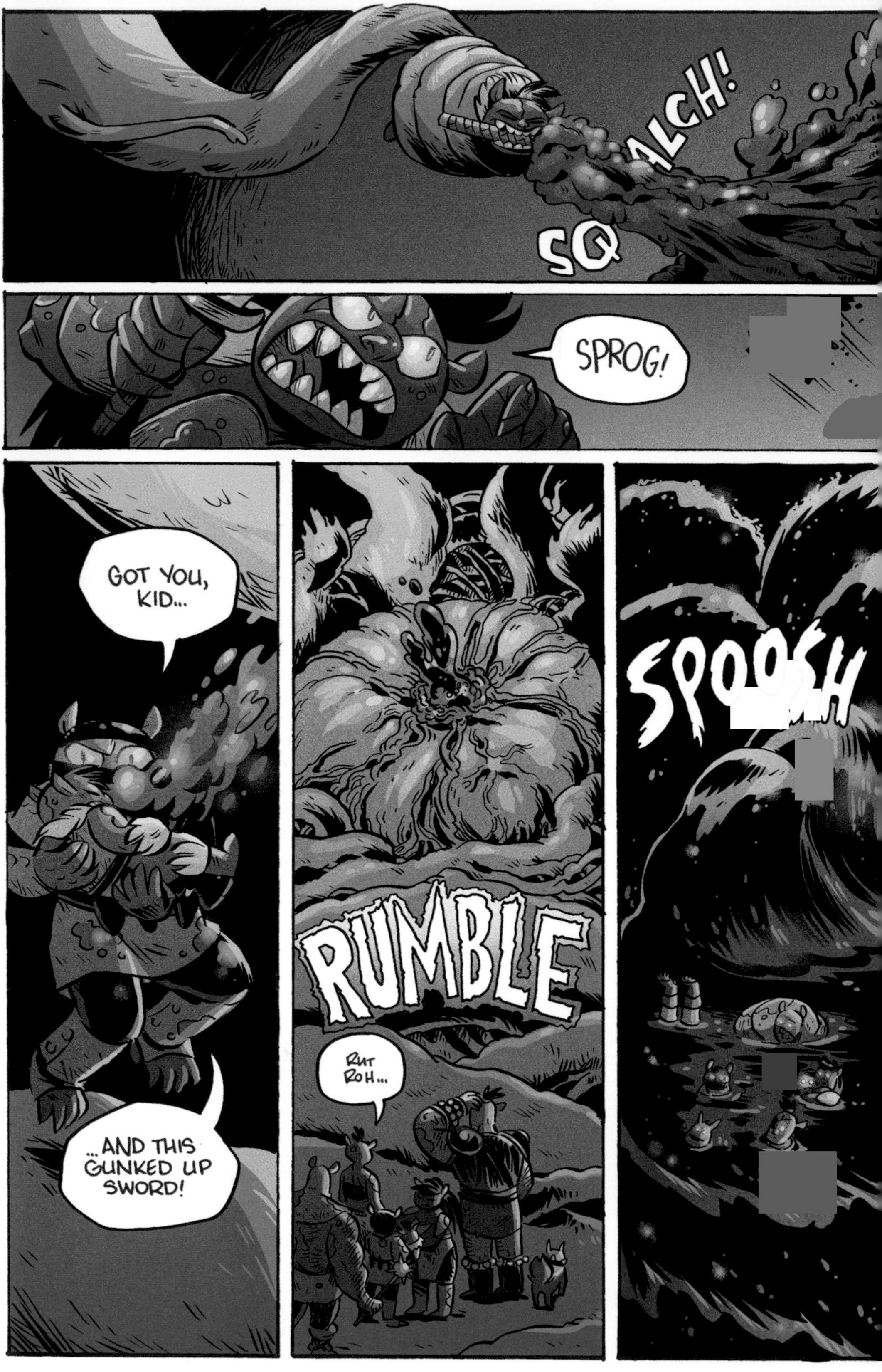
ALCH!
SQ
SPROG!
GOT YOU, KID...
...AND THIS GUNKED UP SWORD!
RUMBLE
RUT ROH...
SPOOSH

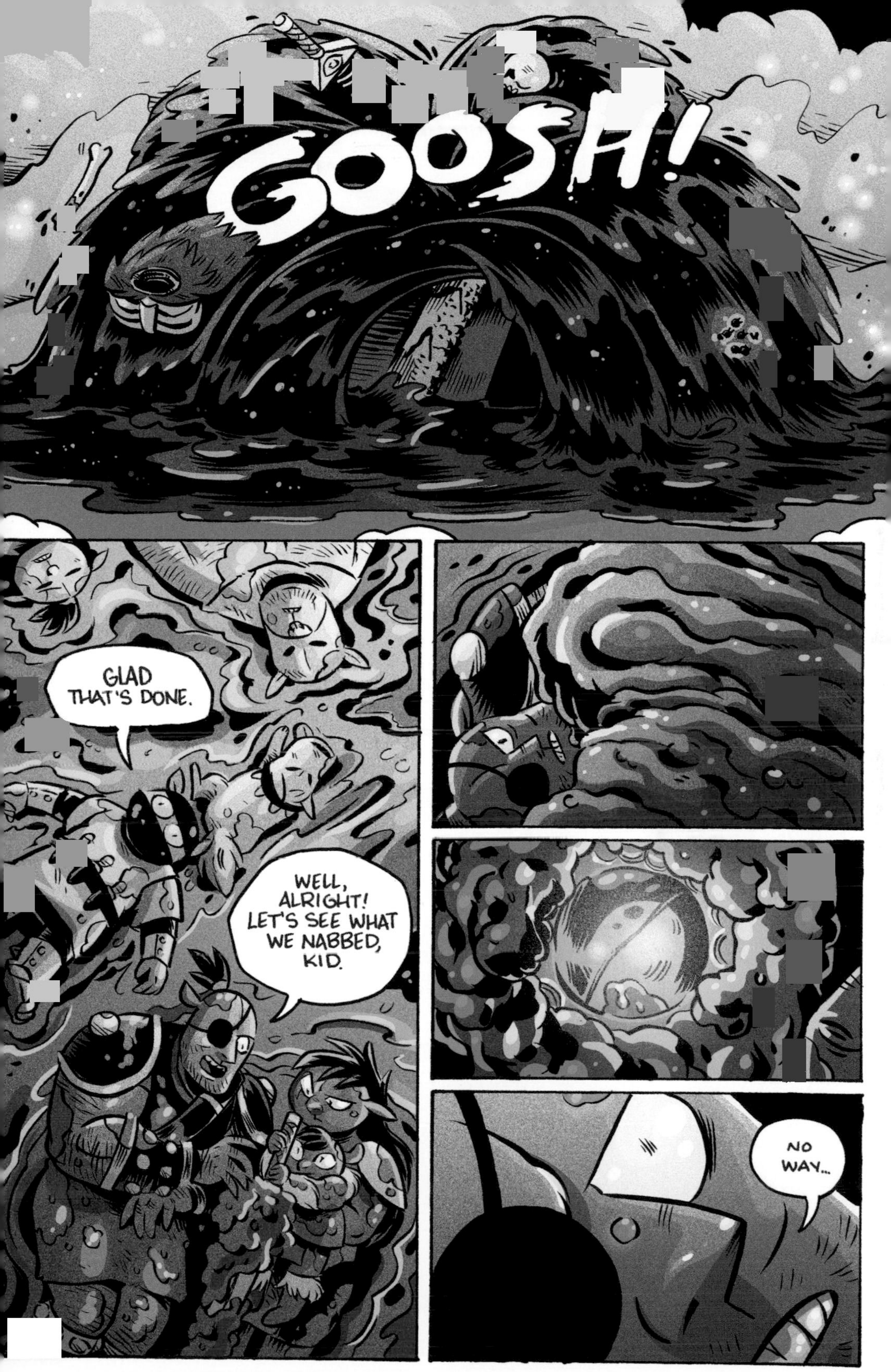
GOOSH!
GLAD THAT'S DONE.
WELL, ALRIGHT! LET'S SEE WHAT WE NABBED, KID.
NO WAY...

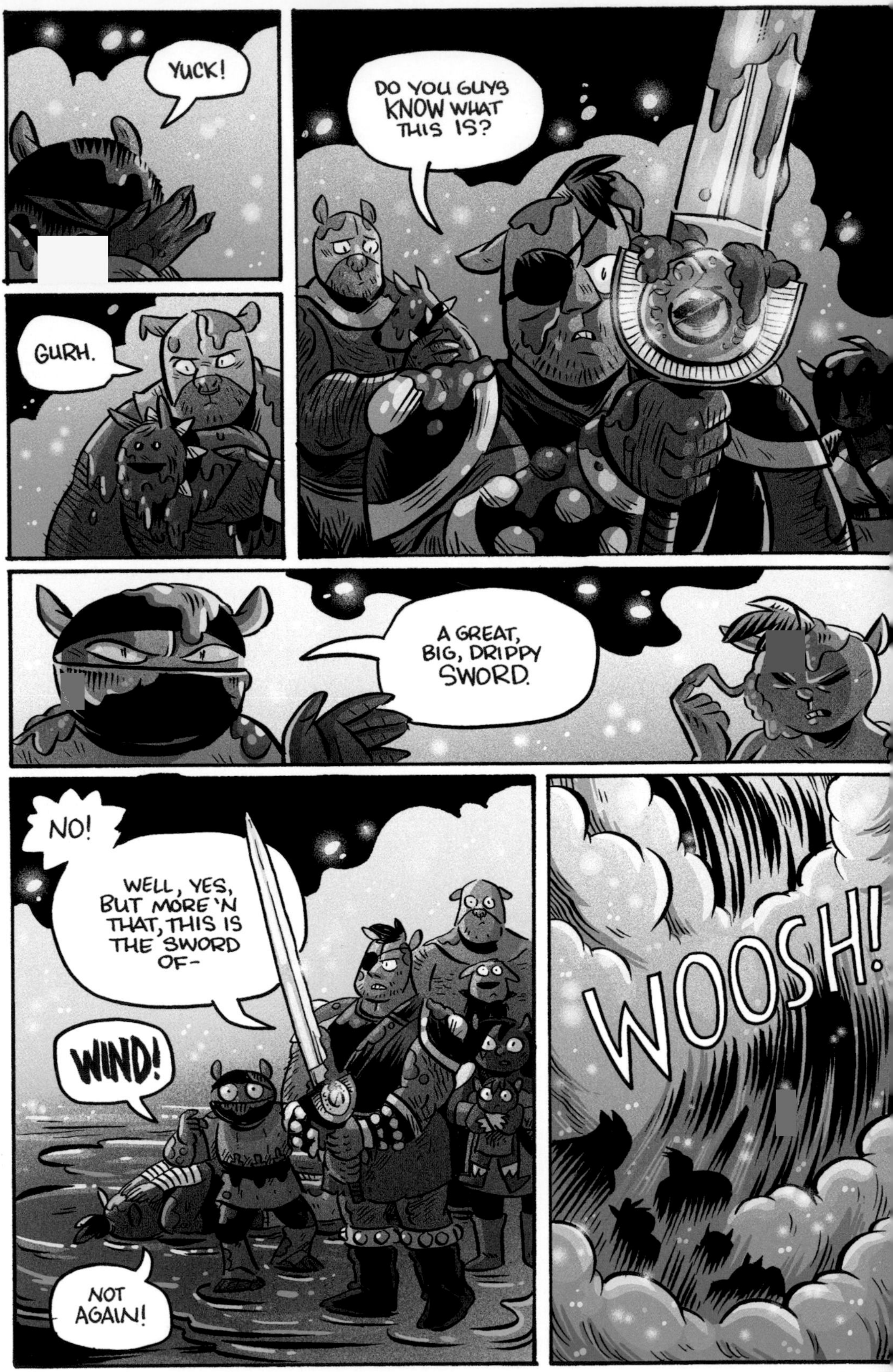
YUCK!
DO YOU GUYS KNOW WHAT THIS IS?
GURH.
A GREAT, BIG, DRIPPY SWORD.
NO!
WELL, YES, BUT MORE 'N THAT, THIS IS THE SWORD OF-
WIND!
NOT AGAIN!
WOOSH!

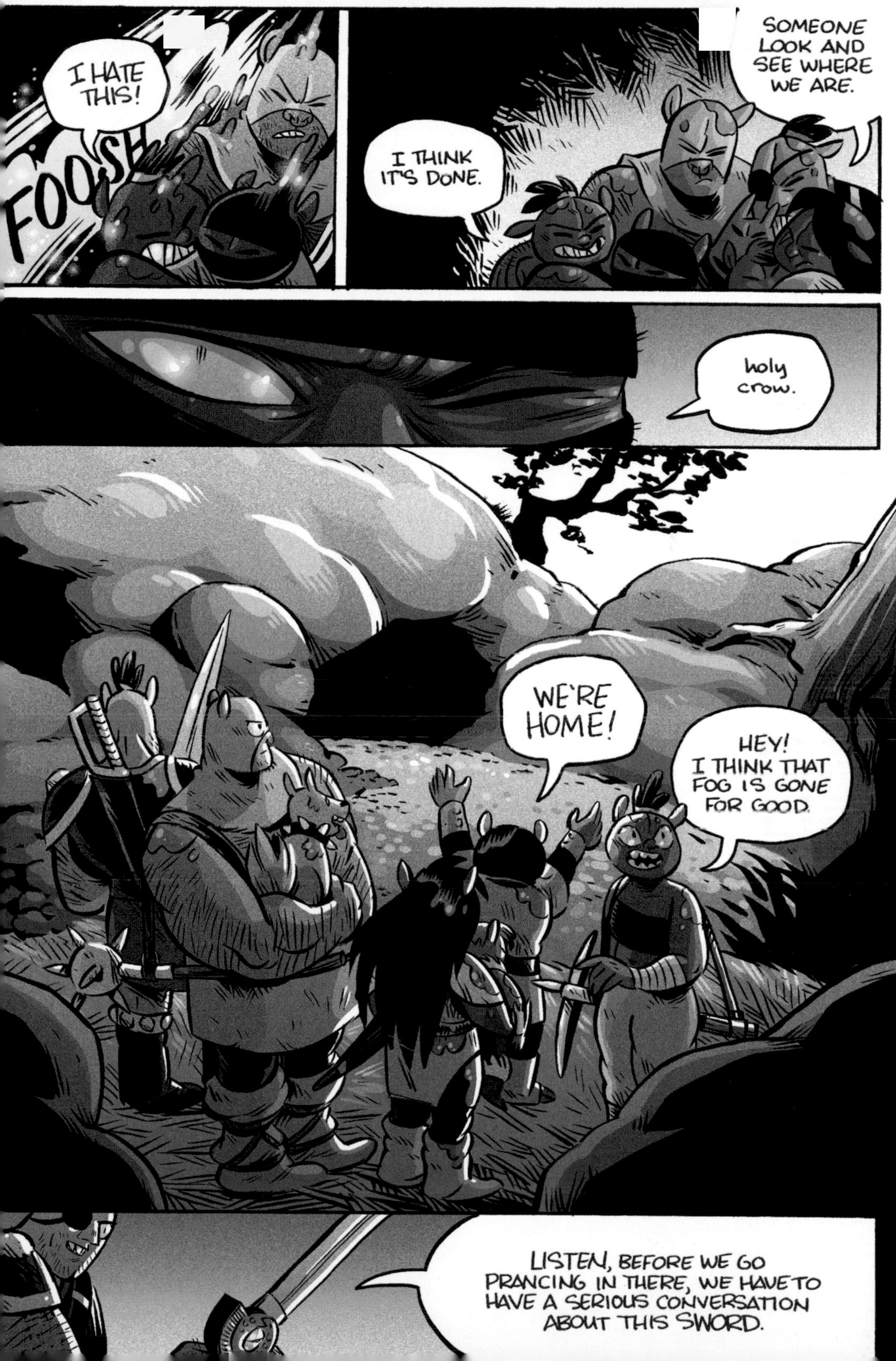
I HATE THIS!
FOOSH
SOMEONE LOOK AND SEE WHERE WE ARE.
I THINK IT'S DONE.
holy crow.
WE'RE HOME!
HEY! I THINK THAT FOG IS GONE FOR GOOD.
LISTEN, BEFORE WE GO PRANCING IN THERE, WE HAVE TO HAVE A SERIOUS CONVERSATION ABOUT THIS SWORD.

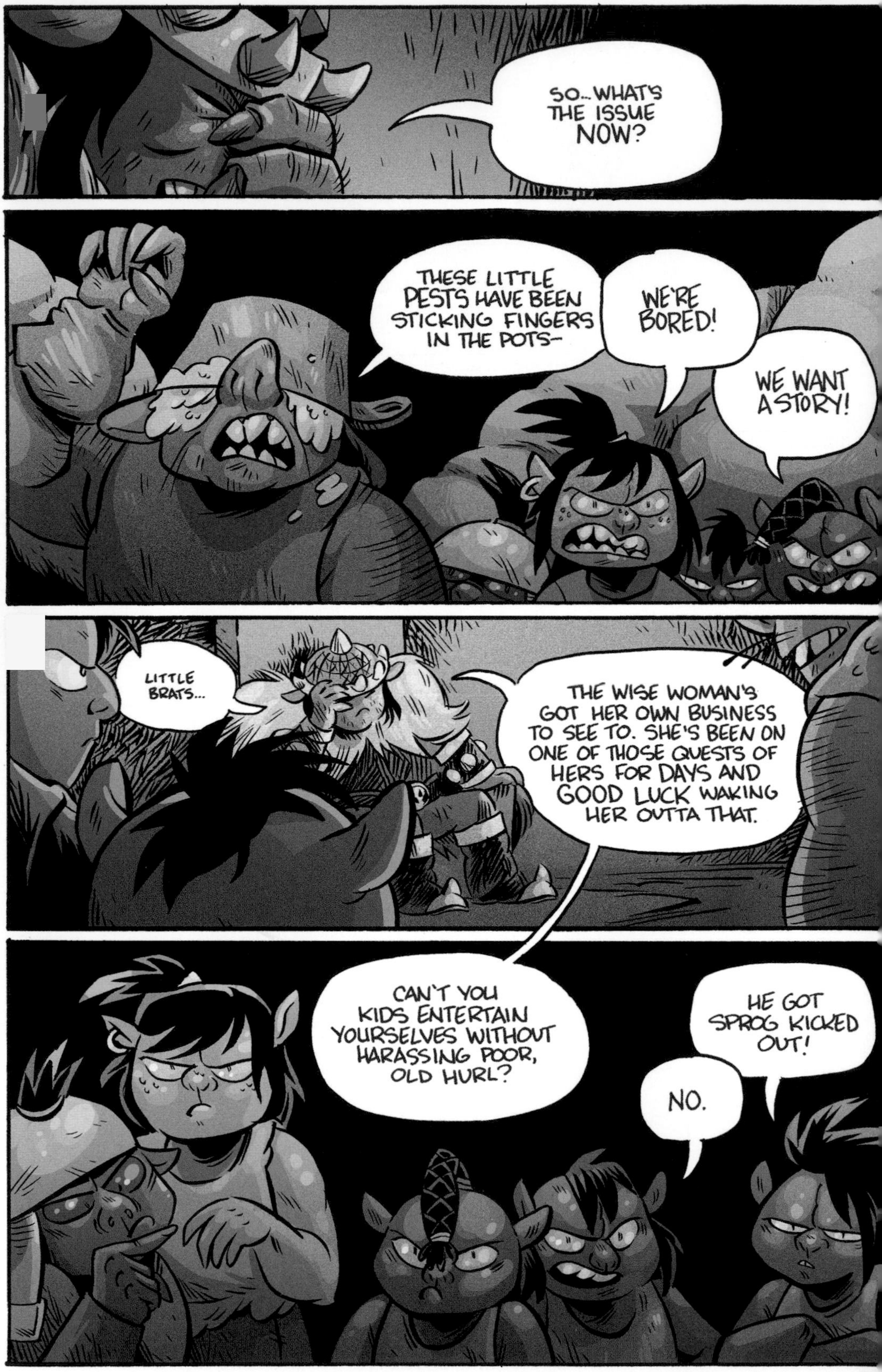
SO... WHAT'S THE ISSUE NOW?
THESE LITTLE PESTS HAVE BEEN STICKING FINGERS IN THE POTS-
WE'RE BORED!
WE WANT A STORY!
LITTLE BRATS...
THE WISE WOMAN'S GOT HER OWN BUSINESS TO SEE TO. SHE'S BEEN ON ONE OF THOSE QUESTS OF HERS FOR DAYS AND GOOD LUCK WAKING HER OUTTA THAT.
CAN'T YOU KIDS ENTERTAIN YOURSELVES WITHOUT HARASSING POOR, OLD HURL?
NO.
HE GOT SPROG KICKED OUT!

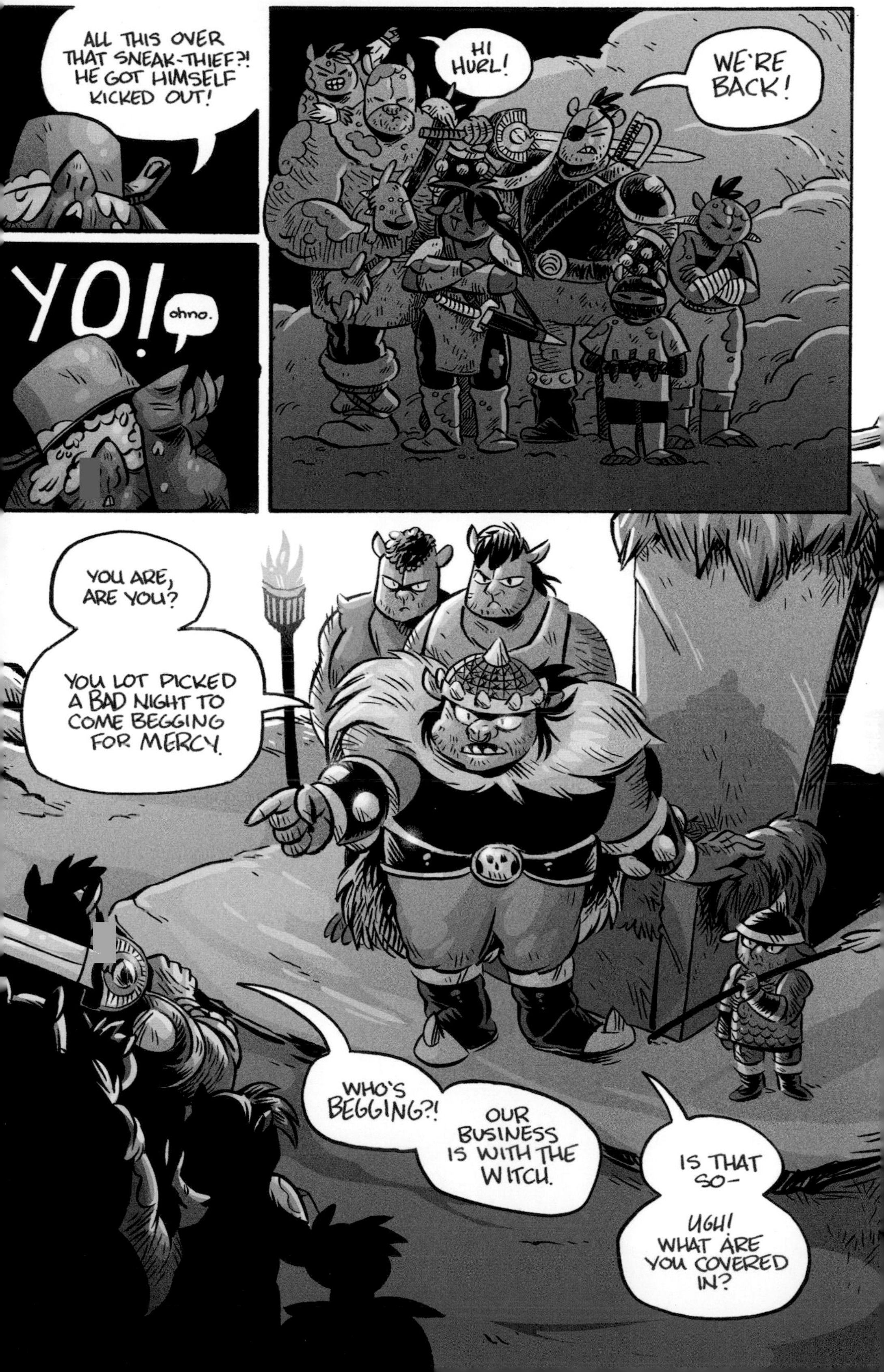
ALL THIS OVER THAT SNEAK-THIEF?! HE GOT HIMSELF KICKED OUT!
HI HURL!
WE'RE BACK!
YO!
ohno.
YOU ARE, ARE YOU?
YOU LOT PICKED A BAD NIGHT TO COME BEGGING FOR MERCY.
WHO'S BEGGING?!
OUR BUSINESS IS WITH THE WITCH.
IS THAT SO-
UGH! WHAT ARE YOU COVERED IN?

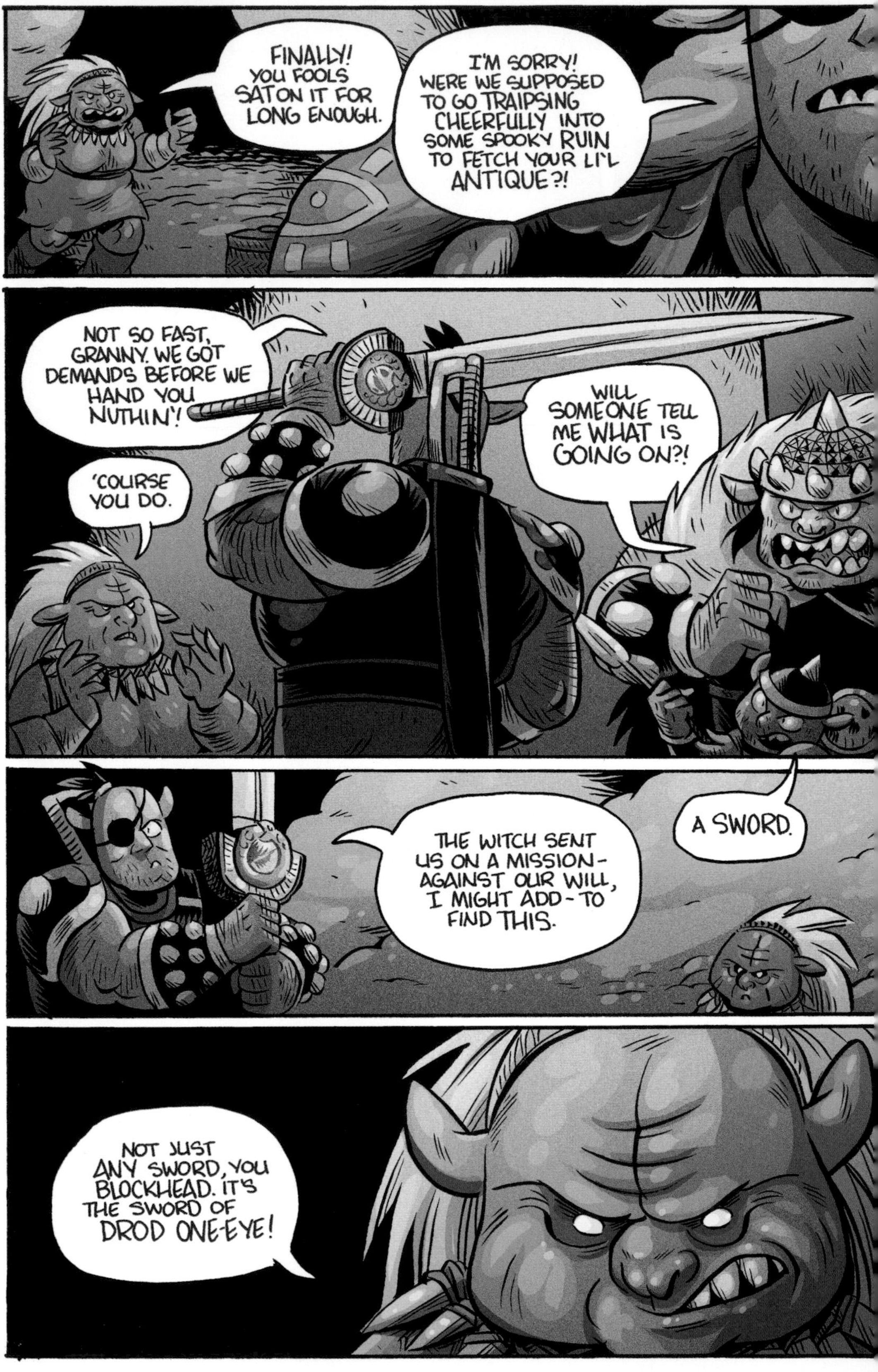
FINALLY! YOU FOOLS SAT ON IT FOR LONG ENOUGH.
I'M SORRY! WERE WE SUPPOSED TO GO TRAIPSING CHEERFULLY INTO SOME SPOOKY RUIN TO FETCH YOUR LI'L ANTIQUE?!
NOT SO FAST, GRANNY. WE GOT DEMANDS BEFORE WE HAND YOU NUTHIN'!
WILL SOMEONE TELL ME WHAT IS GOING ON?!
'COURSE YOU DO.
THE WITCH SENT US ON A MISSION- AGAINST OUR WILL, I MIGHT ADD- TO FIND THIS.
A SWORD.
NOT JUST ANY SWORD, YOU BLOCKHEAD. IT'S THE SWORD OF DROD ONE-EYE!

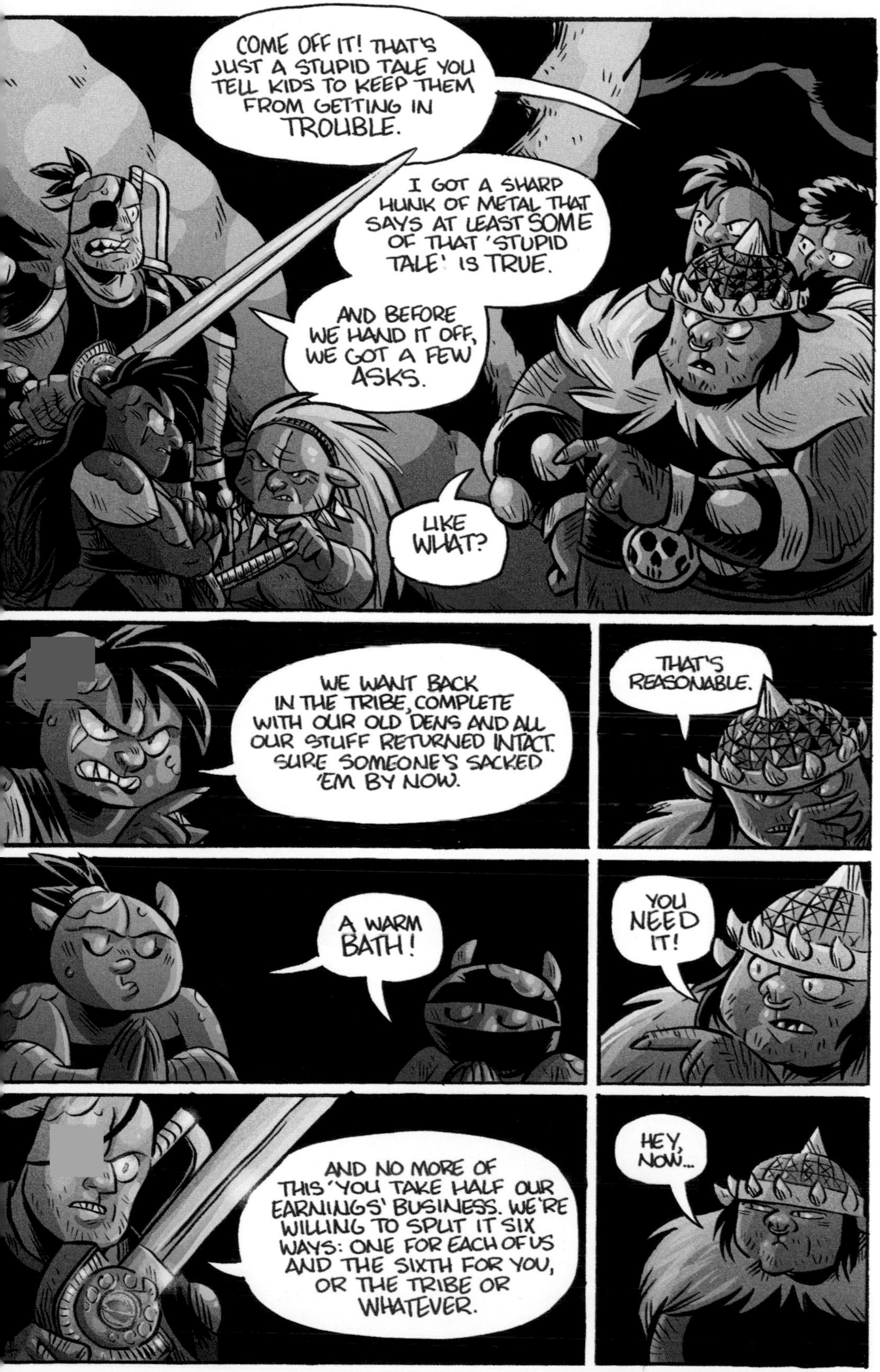
COME OFF IT! THAT'S JUST A STUPID TALE YOU TELL KIDS TO KEEP THEM FROM GETTING IN TROUBLE.
I GOT A SHARP HUNK OF METAL THAT SAYS AT LEAST SOME OF THAT 'STUPID TALE' IS TRUE.
AND BEFORE WE HAND IT OFF, WE GOT A FEW ASKS.
LIKE WHAT?
WE WANT BACK IN THE TRIBE, COMPLETE WITH OUR OLD DENS AND ALL OUR STUFF RETURNED INTACT. SURE SOMEONE'S SACKED 'EM BY NOW.
THAT'S REASONABLE.
A WARM BATH!
YOU NEED IT!
AND NO MORE OF THIS 'YOU TAKE HALF OUR EARNINGS' BUSINESS. WE'RE WILLING TO SPLIT IT SIX WAYS: ONE FOR EACH OF US AND THE SIXTH FOR YOU, OR THE TRIBE OR WHATEVER.
HEY, NOW...

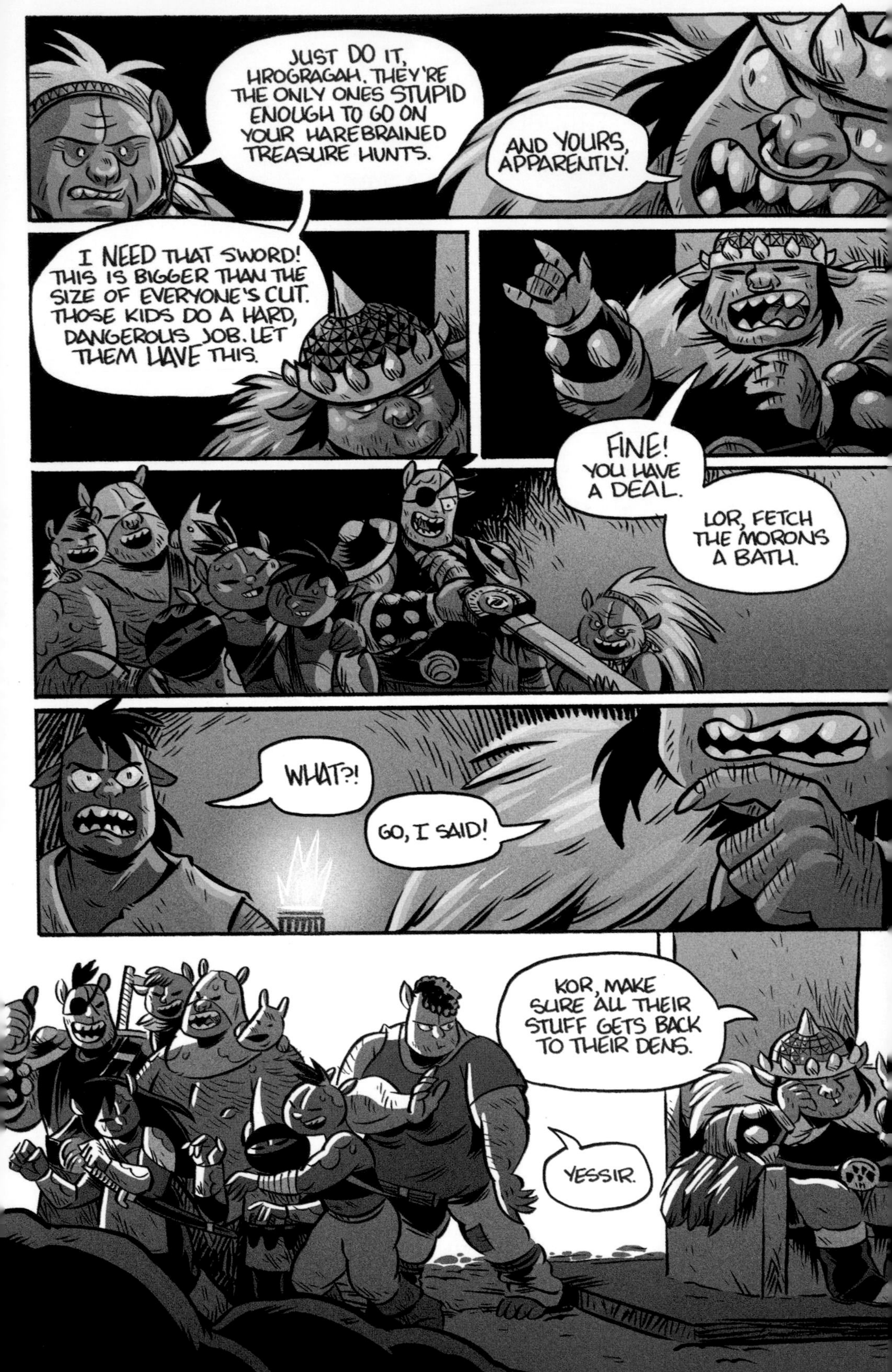
JUST DO IT, HROGRAGAH. THEY'RE THE ONLY ONES STUPID ENOUGH TO GO ON YOUR HAREBRAINED TREASURE HUNTS.
AND YOURS, APPARENTLY.
I NEED THAT SWORD! THIS IS BIGGER THAN THE SIZE OF EVERYONE'S CUT. THOSE KIDS DO A HARD, DANGEROUS JOB. LET THEM HAVE THIS.
FINE! YOU HAVE A DEAL.
LOR, FETCH THE MORONS A BATH.
WHAT?!
GO, I SAID!
KOR, MAKE SURE ALL THEIR STUFF GETS BACK TO THEIR DENS.
YESSIR.

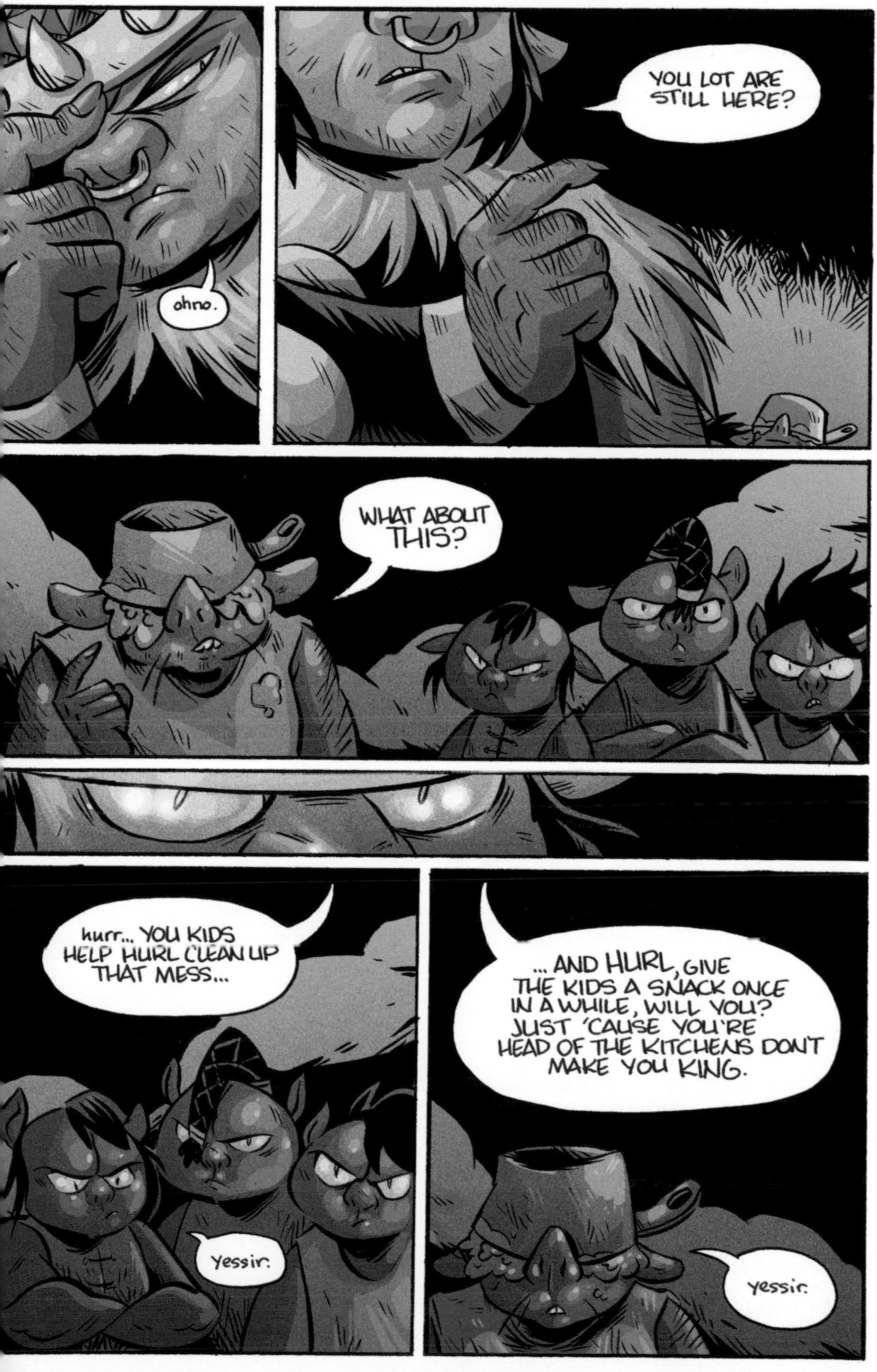
YOU LOT ARE STILL HERE?
ohno.
WHAT ABOUT THIS?
hurr... YOU KIDS HELP HURL CLEAN UP THAT MESS...
yessir.
... AND HURL, GIVE THE KIDS A SNACK ONCE IN A WHILE, WILL YOU? JUST 'CAUSE YOU'RE HEAD OF THE KITCHENS DON'T MAKE YOU KING.
yessir.

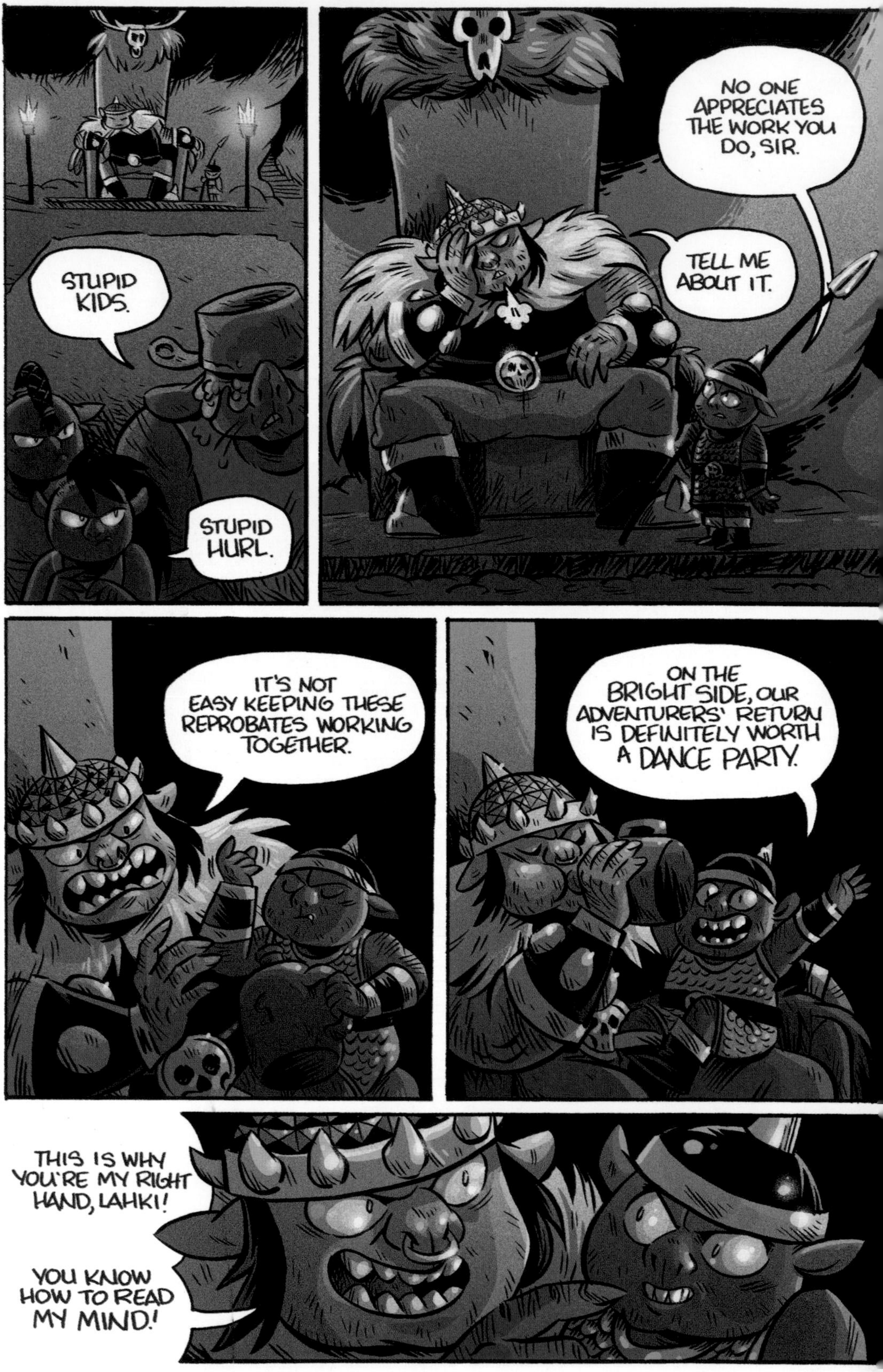
STUPID KIDS.
STUPID HURL.
NO ONE APPRECIATES THE WORK YOU DO, SIR.
TELL ME ABOUT IT.
IT'S NOT EASY KEEPING THESE REPROBATES WORKING TOGETHER.
ON THE BRIGHT SIDE, OUR ADVENTURERS' RETURN IS DEFINITELY WORTH A DANCE PARTY.
THIS IS WHY YOU'RE MY RIGHT HAND, LAHKI!
YOU KNOW HOW TO READ MY MIND!

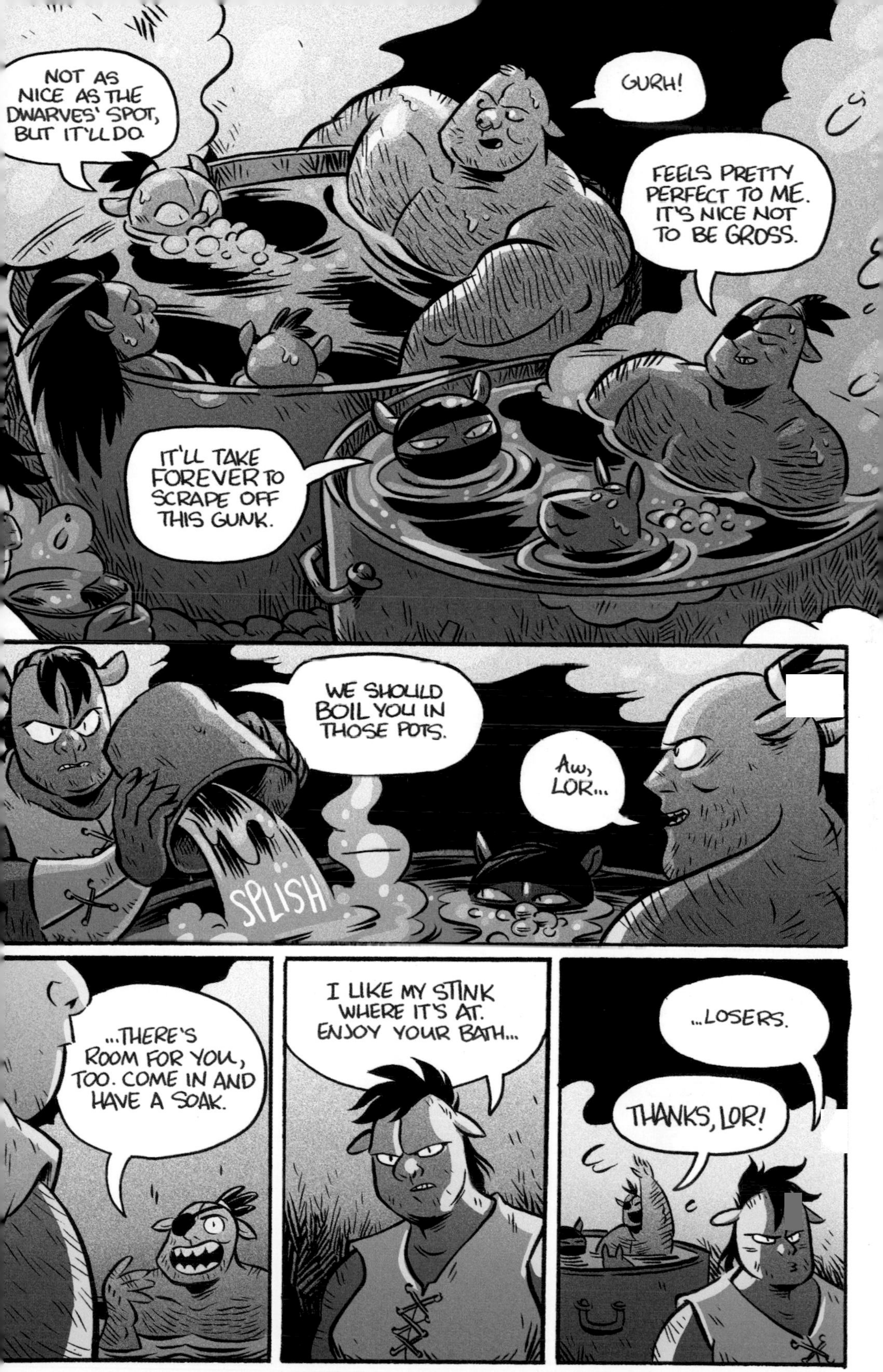
NOT AS NICE AS THE DWARVES' SPOT, BUT IT'LL DO.
GURH!
FEELS PRETTY PERFECT TO ME. IT'S NICE NOT TO BE GROSS.
IT'LL TAKE FOREVER TO SCRAPE OFF THIS GUNK.
WE SHOULD BOIL YOU IN THOSE POTS.
SPLISH
Aw, LOR...
...THERE'S ROOM FOR YOU, TOO. COME IN AND HAVE A SOAK.
I LIKE MY STINK WHERE IT'S AT. ENJOY YOUR BATH...
...LOSERS.
THANKS, LOR!

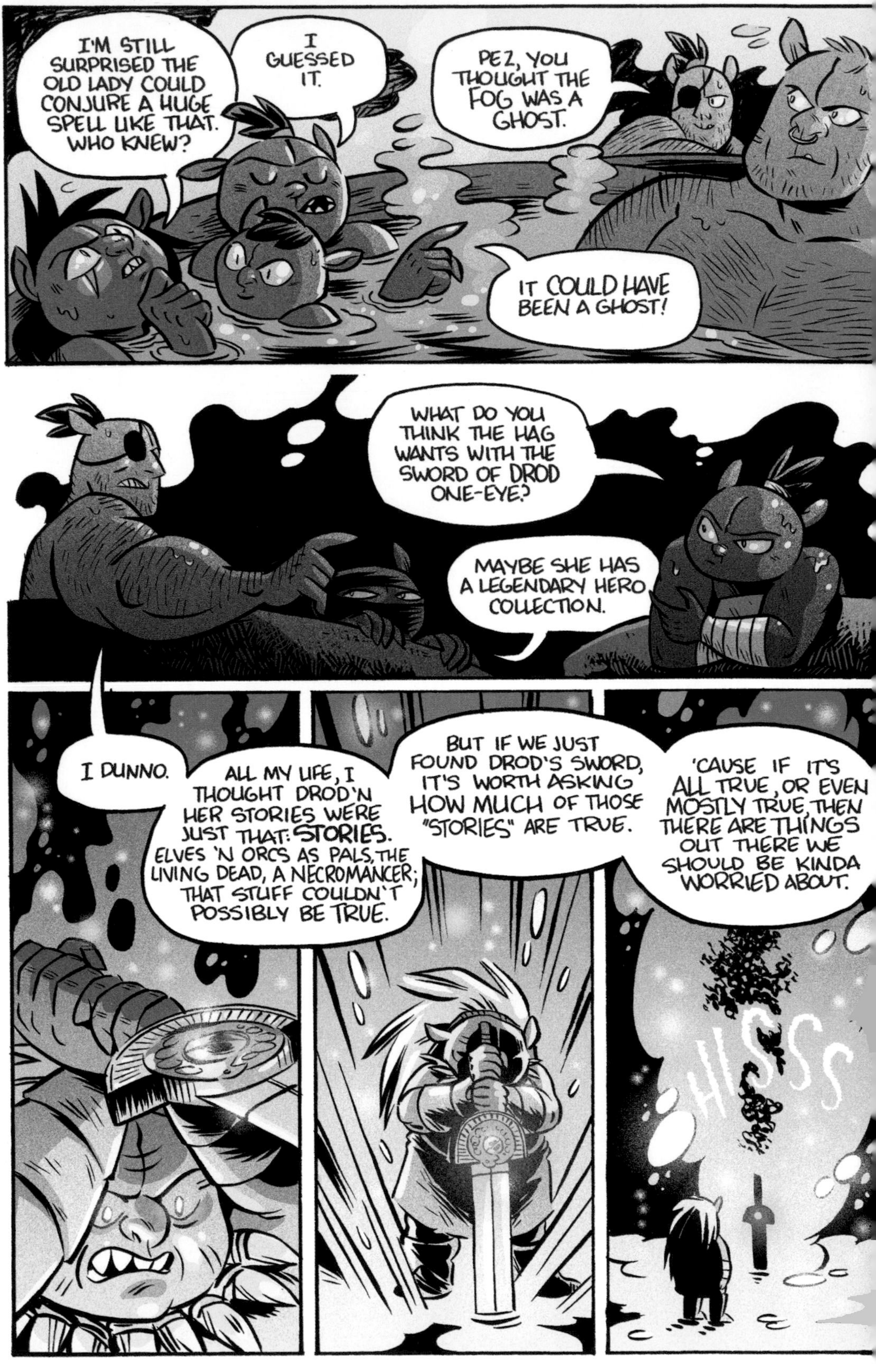
I'M STILL SURPRISED THE OLD LADY COULD CONJURE A HUGE SPELL LIKE THAT. WHO KNEW?
I GUESSED IT.
PEZ, YOU THOUGHT THE FOG WAS A GHOST.
IT COULD HAVE BEEN A GHOST!
WHAT DO YOU THINK THE HAG WANTS WITH THE SWORD OF DROD ONE-EYE?
MAYBE SHE HAS A LEGENDARY HERO COLLECTION.
I DUNNO.
ALL MY LIFE, I THOUGHT DROD 'N HER STORIES WERE JUST THAT: STORIES. ELVES 'N ORCS AS PALS, THE LIVING DEAD, A NECROMANCER; THAT STUFF COULDN'T POSSIBLY BE TRUE.
BUT IF WE JUST FOUND DROD'S SWORD, IT'S WORTH ASKING HOW MUCH OF THOSE "STORIES" ARE TRUE.
'CAUSE IF IT'S ALL TRUE, OR EVEN MOSTLY TRUE, THEN THERE ARE THINGS OUT THERE WE SHOULD BE KINDA WORRIED ABOUT.
HISSS

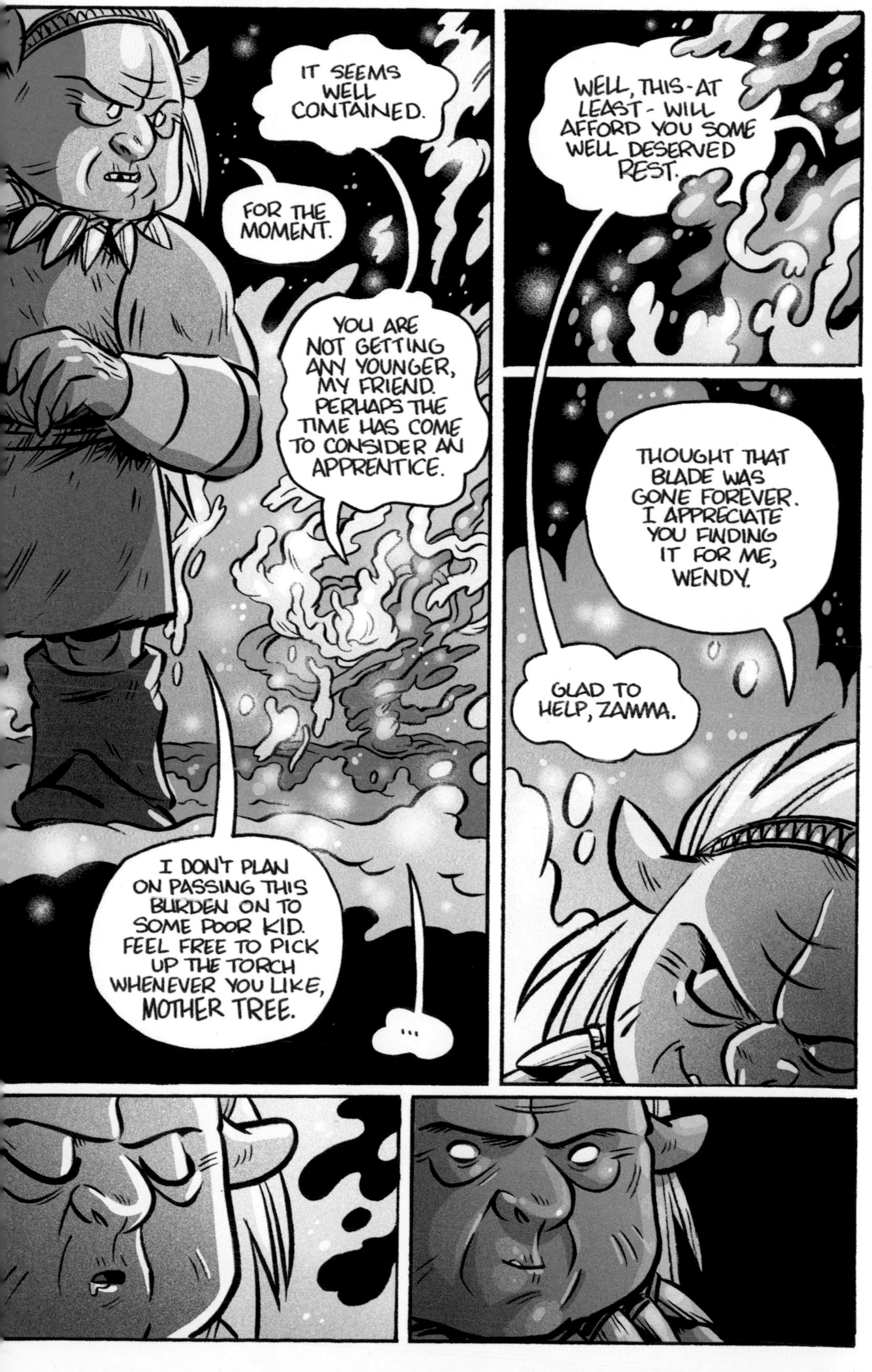
IT SEEMS WELL CONTAINED.
FOR THE MOMENT.
YOU ARE NOT GETTING ANY YOUNGER, MY FRIEND. PERHAPS THE TIME HAS COME TO CONSIDER AN APPRENTICE.
I DON'T PLAN ON PASSING THIS BURDEN ON TO SOME POOR KID. FEEL FREE TO PICK UP THE TORCH WHENEVER YOU LIKE, MOTHER TREE.
...
WELL, THIS-AT LEAST- WILL AFFORD YOU SOME WELL DESERVED REST.
THOUGHT THAT BLADE WAS GONE FOREVER. I APPRECIATE YOU FINDING IT FOR ME, WENDY.
GLAD TO HELP, ZAMMA.

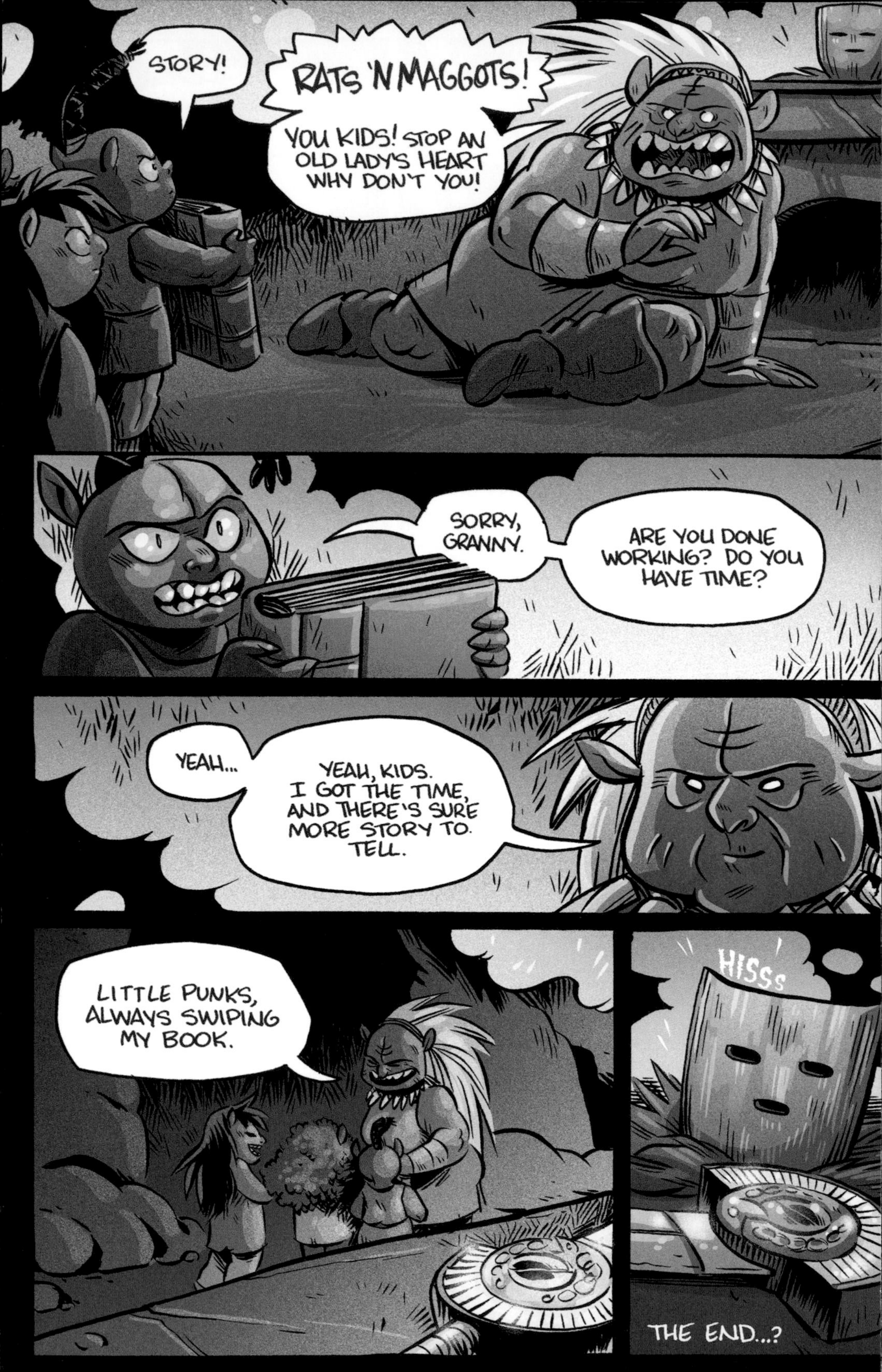
STORY!
RATS 'N MAGGOTS!
YOU KIDS! STOP AN OLD LADY'S HEART WHY DON'T YOU!
SORRY, GRANNY.
ARE YOU DONE WORKING? DO YOU HAVE TIME?
YEAH...
YEAH, KIDS. I GOT THE TIME, AND THERE'S SURE MORE STORY TO. TELL.
LITTLE PUNKS, ALWAYS SWIPING MY BOOK.
HISSs
THE END...?

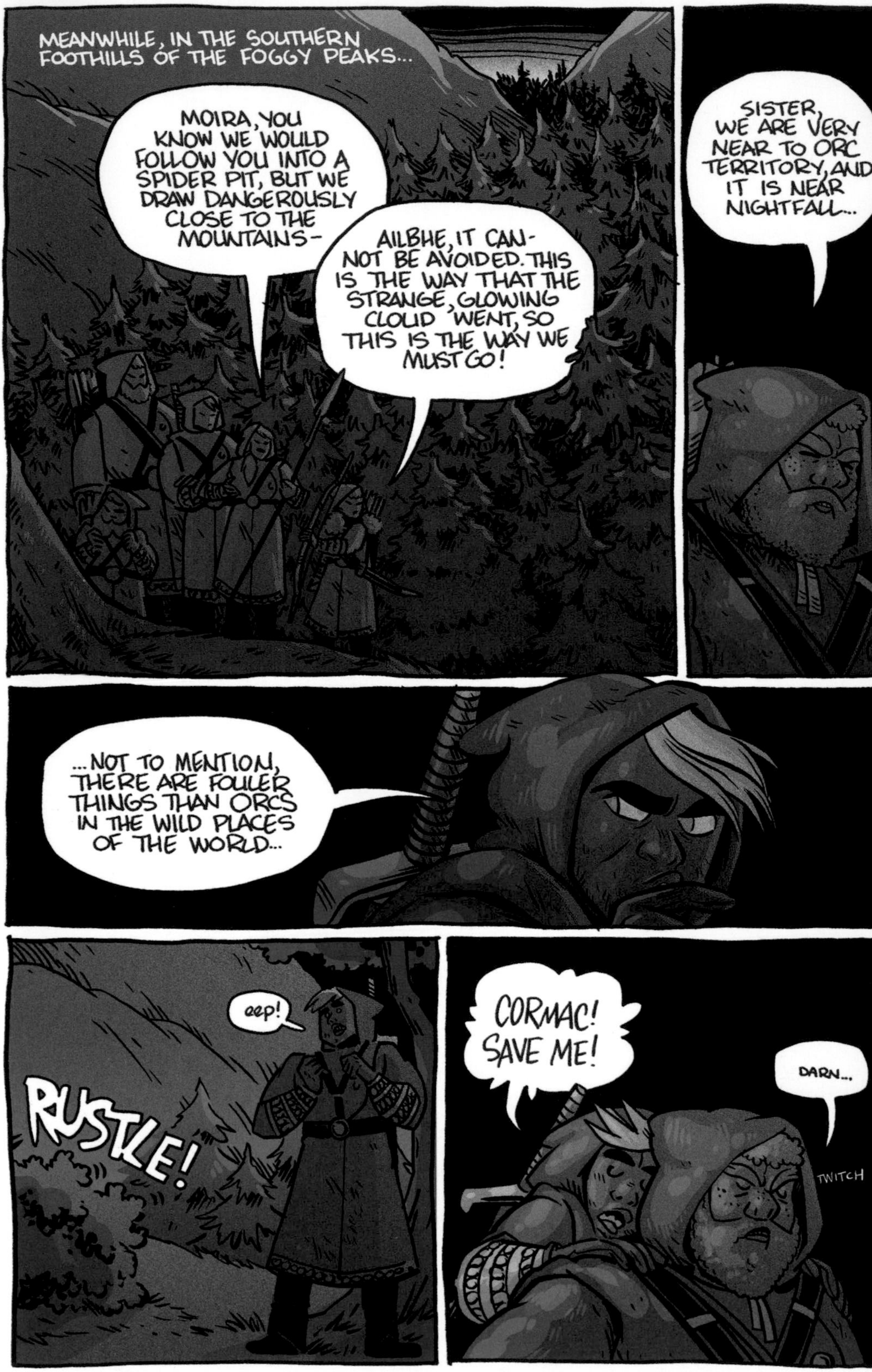
MEANWHILE, IN THE SOUTHERN FOOTHILLS OF THE FOGGY PEAKS...
MOIRA, YOU KNOW WE WOULD FOLLOW YOU INTO A SPIDER PIT, BUT WE DRAW DANGEROUSLY CLOSE TO THE MOUNTAINS-
AILBHE, IT CANNOT BE AVOIDED. THIS IS THE WAY THAT THE STRANGE, GLOWING CLOUD WENT, SO THIS IS THE WAY WE MUST GO!
SISTER, WE ARE VERY NEAR TO ORC TERRITORY, AND IT IS NEAR NIGHTFALL...
...NOT TO MENTION, THERE ARE FOULER THINGS THAN ORCS IN THE WILD PLACES OF THE WORLD...
eep!
RUSTLE!
CORMAC! SAVE ME!
DARN...
TWITCH

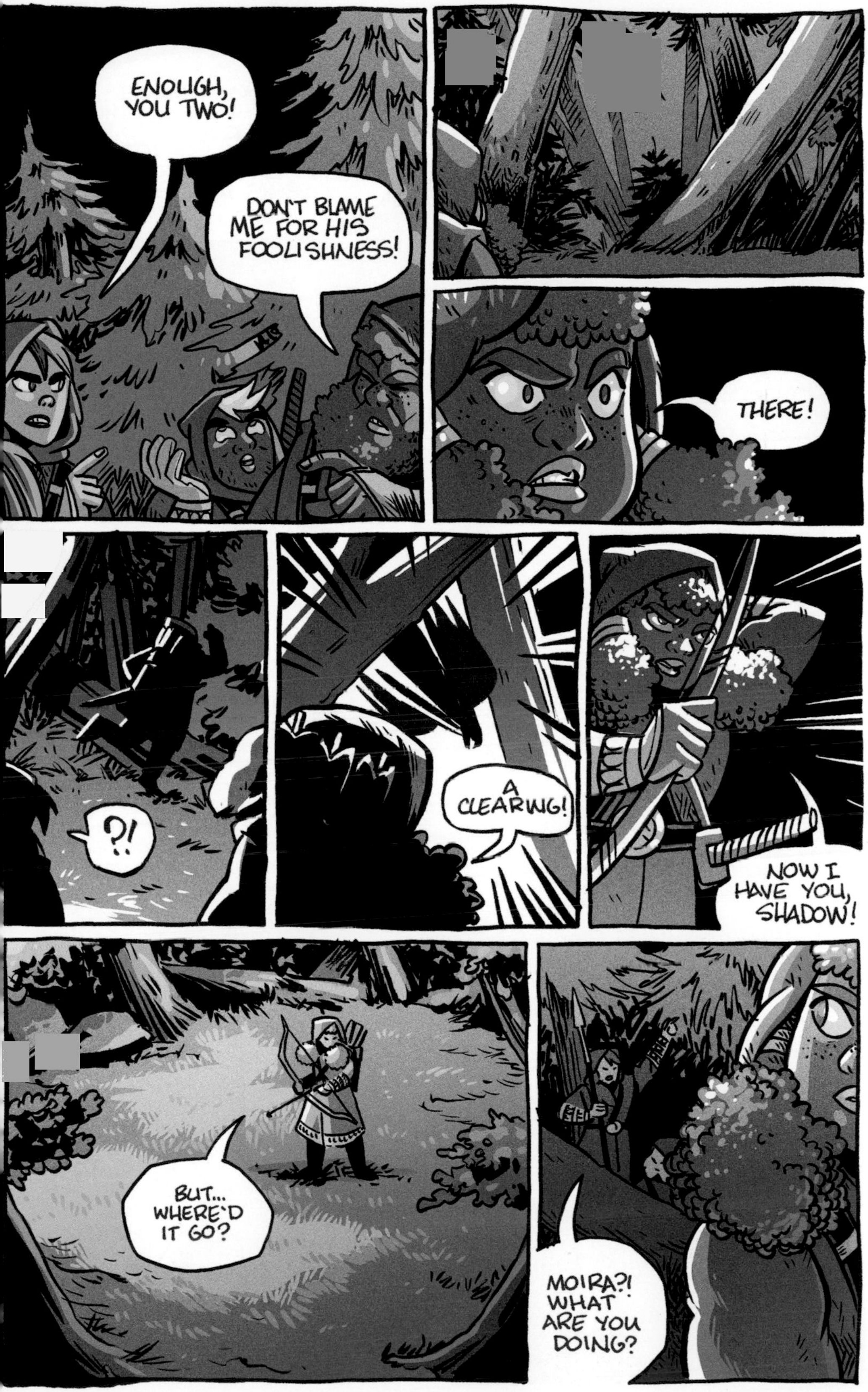
ENOUGH, YOU TWO!
DON'T BLAME ME FOR HIS FOOLISHNESS!
THERE!
?!
A CLEARING!
NOW I HAVE YOU, SHADOW!
BUT... WHERE'D IT GO?
MOIRA?! WHAT ARE YOU DOING?

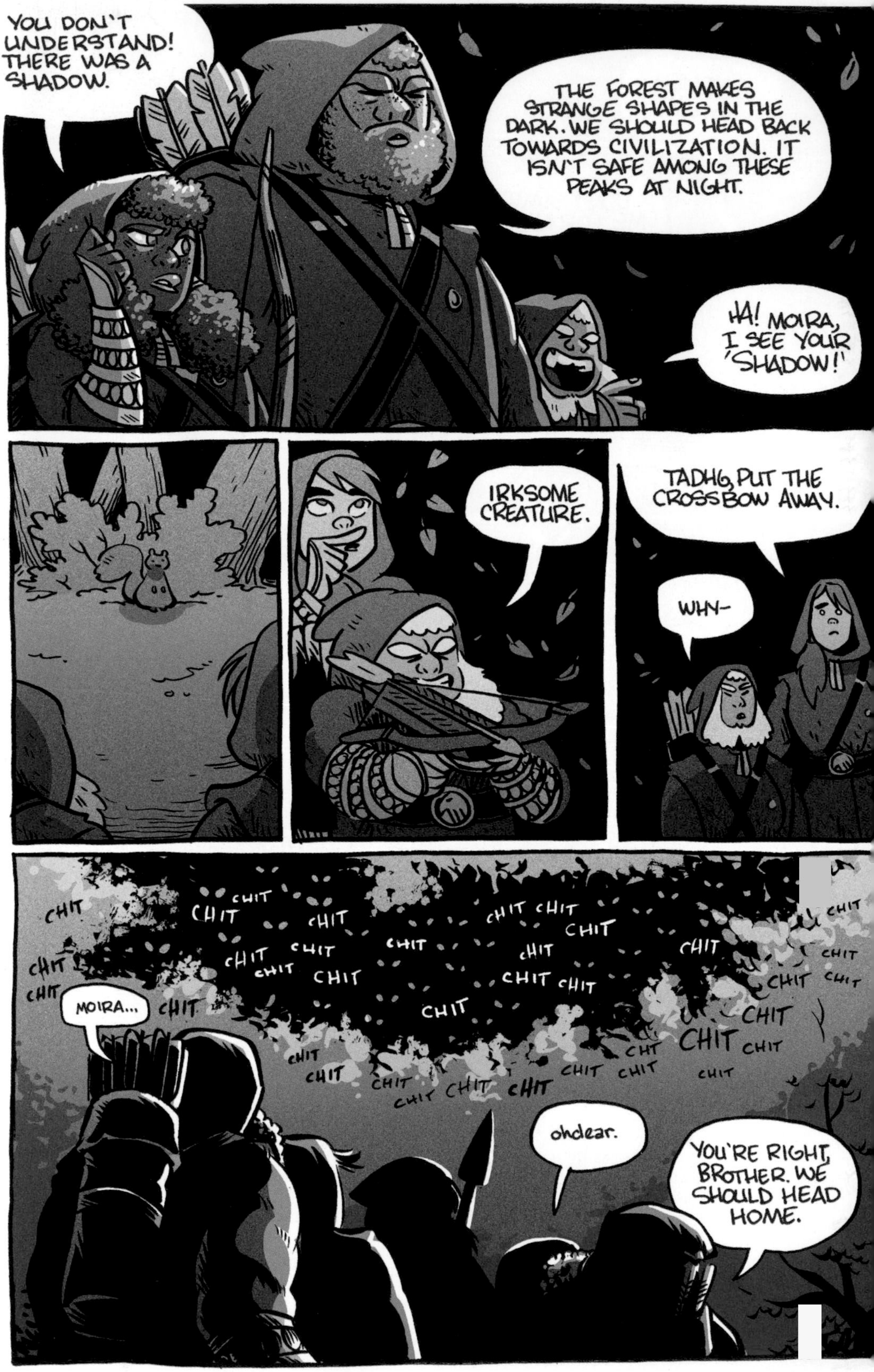
YOU DON'T UNDERSTAND! THERE WAS A SHADOW.
THE FOREST MAKES STRANGE SHAPES IN THE DARK. WE SHOULD HEAD BACK TOWARDS CIVILIZATION. IT ISN'T SAFE AMONG THESE PEAKS AT NIGHT.
HA! MOIRA, I SEE YOUR 'SHADOW!'
IRKSOME CREATURE.
TADHG, PUT THE CROSSBOW AWAY.
WHY-
CHIT CHIT CHIT CHIT CHIT CHIT CHIT CHIT CHIT CHIT
MOIRA...
ohdear.
YOU'RE RIGHT, BROTHER. WE SHOULD HEAD HOME.

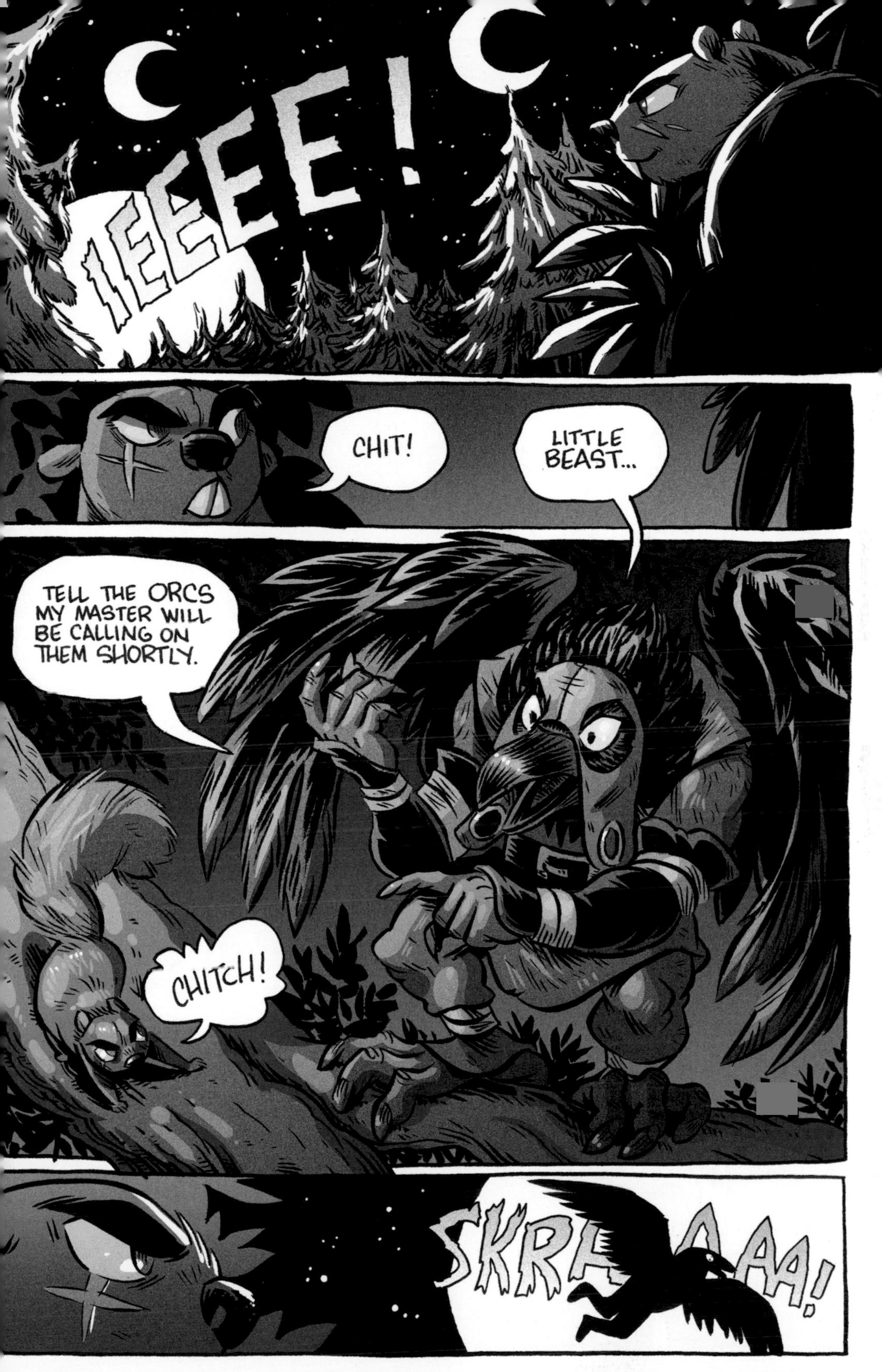
IEEEE!
CHIT!
LITTLE BEAST...
TELL THE ORCS MY MASTER WILL BE CALLING ON THEM SHORTLY.
CHITCH!
SKRA AA!

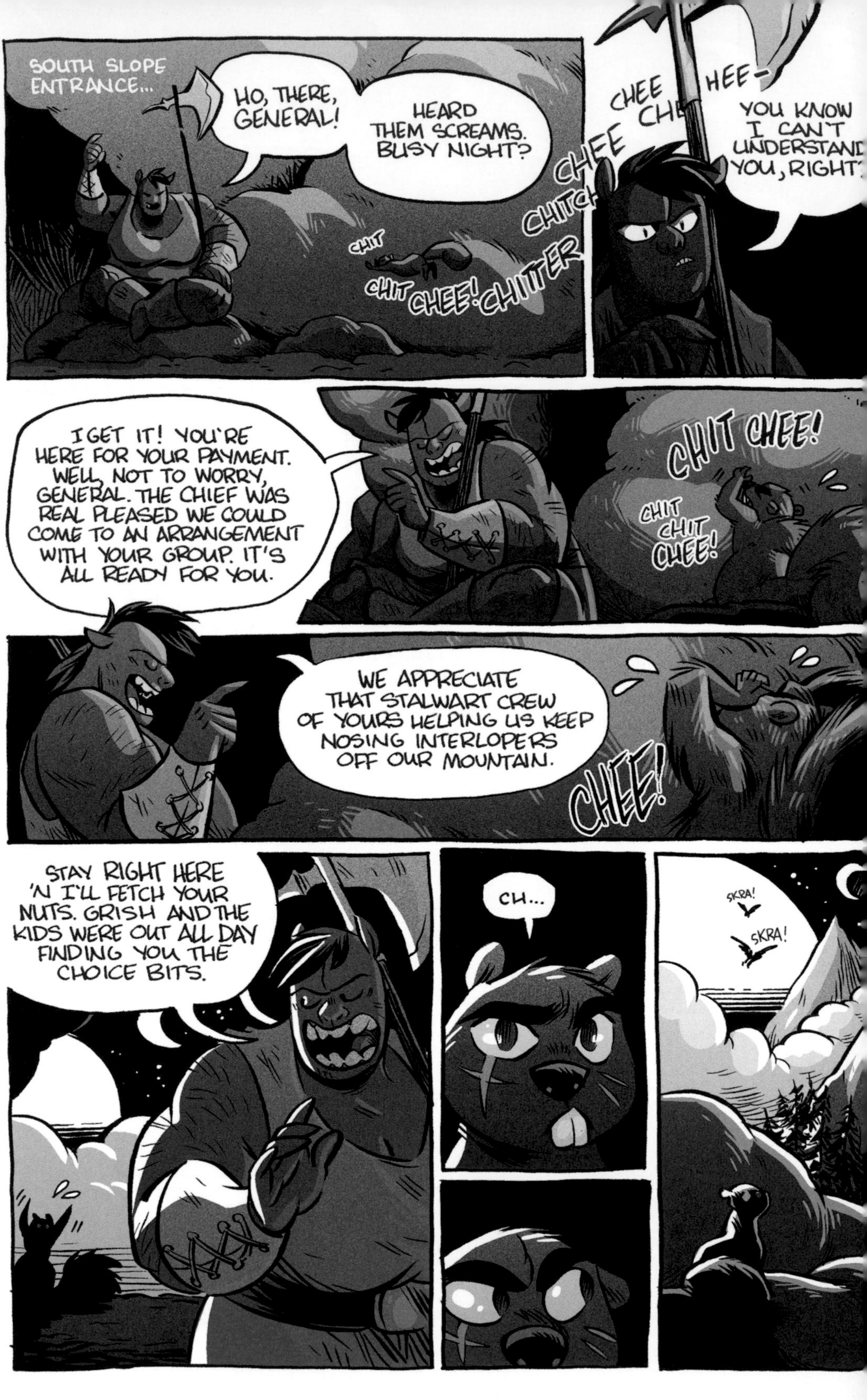

SOUTH SLOPE ENTRANCE...
HO, THERE, GENERAL!
HEARD THEM SCREAMS. BUSY NIGHT?
CHIT
CHIT CHEE! CHITTER
CHEE CHEE CHEE-
CHEE CHITCH
YOU KNOW I CAN'T UNDERSTAND YOU, RIGHT?
I GET IT! YOU'RE HERE FOR YOUR PAYMENT. WELL, NOT TO WORRY, GENERAL. THE CHIEF WAS REAL PLEASED WE COULD COME TO AN ARRANGEMENT WITH YOUR GROUP. IT'S ALL READY FOR YOU.
CHIT CHEE!
CHIT CHIT CHEE!
WE APPRECIATE THAT STALWART CREW OF YOURS HELPING US KEEP NOSING INTERLOPERS OFF OUR MOUNTAIN.
CHEE!
STAY RIGHT HERE 'N I'LL FETCH YOUR NUTS. GRISH AND THE KIDS WERE OUT ALL DAY FINDING YOU THE CHOICE BITS.
CH...
SKRA!
SKRA!

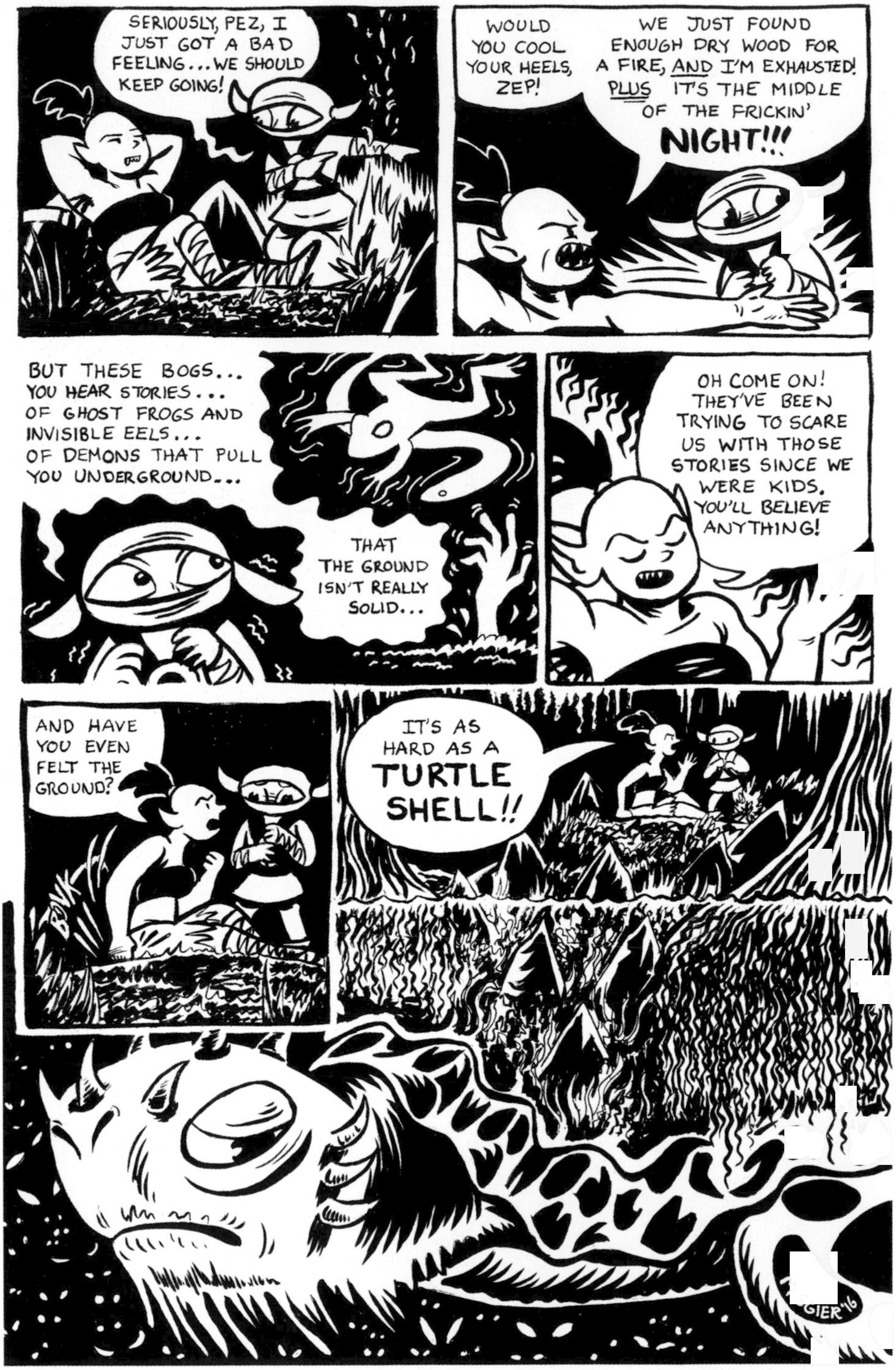
SERIOUSLY, PEZ, I JUST GOT A BAD FEELING... WE SHOULD KEEP GOING!
WOULD YOU COOL YOUR HEELS, ZEP!
WE JUST FOUND ENOUGH DRY WOOD FOR A FIRE, AND I'M EXHAUSTED! PLUS IT'S THE MIDDLE OF THE FRICKIN' NIGHT!!!
BUT THESE BOGS... YOU HEAR STORIES... OF GHOST FROGS AND INVISIBLE EELS... OF DEMONS THAT PULL YOU UNDERGROUND...
THAT THE GROUND ISN'T REALLY SOLID...
OH COME ON! THEY'VE BEEN TRYING TO SCARE US WITH THOSE STORIES SINCE WE WERE KIDS. YOU'LL BELIEVE ANYTHING!
AND HAVE YOU EVEN FELT THE GROUND?
BONK
IT'S AS HARD AS A TURTLE SHELL!!
SGIER '16

PIN-UP BY **MARIE ENGER**

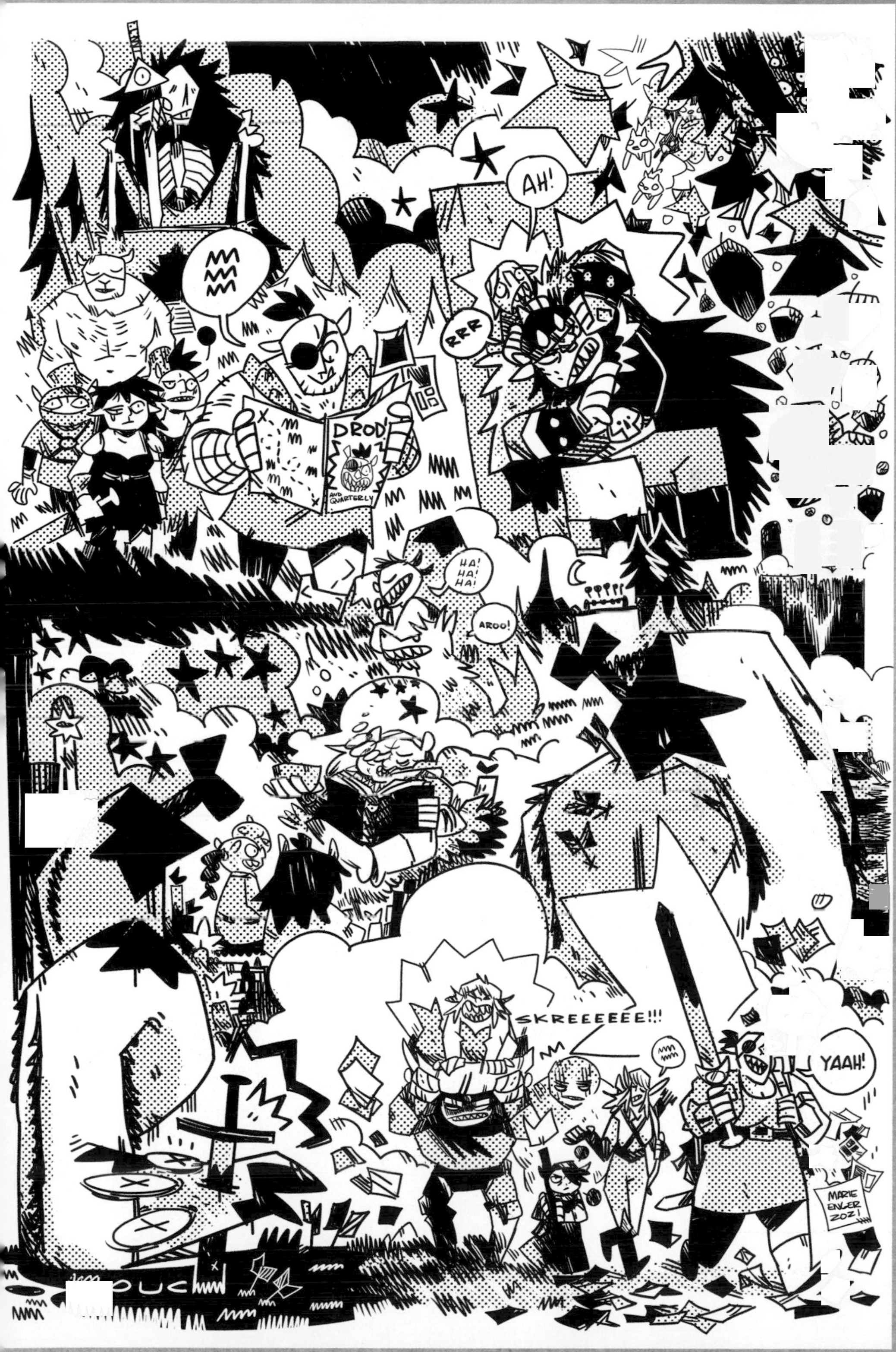
AH!
RRR
DROD
AND QUARTERLY
HA! HA! HA!
AROO!
SKREEEEEEE!!!
YAAH!
OUCH
MARIE ENGER 2021

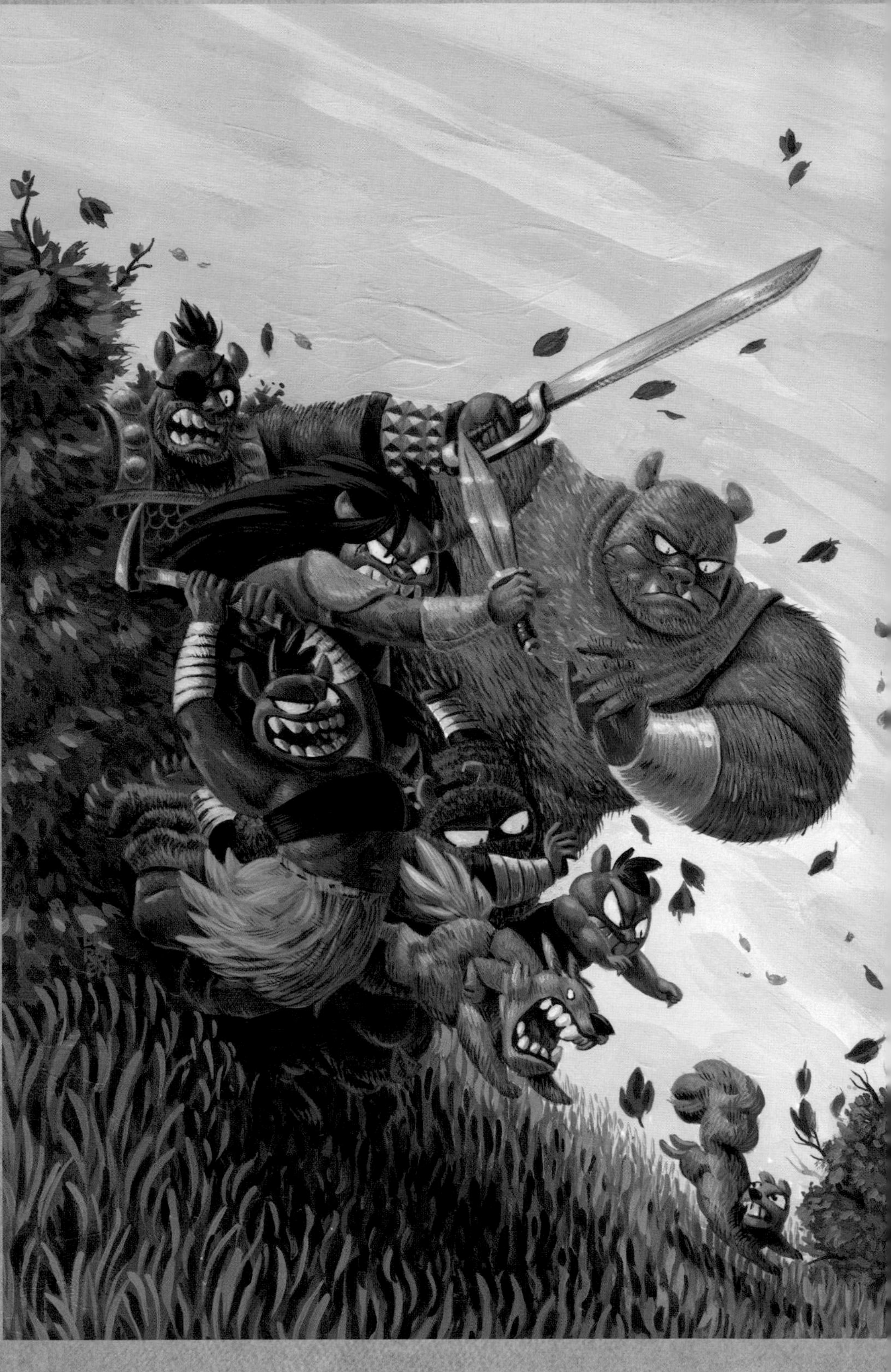

ISSUE ONE MAIN COVER BY **CHRISTINE LARSEN**

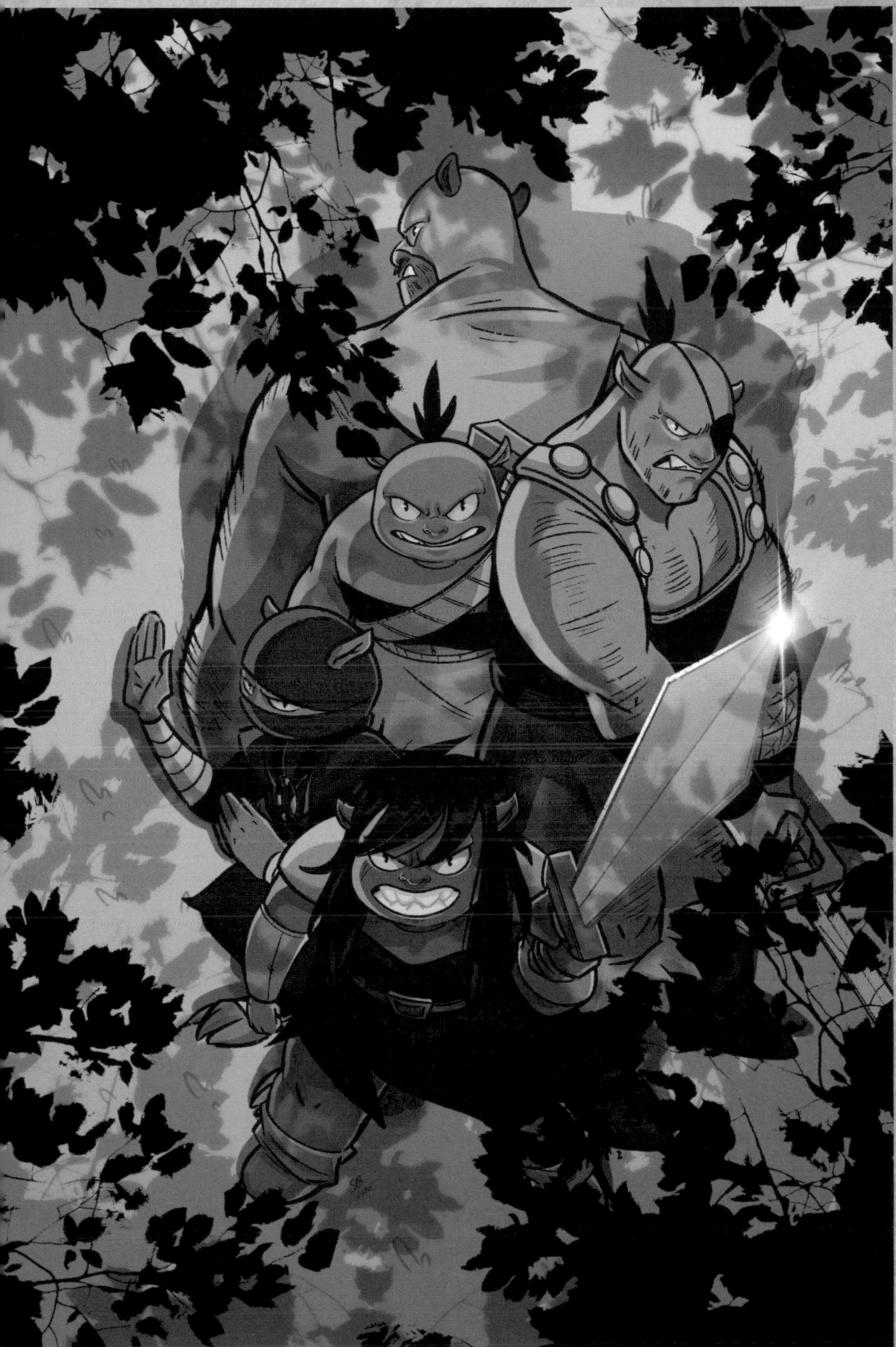

ISSUE ONE VARIANT COVER BY **SWEENEY BOO**

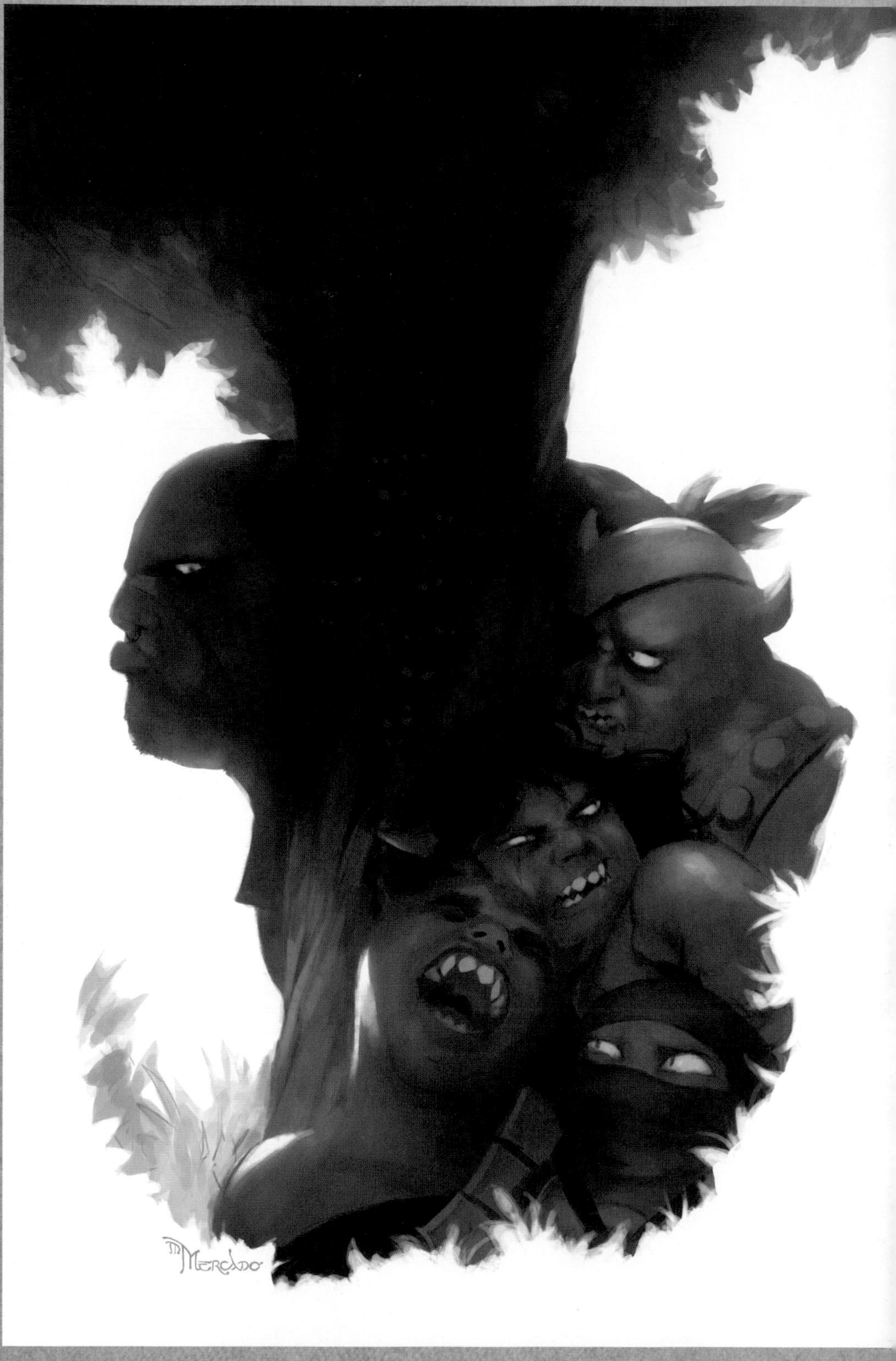
M MERCADO

ISSUE ONE VARIANT COVER BY **MIGUEL MERCADO**

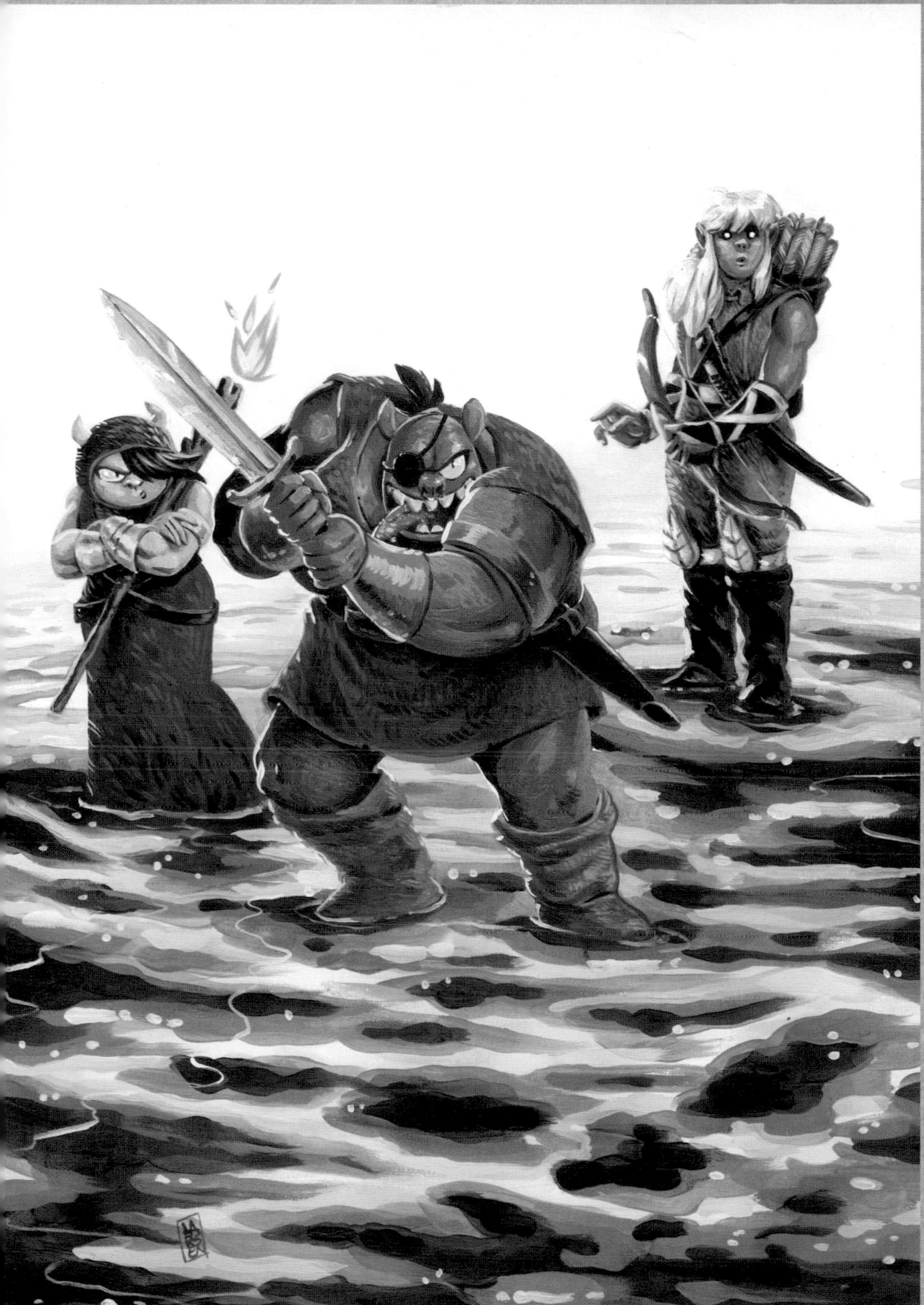

ISSUE TWO MAIN COVER BY **CHRISTINE LARSEN**

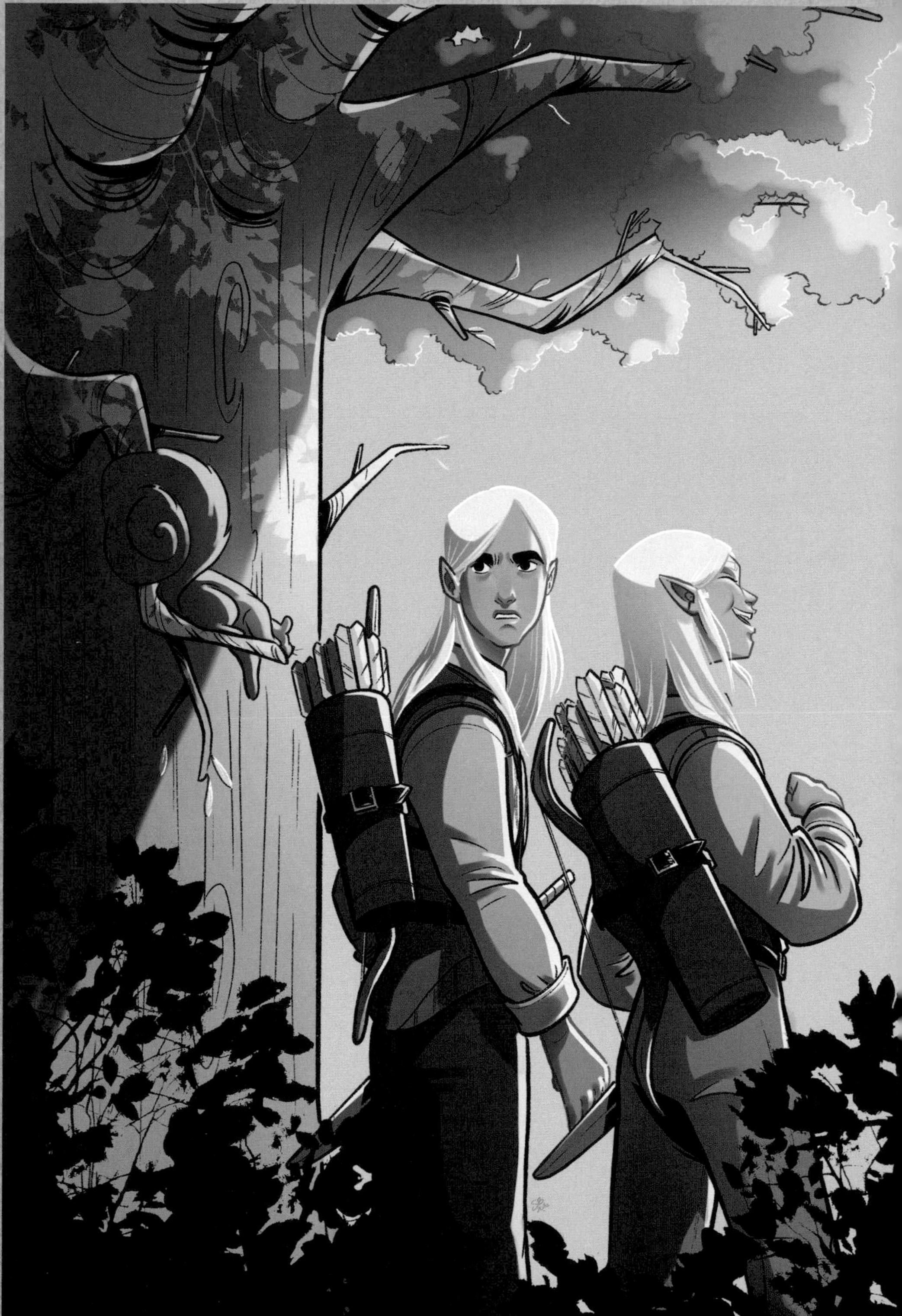

ISSUE TWO VARIANT COVER BY **SWEENEY BOO**

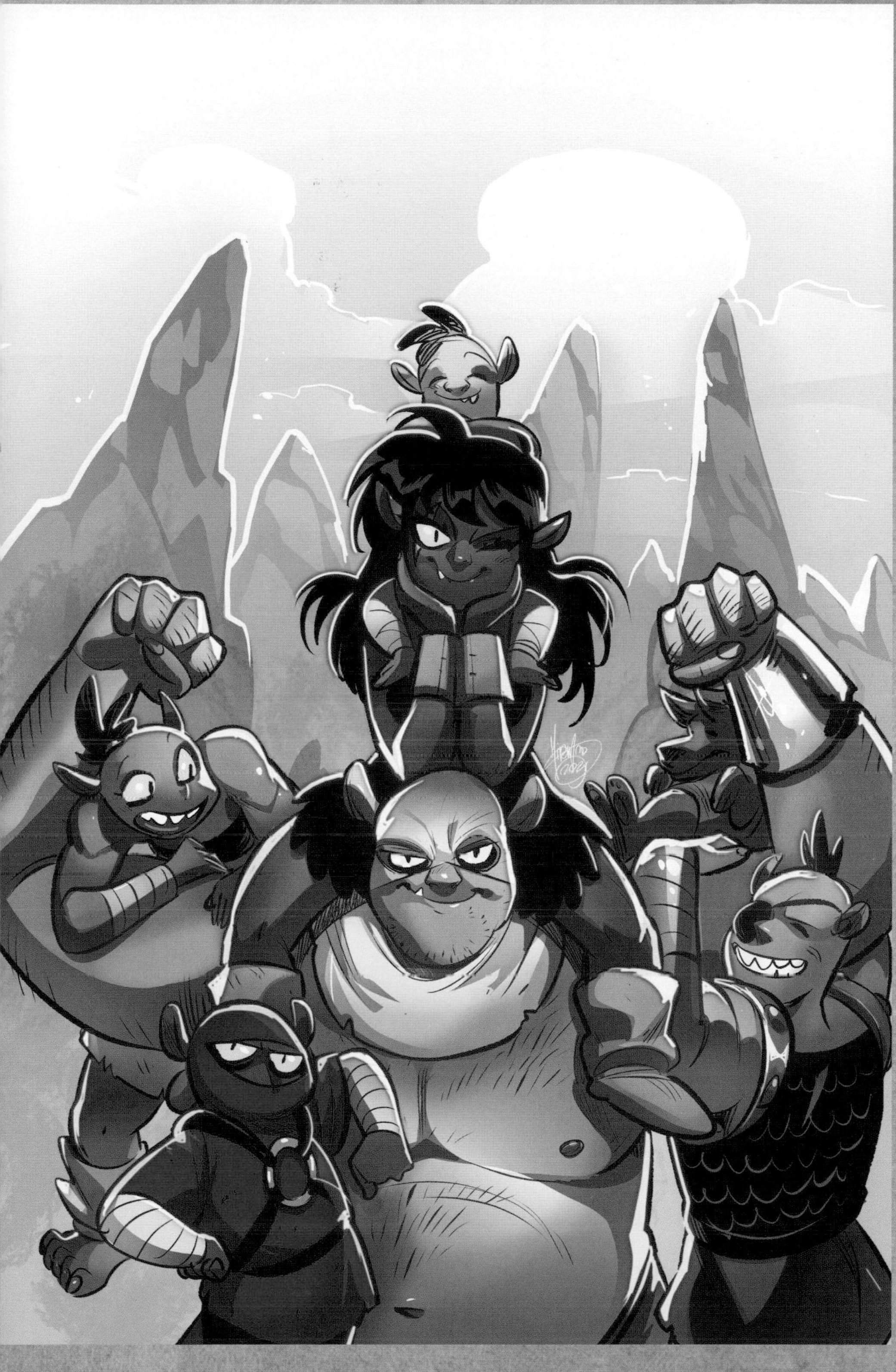

ISSUE TWO VARIANT COVER BY **MIRKA ANDOLFO**

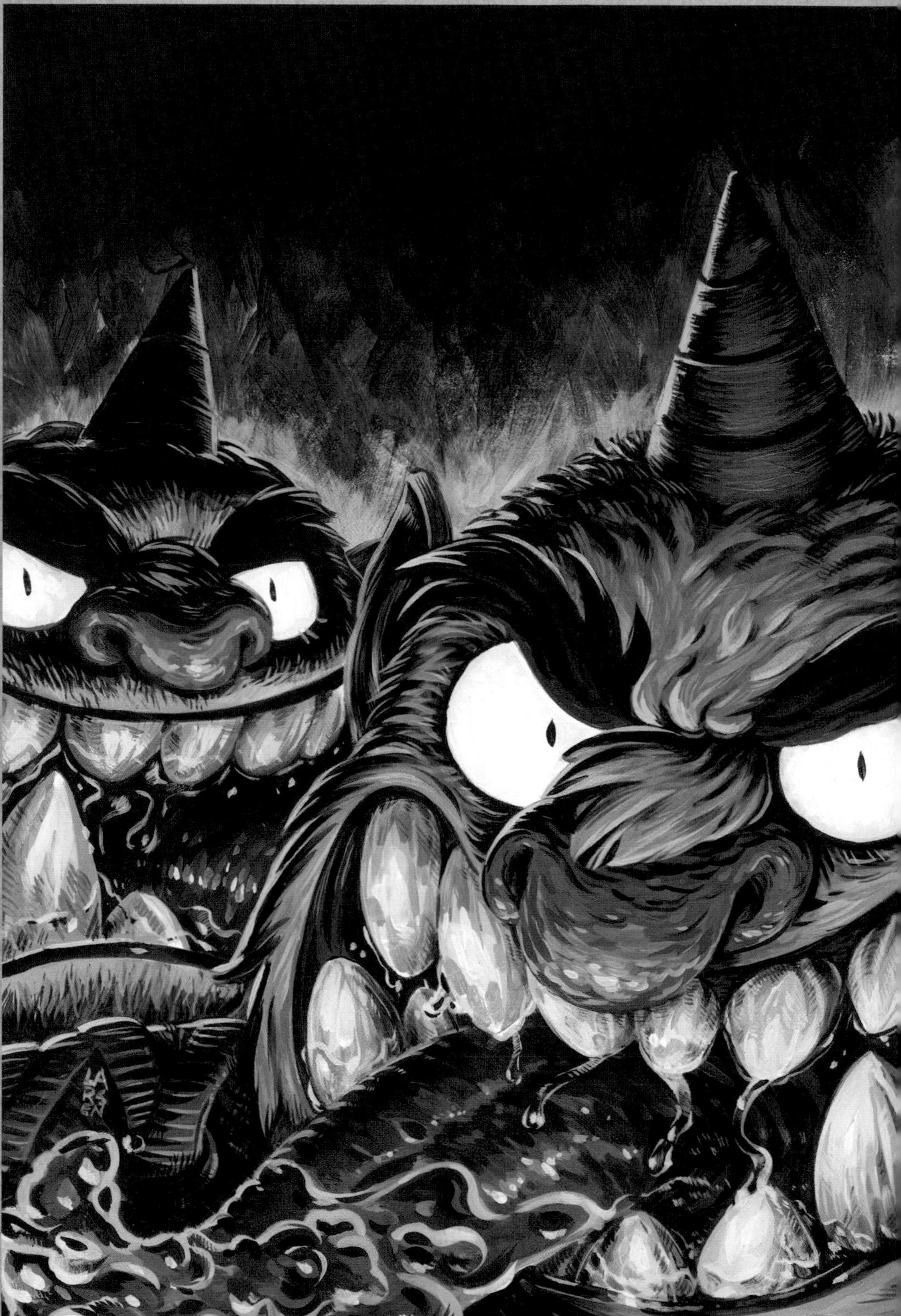

ISSUE THREE MAIN COVER BY **CHRISTINE LARSEN**

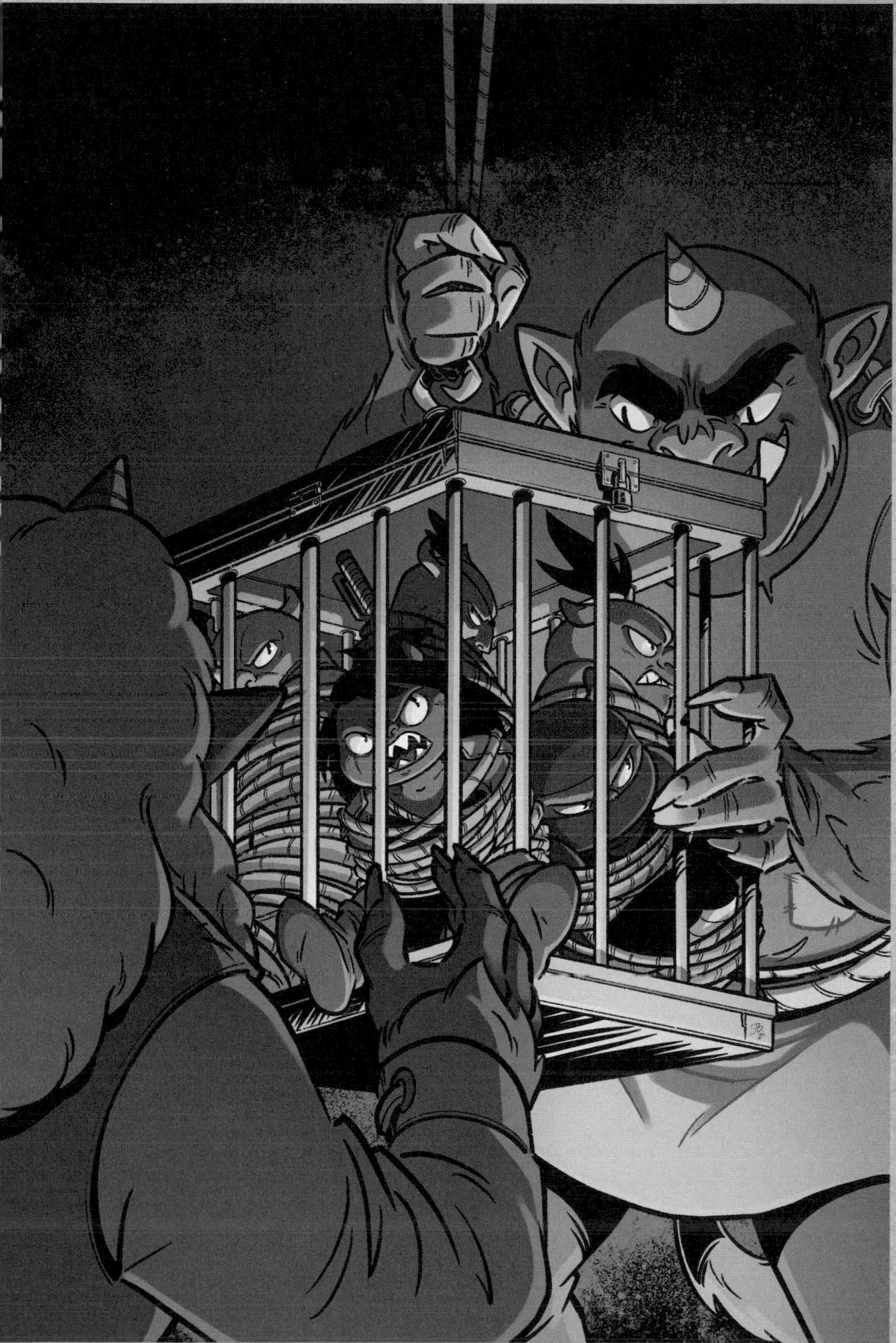

ISSUE THREE VARIANT COVER BY **SWEENEY BOO**

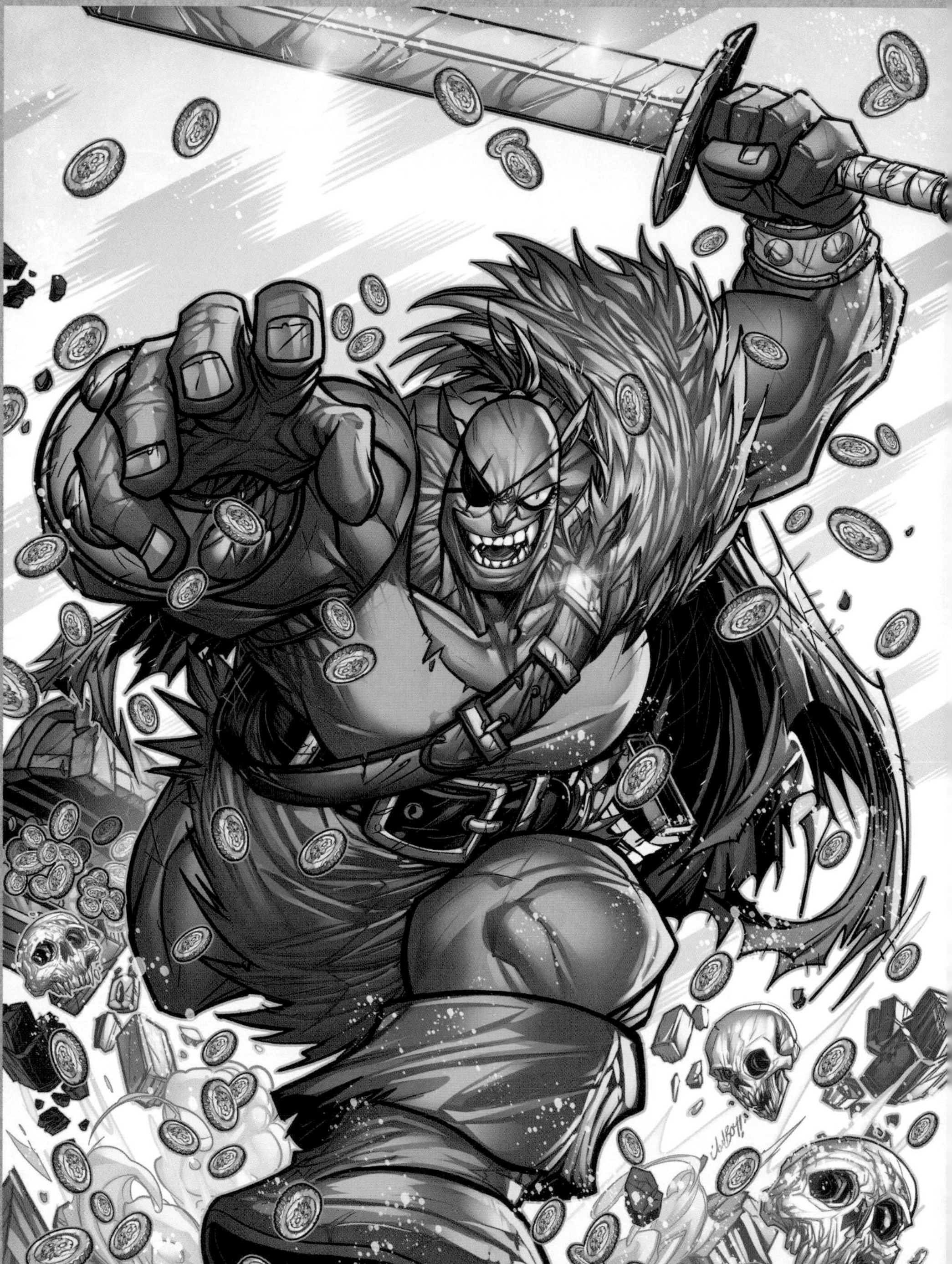

ISSUE THREE VARIANT COVER BY **JONBOY MEYERS**

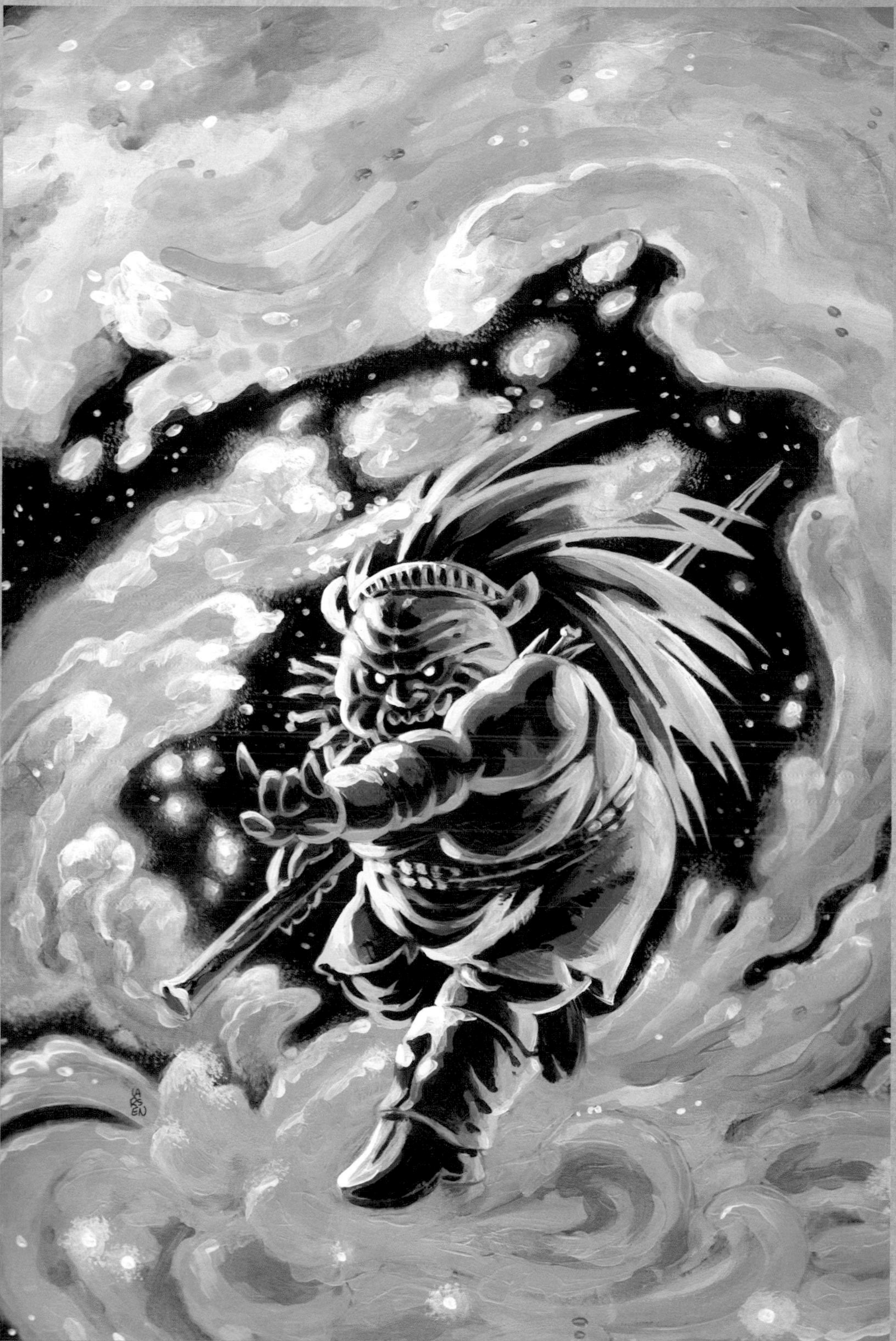
LARSEN

ISSUE FOUR MAIN COVER BY CHRISTINE LARSEN

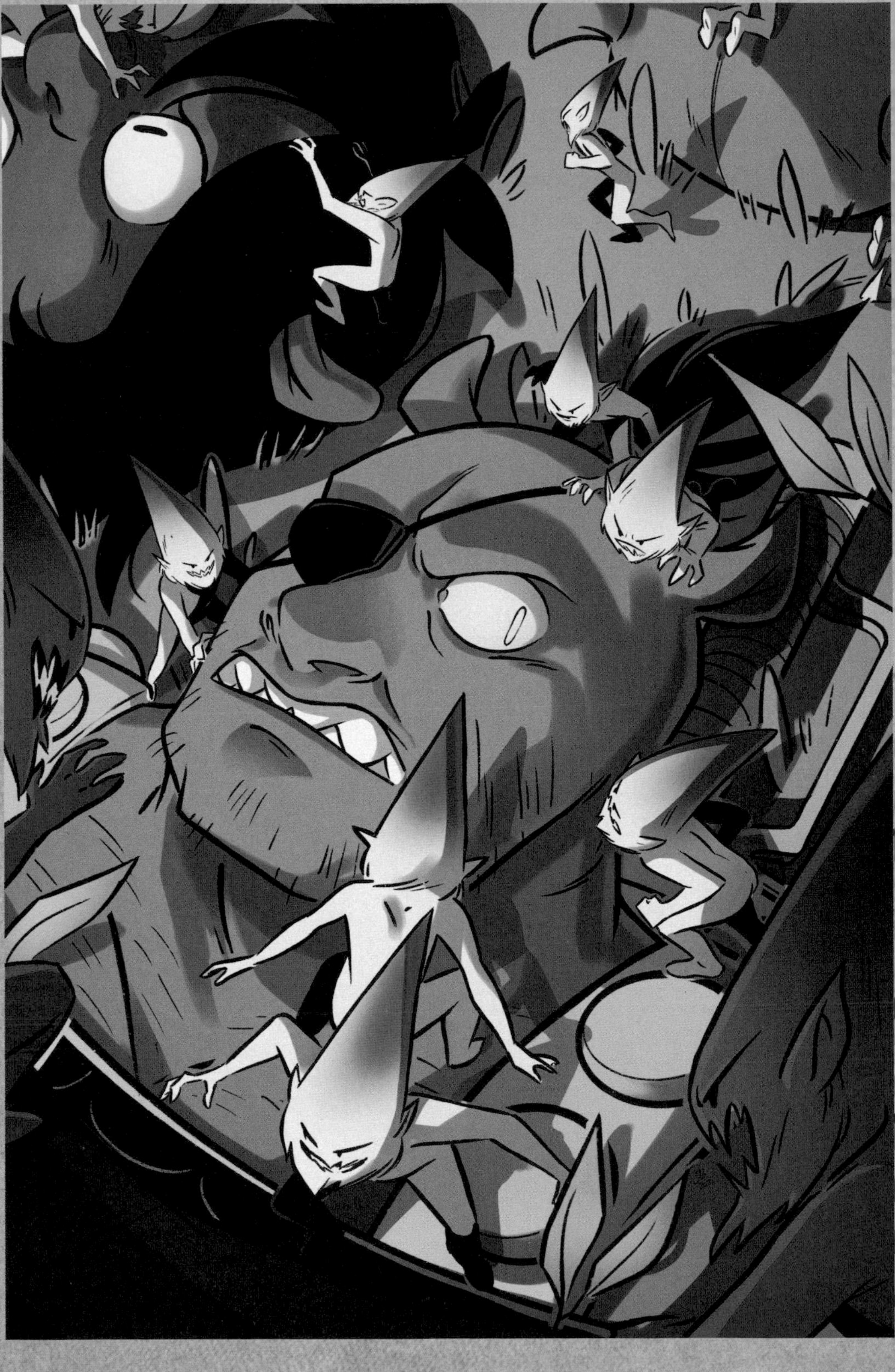

ISSUE FOUR VARIANT COVER BY **SWEENEY BOO**

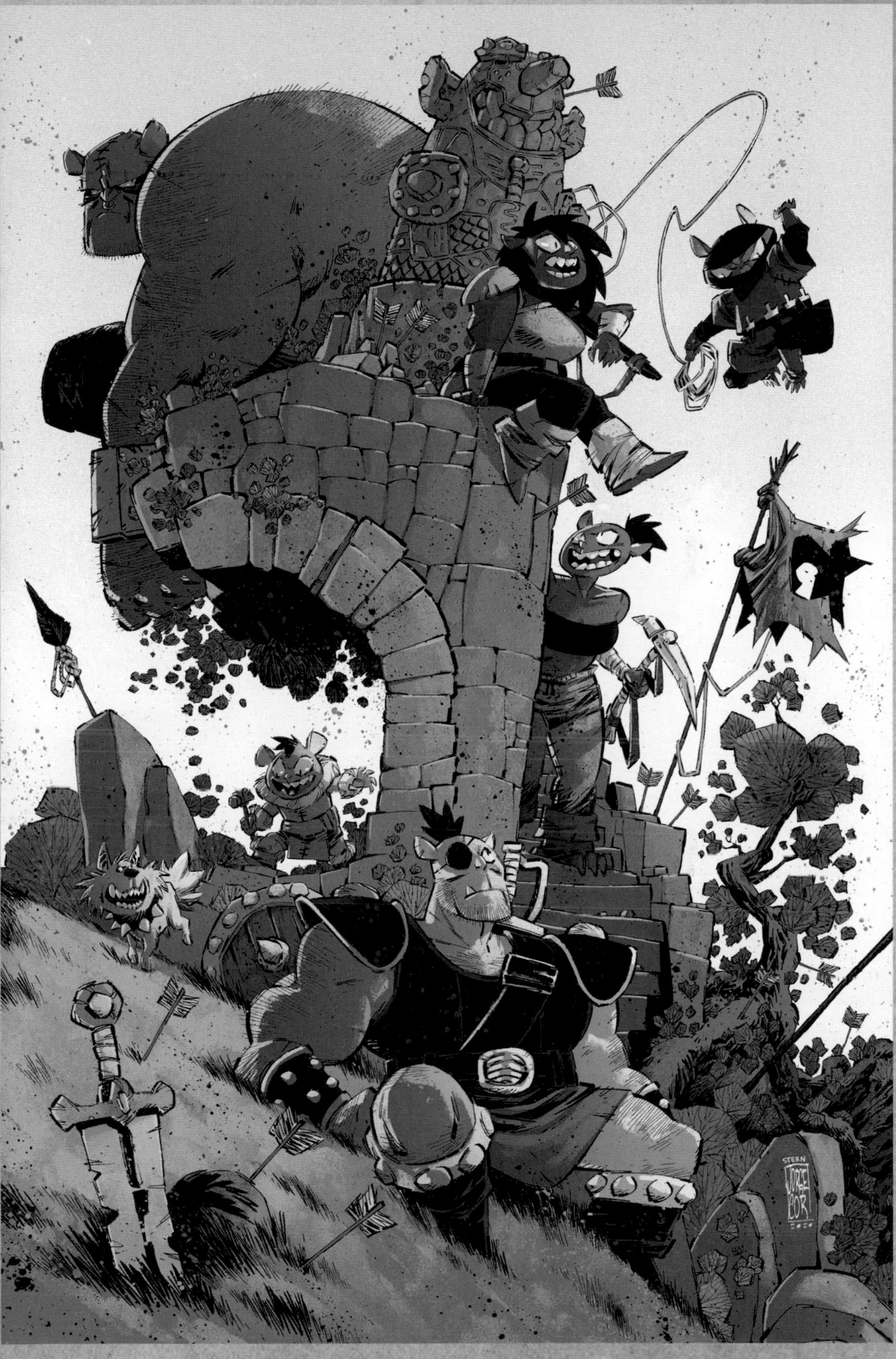

ISSUE FOUR VARIANT COVER BY **JORGE CORONA** WITH COLORS BY **SARAH STERN**

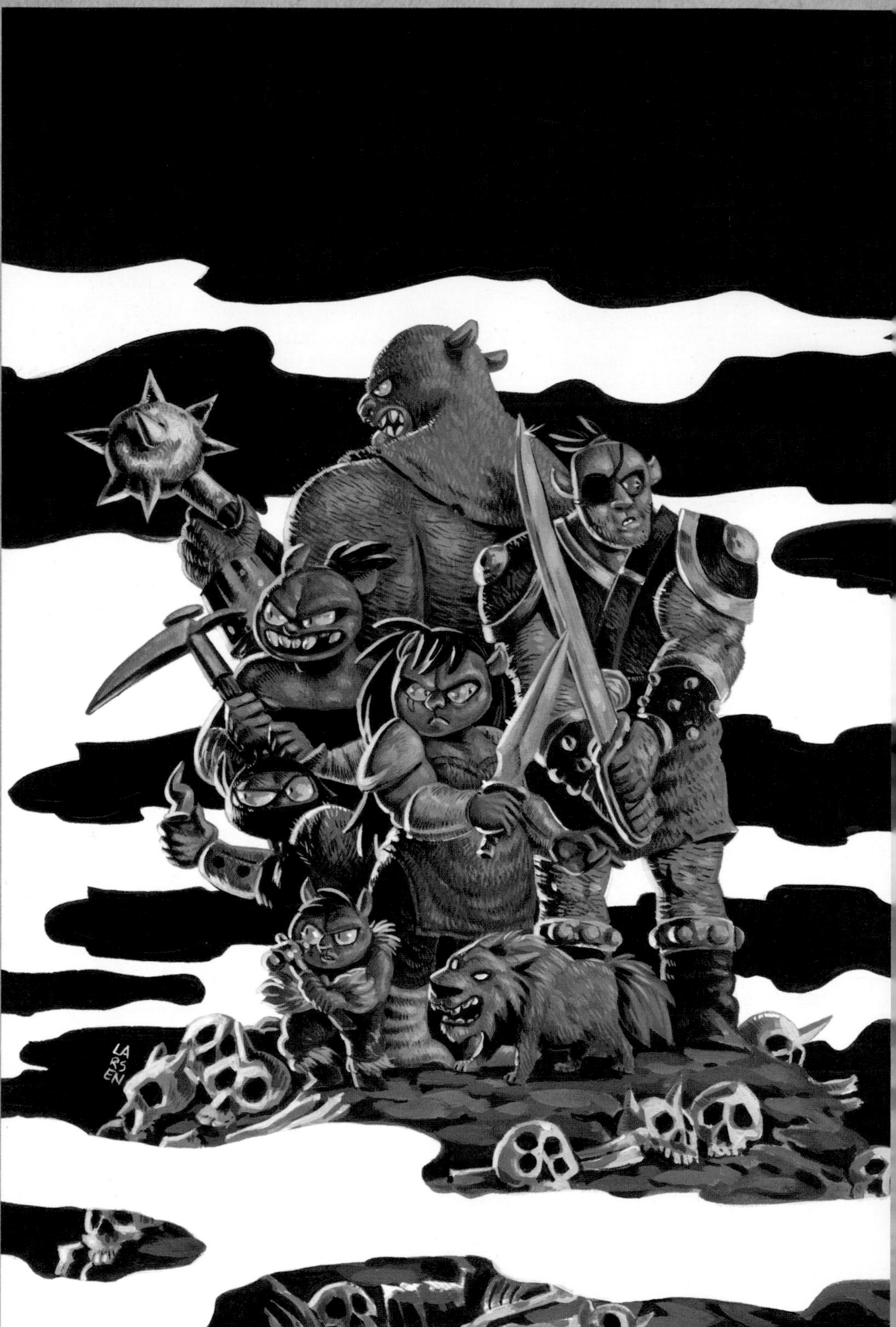
LARSEN

ISSUE FIVE MAIN COVER BY **CHRISTINE LARSEN**

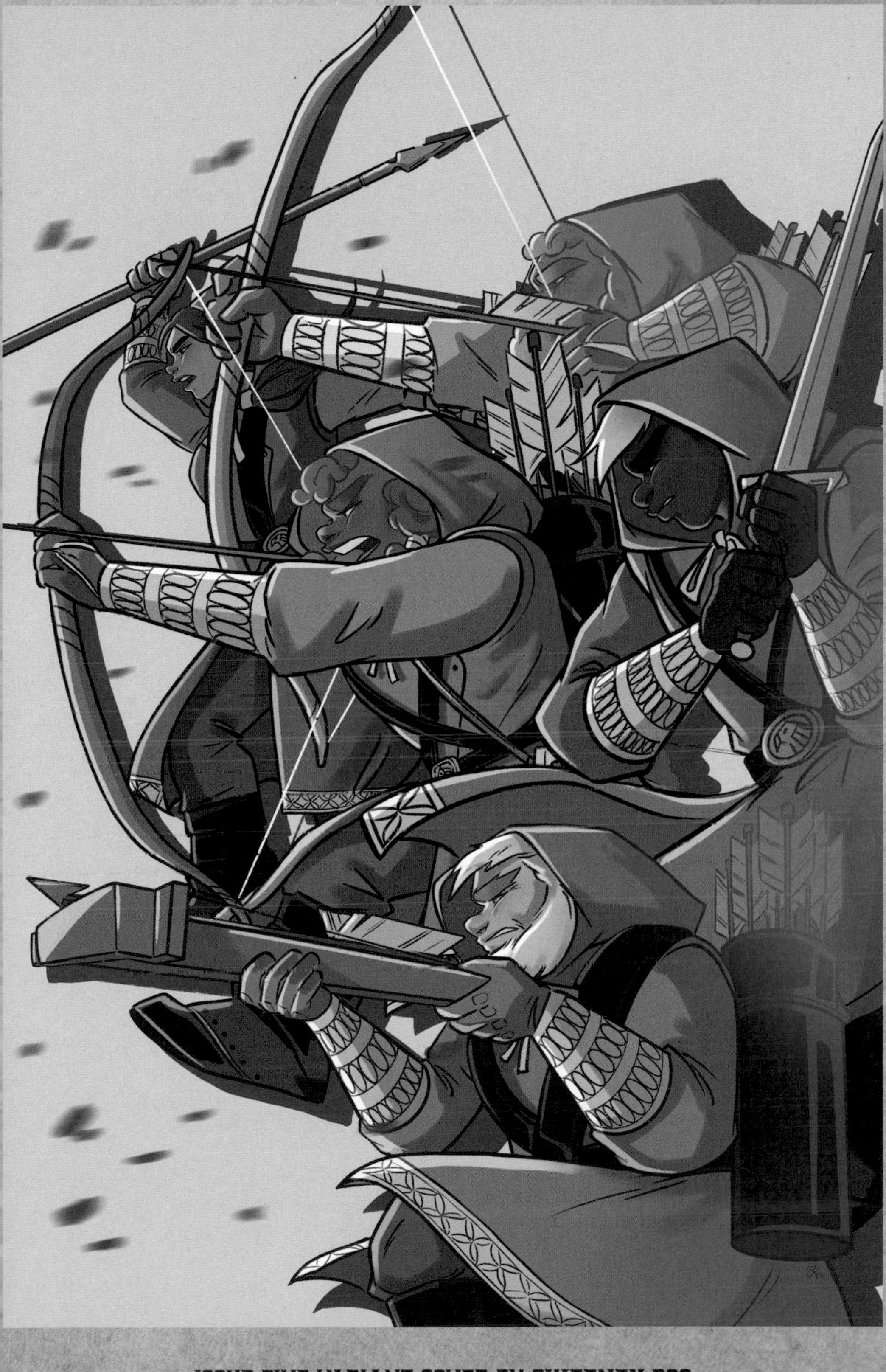

ISSUE FIVE VARIANT COVER BY **SWEENEY BOO**

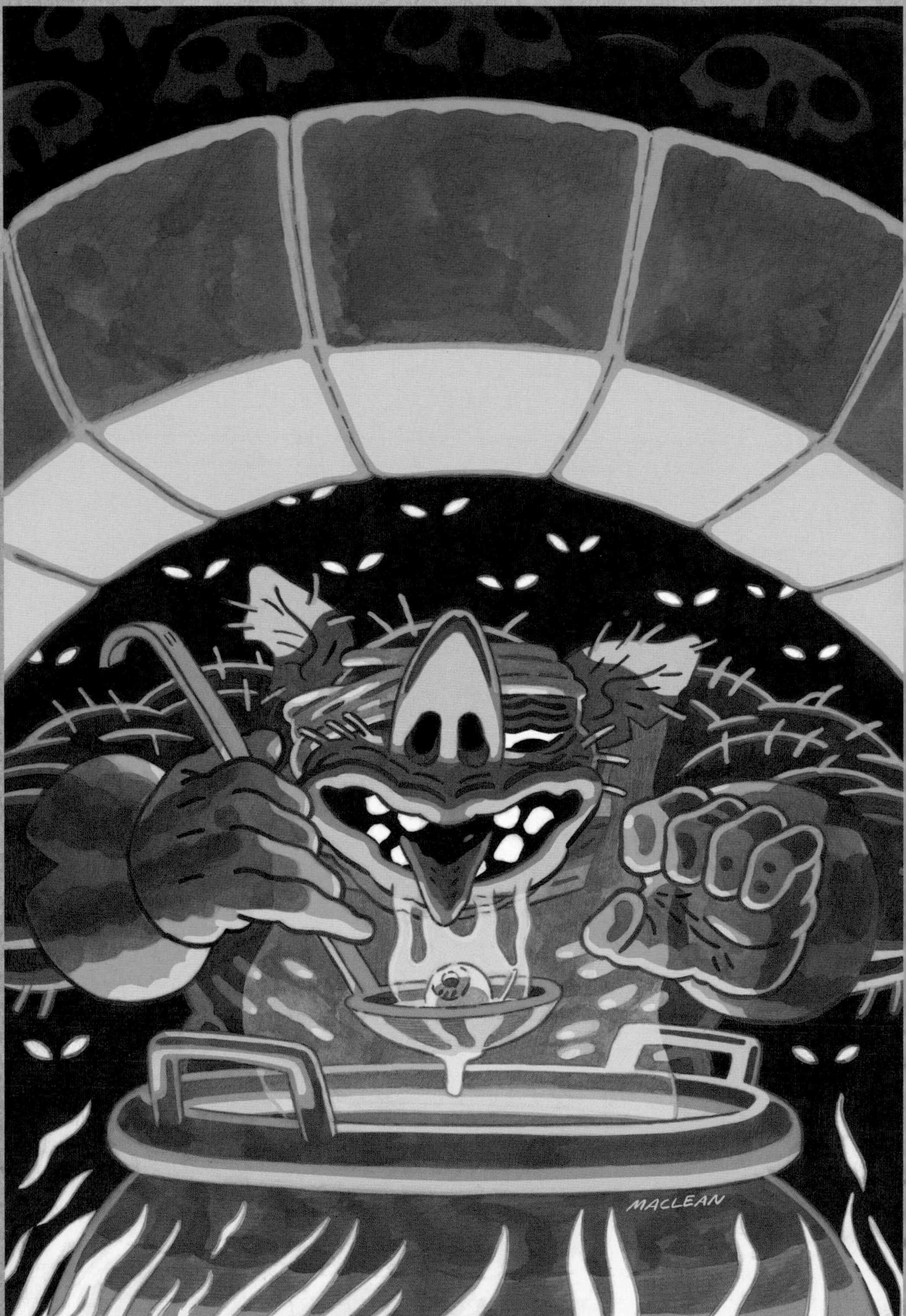
MACLEAN

ISSUE FIVE VARIANT COVER BY **ANDREW MACLEAN**

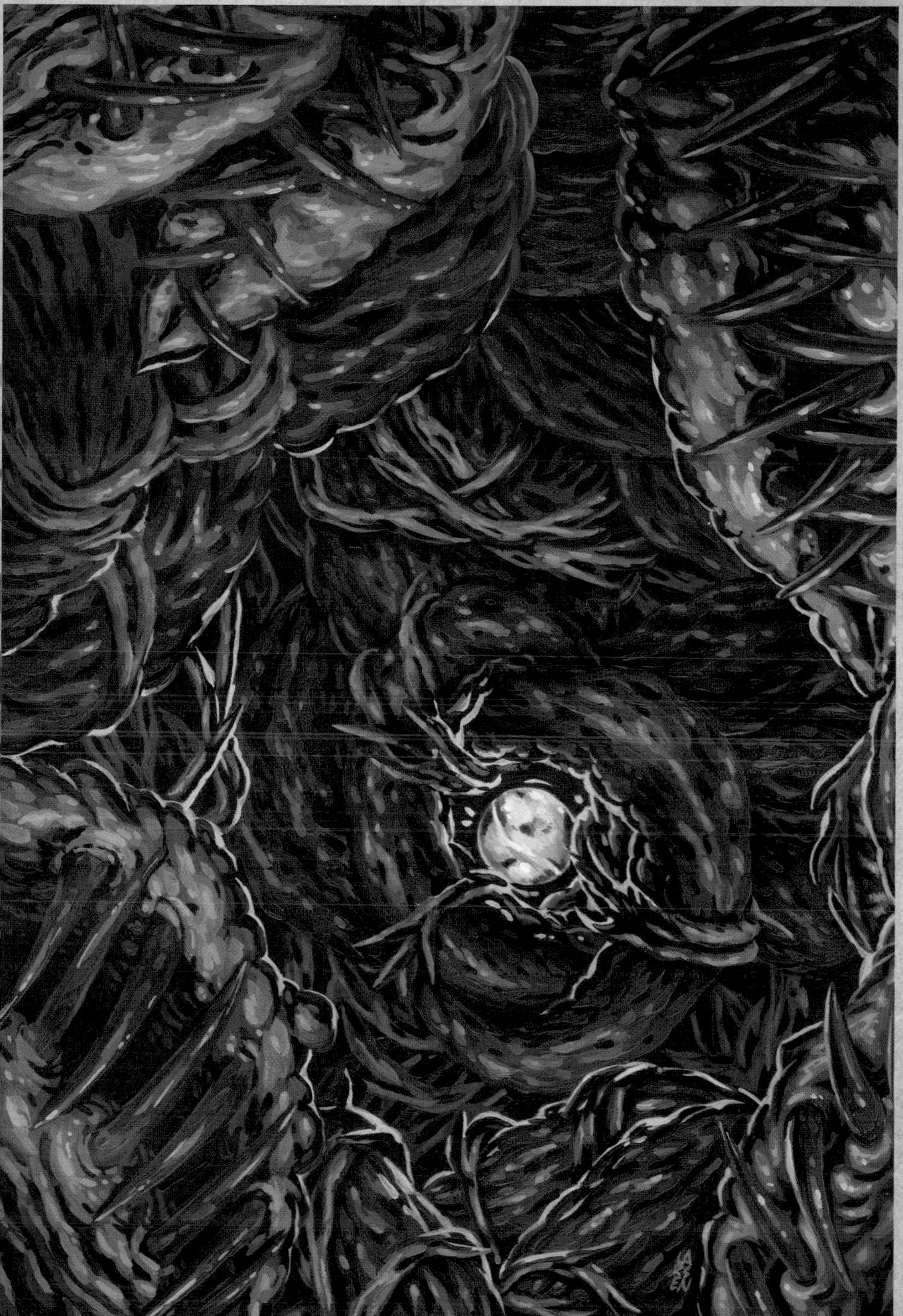

ISSUE SIX MAIN COVER BY **CHRISTINE LARSEN**

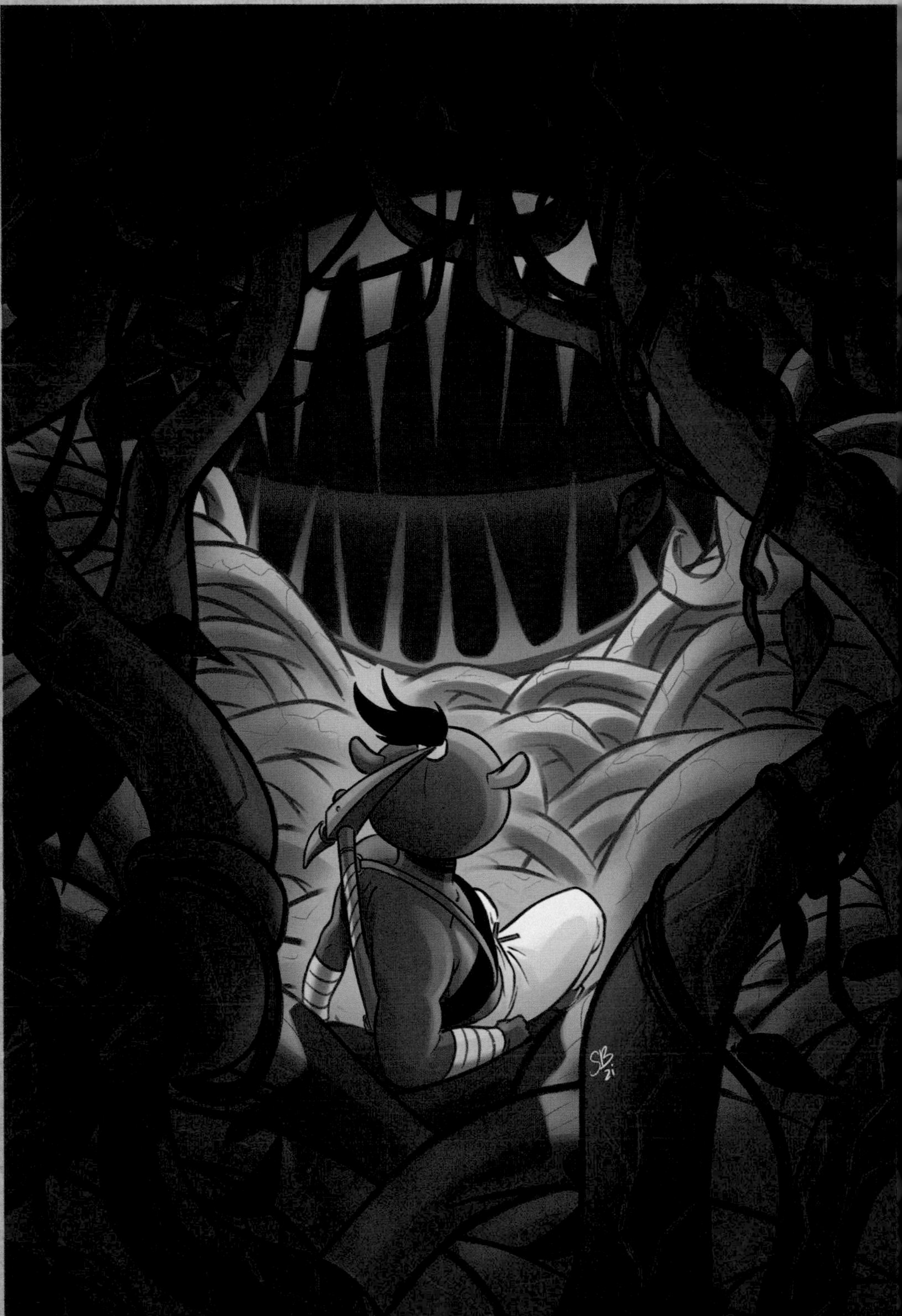
SB
21

ISSUE SIX VARIANT COVER BY **SWEENEY BOO**

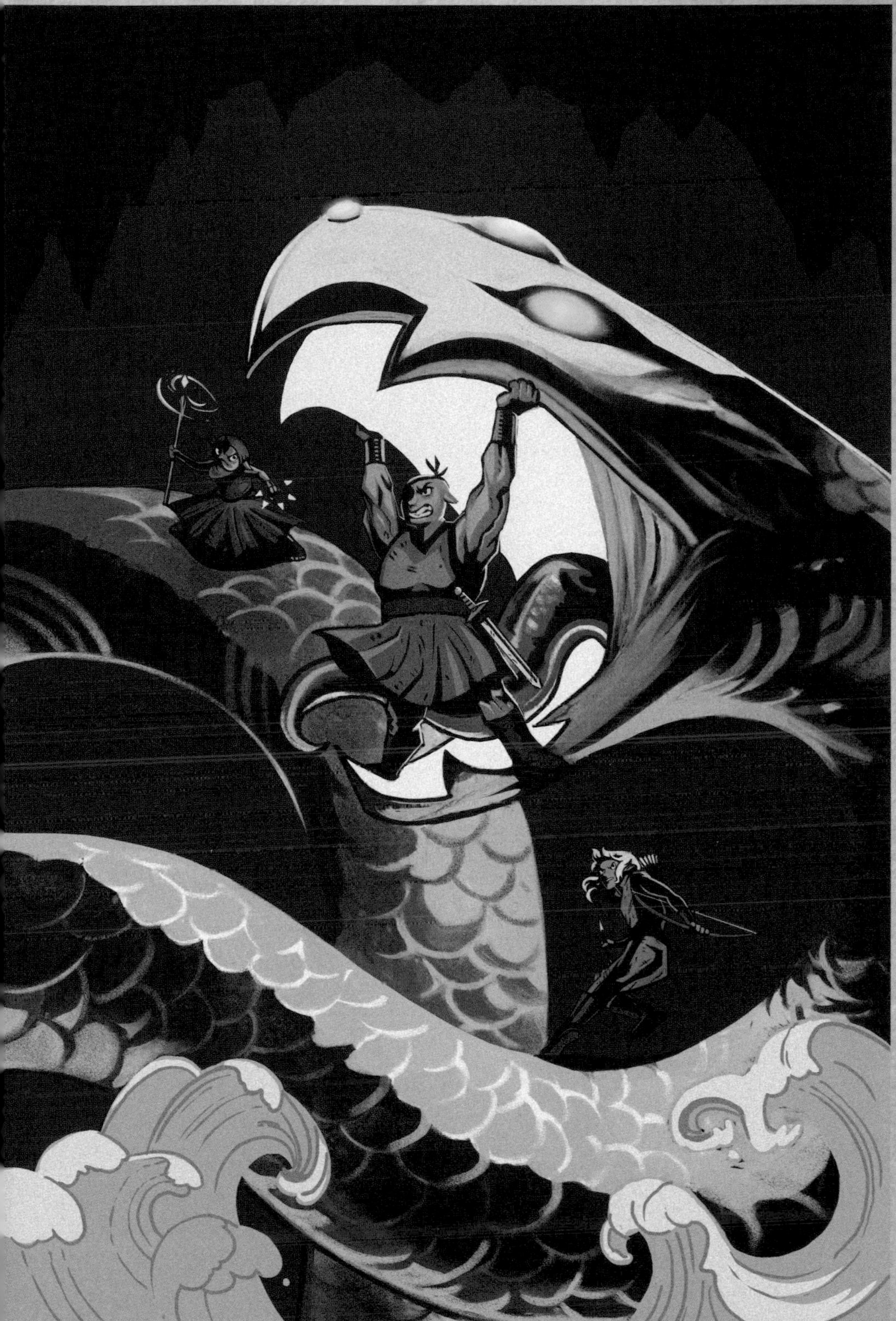

ISSUE SIX VARIANT COVER BY QISTINA KHALIDAH

CHARACTER DESIGNS BY **CHRISTINE LARSEN**

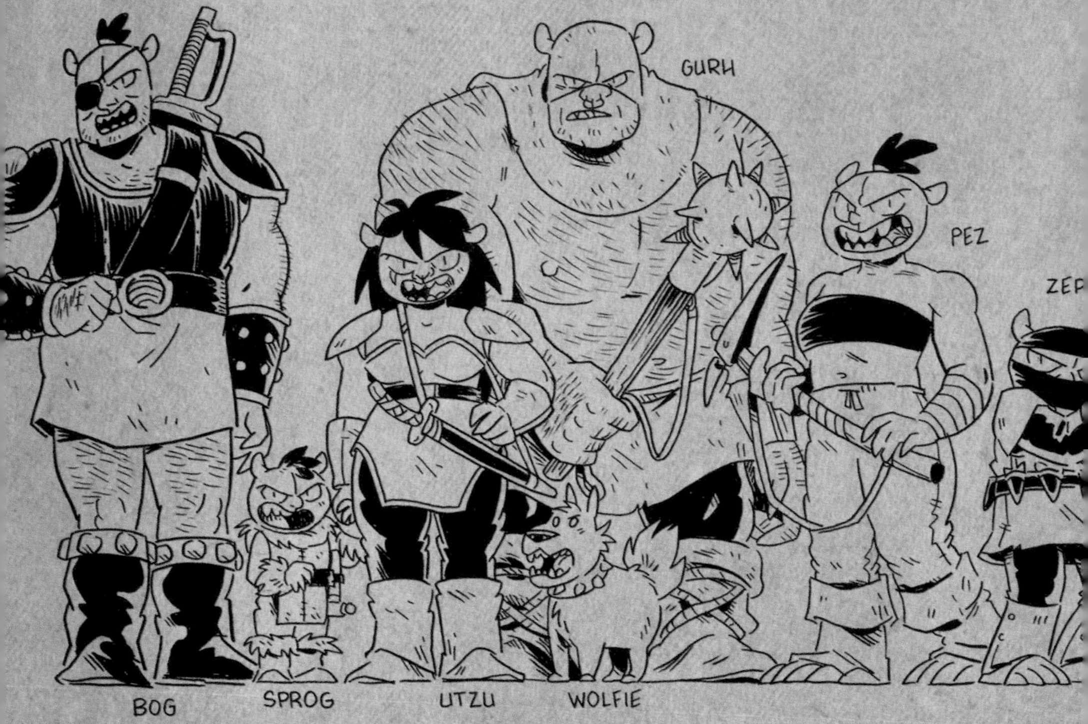
GURH
PEZ
ZEP
BOG
SPROG
UTZU
WOLFIE

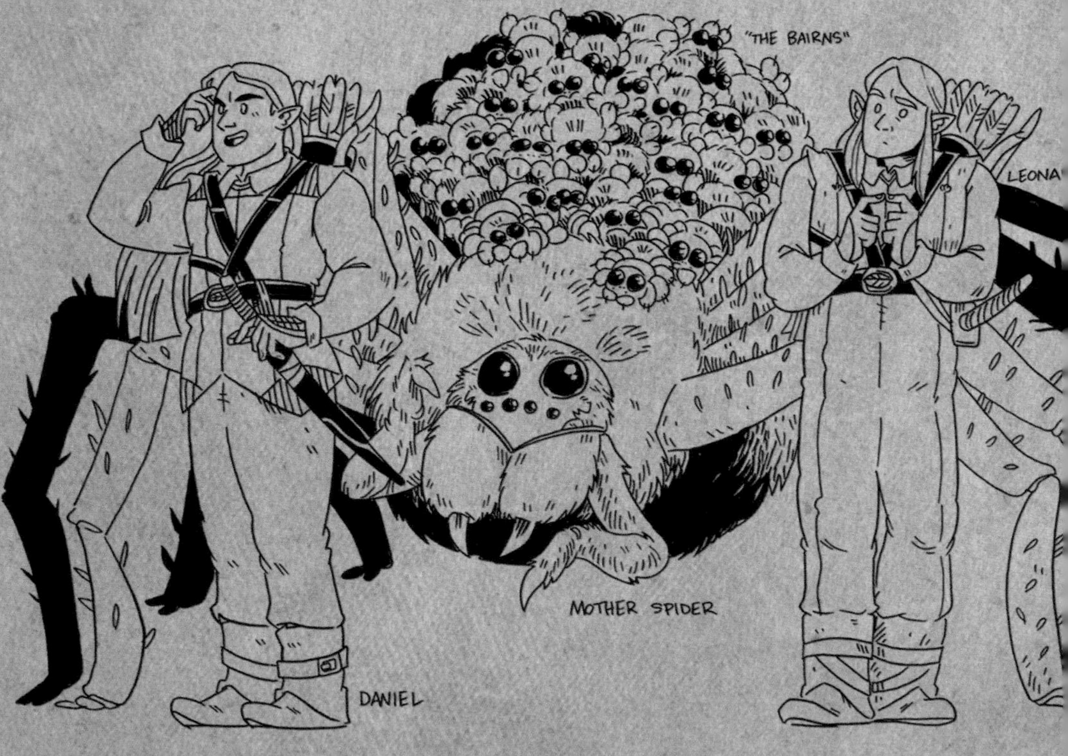
"THE BAIRNS"
LEONA
MOTHER SPIDER
DANIEL

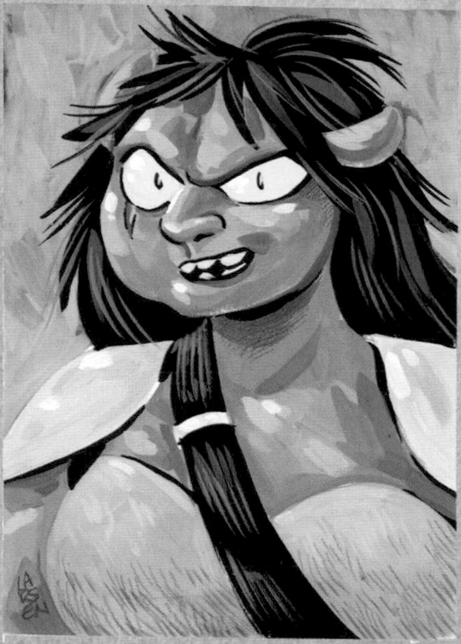

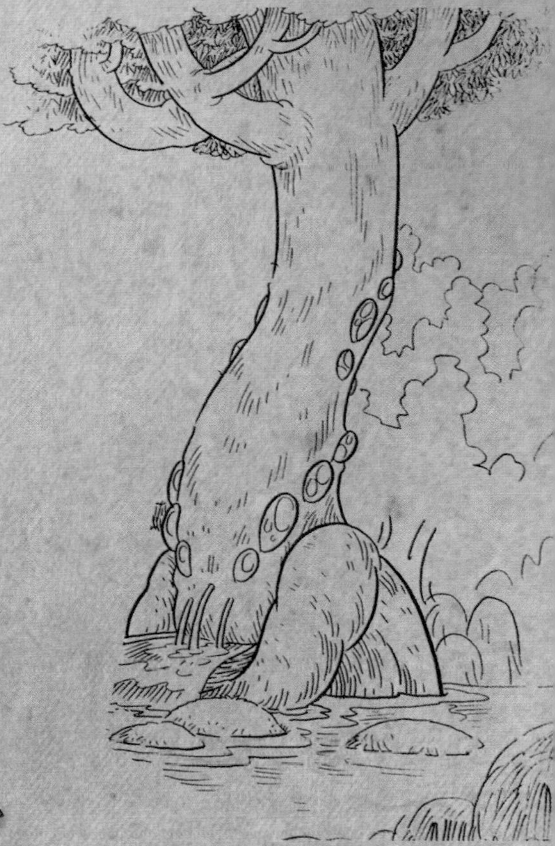

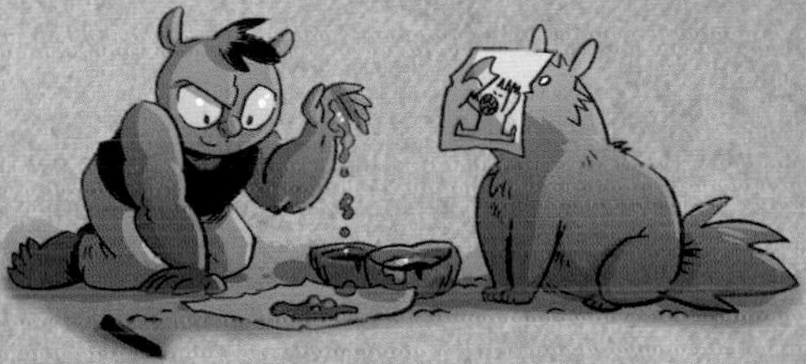

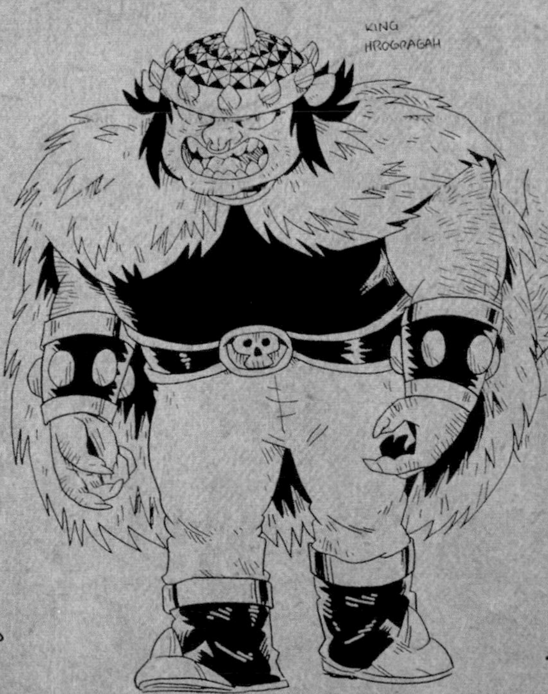
KING
HROGRAGAH

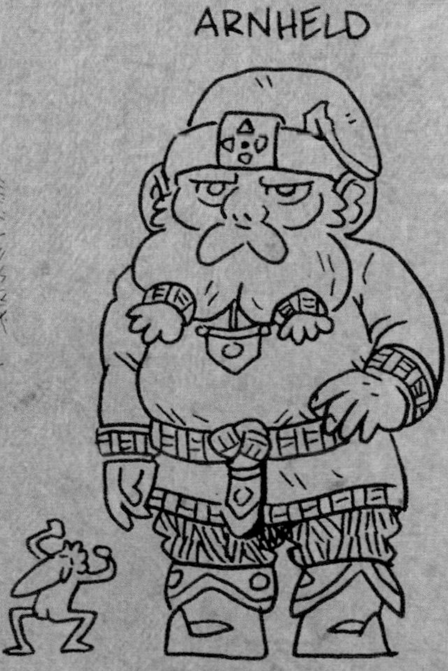
ARNHELD

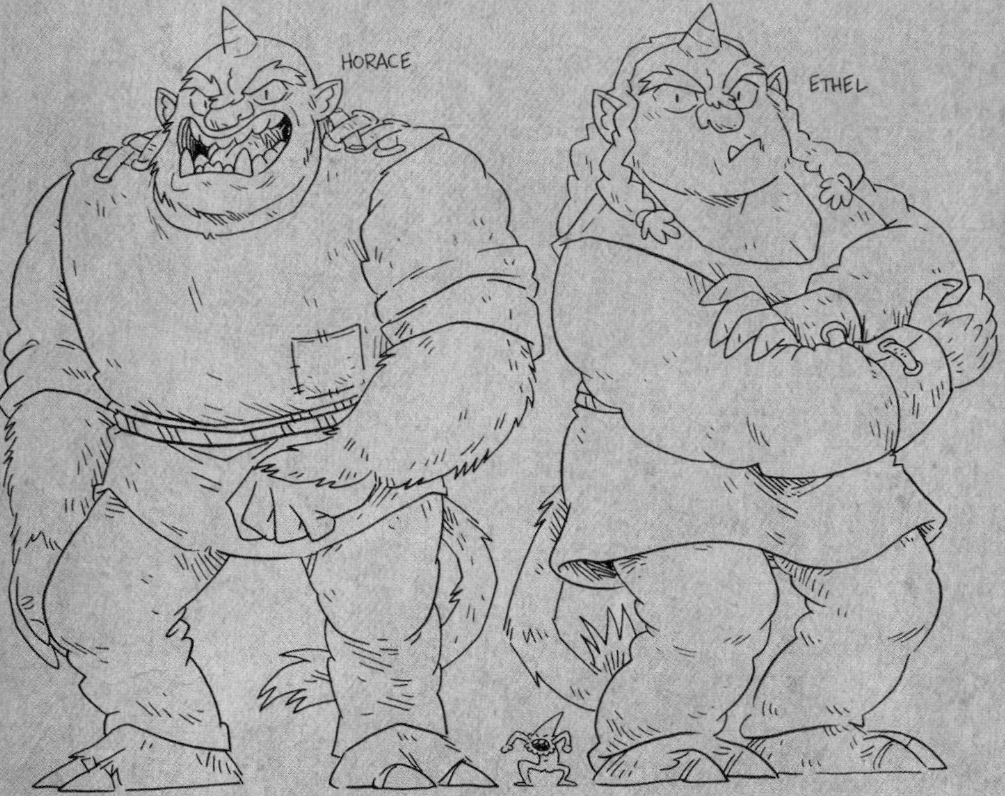
HORACE
ETHEL

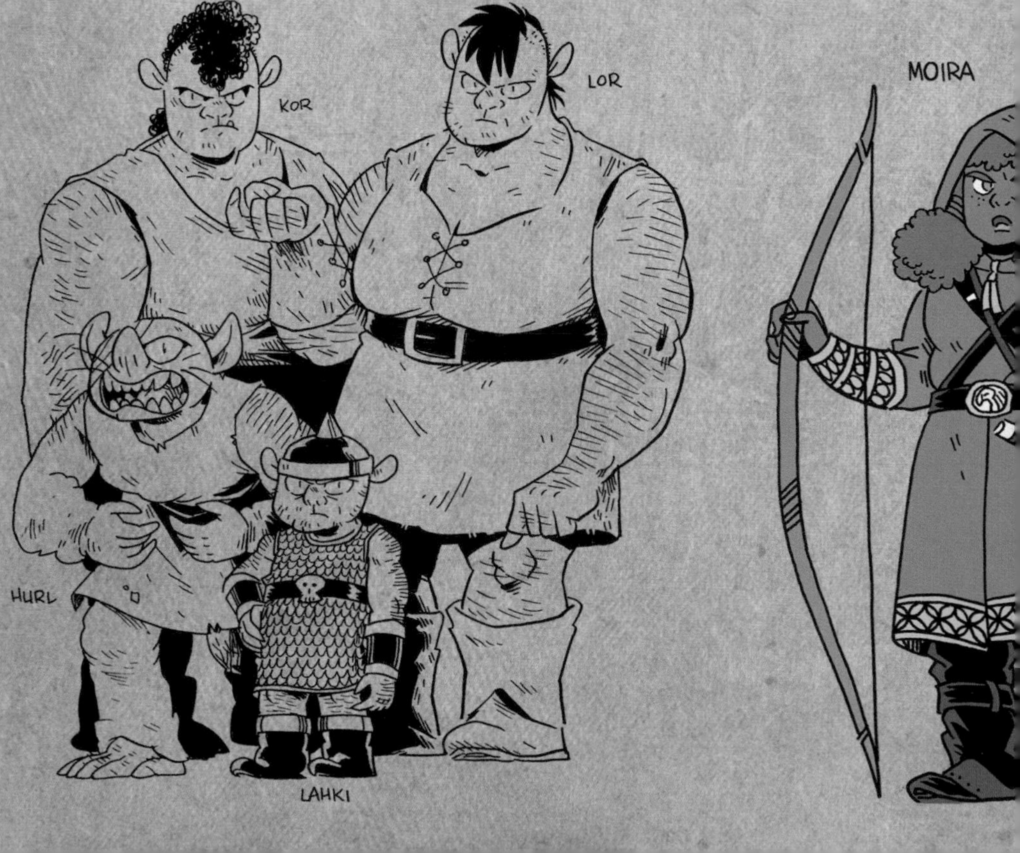
KOR
LOR
MOIRA
HURL
LAHKI

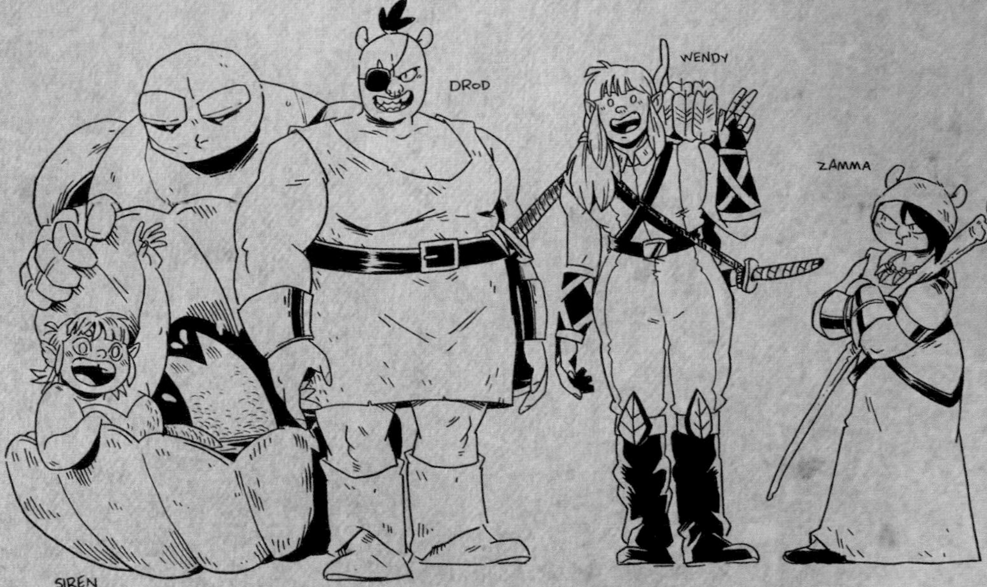
DROD
WENDY
ZAMMA
SIREN

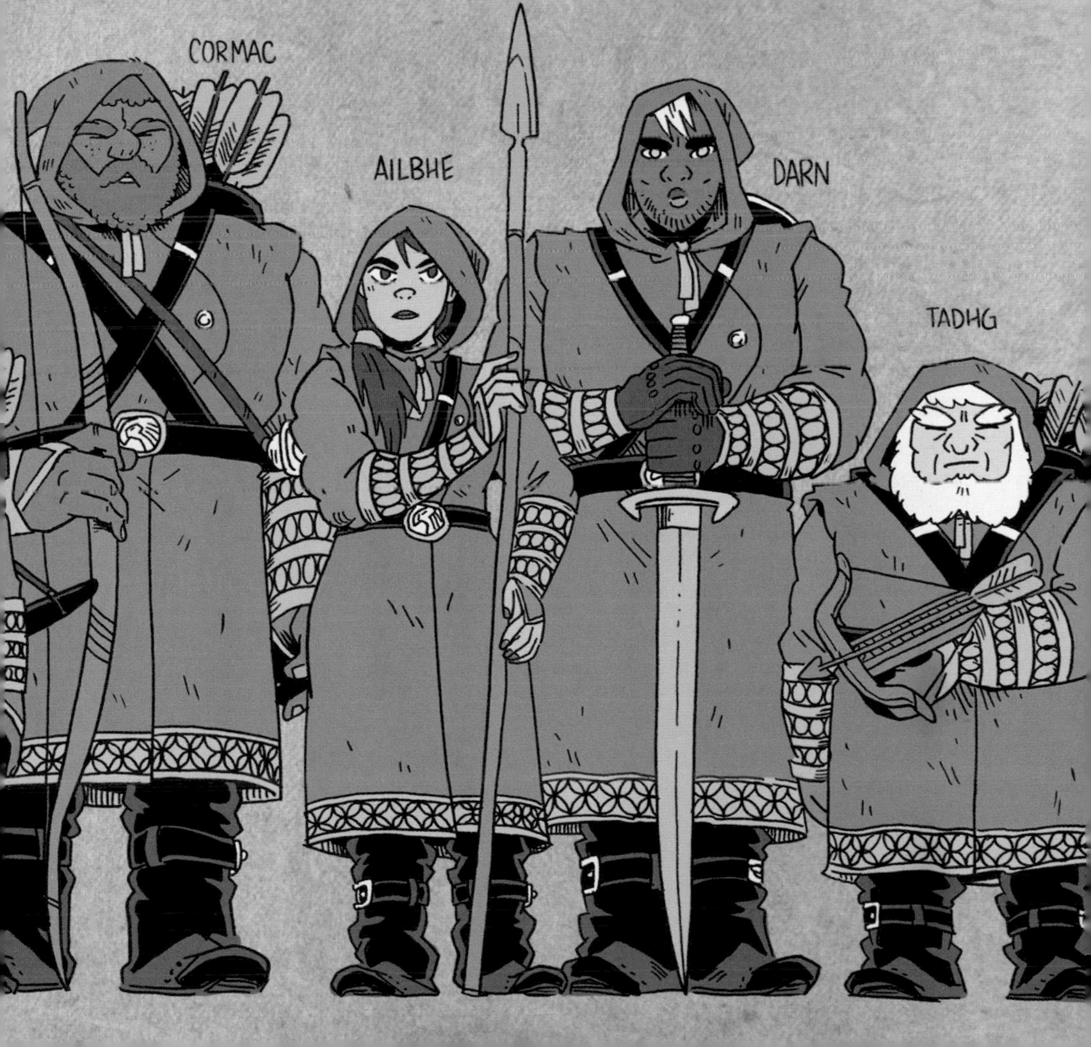
CORMAC
AILBHE
DARN
TADHG

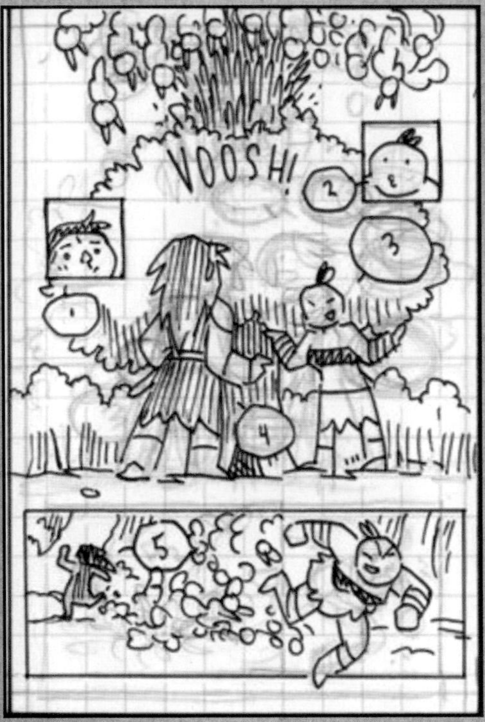
VOOSH!

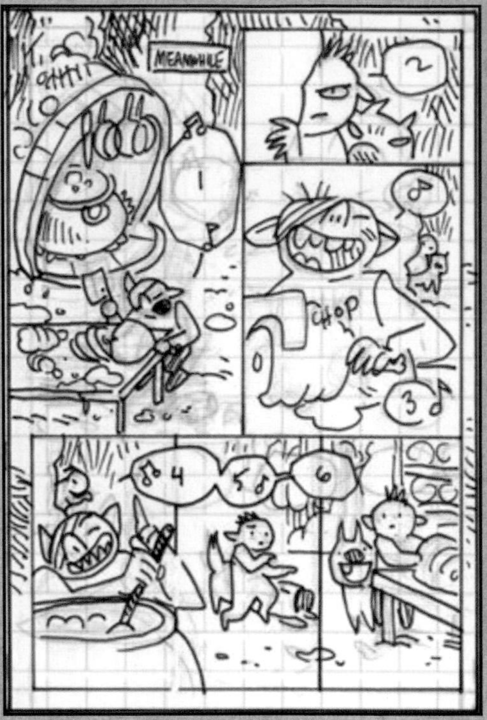
MEANWHILE
CHOP

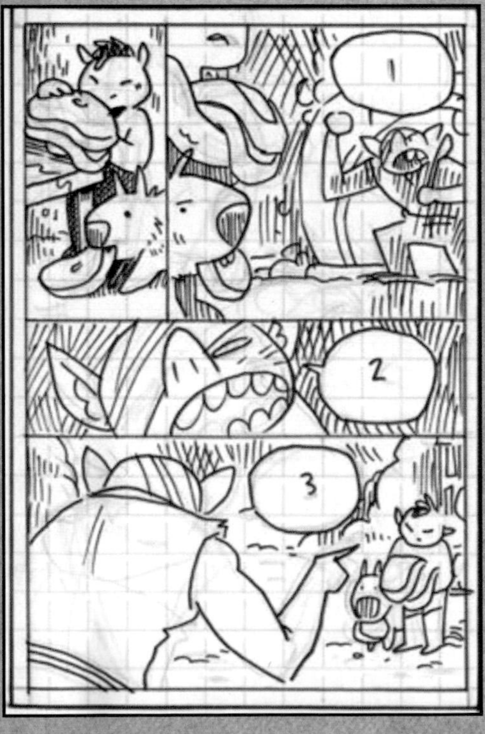

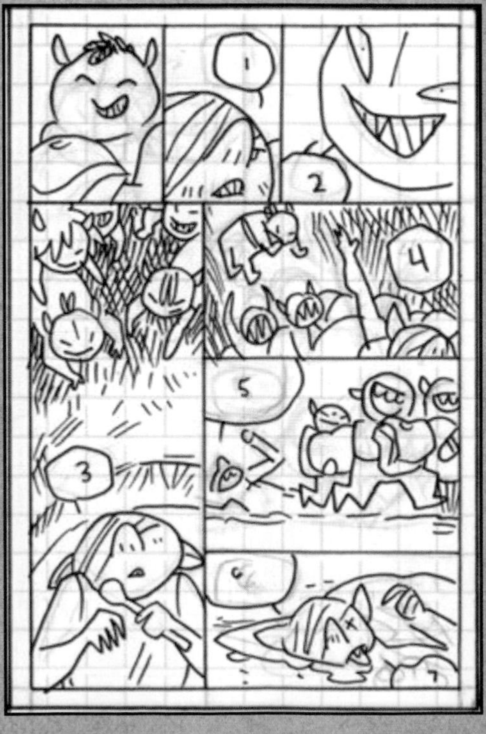

LAYOUTS BY **CHRISTINE LARSEN**

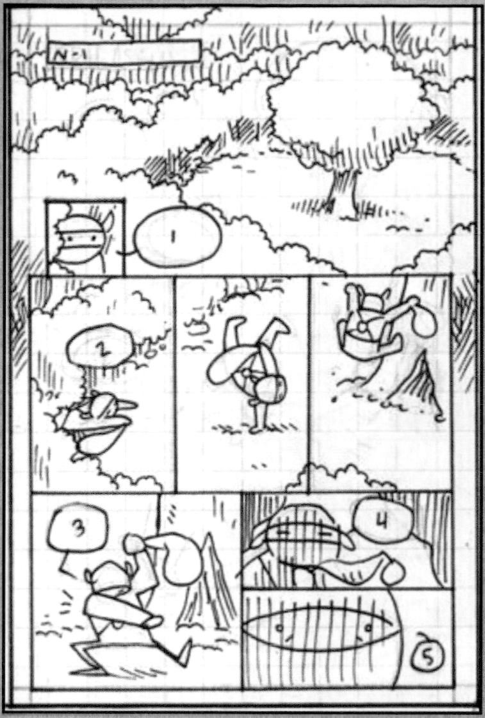

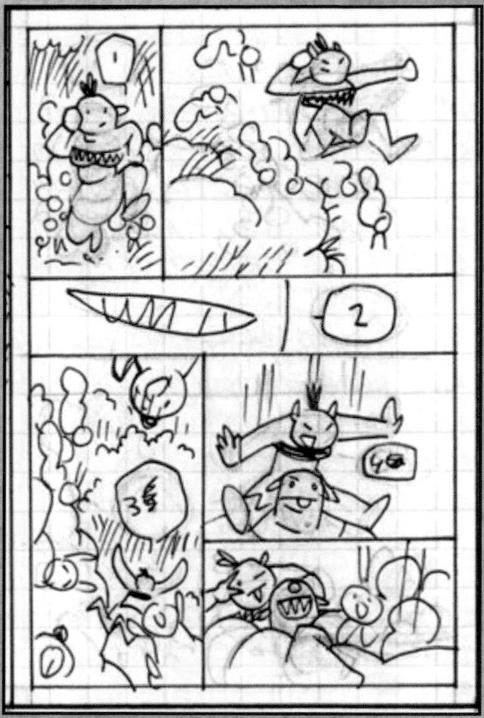

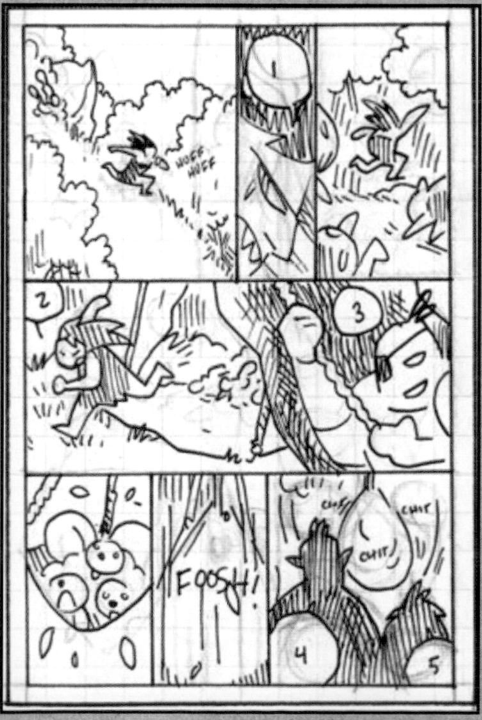
HUFF
HUFF
FOOSH!
CHIT
CHIT
CHIT

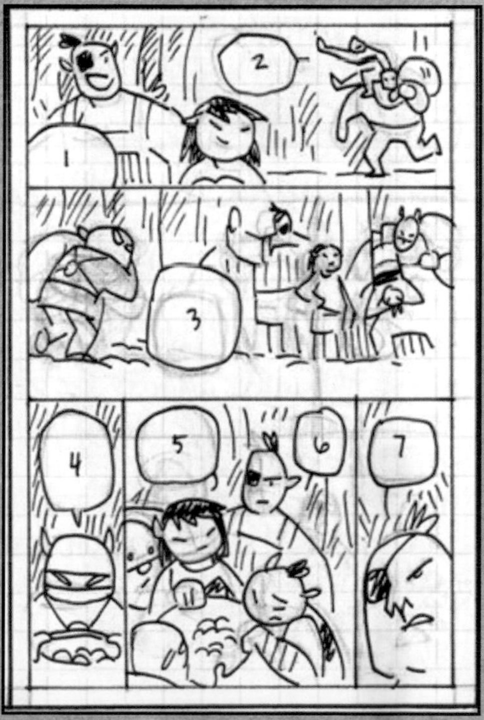

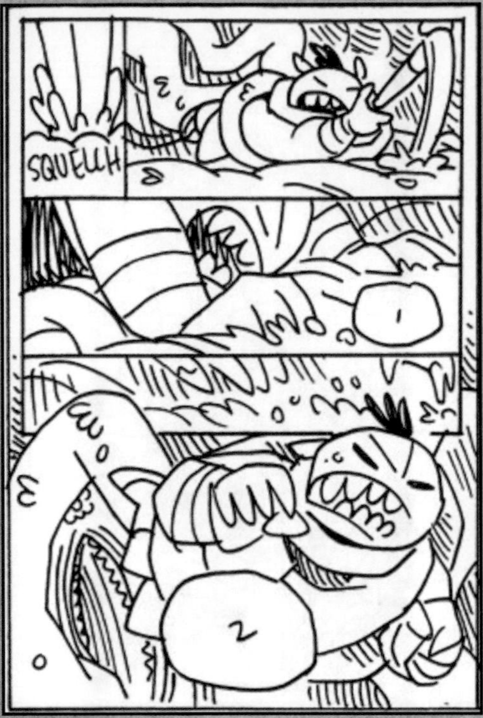
SQUELCH
1
2

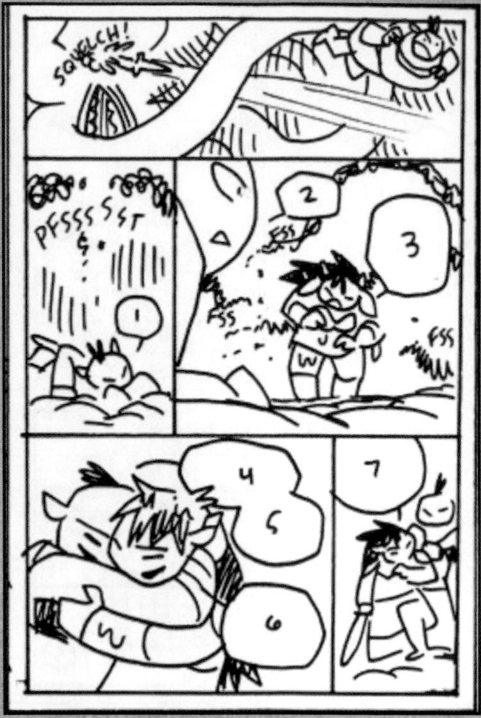
SQUELCH!
PFSSSSST
1
2
FSS
3
FSS
FSS
4
5
6
7

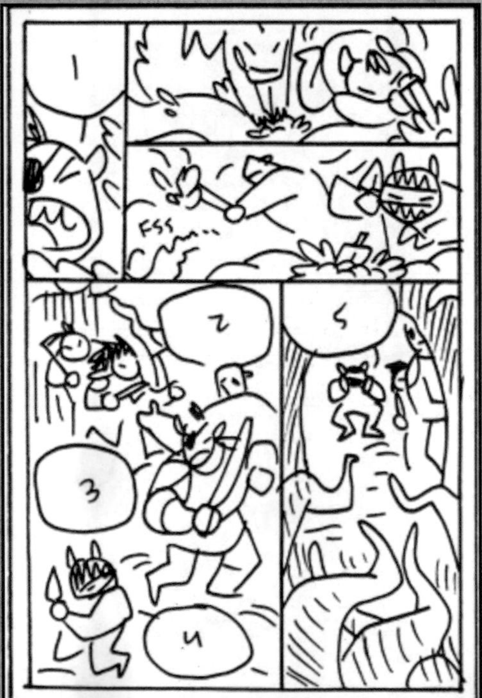
1
FSS
2
5
3
4

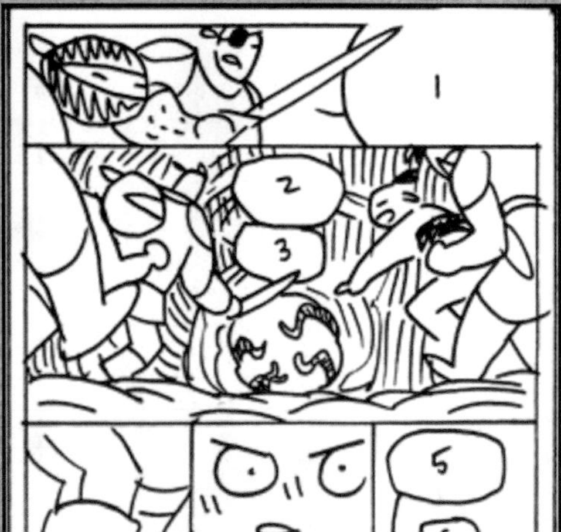
1
2
3
5
6
4
SKID!

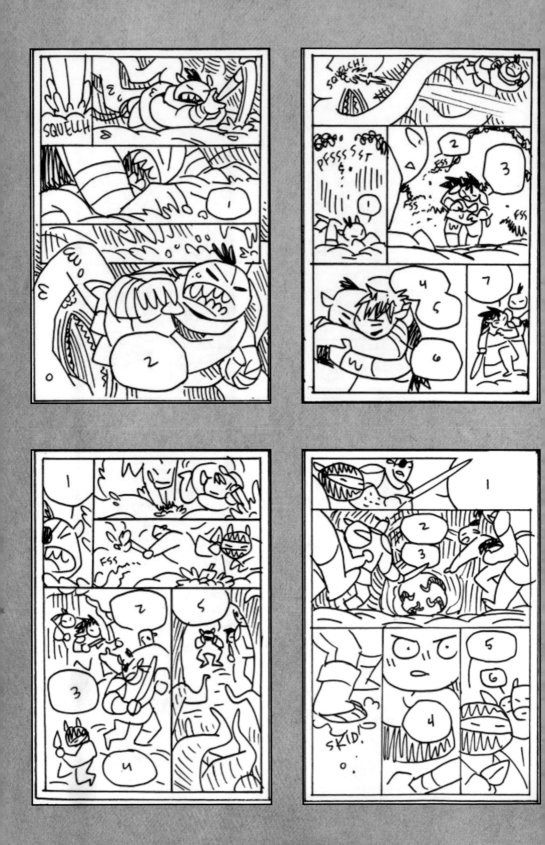

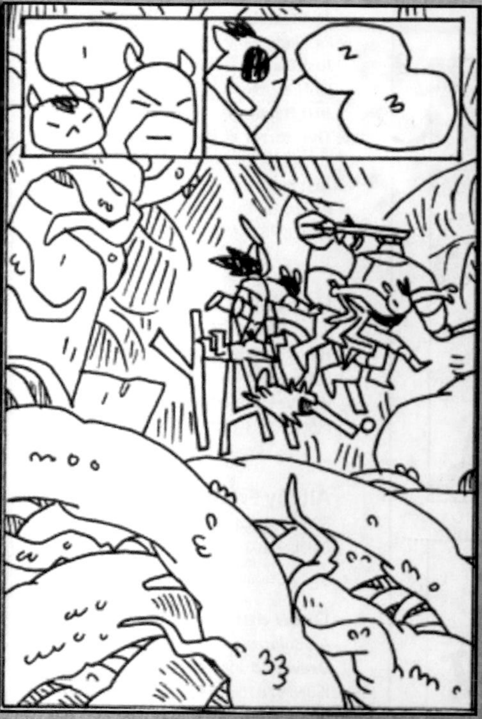
1
2
3

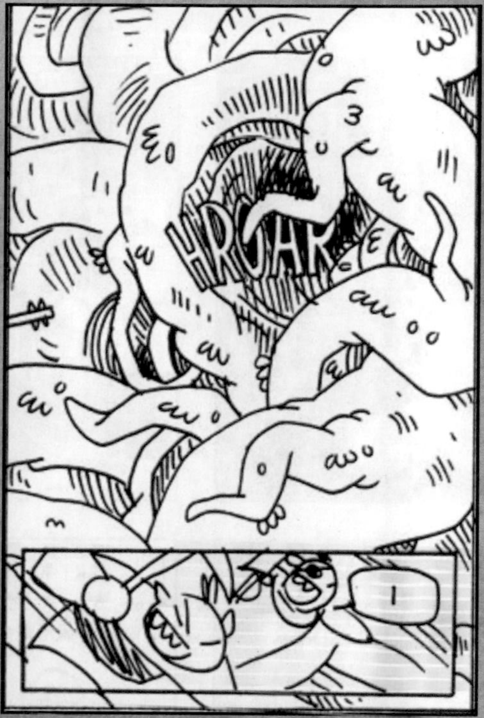
HRUAH
1

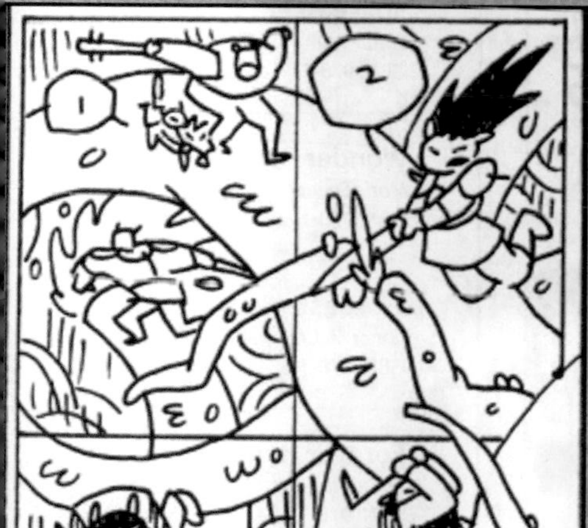
1
2
3

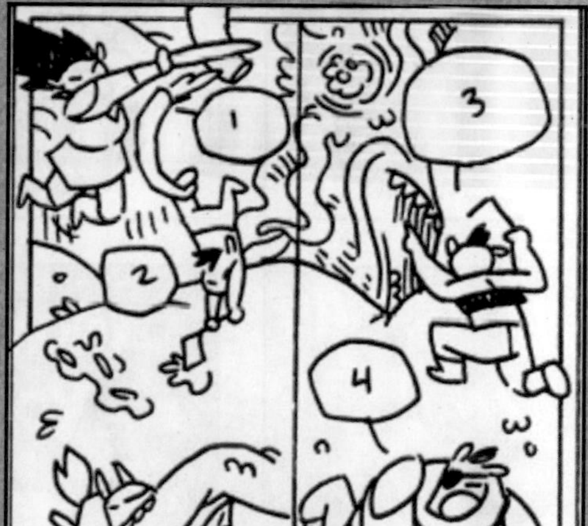
1
2
3
4

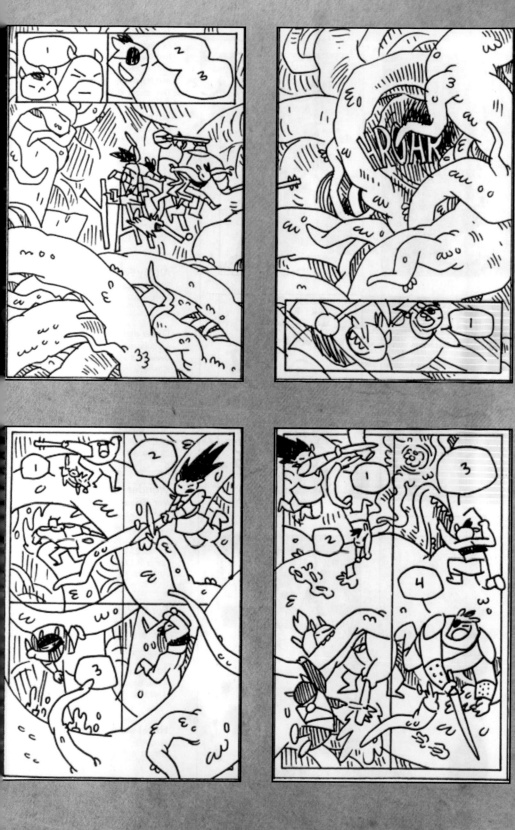

DISCOVER
EXCITING NEW WORLDS

New York Times Bestselling Author
R.L. STINE
JUST BEYOND
THE SCARE SCHOOL

Sam Davies
Hex Vet
Witches in Training

S.M. Vidaurri
All My Friends Are Ghosts
Hannah Krieger

NEW YORK TIMES BESTSELLER
ART BALTAZAR
DREW AND JOT
DUELING DOODLES

SPACE BEAR
ETHAN YOUNG

MARIE SPÉNALE
WONDER PONY

kaboom!

AVAILABLE AT YOUR LOCAL COMICS SHOP AND BOOKSTORE

To find a comics shop in your area, visit www.comicshoplocator.com

WWW.**BOOM-STUDIOS**.COM

Just Beyond
R.L. Stine, Kelly & Nichole Matthews

Just Beyond: The Scare School
ISBN: 9781684154166 | $9.99 US

Just Beyond: The Horror at Happy Landings
ISBN: 9781684155477 | $9.99 US

Just Beyond: Welcome to Beast Island
ISBN: 978-1-68415-612-2 | $9.99 US

Hex Vet
Sam Davies

Hex Vet: Witches in Training
ISBN: 978-1-68415-288-9 | $8.99 US

Hex Vet: The Flying Surgery
ISBN: 978-1-68415-478-4 | $9.99 US

All My Friends Are Ghosts
S.M. Vidaurri, Hannah Krieger
ISBN: 978-1-68415-498-2 | $14.99 US

Drew and Jot
Art Baltazar

Drew and Jot: Dueling Doodles
ISBN: 9781684154302 | $14.99 US

Drew and Jot: Making a Mark
ISBN: 978-1-68415-598-9 | $14.99 US

Space Bear
Ethan Young
ISBN: 978-1-68415-559-0 | $14.99 US

Wonder Pony
Marie Spénale
ISBN: 978-1-68415-508-8 | $9.99 US

The Last Witch: Fear and Fire
Conor McCreery, V.V. Glass
ISBN: 978-1-68415-621-4 | $14.99 US

Forever Home
Jenna Ayoub
ISBN: 978-1-68415-603-0 | $12.99 US

Jo & Rus
Audra Winslow
ISBN: 978-1-68415-610-8 | $12.99 US

Hotel Dare
Terry Blas, Claudia Aguirre
ISBN: 978-1-68415-205-6 | $9.99 US

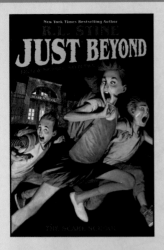

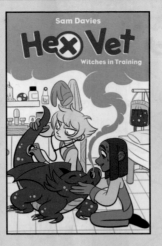

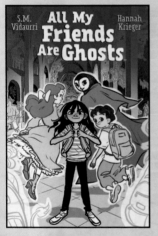

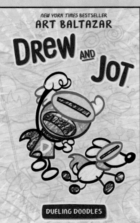

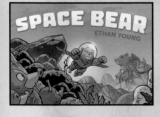

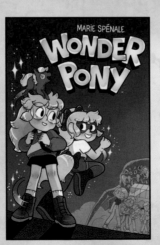

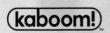